JOHN IRVING

THE LAST CHAIRLIFT

SCRIBNER

LONDON NEW YORK SYDNEY TORONTO NEW DELHI

First published in the United States by Simon & Schuster, Inc., 2022

First published in Great Britain by Scribner, an imprint of Simon & Schuster UK Ltd, 2022

Copyright © Garp Enterprises Ltd, 2022

In essay form, a small portion of the text herein referencing *Moby-Dick*
was previously published in the summer 2013 issue of *Brick*.

Excerpts from *My Father's Dragon* by Ruth Stiles Gannett
are reprinted from the work originally published by Random House,
New York, in 1948. Additional permissions granted by Swift Press.

SCRIBNER and design are registered trademarks of The Gale Group, Inc.,
used under licence by Simon & Schuster Inc.

The right of John Irving to be identified as author
of this work has been asserted in accordance with the
Copyright, Designs and Patents Act, 1988.

1 3 5 7 9 10 8 6 4 2

Simon & Schuster UK Ltd
1st Floor
222 Gray's Inn Road
London WC1X 8HB

Simon & Schuster Australia, Sydney
Simon & Schuster India, New Delhi

www.simonandschuster.co.uk
www.simonandschuster.com.au
www.simonandschuster.co.in

A CIP catalogue record for this book is available from the British Library

Hardback ISBN: 978-1-4711-7908-2
eBook ISBN: 978-1-4711-7910-5
Audio ISBN: 978-1-4711-9207-4

Interior design by Carly Loman

Printed and bound in Great Britain by CPI Group (UK) Ltd, Croydon CR0 4YY

For Dean Cooke

If I must die,
I will encounter darkness as a bride,
And hug it in mine arms.

—WILLIAM SHAKESPEARE, *Measure for Measure*

CHAPTERS

ACT II

THE HONEYMOON ON THE CLIFF

ACT III

RULES FOR GHOSTS

THE LAST
CHAIRLIFT

ACT I

EARLY SIGNS

1.

AN UNMADE MOVIE

My mother named me Adam, like you-know-who. She always said I was her one and only. I've changed some names, but not mine, and not the name of the hotel. The Hotel Jerome is real—it's a great hotel. If you ever go to Aspen, you should stay there, if you can afford it. But if anything happens to you along the lines of what happened to me, you should leave. Don't blame the Jerome.

Yes, there are ghosts. No, I don't mean those ghosts you may have heard were haunting the Jerome: the unregistered guest in Room 310, a drowned ten-year-old boy, shivering with cold and quickly disappearing, leaving only his wet footprints behind; the lovelorn silver miner, whose late-night sobbing has been heard while his apparition roams the halls; the pretty hotel maid who fell through the ice in a nearby pond and (notwithstanding that she died of pneumonia) occasionally appears just to turn down the beds. They aren't the ghosts I usually see. I'm not saying they don't exist, but I've scarcely seen them. Not every ghost is seen by everyone.

My ghosts are vivid to me—they're very real. Some of their names have been changed, but I haven't changed a single essential thing about the ghosts.

I can see ghosts, but not everyone can see them. As for the ghosts themselves, what happened to them? I mean, what made them ghosts? Not everyone who dies becomes a ghost.

This gets complicated, because I know that not all ghosts are dead. In certain cases, you can be a ghost and still be half-alive—only a significant part of you has died. I wonder how many of these half-alive ghosts are aware of what has died in them, and—dead or alive—if there are rules for ghosts.

"My life could be a movie," you hear people say, but what do they mean? Don't they mean their lives are too incredible to be real—too unbelievably good or bad? "My life could be a movie" means you think movies are both less than realistic and more than you can expect from real life. "My life could be a movie" means you think your life has been special enough to get made as a movie; it means you think your life has been spectacularly blessed or cursed.

But my life *is* a movie, and not for the usual self-congratulatory or self-pitying reasons. My life is a movie because I'm a screenwriter. I'm first and foremost a novelist, but even when I write a novel, I'm a visualizer—I'm seeing the story unfold as if it were already on film. Like some novelists, I know the titles and plots for novels that I won't live long enough to begin; like screenwriters everywhere, I've imagined more movies than I'll ever write. Like many screenwriters, I've written screenplays that I'll never see made as films. I see unmade movies for a living; I watch them all the time. My life is just another unmade movie, one I've seen before—one I'll go on seeing, again and again.

They publish your novel, they make your screenplay—these books and movies go away. You take your bad reviews with the good ones, or you win an Oscar; whatever happens, it doesn't stay. But an unmade movie never leaves you; an unmade movie doesn't go away.

2.

FIRST LOVE

I first heard about Aspen from my mother; she's the one who made me want to see the Hotel Jerome. I have my mom to thank, or not, for my going to Aspen—and her to thank, or not, for why I put off going there for a long time.

I used to think my mother loved skiing more than she loved me. What we believe as children forms us; what haunts us in our childhood and adolescence can make us do wayward things, but I don't blame my mom for telling me that her first love was skiing. She wasn't lying.

My mom was an expert skier, though she would never have said so herself. The story I grew up with was that my mother had failed in competition; henceforth, in her estimation, her skiing was no better than "fair to middling." A lifelong ski instructor—she preferred to teach young children and other beginners—my mom wasn't bitter about her failure to compete. As a kid, I never heard a single complaint about her diminutive size—not from her. From my grandmother, and from Aunt Abigail and Aunt Martha—my mother's older sisters—I heard a litany of grievances concerning my mom's size.

"Weight equals speed," was the condemning way Aunt Abigail put it. Abigail was a hefty woman, especially in her hips—more bovine than svelte in a pair of ski pants.

"Your mom was just a little thing, Adam," Aunt Martha told me with disdain. "In the downhill event, you have to weigh more than she ever did—she was strictly a slalom skier, a one-event girl."

"She just didn't weigh enough!" my grandmother would periodically exclaim; in these spontaneous outbursts, her arms reached for the sky, fists clenched, as if she held the heavens accountable.

Those Brewster girls, my mother included, were fond of dramatizing their exclamatory remarks, though my grandmother—Mildred Brewster, whose maiden name was Bates—always maintained that drama was more characteristic of a Bates than a Brewster.

I believed her. Evidence of the dramatic developed slowly in my grandfather, Lewis Brewster. I was told he'd been the principal of Phillips Exeter Academy, albeit briefly and with no accomplishments of significance. Throughout my acquaintance with Principal Brewster, as he preferred to be called (even by his grandchildren), he was retired. As a perpetual principal emeritus, gloomy and stern—bordering on catatonic—the former headmaster seemed destined to live forever. Little seemed to affect him. It would take the heavens to kill him.

My grandfather didn't speak; he rarely did anything. I used to think Lewis Brewster had been born a retired head of school. To whatever was said or done, Granddaddy Lew, as he hated to be called, would respond (when he reacted at all) with no more than a nod or a shake of his head. To engage with children, his own included, seemed beneath him. When he was vexed, he chewed his mustache.

Of course, I was not yet born when my mother told her parents she was pregnant. Before I knew the story, I used to wonder what Principal Brewster had to say about that. I was born one week before Christmas—Dec. 18, 1941. As my unwed mother would never tire of telling me, I was ten days late.

3.

A FIRST-NAME BASIS

My mother was the kind of moviegoer who could not resist likening the physical appearance of people she knew to movie stars. When the Austrian skier Toni Sailer won three gold medals at the 1956 Olympics, my mom said, "Toni looks a little like Farley Granger in *Strangers on a Train*"—a Hitchcock movie we'd watched together. My mom was a Hitchcock fan, but was she on a first-name basis with Toni Sailer?

"Toni almost fell into an open mine shaft in Aspen!" she said in her wide-eyed, exclamatory way. My mother then went on and on about all the ski lifts they were constructing and new trails they were cutting on Aspen Mountain. She said the old mine dumps and the abandoned buildings were being bulldozed, but there were still open pits here and there.

It's also not clear if my mother knew Stein Eriksen, the Norwegian skier; to this day, I don't know if they so much as met. The FIS Alpine World Ski Championships were in Aspen in 1950. "Stein was in first place after the first run," was not quite all my mom had to say about Stein. I'm referring to more than her oft-repeated knowledge of his famous reverse-shoulder technique.

I mean when my mom and I first saw *Shane* together—in 1953, I would have been eleven or twelve—and my mother remarked that Stein Eriksen looked like Van Heflin. "But Stein is handsomer," she confided to me, taking my hand. "And you're going to look like Alan Ladd," she assured me in a whisper, because we were in the movie theater—the Ioka, in downtown Exeter—with the pending violence of *Shane* unfolding before us.

I later pointed out to her that Alan Ladd was blond; whichever movie star I might resemble when I grew up, surely I would remain brown-haired. "I meant you're going to be handsome, in the same way Alan Ladd is handsome—good-looking and *small*," my mom replied, squeezing my hand when she emphasized the word *small*.

My aunts and my grandmother complained that my mother didn't weigh enough to be competitive in a ski race, but I believed she cherished her smallness. My being small was an attractive trait to her. Thus, before my teens, I evaluated Alan Ladd—the solitary but romantic gunfighter in *Shane*—and I imagined I might become a hero, or at least look like one.

Did my mom have an encounter (of any kind) with Stein Eriksen in Aspen? Did she even shake his hand? I know she made the trip; she saved the bus tickets, if only the New-York-to-Denver part. I don't doubt that she was there—in Aspen, in 1950—but she finished nowhere near the podium. Two Austrian skiers, Dagmar Rom and Trude Jochum-Beiser, won the women's events. Stein Eriksen, not yet a household name in international skiing, placed third in the men's slalom. The American racers won no medals. It's verifiable that the FIS Alpine World Ski Championships in 1950 were held in Aspen, but that wasn't the first time my mother was in town.

4.

DETERMINED NOT TO LEARN

The U.S. National Downhill and Slalom Championships were held in Aspen in 1941. It was the weekend of March 8 and 9, only a month before my mother's nineteenth birthday. She kept no bus tickets from that trip—if there were buses from New York to Denver back then. She said she got to Denver on her own; she told me she "hitched a ride the rest of the way with a bunch of Vermonters."

A few members of the Mount Mansfield Ski Club, maybe? Friends she'd skied with at Stowe, most likely. My mom was already a college dropout; she didn't last a semester. "I tried Bennington," as she put it; when the snow came, she went skiing instead.

My mother would have gone skiing at Bromley Mountain. It was close to Bennington. A son in the Pabst Brewing Company family had opened the ski area in 1938. When my mom first skied there, there might have been only one trail—on the west side of the mountain—and I have no idea what Bromley had for a tow.

"They put up their first J-bar between the Twister and the East Meadow runs," I remember my mother telling me. Over the years, when she spouted ski-area statistics to me, I would learn to tune her out.

All the Brewster girls had gone to summer camp at Aloha Camp on Lake Morey in Fairlee, Vermont, allegedly the oldest girls' camp in the state. That summer camp was where my mom made friends with skiers from Stowe. My mother flunked out of Bennington as fast as she could; she didn't stick around Bromley, not for long, not then. With the help of those girl campers from Aloha, she spent her first ski season in Stowe; this went on through the forties and into the fifties, when my mom was helping at the ski area and getting to know Mount Mansfield. My mother would henceforth designate the ski season as her "winter job." Both before and after I was born, she spent most of her winters in Stowe. I felt like I was a ski orphan.

Until July 1956, when I was fourteen, I lived with my grandmother and the principal emeritus. There was much fussing over me by my busybody aunts. I was an illegitimate child, but I was watched over. With two older cousins, I had no lack of hand-me-down clothes—boys' clothes, mostly.

Technically speaking, Nora wasn't a boy. But my cousin Nora was a tomboy; until she was sent off to the school for girls in Northfield, Massachusetts, Nora wore only boys' clothes. My cousin Henrik was a real boy—a real dickhead, it would turn out. Aunt Abigail and Aunt Martha had married Norwegians from northern New Hampshire; my uncles, Johan and Martin Vinter, were brothers. The Vinter family was in the logging and lumber business. Not Uncle Johan and Uncle Martin—they taught at Exeter, which would make my cousin Henrik a faculty brat when he attended the academy. Given that they were daughters of a former headmaster of Phillips Exeter, Abigail and Martha had come of age while paying attention to the young bachelors on the academy faculty—as my grandmother had observed.

My mom, on the other hand, had come of age while paying attention to skiing—or to skiers. Unsurprisingly, Johan and Martin Vinter were skiers. Why wouldn't they be? Their name means "Winter" in Norwegian, and they'd grown up in North Conway—where the Cranmore Mountain ski resort began operations in 1937. Johan and Martin hadn't waited for the first rope tow to be installed. They were telemark skiers on Cranmore before there were any lifts; they put skins on their telemark skis and skinned up Cranmore Mountain before they skied down.

This was how the Brewster girls—my mom, who was the youngest, included—learned to ski. Abigail and Martha met the young Norwegian teachers on the Exeter faculty, and they took my mom with them on the Boston & Maine—"the ski train," my cousin Nora called it. They all went on winter weekends from Exeter to North Conway, where they would be met by carloads of Vinters at the train station. (My mother always referred to the North Conway Norwegians as "carloads of winters.")

Thus did downhill skiing gain a foothold in the town of Exeter—in the seacoast area of New Hampshire, where there are no mountains. Skiing was what the Brewster girls did with their Norwegian relatives on winter weekends. "We went up north," as my mother put it. By the time I was born, the ski season was already my mom's *winter job*. From the age of four, every year I would be given brand-new skis and boots and poles. Yet no amount of new equipment—not to mention the private lessons my mother gave me—would do the trick.

At an early age, in my most formative years, I had decided to hate skiing. I would have preferred a mom who stayed at home with me to one who went skiing from the middle of November to the middle of April every year. I wanted my mother to be around, more than I wanted her to teach me to ski. As a child and a teenager, how else could I have made my point? I was determined not to learn to ski.

As the youngest in an extended family of expert skiers, how could I not have learned? It was impossible not to learn a little. I do know how to ski but I managed to learn to ski pretty badly. No one in the Brewster or Vinter family would call me an expert. I'm a purposely intermediate skier.

5.

BUT WHAT ACTUALLY HAPPENED IN ASPEN?

My mother must have known the seventeen-year-old girl who won the Women's National Slalom Championship on Aspen Mountain in March 1941. Young as she was, Marilyn Shaw was no newcomer; Stowe's "Snow Baby," as she was called, Marilyn Shaw was the youngest downhill skier who ever made the U.S. Women's Olympic Team. It wasn't Marilyn's fault that the 1940 Olympics were canceled because of the war in Europe. Yet my mom, who surely would have skied at Stowe with Marilyn Shaw, was not on a first-name basis with Marilyn—"the Shaw kid," was how my mother referred to her, when she mentioned Marilyn at all, which was rarely.

They were both Vermont skiers; they had to have known each other. And there was more than the Mount Mansfield connection. According to my mom, they'd both been coached by Sepp Ruschp—an Austrian ski instructor. My mother adored Sepp Ruschp. "He took his exam at St. Christoph, under Hannes Schneider," she told me.

"What exam?" I asked her.

"The official Austrian state-certified whatchamacallit, sweetie—his ski-instructor exam!" she exclaimed.

How could I forget the Hannes Schneider–Sepp Ruschp connection? The stem christie, the downhill turn that was the signature of the Arlberg technique—the turn that would replace the telemark turn. I can remember my mother saying, wistfully, how the stem christie itself would be replaced; gradually, it was. By the late 1960s, the parallel turn was more popular. I remember my mom telling me that my old-fashioned stem christie made me look like I was barely better than a snowplower. At the time, my turns *were* barely better than snowplow turns.

What would really kill the stem christie were the parabolic skis of the late 1990s—or so my mother always said. "Those new skis made parallel turns easy," I remember my mom telling me. "Even for *you*, sweetie," she added, squeezing my hand.

It was not lost on me that the Austrian Hannes Schneider came to Cranmore Mountain in North Conway, New Hampshire, in 1939. Sepp Ruschp, who had learned from Schneider, came to Mount Mansfield in Stowe, Vermont, in 1936. And one of Schneider's former students, Toni Matt—the Austrian who schussed the headwall of Tuckerman Ravine (the glacial cirque on the southeast face of Mount Washington, New Hampshire) at an estimated top speed of 85 miles per hour—won both the combined and the downhill events on Aspen Mountain in 1941. Toni Matt had moved to the U.S. from Austria in 1938.

Yet my mom made little mention of Toni Matt that championship weekend in Aspen. Instead, I heard all about the "crude boat-tow ski lift"; my mother said the lift took you only a quarter of the way up. "You had to sidestep the rest of the way," she said; she wasn't complaining. Nor did she gripe about the fact that the participants helped to prepare the course. "Everyone pitched in," was how my mom put it.

I heard so much about Jerome B. Wheeler, I was at first confused; I thought he was one of the skiers in competition. "Poor Jerome," my mother usually prefaced what she said about him. From what I'd heard her say about Roch Run, the first ski trail at Aspen—a challenging run, named for the Swiss mountaineer and avalanche expert André Roch—I assumed poor Jerome was a skier who'd fallen and been badly injured on Roch Run.

But my mother meant "the Macy's man," as she also called Jerome B. Wheeler—she meant the actual president of Macy's, the New York department store. Jerome B. Wheeler was a New Yorker who came to Aspen in the 1880s. Wheeler invested in the silver mines; he completed the first smelter. There was a railroad construction race, between the Colorado Midland and the Denver & Rio Grande—to see which line could beat the other to Aspen, across the Continental Divide. Wheeler put $100,000 into the Colorado Midland. And when prosperity came—when Aspen was a boom town—Jerome B. Wheeler paid for an opera house and the Hotel Jerome.

You would have thought my mom knew Jerome B. Wheeler, to hear how she talked about him. She was definitely on a first-name basis with him. "He was a Civil War hero, you know," she told me. "Jerome rode with Sheridan. Poor Jerome was a colonel, but they busted him to major because he disobeyed some stupid orders!"

"What orders?" I asked her, wringing my hands.

"I have no idea—*stupid* ones!" my mother declared. "Poor Jerome crossed Confederate lines. He rescued a Union regiment—they were starving! Don't wring your hands, Adam—they're small enough already."

"Poor Jerome," was all I could say.

There were a few glory years for the Jerome, but the silver boom would go bust; upon the demonetization of silver and the crash of 1893, the mines shut down. Wheeler's bank was forced to close. In 1901, Jerome B. Wheeler declared bankruptcy; he lost the Jerome for back taxes in 1909. The Wheeler Opera House caught fire in 1912. Poor Jerome died in 1918.

A former traveling salesman who'd been born in Syria became the bartender at the Jerome—this was in the "quiet years" of the grand hotel's decline. Mansor Elisha, the Syrian American bartender, bought the Jerome for back taxes in 1911.

"It's so sad!" my mom would exclaim—she meant poor Jerome and the fate of the hotel. "It's become a shabby boardinghouse, but you can see what a swell hotel it was!" She declared that the Syrian family who took over the Jerome was a family of saints; she said the Elishas always welcomed the townspeople. "André Roch himself stayed five whole weeks at the Jerome," my mother told me. She believed this proved her point: if the famous André Roch had stayed five whole weeks, the Hotel Jerome must have been swell.

During World War II, when the ski troops of the Tenth Mountain Division came to Aspen on cross-country maneuvers, the skiing soldiers slept on the floors of the Jerome. I learned, long after the fact, that many of Stowe's male skiers joined the Tenth Mountain Division. Weren't these men my mother would have seen on the slopes of Mount Mansfield? Maybe some of them were among that *bunch of Vermonters* she'd hitched a ride with, on her way to Aspen from Denver in 1941. She didn't say.

Toni Matt was a Tenth Mountain Division man. A lieutenant in World War II, he was posted to the Aleutian Islands. Toni Matt wasn't married in 1941, when he won two championships in Aspen. Matt was only a few years older than my mom—at the time, he would have been twenty-one or twenty-two.

I've seen photographs of Toni Matt; he looks a little like me. Actually, I think I look a lot more like Toni Matt than I do Alan Ladd, but my mother could not be persuaded of this.

"In the first place, Toni Matt has dark hair," I pointed out to my mom, "and his face is rounder than Alan Ladd's—more like mine. Furthermore, Toni Matt's nose isn't as sharp as Alan Ladd's, and his eyebrows aren't as thick—they're more like mine."

"Toni Matt was never *handsome*, not like Alan Ladd—not to me," my mother added, with a dismissive shrug. "Not like you're handsome, sweetie," she told me.

Once, when I argued with my mom about Toni Matt, she just took my hand and squeezed it. Then she said—with each word, her eyes never left mine—"If you were Toni Matt's son, you would love to ski. Toni schussed the headwall of Tuckerman Ravine," she reminded me. She even knew Toni's time for the four-mile race, from the top to the bottom of the ravine. "Six minutes, twenty-nine and two-tenths of a second," my mom whispered to me; her eyes were locked on mine. "If Toni Matt were your father, no one could have kept you off skis. Leave your little hands alone, sweetie."

But my mom must have been on a first-name basis with *someone* that weekend of March 8 and 9. She never varied from saying I was born ten days late—on December 18 of that year. You do the math. That weekend when Marilyn Shaw won the Women's National Slalom Championship in Aspen, someone got my mother pregnant. Poor Jerome didn't knock her up. That March weekend in 1941, Jerome B. Wheeler was already a ghost.

6.

LITTLE RAY

What I remember of my winters, when I was a child and in my early teens, is that my grandmother was my mother. Nana, my name for Mildred Brewster, was my winter mom. And she was my mother's most devoted apologist—for a while, it seemed to me, her only apologist.

"No one asks to be born," I grew up hearing Mildred Brewster say—to which my audibly breathing aunts, Abigail and Martha, would roll their eyes and breathe more heavily.

"The poor-Rachel routine," Aunt Abigail labeled it.

"Here comes the whaling ship," Aunt Martha would whisper in my ear, "just when we were hoping it had sailed beyond the horizon." But I loved listening to Nana's story about my mother's name. Mildred Brewster had studied English and American literature at Mount Holyoke, a Massachusetts liberal arts college for women; her favorite novel was *Moby-Dick*, the reason my mom was named Rachel.

Nana's copy of the novel was always on the table beside her reading chair. Even as a child, I noticed that *Moby-Dick* was a more constant presence than the Bible; my grandmother consulted the story of the white whale more than she turned to Jesus. "One day, dear, when you're old enough, I'll read this to you," Nana told me, holding the huge book in both her hands. She didn't wait for me to be old enough. I was ten when she started reading the novel aloud to me; I was twelve, almost thirteen, before she finished. It's a slow novel, but the chapters are short. An ocean voyage goes slowly, except for the sinking.

"Keep your eye on the cannibal, dear—Queequeg is important," Nana was always saying. "He's not just any harpooner; Queequeg isn't a Christian. He's referred to as an 'abominable savage' for a reason—not only to get your attention. Queequeg travels with a shrunken head; he's heavily tattooed. And there's his coffin. Please don't forget about Queequeg's coffin!"

How could I forget a coffin? Listening to *Moby-Dick* made me anxious. I was relieved to discover that there was nothing abominable about Queequeg; Melville doesn't even take him to task for not being a Christian. "For all his tattooings he was on the whole a clean, comely looking cannibal," as Melville puts it. Listening to *Moby-Dick*—for close to three years—had a life-changing effect on me. It not only made me want to be a writer; according to my cousin Nora, it essentially shaped and screwed up the rest of my life.

My grandmother was a tireless *Moby-Dick* reader, but I interrupted her, I asked a hundred questions, I was interested in all the wrong things—such as whale vomit, or what makes whales sick in the first place. Chapter 92, the "Ambergris" chapter, raises a lot of gastrointestinal questions. Highly valued by perfumers, ambergris is (in Melville's words) "an essence found in the inglorious bowels of a sick whale!" It is produced only by sperm whales. I made my grandmother explain what would happen to a mass of ambergris that was too large to pass through the whale's intestines. Nana took pains to tell me that such a large mass of ambergris would have to be *vomited* by the whale. Ambergris can float for years, before washing ashore. Lumps have been found weighing as much as fifty kilograms—imagine 110 pounds of whale vomit! This is the kind of thing that distracted me from what was important in *Moby-Dick*. My interest in whale puke drove my grandmother crazy.

But Nana and I understood one thing. We loved Queequeg, the cannibal harpooner. We were thrilled that he was heavily tattooed, and that he traveled with a shrunken head. We were excited that Queequeg wasn't a Christian, because this meant he was capable of doing *anything*. Whatever came into Queequeg's head, he might do it. He might even eat you. The savage from the South Seas was the opposite of an uptight, white New Englander. Nana and I knew what *they* were like.

Years later, when I read *Moby-Dick* to myself, I kept a close eye on Queequeg. My grandmother was right. If you pay attention to Queequeg, the cannibal harpooner, you will appreciate *Moby-Dick*. No amount of whale vomit will turn you against what D. H. Lawrence called "one of the strangest and most wonderful books in the world."

Not being a Christian has a marvelous effect on Queequeg. One day, Queequeg has a fever. He decides he's going to die. Queequeg is right, but it's not the fever that's going to kill him, and he's not the only one onboard the *Pequod* who's going to die. Queequeg asks the ship's carpenter to make a coffin. Queequeg even lies down in his coffin, to be sure he fits. But Queequeg's fever goes away, and he uses the coffin for his clothes. This is not extraneous detail! Not long later, a life buoy is lost overboard. Queequeg hints that his coffin would work as a life buoy—he is a practical cannibal. The ship's carpenter goes to work on the coffin, nailing down the lid, caulking the seams.

"Queequeg sees the world differently than his shipmates aboard the *Pequod*," my grandmother explained. "Only someone like Queequeg would ask the ship's carpenter for a coffin."

I somewhat struggled to make this part fit with Queequeg's not being a Christian. "Does Melville mean a Christian wouldn't ask for a coffin while he's still alive?" I asked my grandmother.

"The ones I know wouldn't," Nana answered me. "That's more in keeping with what a cannibal would request, I think."

Nana and I were a long way into *Moby-Dick* when we got to the moment when Captain Ahab comes on deck and makes whimsical remarks (mostly to himself) about the suitability of putting a coffin to use as a life buoy.

Dedicated lit student that she was, my grandmother often interrupted herself when she was reading aloud to me; she wanted to be sure I had noticed certain things. In the chapter where Ahab is musing to himself on the meaning of a coffin as a life buoy, Nana stopped reading to me and remarked: "I hope you noticed, Adam, that this is the same ship's carpenter who made Ahab's prosthetic leg."

"I noticed, Nana," I assured her.

Moby-Dick is a story about a seemingly unkillable whale. It's also a story about absolute authority—a man who won't listen to anyone. The captain of the *Pequod*, Ahab, is obsessed with killing Moby Dick. The white whale is responsible for Ahab's losing a leg. Nana and I knew that Ahab should just get over it. Ahab refuses to assist the captain and crew of the *Rachel*, another whaling ship. The *Rachel* has encountered Moby Dick; the *Rachel* has lost a whaleboat with all its crew. Won't Ahab help the *Rachel* search for its missing sailors? The son of the *Rachel's* captain is among them. No, Ahab won't help. Ahab only wants to find and kill Moby Dick.

We *know* what's going to happen. Ahab finds what he's looking for—the white whale kills him and sinks the *Pequod*. But wait a minute. There's a first-person narrator. Ishmael is the storyteller. What can possibly save Ishmael? Did you forget that Queequeg's coffin *floats*? It's a good thing not everyone onboard was a Christian. Let this be a lesson to you: never take an ocean voyage without a tattooed cannibal.

"Do you see, dear?" Nana interrupted her reading to ask me. "It is Ahab's refusal to help his fellow men at sea that dooms him—and all hands, but one, aboard the *Pequod*."

"I see," I said. How could I miss it? It took three years.

The white whale sinks the *Pequod*. Everyone, except Ishmael, drowns—"and the great shroud of the sea rolled on as it rolled five thousand years ago," as Melville puts it. That's pretty clear.

Queequeg's coffin, now a life buoy, rises from the sea; it floats by Ishmael's side. And Ishmael says: "On the second day, a sail drew near, nearer, and picked me up at last. It was the devious-cruising Rachel, that in her retracing search after her missing children, only found another orphan."

"Read it again—the whole story," I said to my grandmother, when she got to the end.

"When you're old enough, you can read it again—to yourself," Nana said.

"I will," I told her, and I would—again and again.

But that first time I also asked my grandmother: "You named my mom for 'the devious-cruising Rachel'—you named her for a ship?"

"Not devious in the bad way, Adam—*devious* can also mean wandering, or without a fixed course. And not just *any* ship!" Nana exclaimed. "The *Rachel* rescues Ishmael. Well, dear—truth be told—your mother rescued me."

"You were at sea? You were drowning, Nana?"

"Heavens, no!" my grandmother declared. She explained that Abigail, her eldest, had just been sent away to the school for girls in Northfield; in the following year, Nana told me, Martha would also be sent away. What my grandmother meant was that the birth of my mom rescued her from being left alone with Principal Brewster. While I had not found the principal emeritus to be a lot of fun, I didn't consider him in the same category as drowning at sea.

"Oh," was all I managed to say. I suppose I sounded disappointed.

My mother had chosen to be with her winter job—for almost half the year—instead of choosing to be with me. I know Nana could detect my disillusionment with my mom; after all, she'd been somewhat less than a Rescue Ship Rachel for me.

"Listen to me, dear," my grandmother then said. "Your mother had her reasons for naming *you*—you're not the first Adam, you know." Thus getting my attention, my grandmother maintained—much to my surprise—that my mom had named me Adam for the following reasons: "You're not only the first man in her life, dear; you'll be the only one. You're all that matters to her, Adam—as far as men are concerned," Nana told me.

This completely contradicted my earliest impression of my pretty, young mother. From my sexually innocent perspective—long before I embarked on my own misguided sexual path—I'd presumed that my mom's foremost love was being single. And didn't she choose to be single because she liked meeting men?

I was not yet a teenager—ten, eleven, twelve—when my grandmother read *Moby-Dick* to me. Yet Nana seemed to be saying that my mother wanted nothing to do with men—only me. At the time, the truest thing I knew was this: my grandmother was my mom's most constant advocate; therefore, I didn't entirely believe her.

My *devious-cruising* aunts—I mean *devious* in the bad way—had done their treacherous best to undermine Nana's efforts to make me love and trust her Rescue Ship Rachel.

"Little Ray," Principal Brewster had named my mother. The nickname the principal emeritus had given her was not as astonishing to me as the evidence that the former headmaster had ever spoken.

"But of course he used to talk, dear," Nana told me. "How could a head of school not speak? And Principal Brewster was a teacher before he became— in his own way—a headmaster. Oh, dear—you can't imagine how that man could talk!"

"But what happened to him, Nana?" I asked her. "What made him stop talking?" I must have wrung my hands.

"When you're old enough, Adam," my grandmother began; then she stopped. "Someone will tell you when you're old enough," she said. "Please don't hurt your hands—they're so small."

"Aunt Abigail or Aunt Martha, maybe," I ventured to guess.

"Someone else, I hope," my grandmother said. "Little Ray herself, maybe," she added softly, without conviction.

"Little Ray is a one-event girl—I already told you," Aunt Martha re- minded me, when I asked her to fill in a few missing details. Yes, but Mar- tha's earlier reference to my mom as *a one-event girl* had to do with her being strictly a slalom skier; it was connected to her being small. Now Martha was implying that all three Brewster girls were inclined to one event—in the specific sense that they all wanted one, and only one, child. This was sheer manipulation on Aunt Martha's part. I was used to it, and used to worse from Aunt Abigail—the firstborn Brewster, and proud of it, the cow.

"Little Ray was an accident—an unplanned child. She wasn't meant to be born," Aunt Abigail told me, when I pressed her to tell me what she knew.

"A latecomer," Aunt Martha chimed in. "It's annoying, Adam—how you wring your hands."

You can imagine how confusing this was to me. My mother was named for the *Rachel* in *Moby-Dick*—a rescue-ship girl—and she'd named me after the Garden of Eden guy. According to my grandmother, my mom *was* a one-event girl—but not in either of the two ways Aunt Martha meant it.

Nana meant my mother wanted nothing *more* to do with men. Was my grandmother actually telling me that my mom was *that kind* of one-event girl—namely, had Rescue Ship Rachel chosen the one and only time she would *ever* sleep with a man, strictly for the purpose of giving birth to me?

You can imagine how clumsily I must have formed the words, in order to ask my grandmother exactly what she meant about my being an Adam. I can't remember the tortured way I would have phrased the question; I can't see myself asking my grandmother such a thing in a clear and forthright manner. Such as: "Nana, are you telling me my mother had sex just once—because she wanted a child, just one—and now that she has me, she's never doing it again?"

Can you imagine asking your grandmother that? Well, I did—in no comprehensible sequence of words I can recall.

It's not hard, on the other hand, to summon to memory my grandmother's answer. In a way, I'd already heard it, when I asked her to read *Moby-Dick* again—the whole story.

"When you're old enough, Adam," Nana began, "I'm sure Little Ray would prefer to tell you the story herself—the whole story."

7.

ALL ABOUT SEX

Keep in mind that my mother was the baby in the Brewster family, and then I was—hence the alleged accident of Little Ray's birth was perceived as a precursor to the unplanned nature of my own coming into this world. This was the threefold, presumptive opinion of my aunts: that Little Ray and I were both unplanned; that a resultant chaos attended our births; that an ongoing haplessness would doom the rest of our lives.

To this joyless conviction, steadfastly upheld by Aunt Abigail and Aunt Martha, my grandmother had (albeit briefly) shone on my birth an unverified but undimming light—namely, what if I had been planned? What if I were no accident at all? If Rachel Brewster had intended to have me, didn't that make me the sole reason for my existence? Since I had a mom who chose to spend six months of the year away from me, you can perhaps appreciate why I would cling to this hope.

I don't mean I never saw my mother in the ski season. She never came home for Christmas and New Year's, or for my March break; she was working as a ski instructor, and those were the busiest times in the ski season. However, she came to North Conway to see me—in the week between Christmas and New Year's, and again for the week of my March break.

My Christmases and New Years were spent "up north," in the hearty companionship of the New Hampshire Norwegians. The Vinter side of my family was not universally positive. Uncle Martin and Uncle Johan were ceaselessly optimistic. Robustly busy men, they took charge of us kids—not just waxing or sharpening our skis, and fussing over our boots and bindings, but rallying our spirits when we were tired or hungry or cold. Martin and Johan were endlessly active and cheerful outdoorsmen; they were not the suicidal Norwegians Ibsen brings to mind.

My uncles weren't fjord-jumpers, but they were Norwegians, which once led me to believe they must have seen or read an Ibsen play. They'd named their children Henrik and Nora. As it turned out, Nora would inform me, Henrik had not been named for the playwright, and Nora herself was in no way the Nora in *A Doll's House*. "Though let me tell you," Nora told me, darkly, "if I had three children, I would abandon them. If I had one kid, I'd be out the door."

Nora had her fjord-jumping moments; she was the pessimistic Norwegian on the Vinter side of my family. Nora was the eldest of us cousins, the one and only child of Uncle Martin and Aunt Abigail. In the war Nora bravely waged with her judgmental mother, she won my heart. I thought Nora knew everything, and she was usually forthright to me about what she knew. Those Brewster girls—Nora's mom and mine, and Aunt Martha—were clever at keeping things from us children, and from their own parents. "Maybe even from one another," Nora had hinted to me.

"Why would they keep things from one another?" I asked Nora. She was six years older than I was. As a child and a teenager, I didn't just love her; I idolized her.

"Your mother is the most mysterious—she's the smartest one. My mom and Martha are dolts," Nora said.

I was ten or eleven. Nora would have been sixteen or seventeen; she was already driving. It must have been summer vacation, because we were lying on the beach at Little Boar's Head. It was subversive of everything that had heretofore been implied to me about my mom's intelligence, to hear she was *the smartest one*.

Champion of Little Ray that my grandmother was, even she disparaged my mother's lack of a proper education. While Abigail and Martha had been sent away to Northfield, my mom had refused to leave home.

"Well, truth be told, Adam," Aunt Abigail said, expanding on this theme to me, "Little Ray wasn't much of a student."

"If she'd applied to Northfield, they wouldn't have taken her," Aunt Martha had chimed in.

Mildred Brewster wanted her daughters to go where she had gone. Abigail and Martha would be Northfield girls; they went to Mount Holyoke, too. That my mother insisted on staying home for high school limited her to whatever local education was available to girls. I've read that Exeter's Robinson Female Seminary, which opened in 1867, once had high-minded intentions—an academic school for women, with standards similar to those upheld for the men who attended Phillips Exeter Academy. But most of the girls who went to the school did not go to college. In 1890, the Robinson Female Seminary had reevaluated its curriculum; in the name of domestic science, needlework and the culinary arts were added. My mom never commented on her years in high school. She showed no interest in sewing or cooking. I had the impression that she cared little for homemaking—it was hard to imagine that she'd ever studied it. Maybe the Robinson Female Seminary was where she'd learned to hate domestic science.

That my mother had flunked out of Bennington in record time conclusively proved to my aunts that Little Ray was intellectually subpar. That my mom went to Bennington in the first place was sufficient to relegate her to intellectual inferiority in Abigail's and Martha's eyes.

Bennington wasn't one of the estimable Seven Sisters—the constellation of liberal arts colleges in the northeastern United States, all of them (historically) women's colleges. It had further been suggested to me that my mother might have been "mentally lacking"—these were Aunt Abigail's very words.

"Maybe Little Ray is a little damaged," was Aunt Martha's undermining way of putting it. Martha implied that my grandmother had been too old to get pregnant, or that this was what Nana had believed—meaning my mom had surprised her. Abigail and Martha further speculated that the sperm count of the principal emeritus was "lacking oomph," or perhaps this was what Nana had believed. Nora needed to explain to me what a sperm count was—knowing Nora, she may have made up a good story about the *oomph* part.

"Trust me, Adam," Nora said that summer (I did). "There are ways of being smart without going to the best schools and colleges. Your mother is the smartest of all the mothers."

"You don't mean she's smarter than Nana, too—Nana's also a mother," I pointed out. At ten or eleven, I was no match for my more mature cousin; truth be told, I would never be a match for Nora.

"I *do* mean your mom is smarter than Nana, too," Nora told me. "The conformity begins with Nana. My mother and Martha go along with it—they're conformists. They're *sheep!*" Nora insisted. "But not your mom—she doesn't do what she's *supposed to* do, and she's still not doing it. It's stupid to do only what's expected of you. Your mom has balls, Adam—big ones," Nora assured me.

Nora was my confidante, my most trusted informer, and my ally in a common cause: we both hated the imposed trips up north, though for different reasons. In my case, I had to share a bedroom with Henrik—Uncle Johan and Aunt Martha's one and only. Two years younger than Nora, four years older than me, Henrik had been bullied by Nora, and—without Nora around to protect me—Henrik bullied me.

That I was always wearing Henrik's outgrown underpants seemed to be reason enough for him to revile me. I wore both Nora's and Henrik's hand-me-down clothes, but not Nora's underpants. While Nora was a tomboy, and she dressed like one, Aunt Abigail had made her wear girls' panties. Henrik thought I should have worn girls' panties, too—"especially the ones Nora bled in," as he put it. When I pointed out that Nora's panties had no hole for me to pee out of, Henrik said I had "no penis to speak of." In Henrik's view, I was a mama's boy—I should have sat on the toilet and peed like a girl.

In Nora's case, she shared a bedroom up north with various Vinter girls—her female relatives among those North Conway Norwegians. These blond girls were not tomboys; they were girly girls, around Nora's age. The blondes dressed to seduce boys. "Ski sluts," Nora called them. When the blondes made fun of her for dressing like a boy, Nora beat them up.

"We should share a bedroom," Nora told me. "We're not going to fool around; if you tried, I'd beat the crap out of you. This is more of the Brewster conformity business; this is more of the shit concerning what we're *supposed to* do. Your mom would know better—your mom would let us sleep in the same room. I bet she'd let us sleep in the same fucking bed."

"My mom's not around enough to make the rules," I pointed out.

"You have to get over the part that she's 'not around enough'—that just goes with who your mother is," Nora told me.

I was eleven or so before I accepted Nora's reasoning on this point. I hadn't started at Exeter yet, and Nora would have been around seventeen. We had moved on from the matter of my mom's independent way of thinking to the speculation that Nana was *not* surprised to find herself pregnant with my mother. Both Nora and I believed it was no accident that our grandmother got pregnant with Little Ray. As Nora told me: "The prospect of being left alone with the principal emeritus loomed large for Nana. I'm telling you, Adam, Nana knew perfectly well she *could* get pregnant—I'm sure she *meant* to. Who would want to be left alone with Principal Brewster?"

"Maybe he was more fun when he talked," I suggested.

"I remember when he talked," Nora said. "The old crock of shit never shut up!"

It was my opportunity to ask—as I had asked Nana, to no avail—"What made him stop talking?"

"Your mom didn't tell him she was pregnant—not that I blame her!" Nora exclaimed. "She was nineteen, she wasn't saying who your father was, she had no plans to get married—your mother didn't *want* to marry anyone."

"But my mom told Nana, right?" I asked Nora, who nodded.

"And Nana told the principal emeritus. Knowing Nana," Nora said, "it would have been a long story—if not the whole story."

"The *Moby-Dick* version," I said; Nora nodded again. "And that's when Principal Brewster stopped talking?" I guessed.

"Not quite," Nora answered. "The principal emeritus started to sob; he couldn't stop sobbing. At last, when he managed to get control of himself, he cried out, 'Not Little Ray!' After that, he was done talking—he stopped speaking," Nora told me.

"Why does our family have so many secrets, Nora?" I asked.

"Why do you wring your hands? So what if they're small? When you're old enough, Adam, you'll have secrets," my older and wiser cousin said.

There was another *up north* reason Nora and I were soul mates: our mutual resistance to learning to ski, though we resisted a variety of ski instructors (my mom included) in diametrically different ways. We went to opposite extremes of not learning.

Nora and I would stop short of that fairly common crime among first cousins; we would never have sex with each other. We weren't that brave, but we were partners in crime. Our more timid rebellion—our determination not to love skiing, in a ski-loving family—was what Nora and I did instead of having sex with each other.

I was fourteen, soon to be fifteen, when Nora said the following to me. Keep in mind that Nora was already in her twenties. "If you're not old enough to get this, Adam, you soon will be," Nora began. "The issues we have, about being Brewsters, are all about sex."

When I was falling asleep at night, trying not to think about sex, I would envision myself in the "Let me buy you a drink" scene in *Shane*—that moment when the handsome but *small* Alan Ladd slugs the bigger Ben Johnson, knocking him through the saloon's swinging doors.

When I was still awake, and my thoughts were all about sex, I would think instead of the "lowdown Yankee liar" scene—the shoot-out, when Jack Palance gets gunned down and is buried by the falling barrels.

"Shane, look out!" I could hear Brandon De Wilde calling. In the darkness of my bedroom, I could hear the ensuing gunfire, followed by silence, then the music rising. My thoughts, of course, were still all about sex—as if the sex were what Brandon De Wilde should have been warning Shane about.

HAVE YOU SEEN THEM?

A small geography lesson might help. Stowe is in northern Vermont, closer to Montreal than to Exeter. North Conway is in northern New Hampshire, closer to Maine than to Vermont. And Exeter is in southeastern New Hampshire—Exeter is nearer to the seacoast, even nearer to Boston than it is to Vermont. In New England, the roads running north or south are slightly better than the ones going east or west, but in the 1950s and the 1960s, the roads in New Hampshire and Vermont weren't very good at all. "And if it's snowing," my grandmother used to say, "you can't get anywhere from somewhere else."

In the ski season, this was why my mom never came home to see me. Stowe to Exeter and back was a long drive, and it would be snowing somewhere along the way. But my mother did drive from Stowe to North Conway and back—in those days, not an easy drive but a more manageable trip. The way this worked was my mom would trade places with one of the ski instructors at Cranmore Mountain. The Cranmore ski instructor got a change of scenery (and a chance to ski some new runs) at Mount Mansfield, while my mother gave ski lessons at Cranmore. This way, in the two busiest weeks of the ski season, neither ski area was missing a ski instructor. And this meant my mom had two weeks every winter to teach me to ski.

In elementary school, in junior high school, and in prep school at Exeter, I managed to remain a beginner as a skier. In those holiday weeks, there were mostly little children in my mother's ski lessons for beginners—even after I'd started shaving and had already learned to drive.

The effort this took—the strain on my mom, and on me, of my unwillingness to improve as a skier—required a lot of patience. To stay pleasant, to be positive—we were never unhappy with each other—that was the key. And at night, we were demonstrably affectionate. I truly loved these two weeks every winter of not learning to ski—of staging falls, of letting my perfectly adequate stem christie revert to a sloppy snowplow turn. I think my mother loved these two weeks every winter, too; she not once lost her temper or showed the slightest sign of frustration. "Oh, Adam—your weight on the *downhill* ski would work better, sweetie. But I know it's hard to remember."

No, it wasn't; it was hard, so purposely, to appear I had forgotten. I skied so slowly, perpendicular to the hill, sometimes my skis would just stop—even on a steep slope. Other skiers yelled at me for blocking the trail. When my mom led a line of beginners through their turns, I went last. The eight-year-olds would already be in the lift line when I got to the bottom. In those years when all the parents were afraid of polio, the other mothers asked my mother if I'd been a victim—or they inquired if I had some other handicap.

"Oh, no," my mom answered cheerfully. "My dear Adam just finds skiing potentially dangerous. Adam has always been *tentative*."

There was nothing tentative about Nora, who fiercely upheld her beginner status as a skier by being reckless.

"Skiing *in control* is the goal, Nora," my mother told her futilely—*in control* would never be Nora's goal. She threw herself down the mountain; she hurtled ahead. Nora never was perpendicular to any slope, however steep; she pointed her skis downhill and schussed.

"I'm not into turns, Ray," Nora told my mom.

"My dear Nora," my mother said sweetly, "I'm more concerned that you're not into *stops*."

Nora was more of an athlete than I was, and she was braver; she schussed till she crashed. While my mom was carving her perfect turns, instructing us beginners to turn where she turned—to follow her, if we could—Nora would blow by my mother in a blur.

"In control, Nora!" my mom would call after her. "Oh, that dear girl," my mother would say, turning to one of the eight-year-olds. "That dear Nora was born to do things her way—I just hope she doesn't hurt herself, or someone else. On skis, it's better to be in control."

But hurting herself, or someone else, was of no concern to Nora. She was up to the task. She'd been a big kid—she was a big girl, who would become a big woman. Her professed hatred of skiing had begun with the clothes. Ski pants would never be Nora's friend.

"You'll be happy you have hips aplenty in your childbearing years," Nora's mother had told her. Aunt Abigail had hips aplenty, and boobs galore. But Nora had other plans for her hips—childbearing was not in Nora's plans.

On skis, my mom had observed, Nora was good at keeping her balance or recovering it, and her weight helped her go fast; at high speed, and not losing her balance, Nora could be out of control and get a long way down the mountain before she crashed. Yes, Nora skied too fast; she was too out of control to turn or stop safely. But doing things safely would never be her style.

My mother said Nora was a good enough skier to know when a crash was coming. When Nora knew she was crashing, she would find a guy and take him down with her. It was how she liked to fall, with a young man under her; it was always a hotshot skier, the same type of dickhead who reminded her of her cousin Henrik.

Nora—on the verge of losing her balance—would suddenly crouch down and tackle a skier she'd found offensive, her strong arms wrapped around his hips. I saw Nora knock guys out of their bindings; I saw her separate skiers from their goggles and gloves. Huge hunks of snow slid down the slope, dislodged by the force of their fall. The guy always landed under Nora, cushioning her fall. The tackled skier would be screaming or gasping in pain—or he would lie unmoving, as if dead.

You could tell when Nora wondered if she'd killed someone; she pulled off her ski hat (later, her helmet) and pressed her ear to the unmoving skier's cold lips. "I can hear or feel if the fucker's breathing," Nora told me. "You can't fake not breathing, Adam—not for long."

On skis, Nora liked what she weighed. The house where the North Conway Norwegians lived had a serious-looking scale—the tall kind, one boxers and wrestlers would use. The scale was a hulking presence in the upstairs hall; it was too big for any of the bathrooms. I don't know if athletic-minded Norwegians do things ritualistically, but Uncle Martin and Uncle Johan did. Every New Year's Day, we children were weighed in the upstairs hall. The annual weigh-ins were required of us all: the North Conway Norwegians (those girly-girl blondes), Nora, Henrik, and me. We were always weighed in our pajamas. Nora was the heaviest.

Her senior year in prep school, Nora weighed 170 pounds, minus whatever her pajamas weighed. When Henrik was fully grown, he was taller. Henrik would be over six feet tall; Nora was five-ten, and counting. "I'm five-eleven," was the way Nora put it. And Nora was a very solid 170 pounds; as fast as she skied, when she hit you, she hit you hard.

Legs were broken in these collisions, but not Nora's. Knees needed surgeries, but never hers. In the leather-boots days—long, wooden skis with cable or bear-trap bindings—there were more lower-leg injuries, but not once Nora's. My first skis were wood, of course. I believe they were made by the Paris Manufacturing Company (South Paris, Maine), and they had Kandahar bear-trap cable bindings. Or perhaps these were Nora's first skis.

So much of the past—I mean, my past—has been narrated to me by my older cousin.

Uncle Martin and Uncle Johan were telemark men, free-heelers till their dying days; they loved their nipple-tipped Nordic skis. I remember my uncles telemarking in the 1970s. Most alpine skiers switched to heel-and-toe safety bindings in the 1960s.

"Those old cable or bear-trap bindings caused more than a few spiral fractures of the calf," I remember my mom saying.

Such fractures were not unknown among Nora's victims—along with the upper-body injuries you would expect from such high-speed, hard-impact falls. Separated shoulders and broken collarbones were common, though never Nora's. And if Nora tackled you and landed on you, there might be broken ribs and concussions, too. What made safety bindings safer was that they released when you crashed, and your skis came off. But skis have sharp edges; when two skiers crash together, facial lacerations can occur. Nora was proud of the scars on her face.

One time, her stitched eyebrow opened at night and bled on her pillow; in the morning, Nora's face was stuck to her pillowcase. The girly-girl blondes were shrieking in the upstairs hall, grossed out by all the blood. Another time, Nora broke her nose; her nose was pressed against some guy's sternum when she drove him into the hill. His sternum was cracked—arguably a worse injury than a broken nose.

"It was only a hairline fracture," Nora said with a shrug. "And look at me—I have raccoon eyes. I couldn't pick up a pervert, looking like this," she added, pointing to her two black eyes.

But I had the feeling Nora liked her injuries, if not as much as she liked injuring dickheads. For one thing, if Nora had an injury, she had an excuse not to ski. And there's no doubt that Nora liked looking a little roughed up. In our Cranmore Mountain years, I was not aware of Nora's interest in picking up anybody—not even a pervert. Nora not only dressed like a tomboy; from the moment she'd been sent away to Northfield, Nora had made what her mother called "a haircut statement."

"It's called a crew cut," Nora said; she made a point of not saying this in the exclamatory fashion of those dramatic Brewster girls. "How come when boys have a crew cut, it's no big deal?"

Some guys thought Nora was a guy. When she wore a ski parka that was long enough to hide her hips, or an oversize sweater—it had to be huge to conceal her breasts—the prominent jut of Nora's jaw and her broad shoulders gave her a masculine appearance. And on skis—even when she was just walking on skis—Nora could maintain a manly swagger. Not so off skis, when her hips were involved in the process. With her hips in the picture, or her boobs, it was evident to anyone that Nora was a woman.

As for those hotshot skiers lying under her on a ski trail—in particular, those dickheads who'd had their wind knocked out or were concussed—imagine their surprise when they regained consciousness with their quivering lips pressed against Nora's ear. I'm guessing the questionably erotic confusion of the moment suddenly stood in contrast to Nora's bristling crew cut, her handsome but hard-looking face—the granite jaw, the tight-lipped smirk that passed for Nora's cruel smile.

But I'm making too much of the heroic example Nora set for me. Yes, she helped me endure those winter ski trips up north. But Nora's rebellious antics notwithstanding, what stands out for me are those two weeks every winter when my mother and I were together—in particular, our nights.

"Oh, boy—a sleepover, Adam!" my mom would exclaim, in her little-girl way. "Aren't you excited?"

Yes, I was—at any age. I always was. My mother made me feel that a sleepover with me was her favorite thing; in retrospect, perhaps it was. I know this from Nora: Aunt Abigail and Aunt Martha were ceaselessly disapproving that my mom and I shared a room together during her North Conway visits. For a time, we were given a room with a queen-size bed; to the dismay of my rigidly conventional aunts, my mother and I had sleepovers in the same bed. But that would stop before I became a teenager; when I was eleven or twelve, my aunts persuaded the North Conway Norwegians to give my mom and me a bedroom with two twin-size beds.

"My mother and Martha will even find a way to *die* appropriately," was Nora's response. Indeed, they would.

(I'm a little sensitive to the subject of the deaths of aunts in my novels. Unkind critics have complained how I dispatch, or dispose of, the unlikable aunts in my fiction, but these critics never knew Aunt Abigail or Aunt Martha. Any deus ex machina device would not be too improbable for *them*.)

Aunt Abigail and Aunt Martha interfered with my mom's and my sleeping arrangements. What business was it of *theirs*?

"As much as we like to cuddle, sweetie—even as small as we are—I think we're too big to sleep all night in a twin bed," my mother said; she sighed dramatically. She let me know how sad she was about it. She told me we could always sleep in the same bed together, and we would—provided the bed was big enough.

Even in that North Conway bedroom with the twin beds, we would cuddle together in one of the twins—if only until one of us fell asleep, usually my mom. She'd been skiing all day; when her last ski-school class was over, she took a run or two with Uncle Martin and Uncle Johan. These were black-diamond runs, for experts only. For a few years, the Vinter brothers could keep up with her; then they got too old to try. Abigail and Martha could never keep up with Little Ray.

Skiers at Cranmore Mountain mostly remember the Skimobile—those little cars on the wooden track—and the European-run ski school. But I remember those sleepovers with my mother. How we would talk and laugh. How soon I forgot how much I'd missed her. How quickly my resentment vanished.

My mother didn't drink a lot; she said she was "too small for alcohol." She drank only beer, at most one or two. She told me two beers made her tipsy, but I liked her when she was silly—when her voice was a girlish whisper, or when she giggled like a child. Sometimes, on a two-beer night, the most confounding non sequiturs would slip out, often following a pause in her speech. She would speak in a childlike whisper—secretively, as if someone could be listening to us. We would be lying in the dark, and my mom hadn't said anything for a while; naturally, I was beginning to think she'd fallen asleep. Then her whispering, seemingly apropos of nothing, would start.

This happened in one of those twin beds in North Conway. I don't remember how old I was, but I was already listening to *Moby-Dick*—my paying attention to language was more advanced than the rest of my development. (I had my mom's small hands—and, according to Henrik, my poor penis was like my little finger.) I was in the gentle process of disentangling myself from my mother's arms; I was about to get into the other twin bed, where I would have more room.

"Have you seen them?" my mom whispered in the dark.

I waited until I thought she'd gone back to sleep; it had sounded like something she might have said in her sleep. I felt her lips brush my ear. "You haven't, have you?" my mother whispered.

"I haven't *what?*" I asked her. "Have I seen *whom?*"

"Oh, silly me!" my mom exclaimed. "Was I talking in my sleep?" At the time, I thought she was.

9.

MOVIES, GIRLFRIENDS, FOREIGNNESS, OUTLIERS

Most of the musicals in the 1950s and 1960s were safe for children. I remember seeing *Singin' in the Rain* with my mother, mainly because I recall her saying she would have liked to teach Debbie Reynolds how to ski. I was about ten. I was confused by my mom's remark, because there was no skiing (only singing and dancing) in the movie.

"Debbie may not be a very experienced dancer," my mother explained, "but I can tell she's a good athlete—that's all I mean." My mom liked Gene Kelly, too.

"Because he's handsome?" I asked her.

"Because he can *dance!*" Little Ray exclaimed. "He's handsome enough, sweetie, but not the kind of handsome you're going to be." (Not *small* enough, I guessed.)

The year before, my mother and I had seen *An American in Paris* together. "I think you look a little like Leslie Caron," I told my mom.

"I don't, sweetie!" she exclaimed, kissing me. "But thank you."

I saw other musicals in the 1950s and 1960s—I don't remember with whom. *Brigadoon, Carousel, Oklahoma!* I didn't see these fifties musicals with a date. I was too young or out of it to go with a date. *West Side Story* was later, in 1961. I was nineteen—I might have had a date, but I don't remember taking anyone to see that movie.

"You could've been with one of your unfortunate girlfriends—you know, one of the early ones," Nora reminded me. "On second thought, not the overweight one—she wouldn't have fit in a theater seat," Nora went on. "Didn't Sally get stuck in a shower? Nana told me the shower door had to be removed to get her out."

"I didn't take Sally to *West Side Story*," I said.

"I can't see the clubfooted one having much fun at a musical—poor Rose wouldn't have enjoyed the dancing," Nora said.

"Rose wasn't clubfooted—she just limped, and she was prone to muscle spasms," I said.

"Rose had more like a *lurch* than a limp, as I remember it," Nora pointed out. "She fell down the attic stairs, didn't she?" I just nodded. Nora moved on—to Caroline, who was very strong. Caroline had injured her knee playing field hockey; when we dated, she was on crutches. I'm sure I never took Caroline to a movie theater. She was broad-shouldered and very tall, and her crutches were very long; something awkward would have happened.

Nora moved on to Maud, who was also very tall—a tall and thin cross-country runner. Maud had fallen and broken her arm; her arm was in a cast when we were going out. I knew my mother had told Nora about Maud. My mom referred to Maud as "the virgin." Maud and I had remained friends.

"I didn't *know* Maud was a virgin," I told Nora, as I had told my mom. Nora knew Maud and I were friends.

"I know about first-timers," Nora told me. "I've been with girls who haven't done it. You don't have any idea what'll happen when they do it. But I've never been with a girl in a cast," Nora admitted. She paused. "Your mother said Maud clubbed you with her cast—she said Maud beat the shit out of you," Nora told me.

"Maud got me mostly in my face. She never meant to hurt me," I explained. "Maud was just flailing around. She was basically out of control with a cast on her arm."

"I can picture it," Nora assured me. "It could happen to anyone." She paused again. "I guess the only good thing—I mean, about those musicals in the fifties and sixties—is that they were safe for *virgins*."

"I didn't take Maud to *West Side Story*," I said.

"I don't blame you," Nora immediately said. "With her cast, Maud wasn't safe to take anywhere!"

"I never took Sophie to a musical, either," I volunteered quietly.

"Jesus Mary Josephine—poor *Sophie*!" Nora exclaimed. "She was your first *writer* girlfriend, wasn't she?"

"My first *writer* girlfriend," I repeated sadly.

"All the bleeding!" Nora cried. "It never stopped, did it? A writer who has her period all the time—that's got to be depressing!"

"Sophie was never in the mood for a musical," I admitted.

"The story of a nonstop bleeder is not likely to be adapted as a musical," Nora pointed out. "*Fibroids,* the musical! I don't see it happening."

"My mom still talks about the wear and tear on the washing machine, all our sheets and towels—occasionally, even our pillowcases," I told Nora.

"You know Ray still calls Sophie 'the bleeder,' don't you?" Nora asked me.

"I know, Nora."

"Your mom's not into musicals, is she?" Nora asked me, at last changing the subject from my unfortunate girlfriends—if only "the early ones," as Nora had called them.

"No, Ray doesn't give a hoot about musicals," I said.

My mom was a Hitchcock fan. She loved Westerns and war movies, too. My grandmother and Aunt Abigail and Aunt Martha were enthralled by the "big-band sound"; my mother wasn't. While Nana and my aunts were watching *The Glenn Miller Story* and *The Benny Goodman Story*, my mom and I saw (and loved) *High Noon*, *Stalag 17*, *The Bridges at Toko-Ri*, *The Searchers*, and *The Bridge on the River Kwai*.

My mother and I were sad when James Dean was killed in a car crash in 1955—"He was barely ten years older than you!" my mom exclaimed, hugging me. But regarding James Dean's movies, Little Ray was equivocal. "I wouldn't watch *East of Eden* or *Giant* again—*Rebel Without a Cause*, sure," my mom said.

Ray liked adventure movies. *King Solomon's Mines* may have been the first film of that kind we saw together. (Was I eight? I can't remember.) My mother liked love and war—I mean, together. I might have been nine when we watched *The African Queen*. I'm guessing I would have been ten or eleven when we saw *From Here to Eternity*, which Aunt Abigail and Aunt Martha proclaimed was "*completely* inappropriate."

Going back to Westerns: my mom liked but was upset by *Bad Day at Black Rock*. "I like Spencer Tracy better when he's got both arms," was all she said.

We hated *The Robe* and *The Ten Commandments*. (We agreed that biblical epics were too predictable.) We loved Marilyn Monroe. We held hands during *Bus Stop* and *Some Like It Hot*. We both defended Marilyn's singing in *River of No Return*. "Breathless is just who she *is*!" my mother declared. Marilyn's death would hit us harder than James Dean's.

I'm not a fan of science-fiction films, but my mom and I liked watching them together—both the good ones, like *The War of the Worlds*, and the terrible ones for teenagers necking in drive-ins, like *Attack of the Crab Monsters*, *The Blob*, and *The Wasp Woman*. When my mother and I went to drive-in movies in the summers, we would cuddle together like the teenagers on dates. "How *completely* inappropriate!" my dependably disapproving aunts said, yet again.

Aunt Abigail and Aunt Martha had a hissy fit over *The Graduate*—all because the Dustin Hoffman character is a "college kid" who has an affair with the middle-aged Mrs. Robinson (the Anne Bancroft character) and with Mrs. Robinson's daughter. I would have been twenty-five or twenty-six at the time of *The Graduate*—Nora was already in her thirties. It was 1967, but Abigail and Martha were in a tizzy at the very idea of a movie about an older woman who has sex with a younger man.

"A mere boy!" Aunt Abigail had lamented.

"It should be a crime!" Aunt Martha had chimed in.

"He's a college *grad*—he's not a college *kid*," Nora pointed out.

"I don't see what's wrong with it, even if the boy is a high school kid—not if he *likes* it!" my mother exclaimed.

Yet my mom, who adored Billy Wilder, the Austrian-born director, thought Audrey Hepburn was too young to have anything to do with the aging Gary Cooper in *Love in the Afternoon*—this was in 1957. My mother loved Audrey Hepburn. So did I. When my friends at Exeter said my mom reminded them of Audrey Hepburn, I was embarrassed. I knew their thoughts about Audrey were likely to be comparable to my own. Audrey wasn't the motherly type to me.

All my mom said when we saw *Sabrina*—Billy Wilder again, in 1954— was that Humphrey Bogart and William Holden were "miscast." She must have meant that those old farts were too old to be in a romantic comedy with Audrey Hepburn. Little Ray's disapproval of older men with younger women didn't apply to an older woman, "even if the boy is a high school kid—not if he *likes* it!" As Nora always insisted, Little Ray was her own person.

My grandmother loved those British comedies in the fifties—*The Lavender Hill Mob* and *The Ladykillers*—but Little Ray didn't. My mom was hesitant to travel abroad. She left the United States reluctantly, even in movies.

As much as she liked John Wayne, she didn't like him when he went to Ireland—even in a film. All she said about *The Quiet Man* was: "John Wayne needs to be in the saddle—I mean, in a Western." She believed Westerns were better when they were made by Americans. She liked Clint Eastwood, but she didn't like those Sergio Leone movies: *A Fistful of Dollars*, *For a Few Dollars More*, and *The Good, the Bad and the Ugly*. When I reminded her that one of her favorite Westerns had been directed by an Austrian—Fred Zinnemann directed *High Noon*—Little Ray said something I'm still trying to understand. "Sweetie, Fred Zinnemann was one of the fortunate Jews who left Europe early. They left all their *foreignness* behind." But what about those Austrian ski instructors?

"All their *foreignness*?" I asked her. My mom had been coached by Sepp Ruschp, who'd learned from Hannes Schneider. Weren't the ski schools at

Stowe and Cranmore Mountain teaching the Arlberg technique? Many skiers my mom admired were *foreign*.

"Oh, you know what I mean, sweetie!" my mother exclaimed, but I didn't
understand her.

By the 1960s, I was paying attention to the directors of the films I liked,
but my mom was so American in her tastes—or in her prejudices—that I
couldn't convince her to like Tony Richardson. I loved *The Loneliness of the
Long Distance Runner*. I went to see it a second time. I couldn't wait to take
my mother to see it.

"Well, Adam, I know you like running," she said, "and I guess this is what
they call 'social realism,' which I think you like, too." That was disappointing, but I tried again; I took her to see *Tom Jones*, a different kind of Tony
Richardson. No running, and not as intent on social realism—I mean, not
intended to be realistic to eighteenth-century England.

"Well, sweetie, I guess you like how *bawdy* this movie is," my mom said.
"But were people *ever* into sex this much, even in England?"

"Do you mean, in the eighteenth century?" I asked her. "Do you mean,
were people full of lust *back then?*"

"I said *ever*—I mean, it's not believable to be into sex this much!" my
mother declared.

"When it comes to sex, my mom is more of a Brewster girl than you think
she is," I told Nora.

"When it comes to being stubborn, maybe," Nora replied. "When it
comes to sex, Ray is *not* a Brewster girl, Adam," Nora insisted.

And she wasn't surprised by Little Ray's lukewarm response to Paul Newman. "I thought my mother liked *handsome*—at least, she uses the word a
lot," I complained to Nora. My mom and I had seen *The Hustler*, *Hud*, and
Cool Hand Luke together.

"I'll bet you think Paul Newman is handsome," I said to my mother, after
all three films.

Each time, Little Ray said the same thing: "Too much testosterone."

"That's not weird. That sounds right to me—and it's just like Ray, not
to give a shit about testosterone," Nora said. Here was my grandmother's
theme, albeit worded more coarsely.

It happened that Nora and I and Little Ray saw *The Old Man and the Sea*
together. Given what my mom had said about Spencer Tracy, I expected her
to like him as a two-armed fisherman this time, even though he was three
years older. But my mother fell asleep at the beginning of the film.

"Does she often sleep in movies?" Nora whispered in my ear.

"Never," I whispered back. We watched my mom (sound asleep) as closely as we watched *The Old Man and the Sea*. I hated Hemingway—I mean, reading him. I already knew the fishing story, but Nora hadn't read it.

"I was on the sharks' side, the whole way," Nora said at the end. "And you *slept* the whole way, Ray," Nora told my mother.

"Did I?" my mom asked, in her innocent-sounding way. "Well, there must have been something more interesting happening in my sleep," was all she said.

After the film, Nora said that Ray looked as if she was "on the sharks' side—even in her sleep." Nora and I found the subject of my mother, sleeping soundly through a movie, more engrossing than *The Old Man and the Sea*.

I've forgotten where we were—Nora, my mom, and I—when we saw *True Grit* together. It was the end of the sixties. John Wayne was back in the saddle, where my mother believed he belonged. I guess Hollywood thought John Wayne belonged back in the saddle, too, because they would give Wayne his first and only Oscar for his role as the one-eyed, potbellied marshal.

At the end of *True Grit*, Little Ray gave Nora and me a glimpse of her seemingly obdurate nationalism. Keep in mind that I was almost thirty and Nora was already in her mid-thirties. Nixon had been elected the year before, the same year as the My Lai massacre; both Martin Luther King Jr. and Bobby Kennedy had been killed; and the protests against the Vietnam War were rising. A year later, the Ohio National Guard would shoot and kill those college students at Kent State. Nora and I weren't feeling particularly nationalistic.

"You see?" my mom said to Nora and me, in her little-girl way. We were among the moviegoers leaving the theater, at the conclusion of *True Grit*.

"See what, Ray?" Nora asked.

"John Wayne is old and fat, and he's lost an eye," my mother explained, "but he comes off better than he did in Ireland."

"You don't like Ireland, Ray?" Nora asked.

"I don't think about Ireland one way or another," my mom answered. "I have no desire to go there, or anywhere else that's *foreign*. I like staying here, in America. So should John Wayne." But I knew she loved Austria, home of the Arlberg technique.

"Ray doesn't like anything *foreign*," I explained to Nora. "Except for skiers," I added. "Ray likes Toni Sailer and Toni Matt and Sepp Ruschp and Hannes Schneider—they're foreign, but they're *Austrian*. I guess foreignness in movies is another matter." I paused. I looked at Little Ray, to see how she liked listening about herself in the third person, before I spoke to her. "You don't like foreign films—in particular, the ones with subtitles—do you?" I asked my mother.

"I don't go to the movies to *read*, sweetie," my mom told me.

"You don't like to read *anything*!" I pointed out to her.

"I have read and will read everything you write, Adam—everything you show me," my mother told me, kissing my cheek.

"But, Ray, the movies with subtitles are the ones with good sex," Nora said.

"I don't go to the movies to get good sex!" my mom exclaimed; she laughed, kissing Nora on the cheek. Little Ray had to stand on her toes; she needed to put her arms around Nora's neck to steady herself. On tiptoe, my mother was barely tall enough to kiss Nora's cheek, and I'm guessing Nora bent down to help her. "My dear, dear Nora," Little Ray said. "Not everything is about sex!"

At our age, this was a hard concept for Nora and me to grasp. We knew my mom's aversion to foreignness didn't signify an aversion to sex. On the contrary, Nora and I knew my mother was very selective about sex—she was very particular about it—but Little Ray wasn't averse to it. Maybe her aversion to foreignness was more American than sexual, because my mom was decidedly a sexual outlier. Little Ray and Nora struck me as very comfortable in the outlier role.

Once, when I struggled to say all this to Nora, it came out a little tortured. "The first foreign-language films I saw made me *like* reading a movie," I told Nora. "They made me love all movies with subtitles. Having to read those films made me feel I was writing them, or that I could write movies. It was as if foreign films were made for me," was the way I said it to Nora, who was unimpressed.

Nora shrugged. "That's just who you are, Adam," my older cousin said. "There's a foreignness inside you—beginning with where you come from. The foreignness is *in* you—that's just who you are. You and me and Ray— we're outliers."

Outliers like going to the movies—we can see in the dark. Outliers are looking for other outliers. If you see an outlier on the screen, it's exciting. If you can't find one in the film, it's exciting in another way. When you leave the theater, you're even more of an outlier than you knew.

10.

NOT TARZAN

Not only did I put off going to Aspen for the longest time, but I almost waited too long. Whatever man my mother met in Aspen in 1941 wasn't the only mystery in the area of what happened (or didn't) between my mom and men. Exactly what transpired between my mother and a different man would remain vague, but he became somewhat famous—both famous and infamous—and, at least for a while, everyone knew his name.

An American actor, Lex Barker was best known in North America for playing Tarzan of the Apes. In five years, between 1949 and 1953, Lex Barker starred in five Tarzan movies. Little Ray refused to see them. When I asked her why—I would have been eight—all she said was, "Tarzan *is* an ape, sweetie."

Nora and I saw the first one (*Tarzan's Magic Fountain*) together. By the time we saw the second one (*Tarzan and the Slave Girl*), Nora had heard the stories about Lex Barker and my mother. No one had told me anything.

"Tarzan went to *Exeter*, Adam," Nora informed me. "You weren't born, I would have been a toddler, and Henrik was still shitting in his diapers. Tarzan was three years older than your mom. When Ray was thirteen and fourteen, Tarzan was sixteen and seventeen," Nora said. "You can imagine how my mother and Aunt Martha would have found it '*completely* inappropriate'— namely, that this big gorilla was hitting on Little Ray."

"How did Tarzan get into Exeter?" I asked Nora.

"The *actor*, Adam—not the half-naked man swinging on vines, or fooling around with Jane and that chimpanzee. Lex Barker, the actor, went to Exeter—before he was Tarzan," Nora explained. I must have looked lost. I was eight; the concept of Tarzan *hitting on* my mom surely went over my head. "I don't mean they *dated*, Adam—you know, they never *went out*. I don't know if they ever spoke to each other," Nora said. "But something happened. Maybe Tarzan gave Ray a funny look—he gave her the once-over, in an unwelcome way—or he creeped her out with a certain kind of smile."

Naturally, I was imagining that Tarzan gave my mother one of his ape calls, or he beat his bare chest. Nora always knew what I was thinking. "Adam: Tarzan wouldn't have been wearing just the loincloth, not at Exeter," Nora assured me. "I'm almost certain he had his shirt on when this happened, whatever it was—if anything actually happened. Something about the guy just freaked out your mom. Or the big ape did something that my dumb-fuck mother and Aunt Martha saw, and they were freaked out— probably because they could see that Tarzan had the hots for Ray."

I could imagine that happening, of course. In the area of appropriateness or suitability, it didn't take much to freak out Aunt Abigail and Aunt Martha. For example, Nora was away at school when Lex Barker's third and fourth Tarzan movies—*Tarzan's Peril* and *Tarzan's Savage Fury*—came out. I was nine and ten when those two Tarzan films were playing at the Ioka. Aunt Abigail and Aunt Martha insisted on seeing them with me; they didn't think it was suitable for me to see them alone. Henrik came along, too. In those years, Henrik was thirteen and fourteen. With his mother and Aunt Abigail sitting between us, Henrik couldn't reach around them to punch me in the arm or snap my ear with his fingers, which he was fond of doing.

I remember very little of the two movies. I was distracted by Aunt Abigail and Aunt Martha; they were in their forties, at least a decade older than Lex Barker, and their moral outrage was palpable. Their clenched fists, their heavy breathing, the looks that flashed between them—especially when Tarzan was socializing with Cheetah, the chimp, or cozying up to Jane.

When we were leaving the Ioka after *Tarzan's Savage Fury*, Aunt Abigail said, "Tarzan is more chimp than human."

"I feel for Jane!" Aunt Martha chimed in.

Lex Barker's last Tarzan film (*Tarzan and the She-Devil*) was in 1953. Uncle Martin and Uncle Johan took me to the Ioka to see it. This was the first time I'd ever been in a movie theater with them. Once again, Nora wasn't in town. Now eighteen, she might have been at Mount Holyoke already.

I would have been surprised by my uncles' behavior at the Ioka, if Nora hadn't forewarned me.

"My dad and Uncle Johan are weird—they think everything is a comedy, even tragedies," Nora had told me.

"Is that a Norwegian thing?" I asked her.

"It's just a *weird* thing, Adam," Nora insisted. "They laugh all the way through most movies."

Maybe that was why Henrik didn't come with us to see *Tarzan and the*

She-Devil, which was not a comedy—at least not intentionally. Or Henrik had decided he was too old for Tarzan movies.

The evil ivory hunters burn Tarzan's tree hut, and capture Tarzan and Jane. Tarzan takes the elephants' side, opposed to ivory poaching. Tarzan summons the elephants; they stampede, trampling the villainous Raymond Burr. Lyra, the She-Devil, gets shot. Cheetah, the chimpanzee, provides the only comic relief—he gets caught stealing ostrich eggs. Yet Uncle Martin and Uncle Johan roared with laughter at everything. Parents with small children changed their seats, distancing themselves from the North Conway Norwegians' crazed howls. Jane, held captive by the ivory hunters, provoked the loudest guffaws from Uncle Martin and Uncle Johan.

They were still laughing when we left the Ioka. "Almost as funny as foreign films, Adam," Uncle Martin, Nora's father, told me.

"The ones with subtitles," Uncle Johan, Henrik's dad, chimed in.

"I've never seen a movie you have to read," I pointed out to them politely. Films with subtitles never came to the Ioka.

"We'll soon remedy that!" Uncle Martin shouted.

"There's a French film coming to the Franklin next week, Adam. French films are hysterical," Uncle Johan told me.

I knew Nora would have assured me that not *all* French films were hysterical, but I was eager to see a foreign film with subtitles—even (perhaps especially) a tragedy.

Thus, because I saw *Tarzan and the She-Devil* with my uncles, I was invited to go with them to the Franklin Theatre in Durham to see my first foreign-language film with subtitles. I knew about the Franklin from Nora; her dad and Uncle Johan had taken her to see foreign films there. The University of New Hampshire was in Durham. It was a college town, and the Franklin was the nearest art-house movie theater around.

Nora had told me that Henrik was too impatient to read films with subtitles. Aunt Abigail and Aunt Martha associated all foreign films with sex. Unless they took Nora with them to the Franklin, Uncle Martin and Uncle Johan drove to Durham by themselves. From Exeter, it was a slow half-hour drive. The Franklin Theatre changed my life. Someone said it's now a Thai food place. I don't want to know. I will always remember my first time at the Franklin, and my first trip to Durham.

"Is the French film a comedy?" I cautiously asked Uncle Martin, who was driving.

"Of course it is!" Uncle Johan shouted from the shotgun seat.

I knew from Nora what my uncles thought of comedies and tragedies. As it turned out, my first film with subtitles *was* a comedy, and I laughed as much as Uncle Martin and Uncle Johan.

Directed by and starring Jacques Tati, *Les Vacances de Monsieur Hulot*—in English, *Mr. Hulot's Holiday*—won me over. At twelve, I couldn't tell the Marxist intellectuals from the fat capitalists, or recognize the other proto-types of the French political and social classes, but I understood they were all being mocked. Without meanness, the film makes fun of everyone— Mr. Hulot included.

Jacques Tati was a gentle and intelligent introduction to French cinema and movies with subtitles. The Franklin Theatre would become my film school. Those foreign films I saw in Durham made me want to be a screen-writer. *Moby-Dick* had introduced me to the nineteenth-century novel; I would soon read *Great Expectations*. The Franklin was my introduction to European cinema. In contrast, American movies seemed juvenile.

Take Tarzan, for example. The sexual scandals of many American movie stars outlast the short-lived fame of their films. Yes, I know—sexual infamy lives longer than movie stardom, not only in the United States. But just look at what happened to Lex.

Lex Barker and Lana Turner were married from 1953 to 1957, about as long as Lana usually stayed married. She was married seven times—eight, if you count her marrying Joseph Crane twice (their first marriage was annulled). In 1958, a year after Lana kicked out Lex, Lana's then-boyfriend, Johnny Stompanato, was stabbed to death in the Beverly Hills home Lana shared with her fourteen-year-old daughter, Cheryl Crane. Cheryl stabbed Stompanato with a kitchen knife, either in self-defense or to protect her mother.

"That girl should have stabbed Tarzan!" Aunt Abigail declared, when she heard about the Stompanato killing.

"I'm sure Cheryl must have *wanted* to kill Tarzan," Aunt Martha chimed in.

All my mother said about Cheryl Crane and the Stompanato stabbing was: "Poor Cheryl would have been only ten when her mom married Tarzan. She was thirteen when Lana kicked him out."

"You weren't too young for Tarzan. The big monkey took an interest in *you*, Ray," Aunt Abigail reminded her.

"Meaning you were *way* too young, Ray, but that didn't stop Tarzan!" Aunt Martha chimed in.

"I wasn't *that* young—I wasn't as young as poor Cheryl," my mom said softly. She was almost whispering.

Little Ray was thirty-six when Johnny Stompanato was stabbed. I would have been sixteen, a student at Exeter—old enough to be part of a conversation about scandalous sexual behavior.

"Lana Turner and Lex Barker were guests at the Hotel Jerome," my mother told me, but not when my aunts were around—we were alone. The Hotel Jerome had figured prominently in my mom's conversation, but never concerning Tarzan.

"Lana and Lex were in Aspen when you were there?" I asked her.

"Heavens, no, sweetie—they were guests at the Jerome when they were married, after I was there. I just saw their picture in a movie magazine," Little Ray said. My question hurt her; she misjudged what I was thinking. "No, I never *skied* with Tarzan—we weren't in Aspen together, before the ape married Lana," my mother suddenly said. "Look at yourself, Adam. You must be fully grown, or near to it. You're five feet six; even if you're still growing, I'll be surprised if you get to five feet seven. Lex Barker was six feet four, sweetie. Sometimes I think you don't know me at all. Tarzan *couldn't* be your father."

At sixteen, I knew that Lex Barker couldn't be my father. The ape man had big hands. My father was no Tarzan. I felt badly that I'd asked my mom about him. It was sad how much she hated that she'd ever attracted Tarzan of the Apes.

On one of our trips to the Franklin Theatre, I queried my uncles about Lex Barker's time at Exeter. Aunt Abigail had told me Tarzan looked like a monkey in his 1937 yearbook picture, when he was just a sophomore.

"That monkey never graduated," Aunt Martha had chimed in. The ape man left Exeter without a diploma.

"That monkey looked like a man among boys," Aunt Abigail had said. "Even when he was a *beginning* monkey."

Lex Barker had quite a career in Europe—not only after his Tarzan roles but after Lana. Tarzan spoke French, Spanish, Italian, and German. In 1961, Uncle Martin and Uncle Johan and I saw Barker in Fellini's *La Dolce Vita*. In case you missed him, Lex was Anita Ekberg's fiancé or husband. Martin and Johan burst out laughing when they saw the ape man, tears wetting their cheeks.

Lex Barker made more than twenty films in German, including Karl May's European Westerns. Seven times, the former Tarzan was Old Shatterhand—the German friend and blood brother of Winnetou, a fictional Apache chief.

"Did Tarzan learn all those languages at Exeter?" I asked my uncles. They might have known. Uncle Martin taught French and Spanish at the academy, while Uncle Johan taught German.

"I know he played football," Uncle Martin said. "I know he didn't take French or Spanish with me."

"Tarzan was never in my German class—I know that," Uncle Johan told me. "He definitely did track-and-field."

"Did he *ski?*" I asked my uncles.

"Tarzan on skis!" Uncle Martin cried.

"Skiing in his loincloth!" Uncle Johan shouted. Life was a comedy; my uncles once more dissolved into laughter.

In 1988, thirty years after the Johnny Stompanato stabbing, when Cheryl Crane was forty-five, she published her autobiography, *Detour: A Hollywood Story*. In the book, Cheryl revealed that, between the ages of ten and thirteen, she was repeatedly raped by Lex Barker. When Cheryl told her mom, Lana kicked the ape man out.

In 1988, Lana Turner and Little Ray were sixty-seven and sixty-six, respectively. Lex Barker wasn't alive to read about himself in Cheryl Crane's autobiography. He had died of a heart attack in 1973, at the age of fifty-four. Tarzan was walking down a street in New York City, on his way to meet his fiancée, Karen Kondazian. She was an actress, twenty-three at the time— thirty-one years younger than Tarzan of the Apes. Not counting Jane, she would have been the ape man's sixth wife.

How did my mother respond to the news that Lex Barker had serially raped Lana Turner's young daughter, beginning when the girl was prepubescent? All my mom said, softly, was: "Poor Cheryl."

Later, Little Ray spoke more pointedly—if not in much detail—to me. "I've told you, Adam—please don't ask me again, sweetie. Not Tarzan." This time, I felt badly that I *hadn't* asked my mom about him—not for thirty years.

11.

SMALLNESS AS A BURDEN

Downtown Exeter wasn't much to speak of. At the intersection of Water and Front Streets, there was a bandstand; there were occasional appearances of a band. Below the falls, where the Exeter River ran into the Squamscott, the water was brackish and filthy. Because the Squamscott was a tidal river, the academy crew couldn't row at low tide. Because the Squamscott was polluted, the mudflats stank. A rower would one day tell me: "You can usually spot a beetleskin in the mud at low tide." We called condoms *beetleskins*. The Ioka wasn't much of a movie theater, but it's the only downtown building I remember.

Because I was the grandson of a principal emeritus of Phillips Exeter (or so I thought), the academy—even before I attended it—was my part of town. Front Street bisected the Phillips Exeter campus. I grew up in my grandparents' red-brick house on Front Street, within hearing distance of the bells that heralded the changing of classes. Principal Brewster's house was Georgian—the front door framed by two white columns, white window trim, black shutters. From the cupola window in my attic bedroom, I could look along Front Street and almost see the academy clock tower, where the bells tolled.

When I told her I could see the Roman numerals on the clockface of the tower, Nana said this was an early sign that I had the imagination to become a fiction writer. She knew it was impossible to see any part of the main academy building from our attic.

Nora put it more plainly: my imagining I could see the academy clock tower from my attic bedroom didn't indicate to her that I had a fiction writer's imagination—only that I was a slow learner.

To the Exeter faculty—most of all, to the faculty wives—I was "the Brewster boy," not necessarily because I was the grandson of a mysteriously mute principal emeritus. It was more remarkable that I had my mother's maiden name, and that pretty Rachel Brewster was noticeably unmarried; she was also away for months at a time.

Exeter was a small town, though not as small as the claustrophobic community of a single-sex boarding school. It wasn't unnoticed that Principal Brewster had stopped speaking—at which time, I presumed, he'd been relieved of his headmasterly duties. This was around the time my mom got pregnant, but before she began to show. I don't remember who told me that he'd not been principal for long. I don't remember when Nora told me that he'd never been principal at all. It was only Lewis Brewster's fantasy, all because he believed he *should* have been Exeter's headmaster.

"Those damn Brewster girls indulged him," Nora told me. "In truth, Granddaddy Lew is just another *faculty* emeritus. He was only an English teacher—a strict grammarian, big on rules. When he used to talk, he went on and on about punctuation marks. Saltonstall has been the principal at Exeter since before I was born. Salty will probably be principal forever."

As would always be true of Nora, she was mostly right. William Gurdon Saltonstall was the principal of Phillips Exeter from 1932 until 1963, when he left to direct the Peace Corps in Nigeria. *Salty* appeared to be beloved.

Here was another Brewster family secret I hadn't known. Nora apologized for not telling me sooner. "I thought I'd already told you, Adam; I must have assumed that everyone knew the 'principal emeritus' was deluded, long before he stopped talking." But how would I have known that Granddaddy Lew was delusional? He'd never spoken to me. It unnerved me to think there were faculty members (and their families) who knew more about me and the Brewster family than I did. Other than what Nora told me, I'd been kept in the dark. And after Nora went off to Northfield, and later, to Mount Holyoke, I was alone a lot.

The Front Street house, where I lived with my grandmother and the grammarian emeritus—Principal Punctuation Mark, as I thought of our silent family lunatic—was in easy walking distance of the academy athletic fields and the school gym. Best of all was the Thompson Cage. A 1929 brick edifice with skylights, the cage contained two indoor tracks. On the dirt floor of the cage was a running track; above it, a sloped wooden track circumscribed the dirt track below. I liked to run, but I loved the old cage.

Did I like running because my mother loathed it? Probably, in the beginning. When I began to run, I'm sure this was part of the same perverse psychology that persuaded me to dislike skiing. But the more I ran, the more I liked the aloneness of it. My mom didn't run, but she understood solitary compulsions.

My mother was almost as obsessed with her off-season training for skiing as she was with skiing; she took those exercises very seriously. She did lunges and squats and wall sits, everywhere and all the time. Her lunges never failed to startle the bogus principal emeritus. They were single-leg lunges, which she held for forty-five seconds or a minute (each leg). The squats were deep ones—her butt hit her heels—and the wall sits, which she held for over a minute, were done at ninety-degree angles with her back against a wall and her knees perfectly aligned to her middle toes. "If you can't see your big toes, you're doing it wrong," she would explain to me repeatedly.

The circuit-type training suited my mom's eternal restlessness. She allowed herself no rest between these exercises. "You don't want the lactic acid to clear—you want to increase your lactic acid threshold," she was always saying to Uncle Martin and Uncle Johan, who often tried to do the exercises with her. They couldn't match her pace.

Yet Little Ray hated to run, and she wouldn't ride a bike. All winter, when the academy athletic fields were covered with snow, my uncles would stride over the playing fields on their cross-country skis, but my mother was strictly a downhill skier. She would, occasionally, put on her telemark skis and skin up a mountain, but that was because she liked skiing down.

When it wasn't ski season, my uncles were cyclists. Not Little Ray. "I don't want to be killed by a car," my mom said. "I'm too small—bad drivers won't see me, till they run over me."

I liked running around the academy playing fields, and my uncles had shown me the cross-country running course through the woods. Most of all, I liked running on the wooden track in the Thompson Cage. I liked the sound of my feet on the boards. For the most part, you're alone when you run—even when there are other runners around.

By the time I was old enough to walk anywhere I wanted—when I was also old enough to imagine myself as a student at the academy—I liked watching the older boys playing their sports, and wondering which sports I would play. Most sports didn't appeal to me; team sports were particularly unappealing. So many of the boys on teams appeared to be struggling; the attention paid to balls or pucks seemed stupid, beyond moronically obsessive.

Henrik was a ball-and-puck person; his sports were soccer, hockey, and lacrosse. Henrik started at Exeter in the fall of 1952; he graduated in the spring of 1956, about three months before I would start. Given my negative relationship with Henrik, I had long ago decided against soccer, hockey, and lacrosse.

Because I was small, wrestling tempted me; it was a weight-class sport

(I would wrestle other small boys) and I liked the one-on-one aspect of it. But the wrestlers often competed in a box-shaped gym attached to the cage; the wooden track overhung the wrestling area, and spectators sat on the boards with their legs dangling above the mat. It disturbed me that the wrestlers grappled at the bottom of a gladiatorial pit, with their pitiless fans staring down at them. And I didn't like how the wrestlers ran their laps after wrestling practice—the way their flat-soled wrestling shoes pounded on the wooden track. They jogged half a lap, then sprinted the other half; this meant that I was always passing them, and they were always passing me. Therefore, I somewhat tentatively decided that I wouldn't wrestle. My only sport would be running, I believed. I would run cross-country in the fall, and run the mile in track-and-field—in the cage in the winter, and outdoors in the spring.

I met the snowshoer one winter day, after I'd been running on the wooden track in the cage. I could see him coming toward me. He was crossing the snow-covered baseball diamond, from the infield to the outfield. In the distance, the narrow stone bridge over the Exeter River was obscured by wind-blown snow. I mistook him for a cross-country skier—a very small one, too small to be one of my uncles. The snowshoer had ski poles. His stride was shorter than a cross-country skier's, or he had the wrong wax on his skis. He didn't appear to be getting any glide from his stride. Of course I couldn't see his snowshoes, which I thought were his skis.

In the wind-blown snow, I couldn't be sure he was a guy; he looked smaller than me, even smaller than Little Ray. He was as small as the smallest Exeter student I had ever seen; he was as small as a child, but he didn't move like a child. I saw something decidedly male and adult in the strength of his stride. The way he loped along reminded me of a runner I'd encountered a few times in the warm weather—both outdoors, on the academy athletic fields, and on the wooden track in the cage. He was out of my league as a runner—too fast for me to keep up with, though his legs were comically short. On the sloped boards in the cage, he had lapped me a couple of times in less than a mile. There was a very mature element in how friendly he was; the Exeter students rarely acknowledged me. This made me think he was a very young faculty member, although—in addition to his childlike size—he was absurdly youthful-looking for anyone on the faculty. It was hard to imagine he could command the students' attention.

I was thirteen that February day in 1955. I wouldn't become an academy student until September 1956. I hadn't started to shave; in my estimation, neither had the snowshoer. I couldn't see they were snowshoes until he removed them—old wooden bear paws with leather bindings and rawhide laces. He stood beside his snowshoes in the parking lot of the Thompson Cage, where he brushed the snow off them. They were the long kind of bear paws, shaped like teardrops—nearly a yard long, more than half as tall as the diminutive snowshoer himself. "I thought you were a skier," I told him.

"I'm just a runner," he said, smiling warmly, "either on snowshoes or off them. You're a runner, too, aren't you?"

"I'm just a kid—I'm a kind of faculty brat," I told him. I'd never thought of myself as any kind of faculty brat—not a legitimate one, anyway. I didn't think my being the grandchild of a faculty emeritus counted for faculty-brat status—especially not the grandkid of a deluded grammarian.

"A *kind* of faculty brat?" the exceedingly small snowshoer asked. "What kind of faculty brat are you?" He was too good-natured to be a student; he was definitely a faculty member, but a very unusual one.

I just blurted it all out; I didn't even know his name, but I told him everything. I had never felt as safe with anyone—not even with Nora, occasionally not with my mother. "I'm the illegitimate son of Rachel Brewster—the unmarried daughter of faculty emeritus Lewis Brewster, my insane grandfather," I began, thus capturing the little snowshoer's attention. "Lewis Brewster is a madman emeritus; he has deluded himself into believing he used to be principal of the academy, but he was just an English teacher," I further explained, barely pausing to breathe. "Granddaddy Lew stopped speaking when he learned my mother was pregnant—with me," I added, just to be perfectly clear. "According to my cousin, who remembers when the lunatic emeritus used to talk, all he ever said was stuff about punctuation marks."

"What sort of stuff?" the surprised snowshoer asked. I had the feeling that the part about the punctuation marks was the only aspect of my Brewster family history heretofore unknown to him.

"I don't know," I admitted. "I never heard what he said, because he stopped speaking before I was born," I reminded the snowshoer.

"Oh, yes—you already explained the chronology perfectly," the tiny man told me. "I'm afraid I'm 'just an English teacher,' as you say. I was being overly curious about the punctuation marks." Here the snowshoer lowered his voice, as if he didn't want to be overheard; at a glance, I could see we were alone in the parking lot. "In the area of student writing," the extremely small English teacher said, "some of my colleagues in the department overdo the importance of punctuation."

"You teach writing?" I asked him.

"I do—that is, to the degree that writing can be taught," the little snow-shoer said. He was disarmingly handsome.

"My grandmother read *Moby-Dick* aloud to me—when I was ten, eleven, and twelve," I told him. "When I'm a little older, I would like to try reading it again—to myself."

"That's most commendable," the snowshoer told me. "Perhaps I could suggest another adventure story, also involving a young man—a story that's a little easier to read to yourself?"

"Yes, please," I said, but he could see I'd not once taken my eyes off his snowshoes. All the while I'd been babbling, my mind was racing: the bear paws before me were my escape from skiing; the snowshoer had been running on them, and I liked to run.

Uncle Martin and Uncle Johan had tried to get me on cross-country skis. My mom had tried to get me on telemarks. "Skis are skis," I'd told them. Here before me was an appealing alternative: downhill, uphill, on the flat—on snowshoes, you just ran or walked. With the ski poles, you could go anywhere. On a ski mountain, couldn't you keep out of the skiers' way? Couldn't you go up or down the mountain, off to one side or along the edge of the ski trail?

I'd been talking nonstop to a stranger about my family's darkest secrets, which everyone in the academy community—even the youngest, small-est member of the faculty—knew. Now I couldn't speak. The tiny English teacher must have thought I was overcome at the prospect of reading a young man's adventure story that was easier to read than *Moby-Dick*, but what knocked the wind out of me were the little man's bear paws. I foresaw a way not to ski.

"I confess I knew you were the Brewster boy, but I didn't know about the punctuation marks," the snowshoer said. He added: "Growing up here, as I know you have, I'm sure you must know how people talk." I nodded; I still couldn't speak. The adults I'd grown up with weren't as forthcoming. Here was an honest adult, notwithstanding a small one; I wanted him to teach me how to snowshoe and how to write, but I didn't know what to say. When the words came, I couldn't control what I said.

"My mother is small, like you. She's not as small as you, and she's very pretty, but she is rather small," I blurted out. Consciously, I'd been thinking about his snowshoes, but what came out was all about smallness—his size, my mom's size, their comparative smallness.

"I've seen your mother," the snowshoer quickly said. "No one seems small to me, but your mom is definitely pretty—she's very pretty. I hear she's an outstanding skier."

"I hate skiing," I told him. "Every ski season, it's what my mom does instead of being my mother. She keeps trying to teach me to ski, but I refuse to learn."

"I grew up in ski towns," the little snowshoer said. "My parents are skiers. My father taught me to ski, but I was too small. On the chairlift, he never let go of me. The rope tow was too heavy for me; I couldn't hold on. And there was an equipment problem: a shortage of skis that were short enough, of boots that were small enough, of bindings that adjusted enough. My dad had to shorten my ski poles, thus my poles were custom-made. I didn't *hate* skiing, but it was the first thing that made me aware of my smallness as a burden. My mom got me some snowshoes; they were small enough, and you could make the bindings work with a variety of boots. I already had the downsized ski poles. My mom thought all the poling would make me stronger—then I could hold on to the rope tow, she said. But I *loved* the snowshoeing, and I didn't have to be around all those bigger skiers. I'm very fond of ski towns," the little snowshoer told me, "but I've stopped skiing. I just run, and I snowshoe."

"How tall are you?" I asked him. "My mom is five feet two. Lana Turner is only one inch taller."

"They would tower over me!" the snowshoer declared. His handsomeness was the most grown-up thing about him. "I'm four feet nine—only fifty-seven inches. Too small for Korea; they wouldn't take me. They didn't make uniforms that were small enough, they told me—another equipment problem," the snowshoer added, as if skiing and the military had disappointed him equally. The subject of his smallness as a burden bothered him. "Would you like to try snowshoeing?" he suddenly asked me. There was only one car in the parking lot of the Thompson Cage, a VW Beetle. At the time, did they make anything smaller? As small as a VW Beetle looked to me, I still wondered how the little snowshoer could reach the pedals.

"Yes, please," I answered him. I absolutely believed I was born to try snowshoeing; I also couldn't wait to introduce the snowshoer to my mother. I knew I'd met a man I wanted my mom to meet. I wanted to hear her opinion of how handsome he was—"good-looking and *small*," I could imagine her saying. Before I met the little snowshoer, I believed that destiny only happened in fiction. Yet here was my destiny, and maybe my mother's.

The snowshoer was still talking to me, but I could scarcely hear him; his head and upper body had momentarily disappeared. He was just stowing his snowshoes in the backseat of his VW Beetle. He was telling me he had "other pairs of bear paws"; I heard him say something about the "different shapes," quickly followed by an incomprehensible bit about the boots I would need. "If I have to take you shopping . . ." the snowshoer began, but I didn't catch the rest.

When he emerged from the Beetle, and I could hear him again, he was talking about Charles Dickens. *Great Expectations* was the novel he thought I should read. All of a sudden, it occurred to me, I had my own expectations. How great or small, I didn't know. Expectations for myself were new to me.

"Can I give you a lift?" the snowshoer asked me.

"Yes, please," I answered him.

From the Thompson Cage, I could walk home in about eight minutes; I was imagining I could run home faster than the snowshoer could drive me. It had been a few years since one or more of those Brewster girls had warned me: "Don't accept rides from strangers."

At thirteen, I was about five feet five; fully grown, I would end up just short of five feet seven. In the parking lot of the Thompson Cage, the top of the snowshoer's head barely reached my chin. I accepted the little stranger's offer of a lift home—not only because I wanted to hear more about the aforementioned *Great Expectations*, which the diminutive snowshoer believed I should read, but because I wanted to see how he managed to drive.

I was already acquainted with the interior of a VW Beetle; it was my mother's choice for a car, perhaps owing to her smallness, but I had never seen the driver's seat in such a dramatically forward position. The snowshoer's knees were almost touching the bottom rim of the steering wheel, and he didn't actually sit on the seat. He gripped the wheel so tightly that his fanny never touched the seat. As the stick shift for the Beetle was on the floor, between the two front seats, the snowshoer reached behind him to change gears. I immediately thought that my mom would admire the position the snowshoer maintained while driving. It resembled the ninety-degree angle she held for her wall sits. And although my first trip with the snowshoer was a very short drive, the tensile position he tenaciously held was made more impressive by the small English teacher's recitation of a passage from the opening chapter of *Great Expectations*. My confusion came from my not understanding he was quoting Charles Dickens. I thought the snowshoer was telling me about his own unhappy childhood, not the graveyard circumstances of a fictional character.

"'As I never saw my father or my mother,'" my tiny driver began, reciting from memory, "'and never saw any likeness of either of them (for their days were long before the days of photographs), my first fancies regarding what they were like were unreasonably derived from their tombstones.'" This surely meant his parents had died without his knowing or remembering them—before the time of photography! Or so the snowshoer seemed to be telling me.

"I thought your father taught you to ski, and your mom got you some snowshoes," I interjected. Now, naturally, we were both confused. The snow-shoer's eyes never left the street ahead of us, though he could scarcely see over the steering wheel, which he fiercely gripped in his small but strong-looking hands. I was convinced his mother had been correct in thinking that the ski-poling would make her small son stronger. Yet what was I to make of the snowshoer's telling me that he'd known his parents only by their tombstones?

We had pulled into the driveway of my grandparents' Front Street house, where the smallest English teacher in Exeter history stopped the car. He leaned back in his seat as he regarded me. "That was a quotation, Adam," he told me calmly. "That was the second sentence of the second paragraph of *Great Expectations*. I thought the circumstances of the young, first-person narrator—namely, never knowing his parents—might resonate with you and what little I know of your somewhat similar circumstances."

"I see," I said. The sentence he recited had resonated, all right. I sat in the Beetle while the part about deriving your only knowledge of your parents from their tombstones went on resonating.

There was another car in the driveway—Aunt Abigail's station wagon. Therefore, I was not surprised to see the querulous faces of both my aunts in a dining-room window; those two biddies went everywhere together. Soon my grandmother's benign face appeared in an adjacent window. I could imagine what they were thinking. *Who is bringing our Adam home? Who is that weird little man?* However, Exeter being Exeter, my gossipy aunts would have known all about the handsome but miniature snowshoer. Aunt Abigail and Aunt Martha had made it their business to know everything about everyone.

I could see that the obstacle presented by Aunt Abigail's station wagon was bothering the little snowshoer. There was nowhere to turn around in the driveway; he would have to back up into Front Street.

"Backing up could have become a sticking point in my driving test," the snowshoer was saying, "but I somehow managed." He adjusted his rearview mirror, twice; he kept glancing in his side-view mirror, as if he might have missed something.

Exeter being Exeter, the snowshoer not only knew I was "the Brewster boy"; he knew my first name, too—he'd called me "Adam." I was about to ask him his name, but he was rummaging through the Beetle's glove compartment, where he found and handed to me a tattered-looking paperback of *Great Expectations*.

"Forgive the underlinings, all the marked passages—it's my teacher's copy," the snowshoer said.

"All the better, I'm sure," I told him. It struck me as an unlikely coincidence: the very novel he thought I should read just happened to be waiting for me in the glove compartment of his car. Then the snowshoer explained how he never drove anywhere in the Beetle without what he called "an emergency novel."

"If I drive off the road and am lying upside down in a ditch, unable to move my legs or get out of the car, I want to have something good to read—an emergency novel," Exeter's smallest English teacher explained.

I thanked him, and got out of the car. I hope I was sufficiently sensitive to the little snowshoer's fear of backing up; I made a point of not watching him back out of the driveway. Besides, I couldn't wait to start reading Charles Dickens. At thirteen, I lacked the experience or the suffering to regret anything I'd done. No one close to me had died—not yet. No encounters or interactions with ghosts—not yet. As for *Great Expectations*, I couldn't imagine how a story that begins in a graveyard—about a lonely boy who is accosted by an escaped convict "among the graves"—would become *my* emergency novel.

12.

INTENDED FOR LITTLE RAY AND ME

In July 1956, only seventeen months after I had met the little snowshoer, my mother married him. His name was Elliot Barlow. He was seven years younger than my mom, who was thirty-four on her wedding day. This prompted Aunt Abigail, who was categorically denigrating to older brides, to say: "That makes you the oldest bride in the family, Rachel."

"Just wait and see how old I am," Nora said. At twenty-one, Nora had likened marriage to a terminal disease. She was not known to have had a boyfriend.

"I suppose Nora's waiting for the right fella," was all Aunt Abigail would say in her daughter's defense.

"You can't be fussy about the right fella, Nora," Aunt Martha had chimed in. "You just have to *try* one."

"I'm waiting for one who'll let me cut his dick off," Nora told them. "I'll try that one."

Nora brought a friend to my mother's wedding—a college girl, Nora's classmate at Mount Holyoke. She was an Emily who'd been shortened to an Em. Was Em the name Nora gave her? Was it a way to dominate her? Em was dollish and anxious-looking; she was startled by sudden sounds and movements. Em clung to Nora or hid behind her—at times with her doll-like face buried between Nora's shoulder blades and her locked hands hugging Nora's navel.

To accommodate the out-of-town guests attending the wedding—for the most part, the North Conway Norwegians—my grandmother had reserved several rooms at the Exeter Inn. The inn was a short walk from our Front Street house, where the marriage ceremony and the reception dinner would take place. Aunt Abigail had assumed Nora and Em would stay in Nora's childhood room—in the faculty apartment Nora had grown up in, with her mom and Uncle Martin—but Nora and Em chose to stay in one of the rooms at the inn. "Trust me," Nora told us all, "Em is a noisy sleeper."

"Em doesn't appear to make *any* noise when she's awake!" Aunt Martha had chimed in. In fact, Em didn't talk—not for the entire wedding weekend. Em was as silent as the nonspeaking emeritus.

I questioned Nora about the noises Em made when she was sleeping, although I had to wait for the right moment to ask—when Em went to the bathroom. At all other times, Em was physically attached to Nora in her quiet but clinging fashion. "You said Em is a noisy sleeper—*noisy* in what way?" I asked my cousin. I was fourteen at my mom's wedding. The extremely small groom was twenty-seven, although he looked like an undersize fourteen-year-old.

"Em has ridiculously loud and hysterical orgasms, Adam," Nora told me. "Each orgasm sounds like it's her first or last time."

In 1956, my experience with female orgasms was limited to the cinematic—notwithstanding how vividly I imagined females in orgasm, all the time.

The little snowshoer had driven me to the Franklin Theatre in Durham to see more foreign films with subtitles. These were (and forever would be) a bond between us, in addition to the snowshoeing. My aunts had forbidden Uncle Martin and Uncle Johan to take me to foreign films with female orgasms. I would see my first Ingmar Bergman films with Elliot Barlow. At the time, I was relieved not to have seen Bergman with my laughing uncles. In retrospect, a missed opportunity.

My mother's wedding was the first wedding I attended with Uncle Martin and Uncle Johan, who laughed throughout the marriage ceremony and the reception dinner. In no way did I think of my mom's marrying Elliot Barlow as a comedy. In fact, in my role as a matchmaker, I considered their wedding a triumph. I had worked very hard at it—even harder than I had at the snowshoeing.

I called my mother the night of the same day I met "Mr. Barlow," as I first heard Aunt Abigail and Aunt Martha call him. Not surprisingly, my shrewish aunts had recognized the diminutive driver of the VW Beetle, and they'd cruelly watched him back out of the driveway, inch by inch. My aunts were the head harridans of Exeter's faculty wives; they had fixed opinions of every bachelor on the academy faculty. They'd been on the lookout for an appropriate or suitable bachelor for Little Ray—meaning a marriageable one. For reasons beyond his extreme smallness, my aunts had disqualified Elliot Barlow.

"What on earth are you doing with Mr. Barlow, Adam? He didn't *approach* you, did he?" Aunt Abigail asked me. She and Aunt Martha and my grandmother were still glued to the dining-room windows, watching the small snowshoer navigate the treacherous driveway in reverse. I was thirteen—I was unfamiliar with the implications of the *approach* word. Because I'd spoken to the snowshoer before he spoke to me, I was thinking that I'd *approached* him.

"If Mr. Barlow was too small for Korea, I say he's too small to drive!" Aunt Martha chimed in. She was still looking out the window, as was my grandmother.

"Fiddlesticks, Martha—you can't blame someone for being too careful," Nana said.

"Mr. Barlow is a little light in his loafers, if you ask me," Aunt Abigail said; this expression, not unlike Abigail's usage of the word *approach*, sailed entirely over my head. Though I detected my aunt's derisive tone, I nonetheless imagined she'd noticed (as I had) how nimble on his feet the little snowshoer was. I needed Nora to interpret her mother's homophobic slur for me, which Nora soon would.

"My mom and Aunt Martha think Elliot Barlow is a fairy, Adam—they mean light-footed, like a fag, a queer, a fruit," Nora told me. Their sexual bigotry was consistent with my aunts' convictions that the older, unmarried men on the Exeter faculty were what they deemed *nonpracticing homosexuals*. As for the younger bachelors on the academy faculty, Aunt Abigail and Aunt Martha didn't give a young, attractive man much time to get married. As Nora put it: "If there's a cute guy on the faculty, and he's not hitched up by the end of his first year of teaching—well, he's a homo in the eyes of those witches. That's how those bitches think," Nora informed me. "But you tell me, Adam: How's a guy, even a cute one, going to find a girl he wants to hook up with in *Exeter*? It's an all-boys' school with an all-male faculty, and there's no one to meet *downtown*! Trust me, I know," Nora told me. "I couldn't find a girl to hook up with, not even for a quickie—not *here*!"

"What did little Mr. Barlow *want* with you, Adam?" Aunt Abigail asked me, while she and Aunt Martha were still watching him creep out of the driveway.

"We know what Mr. Barlow *wants*, Abigail!" Aunt Martha chimed in. "More to the point, Adam—what did you two talk about?"

"Snowshoeing," I answered.

"*Snowshoeing!*" Aunt Abigail roared.

Later, when I told Nora about her mother's and Aunt Martha's interrogation tactics, Nora said: "I can imagine how my mother would have said *snowshoeing*—as if you told her that you and Elliot had been talking about *fisting!*"

"What's *fisting?*" I asked Nora, who sighed.

"There will come a day, Adam, when you'll be as grown up as I am—or as grown up as you're ever going to get," Nora said. "Let's leave the *fisting* for another day—okay, kiddo?"

"Okay," I replied. I liked it when Nora called me *kiddo*, an endearment my mom only sometimes used to express her affection for me—only when she felt sorry for me, or when she was saddened by something she wouldn't explain. Nora's pity for me was always apparent, but it became more noticeable near the end of her college years. Maybe what happened to her at Mount Holyoke—where her aversion to men became more politicized— gave her more sympathy for me, her clueless and much younger cousin.

"Mr. Barlow gave me a book," I told my inquisitive aunts, holding up the worn paperback—his teacher's copy.

"A *book!*" Aunt Abigail cried, snatching it out of my hands. "*Great Expectations*—aha!" she exclaimed.

"Are there any pictures?" Aunt Martha asked. Charles Dickens had, at last, drawn them away from the dining-room windows—my grandmother included. Nora later said her mom and Aunt Martha were probably imagining that *Great Expectations* was an illustrated book about penile erections.

"Give the book to me, girls—it's just a novel," Nana told them. "Dickens didn't write pornography."

"There are *underlined* passages," Aunt Abigail said peevishly.

"There's handwriting in it—the midget fairy has scribbled in it," Aunt Martha chimed in.

"It's Mr. Barlow's book—his teacher's copy," I repeated. "I told him you read *Moby-Dick* aloud to me, Nana. I said I would like to try reading it again—to myself," I told my grandmother.

She held up *Great Expectations* almost as reverentially as I'd seen her raise *Moby-Dick*—in a heavenward direction. "Reading this novel would be easier, Adam," Nana said. "And there's a young man finding his way in the story," she added.

"That's what Mr. Barlow told me!" I piped up.

"A young man finding his *way!*" Aunt Abigail cried with alarm.

"What sort of *way*, I wonder!" Aunt Martha chimed in.

"Girls, girls—just stop," my grandmother told them. "This is a *literary* novel."

"Mr. Barlow is a *snowshoer*," I insisted. "Snowshoeing is my answer to ski-ing. I like to run. On snowshoes, I can run on top of the snow," I told them. "And Mr. Barlow teaches writing. I've decided I want to be a writer," I said.

"A *writer!*" Aunt Abigail screamed.

"God have mercy—save us!" Aunt Martha chimed in.

As Nora would one day tell me: "You might as well have said you were going to be a fist-fucker, Adam. Or that you couldn't wait to get fist-fucked," she added. (Yes, this was after the day had come—when I had grown up sufficiently for Nora to illuminate fisting for me.)

But, at the time, I was at a loss to understand the consternation Mr. Bar-low had caused my aunts. I wished I could talk to my uncles about the snow-shoer. I somehow knew they would hold "the runner on top of the snow" (as they called him) in high esteem. Later, when I was able to speak with them, Uncle Martin and Uncle Johan paid Elliot Barlow the utmost collegial re-spect. The little English teacher was popular with his students. As for those students who hadn't taken a class with him, and the ones who were inclined to tease him, Mr. Barlow's good humor would win them over. My laughing uncles were won over by the snowshoer's good humor, too.

At Harvard, Elliot Barlow had declared English as his concentration, Uncle Martin would tell me. The small snowshoer got a bachelor's degree in 1951. Because the U.S. Armed Forces, in their infinite wisdom, said the runner on top of the snow wasn't big enough, or so Uncle Johan told me, Mr. Barlow got his master's at Harvard in 1953. In the fall of that year, the snowshoer started teaching at Exeter. According to my uncles, the only fac-ulty who still raised their eyebrows at the snowshoer's smallness were the old fuddy-duddies.

My aunts kept raising their eyebrows. With their lynch-mob mentality, my aunts had been sounding the homo alarm before the end of Mr. Barlow's first year as a teacher. By the halfway mark of the small snowshoer's second year, he met me. By then, Aunt Abigail and Aunt Martha were in full fruit-alert mode.

As Nora would one day explain to me: "My mother and Aunt Mar-tha were on a faculty-wives' witch hunt; nothing got their rocks off like witch-hunting for fairies." In Nora's opinion, my mom's marrying the little snowshoer saved him. Nora would later modify her opinion: "Ray saved the snowshoer's *job*, anyway."

All I knew, for certain—on the night of the day I met him—was that I had to call my mother. I was waiting for my aunts to leave—to go home to their laughing Norwegians—and for my grandmother to begin her business in the kitchen. "The supper business," Nana disparagingly called her efforts to make dinner for the nonspeaking emeritus and me. My grandmother wasn't a good cook; she didn't enjoy cooking.

What finally persuaded my aunts to leave the Front Street house, to go home to their good-humored husbands, was that my grandmother began reciting from the marked passages she'd been reading to herself in Mr. Barlow's annotated copy of *Great Expectations*.

"Listen to this, Adam—Miss Havisham on the subject of love. Let this be a lesson to you," Nana said, before she began to read aloud. Aunt Abigail and Aunt Martha exchanged dire looks; they were roused to sudden-exit mode. "As follows: 'I'll tell you what real love is. It is blind devotion, unquestioning self-humiliation, utter submission, trust and belief against yourself and against the whole world, giving up your whole heart and soul to the smiter—as I did!' That's Miss Havisham in a nutshell!" my grandmother proclaimed. "The little English teacher knows how to *read*!"

Upon hearing Miss Havisham's proclamation, I was not greatly encouraged by the prospect of *real love*. Through a dining-room window, I observed Aunt Abigail and Aunt Martha's hasty retreat. The very idea of love as *utter submission* was repellent to them. And Nana wasn't finished. In her years with the deluded, now-silent emeritus, my grandmother was used to an audience of one. At least I was a responsive audience.

Another passage the little English teacher had marked prompted Mildred Brewster to keep reciting. "And there's this, Adam," Nana said with gloomy solemnity. "May you be spared such a moment of recognition as this—namely, the conviction that most of your happiness lies behind you, and the lion's share of your loneliness looms ahead. This is poor Pip's view of the marshes at night: 'I looked at the stars, and considered how awful it would be for a man to turn his face up to them as he froze to death, and see no help or pity in all the glittering multitude.' May you be spared such awful loneliness, Adam," my grandmother most solemnly said.

"I'm going to call my mom now, Nana—while you fix supper," I said. Under the circumstances, I tried to sound as hopeful as possible, knowing that the supper business conducted in my grandmother's kitchen rarely turned out well. Still reeling, as I was, from the demands of *real love*, which included giving up my heart and soul to the *smiter*, I was no less devastated by the prospect of freezing to death while receiving no assistance or kindness from the indifferent stars. "What's a *smiter*, Nana?" I asked her.

Handing the little teacher's copy of *Great Expectations* to me, my grandmother was making her stoic way to the kitchen, where I knew her expectations were modest. "A *smiter* is one who strikes a heavy blow, Adam—either with the hand or with an implement," Nana said. It didn't sound good, either way, but I was now alone and could call my mother.

During the ski season, calling my mom in Stowe was not in the devastating category of Pip's seeing "no help or pity in all the glittering multitude"; nevertheless, I faced some uncertainties when I made these calls. In the first place, my mother knew how much I missed her; I had to be careful, especially at the beginning and end of the call, not to make it apparent that my missing her was the reason for my calling her. If she could hear how much I missed her in my voice, she would cry—then we would both feel guilty.

Of lesser importance, yet also of an uncertain nature, was that I had only a vague idea of where she lived in Stowe—not to mention, with whom. She'd told me she had a "bunch of roommates"; usually, when I called, either my mom or Molly answered the phone. "Just picture a kind of dormitory for girl jocks, Adam—that's where I spend the ski season," my mother said. I'm sure she had no idea of the unease and arousal she had conjured up for me, her thirteen-year-old son, lying awake with conflicting images of *girl jocks*— her fellow ski instructors or ski patrollers, and there was at least one female trail groomer in the aforementioned *bunch of roommates*.

Molly was first and foremost a trail groomer. I'd not met Molly. I'd only spoken with her on the phone, when I called for my mom. Little Ray had met Molly at Cranmore, where the mountain had a reputation for "advanced trail-grooming technology," as Molly put it; she'd been a snowcat driver at Cranmore before she took her technique to Stowe. Now Molly was driving what they had for piste machines at Mount Mansfield and Spruce Peak.

I remember when Molly first told me about the "vintage snowcat" she used to drive on the "graveyard shift," when she'd been a night groomer at Cranmore—a 1952 Tucker Sno-Cat. I didn't know anything about working vehicles; Molly had to explain everything. You had to climb up on the tractor treads in order to get in the cab. The Tucker had a stick shift, a clutch pedal, no brake pedal—just a hand brake. Molly had put in the radio and the heater herself. The Tucker Sno-Cat didn't climb very well; Molly had to drive it up the service road and down each trail. She said the Tucker had tipped over a few times when she was going crossways on the hill. Foxes followed the snowcat, chasing the mice the roller scared out of the snow. The slats of the roller broke up and packed down the snow—"the roller leaves the snow looking like skiers have been sidestepping up the trail," Molly explained. She saw the eyes of animals reflected in the snowcat's headlights. "The game wardens say there are no mountain lions in New Hampshire or Vermont, but I've seen them," the night groomer told me. She'd seen mountain-lion tracks in the snow, too; she knew all the animals by their eyes and by their hoof or paw prints. After Molly moved to Stowe, and she was night-grooming, she said she'd been on the lookout for Bigfoot Bob. He was a friend of hers, a nighttime snowshoer. His bear paws left big tracks in the snow—"as if an elephant has been blundering around," Molly said. She was sympathetic that Bob worked all day and could snowshoe only at night, but she didn't want him to be on the trails when she was grooming. "I don't dislike Bob—I don't want to kill him," she told me.

Molly's job sounded exotic. I wanted to go night-grooming with her. My mother told me Molly was the mountain's chief equipment operator. Molly occasionally filled in for the guy who plowed the parking lots and access roads at the ski area. Molly would also sub for the lift operators, and she was in demand as a ski patroller, too.

The night I called my mom to tell her about the little snowshoer, I thought I wouldn't say anything about him to Molly, if Molly was the one who answered the phone. I was worried that Molly might have mixed feelings about Bigfoot Bob.

I often called during Nana's supper business. If my mom answered, I knew Molly had the early shift on the snowcat—"from when the lifts close till midnight," my mother had explained to me. If Molly answered the phone, I knew she was on the graveyard shift, which went from midnight to sunrise— even until the lifts opened, in the morning. Sometimes, when I called my mom at night, she said she was waiting up for Molly. "I like to have a beer with her when she gets home," my mother had told me.

It was around suppertime of the same day I met the snowshoer when Molly answered the phone. "This is Molly," she always said.

"This is Adam," I said back to her, as usual.

"Adam *who?*" Molly always asked. "Is this Adam the Kid—Ray's one and only—or is this some other Adam, up to no good?" (She knew it was me, of course.)

"It's Adam the Kid, Molly," I told the night groomer.

"I thought so," she always said. "Ray!" Molly would then shout. "It's your *kid* on the phone."

Then the girl jocks would chime in; I pictured them, after skiing, stripped down to their long johns, or maybe wrapped in towels, after their showers. "Ray has a *kid?*" someone always cried out.

"How many kids have you got, Ray?" another girl jock yelled.

"I just have my one and only," I could hear my mom say, before she came to the phone.

"Is this my Adam?" my mother always asked, as if—after the hullabaloo my call had caused—I conceivably could have been some other Adam, up to no good, as Molly never failed to inquire.

"I've met someone important," I told Little Ray, not beating around the bush.

"Quiet, please!" my mom called to the girl jocks, who were still horsing around in the background. "Adam has met *someone important,* or so my boy says," I heard my mother whisper, to someone else.

"Uh-oh," a girl jock whispered back—maybe Molly. I also heard the *someone important* part repeated a couple of times.

"Make sure your kid has condoms, Ray!" one of the girl jocks shouted.

"Get your boy out of town, Ray—have him come live with us!" another girl jock called out.

"Yeah, right—Adam the Kid will sure as shit be safe with us," someone (not Molly) said. I couldn't discern more than that from the girl jocks—only their constant murmuring, frequently interrupted by a laugh as short and explosive as a bark.

"Tell me everything, Adam," my mom was whispering. "Who have you met, sweetie? Tell me, tell me."

"A snowshoer!" I blurted out.

"That's funny—Molly almost ran over Bigfoot Bob just the other night," my mother told me. "Trail groomers sometimes have an adversarial relationship with snowshoers," Ray explained, keeping her voice low. Her expertise regarding all matters related or tangential to the ski business couldn't deter me from telling her what I wanted her to know. I somehow knew the snowshoer was intended for Little Ray and me; he was not just *my* snowshoer.

"Go on, go on—tell me everything, Adam," my mom repeated.

I did. My aspirations to be a snowshoer and a writer, which of course became confusing to my mother when I mentioned *Great Expectations*—failing to be clear that it was a novel.

"Sweetie, *wait!*" my mom cried. "What kind of *great expectations* did Mr. Barlow give you?"

When that was sorted out, there were various pitfalls of misunderstanding awaiting us in the area of Mr. Barlow's extraordinary handsomeness. "Are you saying *you* find Mr. Barlow very handsome, sweetie?" my mother asked me.

"I'm saying I think Mr. Barlow will strike *you* as very handsome—good-looking and *small*," I emphasized to her.

"Oh, Adam—are you fixing me up with someone?" my mom asked. "Oh, sweetie—that is the *sweetest* thing!" she cried. It had occurred to me, of course, that I was consciously matchmaking for my mother.

"I think you'll like him," was all I said. "I know you'll think he's handsome—good-looking and *small*," I repeated.

"Adam: promise me Abigail and Martha didn't put you up to this," my mom suddenly said.

"I don't think *they* like Mr. Barlow!" I told her. "Abigail said he was 'a little light in his loafers,' or something; 'the midget fairy,' I think Martha called him," I said.

"Well, that explains why I haven't heard about Mr. Barlow from those two," my mom softly said.

"Mr. Barlow said you were 'definitely pretty'; he called you 'very pretty'—really, he did," I told her.

"Mr. Barlow said that about me?" my mother asked.

"I told him you were 'very pretty,' and he agreed with me—he's *seen* you," I said. I even told my mom how Mr. Barlow drove his Beetle—with both hands holding tight to the steering wheel and his ass not touching the seat, as if he were doing wall sits and driving at the same time.

"Adam, sweetie—just how small is he?" she asked me. "Surely, Mr. Barlow isn't smaller than *me*!" my mother asserted.

I should have known his size would be the clincher. At the time, I didn't know all the reasons why. "Mr. Barlow is *much* smaller than you—he's four feet nine, only fifty-seven inches. He doesn't look like he has to shave," I told her.

"My, oh my," Little Ray said suddenly. There was a shiver in her voice, as if she were cold or had seen a ghost. "Sweetie," my mom whispered, "Mr. Barlow doesn't look as young as *you* do, does he?" She knew by the pause; I was reluctant to tell her. I could hear her teeth chattering. Her voice had given me the shivers.

"Mr. Barlow is small for a thirteen-year-old," I said, speaking strictly as a thirteen-year-old, "but his hands are bigger than mine."

"But how *young* does he look, sweetie?" my mother managed to say. She must have been visibly shaking. There was no more murmuring among the girl jocks, and not a single laugh.

"His handsomeness is the most grown-up thing about him," I told her. "Mr. Barlow is unusually young-looking, if you know what I mean," I added. That was all I could further contribute to our conversation, which had turned stone-cold.

"I know what you mean, all right," my mom said bitterly. "Have you seen any ghosts, Adam?" she suddenly asked me.

"No," I said. "Have you?"

"I have to go now, sweetie," my mother whispered. "We'll deal with the ghosts when the time is right—okay, kiddo?"

13.

THE SNOWSHOER KISS

We meet people who change our lives—in my case, only a few. The little snowshoer was the first person I met who changed my life. The snowshoeing was an acceptable substitute for my learning to ski. My mom accepted snowshoeing, but she had her opinions: snowshoers should stay out of the way of skiers; snowshoers weren't always welcome on ski mountains. From the start, my mother and the snowshoer could talk to each other on this subject—for hours.

It was stupefying to listen to them, but they were animated about where and when—on which ski mountains, at what hours—snowshoeing was allowed. Some ski areas let you snowshoe only when the lifts weren't running, when no skiers were on the mountain.

As for the adversarial relationship trail groomers sometimes have with snowshoers, Molly wasn't the only snowcat driver who almost ran over one. Mr. Barlow and my mom were in agreement: no snowshoeing when the snowcats are on the mountain. "Especially not when the night groomers are working," the snowshoer said. In the ski towns he'd grown up in, he had learned to be political. He'd talked to the trail groomers, the ski patrollers, and the lift operators; he'd occasionally bought lift tickets. "Some ski places make you take the lift up and down. You snowshoe above the tree line, where you're more visible," the little English teacher said.

While my mother believed that beginner or intermediate ski trails were the safest for snowshoers, because the skiers didn't ski as fast on those trails as they did on the expert runs, she also said that the snowshoers would still get in the way of skiers—even if the snowshoers stayed to the side of the piste. "Make the snowshoers stay off-piste, on ungroomed trails—where the climbers and hikers and some telemarkers go," my mom said.

In one of Elliot Barlow's conversations with my mother, concerning what was allowed or not allowed at ski resorts, I learned that Nora had been barred from skiing at Cranmore Mountain. Nora hadn't told me; I assumed she'd stopped coming to Cranmore because she'd had it with the girly-girl blondes, and Nora was old enough to make her own decisions.

"Nora hurt too many people," my mom told Mr. Barlow and me. "The ski patrol barred her indefinitely."

"I've never heard of a mountain barring anyone *indefinitely*!" Elliot Barlow cried. "Not even in Austria."

To my mother, the most enchanting of the ski towns Elliot had grown up in were Austrian: Lech, in the Vorarlberg, and St. Anton and St. Christoph in the Tyrolean Alps. Little Ray revered the Arlberg. She spoke of these three mountain villages and ski destinations in hushed tones, by their full and sacred-sounding names: Lech am Arlberg, St. Anton am Arlberg, St. Christoph am Arlberg. When the little English teacher complimented her pronunciation, my mom admitted that Uncle Johan had helped her with the German.

It is strange to be a teenager before you ever see your mother flirt with someone. Additionally, it was awkward that my mom's first meeting with the snowshoer took place in my grandmother's house. It was unheard of for my mother to have made the long drive from Stowe at the height of ski season, in early February. She came home immediately. Nana did her best, but she failed to keep my busybody aunts away.

"Ray should be forewarned of the *fairy* factor," Aunt Abigail had insisted to my grandmother.

"Mr. Barlow is too small to be *believed*," Aunt Martha chimed in.

"Girls, girls—let Little Ray and Mr. Barlow have some privacy, please," Nana said to the sexually vigilant harpies.

Ah, well—privacy with those Brewster girls was a one-way street. There were the things they wanted you to know; there were the things they kept from you. Besides, my mom and Elliot Barlow weren't afforded much privacy by me—not on the occasion of their first meeting, what my mother would later call her "one and only blind date." Add to the mix the random intrusions of Grandaddy Lew. Even deluded, the mustache-chewing emeritus possibly sensed it was highly irregular to see Little Ray at home in the ski season.

As for the enraptured conversation my mom was having with the little snowshoer, Grandaddy Lew seemed both baffled and outraged by it. The emeritus might have imagined that Elliot Barlow was another illegitimate child Little Ray had given birth to, despite Elliot's repeated efforts to put the delusional mustache-biter at ease.

At each sighting of the indignant-looking emeritus—either peering into or slinking through the living room—Mr. Barlow would bounce to his feet and cry out: "Good afternoon, Principal Brewster!" Thereupon, the affronted old fool would scurry away.

While my grandmother was endeavoring to keep my aunts contained in the kitchen, there were periodic breakouts. Aunt Abigail offering stale crackers and a putrid-smelling cheese; Aunt Martha precariously carrying a decanter of sherry (with very small glasses, the size of eyecups) on a silver tray. I believe it was the same cheese we'd had at Thanksgiving. Only the emeritus ever had the sherry.

"All I drink is beer, and just a little," my mother said to Elliot, as if my aunts had already left the living room or had never intruded.

"I'm just a beer drinker, too," Elliot told her. "Sometimes I can't finish the first one."

"Oh, we're perfect for each other—we could share one beer!" my mom said, batting her eyelashes.

My aunts knew Little Ray was flirting. "Keep your feet on the floor and your hands to yourselves, you two!" Aunt Abigail said to them.

"Keep your knees together, Rachel—remember Adam!" Aunt Martha chimed in. Even I had noticed that my mother was attractively dressed. It was unlike her to pay such close attention to her clothes. Perhaps the tight sweater had been borrowed for the occasion; it might have belonged to one of the girl jocks Little Ray was living with. It was also a surprise not to see my mom in jeans or sweatpants in the winter months. The skirt and the tights were most becoming—like the sweater, borrowed but fetching. That February afternoon in 1955, when my mom and the little snowshoer were first talking about where he'd lived in Austria, I had no doubt Little Ray was flirting with Elliot Barlow. Now I'm not so sure. Hadn't my mother always idolized Austria, not least the Arlberg? Maybe my mom was flirting with the whimsical notion of being there herself. What if the flirtation was all about her imagining herself in Lech and St. Anton and St. Christoph, thus contradicting her previously expressed dislike of foreignness?

As for Charles Dickens and his imagining a pitiless firmament—the vast and distant dome of the uncaring heavens, of no help to mankind—well, Little Ray wasn't a reader. Elliot's love of literature didn't interest her, nor did she give a hoot that my grandmother was impressed by Elliot's parents. "The Barlows are a fine old Bostonian family," Nana had said. What further impressed Mildred Brewster was that Elliot's parents had been college sweethearts—they'd met when he was at Harvard and she at Radcliffe.

"Oh, I get it—the Barlows were sweethearts at *those* colleges," Nora would later comment. In Nora's view, those status-conscious Brewster girls—my mother excepted—were prone to have orgasms over the Harvard-Radcliffe connection. "They get hard-ons for higher education," Nora said. Nora was entitled to her bitterness toward an elite education. Nora never forgot: she'd been a faculty brat at Exeter when Exeter was a boys-only school.

My mom wasn't inclined to higher-education hard-ons; she didn't have an orgasm over the Barlows' Harvard-Radcliffe connection, nor did she give a hoot that Elliot came from a highfalutin bunch of Bostonians. What mattered to my mother was that the snowshoer was a virtual *Austrian*.

"You're practically an *Österreicher!*" my mom told Elliot, breathlessly—showing off her German accent. Her breathlessness was possibly the result of Little Ray's imagining herself skiing at high altitude, which she would have been in Lech, or St. Anton, or St. Christoph—especially in St. Christoph. Maybe my mother was feeling the effects of high altitude at the very idea that the snowshoer had been born in St. Anton, where Hannes Schneider had been a ski guide before the First World War.

Schneider had served as a ski instructor for the Austrian army. After the war, he returned to the Tyrol, starting a ski school in St. Anton, where he perfected his method of instruction—the Arlberg technique.

John and Sarah Barlow had been parents with a plan, even as college sweethearts. The European history and the German they'd studied at Harvard and Radcliffe were as purposeful as Sarah's choosing to get pregnant in St. Anton and have her baby at altitude. Just as she thought all the ski-poling would make her little snowshoer stronger, Sarah Barlow believed she could acclimate her child to altitude if she went through gestation above four thousand feet.

"I *love* your mother for wanting you to be born acclimated to altitude," my mom earnestly declared to the snowshoer, when he told her this story. She suddenly seized one of his small hands in both of hers, holding it to her left breast. Or so it appeared to me, and to Elliot Barlow. "Feel my heart—how it's beating!" Little Ray cried. "It's as if *I'm* at altitude."

"I can certainly feel something," the little English teacher said. In retrospect, I would guess that Elliot had never felt a woman's heart beating above her breast.

I was most impressed that Elliot's parents had planned to be writers—that is, the writing part of their plan was more impressive to me than their intention to live in Austrian ski towns because they loved to ski.

"Well, that's who my parents are—they plan *everything*," the snowshoer said, with barely noticeable exasperation. Even the novels the Barlows wrote were meticulously planned. Between the wars—"in the interwar period," as Elliot Barlow spoke of it—his parents were busily plotting the crime and espionage novels they would write together. They'd received "some graduate-level diplomatic schooling," Elliot said—"whatever Foreign Service training was standard at the time," was the way the little English teacher put it. It was the year Little Ray was born, 1922, when the U.S. Department of State sent the young Mr. and Mrs. Barlow to Germany—first to Berlin, albeit briefly, then to Weimar.

Elliot said his parents had been appointed to Vienna in 1924, only three years after U.S. diplomatic relations with Austria were resumed. Sarah and John Barlow were attached to the office of the chargé d'affaires. The U.S. Embassy had been downgraded to a legation; the ambassador was then an envoy. Not that this lower rank mattered at all to his parents, the little snowshoer maintained. The Barlows acted as liaison officers between the U.S. chargé d'affaires and the Kriminalpolizei, the criminal-investigation department of the Austrian police in Vienna. The Barlows' training and experience in the Foreign Service—and, of course, their German—would be useful to them as writers of international intrigue.

They were already expert skiers. By the ski season of 1927–28, when the Barlows arrived in St. Anton am Arlberg, Hannes Schneider had appeared in seven films—he was already famous—and John and Susan Barlow would become devotees of his ski school. The Barlows were determinedly writing their first husband-and-wife novel. Little Elliot, who would be born in St. Anton in 1929, was also a work in progress.

Ten years later, in 1939, Hannes Schneider would move his ski school to Cranmore Mountain in North Conway, New Hampshire. Prior to his leaving Austria, soon after the Anschluss, he'd run afoul of the Nazis and had spent time in jail. The Barlows left St. Anton in March 1938, immediately following the annexation of Austria by Nazi Germany, but their devotion to Hannes Schneider and the Arlberg was absolute. For the war years, Elliot and his parents lived in North Conway. When the little snowshoer started school in New Hampshire at nine, his German was better than his English. In St. Anton, he'd always been in a German-speaking school.

"We might have met in North Conway, when I was skiing at Cranmore!" my mother exclaimed to Elliot.

"But I was snowshoeing," the snowshoer reminded her, "and you wouldn't have noticed me. You were older," Elliot softly said.

"I would certainly have *noticed* you!" my mom declared.

I knew what the snowshoer meant: when he was nine, Little Ray was sixteen. When the war ended, Elliot was only sixteen; he'd gone back to Austria with his parents. Why would a pretty young woman in her twenties pay any attention to a *kid?* Needless to say, Elliot Barlow must have been an extremely small kid.

"I would have noticed anyone as *handsome* as you," my mother told the snowshoer, "no matter what age you were."

"No matter how *small* I was?" Elliot asked her.

Once again my mother clasped the snowshoer's hand, holding it to her heart—to her breast. "Say *small* again," she told him.

"Small," he said—so softly that I almost couldn't hear him.

"Feel it?" my mom asked him. I saw the snowshoer shudder. He must have felt her heart race. "Small really gets to me, Elliot—like altitude," Little Ray whispered.

If I hadn't been in the living room with them, would they have had sex then and there? I doubt it. That was when Uncle Martin and Uncle Johan barged in, lugging bottles of wine and a case of beer; their eternal kidding around marked the end of what passed for privacy between my mother and the little English teacher.

"Bier, Bier—das Bier ist hier!" Johan sang in German. "Beer, beer—the beer is here!" he repeated in English. Uncle Johan loved to speak German with Elliot. Johan thought the snowshoer's Austrian accent was hysterically funny. Uncle Johan thought all Austrian accents were comedies.

To Johan's credit, he was a reader, albeit not a very discerning one. His love of all things German had led him to read the John and Sarah Barlow crime and espionage novels. "Die besten Kriminalromane! Das Ehepaar des modernen Spionageromans! The best crime novels! The married couple of the modern espionage novel!" Uncle Johan proclaimed.

I could tell that the little English teacher had been embarrassed by this hyperbole before, in German and in English, although the Barlows' first two novels weren't translated and published in German until after the Second World War. After they were translated, the Barlows' historical and political thrillers had bigger sales and a more literary reputation in the German language than they enjoyed in English.

Uncle Martin and Uncle Johan couldn't agree exactly where and when they'd read the Barlows' first novel, which they'd read in English. My uncles were Tenth Mountain Division men. Like Hannes Schneider, they'd helped train the U.S. Army mountain troops, in which Schneider's son Herbert had served.

"Supper is finished!" my grandmother confusingly announced. Nana made it sound as if supper had already been eaten, and we'd all missed it.

Martin and Johan were now in disagreement concerning their whereabouts when they'd both read the Barlows' second contribution to Kriminalliteratur—Uncle Johan's show-off German for the Barlows' spy-noir genre.

The Vinter brothers had been with the First Battalion of the Eighty-seventh Mountain Infantry Regiment at Fort Lewis, Washington, in November 1941, but they'd moved with the First and Second Battalions of the Eighty-seventh to Camp Hale, Colorado, in December 1942. No one was interested in where or when they'd read the Barlows' first two thrillers. I had a hard time imagining how Uncle Martin and Uncle Johan had trained the troops, because my uncles couldn't agree which regiment was where when— or how old they were when the Eighty-seventh was here, or the Eighty-fifth was there.

"In February '44, when the Eighty-seventh returned to Camp Hale . . ." Uncle Martin began, and then stopped, having lost his train of thought.

"The Eighty-fifth Mountain Infantry Regiment was activated at Camp Hale in July '43 . . ." Uncle Johan interrupted—whereupon he paused, the way ahead unclear.

"We were already too old!" Uncle Martin meaninglessly cried out. "I was thirty-eight, Johan thirty-six." He stopped.

"The Eighty-fifth and the Eighty-seventh embarked together, from Hampton Roads in January '45—bound for Naples," Uncle Johan said, rather wistfully.

"I was forty, Johan thirty-eight," Uncle Martin said, his voice trailing away.

What my grandmother meant was that supper was ready to eat. Only the cooking of it was finished. As usual, it was an overcooked casserole of unidentifiable ingredients; it was *mortally* finished, a casserole cooked into submission. Also finished was what remained of my aunts' patience with my uncles' lack of clarity concerning their wartime memories. Aunt Abigail suspected too much beer-drinking was the cause—"Too much fun!" Aunt Martha chimed in.

"Too much gallivanting around!" Aunt Abigail cried, when we were seated at the dining-room table.

"It's a wonder you had time to read!" Aunt Martha chimed in.

Warfare was a young man's game, in my aunts' opinion. My uncles were thirty-six and thirty-four when they started training the mountain troops. Nora and Henrik were six and four, respectively. When the Eighty-fifth and the Eighty-seventh embarked for Italy—from Virginia, in January 1945— Uncle Martin and Uncle Johan went home to their wives and children.

"You were no spring chickens!" Aunt Abigail declared. "And you had *families*—you shouldn't have been gallivanting around!"

"You were having too much *fun*," Aunt Martha chimed in.

"Girls, girls," my grandmother said. My mom gave my hand a quick squeeze under the table. I could tell the word *fun* had affected her, if not as powerfully as altitude.

Elliot Barlow was a brave little man. He tried to describe the plot of *The Kiss in Düsseldorf*, the first of his parents' Nazi-era novels. It was a valiant effort: not to make his parents sound like hacks; not to call their novels potboilers; not to be outmaneuvered by my uncles' interruptions. The intrepid snowshoer began, unwisely, with the eponymous kiss. Two SA men are seen kissing each other during Hitler's speech in Düsseldorf in 1932.

"A two-and-a-half-hour speech—what a kiss!" Uncle Martin declared.

"The SA stands for Sturmabteilung—the Nazi storm troopers," Uncle Johan, ever the German teacher, explained.

"Ernst Röhm and Rudolf Hess were in the SA," Uncle Martin offered. "Röhm and Hess were Freikorps guys originally, before they were Nazis— Martin Bormann was a Freikorps guy, too."

"Right-wing nationalists, they were the bunch behind the stab-in-the-back legend," Uncle Johan interjected. "Die Dolchstosslegende!" he cried, causing the startled emeritus to lose control of his knife and fork. Like everyone else, Grandaddy Lew hadn't really been eating. He'd been picking through his casserole, searching in vain for something recognizable.

My mother was seated between Elliot Barlow and me. Under the table, I could see she'd taken his small hand and was holding it in her lap. They'd scarcely touched the beer they were sharing—their first one.

Whether the hand-holding had distracted the snowshoer, or his grasp of *The Kiss in Düsseldorf* had slipped away, Elliot suddenly said: "One of the SA men seen kissing during Hitler's speech in Düsseldorf is murdered. His killer is alleged to be the SA man who kissed him. Soon other Nazi storm troopers are found murdered, but they never find the kissing killer—that's the plot."

"Ernst Röhm was co-founder and a leader of the Sturmabteilung," Uncle Johan jumped in. "Röhm's homosexuality was well known."

"Hitler had Röhm killed *because* Röhm was a homosexual," Uncle Martin emphatically stated.

"Röhm had fought on the Western Front—he was awarded an Iron Cross," Uncle Johan explained.

"Röhm was wounded—he lost a piece of his nasal bone!" Uncle Martin wanted everyone to know.

"No nasal bones—not when we're eating!" Aunt Abigail ordered.

"Or even when we're *not* eating!" Aunt Martha chimed in. My aunts' interest in the conversation had peaked when the kissing men were mentioned, and when the words *homosexuality* and *homosexual* were used. Each occasion caused Aunt Abigail and Aunt Martha to stare intently at the little English teacher.

"As for the plots of my parents' Nazi-era novels, like their Cold War novels . . ." Elliot Barlow quietly persisted. Then he paused. Everyone's attention was drawn to the childlike behavior of the unfulfilled emeritus. He was not only eating voraciously; he was attempting to feed himself with a serving spoon, which was too big for his mouth. "The plots are all the same," Elliot now resumed. "The killer is never caught. It helps that he's killing bad people—no one's trying very hard to catch him. Cynical characters, bleak nonendings," the snowshoer concluded; his voice petered out. His heart wasn't in it, and what was the point?

Martin and Johan were poised to interrupt him—Johan, in two languages. The hand-holding under the table had not convinced Abigail and Martha that Elliot Barlow was heterosexually inclined. My grandmother was an old-fashioned literary snob; Nana had never finished a single one of Simenon's novels—she said she'd tried. She didn't care for Eric Ambler, either. She claimed she'd never heard of Patricia Highsmith, but Nana had liked the Hitchcock film (*Strangers on a Train*) adapted from Highsmith's first novel. It wouldn't have mattered to my grandmother to hear that Patricia Highsmith, who was born in Texas, was better published and more widely read in German than in English, or that Elliot Barlow's parents had made their living from murder novels.

"Mord, mehr Morde, noch mehr Morde!" Uncle Johan interjected, which he immediately translated into English, thus giving me an insightful glimpse of his repetitive classroom technique. "Murder, more murders, still more murders! The Germans take murder more seriously than we do—I mean, as literature," Uncle Johan explained.

"I want to be completely honest with you," the snowshoer blurted out, speaking directly to my mother and looking only at her.

"Yes, I feel the same way about you!" my mom didn't hesitate to tell him, in her breathless fashion. My aunts had stopped breathing; they were praying for a confession of pederasty from the little English teacher. Even my uncles stopped talking. By the way Elliot Barlow suddenly sat bolt upright at the table, I could tell my mother must have grabbed his knee or his thigh. I'd missed seeing when they finished the first and second beers they'd been sharing—now I saw they had halfway finished their third.

"I love my parents—their writing, not so much," Elliot earnestly said. "Their writing never exceeds the limitation of its genre, no matter what the Germans call *Literatur*; their writing is formulaic noir, but I love my parents nonetheless. I love them anyway." Mr. Barlow's eyes were locked on my mom's throughout his heartfelt proclamation. While this was arguably not the declaration of love Little Ray had hoped to hear, she managed to mask her disappointment with an unfollowable tangent—a tactic familiar to me but baffling to Elliot, who had no previous experience with my mom's method of changing the subject (again and again) until she ended up with the conversation she'd wanted to have in the first place.

Little Ray took the snowshoer's face in her hands, pulling him closer. "Look at me," she commanded him. "I would rather have altitude sickness than read anything. Oxygen deficiency is more interesting than writing—at least you feel *something*!" my mother cried. "Headache, nausea, swelling of the brain, even high-altitude flatulence—at least you can *feel* them!"

"All you can do is avoid alcohol and drink a lot of water," Elliot told her with the utmost seriousness. "I find that eating dried apricots sometimes helps," he added.

"Dried apricots make me fart *more*!" my mom cried.

"I meant that the apricots help with other symptoms of altitude sickness," the little English teacher mumbled.

"I've heard that children born at altitude are abnormally *small*," Aunt Abigail interjected.

"Maybe they just don't *develop*," Aunt Martha chimed in.

"My mother heard this, too," Elliot calmly replied. "But she was also told that this was an old wives' tale. And my birth weight was almost normal, though I was undersize." My mom had not let go of his face. Out of customary politeness, Elliot had tried to look at my aunts when he spoke to them, but my mother wouldn't let him turn his face away from her.

"Listen to me," Little Ray said to the snowshoer. "You're the handsomest man I've ever sat this close to. And you know what *small* does to me," she said in her huskiest voice. Her lips almost touched Elliot's ear. In his wildest dreams, he might have imagined she was going to kiss him. That was when my mom loudly said: "No man can be small enough for me, Elliot—or so I thought, before I met you."

Even to me—at thirteen, a sexually inexperienced boy—it was shocking to hear the smallness of the snowshoer expressed in these terms, in the *small enough for me* way. I hoped no one would ask her to explain. I wished for an irrefutable ending.

That was Little Ray's intention: to make this point, to end exactly here. Like her other tangents, this had been no tangent at all. Didn't she begin by holding the snowshoer's face in her hands? She knew all along she was going to kiss him.

It was a kiss I should have seen coming, but I didn't—no one saw it coming, except my mother. The lawlessness of the kiss made it unwatchable. Everyone but Elliot looked away. It was a kiss you wished someone had given you. The lawlessness of the kiss made you want it. I wanted someone to kiss me like that.

14.

A JUDGMENT CALL

If we hadn't turned away from the snowshoer kiss, we might not have noticed that the infantile emeritus was choking. At the periphery of my fixation on my mom's interactions with the snowshoer, I had seen my grandmother wrestle the serving spoon away from Granddaddy Lew. For several months now, I'd been aware of the periodic appearances of the diaper-service truck in the driveway; the regressive emeritus was turning into a two-year-old. His table manners weren't alone in going backward. The never-a-headmaster had reverted to stuffing his face and shitting in his diapers.

The historic kiss might have gone on forever, but my grandmother had pushed Granddaddy Lew's forehead to the table; standing behind his chair, she'd begun to hit him between his shoulder blades. The blows to the back of the choking emeritus were resounding.

Showing no signs of oxygen deprivation or dizziness, the snowshoer quickly recovered from the kiss. "If that doesn't work, Mrs. Brewster, I know another thing you can try," Elliot Barlow said to my grandmother, as he stepped behind the slumping emeritus. With unexpected strength, the little English teacher clasped his hands above the belly button of the skinny emeritus, jerking him to a sitting position, ramrod straight in his chair. If the never-a-headmaster had been standing, Elliot wouldn't have been tall enough to exert the diagonally upward pressure on the bottom of Principal Brewster's diaphragm. These were abdominal thrusts, exerting pressure on whatever was lodged in the trachea of the toddler emeritus—with a little luck, perhaps expelling it.

"We'll see," the snowshoer said, between thrusts. "I saw a ski instructor in the St. Anton ski school do this, to dislodge some bratwurst—or that's what it looked like, when it came out."

For years, my mother would credit Hannes Schneider with this lifesaving technique—"a kind of Heimlich maneuver before Heimlich," Little Ray liked to call it. Elliot Barlow never made this claim; it was just a trick some young ski instructor at St. Anton happened to know. Elliot would later express his doubts about the Heimlich maneuver. "Personally, I like to start with back slaps—then try the abdominal thrusts, then pound on the choker's chest. I don't count on the first thing working," the little English teacher said.

What Elliot Barlow demonstrated that day was himself as a man of action; even though he didn't initiate the unwatchable kiss, Mr. Barlow got the job done. He'd attracted my mom; with the probable exception of the near-to-death emeritus, no one at the dining-room table would ever forget how Little Ray had kissed the snowshoer. And Elliot Barlow saved the regressor emeritus from choking. Granddaddy Lew would live to die another day.

A great gob of food was expectorated onto the dining-room table. What the infant emeritus had choked on was no more identifiable than it had been before he'd tried to eat it.

"It looks like a potato, but it's probably the pork," Aunt Abigail said. It did not look like a potato; it resembled the first two phalanges of an adult index finger, but it had to be the pork.

In the throes of asphyxiation, the baby emeritus had filled his diaper; in shame, he lowered his head and pouted as Nana led him out of the dining room.

"When was one of you going to tell me about the diaper service?" my mother asked no one in particular, but she was looking straight at her sisters. "Does anyone in this family ever say what's going on?"

"You should talk, Rachel—you of all people!" Aunt Abigail said.

"People in glass houses shouldn't you-know-what, Ray," Aunt Martha chimed in.

Uncharacteristically, my uncles had nothing to say. The kiss they'd seen and couldn't watch was not a kiss anyone had bestowed on them—not even in their Tenth Mountain Division days, when they were alleged to be gallivanting around.

Best of all, my mom and the little English teacher were knocking back the beer and making plans to see each other again. It just so happened that the academy's March break overlapped with mine. "I'll be teaching in the ski school at Cranmore during Adam's March break and yours," my mother was saying to the snowshoer. "Maybe you and Adam can meet me in North Conway!" she said excitedly.

"If we *have* to, we can do something different with the sleeping arrangements," Aunt Abigail informed them, sighing.

"We can put Mr. Barlow and Adam with Martin and Johan, in the boys' bunk room," Aunt Martha chimed in. "Then Abigail and I can sleep with you, Rachel."

"Don't be ridiculous," Little Ray told them. "Elliot knows people in North Conway—Elliot and Adam and I don't have to stay with you."

"My parents know people who have an inn—the innkeepers are European, but the inn is very nice," the snowshoer tried to reassure Aunt Abigail and Aunt Martha. On the subject of my mom's sleeping arrangements, it was clear there was no reassuring my aunts. "When I was at Harvard, I took the ski train from North Station almost every winter weekend. For the snowshoeing," Elliot added; he kept trying. "I did my homework on the train—the same train that stops in Exeter," he said. "I knew some Exeter boys at Harvard; they were boys who'd been teased when they were in school here. One of them had been tormented," the snowshoer added. "When the ski train stopped in Exeter, it made me consider that I might teach here one day," Elliot continued. "I knew I could help the boys who were teased—especially the tormented ones," he told us.

My mother stood up from the table, a little unsteadily. She hugged Elliot Barlow, pressing his face to her breasts.

"You wonderful man—I hope *you* were never tormented!" Little Ray cried, smothering him.

Considering how tenaciously my mom hugged the little English teacher, and the obstacle to his speech and breathing presented by her breasts, he managed to allay her fears. "No, no—I was never tormented, just teased," Elliot told her.

Not wanting to see more wanton displays of affection from my mother, Aunt Abigail and Aunt Martha were busily clearing the table and breathing heavily; their tasks included the stabbing and brisk removal of the partial index finger with a fork.

"Noch ein Bier?" Uncle Johan ambiguously asked the snowshoer or my mom; Johan had already opened another bottle, which he offered to them. The four empties stood as silently judgmental as sentinels between their place mats. My aunts had already removed their beer glasses from the table.

"Yeah, why not?" my mother said, in her girl-jock way, releasing Elliot from her embrace. She was taking a long swig from the fresh bottle when my aunts marched into the dining room from the kitchen; they were carrying clean plates and the dessert, which was always a kind of fruit pie, strangely missing half the pie part. Nana didn't overreach in the kitchen. My grandmother's desserts were better than the rest of her meals, notwithstanding that there was no name for them. No name for *it*, I should say—there was only one.

It was a deep-dish fruit dessert with a thick bottom crust, and no crust on top. "You can't call it a cobbler," Aunt Abigail insisted, "because a cobbler has a thick top crust."

"It's more like a pie than a cake, but sometimes it's vice versa. You never know how the bottom crust will turn out—it's usually burnt," Aunt Martha chimed in.

My grandmother admitted she never made the bottom crust the same way twice; her being a reader had not carried over to her chores in the kitchen, where she wrote nothing down and there were no cookbooks. The bottom crust was flour and sugar and butter, in unspecified amounts and proportions, and Nana threw in some vanilla or rum—or the sherry no one but the infant emeritus drank. Now, since Granddaddy Lew was reliving his infancy, my grandmother hid the sherry from him.

All Little Ray ever said about the unnameable dessert was that the burnt part tasted better with vanilla ice cream on it. She said this to the snowshoer, offering him a swig from the bottle they were sharing. Aunt Abigail, who'd been counting the bottles, chose this moment to say: "Five beers! That's a lot for you, Ray."

"We've been *sharing* the beer—I've had two and a half," my mom told her.

"That's still over your quota, Rachel," Aunt Martha chimed in. "That might explain all the kissing."

"It doesn't matter where you stay in North Conway, Rachel—you should carefully consider the sleeping arrangements," Aunt Abigail said.

"The sleeping arrangements *and* the kissing!" Aunt Martha chimed in.

"I can make my own sleeping arrangements," my mother told them. My aunts gave me their most redoubtable look. I felt incriminated, as if I were positive proof of what came of Little Ray's making her own sleeping arrangements.

By the time my grandmother returned to the dining room, no one was talking. We were silently eating the deep-dish blueberry thing, with vanilla ice cream on the burnt bottom crust. "Girls, girls," my grandmother admonished her daughters. Nana didn't need to hear them to know when they'd been fighting.

My grandmother looked tired and defeated. Real life was not as sensibly or purposely constructed as one of her favorite novels. Mildred Brewster loved all the foreshadowing in Melville and Dickens. She'd not foreseen she would be changing her damaged husband's diapers, and putting him to bed, when there was intelligent company for supper and the unnameable but edible dessert was on the table. On top of that, her children were at war with one another.

"I'm so sorry to have missed a single minute of your company, Mr. Barlow," my grandmother announced. "I was looking forward to talking about books with you."

"I wish someone had read *Moby-Dick* aloud to me, Mrs. Brewster," the snowshoer replied. "I might have paid closer attention and not found it such hard going. I envy Adam his experience."

"No one envies Adam!" Aunt Abigail cried.

"Look how he wrings his little hands!" Aunt Martha chimed in, for good measure. It was evident to my aunts that neither the unexplained indiscretion of my birth nor the interminable exercise of my enduring *Moby-Dick* out loud had led to a single observable virtue in my character or accomplishments. Not yet.

"'It is a most miserable thing to feel ashamed of home,'" my grandmother suddenly said, as if she'd been reading my mind. It was unclear if Nana was speaking to me or to all of us, but I felt certain her remark was meant for me to hear. She'd exposed what I was thinking.

It was absolutely clear that my aunts and uncles were leaving; their mode of departure was familiar to me. My aunts, who saw themselves as pillars of moral superiority, were leaving in a huff; my uncles, in their dickless fashion, were sheepishly following. This had happened before—not infrequently, when my aunts' righteous indignation was aroused by their contemplation of my mother's sleeping arrangements.

It is a most miserable thing to feel ashamed of home—well, yes, it is. But my mother didn't make me feel ashamed. Not what I knew, and didn't know, about her sleeping arrangements—not even the way she'd kissed the snowshoer. My mom never made me feel ashamed.

As for the regressor emeritus, I couldn't blame him for losing his marbles; I didn't hold him accountable for reverting to his diaper days. That can happen to any of us; that Granddaddy Lew was shitting in his diapers only made me feel sorry for him and my grandmother. I regret thinking of him as a diaper man.

What made me feel ashamed was my aunts' intractable hatred of the snowshoer. I was ashamed of *them*—of their obdurate disapproval of my mother, of their steadfast disappointment in me. In Aunt Abigail's and Aunt

Martha's eyes, I was the unwholesome offspring of my mom's unsavory sleeping arrangements.

To a lesser degree, I was also ashamed of my uncles—not of their aesthetic insensitivity, and not of their overall boorishness. Uncle Martin and Uncle Johan were fun-loving goofs, they were good-hearted men; they genuinely tried to boost my spirits and my self-esteem, and they truly liked the snowshoer. What made me ashamed of them was their cowardice; when my aunts were on their moralistic warpath, Uncle Martin and Uncle Johan didn't stand up to them.

"We can give you a *ride*, Mr. Barlow!" Aunt Abigail called from the front hall. Before this loud summons, those of us who'd remained at the dining-room table had heard only the grunting and stomping sounds of my aunts and uncles putting on their boots.

"It's *snowing*, Mr. Barlow!" Aunt Martha chimed in—as if snow in New Hampshire, in February, were an aberration.

"He's a snowshoer," I heard Uncle Martin quietly say.

"I think he likes the snow, Martha," Uncle Johan meekly added.

"Mr. Barlow didn't *bring* his snowshoes, did he?" we could all hear Aunt Abigail ask my uncles.

"Last chance, Mr. Barlow!" Aunt Martha chimed in.

"No, thank you!" the little English teacher called. "I like walking in the snow."

"He's *staying*, Martha!" my mother shouted. "And Adam and I are sleeping together tonight—in his room, in the attic, in the same bed! Under the skylight, where we can see the snow fall. *In the same bed*, Abigail!" my mom yelled.

"Maybe Adam wrings his hands because he's too old to sleep in the same bed with you, Rachel!" Abigail called.

After that, there was more boot-stomping in the front hall—followed by the sound of the front door opening and slamming shut—while my mother told Elliot Barlow (in embarrassing detail) that she and I still liked to sleep together in the same bed, and that she hoped we always would like it.

"Girls, girls," my grandmother muttered, though only one of her girls could hear her.

"It's late—I should be going," the snowshoer reluctantly said.

"Make sure they're out of the driveway before you go, or they'll run over you," my mom told him; she held his arm with both her hands. Little Ray wouldn't let him leave—not when my aunts might see him go.

"'It is a most miserable thing to feel ashamed of home,'" Nana said again, as if—under the circumstances—it bore repeating. "Not a bad way to begin a chapter, is it, Mr. Barlow?" my grandmother asked.

"Chapter Fourteen, I believe," Elliot said. That was when I realized my grandmother had been quoting from *Great Expectations*.

"'Heaven knows we need never be ashamed of our tears, for they are rain upon the blinding dust of earth, overlying our hard hearts,'" Nana now recited to us, as if she were praying.

"What a memory you have, Mrs. Brewster," the snowshoer complimented her. "That's near the end of the first stage of Pip's expectations—Chapter Nineteen, I believe."

"You've marked the passages I most liked when I first read them—you've made me want to read Dickens again," my grandmother told him.

"Oh, I see—you're talking about a book," my mother said, with sudden dismay. "If you're going to talk about books, I'll do the dishes."

I went with her to the kitchen, where we did the dishes together—where we could whisper about the snowshoer without our being heard in the dining room. When we wanted to listen to what Nana and Elliot Barlow had to say about the world of books, we could hear them from the kitchen. Not that we stopped whispering long enough to overhear very much of their book talk; we were too excited about the snowshoer.

"He's the perfect thing—for both of us!" my mom whispered in my ear. "You'll need someone to help you at the academy—your own faculty person, someone you can turn to. Like a father," she added.

"A father?" I asked her.

"I said 'like a father,' Adam—you have to listen to me, sweetie. You aren't a real faculty brat—you need someone on the faculty who treats you like his own faculty brat," my mother whispered.

"I have Uncle Martin and Uncle Johan," I reminded her.

"I said 'your own faculty person'—you're not listening, sweetie," my mom said. "Oh, God!" she suddenly cried out, forgetting to whisper, then clamping her hand over her mouth. "I couldn't keep my hands off that wonderful little man!" she whispered. "I had to stop myself from hugging him!"

"You sure kissed him," I reminded her.

"We'll talk about the kiss later, sweetie," my mother said. "How much is too much, how little is not enough—kissing is a judgment call."

"A judgment call?" I asked her.

"We'll talk about kissing later, Adam," she repeated, taking a swig from the bottle. But was it the fifth beer, the one she'd been sharing with the snowshoer, or was this a sixth bottle? It was just like my uncles to open a beer for Little Ray as they were leaving, when my hawk-eyed aunts wouldn't be around to watch her drink it.

My grandmother and Elliot Barlow could be overheard agreeing about the unfaithfulness of the 1930 film of *Moby-Dick*. "There is scant mention of Ahab's wife in the novel—'a sweet, resigned girl,' she's called," the snowshoer was saying.

"It is a sacrilege that Ahab kills Moby Dick and lives to go home and be happily married—it's not a love story!" we heard Nana cry.

"I hate it that the wife's name is Faith, and she's a minister's daughter," we heard Elliot Barlow bemoan.

"I hate it that there's no Ishmael—they eliminated the main character!" we heard my grandmother wail.

"I don't think I could go out with a guy named Ishmael," my mom whispered in my ear, giggling and spilling her beer—the sixth one, I was pretty sure, or the third for her.

"I love it when Ishmael says 'a whale-ship was my Yale College and my Harvard.' Or, even better, when Starbuck says: 'To be enraged with a dumb thing, Captain Ahab, seems blasphemous,'" the little English teacher was saying.

"I love it when Starbuck tells Ahab, 'God is against thee, old man'—I love Starbuck," we heard Nana tell the snowshoer.

"I love it when Queequeg tries out his coffin, to see if it fits," Elliot was telling my grandmother, "and how Queequeg carves the lid of his coffin, copying parts of his tattoos."

"I love Queequeg, too," Nana said.

"I definitely couldn't go out with a guy named Queequeg," my mother was whispering to me. She had her arms wrapped around me. She was giggling again, and nibbling on my earlobe, when my grandmother and the snowshoer came into the kitchen. Nana never drank—only water. Mr. Barlow had his arms full, carrying the five empty bottles. I took the bottles from him; I knew where the empties went. My mom coyly offered the snowshoer a swig from the beer she was drinking—the sixth one, definitely.

"Come here," she said to him, opening her arms. "You're not leaving without a hug."

I was relieved that Little Ray restrained herself in hugging him; she didn't crush him, or force his face against her breasts. This time, I tried to prepare myself not to watch the way my mother kissed him. I was as surprised as the snowshoer by what a chaste and circumspect kiss she gave him.

Elliot Barlow must have been disappointed, but the little English teacher didn't show his disappointment. My mom was shorter than almost everyone else, but she was five inches taller than the snowshoer. When she bent down to kiss his upturned face, she gave him a quick peck on his forehead—a good-night kiss you might give a child.

"See you up north, snowshoer," my mother told him. At first, I thought I understood what Little Ray was up to: she wanted the snowshoer to remember her first kiss; she wanted him to wonder when she might have more to give him.

In retrospect, I think my mom wanted me to remember the first kiss she gave the snowshoer; I think she wanted me to keep it in mind. When my mother and I had retired for the night in my attic bedroom—*in the same bed,* as Little Ray made a point of telling her sisters, twice—we cuddled together under the skylight, where we could watch the falling snow.

In the summer months, when my mom was home—especially when it was very hot—we slept together in her bedroom, on the second floor. Even though I had a ceiling fan, my attic bedroom got very hot. But we generally preferred to sleep in my bed, under the skylight—where we could see the moonlight and the stars. And when it snowed, we loved how the flakes blanketed the skylight. When the dome was completely covered, my attic room was in total darkness.

My bed was in an alcove; the alcove wall blocked any light from the Front Street end of the attic, where the cupola window was. The cupola was a small, rounded vault with an overhanging roof; it never admitted much light to the room, not even in the day. The only light over the bed came from the skylight, but not when it snowed.

Because my mother wasn't usually at home in the ski season, we didn't have that many nights together in my attic bedroom when it was snowing. In that New England seacoast climate, there were only occasional snowstorms in late October or early November, or in late April—not like up north. It was special for my mom and me—to cuddle together under the falling snow, until the darkness surrounded us. As a young child, alone and far away in that attic bedroom, I had doubts about the darkness.

On the night when my mother met Elliot Barlow, when we first went to bed and were lying under the skylight together, the snow hadn't been falling for very long; some light still lingered in the night sky, and we could still see the snowflakes fall. The dome of the skylight was not yet completely covered.

"I love it when we can still see the snow falling, but the darkness is clos-ing in," my mom whispered. There was no need for her to whisper; there was no one who could have overheard us. "I just love it when the darkness comes," she whispered. It was what she always said—not only under the sky-light, or in the falling snow, but whenever we were waiting for the darkness.

"Why are we whispering?" I whispered to her, as usual.

"Because people in bed together should whisper in the dark, sweetie," my mother always said, but not this time. She was snoring.

"You're already asleep!" I said, loudly enough to wake her.

"It's the beer," she told me, giggling. "I'll be getting up to pee all night," she said. "I hope you'll tell me if I'm farting." She had thrown one of her legs over me, and her head was in the crook of my arm. I could feel her breathing. I waited until I knew she was almost asleep.

"You were saying—about the kiss," I whispered. I waited. I knew she was awake. I could tell by her breathing.

"What about it?" my mom whispered.

"You said we'd talk about the kissing later," I reminded her. The whis-pering seemed to suit our conversation. The snow kept falling, but we could barely see it.

I could feel my mother withdraw the leg she'd thrown over me; she rolled away from me, on her back. I could only dimly see her staring at the dis-appearing skylight. "It's not dark enough to talk about kissing," Little Ray whispered.

"You said 'kissing is a judgment call'—where does the *judgment* come in?" I whispered back.

I had purposely closed my heart to my mom's attempts to teach me to ski. I'd spurned her efforts to make me the kind of athlete she was. I'd shunned the jock in her by not being a jock, but being a jock was a big part of who my mother was. I'd overlooked the jock in her—hence I was always surprised and disarmed by any sudden, explosive display of her athleticism. Even when she'd had a few beers, when I should have been on guard, I was unprepared for the split-second coordination of her strength, her balance, her catlike quickness.

From her back, my mom threw her far leg over me, this time bringing the rest of her body with it. She was suddenly sitting in my lap, with her legs straddling my hips and her hands pressing my shoulders into the bed. I saw only the silhouette of her head and shoulders—now backlit by the diminish-ing light from the disappearing skylight, blanketed with snow.

"Can you still see me, sweetie?" she whispered.

"I can see you a little," I told her.

"Tell me when you can't see me—tell me when I'm gone," my mother whispered.

"Okay," I whispered back.

"Has anyone ever kissed you, Adam?" she asked me.

"Not like you kissed the snowshoer," I told her.

"I should hope not," she whispered. She'd stopped giggling. "The know-ing how much, or how little—that's where the *judgment* comes in, that's where you have to know what you're offering, or what you're getting yourself into."

"I can still see you," I whispered. I didn't want her to kiss me, but I also did. I wanted the kiss she'd given the snowshoer, but I didn't want that kiss from her. Yet how could it have been that exact same kiss if it wasn't hers?

"You're not fooling around when you kiss someone like that," my mom whispered, as she was disappearing in the darkness. "You better know what you mean—you better mean what you're promising—when you kiss someone like that."

"I can't see you—you're gone," I whispered. I know—I might as well have told her to kiss me—I know, I know. And while I truly had lost sight of her in the darkness, I could still see her in my mind's eye, as I will forever see her—the way she stretched her body full-length on top of mine, and the way she kissed me. I have no doubt it was the exact same kiss she gave the snowshoer.

"Like that—that's how you do it," she said, in her girl-jock way, as if the kiss had been routine business for her, as perfunctory as her showing me (again and again) a stem christie or a parallel turn.

She rolled off me. I could no longer see her beside me, but I could hear her breathing. Soon she was snoring, leaving me wide awake in the infinite darkness.

15.

SEEING THINGS

Think of your first good kiss. Was it life-changing, or was it no big deal? Do you remember how old you were? Did it matter, at the time, who gave it to you? Do you even remember who it was?

I'll tell you this: when you're thirteen and your *mother* gives you your first good kiss, you better hope someone matches it or eclipses it—soon. That's your only hope.

I wanted my mom and the snowshoer to hit it off. I even admired the lawlessness of the way she kissed him. But when she kissed me that way, her lawlessness frightened me. Wasn't the way she kissed me a bad judgment call?

At thirteen, I'd been in the habit of telling Nora everything. I couldn't wait to tell Nora about the kiss my mother gave Elliot Barlow. "When you're old enough, Adam, you'll have secrets," Nora had told me. I was old enough. I had a secret I kept from Nora. I didn't want Nora to know how Little Ray had kissed me.

"The issues we have, about being Brewsters, are all about sex," Nora had told me. Does the secrecy in families start with sex? In my case, it started with the snowshoer kiss. My mother's kiss marked the beginning of my having something to hide.

Yes, I felt I was a traitor to my mom. Whenever I found myself thinking that the snowshoer kiss she gave me was *unsuitable* or *inappropriate*, I felt I'd joined forces with my evil aunts. When they called Little Ray a hippie or a free spirit, they were putting her down.

When you're a child, you think childhood is taking too long—you can't wait to grow up. One day, the growing up has happened; you missed it, and you're trying to seize it after the fact. When you keep secrets from people you love, you don't sleep as soundly as a child. That's when you know the growing up has happened, though you still have more growing up ahead of you—I certainly did. That's when my dreams started, when I stopped sleeping like a child.

Now I know they weren't dreams, but I didn't know what to call them then. Can you have premonitions of things that happened before you were born? Now I know that *premonitions* and *dreams* are the wrong words for what I saw in my fitful sleep; nevertheless, I first thought of them as dreams. They began soon after the kiss of questionable judgment. I still see them; I always will.

From the start, they looked like what they were: black-and-white photographs of actual people, places, and occurrences. But they weren't of people I knew, or of places I'd been, or of things I'd seen. How could I have known they were real? I had no idea they were ghosts. There was nothing nightmarish about the first images.

In the passage of time, like recurring dreams, they became as familiar as old friends. Over the years, their predictability grew—like members of your family, they repeated themselves. These eight images were the first ghosts I saw, not knowing they were ghosts.

1. Five rough-looking men are standing or sitting in front of a crudely built shack, a log cabin with an open door. A stack of firewood is beside the cabin; a bucksaw is at rest in a sawhorse in front of the men. Each man is wearing a different kind of hat or cap. Some aspen trees, but more evergreens, are in the background.

2. A trail above timberline—it could be a mountain pass. A mule train is making its narrow way. You can't see what's in the wagons; the heavy-looking loads are covered with animal hides, maybe steerhides. God knows what's being toted.

3. A group portrait—there must be two dozen men, in as many kinds of hats or caps. The men in the back row are standing; the ones in the front row kneel or sit on the ground. There are two children, both bareheaded, and a couple of dogs. On the hillside, which slopes uphill behind this group, is a workplace of shed-roofed buildings made of beams and mismatched stones. Maybe it's a mine.

4. Two men, definitely miners, are working underground. One man holds a sledgehammer over his shoulder; the other man appears to be setting an explosive charge. Crowbars, of various sizes, are strewn at the men's feet. Their boots—like their hats, with crumpled brims—are very dirty.

5. A formal portrait: a close-up of a well-dressed, bearded gentleman. I can't make out what might be an old-fashioned stickpin, perhaps holding a necktie in place; his hair is slicked back and his beard has been purposely trimmed. He's definitely not a miner. Maybe he's the mine owner,

or a banker—an entrepreneur of importance, I deduced from my first look at him.

6. I can't see a name on the façade of the three-story brick building; I can't tell if I'm looking at the front or the back of the building. A horse-drawn wagon, possibly a delivery wagon, stands beside the building, which I first pegged as late-Victorian architecture. Maybe *mine camp* architecture is more apt. It is a massive-looking brick rectangle, with both arched and rectangular windows—impressive, but not pretty.

7. A dark-skinned hotel maid, maybe Mexican, poses with her mop and pail in a hallway between rooms. She has a shy, childlike smile.

8. A boy, or a young man; the first time I saw him, he looked my age, thirteen or fourteen. He is leaning on his snow shovel—a long shovel, or a short boy. The top of the shovel's handle comes to his ear. He is posing in front of a snowbank; he appears to have cleared the sidewalk and the entryway to a building, which has a tall door. Sometimes I think I see skis leaning against the building; the snowbank and an American flag are always there. The boy is handsome, but his smile is childlike. Except for the boy and the hotel maid, the black-and-whites have the look of the 1880s or 1890s. Like the photo of the maid, the black-and-white of the boy with his snow shovel could be from the 1940s. He's wearing jeans and cowboy boots; his ski sweater and hat look like they might have belonged to someone else. The sweater is a little too wide for his shoulders; the pom-pom on the ski hat is girlish, or the pom-pom accentuates something girlish about him. The American flag and the tall door indicate the entrance to a hotel. A hotel guest, a woman, might have given her old hat and sweater to the boy.

When you stop sleeping soundly, you dream more. You're also tired; you can't always discern the difference between your dreams and what you imagine when you're lying awake. When I started seeing the black-and-whites—in the seventeen months between my mom's first meeting with the snowshoer and when she married him, when I still slept in the attic bedroom of my grandmother's Front Street house—my sleep was further disturbed by the smell of human shit. It's an unmistakable smell. You don't dream it; you can't imagine it. When I first woke up to that awful odor, I felt myself under the covers—just to be sure I hadn't had an accident in my sleep. It wasn't me. It was the nightwalker emeritus; he was also detectable by a creak on the attic stairs. The twelfth step, third from the top, invariably creaked. Had my nighttime visitor always come to watch me sleeping under the skylight? When I slept as soundly as a child, I probably didn't hear him—or smell him. Before the prowling diaper man started shitting himself, I wouldn't have smelled him.

One night—it wasn't snowing, and the moonlight was bright—I woke to see the nocturnal diaper man standing in the silvery glow from the skylight. Gaunt as a ghost—naked, except for the loaded diaper—the disassembling emeritus had come to stare at the illegitimate child who'd taken his words away.

"I'm sorry, Granddaddy," I said to him. As the real ghosts would one day teach me, it is difficult to look at someone who is disappearing. I closed my eyes; I didn't open them again until I heard the familiar creak on the attic stairs. The diaper man's smell took longer to drift away. Real ghosts, I would later learn, don't always drift away.

In the seventeen months before their wedding, my mother and the snowshoer got to know each other, and I got to hang out with them. We would spend two March breaks and one Christmas vacation together—all up north, conspicuously not with all the North Conway Norwegians. I can't keep straight the names of the trails on Cranmore Mountain where Elliot Barlow and I were allowed to snowshoe, but Elliot knew all the Austrians there, and he could talk to them in German.

There was an Arlberg run; there was a Skimeister and a Lower Skimeister, too. Of course there was a Kandahar and a Schneider. The names didn't matter to me; I didn't learn them. I never knew the name of the trail we were on. I just followed the snowshoer; up or down, I matched his stride. Elliot Barlow taught me to lengthen my stride—not only on snowshoes, but also when we ran together. Naturally, with my longer legs, I could soon overtake him—as a runner, and as a snowshoer. But, out of respect—later, out of love—I didn't, or I wouldn't, overtake him. You'll remember I had a history of this: even with a good ski instructor, I'd maintained a beginner-to-intermediate appearance.

Elliot Barlow brought my mom and me together; the snowshoer made us a family. Elliot made it possible for my mother and me to separate ourselves from the tyranny of those Brewster girls. I began to see that Nora had been right about my grandmother. Didn't her passivity—Nana's ineffectual "Girls, girls"—enable my aunts' bitchery? Their nonstop scrutiny of my mom's sleeping arrangements was invasive. Aunt Abigail repeatedly asked me about our accommodations at the inn in North Conway.

"We don't care if it's European," Aunt Martha chimed in.

"It's cozy," I told them. "One of the other guests is an Austrian."

"We don't care if it's *cozy*, or about the Austrian," Aunt Abigail said. "Just tell us about your rooms, Adam."

"Just stick to who sleeps with whom, Adam, and in what kind of bed," Aunt Martha chimed in.

I'd read *Great Expectations* twice. I was reading more Dickens; the snowshoer had given me his teacher's copy of *David Copperfield*. I was beginning to imagine myself as a fiction writer.

"Mr. Barlow calls the inn a Gasthaus," I began—this much was true.

"We don't care what Mr. Barlow calls it, Adam!" Aunt Abigail protested.

"Where does Mr. Barlow *sleep*—in what kind of bed, with whom?" Aunt Martha chimed in.

"He has a single bed, a small one. Ray and I have a double bed, in a bigger room. We share a bathroom—it's between the bedrooms," I explained. This was true, too, but I was stalling.

"You're too old to sleep with your mother, Adam," Aunt Abigail said tiredly, for the hundredth time. "Think of your hands."

"My mom visits Mr. Barlow—in his room, almost every night," I said slowly, as if I were writing this sentence. A truthful sentence, nonetheless. After Ray and I had gone to bed—when we'd been whispering together, and had finally run out of things to say—my mother would slip out of bed and whisper a few more things.

"I'll be back soon, sweetie—I'm going to visit the snowshoer," she whispered. "I'll leave a night-light on in the bathroom—okay?"

"Okay," I whispered back.

I would have noticed if she wore a naughty-looking nightie, but she was always wearing her flannel pajama bottoms, or athletic shorts, and a T-shirt—nothing frisky. Sometimes I was awake when she came back to our bed, sometimes not. These are true details, notwithstanding that I knew the conniptions Little Ray's nightly visits would cause my querulous aunts.

"She *visits* Mr. Barlow!" Aunt Abigail cried. "For how long?"

"It wouldn't take long—he's so small!" Aunt Martha chimed in.

"They're not even *engaged*!" Aunt Abigail said scornfully. They soon would be, but their engagement wouldn't matter to my aunts. The inappropriateness of my mom's *visits* with Mr. Barlow would continue to rankle the two most condemning Brewster girls, long after the snowshoer and Little Ray were married.

"Those two have other bugs up their asses—more than the matrimony bug," Nora always maintained, about her mother and Aunt Martha.

"I don't suppose you can *hear* Mr. Barlow and your mom—can you, Adam?" Aunt Abigail asked me. Ah, well—that was the opportunity for fiction writing I'd been waiting for. I was experimenting as a storyteller. I was imagining I could make something up by leaving something out. Dickens would have done it better.

"I don't hear them talking," I started to say. The pause was deliberate. "Well, I can occasionally make out what she says—never what he says, if he ever talks. There's just a lot of grunting and groaning, and laughing," I told them. "The floor shakes, sometimes." My aunts said nothing—that was a first. It was as if they were listening for the grunts or groans, and the lovers' laughter, or they were waiting for the floor to shake.

I didn't tell them that Little Ray and the snowshoer were in the habit of doing her ski exercises together. Their single-leg lunges made the floor shake, and she could hold her lunges longer than he could hold his. Little Ray could also hold her wall sits longer than the snowshoer could hold his. It was during the lunges and the wall sits that she would urge him to hang on a little longer. "Come on, don't quit," I could hear her say.

I also didn't tell my aunts that my mother had found a way to make the squats harder. She made the snowshoer lace his fingers behind her neck, and lock his legs around her waist; then she squatted. She was a big believer in deep squats, but she outweighed the snowshoer by ten or fifteen pounds. When he squatted—with her fingers laced behind his neck, and her legs locked around his waist—he really strained to finish his squats. He couldn't go as deep as she did. "Deeper!" I could hear her urging him. When I could hear them laughing, I knew he'd collapsed or lost his balance—with her still clinging to him—trying to finish too deep a squat.

I thought the way I imitated her overheard dialogue—the "Come on, don't quit" and the "Deeper!"—had the desired effect on my easily scandalized aunts, but their speechlessness deceived me. My early efforts at fiction writing failed. As Nora would tell me later, her mother and Aunt Martha didn't believe me.

"For Christ's sake, Adam—*everyone's* heard Ray doing her lunges, her wall sits, and her squats," Nora told me. "Ray tries to get *anyone* to do them with her—even *I've* done them with her!"

I was ashamed. I thought I'd been creative. I had refrained from telling Aunt Abigail and Aunt Martha how I overheard Little Ray's instructions to the snowshoer concerning the wall sits: "If you can't see your big toes, you're doing it wrong."

"I'm surprised you didn't try to make them believe the wall sits were sexual, too," Nora told me. "My mother and Aunt Martha are convinced that Ray and the little snowshoer are faking it. My mother and Aunt Martha think Ray is looking for a situation that will get you out of the Front Street house, before Nana goes off the rails and the diaper man becomes a fetus emeritus. They say the snowshoer is looking for a way to keep his job. They think Ray is Mr. Barlow's *beard*, Adam," Nora said.

"His *what?*" I asked her.

"Jesus, Adam—I forget you're only twelve or thirteen, or something," Nora said.

"I'm thirteen," I told her.

"A *beard* is a *front*, Adam. In Ray's case, she's pretending to be the girl-friend of a homosexual," Nora told me.

"She's not *pretending*—she really likes him, and he likes her!" I cried. "You didn't see how she kissed him, Nora."

"I haven't met the guy, Adam," Nora said. "Let's leave who's pretending, or not, for another day—okay, kiddo?"

"Okay," I told her.

Naturally, I would find a way to ask my mom about those black-and-whites that were haunting me—whatever they were. One night I phoned my mother in Stowe—at her dormitory for girl jocks.

"This is Molly," the night groomer said, and we went through our *Adam the Kid* routine before my mom came to the phone.

"Is this my Adam?" she said, as usual.

I didn't tell her I'd been having dreams. I said I'd been *seeing things*—usually when I was somewhere between asleep and awake. I told her I'd been *imagining* black-and-white photographs of what looked like actual people, places, and occurrences.

"You're being a little vague, sweetie," my mother said.

"Before it was a ski town, Aspen used to be a mining town—right?" I asked her.

"Silver mining. Describe what you've seen, sweetie."

I began with the guys in front of the shack, the stack of firewood, the bucksaw in the sawhorse; I didn't get to the different kinds of hats and caps. "Sounds like a mining camp in the 1880s—the early days," my mom said.

I got only as far as the mule train carrying heavy cargo above timberline—just the part about the narrow trail the mules and the wagons were on.

"Sounds like Independence Pass—ore wagons, raw silver, going to Leadville over the Continental Divide," Little Ray interrupted me.

I described the men, children, and dogs—their posing in front of the ramshackle buildings. I ended with, "Maybe it's a mine."

"Of course it is, Adam—it sounds like a daytime shift at the Smuggler Mine," my mom told me.

I barely mentioned the two miners underground—the one with the sledgehammer, the other tinkering with what might have been an explosive device. "I've seen those two—they're always setting the black-powder charges. Something must have gone wrong," my mother said.

"You've seen them?" I asked her.

"I've seen their ghosts, sweetie—you're seeing ghosts. This kind of ghost can't hurt you," my mom assured me.

"What about the well-dressed, bearded gentleman? He looks very refined; he looks brave but sad. Is he the kind of ghost who can hurt you?" I asked my mother.

"Poor Jerome," my mom said softly. "Jerome B. Wheeler won't hurt you."

I knew then what the three-story brick building was, without asking. The massive-looking brick rectangle was the Hotel Jerome. I asked my mom about the horse-drawn wagon.

"Oh, that's just a beer delivery," she said. I doubted that the horse's ghost was dangerous. And when I asked her about the shy, childlike hotel maid, Little Ray said, "Oh, I didn't know she died—I think she was Italian."

No—I didn't ask her about the boy, or the young man. His handsomeness, his childlike smile, his smallness alongside his tall snow shovel—that kid from the 1940s, whoever he was. I sensed he might have been a different kind of ghost, the kind who can hurt you. There was something about him that didn't look dead. I'm sure I saw skis leaning against the building.

"I have to go now, sweetie," my mother was whispering. "The ghosts can wait—they're good at waiting."

"Okay," I said. "When will I see you again?" I asked her.

"When the time is right," my mom said.

16.

WHAT HAPPENED THAT NIGHT

I once asked Nora if she brought her girlfriend, Em, to my mother's wedding to create a distraction—to overshadow the evident incredulity toward the unlikely lovers who were getting married. The circulating gossip, which was started by my aunts—namely, that my mom was Elliot Barlow's *beard*—was not as obvious as Nora's decision to be publicly out as a lesbian at a family wedding in her hometown. The submissive demeanor of the dollish and anxious-looking Em was belied by the reputation of her unruly and clamorous orgasms; as Nora had plainly put it, "Each orgasm sounds like it's her first or last time." The wedding guests who were staying at the Exeter Inn were visibly changed by the experience of overhearing Em's ridiculously loud and hysterical orgasms, particularly a contingent of the North Conway Norwegians. The girly-girl blondes, the ones Nora used to beat up, were looking at Nora with newly frightened eyes.

But Nora denied there was any willfulness behind her bringing Em to the wedding. "I don't have that kind of foresight, kiddo," Nora said. She told me she made an easy choice: her childhood bed in Uncle Martin and Aunt Abigail's faculty apartment or a bigger bed at the Exeter Inn, where Nora could have noisy sex with Em. In retrospect, I might have been wrong to ask if Nora had purposely shortened Emily's name to Em—as a rough but abbreviated way of dominating her. So much was violently expended in a single one of Em's orgasms, it's possible to imagine that the last three letters of Emily's name had been lost in the climaxing process.

That the bride wore white did not escape my aunts' condemnation. They were quick to judge both real and imagined violations of Little Ray's virginity and purity.

"A bride who's had a child does not wear white, Rachel," Aunt Abigail told my mother.

"Not to mention a bride who had a child the way you did, Ray," Aunt Martha chimed in.

"Baloney," my mom told them. "I'm wearing a white wedding dress. Molly helped me pick it out."

The wedding was the first occasion any of us had to meet Molly, the trail groomer. If it came to a showdown, the snowcat operator looked as if she could go toe-to-toe with Nora. In the little snowshoer's estimation, Molly and Nora each weighed 175 pounds. They were two big and strong young women. Over the course of the wedding weekend, those two kept eyeing each other—as if they were dying to get into a fight, or into some other trouble.

The sleeping arrangements for the wedding weekend were too confusing for scrutiny; not even my aunts could be bothered with who slept where, or with whom. Those girl jocks from Stowe, used to dormitory living, pitched three tents in the backyard of the Front Street house. My grandmother felt their tents were too near the garden, where the wedding tent was. One of the girl jocks brought her boyfriend; their tent, nearest the ornamental birdbath in the garden, was the smallest one. Two of the girl jocks—the same two who took showers together—had their own tent, too. The biggest tent was for the rest of the girl jocks from Stowe; there were three or four of them, and they pitched their tent on the former croquet court, unused for years. Nana said the tent wasn't safe on the old croquet court, where she predicted someone would come to harm or be killed.

Yes, the croquet court had been improperly cared for, but I doubted it was capable of murder. A mishap had once caused a gardener to quit: an old wicket, lurking just above ground, had wrecked his lawn mower. Years ago, someone had used a croquet mallet to hammer the stakes and the wickets into the lawn. Principal Brewster had been blamed for this, but I'll bet the pounder was Nora, not the principal emeritus—not even before he was in diapers, when he was capable of wielding a mallet. Over time, a few of the wickets had worked their way back above ground—or someone had pulled them level to the lawn. I'll bet the *wicket-puller* was the diaper man; the infant emeritus was the only member of the family who'd played croquet on the backyard lawn.

My grandmother was distraught over the excessive bathroom use by what she called "the tent dwellers," but what were the girl jocks supposed to do— go in the garden? Nana had already accused the boyfriend of peeing in the birdbath, solely on the grounds that she'd seen no birds bathing there since he'd arrived.

I'll admit that the boyfriend, in the tent nearest the birdbath, was a dipshit ski bum. He was a worthless whiner who struck me as too lazy to look very far for a bathroom. He obviously thought I was older than fourteen, because he complained to me about his girlfriend's yeast infection. "I didn't come all this way to sleep in a tent with a girl who can't or won't do it," he told me. "She should have *said* she had a friggin' yeast infection!"

Naturally, I asked Nora what a yeast infection was. I must have been concerned that I could catch it. Nora made me tell her who had one, and how I'd heard about it. "The girl jock with the boyfriend who pees in the birdbath—*she* has it. *He* told me," I confided to Nora. I could see that Em was as fearful of the yeast infection as I was; she buried her face in Nora's boobs and shook against her. That was how the yeast infection made me feel, too.

"Relax, you wimps—you're safe," Nora told us. She then told Molly and my mom about the incident.

The night groomer said she'd handle it. I didn't realize Molly meant she would *handle* the boyfriend—the alleged birdbath pisser—but Molly dragged him out of his small tent when he had only his boxers on, and she held his head underwater in the birdbath. Whatever was in the birdbath, it was clear the ski bum couldn't breathe in it. The girl jock with the yeast infection halfheartedly protested the snowcat operator's way of handling the situation. "You may tell everyone you know about your yeast infection, Nelly," the trail groomer said, "but I don't want Adam the Kid hearing about it." Nelly didn't know her boyfriend had been advertising her yeast infection; she wandered off in the garden, seemingly indifferent to the prospect of the ski bum dying in the birdbath, but Molly had made her point and stopped drowning him. This was the afternoon of the day before the wedding, and Nelly's boyfriend packed up the small tent and his other belongings and left, unceremoniously, before the festivities started. There were two stone sparrows, permanently perched on the rim of the birdbath; throughout my childhood, one of those never-singing songbirds had a chipped beak. Only those sparrows made of stone knew for sure if the ski bum had ever peed in the birdbath. Nelly moved into the big tent on the former croquet court with her fellow girl jocks.

My grandmother was right: the girl jocks took over the bathrooms in the Front Street house. There were wet towels everywhere; those vigorous girls were always taking a bath or a shower. My mom had designated my attic bathroom, adjoined to my bedroom, *off-limits*. She'd moved her things into my bedroom and was sleeping (as usual) in my bed with me. Molly was sleeping in my mother's bedroom on the second floor.

"I'm not antisocial, Kid," the night groomer told me. "I'm just too big to sleep on the ground in a tent with a bunch of women—talking all night about women's stuff." In the terrifying context of the unexplained yeast infection—its cause, its consequences, its potential as a contagion—my fourteen-year-old imagination would make too much of what Molly meant by *women's stuff*. I'm not saying it's the sole reason I waited so long to get married—almost as long as I put off going to Aspen—but, for some years, the repercussions of *women's stuff* seriously affected my imagination.

My mom could sense I was disquieted by these things I was hearing about but not understanding: for starters, the wedding guests whose sleep and peace of mind were disturbed by Em's soul-searching orgasms. And now came the dark and undisclosed mysteries and ramifications of Nelly's yeast infection—the near drowning of the boyfriend who dared to speak of it, and Molly's decision not to sleep in the tent with the girl jocks and their *women's stuff*.

"In the first place, sweetie, you should stop thinking about Em—most of all, the unusual sounds she makes," my mother advised me. "I can only speculate that Nora could be a somewhat traumatizing girlfriend experience—especially if Nora were your first girlfriend." I could see this point, of course, though this did not relieve me from hearing Em's *unusual sounds* in my imagination.

In a similarly dismissive fashion, my mom tried to reassure me about Nelly's yeast infection. "Nelly's going to be okay, sweetie—yeast infections usually aren't life-threatening. Nelly just goes on and on about hers, but every woman has had one or will have one. It's not a big deal," my mother told me. "Okay, there's pain, there's itching, there's the cottage-cheese discharge."

"The *what?*" I asked her.

"From your vagina—you should stop thinking about it, sweetie."

"I can see why Molly doesn't want to sleep in the tent with the jocks, talking all night about the cottage-cheese stuff," I told my mom.

"I need Molly near me, sweetie—not in the tent. I can't get into or out of my wedding dress if Molly doesn't help me," my mother said.

I had seen the white wedding dress. It was hanging from the shower rod in my attic bathroom. My mom said the steam from the shower would keep it wrinkle-free. Yes, it was a complicated dress, but I hadn't realized it was a two-woman job—just to put on the dress and take it off. The business about the girl jocks taking showers day and night—not to mention the two girl jocks who slept in a separate tent and took their showers together—didn't enter into our conversation. My mother could see I was struggling to under-stand the complexities of her wedding dress.

"The dress has to be laced up at the back, sweetie—it has to be as tightly laced as a corset," my mom tried to explain.

I must have nodded, or otherwise pretended to understand. I refrained from asking what a corset was. I decided I should stop thinking about all of it. I would stop asking questions; I would not look puzzled. I decided to adopt an uncharacteristic nonchalance. I would henceforth appear to understand, or be indifferent to, everything.

Yes, it was a pose. It went on for years. In truth, I understood very little; I rarely felt indifferent (or impartial, or unconcerned) about anything. Maybe you're not supposed to be fourteen when your mother gets married for the first time, and of course there were contributing factors, but that wedding weekend, on the evening before the marriage ceremony, I made a choice. I came to a very conscious decision. I would be aloof, detached—even in-curious and uninterested—before I would allow myself to be condescended to. Heretofore, only the snowshoer had never condescended to me. Surely, this was a big part of the reason I wanted Elliot Barlow to marry my mom. Henceforth, I decided, I would only be myself—that is, truthful about who I was and all the things I was curious about—in my imagination. This meant, of course, that I could only be myself—this uncool and searching person—in my *writing*.

What a turning point that wedding weekend was—a watershed weekend for me. My grandmother had asked me to flood the birdbath to overflowing with the garden hose. I knew Nana was hell-bent on ridding her garden of the bad boyfriend's urine, real or imagined. The silent stone sparrows were as disinclined to sing as ever. Whatever they'd seen, there would be no songs about it.

After I flooded the birdbath, I took a closer look at my mom's white wedding dress when I moved it from the shower rod. This was when I was showering and getting dressed for the rehearsal. I could see the row of eyelets, which were loosely laced together at the back of the dress; it appeared that the laces ran along her spine, all the way from her waist to where they were tied between her shoulder blades. Even wrinkle-free and at rest on the coat hanger, it did not look like a comfortable dress. I noted that my mother's shoulders would be bare; I worried that everybody would see the straps of her bra, but I could see there were cups for her breasts in the front of the dress. Did the dress have a kind of built-in bra? Given my newly acquired composure, my adopted insouciance, I was determined not to ask my mom how she would manage her bust in the viselike grip of such a dress.

We spoke instead of the diminishing water pressure we had noticed in our respective showers. My mother had showered and dressed for the rehearsal in her bathroom and bedroom on the second floor; Molly had prevented the girl jocks from using that bathroom. Her shower, my mom told me, had "piss-poor" water pressure, and she had run out of hot water. I was tempted to ask why the girl jocks were always showering, but I resolved to be steadfast in my indifference. I was making up myself, like a fictional character. I was creating the adult I wanted to become, which I saw as inseparable from my becoming a fiction writer. In longing for the infinite powers of detached observation, I was becoming a third-person omniscient narrator—if only in my mind.

No, I hadn't written anything—hence the only fiction I was composing was myself. I'm not generalizing. I don't know if other writers, when they're growing up, go through a similar disconnect between the hesitant teenagers they are and the all-knowing narrators they seek to become.

I practiced my new persona on Henrik at the rehearsal. In my grandmother's garden, the wedding tent was set up for the marriage ceremony—the aisle was the path between the flower beds, and the folding chairs circled the sacred spot where the vows would be exchanged. Henrik was slouched in two chairs—khakis, a blue blazer, a blue button-down shirt, the top button of the shirt unbuttoned, his loosened necktie a statement of indolence. Henrik had his lacrosse stick with him, as if it were needed at the rehearsal.

"The ring bearer is supposed to be a child, Adam—the best man is rarely the offspring of the bride," Henrik informed me.

Never an original boy, Henrik. He had somehow managed to graduate from Exeter. In the fall, he would be attending one of those second-choice schools in the South. Henrik had based his college choice on where he wanted to play lacrosse—his foremost consideration concerned where the weather was warm in the spring. There was no spring to speak of in New Hampshire. At Exeter, at the start of our season for spring sports, the track team had to share the Thompson Cage with the baseball and lacrosse teams. Outdoors, on the playing fields, there was often snow or thawing mud.

As for wedding protocol, Henrik had been listening to Aunt Abigail and his mother—Aunt Martha's perpetual chiming-in.

I sighed—as Nora would have sighed, I hoped. Even Henrik's disapproval was conventional. I tried to convey this in a single sigh. "Oh, Henrik, don't you see? I am the best man because I brought them together,"

I told him. "I am the ring bearer because I'm the youngest child in the immediate family, aren't I?" I asked him. "Even you, Henrik, treat me as if I were still a child."

We were both stunned. Henrik had never heard me speak this way, and I didn't recognize my tone of voice, though I liked the sound of it. The lacrosse stick slipped from Henrik's hands, unbefitting of the tireless midfielder he imagined he was.

"I'm sorry!" Henrik suddenly said, recovering his lacrosse stick but not his jockish self-confidence. "I regret how I treated you, Adam—how I bullied you, when you were a child." I was unprepared for my doltish cousin to be contrite. Contrition was as new to Henrik as the new me was to me. Yet I'd managed to channel Nora's sigh. Luckily, Molly reminded me of my role in the rehearsal in progress. Henrik had distracted me, and I was holding things up.

"Is this Adam the Kid—Ray's one and only—or is this some other Adam, up to no good?" the snowcat operator suddenly said in my ear, bending over me.

"It's Adam the Kid, Molly," I answered her, as I was used to answering her on the phone.

"Well, Kid, if I'm the maid of honor and you're the best man, we have some rehearsing to do," Molly reminded me. I'm guessing that the dick-shrinking look the trail groomer gave to Henrik and his irrelevant lacrosse stick only further contributed to Henrik's transformative act of contrition. Molly could shrink your dick with a look.

As for wedding protocol, there were many more bridesmaids than there were groomsmen. I'm sure Aunt Abigail and Aunt Martha had something to say about the inappropriateness of this imbalance, but I never heard what those two had to say. One of the things I most enjoyed about my mother's wedding was that my aunts were rendered relatively speechless—no doubt they were aghast that the wedding was happening at all, whatever the protocol.

Molly was the maid of honor, but all the girl jocks were bridesmaids. My mom had asked Nora to be a bridesmaid, but Nora declined. All Nora said about it was: "I better not leave Em alone. She gets a little strange in a crowd, when she's not with me."

"Then it's best not to leave her alone, dear," my mother told Nora. In time, I would see how Em behaved in a crowd when she wasn't with Nora.

There were only three groomsmen. My aunts, I'm sure, were critical of the snowshoer's choices. Aunt Abigail and Aunt Martha probably thought

that Mr. Barlow was ingratiating himself to the Brewster family by choosing Uncle Martin and Uncle Johan, but the snowshoer genuinely liked my
uncles, and they liked him. I did not yet understand why Elliot chose the
academy wrestling coach as his third groomsman. I didn't know the snowshoer was a wrestler. The coach was a handsome, wavy-haired man with a
winning smile. He and Elliot seemed to be good friends. The wrestling coach
was broad-shouldered, barrel-chested, and bull-necked. Nelly, the girl jock
with the yeast infection, mistook him for the wedding bouncer.

"Do you have yeast on the brain, Nelly?" Molly asked her. "Nora and I
are the wedding bouncers." I noticed this made Nora smile, and Em clung
all the closer to her.

When I asked my mom if she thought the wrestling coach was handsome,
I already knew what she would say.

"Yes, but . . ."

"But he's too big?" I asked her.

"Yes," Little Ray said softly.

We got our first look at Elliot's parents, John and Susan Barlow, at the
rehearsal. "Handsome and *small*," my mother whispered to me.

"You mean him?" I asked her, with a nod to John Barlow.

"I mean both of them," my mom whispered.

We couldn't have cared less about Nana's opinion—namely, that the Barlows were a fine old Bostonian family. I knew my mother was infatuated with
anything or anyone Austrian; there was more about the Barlows that was
European than anything that spoke of Boston. I knew Elliot had distanced
himself from his parents' crime and spy novels, but the Barlows' Foreign Service training—their diplomatic schooling and international experience—
stood out. An aura of intrigue emanated from them. A mountaineering life
had made them fit and permanently tanned.

Not even my aunts could have bitched about the Barlows' embrace of
wedding protocol. It was completely appropriate that the groom's parents
were hosting the rehearsal dinner at the Exeter Inn. Nor could the Barlows
be blamed for Uncle Johan's insistence in speaking German to them, or
Uncle Martin's incessant admiration (and reiteration) of the plot of *The
Kiss in Düsseldorf*. It wasn't the Barlows who were lecturing nonstop about
Kriminalliteratur and the underappreciated brilliance of the modern espionage novel.

That I was both the best man and the ring bearer was a mere glitch in
wedding protocol. The real problem was the infantile father of the bride.

How could the diaper man manage to give the bride away? The phony emeritus appeared not to know that Little Ray was getting married, or even what a wedding was.

My grandmother had hired a live-in nurse. Dottie was no fool. A flinty woman my aunts' age or older, Nurse Dottie was from New Hampshire's neighboring state of Maine; yet the way Dottie spoke of her home state made us feel there was an ocean and a different language between us. The idea that the diaper man could fulfill his function as father of the bride was not to Dottie's liking.

"Could a baby give a bride away, Mrs. Brewster?" the nurse had asked my grandmother. I took Dottie's side. I was also grateful to Dottie that (in her care) the diaper baby was no longer permitted to wander the Front Street house at night; since her arrival, I hadn't seen or smelled him in my attic bedroom, or heard his creak on the attic stairs. Yet Nana and my mom wanted the deluded diaper man to be at the wedding, whatever came of it. What for? To stand in close proximity to the wedding vows, which the infant emeritus couldn't possibly comprehend?

As Dottie said to me at the rehearsal: "It's not what we *woulda done* in Maine." She'd managed to dress the diaper dad for the occasion—a dark suit, a white shirt with cuff links, a matching pocket handkerchief and necktie. It wasn't Dottie's fault that Principal Brewster put his necktie in his mouth, or stuck the tip of it up one of his nostrils—or took off his cuff links and played with them in the birdbath. In Nurse Dottie's opinion, this harmless child's play was to be expected. We were lucky, Dottie pointed out, that the diaper guy hadn't taken off his diaper and played with whatever was in it.

"What I don't like, Adam," Dottie confided to me, "is how the poor fool keeps eyeballin' your mother—like he don't trust her, or somethin'—and, if looks could kill, how the diaper baby keeps lookin' at that little groom!" I'd seen those looks—delusional, to be kind. It's a wonder to me how we got through the rehearsal without a hitch—worse, with no forewarning of what would happen at the actual event.

The diaper man did not attend the rehearsal dinner at the Exeter Inn. The befuddled emeritus was left at the Front Street house, where Dottie could take charge of him—where we could, for the moment, forget about him. There was a tent outdoors at the Exeter Inn, too—the rehearsal dinner would be there.

It was a warm July night. I have no idea if the Exeter Inn had air-conditioning in 1956—likely not, because many of the guest-room windows were open. Before the music started in our tent, we could hear snippets of conversation and occasional laughter from the open guest-room windows of the inn.

As for the music we awaited in our tent, Nora had forewarned me that her dad and Uncle Johan were providing it. Thank goodness they weren't performing it, but the music was their idea. Nora and I knew this was a dangerous plan: to match my uncles' deplorable taste with the Barlows' European refinement. Nora had predicted strippers from Boston, grinding to country music. But the musical entertainment had not arrived. Em and Nora were nowhere to be seen. Nora might have been dreading the musical entertainment, or so I imagined.

Not so. Nora told me later that they'd gone to their room in the inn because Em wanted to get a jacket or a sweater—something to put on if the weather turned cooler later, under the tent—and while they were in their room, they started fooling around. I guess one thing led to another. Suddenly we heard the keening cries of Em's orgasm; I'd heard nothing like it, not even in foreign films with subtitles. Not even Uncle Martin and Uncle Johan thought Em's orgasm was funny—they weren't laughing. This was a climax that could end the world. Em's orgasm went on and on—it just kept going. One of our waitresses under the tent appeared to be mentally disordered by how long the ecstatic screams lasted—she lost control of her tray, a water pitcher was spilled, and the waitress dropped to her knees to recover her equilibrium.

"Merciful God!" Aunt Abigail cried.

"Someone should call the police, and an ambulance," Aunt Martha chimed in.

In the context of what was going on, it was not clear if their remarks concerned Em's orgasm or the unbalanced waitress. My grandmother had covered her ears with both hands, her lips silently repeating a passage she'd memorized and only she could hear—from Moby-Dick, I'm certain. The white whale wouldn't have survived an orgasm of this kind; harpoons were no match for it. At long last there came a gasp, a sorrowful inhalation all of us heard; we held our breath in anticipation of the crescendo, but no cry came. Em had reached her peak. We were surrounded by a shattering silence.

"You should stop thinking about it, sweetie," my mother whispered to me. I still can't stop thinking about it. My mom was seated at the dinner table between Molly and me. We were across the table from the Barlows, the three of them. Elliot was the littlest one. He sat, like a happy child, between his parents.

"That was no quickie," the trail groomer said, to no one in particular. The little English teacher was beaming.

"That's the kind of thing you would expect to hear more frequently in Italy—on a summer night, with the windows open," John Barlow said. He spoke as if he had already written these words.

"Oh, once or twice—when we were in Italy," Sarah Barlow said, with a wave of her small hand. "But, honestly, John, I can't remember ever overhearing anything quite like that—not even in Italy."

"Not even in Italy," the snowshoer repeated reverentially, smiling sweetly across the table at the three of us—my mother and the snowcat operator and me.

All of us were transported in the throes of Em's orgasm. No one noticed the arrival of the solitary and elderly musician, though someone should have spotted the lederhosen he was wearing—not to mention the Tyrolean hat with the feather—and the instrument the old man was carrying was not your everyday stringed instrument. We should have seen the small table and single chair that stood apart from the dinner tables under the tent; a microphone was affixed to the side of the table facing the dinner guests, and the periphery of our tent was here and there surrounded by amplifiers. Yet not even Uncle Martin and Uncle Johan saw the zither player enter the tent and take his seat at that little table, and those two were expecting him. Those two had found him and hired him. As Uncle Martin would tell me, years later: "You can find anyone you're looking for in New York, Adam." Even an old Austrian zither-meister.

"Just the man to entertain the Barlows, with their postwar background in occupied Vienna!" Uncle Johan told me later in the evening. "And who better to play the 'Bridal Chorus'—'Treulich geführt'!—at the snowshoer's wedding? Wagner's *Lohengrin* on a zither!" Uncle Johan cried.

Only my uncles would have thought of and found a zither player. Hadn't Uncle Martin and Uncle Johan taken me to the Franklin Theatre to see Carol Reed's *The Third Man*? It was one of those nights when the Franklin was showing a classic. *The Third Man*, from Graham Greene's screenplay, was released in 1949, when I would have been too young to see it, but during exam periods at the University of New Hampshire, the Franklin occasionally revived these great old films—the films that everyone should see.

The poor Barlows! How many of their American friends and acquaintances had imposed "The Third Man Theme" on them—or "The Harry Lime Theme," as the famous zither creation of Anton Karas was also known? For many Americans, as the three little Barlows well understood, *The Third Man*—that movie with its melancholic music—amounted to all we knew about Vienna. All Little Ray knew about Austria was the skiing and the skiers, but even my mom had heard "The Third Man Theme"—even my mother remembered the scene at the Viennese Ferris wheel (das Wiener Riesenrad, as Uncle Johan would have called it) and those wet sewers under the city, where Harry Lime pays for his terrible crimes.

When the music started in the rehearsal dinner tent, only the little Barlows bowed their heads—not in reverence but out of their painfully repeated exposure to that unhappy song. I'm sure they could have closed their eyes and seen the credits roll over that close-up of a zither's strings. And who can forget the haunted instrumental playing over that story of doomed love and unspeakable crimes? Just what you want to hear when you're tying the knot!

"*Der Dritte Mann!*" Uncle Johan cried—as if Anton Karas himself were playing the zither, or Harry Lime had escaped the sewers and was slithering into our tent. For once, I'm ashamed to say, I had to agree with my aunts.

"What were you thinking, Martin? 'The Third Man Theme' isn't *wedding* music, you moron!" Aunt Abigail abused Uncle Martin.

"Nobody gets married to a *zither*, Johan," Aunt Martha chimed in, but my uncles didn't hear their disapproving wives. Uncle Martin and Uncle Johan were doubled over with their typically inappropriate laughter, while the elderly Austrian zither-meister kept playing that inescapably sad song.

Nora had reappeared with Em. "Where are the strippers?" Nora whispered in my ear. "Even strippers from Boston would have been better than this." No one dared to look at Nora—except for Molly, who was looking Nora up and down—and the meek, nonspeaking Em shrank from the looks she was getting, hiding herself behind Nora's broad back. "Leather shorts with suspenders would never be my choice," Nora was saying, scrutinizing the old Austrian in the lederhosen with the Tyrolean hat—a green felt hat with a wide brim and a crown that tapered to a point. "I'm betting a pheasant was killed for that fucking feather," Nora added to her assessment.

As befitted proper wedding protocol, John and Sarah Barlow gave a gracious speech, welcoming my mom and me to the little Barlow family; there were other speeches, but I don't remember most of them, only that Uncle Johan spoke in German. Henrik grew more profuse in his apologies to me for his formerly loutish behavior. The only signs of the Henrik I remembered were his repeated efforts to get Em's attention by doing dumb tricks with his lacrosse stick. This included tossing a dinner roll to her, but Nora caught the roll and rifled it back at her cousin. Em, clinging constantly to Nora, showed no interest in Henrik or his stupid lacrosse stick.

The repertoire of the zither-meister was no match for Anton Karas. The only songs I heard, over and over again—I mean, in addition to the countless repetitions of "The Harry Lime Theme"—were also recognizable to me from *The Third Man*. The slow "Das alte Lied" ("That Dear Old Song"), the more sprightly "The Café Mozart Waltz," and the most lugubrious "Farewell to Vienna." That last one plays over the ending of the film, the saddest song of all—when Anna (Alida Valli) leaves the cemetery where Harry (Orson Welles) has been buried, leaving Holly (Joseph Cotten) loveless and alone.

"How are we going to dance to this shit—isn't there dancing tomorrow?" Nora asked me. Yes, there would be dancing, I knew—after the marriage ceremony, and both during and after the reception dinner—or so I'd been told. I was aware of the infinite preparations: the choreography required to rearrange the folding chairs from the ceremony for the dinner tables; the necessary steps to keep the elevated platform for the dancing accessible under the wedding tent; where the amplifiers for "Here Comes the Bride" should be located; and, now that I knew there was a zither, where the zither-meister should be seated. The thought of Wagner's "Bridal Chorus" from *Lohengrin* on a zither concerned me more than what we were going to dance to, but I merely reminded Nora of the waltz in the old Austrian's repertoire.

"What waltz, Adam? You heard a waltz?" Nora asked me.

I pointed out that the zither man had played "The Café Mozart Waltz."

"It went over my head," Nora said. "Did you hear a waltz?" she asked Em, who violently shook her head and squinted her eyes shut. I wish she hadn't done that, but I no longer imagine her climaxing this way—at the frightening apex of her screams, or during the gasping inhalation all of us heard, before her toe-curling silence.

I remember Molly's speech. It seemed impromptu, but it was incisive and short, and the snowcat operator had waited for the end of the evening. There was a moment when the zither man was quaffing a beer, when the abiding sorrow of our musical entertainment fell silent. The only one moving between the tables was that waitress who'd been brought to her knees by the keen of Em's orgasm agonies. The waitress had somewhat recovered herself, we'd all observed. She was moving very slowly and carefully among the dinner tables, gathering up the dessert dishes and empty glasses.

At this lull in the evening's festivities, the trail groomer stood. The clarity of her dessertspoon striking her water glass brought us to attention, briefly causing the old zither-meister to choke on his beer.

"I want to say something," Molly told us; she put one hand on my mom's shoulder, while pointing to the little snowshoer with her dessertspoon. "These two are meant for each other," the night groomer said. "If there's anyone here who thinks otherwise, you should talk to me." Yes, Molly was used to being on a mountain in a snowcat when everyone else was asleep—she was not afraid of the dark, or of much else. She kept her hand on my mother when she spoke, and she'd pointed to the snowshoer, but the trail groomer was looking at Aunt Abigail and Aunt Martha, who quickly looked away. When Molly sat down, I was thinking it might be a good time to leave—knowing we had another night of reveling to the zither ahead of us. Other people were leaving.

That was when Henrik, cradling a cupcake in his lacrosse stick, took a sidearm shot at Em—an errant shot, but one with a lot of zip on it. The untouched cupcake was chocolate with a cranberry frosting. It struck the white apron of the waitress who'd already been emotionally shattered by Em's orgasm. The zooming cupcake hit her in the area of her lower abdomen, below the tray she was carrying.

"Oh, that poor girl—she's having a rough night," my mother said, squeezing my hand at the clatter of the falling tray with the dessert dishes and empty glasses. The zither-meister misinterpreted the meaning of the clamor—he instantly resumed playing.

Naturally, the waitress had screamed. To the dinner guests who hadn't seen the flying cupcake, she sounded as if she'd been shot. The waitress hadn't seen the cupcake, either. Once more, she'd fallen to her knees—this time, she was clutching her lower abdomen. Of course the cupcake had rolled away, but the cranberry frosting was prominent on the waitress's white apron. The dark-red, sticky stuff was smeared on the waitress's hands. She may have thought it was blood.

What I said to Nora, when more people were leaving, was not intended to be unkind. Yes, now I know it was thoughtless of me not to consider how my remark might be misunderstood by Em. "After a night like this," I said to Nora, with Em hugging her, "it's hard to imagine that the wedding won't be an anticlimax." Em responded with another scary inhalation.

"Merciful God!" Aunt Abigail was soon crying, again.

"Someone should call the police, and an ambulance," Aunt Martha once more chimed in.

As before, given the hysteria at hand, it was difficult to know if my aunts were anxious about the fallen waitress—now wailing to herself in a fetal position—or if they were more concerned for Em's fragile state of mind. Em had dissolved into tears—she was sobbing inconsolably in Nora's arms.

For my inadvertent role in making Em unhappy, I felt very sorry. Nora knew I hadn't meant anything judgmental by my anticlimax remark. What did I know about female orgasms? At fourteen—actually, at any age—I would never have judged Em for hers. But that's how it was. This is what happened that night at the Exeter Inn, and it was only the rehearsal dinner.

17.

SON OF THE BRIDE

I said too much to Nora about the snowshoer kiss. The beginner writer in me had been trying too hard. I overdescribed the way my mom kissed Elliot Barlow at the Front Street dining-room table. Too much detail. I overdid the part concerning the effect of that lingering kiss on the snowshoer. This was pure speculation on my part—my teenage skills at storytelling were amateurish. I never wanted Nora to know how my mother had kissed me when I was thirteen, but Nora knew there was something I hadn't told her. The way I wrung my hands gave me away.

The night of the rehearsal dinner, I made plans to meet Nora and Em for breakfast at the Exeter Inn on the following morning, the day of the wedding. I knew the girl jocks would be competing with the caterers in the Front Street kitchen. My mom and Molly had forewarned me that I should stay out of the girl jocks' way when they were making breakfast. It would be chaos in the kitchen, where the caterers were eager to get an early start on the reception dinner.

On a July Sunday morning, Nora and Em and I were ahead of the brunch crowd. Our rehearsal-dinner guests were sleeping in or having room service. The sophisticated little Barlows struck me as a couple attuned to room service. Like some other Norwegians I would later know, the North Conway contingent were hearty drinkers—they were definitely sleeping in. The girly-girl blondes were no doubt hiding themselves from Nora and Em.

The three of us were virtually alone in the dining room of the inn, where we were relieved not to see the twice-stricken waitress of the night before—the impressionable young woman who'd been dropped to her knees, first by Em's orgasm, then by Henrik's cupcake. I hoped the much-abused waitress was sleeping in, if she wasn't already in therapy.

Our only companion in the dining room was the solitary Austrian musician. He'd brought his zither to breakfast, where we feared he might start strumming the strings. The lederhosen and the Tyrolean hat made us think the Austrian was fanatical—maybe he couldn't go for as long as an hour without playing "The Third Man Theme" to himself. His waiter, an older man, had removed the place setting opposite him. Thus the beloved instrument was in reach across the table from the musician, though he not once touched it or spoke to it. They sat together without a word between them. They resembled an elderly, long-married couple—devoted to each other without conversation. I knew we still had to get through the "Bridal Chorus" on a zither, but I was overlooking what else might be Wagnerian about my mom's marriage ceremony or its immediate aftermath.

At fourteen, I lacked the perspective to see our suddenly expanding Brewster family in comparison to other families. Given the dramatic effects on our rehearsal dinner caused by Em's enduring orgasm and Henrik's cupcake missile, I was naïve to imagine that my mother's wedding could be anticlimactic. Considering what happened with Nora and Em after our breakfast, I should have known the day ahead would be no less awkward.

Nora—in the act of paying our waiter, the older man—spoke to me (almost casually) while she was looking at Em. "About the snowshoer kiss, as you call it, Adam—Em and I have had a hard time visualizing it, for more than a year." I was further disconcerted by Em's frown, and the way she nervously nodded her head. I couldn't look at her, or at Nora. "We just can't see it, kiddo," Nora told me, taking my hand. "If we go upstairs to our room, maybe you can show us."

I noticed the plural. Holding my hand, Nora led me upstairs. Em followed. I wouldn't have dared to say Nora shared any genetic traits with those Brewster girls. Like the hips Nora had in common with her mother, an off-limits subject, I would have been risking my life to suggest that Nora was similar to her mom and Aunt Martha in other respects. Yet Nora had autocratic tendencies. Her sexual politics may have been at the opposite end of the spectrum from my aunts' beliefs, but Nora was a sexual autocrat and a bully. The complicated part, for me, was how much I revered her—and agreed with her.

It was with the greatest trepidation that I entered the room Nora and Em were sharing at the Exeter Inn. The view of the tent for the rehearsal dinner was the first thing I saw out the open window. Apparently, the tent wasn't going to be removed on a Sunday. I tried not to look at the unmade bed, the sight of which recalled Em's plaintive wails. The rumpled bed represented a gladiatorial arena where Em had been sexually slain, repeatedly.

"What I don't get, Adam," Nora was saying, "is how you could know so much about a kiss by just watching it. I mean, there's a limit to what you can see—isn't there, kiddo?" I saw that Em had opened her mouth; she was pointing to her tongue. It was unnecessary for Nora to tell me what Em meant, but she did. "There's a lot of kissing that happens inside the mouth, Adam," Nora explained. I knew I wasn't in the same league with Nora or Em when it came to kissing. All I could think was that Em had the tiniest teeth and the pinkest tongue. "Don't even think about kissing me, Adam," Nora suddenly said. I wasn't. "You can't kiss me, kiddo—I'm your cousin." I was relieved to hear this, but not for long. Em suddenly moved closer. She'd shut her eyes and had lifted her face to me. She wasn't exactly grimacing or squinting—her lips were only slightly parted. Em wasn't so much waiting for me to kiss her as she was resigned to it. She and Nora must have talked about it, and Em appeared to be bracing herself for it. "Go on, kiss her," Nora told me. "Show her how Ray kissed the snowshoer—then Em will show me how Ray did it."

I'd only recently decided to be cool and detached. I was experimenting with being aloof and uncaring. This new act didn't fit very well with my most vivid memory of the snowshoer kiss my mom gave me, which I did my best to demonstrate on Em. Em was a pretty but meek-looking mouse to behold, even with her eyes closed and her lips open. I could not dispel a conflicting image I had of the compliant and nonspeaking Em—specifically, the roaring lioness I knew was alive inside her. Of course I was attracted to her.

When it came to the meeting of mouths for a kiss, I was a novice. When I made contact with Em's expectant mouth, I didn't know where our noses should go. Even with her eyes closed, Em managed to show me. Since Em had shut her eyes, it seemed disrespectful to keep mine open. Furthermore, I wasn't used to looking at anyone this closely. However, when we started kissing and I closed my eyes, I was upset by a sudden and unwelcome flashback— my mother athletically straddling me, pinning me to my bed in the attic. Here was another conflicting image to brush aside, in order to concentrate on the kissing.

Em didn't respond to my kiss, not even a little. I touched her tongue with my tongue, but her tongue never moved on its own—only because I was pushing it around. If Em leaned into me, just a little, that was because I pressed myself against her—as my mom had pressed herself against me. Em was merely pushing back.

It would be wishful thinking on my part to say that Em's breathing quickened, or became irregular in any way. It didn't. There was an ever-steady flow of air from Em's nostrils, soft and warm against my cheek, while I went on kissing her. I believe I was being faithful to the way my mother had kissed me, but I didn't remember (or I'd lost track of) how she'd stopped. As for my remaining cool and detached, I didn't. Once I started kissing Em, I couldn't stop.

"For Christ's sake, kiddo, that's enough—you're going to hurt yourself," Nora said. Em was nodding her head in that irritating way she had. I was not aware I'd been straining, though as soon as Nora spoke and I stopped kissing Em, I suddenly felt I had pulled a muscle in my neck.

I was unprepared for the way Em hurled herself into Nora's arms—not to mention how aggressively Em began to kiss her. It was hard to be a bystander to such an assault. Surely I hadn't kissed Em as savagely as Em was kissing Nora, or had I? Now my tongue was numb, as if I'd suffered a protracted dental procedure with repeated procaine injections. Or perhaps watching the way Em kissed Nora had numbed my tongue. I wanted Em to kiss me like that.

"That's enough, Em—for Christ's sake, *stop!*" Nora said, turning away from her. Set free from performing the snowshoer kiss, Em was panting like a dog—the kiss had winded her.

"There's no way you just *saw* your mom plant that kiss on the snowshoer, Adam—don't try to bullshit me," Nora said. "Did Little Ray plant that kiss on *you?* Don't lie to me, kiddo." Em was nodding again, in her fashion. I was exposed, or my mother was, and I knew it.

"My mom just wanted to show me how you do a kiss like that. She was just showing me—she didn't mean it!" I blurted out.

Nora held out her arms to me; she spoke very gently. "Come here, sweetie," she said, my mother's word for me. I went to Nora and let her hug me; I needed someone to hug me. To my surprise, Em came closer and hugged me between her and Nora.

"My mom said you're not fooling around when you kiss someone like that," I told them. I was crying. "Ray told me you better know what you mean—you better know what you're promising—when you kiss someone like that," I went on (and on) to them. I could feel Em's head nodding against my back, and Nora hugged me harder.

"That's all true, Adam," Nora said softly. "But maybe Ray shouldn't have kissed *you* like that, kiddo."

"Maybe she shouldn't have," I whispered. I could feel Em nodding her head harder, but she no longer irritated me—she meant well. It was a lonely but strangely comforting feeling, to realize that Nora and Em were the closest friends I had.

Nora and Em were a little extreme, but—in my extended family—who wasn't somewhat extreme? My laughing, backslapping uncles—the North Conway Norwegians—were weird. My harridan aunts would have felt at home with their Puritan forebears at the Salem witch trials, lending their shrill voices in favor of executing the accused. Lewis Brewster—a former English teacher, faculty emeritus—had invented himself, stopped talking, forgotten who he was, and regressed to infancy. The diaper man had never made much of an income, but the Front Street house looked like money. Even the Brewster family's money was a secret, if there was family money. My grandmother had been a Bates. Did the Front Street house speak of Bates family money? Certainly, my mother didn't make any money. She was, as she'd always been, a ski instructor—a seasonal job.

It seemed beside the point, but because Nora and Em were still hugging me, I took advantage of their sympathy and asked Nora where our money came from. All Nora said was: "Money doesn't make you normal, kiddo." I would always be catching up to Nora.

I couldn't help thinking that the Barlows' money at least came from a visible source: notwithstanding what Elliot thought of his parents' subliterary stature, John and Susan Barlow wrote bestsellers. I didn't share my grandmother's esteem for the Barlows as a fine old Bostonian family. I didn't care how little money the snowshoer made as a schoolteacher. What impressed me was that the Barlows' family money came from *writing*. That thrilled me.

But Nora took off on a tangent, on the subject of where our moral superiority came from—and both the Brewster and the Bates sides of our family got blamed. This concerned Nora more than what was secretive or unknown about our family money. Nora never failed to find Nana at fault. More than I ever did or would, Nora blamed our grandmother for our family's air of entitlement.

It was with Nana in mind that Nora now stopped hugging me. As suddenly, she said to me—to Em, this came completely out of the blue—"You're always letting her off the hook, Adam, but what sort of woman reads *Moby-Dick* aloud to a ten- or eleven-year-old boy?" I'd heard this before; I'd stopped answering this question. Nora knew I had loved it when Nana read *Moby-Dick* aloud to me, and Nora knew I was twelve by the time Nana finished reading to me.

But Em gave an audible gasp. Poor Em was confused. After all, we'd been talking about my mother and the questionable kiss she gave me when I was a thirteen-year-old. Em didn't know Nora was now talking about our grandmother. In the context of the snowshoer kiss, it's understandable that Em might have been overthinking the impropriety of my mom's behavior. Now there loomed the imagined horror of her reading *Somebody's Dick* aloud to a child. It is hard to imagine that any young woman could go to a college as good as Mount Holyoke and not have heard of *Moby-Dick*—at least enough to know it wasn't pornography. Maybe Em had misheard how Nora said the title; Em had heard the *dick* word, clearly.

"No, no, no—*Moby-Dick* isn't porn," Nora quickly told Em. "It's just really long."

I can see why what Nora said failed to put Em at ease—there was a *dick* in what was read aloud to a ten- or eleven-year-old, and it was *really long*. Under the circumstances, I could appreciate why Em gave me another hug. I was touched by Em's sympathy for me, and Nora's. As you might imagine, it took a while to work out who'd read what aloud to me when I was ten, eleven, and twelve: that the accused reader was my grandmother, not my mother; that the eponymous Moby Dick was a whale, not a penis.

"No, Em, not 'a whale of a penis'—an *actual* whale," Nora had to explain. It was hard for me to know what Em was thinking, because she never spoke—not once, not in my presence, the entire wedding weekend. Nora knew what Em was saying with her body—Em pantomimed what she meant. And Nora had told me that Em could talk—"only when she really gets to know you." It seemed that my giving Em the snowshoer kiss had not helped her to get to know me.

Em wasn't the first person to be confused by the hyphen, once we'd sorted out what kind of dick Moby Dick was. I'll never know what made Nora mention the hyphen; that the title of the novel was hyphenated, and the white whale itself wasn't, made Em shake her head violently and squint her eyes tightly shut.

I would read *Moby-Dick* twice in a classroom with a teacher—once as an undergraduate, in an American literature class, and again in a master's program. I don't recall what was said about the hyphen in the title, or its noticeable absence in the novel when Melville refers to the white whale by name. The astounding way Nora explained the meaning of the hyphen to Em has stayed with me, though I doubt that Nora ever heard this theory explained in a classroom, or that she read about it. I would be surprised if Nora ever studied *Moby-Dick*, at either Northfield or Mount Holyoke. I'm not convinced that Nora actually read the novel. I believe she came to her own conclusions about the hyphen around the time Nana was reading *Moby-Dick* aloud to me. Nora would have been in her mid-to-late teens at the time.

"That book *is* an undying whale, Adam—it took Nana three years to read it to you," Nora always said. Nora claimed that it drove her crazy to overhear Nana reading *Moby-Dick* aloud to me. Nora said Nana's reading that novel to me amounted to child abuse.

It is my fondest, most enduring memory of my grandmother, but Nora cited this as exemplary of how little Nana liked or understood children. To Nora, Nana's reading *Moby-Dick* to me was an example of her selfishness. "Reading *Moby-Dick* was what Nana wanted to do, to entertain herself—she should have tried *playing* with you, Adam!" Nora always said. "It made me nuts to listen to her reading to you—I had to force myself to think of something else, kiddo."

"So you thought about the *hyphen?*" I asked Nora. Poor Em! First the *dick* word had misled her to imagine a pornographic whaling adventure; now Nora had sidetracked her with a hyphen.

"Here's all you need to know, Em—I'll be brief," Nora began. "If there's no hyphen in 'Moby Dick,' there are other white whales in the Dick family— Moby's just one Dick among many. There's a Harry Dick, a Joy Dick—even a Richard Dick, for all we know. In other words, it's no big deal that there's a white whale named Moby—there are other white Dicks swimming around." I was as stunned by this less-than-comforting plot summary as Em was. It was bad enough to imagine one Moby Dick—a *sea* of white Dicks swimming around was another matter. "However," Nora suddenly said, "put a hyphen in 'Moby Dick,' and what do you get?" Em and I just looked at each other fearfully. We knew what porn was, but this could be worse. We had no idea where Nora was going with this. "That hyphen makes Mr. Moby a one-and-only white whale; that hyphen means Moby isn't part of a family; that hyphen makes Moby a one-of-a-kind Dick; that fucking hyphen means Moby-Dick is *immortal*," Nora said. Em shivered.

"An unkillable Dick—is that your point?" I asked Nora.

"*Unkillable* means *immortal*, kiddo," Nora told me.

"But it's both ways, Nora," I reminded her. "In the novel, Moby Dick, the whale, has no hyphen—only the title is hyphenated."

All Nora said was: "Maybe Melville was being ambiguous." Maybe Nora *did* read the novel, I was thinking. I would never get a committed answer out of her, not on this subject. The way Em went on shivering made me think she thought being ambiguous was as bad as reading porn aloud to a ten- or eleven-year-old. Em did not look like a woman in a hurry to read *Moby-Dick*, and it would be a while before I had a chance to ask Nora if Em ever said anything about *Moby-Dick* or Melville's ambiguous use of a hyphen.

"A bad name for a whale or a novel, hyphen or no hyphen," Em had said, or she somehow pantomimed this. In Nora and Em's room at the Exeter Inn, we didn't talk about it.

In a confounding non sequitur to Nora's speculation that Melville was being ambiguous, Nora began to unbutton her blouse. "Come on, Em—we should get ready for the main event," Nora said. Em appeared to be paralyzed with uncertainty. I was already edging toward the door to the hall, when Nora noticed the consternation she had caused. "The main event, you morons—the marriage ceremony, the reception dinner. *That* main event. We have to get into our *dancing* clothes!" Nora exhorted us.

At the *dancing* word, Em jumped on the bed, where she began an off-balance dance of a kind unknown to me. I kept edging toward the door. I remembered what had happened in that hotel room the night before, prompted by an innocent changing of clothes—that's how the fooling around had started, and one thing led to another.

Besides, it was time for me to get dressed for the main event. I also wanted to see what the girl jocks were up to, and I was curious to know more about the two-woman job of getting my mom into her complicated wedding dress. I knew my mother needed Molly's help to get into or out of the white wedding dress. I was still struggling to understand the corset concept, how the trail groomer would go about stuffing my mom into that dress—not least, the night groomer's technique for loosening those laces at the back and getting the dress off her. Nora (now taking off her blouse) and Em (still dancing on the bed) did not notice when I slipped out of their room.

As I walked along Front Street from the inn to my grandmother's house, I was joined on the sidewalk by the Austrian zither-meister. He was carrying his instrument in both arms, as if the zither were a sleeping baby. The zither man was wearing a sky-blue shirt, embroidered with white flowers. Given the jaunty feather in his Tyrolean hat, and the lederhosen, his flowery shirt gave him a festive but rustic appearance. "Edelweiss," the old Austrian said. With a glance, he indicated the flowers from his beloved Alps. "And you, young man, are . . . ?" the zither man asked me.

"Adam," I told him. He seemed to consider this carefully. The snowshoer had told me that Austria was a Catholic country. I didn't know much about Catholics. I consequently wondered if the Austrian musician was

giving my name some curiously Catholic consideration. I didn't know if
there was (or ever had been) a Saint Adam. Maybe, because of the Garden
of Eden business, Adam was not an allowable name for a saint? I'd been
an irregular churchgoer. Nana was a Congregationalist, but she stopped
making me go to church when I was old enough to be left at home alone
on Sunday mornings.

According to Nora, Congregationalists were among the least religious
Protestants—"they're the kind of Protestants who believe in almost nothing," was the way Nora put it. The Congregational Church was a plain white
building within view of the bandstand in downtown Exeter. The church was
called the Congo, and the worshipers did their praying and hymn-singing on
the second floor, which backed up what Nora said, but I didn't know much
about Protestants, either.

As it turned out, the Austrian musician wasn't mulling over anything
Catholic in his consideration of my name. "*Son of the Bride*," he said to me,
in a thoughtful and respectful way, as if this were my official title. "Your
mother is going to be a beautiful bride," the zither-meister told me. "You
know, she looks a lot like Valli," he solemnly said. At the time, I'd seen
Alida Valli only in *The Third Man*, where she is certainly beautiful, but very
sad. "In real life, Valli is a baroness," the edelweiss man intoned. "She was
christened Baroness Alida Maria Laura Altenburger von Marckenstein und
Frauenberg."

I was at a loss concerning what to say about this endless name. Instead I
told the old Austrian that my mom would be wearing a complicated wedding
dress. It had to be laced up (and unlaced) at the back—such a strenuous task
that the maid of honor had to wrestle the dress on and off her.

The zither man smiled at me, shaking his head. "That's not for us to think
about, Son of the Bride," he gently informed me. We had arrived at the wedding tent in my grandmother's garden. Those stone sparrows, unmoving on
the rim of the birdbath, gave no indication that they'd noticed the bustling
activity in the backyard of the Front Street house. Out on the croquet court,
the caterers had already lit a cast-iron barbecue as big as a small car—beside
it was a wheelbarrow full of briquettes. The caterers were worried about the
weather forecast: late-afternoon or early-evening thunderstorms were predicted for the New Hampshire seacoast. If they could serve the food in the
wedding tent before the rain started, it wouldn't matter if the rain put out
the fire in the barbecue.

"I just don't want to be flippin' burgers with a metal spatula when there's lightnin' strikin' the whatchamacallit," the barbecue chef said to my grand-mother.

"The croquet court," Nana reminded him.

Crawling around the big barbecue, on all fours, was the infantile Princi-pal Brewster. He was not yet wearing his father-of-the-bride clothes, only his diaper. Dottie was in charge of him, keeping him away from the fire.

"Why is Granddaddy on his hands and knees?" I asked my grandmother.

"The principal emeritus has picked today to stop walking and start crawling—he has regressed past toddlerhood," my grandmother said. I was wondering how the father of the bride could manage to hand over my mother to the snowshoer on all fours, but Nana must have read my mind. "Your grandfather can still stand, Adam—he only crawls when he wants to go somewhere, or leave somewhere."

As for the procession down the aisle to Wagner's "Bridal Chorus," the decision had already been made not to allow the infant emeritus to escort the bride. Little Ray would be escorted by my uncles. The diaper man, positioned between Dottie and my grandmother, would be waiting for my mom at a safe distance from where the snowshoer would be standing; my grandfather believed the little groom to be another of Ray's illegitimate children.

"A little unusual, maybe," Uncle Martin had admitted.

"But a necessary precaution, perhaps," Uncle Johan had chimed in. Om-inously, I thought, my aunts had said nothing.

I saw that the edelweiss man had located the small table with the single chair in a strategic corner of the tent. He had placed his holy instrument on the table and was checking out the microphone and amplifiers. The min-ister from the Congregational Church came early. He may have been a lot less religious than other Protestants, believing next to nothing, but he had plenty of opinions, which he hastened to express to my grandmother. The front row of folding chairs, already unfolded and gathered in place for the marriage ceremony, should not be too close to where the bride and groom would say their vows.

The caterers had expressed a contrary view of the assembled chairs; they wanted more room at the back of the tent for the folding tables. The cere-mony couldn't be over soon enough, not in the caterers' opinion. After all, they had to rearrange all the chairs around the unfolded tables, setting up the tent for the reception dinner.

Meanwhile, the action on the croquet court took an unpleasant turn. The two girl jocks who slept in their own small tent and took showers together had just taken a shower. They were both wrapped in undersize towels and brushing each other's hair in the sun, in an effort to dry their hair before they got dressed for the wedding. Thus scantily wrapped in their too-small towels, and up to their own business, the two athletic-looking young women had attracted the attention of the not-very-bright barbecue chef. While waving his spatula over the preheating barbecue, and being careful not to step on the crawling diaper man, the barbecue chef kept giving sidelong glances to the two girl jocks in their skimpy towels.

There was nothing sidelong about the looks Henrik gave to the girl jocks in their fetching towels. Henrik, dillydallying with his irrelevant lacrosse stick, gawked at the girls from the stance he'd taken in the middle of the croquet court, where he aggressively occupied the space between the smoking grill and the big tent belonging to the rest of the girl jocks—wherever they were. I suspected they weren't in their big tent, where they would have been sweltering. It was a hot, sunny day—typical of an early afternoon in July.

The girls drying their hair ignored Henrik, who kept leering at them. Henrik was cradling an old croquet ball in his stupid lacrosse stick, as if he were fondling one of his own testicles. The croquet ball—a faded maroon, long exposed to all kinds of weather—must have been lost in the bushes, where Henrik had dug it out with his lacrosse stick. It was barely recognizable as the brightly colored ball it once had been, but the crawling diaper man recognized it. The infant emeritus may have stopped speaking and lost the ability to walk, but—even on his hands and knees—the diaper man knew one of his old croquet balls when he saw it. Circling Henrik on all fours, Principal Brewster bit the distracted midfielder in the area of his Achilles tendon. Possibly Henrik's habit of wearing unmatching socks had further enraged the principal emeritus. We'll never know. What could the diaper man tell us?

Dottie had a harness with her, and a short leash—of the kind attached to Seeing Eye dogs. Thus was the diaper man dragged away. If a look could speak, it was easy to interpret the cursory glance Dottie gave to Henrik, who'd lost control of his lacrosse stick when he'd been bitten. Dottie's glance gave Henrik some idea of what Dottie *woulda done* in Maine, where she would have bitten his throat. The croquet ball had briefly rolled free, but not for long. The baby emeritus had grabbed it and stuffed it in his diaper.

I wished I could read lips. I wanted to know the unspoken words the diaper man was mouthing, as Dottie led him (still on his hands and knees) to the Front Street house. Whatever the infant in reverse kept repeating to himself, he seemed sure about it.

"Son of the Bride," the old Austrian musician whispered to me. "You're not a lip-reader, are you?"

"No," I answered him. He was returning to his small table and unattended zither.

"I am," the zither man said, almost indifferently. "Your grandfather was saying, 'My ball, my ball'—over and over again."

I didn't know if I believed the zither-meister. It was too easy to guess that's what Granddaddy Lew had been thinking, though how would the edelweiss man have known that Principal Brewster was the only croquet player in the family?

My grandmother had left the wedding tent immediately after the biting. She'd told me she was going to rescue the caterers from Aunt Abigail and Aunt Martha, who were poking their noses into everything in the kitchen. I decided to leave the wedding tent, too, upon the appearance of my aunts on the croquet court, where they'd arrived with a first-aid kit to attend to the wound in Henrik's Achilles tendon. Henrik sat cross-legged on the court while my aunts fussed over him. One of the girl jocks had picked up Henrik's lacrosse stick. She was handling it like she knew what she was doing. The other girl jock had her hands on her hips while she stood over Henrik, looking down at him. The two girl jocks seemed to enjoy my aunts' disapproval of the girls' skimpy towels—not to mention how the fallen Henrik had been humiliated by a biter on all fours in a diaper.

The not-very-bright barbecue chef had gone off somewhere, taking his spatula with him. The big barbecue was smoking up a storm, but all the food was still in the kitchen of the Front Street house or laid out on the dining-room table. There were two huge Westphalian hams and giant bowls of German potato salad. There was a pantry, between the dining room and the kitchen, where the caterers were keeping the wedding cake hidden. There was no hiding the washtub of beer on ice from Uncle Martin and Uncle Johan, who were already drinking beer and laughing loudly about the platter of uncooked food that was going to be barbecued—salmon steaks, chicken breasts, and burgers. Apparently, my uncles found these food choices as funny as foreign films with subtitles.

I slipped upstairs to the second floor, where it seemed likely I would discover the rest of the girl jocks. Fresh from their baths and showers, with wet hair and wearing only towels, the spanking-clean girls made a formidable barricade on the bottommost steps of the stairs leading to my attic bedroom. I couldn't step over them or make my way through them.

"Sit here, Kid," one of the girl jocks said. She moved over and I sat on the stairs beside her, with my back against the knees of the girl jock on the step above me.

"We can't let you go up there, Adam—there's a battle with a dress going on," said the girl jock sitting behind me.

"You're killing me, Molly!" we could hear my mother screaming.

"Stop holding your breath," the trail groomer told her.

"I'm not holding it—I can't breathe!" my mom shouted.

"You're being dramatic, and it isn't helping," we heard the snowcat operator say.

"Your wedding clothes are laid out for you on the bed in your mom's room, Adam," Nelly told me. I was relieved to see no visual evidence of her yeast infection. "You're supposed to shower in your mom's bathroom," Nelly added.

"Then we'll help you get dressed, Kid—all of us!" said the girl jock sitting behind me. She bumped me with her knees, and the other jocks laughed.

"That's okay—I can manage by myself," I told them. I knew they were kidding, but I was both agitated and excited by the prospect of all of them dressing me. "Do you have to get dressed in the big tent—all of you?" I asked them.

They all groaned. "It'll be a sauna in there," one of the girl jocks complained.

"We can all get dressed in Ray's room, with Adam," Nelly suggested. The girls all laughed again, but I had to restrain myself from saying what I wanted to say to them. I would have loved it if they all got dressed (or undressed) with me.

"Ow! That's my rib, Molly—one of them, anyway," we could hear my mom saying.

"If I don't make it tight, Ray, your dress will slip down—there's nothing but your boobs to hold it up, and you don't exactly have humdingers," the night groomer told her.

"I didn't know that's how you felt about my boobs, Molly," we could hear my mother saying, "but it doesn't matter what you think of them—you're *crushing* them!"

"I'm very fond of your boobs, Ray," we heard the snowcat operator say.

"I'm just telling you that your boobs can't keep your dress from slipping down—not all by themselves."

"Ow!" my mom cried out again. "That's my nipple, Molly, or what's left of it—one of them, anyway."

"Dressing you will be a lot easier than this, Adam," one of the girl jocks told me.

"Yeah, I could dress Adam in under a minute, start to finish—the necktie and everything," Nelly said.

"You could *undress* Adam in under a minute, Nelly—I don't doubt that," said the girl jock sitting behind me.

"It'll take you more than a minute to tie the necktie, Nelly—everything else, in under a minute, is easy," another girl jock said.

"I could use a little help with the necktie," I told them. "I don't need help with anything else."

"Listen to me, Kid," Nelly said. "When you get dressed, except for the necktie, come find us. We'll take care of the tie. Then we'll get into our bridesmaids' dresses in your mom's bedroom. Got it?"

"Got it," I said.

"Ow!" my mom cried.

"I almost have it, Ray," the trail groomer told her.

I went along the hall to my mother's bedroom, where I found my clothes neatly laid out on the bed. My mom's clothes, and Molly's clothes, were everywhere else. The night groomer's clothes looked huge in comparison to my mother's small things. On the dressing table, in front of my mom's makeup mirror, was a very big bra. I knew it was Molly's bra—she had humdingers.

There were two razors in my mother's bathroom, but I didn't have to shave. To my disappointment, I was showing no signs of a beard. My mom liked to run her finger over my upper lip, because she said it was so smooth. "Don't ever grow a mustache, sweetie," she would tell me, but I wished I could grow one.

After my shower, when I was getting dressed, Molly's bra watched me and I stared back at it. The trail groomer's humdingers were even bigger than Nora's, I was imagining. The bedroom windows were open, and I could hear the zither-meister warming up—just the first few chords of "The Third Man Theme," as if Harry Lime were alive and lurking under the wedding tent in my grandmother's garden.

Unquestionably, a mood of intrigue and melancholy comes across in

"The Harry Lime Theme" on a zither; yet it was an unusually tranquil moment in the midst of my mother's wedding weekend. At that moment, alone with the night groomer's captivating bra, I was thinking that the lion's share of the drama was surely over. At fourteen, I hadn't learned that the things you imagine when you're alone with a bra can deceive you.

18

WHAT THE STONE SPARROWS SAW

Certain families have an aura of arrival. I don't mean an annoying punctuality—the opposite of the haplessness of always being late. Our Brewster family's aura of arrival was borne of anxiety, bordering on dread. We sensed that something bad was about to happen. We had forebodings of doom—we could intuit when the doom was due to arrive—but we never knew who or what was doomed.

The snowshoer and I had talked about the terms of his adopting me. I could become Adam Barlow or remain Adam Brewster. "If you want to be a writer, Adam, I don't recommend becoming a Barlow," Elliot said; he really held his parents' genre against them.

My mom was thirty-four on her wedding day. "I've been Rachel Brewster too long to become Rachel anybody else," she'd told me and the snowshoer.

Naturally, Nora reported to us concerning the name business. "In my mother's and Aunt Martha's eyes, your being a Barlow will never legitimize you, Adam," Nora told me, "and Ray's becoming a Barlow won't redeem her from having disgraced herself as an unwed mother." I could hear in Nora's reiterations, of course, exactly how Aunt Abigail and Aunt Martha must have expressed themselves on this subject; their righteousness was tireless.

All this is fair to say, but the real reason my mom and I were right to remain Brewsters is that you can't change a family characteristic as easily as you can change your name. Curse or blessing, we Brewsters were stuck with our forebodings of doom. An aura of arrival was our thing.

In my mother's bedroom, the afternoon of her wedding, Molly's big bra had distracted me from my sense of foreboding. That nothing went wrong with the marriage ceremony was further misleading. Not even the sound of Wagner's "Bridal Chorus" on a zither forewarned me. Did I imagine *Lohengrin* had a happy ending?

I didn't screw up the rings, although both were small. Moreover, Dottie had found a way to bribe and pacify the diaper man with the old croquet ball. If the big baby stood (and remained standing) between Dottie and my grandmother, Dottie let him hold the sacred orb. If the infant emeritus dropped to all fours and started to crawl, Dottie took away his croquet ball. For a while, it worked.

Who cared that Henrik was limping? Henrik had no duties that required him to walk or stand; he had his lacrosse stick to use as a cane or a crutch when he hobbled around. The girl jocks were glad that he wouldn't be asking them to dance.

In their bridesmaids' dresses, the bare-shouldered girl jocks looked lithesome and strong. They were the fittest bridesmaids I've ever seen, especially for an older bride, and Molly was a strapping physical specimen among maids of honor. The night groomer didn't just loom large. The décolletage of the bridesmaids' dresses was cut exceedingly low, but Molly was showing the most cleavage.

Of course, my mom's dress was the whitest and the prettiest; she may not have had humdingers, but that tightly corseted dress made the most of them. The neckline was an unusually low one for my mother. For such a small person, Little Ray was showing what amounted to a lot of cleavage for her. Even in the shade of the tent, the brightness of my mom's white dress was dazzling. I suddenly saw what the zither man had seen in her: my mother was as beautiful as Alida Valli in *The Third Man*. In another world, if not in New Hampshire, Ray Brewster could have been a baroness.

Yet how could I have overlooked the aura of arrival that emanated from my aunts? Aunt Abigail and Aunt Martha had not neglected their foremost family characteristic—their sense of foreboding was as keen as ever. If those two didn't see doom coming, they went looking for it. Nora told me later that her mother and Aunt Martha had been on the rampage in the Front Street house shortly before the ceremony started. Those two were opening every closet door and peering inside, hoping to catch the snowshoer with his pants down—"caught in the act of sodomizing someone, or being sodomized by someone," as Nora put it.

When Little Ray, beautiful and radiant in white, was escorted down the aisle—looking like a baroness between my broad-shouldered, admiring uncles—Aunt Abigail and Aunt Martha glared at her from their front-row seats. Those two did more than suffer our family's forebodings of doom. In my mom's case, Aunt Abigail and Aunt Martha prayed for an unforgiving doom to befall her. There's no measuring the harshness of the moral come-uppance or just deserts my aunts imagined my mother had coming to her.

For Aunt Abigail and Aunt Martha, their aura of arrival was entwined with what they wished for.

I saw how those two were looking at their younger sister—on Little Ray's wedding day, my aunts were wishing her dead. But nothing untoward happened; the ceremony was never interrupted. My own aura of arrival may have been asleep, but even I was half expecting a long-imagined interruption: a stranger—unrecognizable to everyone, except my mother—leaping to his feet and pointing to me. "He's *my* son!" the angry man would declare. Then, pointing to the bride, his voice breaking, the stranger would say, "Remember me, Ray? Aspen, the Hotel Jerome, March '41?"

But no such stranger came forth to stop the marriage ceremony—not even the one my aunts must have been imagining, the one they so ardently wished for. A pretty boy—a screaming young fairy, as my aunts would have labeled him—standing on his chair and showing us his member of the Dick family, as Nora no doubt would have embellished it. This, of course, would have been the snowshoer's last lover—a jilted soul. Wouldn't a pretty boy like that have been a surefire wedding stopper? But no such screaming fairy showed up and stood on a chair—alas, leaving my aunts with an undying disappointment and inner sorrow. No detectable disappointment or symptom of sorrow was evident in my jolly uncles, who laughed throughout the ceremony and burst into cheers during the vows.

The croquet ball almost kept the diaper man standing and calm. The sacred orb seemed to soothe him. When the Congo minister asked his "Do you, Rachel . . ." and his "Do you, Elliot . . ." there was no hesitation from Little Ray or the snowshoer, and their answers were crystal-clear. Yet I saw something change in the innocent and roaming attention of the principal emeritus. When my mom said, "I do," the diaper man's expression darkened. Something cognizant and distrustful crept into the standing child's face.

Since he'd stopped speaking, and the retired grammarian began his slow drift toward infancy, Principal Brewster's sole means of expressing himself was to chew his mustache. But Dottie had shaved it off when he was sleeping—no doubt, what Dottie *woulda done* in Maine. His beard had stopped growing anyway, and the hairs of his mustache were falling out—or the infant emeritus was pulling them out, and eating them. Dottie's justification for shaving him, as she so frankly expressed to my grandmother, was neither profound nor illogical, but—to Nana's thinking—it was vulgar. "The poor fella is becomin' a baby, Mrs. Brewster. I don't see babies havin' much use for any kind of pussy-tickler." Once Granddaddy Lew's mustache had been labeled with such a vulgarism, my grandmother did not regret his losing it.

However, when the kiss-the-bride business began, I saw how the infant emeritus reacted. A moment of adult recognition or recollection deepened the diaper man's frown. My mom had leaned over the snowshoer. She bent him backward when she kissed him, holding him tightly. There were oohs and aahs from the wedding guests, though I thought the kiss my mother gave Elliot Barlow was a tame version of the snowshoer kiss—a PG-13 kiss, we might call it nowadays. But there was something about the way Ray Brewster had delivered her "I do" and the kiss. I saw that the backward-traveling diaper man was flat-out racing through time. The infant emeritus appeared to be fast approaching his time as a father, albeit from light-years away. He seemed suddenly surprised to be holding the old croquet ball, which he dropped at his feet and kicked away from him—I thought the ball rolled under the front row of chairs. The diaper man touched his upper lip, as if feeling for his missing mustache, and I distinctly saw his lips move. Once more, the principal emeritus was mouthing unspoken words, which I could neither hear nor read.

This time, the zither-meister was too far away to read the diaper man's lips. Besides, the zither man was busy. From the far end of the tent, at the rear of the assembled chairs, nearest the elevated platform for the dancing, the old Austrian was hell-bent on strumming his strings. He was heralding the sacrament of marriage, now sealed by the less-than-snowshoer kiss—the edelweiss man had no time for lip-reading. The wedding guests stood and applauded.

Well, not everyone. When Aunt Abigail grudgingly rose from her front-row seat, her feet flew out from under her. Reaching for someone to grab hold of, she dragged Aunt Martha to the ground with her. "The croquet ball," the Congo minister whispered in my ear, while the zither recessional played on. Arm in arm, the snowshoer and Little Ray were proceeding up the aisle between the assembled chairs. I saw the moment when the puerile principal emeritus lost sight of the married couple. At that instant, Granddaddy Lew seemed stricken with a frightened father's crazed anguish. I couldn't read the unspoken words the diaper man mouthed, but I saw in his lunatic expression everything my infantile grandfather feared: his youngest daughter had just married one of her misbegotten children, and Principal Brewster had been powerless to prevent it!

That was when the diaper man reverted to his inner dog. While Uncle Martin howled with laughter and Uncle Johan actually barked, Granddaddy

Lew dropped to all fours and began biting. On his hands and knees, the pos-
sessed infant scurried up the aisle, snapping at ankles and Achilles tendons.
Dottie pursued him, holding fast to her Seeing Eye dog equipment. "Poor
Lew," my grandmother said wearily, squeezing my hand. "The bats in his
belfry have taken over, Adam—it's a good thing we've dispensed with the
receiving line."

We could see the wedding guests dropping and hear their cries—it was
hard to tell who'd been bitten by the angry infant and who had merely stumbled and fallen into one of the flower beds. My grandmother's garden was an
obstacle course in transition; the caterers were unfolding the tables for the
reception dinner, and they were rearranging the chairs around the tables.
Platters of the sliced ham were carried to the tables, together with bowls of
the German potato salad. There were still too many people standing under
the tent for Nana and me to see what was happening out on the croquet
court, but the smell of cooking was in the air. I would have bet that the
barbecue chef began grilling before the ceremony started. Wagner's "Bridal
Chorus" had mercifully ended—the zither-meister was taking a break. I
could see that Nora and Em were talking to the old Austrian—well, Nora
was doing all the talking, and Em was nodding her head off.

"I think that went pretty well, all things considered," the Congo minister
was saying, albeit tentatively, to my aunts.

"That kiss was *completely inappropriate*—it lingered much too long!" Aunt
Abigail retorted. She'd turned her ankle on the croquet ball; she was limping, and leaning on Aunt Martha for support.

"That dress was much *too low*—not to mention, *too white!*" Martha
chimed in.

"Girls, girls," my grandmother muttered, more to herself than to my condemning aunts. My uncles were woofing like dogs and pretending to bite
each other.

Speaking of *too low*, I spotted the maid of honor and her most revealing
décolletage—even from afar. Molly and her cleavage stood out. She was
standing at the periphery of the milling crowd. The caterers were still setting
the dinner tables, where only a few of the wedding guests had taken their
seats. Fewer people were falling and crying out—mere blunderers, felled by
the flower beds. I was confident that Dottie had harnessed and leashed the
dog man. She likely had the biter under control.

Yes, I was drawn to the night groomer. Molly commanded the attention of
every alert male under the wedding tent. Maybe that was why she'd stepped

away from the ongoing fray? The trail groomer was the tallest woman standing, and she was showing the most cleavage. As I cautiously approached her, I was wondering if I would ever recover from encountering her bra. But when I got closer to her, I saw she'd been crying. Unmindful of her tears, Molly was as vividly transported by her thoughts as the diaper man was muddled by his.

Yet when Molly noticed me standing next to her, she immediately snapped back to the reality of the moment and the matter at hand. "You're right on time, Adam the Kid—you have just what I need," the night groomer said, taking the handkerchief that matched my tie from the breast pocket of my suit jacket. "Why do you think I put it there?" Molly asked me, wiping the tears from her face with my handkerchief, which she matter-of-factly returned to my breast pocket.

"You put it there?" I asked her. It was difficult to speak, at eye level to her cleavage.

"When your mom and I were laying out your wedding clothes, I asked her for a handkerchief to put in your pocket—I knew I would be bawling my eyes out, and I was going to need one," the trail groomer told me. "They are not just the cutest-looking couple I know, Kid," Molly said. "Of the couples I can think of, I'll bet your mom and the snowshoer last the longest—I'm betting they go the distance."

I was so suddenly moved to tears by Molly's remarks that the snowcat operator hugged me. The bridge of my nose was flattened against her breasts, and I remembered my mother's tearful shouting ("I can't breathe!") from my attic bedroom. My aunts' awful aspersions must have affected me more than I realized. To have someone as stalwart as the night groomer speak with such authority about the veraciousness of my mom's marriage to the little snowshoer—well, it truly mattered to me. I needed to hear it.

"My aunts say my mom is Elliot's *beard*—Nora told me they think he's a little light in the loafers," I said to Molly. She was using my handkerchief again—this time, to wipe the tears from my face.

"You should listen to Nora, Kid—you can trust her," Molly said. "But your aunts wouldn't understand a *beard* if they grew one. You can count on your mom and Elliot to be there for you, Adam—you can trust me, too," the trail groomer told me. I did. I actually began to relax a little.

Only the occasional fool, not watching his or her feet, was falling into the flower beds and thrashing around in the flowers. Henrik, already disabled, had his eyes on the girl jocks when he tripped on his lacrosse stick and flailed away in the blue hydrangea bushes. "Blame that one on the décolletage of the bridesmaids' dresses," was all the night groomer said. I saw she had her eyes on Nora and Em, who were still seeking to influence the zither man in an apparently musical direction. Em was dancing for the zither-meister while Nora appeared to be singing to him. For his part, the edelweiss man would strum a few strings—perhaps to demonstrate that he knew the tune of the song Nora was singing to him. "It looks like Nora and the screamer want something they can dance to," Molly was saying. "Those two came dressed to do some dancing."

More of the wedding guests had found seats for themselves at the tables. I could plainly see what Nora and Em were wearing. Short skirts, the pleated kind—skirts that flared when you spun around, skirts that showed a lot of your legs and your panties. Both Nora and Em were wearing slinky blouses. There wasn't much support in the bras they were wearing. "I think that's as close as you can get to the no-bra look and still have a bra on," the trail groomer told me in her matter-of-fact fashion. Molly's nonjudgmental tone contrasted sharply with the way my aunts spoke of women who flopped around without bras or aspired to the no-bra look. "What kind of music does Nora like to dance to?" the night groomer asked me.

"Nora has never danced with me," I quickly said. "I think she likes Elvis, but Nora says Elvis should have been a woman."

The snowcat operator nodded. "There's something about Elvis—his gender is all over the place," was the way Molly put it. "Elvis or no Elvis, Kid—when the dancing starts, you find me. I'll dance with you."

"I've never danced with anyone except my mother—I'm not much of a dancer," I told the trail groomer.

"It'll be easy, Kid—I lead, you follow," Molly said.

"Okay," I told her.

"I guess we should look for our seats—I don't know if there's somewhere we're supposed to be sitting," the night groomer said.

We had a clear view of the croquet court, where the barbecue chef was brandishing his spatula. He was conducting a virtual orchestra of salmon steaks and chicken breasts and burgers, while waiters and waitresses and sous-chefs assisted him or tried to stay out of his way. We could also see the determined diaper man, down on all fours and fiercely digging for something on the croquet court. Dottie had him harnessed and was letting him dig. Nana had told me that Dottie was going to feed the infant emeritus in the kitchen. Maybe the biter was beyond doing more damage to the festivities.

Molly and I sat at the table with the girl jocks, and with Nora and Em. It was okay with me that I was the only guy at the table. There were speeches, of course, but I don't remember them. The zither man took his time, getting up his nerve to tackle Elvis. The Austrian began with the oldies in his repertoire, familiar to us from the night before. My mom and Elliot started the dancing to "The Third Man Theme," which is what Molly and I first danced to. The trail groomer threw me around and crushed me against her. She led and I followed her through the zither-meister's liveliest and most lugubrious numbers. Fast and slow, from "The Café Mozart Waltz" to "Farewell to Vienna," I danced with all the girl jocks, and with Em, but Molly was my main dancing partner. Molly had noticed how Em lifted my chin and pointed to her eyes, indicating where I should look when we were dancing—not at her breasts, Em meant. "Em can read your eyes, Kid—she knows what you're looking at," Molly told me.

The reception dinner was over—the wedding cake had been cut and served—before the edelweiss man worked up the courage to give us the zither version of "Heartbreak Hotel" and "I Forgot to Remember to Forget"—as Nora put it, "Elvis to grind to, and Elvis to hug to."

"For an old guy in leather shorts, and a hat with a feather, two by Elvis is pretty good," Nora said. At our table, everyone was laughing, and everyone kept getting up to dance. The girl jocks knew the lyrics to "Heartbreak Hotel," which they sang along with the zither.

The only words I knew were "so lonely" and "could die," and I never forgot the "Lonely Street" location of the hotel. When Molly and I were dancing to "I Forgot to Remember to Forget," she sang the beginning of the song to me. But even when Molly was dancing with me, I was aware of her keeping an eye on my mom and the snowshoer. The night groomer also kept an eye on the night. Molly knew there was a storm coming—she knew my mother and Elliot had a drive ahead of them.

"No beer," I'd heard Molly tell the newlyweds. "You've got a honeymoon coming up, and you still have to drive there."

The honeymoon hotel was somewhere on the coast of Maine. "It's on a cliff, I think," Nelly had said.

"In case the honeymoon doesn't work out, there's always the cliff—I'm just kidding, kiddo," Nora said to me. Nora knew me.

After nightfall, the air was still but the rain didn't come. The air just felt like the rain was coming. Now that the zither man was in his Elvis mode, we wouldn't have heard the distant rumbles of thunder. Under the tent, how could we have seen the blinks of approaching lightning?

Elliot's parents had reserved two rooms at the Exeter Inn for the wedding weekend. They'd wanted their son to be near them, and it was easier for Elliot. The inn was closer to the Front Street house than the snowshoer's faculty apartment. Elliot had already left the reception dinner; he'd gone to the inn to change his clothes, and to pack up his things for the honeymoon.

Meanwhile, Molly was impatient to "start the fight"—she meant the struggle to get my mom out of "that killer dress."

"Will it be as hard to get off as it was to put on?" I asked the night groomer.

"Maybe harder, Kid—the way I laced up that dress, your mother might have to starve herself to get it off."

A few of the older folks were leaving. The younger crowd had a higher tolerance for Elvis on a zither, and for the way Nora and Em were grinding together. By this point in the evening, everyone had seen a lot of Nora's and Em's panties—those two had been dancing so hard, they were sweating nonstop. The writing team (both Barlows) had gone with Elliot to the inn, and at first I thought my mom was dancing with the wrestling coach.

"They're not dancing, Kid—Ray's showing him her single-leg lunges," the trail groomer more accurately observed. It was clear the coach couldn't hold his lunges as long as my mother could hold hers.

"Come on, don't quit," we could hear my mom urging him.

"We're lucky, Kid—there's no wall for Ray to show him her wall sits," Molly said. "If she tries to show him her squats, that dress will cut off the blood supply to her heart and lungs."

That was when the night groomer went out on the dance platform and persuaded my mother to call it a night.

"Look—Molly's cutting in on the single-leg lunges," Nelly said. She'd had a lot of beer, I knew. She'd been a little unsteady when we were dancing, and that had been a while ago.

"Molly wants to get my mom out of that dress—Molly is thinking about the honeymoon," I told Nelly. Most of the other girl jocks were at the table. They just looked at me, not saying anything. "Molly is worried about the weather," I went on. "She's thinking about the drive to the honeymoon hotel," I further explained to them; they just looked at one another, still not saying anything. I didn't know what might have made them suddenly so uncomfortable. The trail groomer, we could all see, had already ushered my mother into the Front Street house—not that many of the remaining guests had noticed. Nora and Em were providing a more watchable distraction.

"Well, it's a good thing it's not my honeymoon—not with my yeast infection," Nelly said. She was attempting to lighten the mood of the moment, I thought, but I felt it would have been rude to laugh, and the other girl jocks still seemed uncomfortable. I thought they were just tired of hearing about Nelly's yeast infection. "You know what the next best thing to a honeymoon is, Adam?" Nelly was asking me.

"No, what?" I asked her.

"Dancing with you, Kid," Nelly said, taking my hand—she led me, more than a little unsteadily, to the dance platform. That was why I happened to be in close proximity to the zither-meister when the first flash of lightning lit up the night sky. The bright-white light illuminated every detail of the unattended barbecue out on the croquet court. The boom of thunder was much louder and closer than anyone expected. We hadn't heard the far-off rumbles, because of Elvis on the zither. Under the tent, we definitely didn't see the faraway flashes of lightning. Now, even over the constantly repeated Elvis songs, we could hear the rain drumming on the wedding tent. Nelly and I could hear it pinging on the iron barbecue, once more in total darkness, out on the croquet court, where my grandmother had predicted someone would come to harm or be killed.

I had doubted this. I didn't think anything was wrong—nothing seemed amiss. Even drunk, and stepping on my feet, Nelly was fun to dance with—I'd lost all fear of her yeast infection. That was when the lightning flashed again, so bright that everyone under the tent seemed exposed, their motion arrested—the way flash photography can both blind and freeze its subjects with unnatural clarity. There were Nora and Em: their mouths weren't mashed together, but their tongues were touching, and their hands were groping each other under their slinky blouses. There were Uncle Martin and Uncle Johan: for some reason, they were no longer singing (for the hundredth time), "Bier, Bier—das Bier ist hier!" That was because Uncle Johan was choking. Uncle Martin had thrown him full-length and facedown on the dinner table, where Martin pounded away on his brother's back. With the snowshoer still at the Exeter Inn, we were in need of a choking expert. "Go get Dottie—she's putting the principal to bed. Dottie will know what to do," my grandmother said, to either Nora or me.

"I'm faster," I told Nora, who was still entangled with Em.

To no one's surprise, Dottie did know what to do. When we returned to the tent, Uncle Martin had been joined by Henrik, who was whacking his father on the back with his lacrosse stick. "Give me that thing you're always playin' with," Dottie told Henrik, who handed his lacrosse stick to her. She slid the stick sideways, under Uncle Johan, kneeling on my prone uncle's lower back. Dottie wrenched the lacrosse stick upward, just below Uncle Johan's diaphragm, holding the stick in both her hands. What my uncle disgorged defies description: a slab of Westphalian ham, the size of an adult's shoe, doesn't cover it—no small amount of wedding cake was involved, and lots of beer. It crossed my mind to wonder what Dottie *woulda done* in Maine, in lieu of using a lacrosse stick—a clam rake, maybe—but Dottie wasn't one for idle conversation. "I gotta be gettin' back to the baby man, Mrs. Brewster—he wasn't sleepin' like he shoulda been when I left him," was the way Dottie put it to Nana.

"Bier, Bier—das Bier ist hier!" Uncle Johan started singing, weakly. Uncle Martin was once more laughing when the lightning struck yet again, even brighter and closer than before, and the thunder came crashing down upon us. The amplification system for the music momentarily cut out, and the edelweiss man stopped zithering. How was it possible that we still heard some music? There was suddenly, however remote, a rhythm section. From the darkness of the croquet court came the reverberating rattle of a snare drum, a metallic drumming.

"Oh, shit," Dottie said softly—just seconds before the lightning struck once more, showing all of us the drummer. The standing diaper man was naked, except for his lightning-white diaper. The infant emeritus had not dug those rusty wickets out of the croquet court only to abandon them in the downpour. The wire wickets, which he'd been beating against the gleaming-wet cast iron of the barbecue, must have made music only the diaper man could understand. When the lightning struck him, the principal emeritus was mouthing the same words I'd seen him repeating to himself when the bride kissed the little English teacher.

There was a crack, or at least a loud click, coincident to the lightning strike and only a second before the boom of thunder. I saw that the zither man had seen my grandfather's last words, although no one had heard them. "What was he saying?" I asked the old Austrian.

"Sweetie," Nora suddenly said, again using my mom's word for me. Nora and Em had moved between Nelly and me—I'd only just come back to the dance platform. "You don't need to read lips, kiddo—you know what Grand-daddy was saying."

"It looked like 'Not Little Ray!'—that's what I saw," the zither-meister said.

"That's what you saw, all right," Nora told him. The croquet court was in darkness again. Dottie and my grandmother, followed by my uncles (who were not laughing) and the limping Henrik, were the first to venture into the darkness.

"Lew, Lew—you poor thing," Nana was saying. Aunt Abigail and Aunt Martha—histrionically, of course—were wailing.

"Son of the Bride," the edelweiss man said gently. "You should go find your mother—you have to tell her."

"No, don't *you* go—I'll tell her, kiddo," Nora said, both too quickly and too loudly. But I was already off and running.

"I'm faster," I told Nora, for the second time that night.

"Let *me* do it, Kid!" Nelly called after me.

"No, no—Kid!" I heard two or three of the girl jocks shouting. But I had the snowshoer to thank for my being a better runner than I used to be. I had a head start, and no one could catch me or stop me. I ran through the Front Street house, which was virtually empty and silent—only the rain was beating down. The rain made it hard to hear anything on the second floor, and the rain was even louder as I ran up the attic stairs, taking two steps at a time. I skipped the step with the creak in it, near the top of the stairs.

Yes, I thought it was curious—not to hear a word of dialogue between my mom and Molly. Was the wedding dress not as difficult to get off as it had been to put on? To my surprise, I saw the white dress lying on the attic floor—flung far from the bedroom, where my view of the bed was blocked by the half-open bathroom door. Yet I could see my mother and the night groomer reflected in the skylight above my bed. They were naked and locked in an upside-down embrace, their faces buried between each other's legs, their hands holding fast to each other's buttocks. At fourteen, this was an unfamiliar embrace to me. I wasn't sure what I saw, but I knew I wasn't supposed to see it.

When the lightning flashed, the skylight above my bed glared a blinding white. The reflection of my mom in the snowcat operator's grasp vanished as suddenly as I had seen it. When I went back down the attic stairs, I was still half-blinded by the skylight's glare—that was why I stepped on the step that creaked.

"Adam?" I heard my mother say, a little breathlessly. "Is that you, sweetie?"

I saw Nora and Em standing at the bottom of the attic stairs—Em had her fist in her mouth and was biting the big knuckle of her index finger. It was pretty clear that both of them knew what I had seen—they'd known what I was going to see before I saw it.

"I tried to stop you, kiddo," Nora said quietly to me, when I got to the bottom of the stairs, but I couldn't speak.

"Nora? Is that you, Nora?" we heard my mom asking.

"Granddaddy Lew is dead, Ray—he got hit by lightning," Nora called upstairs to her.

"Where is Adam?" my mother asked. Nora had gone halfway up the attic stairs, where she'd stopped, looking back at me. Em had her arms wrapped around me. I could see the length of the second-floor hall, where the girl jocks were waiting for me. I was angry and near tears. I knew that all of them had known about my mom and Molly.

"Adam got here first, Ray—he saw you and Molly," Nora told my mother.

"Sweetie! Adam?" my mom kept calling, but I still could not speak. There was nowhere to run—the girl jocks had me surrounded. It was no wonder I'd made them uncomfortable when I went on and on to them about how Molly wanted to get my mom out of that dress, and how Molly was thinking about the honeymoon. The girl jocks were still uncomfortable, and Em had locked her hands around my waist. There was no getting away from Em, either.

Nora came back down the attic stairs. She found us all in the second-floor hall. I suppose we looked like we didn't know what to do with ourselves— I certainly didn't. "We should let them get dressed, for Christ's sake," Nora said. "We're not doing anyone any good here," she told us.

Naturally, back under the wedding tent, the mood was tense in a different way. The diaper man lay covered with a sheet on the same dinner table where Uncle Johan had been saved from choking. I hoped there'd been time to clean up the disgorgement before the body was brought to the table. The snowshoer and his parents were back at the party. Elliot was more casually attired—in his honeymoon clothes, I was thinking. "Does your mom know— have you seen her?" the little English teacher asked me. I was wondering if I would ever speak again, but Nora spoke for me.

"Ray knows—Adam saw her," Nora told the snowshoer. I was glad the girl jocks didn't say anything to Elliot about what a bugger it was to get my mother into that wedding dress, or to take it off her.

"We understand that you would like to be a writer, Adam—either a novelist or a screenwriter, or both," John Barlow suddenly said to me.

"Yes, we're so sorry we didn't get a chance to talk to you about *writing*," Susan Barlow told me.

In addition to my having no confidence that I could speak, it was awkward to know what to say to Mr. and Mrs. Barlow. They were standing across the table from me, with the body of the diaper man under the unmoving sheet between us.

"Perhaps now isn't the time," the snowshoer said to his parents.

"But now is so *noir*—it's the perfect time, dear," Mrs. Barlow said to her little son.

"The Western will be replaced by the gangster film, because noir is the most original thing in American writing," Mr. Barlow told me.

"I think Melville and Hawthorne are the most original things in American writing," the little English teacher said to his parents. "I suppose they were somewhat noir."

"Oh, you and your Melville and Hawthorne, dear," Susan Barlow said to her son. "We write novels *and* screenplays, Adam," Mrs. Barlow reminded me. I knew that Elliot didn't like his parents' movies any better than he did their books. "While our sensibilities are certainly European, our feeling for noir is very American," Mrs. Barlow said.

"America will always be a frontier country, Adam," John Barlow told me, "and noir is the tone that best captures the frontier—*any* frontier." Mr. Barlow had leaned forward on the table, as if the covered body between us was proof of what was noir about America—as if the diaper man himself, from his infancy to his electrocution, had been a noir frontiersman.

"Sweetie!" I heard my mom calling. Understandably, Mr. and Mrs. Barlow believed my mother was hailing her darling husband. The writing team seemed surprised when my mom flung her arms around me instead of the snowshoer. "Oh, Adam, don't worry, sweetie—everything's going to be fine," she whispered in my ear. "You just can't sleep alone in this house, not until we know what kind of ghost Granddaddy is going to be," she told me. "But don't worry, sweetie—I told Molly to sleep with you."

Under the circumstances, it was difficult to find the prospect of sleeping with the night groomer reassuring. "Molly says she doesn't see ghosts—she doesn't believe in them," my mother went on whispering. "Maybe we're the only ones who see them, sweetie. I don't know if I believe in them, but I sure see them," my mom told me.

This wasn't exactly reassuring to me, either. It made me wonder what else ran in the family. I could see Nora giving me her most reassuring look—not that Nora was much inclined to be reassuring—and Em was nodding her head to me, as if Em could hear (and completely agreed with) everything my mother was whispering.

That was when my mom suddenly exclaimed, "I don't see him! Where's Daddy?"

"He's under the sheet, Rachel—it should be *you* lying there!" Aunt Abigail declared. She was still limping, and leaning more heavily on Aunt Martha for support.

"Yes, Ray, *you* did it to him—*you* killed him!" Aunt Martha chimed in.

"He was killed by lightning—the *heavens* did it to him, you raving assholes," the trail groomer told my aunts.

"Is he charred black—is he all burned up?" my mother cried, pointing to the sheet. I confess I wanted to see how he looked. The diaper man had spent half his life changing who he was. Who wouldn't have wanted to see how the infant emeritus ended up? But no one would answer my mom—no one lifted the sheet. I learned later that the wrestling coach had carried Granddaddy from the croquet court, but the coach didn't speak up, or he'd since gone home.

The snowshoer had locked his hands around my mom's waist, hugging her from behind, where she couldn't see him, but she knew his small hands and clasped them tightly, closing her eyes and leaning against him. "Yes, take me away, dear Elliot," she told him. "Let's go look at that cliff together—just keep hold of me."

"I've got you, Ray," the snowshoer told her. There would be no confetti thrown at them. When they left, I can't remember which of them was driving. Em hugged me from behind, the way Elliot had comforted my mother. Maybe Em liked holding me that way, if only because she knew I couldn't kiss her or look at her breasts with my back turned to her.

I remember what Nora told me: "You have to trust them, Adam—I mean all of them, kiddo."

"All of them?" I asked her. It wasn't a lot to say, but at least I'd spoken.

"You have to trust Ray and the snowshoer—you should trust Molly, too," Nora told me. There was Em's head, thumping me between the shoulder blades, but I was having a hard time with the concept of trusting anyone.

Not even Dottie had anything to say. If Dottie knew how the diaper man looked after the lightning struck him, I suspect she also knew how they *woulda described* his final appearance in Maine, but she spared us those details. My grandmother was talking only to herself—her lips mouthing what looked like a short, declarative sentence. Fortunately, or unfortunately, the edelweiss man was standing beside me. I didn't have to ask him for a translation. "Son of the Bride," the zither-meister said, "what your grandmother keeps telling herself is: 'The drama's done.' Of course, that could be the truth or just wishful thinking."

It was neither, I knew—it was only the first sentence of the Epilogue to *Moby-Dick*. (Queequeg's "coffin life-buoy" has not yet risen from the sea; Ishmael has not yet found his safe passage through the "unharming sharks"; the "devious-cruising Rachel," Ishmael's rescue ship, has not yet "only found another orphan.") All I knew was that I wanted to grow up and leave home, forever. If I could have accomplished this overnight, I sincerely would have.

Mr. and Mrs. Barlow were talking about the gangster film as the epitome of noir. They were expounding to anyone who would listen. They'd just seen a new gangster movie—"a rough cut," in New York. The snowshoer told me that his parents often saw films before they were finished, long before their theatrical release. Elliot implied that the writing team enjoyed talking about a movie they'd seen, but no one else could have.

"It's called *The Wrong Car*—it's not a great gangster movie," John Barlow was saying.

"But the guy who plays the driver of the getaway car is *really* noir—he's someone special," Susan Barlow weighed in. "I know we're going to be seeing more of him."

"His name is Paul Goode—with an *e* on the end, that kind of *Goode*," Mr. Barlow was telling a small audience.

"And the getaway driver is *really* handsome—small but handsome. I think he looks a lot like our Elliot," Mrs. Barlow was saying.

"Well, he's not *that* small, darling," Mr. Barlow said.

"He's *that* handsome," Susan Barlow insisted. When a mother says another man is as handsome as her son, you remember it. That's why I would remember the actor's name. Indeed, we would be *seeing more of him*, as the snowshoer's mom had said, though I wasn't really listening to the Barlows' off-the-cuff conversation.

"Think of a very young George Raft," John Barlow was suggesting.

"If George Raft were *really* handsome," Susan Barlow added. Ironically, my mom and I didn't think George Raft could ever be handsome; we didn't much care for gangster films, either. But I would remember the singling out of the getaway driver.

That was when the snowcat operator spoke to me. "Is it Adam the Kid?" she asked me. I know, I'd been able to speak to Nora, but I couldn't quite manage to speak to the night groomer. I was barely capable of nodding to her. "I'll be seeing you later, Kid—ghost or no ghost," Molly told me.

"Okay," I managed to say to her.

"When shit like this happens," I heard Nora saying to the zither man, "some people call it a night—they just pack it in." I saw Em crazily shaking her head, not wanting to be mistaken for one of those craven people. I could see where this was going.

"I'm guessing you and your friend just want to keep dancing," the zither-meister said to Nora and Em.

"Shit or no shit, we keep dancing," Nora told the Austrian. My aunts and uncles had called it a night. Foreseeing no prospects of dancing, Henrik had packed it in with them—he'd hobbled off. No one could recall when the girly-girl blondes and the rest of the North Conway Norwegians had departed for the inn—perhaps before the fatal lightning strike, and what was for me a life-changing aftershock.

When I said my good-nights to Nana and Dottie, who were sitting at the far end of the table from the infant under the sheet, Dottie told me they were "waitin' up for the authorities—them usual lamebrains in charge of anythin'," as she put it. The girl jocks made a to-do over my going to bed, hugs and kisses galore. The night groomer definitely knew when I was calling it a night. Molly blew me a kiss as I was leaving the wedding tent.

There weren't many partyers under the tent when the edelweiss man resumed zithering. Nora and Em were out on the dance platform, where a few of the girl jocks were dancing with one another. Small groups of people were gathered at the near-empty tables, just talking or drinking. With the tables cleared, I could more clearly see the floating candles. These misbegotten candles had been the idea of our local fire marshal: candles afloat in bowls of water. If someone knocks over a candle, you have a bowl of water handy to douse the flame. But of course the candles kept getting submerged in the water bowls. Then the wicks were wet, and it was hard to relight them. (Dottie doubtless would have included our local fire marshal among the lamebrained authorities.)

A wedding guest, bored and brainless—Henrik, maybe—had placed one of the floating candles in the birdbath. Thus I went to bed with a larger-than-life image of the stone sparrows perched on the rim: the floating candlelight had cast giant shadows of the birds' heads and beaks on the roof of the tent above the birdbath. More disturbing than the huge size of the birds was that they appeared to be moving—twitching slightly, or preparing to peck. The candle afloat in the birdbath was never still—it kept moving, just a little. It was an unsettling image to take to bed—enormous, predatory sparrows—but I was relieved to have something else (anything else) to think about.

I needed to stop thinking about what I'd seen, and what it meant. Was it immaterial that my mom either was or wasn't Elliot Barlow's beard, now that the snowshoer evidently was a beard for my mother? Just what kind of honeymoon could my mom have with the little snowshoer, now that I'd seen the honeymoon she'd been having with the very big trail groomer? If good-looking and small were the features my mother found most attractive in men, what was I to make of Molly, who was beautiful but big?

These were the troubling thoughts that consumed me as I climbed the attic stairs to my bedroom. I wasn't afraid of a nighttime visit from my grandfather's ghost—with or without the night groomer to protect me. I even welcomed a haunting from the diaper man's restless spirit. If the ghost of the infant emeritus came creeping up the attic stairs, at least I would have someone else to think about. I didn't know what to think about my mom and Molly and the little snowshoer—I kept trying to imagine them in the rest of my life.

Now on a hanger—on a hook, on the inside of my bathroom door—my mother's blameless wedding dress regarded me with unlaced simplicity. The bed was neatly made for me. No naked bodies, locked together in an upside-down embrace, were reflected in the skylight. No rain, no thunder, no lightning—the storm had passed. I left a light on in the bathroom, with the door ajar—a night-light for the night groomer—and got into bed in my boxers. The skylight, partially open, was tilted toward my bed. I heard a moth, flapping against the screen, no doubt drawn to the light from my bathroom. I could also hear the zither—a zither makes ghostly music when you hear it from far away, especially "The Harry Lime Theme."

The tread I heard on the attic stairs was too heavy a footfall for Granddaddy's ghost—at the time of his death, the diaper man didn't weigh as much as Little Ray. But then I reconsidered: Why should you hear a ghost's footsteps at all? When that telltale step sharply creaked near the top of the stairs, I heard the trail groomer say, "Don't worry, Kid—it's just me." Under the circumstances, this wasn't entirely reassuring. At the time, I may have been more afraid of Molly than I was of anybody's ghost. Molly was wearing some workout shorts and a tank top without a bra, what my mom might have slept in on a warm summer night, and the night groomer got under the sheet with me as matter-of-factly as my mother would have—notwithstanding that the final resting place for my grandfather, whose ghost we awaited, had been under a sheet.

"I don't think Granddaddy's ghost will be charred black, or even a little bit burnt," I said to Molly. "Do you think ghosts look like they looked at the moment they died?" I asked her.

"I don't think about ghosts—I don't see ghosts, no matter what they look like or how they died," Molly said. "I think some people see them, and some don't," she added.

"My mom sees them, and she's always asking me if I've seen them, but I've only started to see them," I explained to Molly.

"I just know I'm not going to Aspen, or nowhere near that hotel your mother never stops talking about. There are plenty of other ski towns and hotels to go to," the night groomer told me.

"The Hotel Jerome," I said—as reverentially as possible, given the history.

"You couldn't get me to go there for breakfast," Molly said.

It's too simple to say that people who don't believe in ghosts don't see them. Nana said she'd seen enough of Granddaddy when he was alive, not least when he wasn't speaking and in a diaper. Nana said she didn't need to see his ghost.

Only God knows how Aunt Abigail and Aunt Martha really felt about ghosts; only time would tell if my aunts were susceptible to seeing them. I would venture a guess that Aunt Abigail and Aunt Martha basically disapproved of ghosts; I always believed they would express their moral indignation upon seeing one. Only God knows what form that moral indignation would take. Only God would be there, upon their apparent ghost sighting.

If Uncle Martin or Uncle Johan ever saw a ghost, I'm sure their response would be completely inappropriate. My uncles, and other people who can't distinguish between comedy and tragedy, probably shouldn't see ghosts.

Surely Henrik lacked the imagination to see or believe in ghosts. He would one day be elected to the U.S. House of Representatives from a southern state—the same state where he went to college, to play lacrosse. At the time of my mom's wedding, Henrik had not yet revealed his political inclinations, but given Henrik's habit of expressing his desire for Em with his lacrosse stick, we should have known his politics wouldn't be altruistic. A future Republican, Henrik was too self-interested to adapt to ghosts.

It suffices to say that my thoughts about ghosts were wandering while I waited for Granddaddy's ghost to appear. It's true that the ghost of the bogus principal emeritus wasn't the first ghost I saw, but the diaper man was the first ghost I had known when he was (more or less) alive.

Then I saw Lewis Brewster's ghost. He was nicely dressed, in a jacket and a tie—a much younger man than I'd ever known, and he seemed to take a frank and kindly interest in me, which he'd never taken. "My dear boys," the youthful-looking English teacher said to Molly and me. Ghosts didn't see very well, or this one didn't. "Punctuation doesn't have to be this difficult," young Mr. Brewster assured us. I'd only seen photos of him at this age.

"What is it, Adam?" Molly asked. She'd put her arm around me. I must have made some sudden, startled move beside her when I saw the ghost. The young English teacher was standing under the skylight, as if he'd descended from the heavens.

"It's him—he's not burnt," I told Molly. "It's him, before I was born."

"I've got you, Kid," the night groomer said, putting both her strong arms around me.

"Remember one thing, boys, about the much-maligned semicolon," my youthful grandfather was saying to us. "The clause following a semicolon should ideally be a complete sentence; the part about a complete sentence is what distinguishes the semicolon from the dash," the youthful Mr. Brewster further explained to us. "What follows a dash can but needn't be a complete sentence—just an aside, perhaps a random interjection. Do you see, my dear boys?" Granddaddy's ghost asked. When I nodded, I could tell that the trail groomer had gone to sleep—with one heavy leg thrown over me. The young English teacher went on and on, until I fell asleep, too. It was "I Forgot to Remember to Forget" that the zither man was playing when Molly and I woke up hugging each other.

"Is the damn ghost gone?" the night groomer asked me. He was. The punctuation lecture was over. When I tried to tell Molly what the ghost had taught me, all she said was: "I'm still not going to Aspen—not even if the conversation is about punctuation. Besides, we've got more important things to talk about, Kid."

She sang the beginning of the Elvis song to me again—just a few lines from "I Forgot to Remember to Forget."

I just started talking—I told Molly everything. How my mom had shown me the way she'd kissed the snowshoer—how I'd shown Em, who showed Nora, what kind of kiss it was. I even told the night groomer what I'd seen reflected in the skylight above my bed, and how little I understood what

I saw. Molly kept holding me, but she just listened. By the time I finished everything I had to say, the zither-meister had stopped playing. Molly and I saw a predawn glow in the skylight. I'd told the trail groomer my most troubling thoughts—all the stuff about who was whose beard, and my mother's apparent fondness for small, good-looking men and big, beautiful women. I mean truly everything.

"Here's what I know, Kid—I love your mom for how she just does certain things without any forethought, because if you truly love someone, you have to love everything about them. Even the things that hurt," Molly said. "As for a *beard*, it's a hateful word the way your hateful aunts use it—in their eyes, a beard is all about the deceit. But two beards are better than one, Kid," the night groomer assured me. "Your mother and the snowshoer aren't deceiving each other. They love each other, in their own way. It doesn't have to be the same way your mom and I love each other," was the way Molly put it. "There's more than one way to love people, Kid." All through the night, we'd held on to each other, and I thought of the honeymoon my mom and the snowshoer were having in Maine—how they were looking at that cliff together, how my mom had told Elliot to keep hold of her.

When there's an event that changes your life forever, you know how the afteryears go by—how some people change, and some don't. As I lay in the night groomer's arms, I was hoping that this precarious triangle—that these three beloved people—would never change. Not Molly, not my mom, not the snowshoer. *Please stay on the cliff,* I was praying—to all three of them, for all four of us. *Please keep hold of me, and of one another,* I prayed.

ACT II

THE HONEYMOON
ON THE CLIFF

19.

"I SAW ME IN YOUR EYES"

For another thirty-five years, I wouldn't go to Aspen; I didn't set foot inside the Hotel Jerome. "You couldn't get me to go there for breakfast," as Molly said. But you should be careful what you purposely put off doing; over time, the importance of doing it grows. I also put off falling in love and getting married. At first unconsciously, then consciously, I chose unmarriageable girlfriends. Naturally, most of my girlfriends didn't know I thought they were unmarriageable. You should be careful about that, too.

I was almost fifty when I first got married; my much younger wife was only thirty-four. In my years of unmarriageable girlfriends, I'd learned to avoid younger women; they were more likely to be marriageable. When you make a point of not looking for the girl of your dreams, this has consequences. When you go out of your way to avoid any woman who looks like she might lead to a serious relationship, you get used to lying to yourself. I got used to being attracted to girlfriends who didn't attract me.

My mother met my future wife before I did. My mom gave her ski lessons. Little Ray and the snowcat operator decided that this young woman might be the one for me. My mom and Molly would hold on to each other—no falling off the cliff for them.

"Now that you've met the right woman, don't ever lie to her, Adam," my mom would say. "Lies of omission count as lies, sweetie—they can be the worst ones." This really rubbed me the wrong way.

What a hypocrite my mother was. Imagine her telling me that lies of omission counted as lies. Hadn't she demonstrated that lies of omission could be the worst ones? She'd not told me about her and Molly! She'd let me discover them as a couple—in their unforgettable, upside-down embrace. "Molly and I were thinking of the best time to tell you, sweetie—we thought *after* the wedding would have been best," was how my mom put it.

"That was an apology, kiddo—just get over it," Nora would tell me, but not even Em would nod her head to that. Em and I were on the same page when it came to a lie of omission of that magnitude. My mother should have told me about her and Molly. This was why I didn't heed her advice about lies of omission. Nora had tried to set me straight: "No one knows more than Ray about lies of omission. You should listen to her on the subject, kiddo."

The past is everlasting. In my new life, with my new wife, I got off to a bad start. I should have forsworn the lies of omission, including how I put off telling her about the ghosts. In my defense, I was remembering my experiences with some previous girlfriends—the ones I told about the ghosts. With a few of my most unmarriageable girlfriends, telling them about the ghosts was a good way to initiate the process of breaking up with them. Usually, they thought I was kidding. If I insisted that I was one of those people who saw ghosts, they thought I was crazy and broke up with me.

There were the disbelieving girlfriends who asked me to prove it. When my grandmother was still alive, I took the disbelievers to the Front Street house. When the semicolon emeritus appeared, there were mixed reactions to him. Like Molly, there were women who didn't believe in ghosts, or they simply didn't see them; in their eyes, I was a nutcase. This is a relatively painless way to break up with someone. Yet when the disbelievers saw Granddaddy's ghost, of course I would be blamed for their paranormal experience—as if the supernatural manifestations were all my fault.

"When you want to break up with someone, you're going to get blamed for it—no matter how it happens, sweetie," my mother told me. She had a point, but I took her advice on this aspect of love *with a grain of salt*—as Dottie said they were always saying in Maine.

In poor Sally's case, I was not trying to break up with her when I took her to my attic bedroom and she saw the spirit of punctuation perfection. Sally was my first girlfriend. I was very fond of her. I didn't want to break up with her. I just wanted to make out with her, and I knew Nana and Dottie wouldn't intrude; those two were fussing around in the kitchen, where my grandmother was struggling over one of her mystery casseroles. "When you're in your attic bedroom, I'm leavin' you to your own business, Adam—if I need ya, you'll hear me hollerin' from them attic stairs!" Dottie had told me.

I suppose I was hoping to impress Sally. I'd told her that my grandfather was a ghost; she said she wanted to see him. She wasn't challenging me—she sounded like she believed me.

Nora had a way of compartmentalizing my girlfriends—"the overweight one" was Nora's shorthand for Sally. "Didn't Sally get stuck in a shower?" Nora was always asking me—thus pigeonholing one awkward moment as the epitome of my "fat-girl infatuation," as Nora referred to my first girlfriend experience.

This seemed unkind of Nora, who was (as she'd always been) a big girl. But I'd already noticed—at fourteen, going on fifteen, when I was a first-time student at the academy—how overweight girls were discriminated against, often cruelly. I took their side; I felt sorry for them, but I was truly attracted to them. Did their bigness in juxtaposition to my smallness have something to do with my attraction to them? My mom said she thought so.

"Duh!" Nora said, when I asked her about it.

I met Sally at a high school dance. There were dances in the gym at Exeter High School on the weekends. The students were the same kids I'd known in elementary or junior high school, but now that I was attending the academy, I felt ostracized at those dances. The high school kids either ignored me or they treated me as if I'd snubbed them.

The pretty girls were always with someone; they were already dancing. Before I went to my first dance, the snowshoer warned me about cutting in. "The townies who go to the academy are not very welcome at the high school dances, Adam—just don't cut in," Elliot had told me.

The not-so-pretty girls were dancing with one another, or they sat waiting to be asked to dance. I noticed that no one asked the overweight ones, and the heavier of them were disinclined to dance with one another; maybe they thought dancing together would just call attention to how big they were. I saw Sally sitting by herself. Even when she was sitting down, I could see how big her boobs were and how tall she was. I knew I would come up only to her collarbones.

Our first dance was a slow one. I was slow-dancing at eye level to Sally's boobs to "Old Shep" or "How's the World Treating You?" —'56 was a big year for Elvis. A few of the cooler couples were quick to laugh at us.

"They're laughing at us because I'm small," I said to Sally.

"They're laughing at us because I'm fat," Sally told me, without hesitation.

"I don't think you're fat, but I know I'm small," I told her.

"I know how to shut 'em up," Sally said, pulling my head to her breasts and holding me there. This was when I got the idea of making out with her in my attic bedroom; this was also when the disc jockey decided to switch from slow Elvis to fast Elvis.

First my face was pressed against Sally's boobs, and we were dancing to a dead-dog dirge; then Elvis was singing "Blue Suede Shoes" or "I Got a Woman," and I was trying to hang on.

Fast-dancing with Sally was an exercise in staying out of her way. I soon realized Sally was intent on doing damage to the couple who'd laughed at us the quickest and the loudest. Sally hit the couple hard, mid-twirl, hipping them across the gym floor, where they fell together in a tangled heap. "Oops!" Sally said, twirling back to me. I realized she was more agile than she looked.

I liked her so much, I even introduced her to my mother and the little snowshoer—this was in the fall, before the ski season, of course. But there was nowhere Sally and I could have made out in Mr. Barlow's faculty apartment; it was a small apartment in one of the academy dormitories. I would have had to bring Sally into the dorm, where all the Exeter boys could get a look at her. I was afraid of the comments one of those cruel boys might have made. I was brand new, as both a faculty brat and an academy student. Many of those Exeter boys were smarter and more sophisticated than I was. I felt I was an outsider among them.

I liked how clear Sally was about the rules for making out; she was exceptionally clear about the guidelines. Compared to Sally, my later girlfriends would be vague or misleading or self-contradictory about the regulations regarding touching or no touching. "We keep our underwear on—there's no touching anything that's inside our underwear," Sally told me, as we were going up the attic stairs. "*Rubbing* is okay—we can rub against each other, anywhere we feel like it," Sally said.

"Okay," I said. At fourteen, who wouldn't be okay with that? And what if I hadn't said a single word to Sally about Granddaddy's ghost? What if the never-a-headmaster had just shown up, blathering about punctuation marks? It's hard to imagine that would have turned out any better. Exeter is a small town. Everyone knew Lewis Brewster was dead; everyone had heard how he'd died.

Like many things, ghosts are a cultural problem. People who haven't seen a ghost expect to see their prevailing fantasy of a spirit: a gauzy shape, a vague presence, or the mere sensation of a spiritual life; a bodiless voice, a cold draft, a chair that moves. People who don't know ghosts aren't expecting a person who seems real.

There we were, in our underwear in my attic bedroom, Sally and I, rubbing each other everywhere; we were kissing and touching everything, except those parts of ourselves that were inside our underwear. It was twilight, and we were writhing around under the skylight. This time, the late Princi-pal Brewster was talking about commas.

"Boys, boys," he began. (Trust me: Sally didn't look like a boy.) "The poor comma can't do everything, my dear boys—you expect too much of it," my youthful-looking grandfather said.

I noticed that Sally had stopped rubbing herself against me; she'd stopped touching me, too. This could mean that Sally was sexually satisfied—more likely, she'd lost interest in me, I was thinking. I didn't notice that Sally had stopped breathing.

"A comma fault, also called a comma splice," Granddaddy's ghost was saying, when Sally caught her breath and started screaming. Her screams were of no concern to the deceased faculty emeritus, who decided to sit beside us on the edge of my bed.

Sally ran screaming into the bathroom—a very small bathroom—formerly the attic closet. When I was born, there was no bedroom in the Front Street house to accommodate a live-in grandchild. Once there was a bedroom for me, in the attic, the closet was converted to a bathroom. It was too small a bathroom, to begin with; the shower stall was even smaller. "It doesn't matter how small the shower is," my mother told Nana. "My one and only is going to be small!"

It was too small a shower stall for Sally. What was she thinking when she got in the shower in her underwear? In the first place, Sally never meant to turn the water on; she wasn't trying to take a shower. Sally was trying to get away from the ghost. She sized up the shower as entirely too small for the ghost to get in with her.

Sally's nonstop screaming had started a debate between my grandmother and Dottie in the kitchen, two floors below.

"I hope that's not a loss-of-virginity scream—that girl is much too young," Nana had said. (Dottie would tell me—not then, but later—how she'd an-swered my grandmother.)

"That sure as shit sounds like too much caterwaulin', and the wrong kind of caterwaulin', for a loss of virginity to me, Mrs. Brewster," Dottie told my grandmother. Sally's prolonged screaming had sounded like "a toolbox situation" to Dottie, who was prescient enough to have brought her toolbox, when she called up to me from the bottom of the attic stairs. "Is there some-thin' or someone in need of fixin', Adam?" Dottie called.

By then, the situation in the shower stall had worsened. Poor, overweight Sally had slipped and fallen; before she fell, she'd inadvertently turned on the shower. The cold water must have surprised her; then the hot water had scalded her. She'd contorted herself to get away from the stream. She lay wedged against the door—I couldn't open the door because she was pressed against it. Her bra and panties were thoroughly soaked, and thoroughly transparent. "Don't *look* at me, Adam!" Sally wailed. "Don't let the ghost get in here!" she cried.

But Granddaddy's ghost had vanished; he'd heard Dottie calling from the bottom of the attic stairs. Not even death had saved the infant emeritus from his fear of Dottie and her Seeing Eye dog harness.

"You're going to need your toolbox!" I was calling to Dottie. I could hear her clomping up the attic stairs.

"I could tell by all the caterwaulin'—I know a toolbox situation when I hear one, Adam," Dottie was saying.

"Dottie will help you," I said to Sally. "Dottie isn't a ghost." The way she was wedged in the shower made me reconsider Sally's agility.

"You've seen too much of me, Adam," Sally moaned. "When you think of me, you'll remember me this way," she added. I knew it was true; I couldn't refute it, then or now.

"Holy shit," Dottie said, when she saw what the toolbox situation entailed. "You get out of here, Adam—go talk to your grandmother, or somethin'," Dottie told me. "Don't you worry, sweetheart," Dottie said to Sally. "This stupid shower wasn't built for a full-size person, but there ain't a door I can't get off," Dottie said. I put on my clothes and left the two of them, with Dottie at work removing the hinges to the shower door.

"My nipple got burned by the hot water—just one of them," I could hear Sally telling Dottie, as I went down the attic stairs.

"Don't you worry, sweetheart," I heard Dottie say. "I know what works for a scalded nipple—I just gotta get this fuckin' door off first."

I helped my grandmother in the kitchen and the dining room while Dottie was attending to Sally. I was surprised how relieved Nana was to hear what had happened to poor Sally. I felt awful about Sally's humiliation in the shower, and her scalded nipple. Not knowing, at the time, about Nana's conversation with Dottie, I was unaware that my grandmother had imagined far worse. Now, in retrospect, I'm not at all sure that Sally's loss of her virginity would have been worse.

"I saw me in your eyes—what you were thinking," was all Sally would say to me about it, ever. I knew, even before Dottie brought her downstairs to the dining room, that Sally and I were finished. Her blouse was a little too sheer to wear without a bra, but Sally sat through dinner while we listened to her underwear in the dryer. You couldn't quite see her nipples through her blouse, but the Band-Aid covering the scalded nipple was very clear. Dottie wouldn't tell me what Down East remedy for relief she'd put on the nipple, or on the Band-Aid. "Just a dab of somethin'," was all Dottie would say. For a big girl, poor Sally didn't eat much of Nana's mystery casserole while we listened, interminably, to the clicking sound made by Sally's bra in the dryer.

Mr. Barlow suggested I write about it. "Your first girlfriend, your first heartbreak, and hers—that's a short story, Adam," the little English teacher told me.

I called the short story "I Saw Me in Your Eyes"—Sally's title, of course. What Sally had seen in my eyes was pity; once she'd seen how I pitied her, I could never take it back.

"You should save your pity for your fictional characters, Adam—pity is a good thing, in fiction," the little snowshoer said. "Real women, on the other hand, do not take kindly to your feeling sorry for them—real women want to be loved, not pitied," Mr. Barlow told me.

It meant a lot to me that the snowshoer liked my short story, and the title. I admitted to Mr. Barlow that I'd been tempted to call the story "The Scalded Nipple," but I chose Sally's title (as I thought of it) instead. The snowshoer assured me that I'd made the right decision.

"There's more pity in Sally's title," Mr. Barlow said.

20

A LITTLE BEHIND GIRLS HER AGE, SOCIALLY; DEFINITELY AHEAD OF; DEFINITELY BEHIND

I decided the high school dances were off-limits, not wanting poor Sally to see in my eyes how she'd looked when she was wedged in the shower. Besides, who was I going to ask to dance? One of those girls who was dancing with another girl? They looked like girl jocks to me; maybe they were teammates, field hockey players or cross-country runners. Was there a protocol concerning cutting in on girls who were dancing together?

I asked Mr. Barlow, but he deferred to my mother and Molly. "Ask them—they know more about what enrages girls than I do," the little English teacher said.

"The problem is the one you *don't* ask to dance—she'll hate you, sweetie," my mom said.

"Eventually, if they're teammates, *both* of them will hate you, Kid," Molly told me.

I complained to the snowshoer that the hatred my mother and Molly had predicted from the dancing teammates didn't sound logical to me. "Then it's definitely true—hatred isn't logical," Mr. Barlow said. "A wallflower might be safer than a girl jock," he advised me. I considered the word *wallflower* already old-fashioned, even in the fifties. Wasn't it a word more in keeping with my grandmother's generation than the snowshoer's? And if a wallflower was a person who remained on the sidelines of any activity—out of shyness or unpopularity, or the lack of a partner—wasn't Sally, who was overweight, a wallflower?

Surely I was just a different variety of wallflower—hence I felt a natural attraction to other wallflowers. As a new boy at the academy—one who was perceived as an interloper when I intruded upon the public school kids— hadn't I become an outsider in the town I'd grown up in?

I didn't meet Rose at a dance—"the clubfooted one," Nora called her.

"The *kinda* clubfooted one," was the way Dottie put it, which seemed no less unkind.

"Rose isn't clubfooted," I insisted. "She just has a right foot that goes awry."

"It sure as shit went awry on them attic stairs!" Dottie had exclaimed.

"That's enough, Dottie—please don't. Poor Rose," my grandmother always said.

"And the strong one on crutches, and the tall one with her arm in a cast!" Dottie declared, rolling her eyes.

"They were jocks—they just had injuries, temporarily," I told her.

"As I recall, Adam, you only went out with 'em when they was injured—temporarily," Dottie told me.

"Please, Dottie—that's enough," my grandmother repeated.

I met Rose in the library, where you might expect to encounter a wallflower. This was the town's public library, not the academy library. Rose was such a wallflower, I didn't even know she was a faculty brat; most faculty daughters went away to private schools. In an all-girls' school, her parents had feared Rose would be teased, because of her limp—her *lurch*, Nora had labeled it. I didn't think it was a drastic limp, though the first time you saw it, you thought Rose had tripped and was going to fall. It may not have been a congenitally misshapen deformity, but something went wrong with the right side of Rose's body when she walked. She spent much of her time in the library doing research on limps, and reading about surgical mishaps.

The old librarian, Mrs. McNulty, who walked with a cane, always put her index finger to her lips when she looked at us—as if to shush us, although Rose and I never spoke in the library. We wrote each other notes. Mrs. McNulty must have thought that teenagers couldn't be trusted to keep quiet in a library. Mrs. McNulty also appeared to disapprove of our writing each other notes.

"You're always writing, usually not reading. What are you writing?" was the first note Rose wrote to me.

I had to tear several pages out of my notebook in order to explain that I was trying to be a fiction writer; I was making things up. I didn't like to write in the academy library, because there were students (usually older boys) who grabbed my notebook to see what I was writing. Rose confided to me that faculty daughters in their teens were considered a distraction to the boys in the academy library. When the boys saw her sitting at one of the tables, they flirted with her—until she had to walk somewhere, and the boys got a look at her limp. Thus was I forewarned of the limp before I saw it. Rose and her parents were undecided about the corrective surgery proposed for her limp. "What if the surgery makes the limp worse?" was the way Rose had written it.

Mrs. McNulty was a bitch about the sound I made when I tore pages out of my notebook. I stopped writing in spiral notebooks. I began to use a loose-leaf notebook, the kind with rings. If you were careful, you could open and close the rings without making a popping sound. Mrs. McNulty had nothing better to do than watch me when I opened and closed the rings, in her hawklike anticipation of the *pop*. It took me a few weeks to get up the nerve to write Rose the note about the attic bedroom in my grandmother's house. "It's on the third floor," I felt it was necessary to say. I'd still not seen Rose walk. I didn't know if she could manage stairs.

"If there's a banister, I can do stairs—no problem," Rose wrote me back.

The first night I walked her home from the town library, I did my best not to gawk at her limp. There were academy boys who imitated the way she limped, Rose told me. Her parents' faculty apartment was only on the second floor of one of the student dormitories, but when Rose was limping upstairs, or down, there were boys in the dorm who purposely stayed behind her on the stairs—they watched her limp. Such cruelty was unimaginable to me. I found her very pretty—in a kind of literary, damaged, tragic way.

Rose was a year older, and a year ahead of me in school; she was fifteen, almost sixteen, but she didn't have her driver's permit. "I'm not allowed to learn to drive," Rose told me. "My right foot is my *accelerator* foot," she said, "and sometimes I get muscle spasms when I'm sitting or lying down." I remember how she paused before she kissed me; she was more tentative about kissing than Sally.

There are things you hear that you only later realize you should have listened to more closely. The quiet way Rose said, before our first kiss, that her muscle spasms were worse than her limp; or the first time she let me touch her small but pretty breasts, when Rose told me she was a little behind girls her own age, socially. (She did not mean the size of her breasts, I would only later realize.)

I didn't wonder, as I should have—seeing how she struggled with the steepness of the attic stairs—why Rose hadn't stated what the rules were for making out. The "touch this (but not that)" business had not been made clear. It wouldn't have occurred to me to imagine that Rose might not have made out before. She was such a pretty girl, and she was a year older than me.

Why risk spoiling everything by telling her about Granddaddy's ghost? I was thinking. Weeks would pass without the punctuation maven showing up. I thought of reassuring or dismissive things I could say if the infant-brained spirit suddenly appeared. "Pay no attention to this tiresome fool" was too cavalier to say about a ghost. I decided it would be better if I gave the phantom English teacher a direct command. Such as: "Get out of my bedroom!" Wouldn't my taking charge of the apparition be the most reassuring to Rose? Clearly, at fourteen and dying to make out with Rose, I'd not considered the unlikelihood of my taking charge of a specter. Granddaddy's ghost, especially as an English teacher, was not in the category of a headless horseman—or so I thought. When you're young and inexperienced, it's easy to underestimate the power of the supernatural—or of muscle spasms.

I took off my clothes first, leaving my boxers on; Rose just watched me, doing nothing. "Our underwear stays on, right?" she asked.

"Right," I answered her. She sat on the edge of the bed, slowly taking her clothes off. I didn't watch her; I had my eye on that spot under the skylight where you-know-who had a habit of just appearing. When Rose and I were kneeling together on the bed, she was still taller than I was—even on her knees. When we were lying down and kissing, and feeling each other up, I truly thought Rose was the right girlfriend for me—certainly not because I pitied her.

I mistook the muscle spasm in Rose's right calf for her first sighting of the infant emeritus. Rose emitted a bloodcurdling cry, worthy of a first-time ghost sighting. Her right foot flopped crazily all around, and Rose grabbed the back of her right thigh—then, suddenly, the right cheek of her buttocks. She'd not told me her muscle spasms had a ripple effect on the right side of her body; the ripples ran from her calf to her hamstring to her gluteus maximus. Rose had writhed off the bed and was propelling herself with her heels, on her back, across the bedroom floor. I was looking everywhere for the diaper man, but I couldn't see him. I had no doubt that Rose must have seen him.

As with Sally, I would only belatedly learn the gist of what Dottie and my grandmother were saying in the kitchen, where Rose's piercing screams had reached them. "Heaven have mercy—they can't be having sex, can they?" Nana asked Dottie.

"That sure as shit don't sound like sex to me, Mrs. Brewster—not in any of the usual positions I can think of," Dottie answered her.

Maybe the faculty emeritus had been lurking in the open doorway of my attic bathroom, and Rose had seen his reflection in the skylight? Although I couldn't see Granddaddy's ghost, I didn't hesitate to speak sharply to him. I never imagined that poor Rose would think I was speaking to *her*.

"Get out of my bedroom!" I said (I thought) to Granddaddy's ghost, who (of course) wasn't there. Nana and Dottie didn't hear what I said—not over Rose's heart-stopping scream, not as far away as the kitchen—but, from Rose's heartrending expression, I had no doubt that Rose had heard me.

"No, not *you*—I meant the *ghost!*" I said to Rose, which my grandmother and Dottie also didn't hear; Rose clearly did. The *ghost* word, and her perception that I was rejecting her, gave a new urgency to Rose's backpedaling across my bedroom floor. She'd called her wonky right foot her *accelerator* foot—the stated reason Rose was not allowed to drive a car—but the way she propelled herself with both her heels, on her back, down the attic stairs, suggested to me another reason not to let Rose drive. In the middle of a muscle spasm, Rose's capacity to accelerate in reverse would have been more hazardous (and frightening to behold) in a car.

From the attic, I could only watch in horror Rose's headfirst and rigidly supine descent of the stairs. Dottie was there—she was able to soften Rose's fall at the foot of the stairs. Rose's panties had been pulled down to her knees—step by step, an inch or two at a time, in the course of her harrowing descent. Commanded to get out of my bedroom in the agony of her muscle spasm, and being abruptly told there was a *ghost*, poor Rose had seen me at the top of the stairs. She not only knew I'd watched her fall; she saw the exact moment of my seeing her so crudely exposed.

You can't control how you look when you see someone revealed that way. I can't imagine the expression on my face, or how poor Rose would ever forget it. At that moment, my pity for her was apparent. As with Sally, it wasn't a look I could take back.

In my boxers, I started down the stairs; Dottie stopped me before I got to the step that creaked. "Get dressed, Adam—then bring me this young lady's clothes," Dottie said. Rose had managed to pull her panties up, but she clung to Dottie, with her face turned away from me.

After Granddaddy's death, when I was asked if my grandmother had a servant, I answered truthfully and without hesitation: "Not exactly." During the diaper man's decline, Dottie had taken charge of him. As my grandmother aged, I could foresee Dottie taking charge of her. Now, on the evening of Rose's muscle spasm, Dottie certainly took charge of Rose. Dottie got Rose dressed for the dinner table. Dottie gathered Rose's wits together for her.

At dinner, after my grandmother served the casserole, all eyes were on the recovered but clearly shaken Rose. "I don't like to take the muscle relaxant, because it makes me sleepy," Rose was telling us. "I take it at bedtime, so I don't get a cramp in my sleep, but during the day—well, you know, I just take my chances." She shrugged.

The shrug seemed to trigger the first twitch. Her fork, in her right hand, had been pushing the tuna casserole around, with no apparent purpose. When Rose's right biceps contracted, her fork grazed her right cheek—it came close to poking her in the eye. An errant glob of tuna, pasta, and cheese sailed over Rose's right shoulder. "Limping is safer for me than sitting, and lying down is when I get the worst ones," Rose explained. She was doing her best to remain detached from her body's behavior.

Her right knee suddenly struck the underside of the table, making our water glasses jump—the fork flew out of Rose's right hand. "Or when I'm nervous, like when everyone is staring at me," Rose blurted out. "Like when everyone is waiting for me to have a major muscle spasm, if I just *twitch* or something," Rose said, twitching. It was hard to look at her, but it was harder not to.

I looked under the table for Rose's lost fork, but Dottie had already gone to the kitchen to get a clean one. The lost fork wasn't under the table. What caught my eye was Rose's right foot; Rose had told me her right foot had a mind of its own. Under the table, I saw her right foot keeping time to a tune no one could hear.

I would walk Rose home. Knowing that limping was safer for her than sitting down, we had a peaceful walk, but we both knew that would be the end of it. "I'm so sorry that, if only for a moment, you thought I was telling *you* to get out of my bedroom," I said to her, but she wouldn't even hold my hand.

"I can't believe you didn't warn me about the ghost," was all Rose had to say.

When I told Mr. Barlow about it, he was full of sympathy for Rose. "If you didn't prepare her and she saw the ghost, it's not pretty to imagine the muscle spasm Rose might have had," the snowshoer said.

I tried not to imagine the muscle spasm the ghost of the infant emeritus might have provoked in Rose. I told Mr. Barlow I was in no hurry to write about it. "Yes, it would be better to wait. The worst stories get worse over time—you're wise to wait," the little English teacher said, but he couldn't refrain from opening the Pandora's box of possible titles for Rose's story.

Of course Nana and Dottie had already provided the snowshoer with their details of Rose's muscle spasm and her indecent exposure on the attic stairs. My grandmother couldn't say her name without turning her into a title: "Poor Rose." Dottie referred to Rose in three ways. "The Kinda Clubfooted One" was the least sympathetic as a title, in Mr. Barlow's opinion, although I thought "The Twitcher," which was Dottie's favorite, would have been worse. The snowshoer and I agreed that the closest Dottie came to pity was when she called Rose, almost neutrally, "The One with the Limp."

"I have a hard time hearing much sympathy in any title with *muscle spasm* in it," the little English teacher told me. I did not tell Mr. Barlow what Rose had said the first time she let me touch her breasts. I was ashamed—I *am* ashamed—I misunderstood her. When Rose told me she was *a little behind girls her age, socially,* I should have known she was trying to tell me she was sexually inexperienced. How could I have thought poor Rose was referring to the smallness of her breasts?

I got off to a rocky start with my first two girlfriends, but they weren't bad girlfriends. I was truly attracted to Sally and Rose; what went wrong wasn't their fault. Not only in my adolescence, but continuing through college, I seemed to be attracted to a succession of girlfriends who were predisposed to tragedy, giving credence to Nora's (and my mother's) speculation that I was drawn to doom in my girlfriend-selection process.

My empathy for my next three girlfriends is as various as they were. "The Strong One on Crutches," "The Tall One with Her Arm in a Cast," "The Bleeder"—were they tragically inclined? In their varying ways, yes. But I was young, and so were they. Even my grandmother—even Dottie—cut me some slack because of my age, and the age of those girlfriends.

I didn't dare go to the dances in the Exeter High School gym until someone told me Sally had been sent away to boarding school. By then, I had my driver's license. Mr. Barlow had taught me to drive; I'd passed my driving test in his VW Beetle. During the exam, when I felt my grip on the steering wheel overtighten, I remembered to remain seated—as the little English teacher had advised me.

As for the girl jocks who were dancing with one another, I knew better than to cut in. It hadn't occurred to me that the loners among them—the girl jocks who weren't dancing—would be the ones who were injured. I certainly knew better than to ask a girl on crutches to dance. I first saw Caroline standing on her crutches at the periphery of the dance floor; later I saw her sitting alone in one of the folding chairs, with a second chair supporting her injured leg. On crutches, she'd appeared hulking—even sitting down, she looked very strong. When I sat down in the empty chair beside her, her broad shoulders made me feel especially small. From where I sat, her crutches—leaning against the gym wall, behind her—seemed taller than I was.

I thought Caroline was a little vague about her knee injury. "Some rotational force was applied to my right knee when all my weight was on that same leg," was the way she put it. I had trouble visualizing this, but I don't know field hockey at all. Caroline was still angry that the opposing player hadn't drawn a penalty for the hit.

As for the surgery, she was somewhat more specific. "Torn meniscus— they took the whole thing out," Caroline said, shrugging her big shoulders. She had stitches, a gauze bandage, and an elastic compression bandage over the gauze bandage. They'd instructed her not to bend her knee and to keep . her right leg elevated, but she wasn't in a cast. I thought the jocks I knew at the academy, the ones who'd had a meniscectomy, were in casts, but Caroline assured me the ACE bandage was sufficient to remind her to keep her right leg straight.

"It's a pain in the ass to keep the stitches dry," she told me. If she took a bath, she had to hold her right leg above the tub. If she took a shower, she had to enclose her right leg in a plastic garbage bag; she had to find a rubber band big enough to make the garbage bag watertight, in the area of her upper thigh. "I don't have a small upper thigh," Caroline pointed out, showing me. She indicated her thick leg, supported by the chair.

I couldn't imagine we had anything to talk about, nor would Nana and Dottie allow this hulking brute on crutches anywhere near the attic stairs. If poor Sally had managed to wedge herself in my small shower stall, I couldn't conceive how Caroline could fit through the shower door—certainly not with her right leg in a plastic garbage bag. Dottie still complained about the shower door. "It was easy as fartin' to take off," Dottie said, "but it was a bitch to put back on."

I was about to wish Caroline all the best for her knee and call it a night when Caroline suddenly said, "You're the skier's kid, aren't you? I wonder what that's like." I asked her what she meant; she shrugged again. "I just heard about her—girl jocks hear about other girl jocks," Caroline said, in her vague way.

When her dad had been in the military, her family was always on the move; Caroline had lived all over the place. Now she missed the moving around. Never getting out of the town of Exeter was boring; since her knee injury, Caroline even missed the road trips on the team bus. I got the feeling that Caroline was probably ahead of girls her age, socially. I began to think about a road trip we might take together.

My mom was already in Vermont for the ski season—there was snow there by mid-November. I knew the snowshoer would let me borrow his VW Beetle. Caroline had to keep her knee elevated; she could have the whole backseat to extend her right leg. My mom and Molly had a big futon in their TV room; I explained to Caroline that we could sleep on the futon on the floor of the TV room. It was a long drive, but we had some free time during the long Thanksgiving weekend.

When I spoke to my mother and Molly about our visit, they seemed more interested in Caroline's knee surgery than they were curious about our relationship. Molly said a torn meniscus wasn't the skier's friend. So-called open meniscal surgery meant removing the entire meniscus—"often for pain not related to the meniscus," she said. "When you take the meniscus completely out, there are complications—you can cut the medial collateral ligament, and there's all the bleeding," Molly said. "One day, orthopedists will come up with a less invasive, less destructive procedure for repairing an injured meniscus—now they remove all of it."

I said that Caroline wasn't in a cast, just an ACE bandage, but Molly didn't sound concerned. "Immobilizing the knee allows scar tissue to fill the void left by the meniscectomy," Molly said. "Your friend just has to be careful not to flex that knee, or she could tweak it."

I told Molly that Caroline would still have stitches when we came for a visit, but Molly didn't seem to think the stitches were a big deal. "She'll just have to be careful not to put any direct pressure on her stitches, not to tweak them," Molly said. Jocks were fond of the *tweak* word, I was thinking.

When Molly asked me about the "injury mechanism" that led to Caroline's meniscal surgery, I said Caroline had been a little vague concerning how the injury had happened. "For a torn meniscus, a twisting force on a loaded leg is common," was all Molly said about it.

Jocks had their own language, I was thinking. My interest in Caroline's knee was limited. Only later would I realize that the way Caroline had described her injury—as a rotational force applied to her right knee when all her weight was on that same leg—was pretty close to what Molly meant by "a twisting force on a loaded leg." Maybe I'd misjudged Caroline; maybe there was nothing *vague* about her.

There was no vagueness about the way Caroline undressed, after Molly and my mother had gone to bed and left us to sleep or fool around on the futon in the TV room. Having heard truly *all* about her knee, I was not expecting there would be much making out with her. I was unprepared for

Caroline to take everything off, except her ACE bandage. I made no effort to resist her when she stripped naked, but I was clearly not ready.

"Oh, cute!" Caroline said, when she got a look at me. "Don't worry—you'll get bigger." When she was putting the condom on me, I suppose I got a little bigger. "This is a new experience for you, isn't it?" she asked me. I was thinking she probably meant more than the condom part of the process, but I couldn't speak. I barely managed to nod, before she proceeded to arrange me on the futon in an orderly fashion. The way she wanted me to lie down, on my back, suggested to me that she was carrying out a plan that she'd carefully considered. I decided that Caroline was definitely ahead of girls her age, socially. To safeguard her knee, however, Caroline had conceived of a new way to have sex—as new to her as having sex, in any fashion, was to me.

"You're on the bottom, I'm on top—it'll work," she said. The superior position Caroline tried to master would have been more easily achieved by a lithe little yoga woman; there might even be a name for it. But Caroline was neither lithe nor little. When she straddled me—kneeling on her left knee, with her right leg fully extended in front of her—her ACE bandage brushed softly against my ear. It had a medicinal smell. My elbows were tucked against my chest, my hands pressed together in a prayerful position, while Caroline precariously lowered herself onto me. She looked a little off-balance to me, and she seemed to be having some difficulty locating where my penis was—not that I knew where it went or what to do with it.

Jocks are inclined to postgame analysis. Caroline would later analyze what she called the "challenging angle of entry," and what went wrong; at the time, however, she just said, "You have to help me put your thing in the right place." In my pinned-down position, it was unclear to me exactly where *her* thing was. "Not *there*!" Caroline sharply said. I tried not to think of poor Rose's *thing*, descending the attic stairs. "Yeah, that's it," Caroline told me, matter-of-factly. Even under such stressful circumstances, I suddenly wondered (albeit briefly) when I had ever been this happy.

Caroline's postgame analysis did not include exactly what went awry after we were blissfully connected; her criticism concerning the "challenging angle of entry" didn't explain the sudden jackknifing of her upper and lower body. The throes of sexual excitement? Had she first felt a tug on her stitches or a twinge in the joint of her right knee? Did an unexpected ecstasy cause Caroline to abandon the contortions she'd attempted to safeguard her recovery from knee surgery?

"You screamed as loudly as she did, Kid," Molly would tell me, in *her* postgame analysis. The bruise on my cheekbone, where Caroline's right knee made contact with my face, was an after-the-fact discovery; it wasn't why I cried out. When Caroline jackknifed her body, and then rolled off me, my penis was bent in a way that penises aren't meant to bend. It seemed to me that my penis had suffered an unnatural wrenching. In jock terms, it was a serious *tweak*, but Caroline was the one with the knee injury. When my mother and Molly rushed into the TV room, Caroline was their chief concern. I was aware my mom had noticed the condom by how quickly she looked away.

"Come into the kitchen with me, sweetie—let Molly have a look at Caroline's knee," my mother said. I put on my boxers and a T-shirt, not knowing what to do about the condom. I sincerely hoped my mom didn't intend to take a look at my penis, although I was in sufficient pain to imagine that the condom could be the only thing holding the torn or severed parts together.

"I want to unwrap that ACE bandage and take the dressing off—I want to see if there's any bleeding where the stitches are, or if there's any swelling," I could hear Molly saying.

My mother was whispering to me before we got to the kitchen. "You shouldn't have sex with a girl on *crutches*, sweetie—Caroline is on crutches because she's *injured*. You don't have sex with someone who's just had *surgery*, sweetie!"

This had not been my mother's reaction when she first heard the screaming, Molly later said. "That's my one and only—Caroline has rolled over and crushed him in his sleep!" my mom had cried.

"I heard Caroline scream, too, Ray," Molly had pointed out.

In the kitchen, my mother went on whispering. Her concerns, I thought, were not entirely focused on the well-being of her one and only. "Frankly, sweetie, I wouldn't want to watch Caroline play field hockey, for the same reason I don't like to imagine her having sex—because someone's going to get injured in the process!" my mom whispered.

That was when Molly came into the kitchen. "Do we have any large garbage bags?" she asked my mother.

"Of course we do," my mom answered her. "Do you see, sweetie?" she asked me; she was back to whispering. "That's what happens when you have sex after surgery—now Molly has to throw Caroline's leg away or something."

"Caroline just wants to take a shower, Ray," Molly told her. "Maybe you can help Caroline get in and out of the shower. Caroline and I are a little too big when we're together," Molly explained.

"I'm not going to take a shower with Caroline!" my mom whispered.

"I think her knee is okay," Molly told us. "No bleeding around the stitches—no swelling that I can see, but I'll take another look in the morning. You just have to help her in and out of the shower, Ray," Molly whispered.

I was alone with Molly in the kitchen while Little Ray was dealing with Caroline and the garbage-bag business in the bathroom. "Are you okay?" the trail groomer asked me. I knew that as a ski patroller, Molly had had emergency medical training. But wouldn't a penis injury be an uncommon skiing mishap?

"My penis was bent in an extreme sort of way—it still hurts," I whispered. "Maybe I just pulled a muscle in it."

"I don't see a lot of penises, injured or otherwise, but I suppose I should take a look at it," Molly told me. I showed her. "There are no muscles in a penis, Kid—just tubes and blood vessels," Molly said. "I have no penises to compare this one to, but it looks okay to me, Kid. I'll take another look at it in the morning—to see if anything has changed."

"What sort of changes are you looking for?" I asked her.

"You can break the blood vessels in a penis, Kid—I'll be looking for a hematoma, the result of broken blood vessels. The trauma can heal with scar tissue—it's not erectile, it can't expand or stretch," Molly explained. "You get a hard-on, there's a kink—your penis curves, Kid. That'll hurt—then you need a surgery." Since Molly seemed to know quite a lot about surgeries, I asked her to tell me what was entailed in penis surgery.

"I know more about knee surgeries, Kid. As a patroller, I've not seen a ski injury involving an erect penis. The only permanently bent penis that needed a surgery—the only *totally wrecked penis* I ever knew of personally— was one of Nelly's former boyfriends, before her yeast-infection boyfriend," the snowcat operator told me.

"Was it a sex injury?" I asked her.

"Of course it was, Kid," Molly said. In the ensuing silence, she saw I was worried about a possible penis surgery. "I'm sure it's a better surgery to have than a meniscectomy," Molly told me, just as my mother came into the kitchen.

"It's a better surgery for a *boy* to have," my mom said inexplicably. I thought she must have overheard us talking about penis surgery, and she was making a senseless penis joke; in retrospect, I think all my mother heard was the *better* word and the *meniscectomy*.

Molly was unfazed. "We were talking about a meniscectomy, Ray," Molly told her.

"I know you were," my mom replied, "and *I* said, 'It's a better surgery for a *boy* to have'—not to repeat myself." While this made no sense at all, I was relieved not to share my pending penis surgery with my mother, and Molly simply changed the subject.

"How's it going with the garbage bag, Ray?" Molly asked.

"Well, that Caroline is a big girl, all right," my mom said, "and it's a good thing she brought her own rubber band—a *big* one."

I left them talking together in the kitchen. I didn't need to hear (again) the list of the complications Caroline faced in efforts to keep her stitches dry. I hoped I might fall asleep on the futon, before Caroline lumbered back to the TV room on her crutches, but my penis was throbbing—in pain, not in an arousing way—and even if I'd been sound asleep, I would have woken up when the full-bodied Caroline stretched herself, giggling, beside me. "Did your dick get tweaked when I kind of went crazy with you inside me?" she whispered. When Caroline spoke in a whisper, there was something insincerely little-girlish in her voice.

"It got a little tweaked," I told her, trying to downplay the drama of the hematoma I was certain I would see in the morning, and the subsequent surgical straightening. My penile procedure would soon be a fait accompli. I could feel myself losing consciousness, as the anesthetic rushed through my veins.

Caroline couldn't stop giggling. "Just imagine how *I* felt—stark naked with a couple of lesbians!" she whispered, in the unlikely voice of an annoying little girl. I didn't like the *lesbian* label. As disapproving as Aunt Abigail and Aunt Martha were, those biddies didn't use the word. The way Nora said *lesbian*—in a relaxed, offhand manner—it wasn't a label.

"You're the skier's kid, aren't you?" Caroline had asked me. "I wonder what that's like," she'd said. Of course I'd asked her what she meant, but all Caroline had told me was that she'd just *heard about* Little Ray—the way girl jocks hear about other girl jocks, she'd said. But what did *that* mean? I wondered now—*what* had Caroline and the other girl jocks *heard about* my mother, in the smaller-than-Chihuahua-shit town of Exeter?

I was lying beside the injured giantess—hating her, but resisting the impulse to roll onto her right knee—when I realized Caroline had conked out, leaving me to ponder what I should have said about the *lesbian* label.

In the morning, very early, there would not be many moments condu-
cive to meaningful conversation. Molly wanted to have a look at Caroline's
knee, but there'd been no bleeding around the stitches, and the joint wasn't
swollen. Caroline couldn't point to the place where she'd felt a twinge; she
felt no pain now.

Meanwhile, when Molly was examining the surgery site, I slipped into
the bathroom and examined my injured penis—from various angles, in multiple mirrors. It wasn't bent, but it wasn't erect—no hematoma, no sign of
bleeding or bruising. When I had a moment alone with Molly, I told her it
wouldn't be necessary for her to take another look at my injury.

"Keep an eye on it, Kid—show it to a doctor, if you see any discoloration.
I don't like to think of you with an L-shaped penis, looking like an Allen
wrench," the snowcat operator told me. Leave it to the trail groomer to know
more about tools than most guys did—more than I knew, anyway. We were
in the kitchen, where Molly found an Allen wrench in the tool drawer, and
she showed it to me.

That was when my mother came in. She was wearing her long johns, and
she was in the act of putting on her other ski clothes (while she was trying
to drink her coffee). "What do you need an Allen wrench for, sweetie?" she
asked me.

"I was just showing him what one looked like, Ray," Molly told her.

It was early on Sunday morning of the Thanksgiving weekend, but it was
a workday for Molly and my mother—a busy day on a ski mountain. They
were rushing around, putting on layers of clothes or stuffing more layers in
their backpacks; even dressing for skiing is a pain in the ass. I didn't expect
Molly or my mom to inquire if my painful and completely unplanned coitus
interruptus, coincident with Caroline's twinge in her knee, amounted to my
one and only time.

Nobody seems terribly concerned with the ways boys lose their virginity, I was
thinking, when Molly—shouldering her backpack and leaning over me, as
we were casually passing each other in the narrow hall—whispered in my ear.
"Don't worry, Kid—if that was your first time, the next time will be better,"
the night groomer told me. Although my view of my mother was partially
blocked by Molly's big shoulder, I saw that she was watching us.

When my mom kissed me goodbye, she also whispered in my ear. "It
doesn't matter to me, sweetie—whatever secret you and Molly are keeping
from me—I'm just so happy you have your driver's license. Now you can
always come see me, even in the ski season!"

There wouldn't be much scintillating conversation with Caroline on our long drive back to New Hampshire. The sidelined field-hockey player slept the whole way, with her right leg fully extended on the backseat of Mr. Barlow's VW Beetle—her post-op knee never gave her a twinge. I was a little disappointed that my penis had stopped hurting, too. Wasn't it a small tragedy that there was so little to remember about the loss of my virginity? Not even the pain had lingered.

Caroline didn't wake up until I pulled into her driveway, where I presume it was her parents I saw staring at me through a ground-floor window. I could tell they weren't going to venture outside to meet me—they just wanted to get a look at the skier's kid. Probably, Caroline's parents had also *heard about* my mother. Their condemning faces in the window informed me of their thoughts. *Look, it's that lesbian's boy—that woman with the little husband and the big girlfriend, the one who's away all winter.* Or was their presumed homophobia (and Caroline's) only in my mind?

"So long, Adam," Caroline was saying. Because she was on crutches, I fully intended to carry her backpack, but she'd already secured the straps on her shoulders, and the crutches were under her armpits—she was ready to go.

"So long," I said. I half expected her to say that she hadn't had *this* much fun on a road trip since her knee was injured. (It had been at an away game, Caroline had told me, and they'd packed her knee in ice and had stretched her out on the dirty floor of the team bus for the painful ride home.) But her *So long* to me, and mine to her, would suffice. It was pretty clear we'd had an awful time. Her parents' faces in the window—perhaps condemning, maybe merely inquisitive—now looked relieved to see the obvious lack of affection in our parting.

The snowshoer cautioned me that I couldn't be sure about Caroline and her parents—their sexual hatred seemed obvious to me, but Elliot told me that bigots could be "slippery" if you accused them outright. Caroline could say she was just kidding or that I had no sense of humor. Her parents might say I'd misread their expressions—or that I was paranoid, or I was projecting. The snowshoer had heard lots of excuses for sexual bigotry at the academy. Those Exeter boys were very smart—they could be "slippery" in ingenious ways, the little English teacher told me.

In those days—the end of the 1950s—I don't believe I ever heard the word *homophobe.* There were clearly a lot of homophobes around, but the word wasn't in use yet. If anyone had known it, it would have been Mr. Barlow, but not even he was saying it.

There may have been no name for them, but the snowshoer and I both suspected there might be more homophobes at the dances in the public high school gym than there were at the academy, although there surely were a lot of homophobes at an all-boys' school—there were a lot of them *everywhere*, and they were definitely "slippery," the little English teacher and I decided.

Meanwhile, Mr. Barlow had met a girl he thought I should meet. "I'm not in the habit of inserting myself as a matchmaker, Adam," the snowshoer assured me. "In poor Maud's case, however, I believe she is without prejudice, or at least disinclined to prejudge anyone—given the recent ridicule and derision she has suffered. Talk about 'adding insult to injury,' as they say!" the little English teacher declared.

The abused girl Elliot had met was the tall one with her arm in a cast— my last girlfriend, ever, from the smaller-than-Chihuahua-shit town of Exeter. That poor Maud had been injured made me anxious, even before I learned how. Given poor Rose—her limp, and the resultant muscle spasms. Given Caroline—the twinge in her knee, and the consequent bending of my penis, which would forever define the loss of my virginity. "What happened to Maud—how was she injured?" I asked the snowshoer.

It's what comes of writing plot-driven novels: my mind always races ahead to the end of the action, or to the aftermath. I'm thinking of the conversation with Molly and my mother in their Vermont kitchen, when poor Maud was in the bathroom—recovering, or trying to recover. I was sitting at the kitchen table, where Little Ray was dressing my facial wounds—there were a few small lacerations, a few more abrasions. "Hold still, sweetie," my mother kept saying, but the antiseptic hurt, and the condom (once again, under my boxers) was very uncomfortable. Molly just sat with us at the table, waiting—the can of white paint and the paintbrush in front of her. Molly was waiting to paint over the bloodstains on Maud's cast, as soon as Maud managed to recover in the bathroom. "You *never* screw someone in a cast, sweetie—you just *don't*!" my mom was whispering.

"Maud wasn't the one who got hurt screwing, Ray," Molly said.

"A cross-country runner breaks her *arm*—that should have told you something, sweetie," my mother whispered. "Please hold still."

"Anyone can trip, Ray," Molly pointed out.

"Maud just fell—anyone can *fall*!" I told my mom.

"Maud took out the field of runners when she fell, sweetie. What did you think she would do when she had sex? It was her first time!" my mother cried, her voice rising slightly above a whisper. "Don't move," she whispered.

"I didn't know Maud was a virgin—she didn't tell me," I said.

"I don't think you usually *tell* someone, sweetie. Did you ask her?"

"I don't think you usually *ask* someone, Ray," Molly said.

"Someone with the capacity to wipe out an entire *event*—I would definitely ask her, Molly!" my mom whispered harshly. "Hold still, sweetie," she said, sighing.

But the way Mr. Barlow had met Maud was innocent—the snowshoer didn't have the advantage of sexual hindsight. He'd only *heard about* Maud as a runner. Like poor Rose, with her stigmatizing limp, poor Maud was a faculty daughter who lived in virtual hiding in academy housing. Unlike Rose, Maud had left Exeter to attend an all-girls' boarding school, where things went haywire and she'd been sent home. Among the mixed truths and rumors Elliot Barlow had *heard about* Maud: she was sitting out the remainder of the academic year; she was busy making applications to other all-girls' boarding schools; she was recovering from a nervous breakdown; she was either completely at fault or she'd been most unfairly blamed for the debacle at the start of a varsity girls' cross-country race, a New England championship for independent schools.

Even I had heard about an unnamed faculty daughter who was temporarily out of school because of a nervous breakdown. Aunt Abigail and Aunt Martha were quick to presume an unwanted pregnancy. In their judgment, there could be no other reason for severe emotional and mental disorders among girls. In their judgment, such girls should be kept away from the academy boys. These wayward girls had demonstrated their proclivity to get themselves in trouble. Now there was one living in a faculty apartment in an academy dormitory. What would prevent such a mental case from roaming the halls of the dorm, seeking to make herself pregnant again?

The snowshoer foresaw no such proclivity in poor Maud. He'd met her on the Exeter boys' cross-country course—at such an early hour of the morning, the academy dining halls hadn't yet opened for breakfast. Maud was most unlikely to find a boy to make herself pregnant there and then; the boys who ran cross-country at Exeter ran in the afternoons. Maud wasn't startled by the appearance of the little English teacher on one of his early-morning runs. With a cast on one arm, and in a sling—one empty sleeve of her sweatshirt flapping, as if she'd lost an arm—Maud was walking the course, not running, and (as a good English teacher would notice) she was carrying a good novel in her only visible hand.

Tall and thin, Maud had the prototypical build of a long-distance runner.

As the snowshoer first described her to me, "Her pretty face has an edge to it, as if she accepts her propensity for sadness, while at the same time she stands in defiance of being blamed for her public humiliation." The novel Maud carried with her—Charlotte Brontë's *Jane Eyre*—identified poor Maud to Mr. Barlow as conclusively as her cast. The snowshoer knew immediately who Maud was. "Not many nice young women in English literature were persecuted as entirely unjustly as poor Jane," the little English teacher told me.

Maud had grown up running on the Exeter cross-country course—"Never when the boys were running," she told Mr. Barlow. She knew who Mr. Barlow was; everyone who ran had seen the little snowshoer, who was always running. Maud told him that she reread *Jane Eyre* whenever she was feeling sorry for herself. "Worse stuff happens to Jane," was how Maud put it. Jane Eyre, however, had not tripped and fallen at the start of a cross-country race.

Maud admitted to Mr. Barlow that she had a tendency to flail her long arms—"to reach out for things"—when she was falling. With her long legs, Maud made giant strides in an effort to regain her balance—"super lunges," Maud said. Maud admitted that she "went on falling for quite a while." Observers claimed that Maud's long arms dragged down the runners around her; her long legs trampled over the runners ahead of her, as Maud stumbled forward. On the cinder track, where the race started, Maud's fall had a bowling-pin effect on the closely concentrated field of runners. When Maud went down, an estimated three-quarters of the entries fell with her.

Surely some of the blame belonged to the organizers—for starting a race with a crowded field on the cinder track. Okay, let the race *finish* on the track, when the field of runners is more spread out, but the girls should have started in a more open area—on one of the playing fields, where the runners wouldn't have been in such close contact with one another. "I was tripped—then I was pushed, more than once," poor Maud had told the little snowshoer, who'd read what some of the other runners had to say.

"Maud is very free with her elbows—when she's passing you, or you're passing her," one girl had complained.

"She's so tall, her elbows get you in the face," another girl said.

A Boston newspaper that was not normally known to cover secondary-school sports, especially not sports for girls, published a photo of the catastrophic start. All you could see was a pile of girls, their entangled arms and legs every which way on the cinder track, where the elderly gentleman holding the starting gun appeared to be overcome with shock or dismay—as if he'd somehow managed to kill them all with a single shot. Nowadays might have been worse; the video-sharing possibilities could have made poor Maud a spectacle of clumsiness, a YouTube sensation in the category of funniest fall. Never mind that Maud's arm was broken when she fell, or that her hair was pulled, her face was scratched, and she was kicked. In the pile of girls, one of the fallen runners bit Maud's ear—after calling her "a stupid cow."

But, as Maud herself insisted to the little English teacher—as Maud later reiterated to me—Jane Eyre suffered worse privations and emotional abuse. If *Great Expectations* became my emergency novel, *Jane Eyre* served such a purpose for Maud. The unnamed school where Maud had suffered her nervous breakdown was not as bad as poor Jane's mistreatment at Lowood Institution, where Jane's best friend, Helen, dies in her arms. (Maud admitted she'd had "a Helen-like friend," but Maud's friend hadn't died—she was merely expelled.) Not even Maud's loneliness at Exeter, where she was an out-of-school girl in a cast—in a third-floor faculty apartment, in an all-boys' dorm—could compare to Jane's agonies over Mr. Rochester at Thornfield Hall. "I'm not in love with a man who keeps his mad wife in the attic—I'm not likely to marry a blind guy, who has also lost one of his hands," said the stoic Maud.

Maud did not tell Mr. Barlow that she may have been in love with Helen—only that Helen was her best friend and she'd been expelled from school—but Maud told me, in our first meeting. "The cast is coincidental," she told me—swinging her arm back and forth above the table, spilling the sugar bowl at The Grill, where we were having a cup of coffee. The Grill was an Exeter student café. A faculty daughter—especially a tall and pretty one, with her arm in a cast—was a rarity there. "That I was blamed for the start of a race, where a bunch of girls ganged up on me, doesn't matter. But poor Helen was thrown out of school—just when Helen and I were on the verge, you know," Maud told me. Her left arm, in the cast, was restless—she swung it suddenly over her head.

"On the verge of what?" I asked Maud.

"*You* know!" Maud said, clutching my hand. "I was about to find out if I was a lesbian or not, but they threw Helen out. She'd slept with another girl, but it was history—it was old news, you know. Someone ratted," Maud said, shrugging.

"So you still don't know if you are or you aren't," I ventured to say. I admired her. She was philosophical in the face of unfairness, ridicule, and falling in love—like the beleaguered heroine of a nineteenth-century novel. I hadn't loved *Jane Eyre*, but I'd liked it. I had liked the *Wuthering Heights* Brontë sister better.

Maud tapped my forehead with the rough plaster of her cast. "I'm not going to find out *here*, am I?" she asked me. The surrounding Exeter boys were sizing us up—at what might have appeared to them as the impromptu faculty-brat table in The Grill. And what *were* we, exactly, my fellow Exeter students were wondering—childhood friends, just catching up, or would-be lovers? I suppose Maud and I were wondering what we were doing together, too.

"Helen was like a character you meet in a novel," Maud was saying. "You know, you love her, you want to know everything about her, but then the book is taken away—you never know what happens to her, or what might have happened to the two of you," Maud told me.

"I *know*," I earnestly lied to her, knowing nothing at all—not having a clue of what emotions might remain unlocked in Maud and Helen, or what emotions Maud might (or might not) feel for me. What was true, what I truly did know, was that I thought Maud was like a character you meet in a novel—a character *on the verge*. If Maud had been on the verge with Helen, and Helen was taken away, wasn't Maud still on the verge? (On the verge of what, of course, remained uncertain.)

What was clear, from my first look at Maud, was that she could outrun me. Maud looked made to run. How awful for her that she might not feel welcome to compete as a cross-country runner again—at least not in those New England schools for girls Maud was applying to, where they'd all heard of "the angry stork." She'd also been called "a heron on the attack"; these cruel appellations were attached to Maud by coaches on opposing cross-country teams. At the time, I was only running JV cross-country at Exeter. I had no doubt that Maud could have outrun me in her cast.

I might have paid closer attention to the way Maud wielded her cast, as if she thought of her broken arm as a weapon—not unlike a knight-errant exhibiting his prowess with a mace in the Middle Ages. But I didn't dwell on this fleeting image of Maud with a mace. It was preferable to imagine taking her to Vermont to meet Molly and my mother. I'd met a girl who not only wouldn't *label* my mom and Molly, but would likely think they were cool. Maybe my mom and Molly would think I was exceptionally sophisticated, or at least very grown up, to be friends with a young woman whose sexual predilection was undetermined.

As positive as Mr. Barlow had been about my meeting Maud, he cautioned me not to make sexual presumptions. "Not only about Maud," the snowshoer added. He seemed to be saying I shouldn't presume my mother and Molly would welcome my spending a night on the futon in the TV room with Maud, simply because Maud had fallen in love with a girl at school.

In fact, when I first proposed bringing Maud to Vermont for an overnight during the Christmas holidays, my mom sounded somewhat less than welcoming over the phone.

"You don't have sex with a girl who's recovering from a nervous breakdown, sweetie," my mother told me. "And Maud is still in a cast—she's still *injured*, right?" My mom must have talked to Elliot—Little Ray may even have heard what Aunt Abigail and Aunt Martha were saying about Maud, I thought.

"Maud likes snowshoeing," I said. "She can use one ski pole—that'll be fine, if we go where it's not too steep."

"You don't have sex with a girl who thinks she may like girls, sweetie. Let me tell you: if Maud isn't sure, that's really asking for trouble," my mom said.

"We're not having sex—we're just friends!" I cried. "We talk about *books*!" I might have more truthfully declared that Maud and I had no idea what our relationship was.

"I'm sure she's a very nice girl, sweetie," my mother said. Maud *was* a very nice girl. She'd also had a nervous breakdown—Maud was definitely still on the verge.

What I shouldn't have presumed was to think that Maud had any sexual experience with boys. She'd no more tried anything with a boy than she'd had a chance to try anything with Helen. Why did I assume Maud had fooled around with boys, at least a little? I guess I imagined she'd been underwhelmed by boys—hence her interest in Helen. The truth is Maud hadn't fooled around at all, with anyone. Reading good novels can make young readers seem more experienced about relationships than they are.

I had no expectations that I would make out with Maud—I wasn't even going to try. My penis bender with Caroline was recent enough to make a platonic relationship with Maud imaginable. Reading good novels can make almost anything seem imaginable.

Maud was in the bathroom when my mother gave me a handful of condoms in the kitchen. "Just in case, sweetie," my mom whispered. I could see Molly in the background—I could read her lips.

"Sorry, Kid," Molly's lips were saying. Maud was in the shower—she didn't need any help keeping her cast dry with a garbage bag. We'd had fun snowshoeing, though I'd struggled to keep up with her, and I had two ski poles.

"It's just because my legs are so much longer—you're a good snowshoer," Maud had told me nicely.

"Maud really *is* a nice girl, sweetie," my mother went on whispering in the kitchen. The handful of condoms I'd stuffed in two pockets of my jeans seemed to contradict how nice Little Ray thought Maud was.

Maud was very shy at dinner. She became more animated when she started talking about *Jane Eyre*. Molly remembered reading the novel in high school, but my mom hadn't read it. When Molly said she remembered Grace Poole getting drunk, my mother thought Grace was someone Molly had known in high school—not the nurse hired to look after the mad wife in the attic. When Maud carried on about poor Helen, who died in Jane's arms, I could see my mom was confused. Little Ray was thinking of the Helen who'd been thrown out of school, the girl Maud didn't get to sleep with—not the Helen who dies in *Jane Eyre*. Because my mother wasn't a reader, she became agitated and distracted when people talked about characters in novels as if they were real people.

It is hard to know where to hide half a dozen condoms in a TV room, so I just left them in the front pockets of my jeans. There we were, on the futon in our underwear—we hadn't even kissed—when Maud (lying as still as a cadaver, on her back) said to me, "You know, I just love Molly and your mom. I love your stepfather, Mr. Barlow, too."

"I love them, too," I told her, as clueless as ever.

"You know, I've never done this," Maud suddenly blurted out; she sat bolt upright, whipping off her bra. "I've been dreading doing it the first time, with a boy *or* a girl—with *anybody*," she said, sighing, and lying down again. Maud arched her back and wriggled out of her panties. She was once more lying as motionless as a cadaver, but her eyes were tightly closed and she was grimacing. "I might hate it, you know—you may have to stop, if I hate it," Maud told me. "Just go kind of slow, at the start—I'll let you know how it's going," she said.

"We don't have to do anything, Maud," I told her—hoping this didn't make her feel that I found her unattractive, because I thought she was very attractive.

"Please don't go away, don't be a Helen," Maud said bitterly, biting her lower lip. Her eyes were still tightly closed—she was still grimacing. My mother's preparedness notwithstanding, I didn't have a presentiment that this might be a six-condom night. *Surely one condom will suffice,* I imagined, proceeding slowly and uncertainly—having only Swedish and French films, with subtitles, to guide me. I'm guessing that the missionary position was never as conventionally or boringly upheld, but I was determined not to deviate from the norm. I was opposed to taking a position even remotely reminiscent of Caroline's gymnastic penis bending. Of course I fully understood the risk I was taking—namely, that of providing poor Maud with good reason to follow her lesbian inclinations.

I expected Maud's first-time experience might be conflicted, but how Maud manifested her sexual turmoil was somewhat surprising. I was unprepared for her to wrap her long legs around me, and arch herself into me. She certainly appeared to be enthusiastic—she was humping me harder than I was humping her. Yet Maud was also beating me, in the area of my head and face, with her clublike cast. She wielded her cast like the mace of a knight-errant in the throes of battle, and the words she grunted—with each thrust and blow—were more explicit and contradictory than anything I could recall in *Jane Eyre*. "Yes! No! Yes! No!" Maud kept grunting—as she arched her body into mine, as she clubbed me with her cast.

It was my mom who unwrapped Maud's legs from around me, and pulled me off her. Molly managed to get hold of Maud's arm in the cast, gently pinning it to the futon. More slowly, Maud managed to stop arching her back—to stop humping. Maud's yes-no mantra trailed away to a sorrowful memory.

"That wasn't the *next time* I had in mind, Kid," Molly told me, while my mother was attending to my facial wounds at the kitchen table; Maud was in the bathroom, recovering from her conflicted experience. When Maud joined us at the kitchen table, I'd waited too long to tell Molly my thoughts: my bleeding face and ears aside, having sex with Maud had been much better than the penis bender with Caroline; the *next time* truly had been better, as Molly had predicted. But I said nothing. My mom didn't know Caroline had hurt my penis, and Maud didn't know about Caroline at all.

Besides, Maud was all wound up—she was the one with a lot to say. While Molly painted over the bloodstains on Maud's cast, Maud gave us the *Jane Eyre* version of her sexual awakening—a first-person narrative of intense psychological consciousness. "I actually like sex, more than I thought I would—more than I thought I would with a *boy*, anyway," Maud began. "As I told Adam, I was *dreading* doing it the first time, but I really, *really* liked it!" Maud exclaimed. I nodded, but this interfered with my mom's iodine applications—or whatever antiseptic she was using on my ears and face.

"Hold still, sweetie," my mother said.

"But, at the same time," Maud went on in her intimate, stream-of-consciousness fashion, "I had very contradictory feelings—*at the same time* I was liking it, you know?"

"I know," I said, trying not to move my head, but I must have nodded a little.

"We know," Molly said, more softly.

"You're moving, sweetie," my mom told me.

"I don't really like to lose control—I really, *really* don't like it!" Maud declared.

"That's a potential contradiction, all right," Molly told her.

"Losing control kind of goes with the territory of liking sex," my mother said as nicely as possible.

"That's exactly what I mean!" Maud shouted, both her long arms flying up from the table. With her good arm, Maud almost spilled the can of white paint; she hit Molly in the chin with her bloodstained cast. "Sorry!" Maud said to Molly. "You won't tell anyone what happened, will you?" Maud asked me. Naturally, I shook my head.

"Hold still!" my mom shouted. There was a moment of industrious silence, while my mother was bandaging my wounds and Molly was painting over the blood on Maud's cast.

"Now it itches like crazy where I can't scratch it!" Maud suddenly cried out. A look of uncomprehending horror must have crossed my unmoving face. Little Ray and Molly exchanged an inquiring glance. "I mean my *arm*, under the cast—where I can't get to it," Maud explained. "Maybe if I had a long knife—or one of those skewers you use to put shrimp on the barbecue, you know," Maud said distractedly.

"No, no, no!" my mom cried. "Don't you dare stick anything sharp under your cast—just *don't*!" my mother said. Now that I understood what itched, I must have violently shaken my head. "Hold *still*!" my mom cried.

"I've had casts, you know, Maud—they itch," Molly told her. "You just wait till they take them off. Then you can go nuts scratching yourself," Molly said. We all sat at the kitchen table, considering that to go nuts scratching herself might never be a safe activity for Maud.

"On second thought, Maud," my mom said, "start out scratching yourself slowly."

"It should have been Helen, my first time," Maud suddenly said. "I was thinking it should be her—I was *wishing* it was her—while I knew it was you, Adam," Maud told me. I kept still.

"You should let Helen know how you feel, Maud," Molly said softly.

"Is Helen still alive?" my mother asked. "She didn't die?"

"That was the Helen in *Jane Eyre*, Ray—she's the Helen who died," Molly explained.

"Fucking *books*!" Little Ray exclaimed. "You should definitely let the Helen who's alive know how you feel, Maud—maybe after you get your cast off."

"I know," Maud said, sounding subdued. "You're my friend for life, if you want to be, Adam," she told me. "There are worse ways to have sex the first time, you know."

"He knows," Molly told her.

"There are worse ways," I agreed. "Friends for life, if you want to be," I said to Maud. She wasn't the right girlfriend for me, clearly, but the older you get, your friends for life mean more to you than the girlfriends or the boyfriends. In the passage of time, Maud and I would retain the awkwardness of the awkward age we were when we met, but we would stay friends. I would go on loving the tall runner with her arm in a cast, in an entirely *Jane Eyre* kind of way.

21.

IN CONTROL

I developed a preternatural interest in what passed for physical affection or intimacy between my mother and the snowshoer. I was pulling for them, from the start. Whatever was between them, I wanted it to work—regardless of what was between my mom and Molly. I wasn't privy to the conversations my mom and Elliot must have had. I didn't know what choices were available to them in the area of Exeter faculty housing.

Mr. Barlow was obligated to do dorm duty. He'd been living in a bachelor faculty apartment in Bancroft Hall—or was it Webster? I can't remember. The newlyweds and I would move into a two-bedroom faculty apartment on the second floor of Amen Hall. Amen was not a dorm devoted to prayer; it was named for Harlan Page Amen—for eighteen years, an actual and distinguished principal of Exeter. Unlike the diaper man, Principal Amen didn't retire—in 1913, he died on the job. A far cry from the infant emeritus, electrocuted in a lightning storm while making music on a barbecue with croquet wickets—struck down while imagining his youngest daughter had married one of her illegitimate children.

Our sleeping arrangements in Amen Hall would not escape scrutiny. I'll bet my mother and the little English teacher took my aunts' sexual surveillance into consideration. Our two bedrooms in Amen were similar in size and configuration. Each had a queen-size bed and an adjoining bathroom—one with a shower, one with a tub. My mom insisted on my having the bathroom with the shower. "No boy your age takes baths," she told me. I was fourteen, not likely to drown in a bathtub. To Aunt Abigail and Aunt Martha, Little Ray made a different point. "Elliot and I are so small," she told them, "we can fit together in the tub."

Yes, those two could have fit together in that bathtub—this is true. Did they purposely let me hear them splashing and fooling around in the tub together, or were they only pretending to fool around? There was no denying their physical affection for each other. Everywhere they went, they held hands. Anywhere there was a couch, they would curl up together on it.

In our faculty apartment, the kitchen and the dining room (or the living room) was one room—not a big one. I guess we were supposed to choose which room we wanted to have, either a dining room or a living room. We chose both, or neither. There was one couch and one comfy chair. They faced the TV, which was always on with the sound off. There was a table between the kitchen and the end of the room designated for silent television watching. We called it our kitchen table.

In the evenings, the snowshoer lay reading on the couch—his head in my mom's lap, where she played with his hair. She watched old movies with the sound off, her lips sometimes in sync with the remembered dialogue. If they were movies she hadn't seen or didn't remember seeing, she said she preferred to guess what the characters were saying—she believed this was better than hearing their actual dialogue. She watched TV Westerns with the sound off, too. "You don't need to know what they're saying in Westerns," my mother said. Given *Gunsmoke*, *Cheyenne*, and *The Life and Legend of Wyatt Earp*, I don't doubt that this was true.

My mom didn't watch most of the TV shows that my grandmother saw in the Front Street house. It depressed me to see Nana slumped in her reading chair, not reading. *The Milton Berle Show*, *The Red Skelton Show*, *The Jack Benny Show*, *The Ed Sullivan Show*, and (especially) *The Lawrence Welk Show* really depressed me. *Walt Disney's Wonderful World of Color* was a crapshoot. What had happened to the wonderful woman who'd read *Moby-Dick* aloud to me? My grandmother sat as if she'd been poleaxed in the chair she used to read in. The blank way she watched TV suggested that television was killing her. Fortunately, Nana's stupor didn't endure; she would eventually go back to *Moby-Dick*.

The occasional good stuff on TV perked up Nana's and my mother's attention. Little Ray turned on the volume for *The Honeymooners* and *Alfred Hitchcock Presents*. But, for the most part, our faculty apartment in Amen Hall was a sanctuary for silent television. In my Exeter years, I did my homework at our kitchen table, where Mr. Barlow would join me when he was grading papers. The ever-changing light from the soundless TV glowed or flashed over us—a distant war in a foreign country, sanitized, void of suffering.

Even in the ski season—in the long winter months when my mom was away—Elliot and I kept the quiet television on. We went to the extreme of reading *TV Guide*. We wanted to be sure our TV was on the channel Little Ray would have been watching. We missed her, but it was easier for me that

I had company in missing her. The academy was hard—the schoolwork was overwhelming. I was busier, but more engaged in a good way, than I'd ever been before.

Outwardly, my mom and Elliot Barlow were the lovebirds on the Exeter campus. In those months they were separated, not counting the ski holidays, did they sincerely miss each other? Was that why they seemed so in love whenever they were together? "They're not like a married couple," one of my friends would tell me. "It's like they've just met, and are head over heels in love." I'm not sure I know what my mother and the snowshoer were really like. I just know that I loved the way they were together, and I loved our family of three. Four, counting Molly. It was the snowcat operator who said that Little Ray and the snowshoer never stopped looking like newlyweds.

"They give you hope," another of my friends told me.

"What hope?" I asked him.

"Hope you'll meet someone you can't keep your hands off—hope she's someone who can't keep her hands off you. *That* hope," my friend said.

I would wrestle at Exeter. The snowshoer was not wrong to recommend it. He regretted he hadn't wrestled, but he'd grown up in ski towns in Austria and New Hampshire—not exactly hotbeds of wrestling. Elliot Barlow's first opportunity to wrestle would have been at Harvard. He thought it was too late to start. Besides, he couldn't have competed. The snowshoer didn't weigh enough for the lightest weight class. If you asked him what he weighed, he sounded indifferent about it. "Right around a hundred pounds," Elliot said—he always shrugged. But I knew he weighed himself obsessively. Only occasionally, when he weighed as much as 105, did the little English teacher say he was too big.

My mom was always weighing herself, too. When she weighed as much as 120, she said she was over her limit and going on a diet. Her normal weight was 110 or 115 pounds. In our faculty apartment in Amen, there was a scale in the bathroom with the tub—in *their* bathroom, as I thought of it. But for most of the night, when it wasn't the ski season, my mother slept in my bed with me.

Was it only for the sake of appearances that my mom kept her clothes in a closet and chest of drawers in their bedroom? No, I don't think so. I believe that Little Ray knew it was more appropriate for her to dress and undress in front of the snowshoer, regardless of what their real relationship was. Of course, she kept a toothbrush and some of her other toiletries in my bathroom, and sometimes she took a shower there, but she never dressed or undressed in front of me. Whatever was innately lawless about my mother, she had her own rules about dressing and undressing.

The first Christmas they were married—my first Christmas as a wrestler— Elliot Barlow gave me a scale for my bathroom as a Christmas present. The snowshoer knew I would soon be weighing myself obsessively, as wrestlers do. He was also being discreet. I'm sure he knew that Aunt Abigail had deemed him a little light in his loafers. My aunts were outraged that my mom would marry Mr. Barlow and then leave me alone with him in the ski season. But I would always be safe with the snowshoer. The little English teacher had his own rules about dressing and undressing, too.

I don't think my mother could be in the bathroom, Elliot's or mine, without weighing herself. It was another bond between us; weighing ourselves was something the three of us shared. There are worse obsessions. The way I kept thinking about Em was one. Molly was my other.

Many of my wrestling teammates had observed, with heartfelt longing, that my mom and Mr. Barlow couldn't keep their hands off each other. Wrestlers are creatures of constant physical contact. Okay, I know—wrestlers aren't necessarily known for hugging and kissing one another, or for holding hands.

As for public displays of their year-round training, not solely indicative of their physical affection, the snowshoer and Little Ray took turns giving each other piggyback rides every time they encountered a flight of stairs. We had piggyback races in the wrestling room, carrying a workout partner in our weight class or near it. It was integral to our training, to lift and carry a body weight comparable to our own. It seemed natural that my fellow wrestlers would notice the athletic or competitive nature of the physicality between my mother and Mr. Barlow. Leave it to wrestlers to notice that Little Ray and the snowshoer were like workout partners who happened to hug and kiss each other, and hold hands.

Elliot Barlow had been a regular in the Exeter wrestling room since he came to the academy. In my first wrestling season, the winter of 1956–57, Elliot's skills were better than those of a third-year wrestler. He was as experienced as the four-year seniors in the room. In his late twenties, the snowshoer was exceptionally fit; pound for pound, he was also stronger than anyone in our wrestling room. He'd shown up for his first wrestling practice in the 1953–54 season. He knew there would be a few little kids in the room, "right around a hundred pounds." In those days, the lightest weight class was 110 pounds. In three years, the little English teacher would be competitive with the best lightweights in the room. By the time I was wrestling at Exeter, Mr. Barlow was treated as an assistant coach.

But the reason Elliot tried wrestling in the first place, and the foremost reason he wanted me to try it, was the coach. Mr. Dearborn had been a Big Ten champion and a two-time All-American at Illinois. An NCAA runner-up, he was overqualified for the job of coaching wrestling at Exeter— his teams dominated New England interscholastic wrestling for years. The snowshoer wanted me to try wrestling because he knew Mr. Dearborn was a good coach. My mom had wanted me to have my own faculty person at the academy, someone "like a father"—someone who treated me like his own faculty brat. Elliot Barlow was a good stepfather to me, from the start. His instinct to match me with Coach Dearborn was the first instance of the snowshoer's steering me through Exeter.

I'd missed seeing the coach carry the diaper man's body from the croquet court, but I remembered his doing lunges with my mom at her wedding— when I'd mistaken their lunges for dancing.

"You'll need someone to help you at the academy," my mother had told me. Elliot found the good teachers for me—he put me in their hands. *Substitute Fathers*, I would title an early novel—a bad title for fictional amalgams of my teachers and coaches. I changed it.

Coach Dearborn was an honest man. He said I wouldn't ever be better than "halfway decent" as a wrestler—not for lack of good coaching, or good workout partners. I just wasn't the athlete my mother was. "That you're not very talented needn't be the end of it," Coach Dearborn told me. When I was a beginner as a writer, with no confidence in my talent for storytelling, I took what my first wrestling coach told me to heart. I never believed I was very talented, but that wouldn't be the end of it.

When I started wrestling at Exeter, the wrestling room was in the basement of the old gym. The rope we climbed every day, before and after practice, hung from the low ceiling. Some of the smaller wrestlers, Elliot included, had to be lifted up to reach the chinning bar. I began wrestling on horsehair mats, which were covered with a filmy plastic sheeting—a preventative but ineffective measure against mat burns. The shock-absorbing abilities of those old horsehair mats were nonexistent in comparison to the new Resilite mats, which arrived at Exeter in my second or third year. I can't remember exactly when this happened, but we were excited to move to our new wrestling room. It was on the upper level of the Thompson Cage—where the wooden track was. We had a higher ceiling for our rope climbing. We had more than one chinning bar. Mr. Barlow was still the best rope climber in the room—he could do the most chin-ups, too.

Coach Dearborn wasn't very enthusiastic about lifting weights. "You want to lift, just wrestle more," he would say. Maybe it was an Illinois or a Big Ten thing, but Coach Dearborn believed that rope climbing and chin-ups were the best strength training for wrestlers. "There's more pulling than pushing in wrestling," he said. Coach Dearborn wasn't impressed by the bench press. "Just stay off your backs," he liked to say.

All the ski-poling had helped the snowshoer as a wrestler. Hand strength matters—wrestling is a squeezing sport, too. As for our piggyback races in the wrestling room, Elliot was no slouch at carrying kids who were heavier than he was. He'd been lugging my mom around, and Little Ray usually outweighed him by ten or fifteen pounds.

In my third year at Exeter, the wrestling season of 1958–59, I became the varsity wrestler in my weight class, the starter at 133 pounds. In schools, wrestling is a winter sport. I was competing in the ski season. But now that I was facing outside competition, my mother—at first, only occasionally—came to see my matches against wrestlers from other schools.

What made this possible was that she was no longer as far away as Stowe. My mom and Molly had moved to Bromley—it was a smaller mountain and ski area, but Bromley treated them well, and they liked living in southern Vermont. My mother and the trail groomer bought a small house in Manchester. They liked the town, and the drive to Exeter was a lot less formidable than that from Stowe. (This was why I was able to take Caroline and Maud from Exeter for an overnight with Molly and my mom, but it was still a long drive.)

Some of my away wrestling matches were at schools nearer to Manchester, Vermont, than Exeter was. My mom came to see a few of my matches at other schools, but she preferred the Exeter home matches. That way, she and I could have a sleepover together in the bed we shared in Amen Hall. Exeter had wrestling matches on Wednesdays and Saturdays. In the beginning, my mother came only to the Wednesday matches—weekends were the busiest days in ski areas. But soon she was coming to see my Saturday matches, too, even though this meant her leaving Exeter at four or five o'clock on Sunday morning, in order to be at Bromley before the ski lifts started running.

I was surprised when my mom became a wrestling fanatic, but this was no surprise to Molly. "Your mother is small but strong, Kid," the trail groomer told me. "Wrestling is a weight-class sport—you get to beat up people your own size. What's not to love about that?"

My mom's fanaticism for wrestling didn't surprise Nora and Em, either. "Why wouldn't Ray love the idea of beating up someone, even at the risk of being beaten up?" Nora asked me. "Look how awful my mother and Aunt Martha were to her, Adam—and Ray hated school, right?" I nodded, if not as vigorously as Em, who saw and understood the connection to hating school more clearly than I did. "The bitchy girls who turn against you, because you're not getting wet over boys," was the way Nora put it. "What's not to hate about that?"

Em was in her advanced pantomime mode. She had studied—later, she taught—in workshops for pantomimists in Italy. If I'd not seen her enactment of vomitous retching a few times before, I would have thought she really was vomiting. "All those years they made us ski, kiddo," Nora suddenly said, while Em retched, "don't you think I would have liked wrestling better?"

I knew wrestlers who loved wrestling because it was an outlet for their anger, but they weren't the norm. It wasn't what I loved about wrestling, or about writing. In both cases, I loved the act of perfecting. What the snowshoer and I admired about Coach Dearborn was that he was a perfectionist. He sized you up and taught you what worked for you, and what didn't.

For wrestling, good balance is important—good balance is also uncoachable. I'm slow to recover my balance when I lose it. Coach Dearborn said this was my chief weakness as an athlete, a sizable liability for a wrestler. For a skier, too, my mother had taught me—it was why I struggled with parallel turns, she'd said. "Your balance isn't very good, sweetie," was how she put it, as nicely as she could.

Coach Dearborn taught me to be in control. A mix-up on the mat—a scramble, a free-for-all—favored the better athlete. I learned to keep the score close; I learned that mayhem wasn't my friend. "In a scramble, Adam, you're not likely to end up on top," was the way Coach Dearborn put it, as nicely as he could.

But who told me to apply this principle to writing? No one said I lacked talent as a writer—I just assumed it. From wrestling, I learned to be strategic—I was never spontaneous and I kept myself under control. If I could navigate a wrestling match, why not a novel or a screenplay? In a wrestling match, chaos is the best friend of the better athlete. But why would mayhem be the friend of any writer? Doesn't a plot imply that you know where you're going?

As a ski instructor, my mom taught beginners (mostly children) to ski in control. But I didn't know her when she was a racer. I wasn't good enough to ski flat out with her. When I saw how my mother reacted to wrestling, I had a picture of her as someone who skied on the edge. When we watched ski races together, she liked the skiers who took the most risks, the ones who looked reckless to me, those downhill racers and slalom skiers who looked off-balance, at times on one ski, borderline out of control.

My mom and Molly and I watched Franz Klammer's gold-medal down-hill run at Innsbruck—the 1976 Winter Olympics. Klammer looked to me like he was on one ski, and about to crash, the whole way. He came close to hitting the hay bales at the edge of the piste. On one of their trips to Austria, only a year or two before Klammer's run, the snowshoer had taken my mother to Innsbruck—she wanted to see the Patscherkofel course. Molly and my mom and I watched Klammer's win-or-crash run on TV in Man-chester, Vermont. Little Ray was screaming for Franz Klammer, all the way. "That's how your mom likes to ski, Kid," the trail groomer told me. "Not the way she teaches the beginners." It was the first I'd heard, from anyone, about how my mother liked to ski, but the way Little Ray behaved at wres-tling matches had tipped me off. Yet hadn't she hidden her anger and her daredevil recklessness from me? Weren't these aspects of her nature also in the category of lies of omission?

"There's no end to her secrets," I remember saying to Nora. (This was right after the 1976 Winter Olympics.)

Nora gave me her tell-me-something-I-don't-know shrug. "There's a title in what you say—*No End to Her Secrets*. Maybe you can use it, kiddo," was all Nora said. It was a better title than *Substitute Fathers*, I knew. I didn't have to look at Em to know she was nodding.

I was in my thirties when Franz Klammer's gold-medal run made my mother exclaim, "If I'd been your size, Molly, I would have been a downhill racer—slalom is baloney!" My mom and Molly were in their fifties. It was the first time I'd heard Little Ray disparage her own smallness. I'd adjusted to my mother's falling in love with a woman as big as the night groomer, but I'd not heard her say she wished she'd been bigger herself—not even as a skier.

The next winter, in December—on the same TV in Manchester, Vermont—my mom and Molly and I were watching a women's downhill race at Cortina. Franz Klammer, who was only twenty-three, would win the men's downhill at Kitzbühel a month later. Another Austrian, Annemarie Moser-Pröll, won the downhill at Cortina. Molly had picked Moser-Pröll to win, but my mom was cheering for Monika Behr—Moser-Pröll's hotshot teammate. As you may remember, if you saw her fall, that would be Monika Behr's last time on skis.

Yes, we'd seen Monika Behr fall before. Who hadn't? More than one of her falls—not just her last one, on that course in Italy—is repeatedly shown in video highlights, whenever winter sports are on television. Monika's career as a downhill racer ended at Cortina in December 1976. She was Franz Klammer's age, but she would watch herself falling in video highlights for the rest of her life. She was a crash-or-win downhiller, but mostly a crasher. Monika was an all-out, go-for-broke girl. Molly and I did not share my mother's affection for Monika Behr. The way that Austrian downhiller skied was the way she did everything else.

After a World Cup race at Val d'Isère in 1974, she had been arrested by the French police for assaulting a photographer. Monika had hit his telephoto lens with the heel of her hand, driving the camera into the photographer's face, injuring his eye and cutting the bridge of his nose.

She'd crashed in World Cup races at Garmisch and Jackson Hole in 1975. Both times, she'd been accused of assaulting the medics who attended to her after she was airlifted from the course. The way Monika Behr skied, she kept crashing, but she was not airlifted again until they lifted her lifeless-looking body from the course in Italy. She'd bounced from one hip to the other in that final crash, and had not appeared to be conscious after her initial contact with the piste—on the back of her neck.

There was other trouble before the Cortina crash. A fistfight with a downhiller on the U.S. women's team at a World Cup race at Wengen in 1976—two big girls throwing punches and kicking each other with ski boots, in that restricted area behind the starting gates. Monika Behr had been screwing the boyfriend of the U.S. skier, a brash young man on the U.S. men's team—he was not without troubles of his own. Then, just two months later, during the World Cup events and festivities in Aspen, Monika Behr had been arrested for lewd behavior in the car belonging to that same male skier; the unfortunate Monika got caught with her panties down, still screwing the guy.

No matter what you thought of Monika Behr, it was hard to watch how she fell at Cortina, or how she looked when they airlifted her that last time—she looked dead.

"Oh, my God, that poor girl—she broke her neck!" my mom cried, shielding her eyes with her hands. She wouldn't watch the replays. Molly and I were riveted—we watched Monika Behr fall, again and again. If you'd ever skied at all, it was as hard not to watch how she fell as it was to watch.

"If not her neck, maybe her spine," the night groomer said, after the replays. They'd made Molly a full-time ski patroller at Bromley—at first, in addition to putting her in charge of the trail grooming. Later, when they made her the director of the ski patrol, she was given a backup role in the snowcat operations. When she was over fifty, Molly was only occasionally a snowcat operator on the mountain. "I'm a night groomer when I want to be, Kid," was how she explained it to me, "or when one of the regular fellas is sick or needs a break."

Molly was not a neurosurgeon, but the trail-groomer-turned-ski-patroller was pretty much right in her analysis of Monika Behr's crash at Cortina—it was a spinal injury, resulting in paralysis of both lower limbs. In her early twenties, Monika Behr became a paraplegic—a big woman, bordering on homely, in a wheelchair.

"Oh, my God, that poor girl—she's not even pretty!" my mother lamented. Yes, I know—I'm leaving too much out. Writing screenplays will do that to you. And this was the leap I should have seen coming, but I didn't.

Molly did. "Don't, Ray," the ski patroller started to say.

"Poor Monika Behr—she'll become like one of your unfortunate girl-friends, Adam!" my mom declared. "Too big, always fighting her weight, and never was or will be good-looking—I'm talking about the *younger* ones, sweetie, the ones even close to your own age," my mother said. "The kind of women you look at, but then, more quickly, you look away from—those poor women you know you'll never stay with, not for long. Poor Monika Behr will become your *type*, sweetie!"

"Stop it, Ray," Molly told her.

"I'm not even talking about your *older* girlfriends, Adam. I know you're not inclined to introduce Molly and me to the older ones, but I can manage to get a few details out of Elliot—that oh-so-discreet man!—and your grandmother occasionally slips up. Dottie isn't exactly discreet, you know. Poor Jasmine," my mom said, after a pause.

"Sorry, Kid," the trail groomer told me.

There was something disingenuous about how softly my mother said the *Poor Jasmine* part, her hushed voice sounding somewhat falsely sympathetic to Jasmine. I was thirty when I went out with Jasmine, who was fifty. Tellingly, Jasmine was a year older than my mom—closer to Molly's age. Jasmine was one of the divorcées I dated. She liked to call her ex-husbands or former boyfriends just to give them a piece of her mind. She liked unloading her grievances on anyone who answered the phone—a new wife or girlfriend, or even a child.

Jasmine would end up being my second-most unmarriageable girlfriend. When I was ready to break up with her, I took her to the Front Street house, where my grandmother (who was eighty-nine) tried to warn me that Jasmine might be "especially susceptible" to seeing ghosts.

"It's not just that Jasmine is as old as your mother, dear," Nana began.

"Jasmine is *older* than Ray, ya know, Adam," Dottie said.

"I know," I told her. I'm not sure how old Dottie was—I never really knew. If Nana was eighty-nine, I'm guessing Dottie was in her seventies.

"Furthermore—Adam, dear—I don't believe Jasmine knows you think she's unmarriageable," my grandmother pointed out. "Jasmine still thinks of herself as marriageable."

"Jasmine just keeps marryin' and marryin', don't she?" Dottie asked me.

"I know," I said. The three of us were in the kitchen of the Front Street house, where we were washing the supper dishes. Dottie had already pointed out that Jasmine was the first of my unmarriageable girlfriends to have cleaned her plate of one of Nana's gloppy casseroles. We could hear Jasmine talking on the phone, all the way from the living room. She was unloading her bitter feelings on a former boyfriend, or one of her ex-husbands—not the ex-husband who had died, I hoped. Jasmine hadn't told me that she'd *seen* her ex-husband who'd died, but Jasmine had confided this to Dottie and my grandmother.

"In those restaurants in New York, where they used to go together—that's where Jasmine has seen him," Nana told me.

"Jasmine said he's usually with another dead person—so she sees *other* ghosts, ya know," Dottie added.

"And this is what makes you think Jasmine might be 'especially susceptible' to seeing ghosts?" I asked my grandmother. Dottie just rolled her eyes. "Granddaddy's ghost just talks about punctuation—he's never scary," I pointed out to them.

"It's nothin' special, I suppose—seein' your dead husband, with a bunch of dead fellas ya used to know," Dottie said, shrugging.

"Adam, dear," Nana began, "I think Jasmine believes in eternity." I had no idea why Jasmine's belief in eternity—her own immortality, most of all—should concern me, but my grandmother had given more consideration to Jasmine's spirituality than I had. "I don't think a woman like

Jasmine will necessarily find this kind of encounter with a ghost soothing, dear."

"*Soothin'!*" Dottie exclaimed. "When she calls them ex-husbands and old boyfriends, she tells 'em how much sex she's havin' with you—ya know, Adam," Dottie said.

"I know," I said. We were aware of Jasmine's voice growing louder in the living room.

"A woman as old as your mother, Adam, dear, should not see the deluded, departed infant man in the bedroom of a *much younger* man she's sleeping with!" my grandmother declared. "This could cause Jasmine to become un-hinged," she added.

"If you ask me, Mrs. Brewster, Jasmine *is* unhinged," Dottie said.

"I'm with a young guy right now, Harold—he wants it all the time!" we could hear Jasmine yelling from the living room.

"When you break up with her, dear, she'll be calling *you*, you know," Nana told me.

"I know," I said.

"He never tells me he can only get it up with *prostitutes*, Harold!" Jasmine yelled.

"She's *unhinged*, all right—her pussy can't be so special to all them fellas," Dottie told us.

"I know," I said.

"You mouse-dick, Harold—you squirrel-dink!" Jasmine shouted. Nana and Dottie just looked at me.

"I know, I know," I said.

"You *hamster*-penis, Harold!" Jasmine screamed. The sound of her hang-ing up the phone in the living room was very audible in the kitchen.

"A *hamster* is a new dick to me," Dottie told us.

I was considering that the eternity Jasmine believed in was of the damna-tion kind. What I should have remembered was that Nana had long been a pillar of prescience. Hadn't she predicted that someone would come to harm or be killed on the old croquet court? And while my grandmother didn't ex-actly tell me about my mom and Molly, didn't Nana (in her ambiguous way) imply to me that my mother wasn't living the bachelorette life my aunts and I had once imagined? "You're not only the first man in her life, dear; you'll be the only one," my grandmother had said. "You're all that matters to her, Adam—as far as men are concerned," she had told me. In her beat-around-the-bush fashion, hadn't my grandmother told me my mom was a one-event girl—hadn't Little Ray chosen the one and only time she would *ever* sleep with a man, strictly for the purpose of giving birth to me?

I see now how the ill-starred girlfriends in my life reached an unwelcome pinnacle on that night in my attic bedroom of the Front Street house with Jasmine. I see now how all my girlfriends look ahead to my misguided encounter, years later, with Monika Behr.

22.

MY SECOND-MOST UNMARRIAGEABLE GIRLFRIEND

In my life as an unmade movie, I'll refrain from showing you a flash-forward of my ill-timed meeting with the paraplegic Austrian downhiller, but I can't avoid the flashback to my night under the attic skylight with Jasmine. If my life were ever a finished film, I would insert here my mother's voice-over—both her *Poor Monika Behr* routine and her more softly spoken *Poor Jasmine*. I would end my mom's voice-over with her hushed uttering of Jasmine's name, just as Jasmine—at fifty—slips into bed with me.

I was thirty. I'd purposely left my bathroom light on, with the door ajar. There was a path of light on the floor by my bed, and it was a starry night. A silvery glow of starlight descended from the skylight. I was worrying about Nana's presentiments—specifically, that a sudden sighting of Granddaddy's ghost could cause Jasmine to become *unhinged*. I was seeing Jasmine anew, through my grandmother's eyes. I'd not been critical of the negligee Jasmine wore to bed, until now. She always wore one, something sheer but not fully revealing. Thus partially concealed, Jasmine got into bed, taking the garment off just before we had sex, if we were having sex.

Because we were in my attic bedroom for the express purpose of seeing a dead man, I saw no prospect of having sex—the negligee remained on. I was relieved for that, but not by Jasmine's recurring bedtime recitations—her incessant repeating of what she'd said on the phone to this or that ex-husband or former boyfriend.

I began to understand my folly. When I dumped Jasmine, only her death would free me from her; she was fifty, old to me, but she likely had a few years to go. Jasmine would never stop phoning me. Only now did I see what Jasmine saw as her station in life, not only because her dead ex-husband had been a wealthy one. While Jasmine generally maintained an erect posture—she did not round her shoulders, nor did her upper back show any signs of her developing a dowager's hump—she definitely had a dowager's air of social position. Nana tried to warn me.

"Adam, dear," my grandmother had said, "those restaurants in New York, where Jasmine is always seeing her dead ex-husband—well, those restaurants speak to me of how inseparable Jasmine is from what she sees as her *station in life*."

Whoever the more recent ex-somebody was, Jasmine told me he'd been given an earful. It was clear Jasmine didn't move on; she continued to keep score. I foresaw that it would be all uphill—to prepare Jasmine for the always-sudden visitation of Granddaddy's ghost.

"He's usually well dressed," I began.

"Who is?" Jasmine asked.

"My grandfather's ghost," I reminded her.

"Oh, him," she said. In her perfunctory fashion, Jasmine took my hand and put it under her negligee, where she held it to her bare (only slightly sagging) breast. With her other hand, Jasmine pushed my face into her fragrant (not noticeably wrinkled) neck. How many men before me had been similarly guided, and how many of them were still changing and unlisting their phone numbers?

"I'm just not interested in your grandfather's ghost, Adam," Jasmine was saying. "My ex-husband, the one who died, is no more interesting dead than he was when he was alive—he still hangs out with the same old friends. They were *always* dead! They were always as boring as he was," Jasmine said.

"I don't think Granddaddy had any friends, only obsessions," I told Jasmine. "It can be startling how he suddenly shows up, but there's nothing scary about him. He never has anything shocking to say about punctuation," I said. It was the first time I'd acknowledged the emeritus as friendless. It made me pity him. It made me afraid of him, too, but Jasmine just wasn't interested in him. She lifted her negligee and straddled me.

"What if we were fucking when he suddenly showed up?" Jasmine asked me. "That might rattle the old boy's commas," she said, rubbing herself against me.

It was the first time I considered that fucking in front of ghosts was probably a bad idea. Certainly, I'd heretofore acknowledged that fucking in front of anyone was disrespectful—and Jasmine had further irritated me. She'd mounted me at a ghost sighting.

With Jasmine grinding away on top of me, I was unable to see the area of my bedroom floor I'd taken pains to light. The way I'd been mounted, I couldn't see the star-bright spot under the skylight where the diaper man's ghost usually appeared. I'd long stopped listening for the creak from the step on the attic stairs. I assumed ghosts were weightless, or they didn't need stairs. I'd not yet learned not to jump to conclusions regarding rules for ghosts. I would later learn that ghosts like elevators, or that some ghosts ride in elevators for unknown reasons.

"Don't be afraid—he's just very schoolteacherish," I tried to both fore-warn and assure Jasmine.

You should never generalize about ghosts. But what did I know? In the years since the infant emeritus was struck by lightning, he'd steadfastly been only an uninterruptable English teacher—obliviously addressing both sexes as *dear boys*. There'd been nothing to fear about his behavior.

In the passage of time, those other ghosts—those recurring dreams I first mistook them for—had indeed become as familiar (and as unthreatening) as old friends. What is safer than black-and-white photographs of people, places, and occurrences in the past?

Those same five men in an early Aspen mining camp; the mule train, ore wagons, crossing Independence Pass; what my mom said was probably an afternoon shift at the Smuggler Mine; two miners underground, setting black-powder charges; the formal portrait of the brave- but sad-looking Jerome B. Wheeler; the horse-drawn wagon, a beer delivery, at the Hotel Jerome; the dark-skinned hotel maid, maybe Mexican (Little Ray thought she was Italian). No, I'm not forgetting the boy or young man I didn't de-scribe to my mother—I still hadn't described him to her. That kid from the 1940s, handsome but childlike, a short boy with a tall snow shovel. I'd sensed—I still sensed—he might have been a different kind of ghost, the kind who can hurt you. Or maybe he was just a recurring dream, but I didn't think so. What was slightly off about him haunted me: his ski sweater and the hat with a pom-pom. The sweater was too big for his shoulders; the pom-pom on the ski hat was girlish, or it accentuated something girlish about him. A hotel guest, a woman, must have left her hat and sweater behind. In the passage of time, these images never changed—old black-and-white photographs don't lie, do they?

There'd been another image, more disturbing than the rest. I'd talked to my mom about it.

"Oh, those guys," she said, unconcerned. "The white guys are Aspen volunteers—I think they put down a Ute uprising."

In a telephone conversation with a helpful person at the Aspen Histor-ical Society, I said I was trying to understand what was going on in a black-and-white photo I'd seen: armed white men are posed with the bullet-riddled body of a dead Ute. One of the white men's dead companions is propped up in a more dignified position than the splayed-out body of the disrespected Ute. Aspen was once called Ute City, a silver camp in the Roaring Fork mining district. The Utes were removed to Utah in the 1880s. There'd been a Ute uprising in 1879, and another one—a small one, maybe the last—in 1887. The historical society had no record of the photo. I don't know which Ute uprising I got a glimpse of. Does it matter? They're all ghosts now, not just the two dead guys. Only the disrespect remains.

Now I know I shouldn't have spoken so presumptuously to Jasmine about Granddaddy's ghost. I never meant to mislead her, but a well-dressed young English teacher was not the ghost she saw. I felt Jasmine stop breathing in the same split second her hands flew all around, as if she were warding off an unseen swarm of bees—in the same split second I felt her hot urine flood over my thighs, and I heard the diaper man bellow, "Not Little Ray!" Not his classroom voice. Even before I could manage to see him, I knew the emeritus had moved on from punctuation. There was nothing schoolteacherish about this ghost. This was the infantile shitter, on the verge of electrocution.

I had to shield my face from Jasmine's flying hands. Her rings were cutting me, everywhere. There was a clunky, glitzy ring on each of her fingers—except the wedding one. "That woman's hands were mostly diamonds, dear—big ones," Nana told me later. (Sharp ones, I can attest.)

"Not Little Ray!" the enraged diaper man kept shouting. He didn't need a lip-reader to be understood now. I saw he was the infant in extremis, the infant terribilis, the near-death diaper man—the scrawny lunatic emeritus, naked except for the diaper, clutching a fistful of croquet wickets in his wizened hands.

"Not Little Ray!" Jasmine was now wailing—she was doing her best to convince the ghost she was on his side.

"Not Little Ray!" they now screamed at each other. If my grandmother didn't hear (and couldn't see) Granddaddy Lew, she of course could hear Jasmine screaming the unmentionable.

"I got this, Mrs. Brewster!" I heard Dottie calling.

Our neighbors must have heard Jasmine screaming, "Not Little Ray!" The raving bed-wetter was now standing on my bed, where her soaked negligee clung to her. In truth, although Jasmine was slightly younger than Molly, she looked a lot older than the ski patroller in these circumstances.

"Little Ray is my mom," I felt compelled to say, since Jasmine wouldn't stop shrieking her name. For no known reason, what I said appeared to upset

Jasmine more. At that moment, the diaper man stopped shouting. A passing semblance of sanity crossed his face. He squatted, grunting. Could ghosts crap? Did they? I'm done with generalizing. All I'll say is that the diaper man appeared to be trying to fill his diaper. Not to be outdone, or having abandoned what remained of her reasoning, Jasmine—still standing on the bed—let her bowels go. Or she let go of both her bowels and her sanity, in no discernible order.

Yes, Jasmine shit in my bed. No, this never happened with another girlfriend—marriageable or unmarriageable. Such a spontaneous act of defecation defeated or outdid the diaper man. He disappeared, which ghosts can do as suddenly as they can show up.

"Look what you've done to me, Adam—just see what you've done," Jasmine said. She knelt, beshitted, in my bed.

"Don't you be goin' up them attic stairs, Mrs. Brewster," I heard Dottie saying. "I'm the fix-it person in this house, and this sure as shit sounds like a situation in need of fixin' to me."

"This is not the woman I am, Adam—this is entirely your doing," Jasmine was telling me.

I foresaw what would become the theme of her unceasing phone calls. Jasmine would never completely recover her sense of herself. When a woman of a certain age—and, as Nana had noted, a presumed *station in life*—shits in bed, and all over herself, this can only be someone else's doing.

When I heard the familiar creak on the attic stairs, I saw Jasmine flinch. She sprang to her feet, covered with shit, teetering on my bed in anticipation of the next ghostly visitation. All I had time to say was, "Don't worry—it's not a ghost."

It's not my fault I never knew how Dottie readied herself for bed. Her face cream, thickly applied, was the lifeless color of the moon—it had a wet, otherworldly shine. The halo that encircled Dottie's face, like a lampshade, was intended (she later told me) to prevent her from rolling over and smearing her face cream on her pillow. What Dottie did to herself, nightly, meant that she slept unmoving on her back. Her halo, her thickly creamed face, and the stark severity of her black bathrobe gave Dottie the appearance of the Angel of Death.

Upon my graduation from Exeter, Elliot Barlow had given me a book of Ingmar Bergman's screenplays—*The Seventh Seal* among them, my favorite Bergman film. That was the first screenplay I read. I don't believe I've read a better one. When I saw Dottie step into the path of light, leading from my open bathroom door to the beshitted Jasmine standing on my bed, I thought Dottie was Death—a frightening female version of the moon-faced Bengt Ekerot, the black-cowled, medieval monk who personifies Death in *The Seventh Seal*. Dottie told me later that I whimpered when I saw her.

If Jasmine could have evacuated more, I'm sure she would have, but Jasmine gave up. Resigned to her fate, she curled into a fetal position in the bed and lay trembling in her terrible waste, waiting for Death—with a Down East accent—to finish her off.

"Holy shit—was it the casserole?" Dottie asked me.

"It was Granddaddy's ghost, near the end—he was wearing just the diaper," I told her.

"Looks like your *lady friend* shoulda been wearin' the diaper," Dottie replied. (You have to admire the old-timers from Maine, the ones who take charge in a crisis.) "You should see yourself, Adam," Dottie told me. "Go clean yourself up in your mom's bathroom. I'll clean up this mess and attend to the lady."

As politely as possible, I tried to indicate to Dottie that she should take off her terrifying halo and do something about her moonstruck face cream. "Well, sure as shit, I intend to take this stuff off," Dottie said, somewhat indignantly. "What with all the caterwaulin', Adam, I didn't think I should *dillydally* about gettin' here."

"Dottie will take care of you," I said to Jasmine. I definitely sensed there would be no more constructive conversations between us. Given that shit of this magnitude had happened, I knew there would be only Jasmine's incriminating phone calls.

23.

"ALMOST PERFECT" OR "NO STRINGS ATTACHED"

I've not described in what way my mom became a wrestling fanatic. I know I haven't given you a picture of how she behaved at wrestling matches. My teammates loved her and her behavior, but she embarrassed me. That several of my teammates were in love with my mother—not least, the smallest of them, our starting 110-pounder—further embarrassed me. I doubt that Coach Dearborn had a crush on my mom. The coach wasn't flirting with her on the dance platform at the Front Street wedding—their single-leg lunges were just lunges to him.

Coach Dearborn never lost his temper—he would reprove us when we lost ours. "Getting angry is a distraction for wrestlers," he told us. Yet he was as delighted as my teammates when Little Ray lost her temper at wrestling matches; she mostly vented her frustration at referees. Speaking diplomatically, as he was inclined to, Coach Dearborn said, "The quality of refereeing in New England is not what I was used to in the Big Ten."

I once asked Molly if my mother had been cheated by a low score when she'd been a slalom skier, in competition. Or, in some other way, had Little Ray been unfairly judged by a racing official? "I didn't know her when she was competing, Kid," was all Molly said about it.

There was an episode at an away match—in the James Gym at Mount Hermon, where Little Ray kept calling the referee "Baldy." The ref was beyond bald. He was also guilty of not penalizing—of not even warning—the Mount Hermon wrestler for stalling. The wrestler kept crawling off the mat. He was making no effort to get off his belly and his elbows. He was losing the match, just trying not to get pinned. It was the first match of the day—in those years, the lightest weight class always wrestled first—and my mother knew our 110-pounder had the hots for her. When I'd introduced them to each other, Matthew Zimmermann couldn't look at her—he could barely speak. My mom was flirting with him when she told him—in her wide-eyed, exclamatory way—they were in the same weight class.

There are a preternatural number of wrestlers named Matthew. As you might guess, they're all called Matt. Not Zimmermann—we called him Zimmer or Zim. In those years, at an all-boys' school, last names were the norm. The teachers addressed us by our last names. We called our close friends by their last names.

Zimmermann was a scrappy 110-pounder, but my mother thought he lacked the requisite killer instinct. When he was winning on points, he was content to coast—he didn't go for the fall. When he was being beaten, he stopped trying to win—he just tried to stay off his back. Zimmer's lack of aggression could cause my mom to yell at him. ("You can kill this guy, Zim— just *kill* him!" she would scream.) But she saved the worst things she was capable of saying for the referees. "You need glasses, Baldy, if you can't see he's stalling!" she hollered at the ref at Mount Hermon. He heard her—I'm pretty sure everyone heard her. When the wrestlers went off the mat, the ref blew his whistle. While the wrestlers were returning to their positions in the center of the mat, the ref stared at my mother. My mom stared back. The whistle was still in the bald referee's mouth, but he hadn't blown it, when Little Ray said, "Maybe glasses and a wig."

It was very quiet in the old James Gym while Coach Dearborn and the beyond-bald ref were talking. When the coach went over to the bleacher seats, where my mother was sitting—in the front row, at mat-side—he invited my mom to come sit on the bench with the Exeter team. There was scattered applause from the Mount Hermon crowd when my mother joined me and my teammates on our bench—my teammates applauded, too. Coach Dearborn made my mom sit next to him. I was relieved that the snowshoer wasn't with us at Mount Hermon. Mr. Barlow was traveling with the JV team.

"We're happy to have you sit with us, Ray," Coach Dearborn told her, "but you can't talk to the referee from the team bench."

"So I can't tell him that refs wear black-and-white-striped shirts because they have sex with zebras?" my mother asked.

"Not from the team bench, Ray," Coach Dearborn said, smiling at her. It was clear the ref had only partially heard her. She'd raised her voice when she mentioned the black-and-white-striped shirts, and again when she said the *zebras* word. She behaved herself for the rest of Zimmer's match. When the referee actually warned Zim's opponent for stalling—it was just a warning, not a penalty—Coach Dearborn gave my mom a cautionary look.

"Finally," Little Ray said quietly—to the coach, not the ref.

When the matches were over, there was the usual milling around on the mat. Some of the wrestlers were shaking hands with their opponents, some weren't. I was nervous when I saw my mother approach the referee. Technically speaking, she wasn't talking to him from the team bench, but Coach Dearborn and I—and, of course, my teammates—were listening closely.

"I'm so sorry I called you 'Baldy'—that was just mean," Little Ray told the ref. I know my teammates felt a little let down.

Later, in the basement of the old James Gym, by the lockers for visiting teams, Coach Dearborn took me aside. "I'm very fond of your mom—as are your teammates, Adam," the coach began. "But I believe Mr. Barlow would agree with me—as a rule, she shouldn't sit with the team. We'll see this ref again, and the way he calls stalling isn't likely to change—if you know what I mean."

"I know what you mean," I told him. I was nodding my head off, in a way that would have made Em proud. Not counting my uncles and the snowshoer, most of the Exeter faculty didn't call me Adam—I was more commonly called Brewster. By calling me Adam, Mr. Dearborn made me feel like family. A wrestling team can be a family, if not exactly like my family.

I loved my family of four, counting Molly. Of course I knew there were other families who would consider us strange, but we were not strange to me—just different. I try to apply this principle when I consider my mom as both an object of desire and a substitute mother to my wrestling teammates—those physically self-abusing boarding-school boys away from home, missing their mothers and without any girls their own age around. Mothers—I mean someone else's mother—can provide lonely young boys with a lot of erotic stimulation. Little Ray was small and sexy, and my wrestling teammates weren't used to girl jocks. The wrestlers were also undone by how flexible and strong my mother was.

Before she met Molly and Elliot, I'd not seen my mom flirt with anyone. After she married the snowshoer, and she was living with the snowcat operator, I never saw Little Ray flirt with anyone her own age or older. But my mother flirted with my wrestling teammates. She was very aware of her effect on boys and younger men. Don't think *I'm* fantasizing—fantasizing about older women is what boys and younger men do.

Coach Dearborn invited my mom to wrestling practice. You're always changing your level or your angle in wrestling. Coach Dearborn had seen my mom's single-leg lunges; he wanted her to show my teammates how she did her squats and wall sits, too. That's how the practice started—innocently enough, with my mother in sweatpants and a T-shirt, just demonstrating her ski exercises to the wrestlers. Explosiveness counts, in skiing and in wrestling, but before long my mom was rolling around with the other light-weights in the wrestling room—not just with the snowshoer. Little Ray took down Matthew Zimmermann with a picture-perfect double leg—what nowadays is called a freight-train double. She dropped her shoulder lower than Zim's waist and drove through him—her hands holding both cheeks of Zimmer's butt, her head tucked under his rib cage, as she stuck our starting 110-pounder on his back.

"I see someone's been paying attention to her takedowns—that's how to hit a double leg," Coach Dearborn said.

"I told you," the little English teacher said. "Ray would have been a heck of a one-ten-pounder."

Zimmermann had the wind knocked out of him—he lay gasping on his back. My mom's ministrations to him were a weird mix of more than moth-erly affection and training-room talk.

"Zim, listen to me," she was saying as she bent over him with her hair falling in his face. "You got to breathe in through your nose and out through your mouth, or you'll hyperventilate."

The way she'd straddled Zimmer reminded me of the night she'd shown me the snowshoer kiss. I doubted this was the best way for Zim to regain normal breathing.

"No, no—purse your lips and blow out like this," my mom was telling our gasping 110-pounder as she blew in his face. Was I the only one in the wrestling room who noticed Zimmer had a hard-on—not a known symptom of hyperventilation—or were his sweatpants just bunched up from the way Little Ray had driven him to the mat?

Before I knew what became of Matthew Zimmermann, I used to be afraid of what would become of him. What if Zimmer married an older woman, a dead ringer for Little Ray? I pictured poor Zim as attracted to older women who drilled him with freight-train doubles. Then they blew in his face and gave him hard-ons while he gasped for breath.

As for the beyond-bald referee, the one with a limited understanding of stalling, it was a home match, at Exeter, where we saw him again. It was the first time Molly had come to see me wrestle, or maybe she'd come to have a look at how Little Ray behaved around the wrestlers. My mom and the night groomer were not sitting on the team bench; they were at mat-side, in the front row of bleacher seats. We were wrestling in that gladiatorial pit in the Thompson Cage. The legs of our fellow students dangled above us, their faces peering down at us from the board track above. The students sat on the L-shaped entrance to the wooden running track that circumscribed the dirt track below. From the mat, we could hear the starting gun for the runners and the hurdlers in the cage.

This was the first time my wrestling teammates had seen Molly, even from a distance. It was winter—the snowcat operator and my mom were wearing their après-ski stuff, not the most flattering attire. Even so, because the trail groomer was a goddess in my eyes, I was shocked that my teammates had eyes only for my mother. You can learn a lot about point of view from writing, and from sexual desire.

"Who's the big blonde with your mom, Brewster?" one of my teammates asked me.

"That's Molly—she's my mom's best friend. Of course she's a skier," I said.

"She's a humongous friend and skier," Zimmermann observed, speaking strictly as a 110-pounder. He'd been skipping rope and was sweating—what he liked to do to get his heartbeat going, just before he stepped out on the mat.

Fittingly, it would be Zimmer's match—as usual, the first of the day—that exposed the beyond-bald referee's failure to warn or penalize for stalling. Zimmermann's opponent got taken down twice and decided to stop wrestling. Zimmer took him down, let him go, and quickly took him down again. It was 4–1, only halfway into the first period. Zim's opponent, on the bottom, turned himself into a table. On all fours, head up, the guy spread his hands and knees apart—he was unbudgeable. Keeping his arms and back straight, the staller blocked every move Zimmer made on him.

"What's he doing on the bottom?" Coach Dearborn calmly asked the ref, who did not respond. Zim cranked on the guy's arms. He jacked up the guy's ankles and ran him forward like a wheelbarrow. But the staller would not be broken down—he was committed to being a table.

"Stalling on the bottom?" the snowshoer suggested to the referee, but the ref remained oblivious to stalling.

"This is baloney, ref—he's stalling on the bottom!" my mother screamed. At least she didn't call him *Baldy*.

"Cross-face cradle, Zim!" Coach Dearborn barked. That's what I'd been thinking, but Zimmermann was a little frustrated. He was on his toes, his chest on the guy's back, slapping the guy with the cross face—first one side of his face, then the other.

When the ref blew his whistle, he penalized Zim for unnecessary roughness—one point for the staller. Zimmer was still ahead, 4–2.

"Zim!" Coach Dearborn said sharply. "Let him go. Take him down again." Zimmer gave the guy the escape. It was 4–3 at the end of the first period. Sometimes the crowd quieted down between periods. There was some murmuring on our team bench—to the effect that penalizing Zimmermann for unnecessary roughness missed the whole point about him.

"Zim is more of an *insufficient* roughness guy," one of my teammates said.

Then Little Ray jumped to her feet and shouted point-blank at the bald ref. "Not even a zebra would fuck you!" my mom told him.

Yes, the zebra-fucking idea had a context—not that everyone who heard her knew the context, and everyone had heard her. I was sitting next to Coach Dearborn, who quietly said, "That pretty much sums it up, Adam— not even a zebra."

"Not even a zebra," the snowshoer said, so softly that it sounded reverential.

We could all see that Molly had her arm around my mother. The trail groomer was guiding my mom toward the exit. I would only later consider that the night groomer knew something about the nature of competition. Molly didn't want to leave anything in the hands of a bad official. The ref couldn't throw out Little Ray if she was already leaving.

"Not even a zebra!" some students in the crowd were shouting.

"We're witnessing the birth of a mantra," Elliot Barlow said, as Zimmer built a lead against his flagging opponent. Zim just kept taking the guy down and letting him go. Two points for a takedown, one point for an escape—you can build a lead fairly fast.

I was warming up for my match when Zimmermann spotted my mother and Molly. Zim had taken my seat on the team bench, where he'd been looking all around for my mom. Little Ray and the trail groomer were sitting with the students on the board track above us—"the outfield seats," my mother called them. She'd told me she liked being at mat-side, where she could see the wrestlers sweat and hear them breathing.

I'll always remember that day. Seconds before I stepped out on the mat, I saw Zimmer wave to my mom, who waved back. Molly still had her arm around her. It was the day *Not even a zebra* started gaining momentum. Among my teammates, it would one day acquire the status of a sacred chant.

In a book almost no one read, I told the zebra-fucking story—only I had someone else's mother say it. I thought my mom would appreciate that I'd changed the story to protect her. But Molly later told me that I'd hurt my mother's feelings. "Ray thought you didn't give her credit, Kid," the snowcat operator said.

Over time, a pattern was established. Molly would be the one to tell me what my mom thought of something I'd written. Apparently, Little Ray wondered why I *didn't* write about her. "Who are all these other mothers? They're not *me*!" she would wail to the night groomer. "There are always mothers, but who *are* these women? Did I make no impression at all on him?" my mom asked Molly, who would report to me.

"Does my mother really want me to write about her?" I asked Molly repeatedly.

"No, of course not, Kid," the trail groomer told me. "Ray doesn't understand fiction. Ray doesn't read fiction. Except yours."

This pattern of behavior was a two-way street. I learned I could complain to Molly about those things my mom wouldn't tell me about; for example, I thought Molly could persuade my mother to tell me who my father was. Or suppose Little Ray told the night groomer first? Maybe then my mom would let Molly tell me.

The night after *Not even a zebra* was when the idea of Molly as a go-between blossomed. When Molly and my mom came back to Exeter together—usually, to see me wrestle—the sleeping arrangements were different. The snowshoer's apartment in Amen Hall didn't work with four of us. If my mother and Elliot slept together, that meant Molly had to sleep with me. After the wedding night, there seemed to be some ambiguity concerning the consequences of my being in the same bed with the snowcat operator— perhaps not the healthiest thing for a teenage boy.

In those years, when my mom and Molly had an overnight in Exeter, they stayed in my mother's bedroom at the Front Street house. Naturally, my mom slept in my attic bedroom with me. Of course I knew Little Ray would leave me alone, at times—when she was visiting Molly, or when we were disturbed by an impromptu punctuation lesson from the ghost of the semicolon emeritus. My mother didn't enjoy Granddaddy's ghostly visits. It was hard for her to be reminded of the time when he still talked. I understood why his monologues upset her. She didn't care to remember how the faculty emeritus had doted on his Little Ray, before her pregnancy rendered him speechless. It was after one such haunting—"Boys, boys," the ghostly grammarian began—when my mom got out of my bed and stomped down the attic stairs.

"I'm not a *boy*, Daddy—I never was—which, you may remember, is why I could get *pregnant*!" Little Ray was calling, all the way down the stairs. The diaper man's ghost continued to address me in the plural. I'd fallen asleep when the night groomer got into bed with me, maybe at my mom's prompting.

"You can tell me what's on your mind, Kid," Molly said in the dark. "Only if you want to tell me."

I had plenty to say. I'd not stopped wanting to know who my father was—I'd just stopped asking my mother. "I know the snowshoer has asked her—she won't tell him anything," I told Molly.

"I'm in the club, Kid," the snowcat operator said. "Ray won't tell me, either."

Elliot Barlow had long been a go-between for me. Now I had two. I was already telling the snowshoer what I wished my mom would tell me. "You have to give Ray more time, Adam," Elliot had said. "It might be easier for her to tell me or Molly first."

The night when Molly told me she was *in the club*, I began to understand what the little English teacher had meant. Like Little Ray, I was keeping a secret. I hadn't even told Nora and Em. If I told anyone, I was beginning to think, it might be easier for me to tell the trail groomer first.

I knew the snowshoer wore my mother's clothes. Okay, he missed her— we both did. But, even when my mom was away, I didn't wear her clothes. Yes, they were close to the same size. Although Elliot had to stand on his toes when he kissed her, and Little Ray had ten or twelve pounds on him, her clothes fit him.

I know, I know—my mother kept her clothes in the snowshoer's bedroom in Amen Hall. I could understand his temptation to wear her clothes to bed. But—by the wrestling season of my third year at the academy, when I was seventeen—Elliot was in the habit of dressing himself in Little Ray's clothes whenever he was in our faculty apartment. In the evening, students often knocked on our door—wanting the snowshoer's help with their homework, or because they had other problems. What if one of the students saw the little English teacher dressed as a woman?

Because my mom was a jock, a lot of her clothes weren't very feminine, but Elliot was into her makeup, too. Little Ray kept most of her makeup in the snowshoer's bathroom. Elliot liked her lipstick, her eyeliner, her eye shadow. When he put on her face powder, every trace of his beard disappeared. He had a light beard.

When you love someone who's different, you worry about them more—you're always looking out for them. In my childhood, I was aware of my grandmother's efforts to protect my mother. I was conscious of trying to protect her, too. When I was a student at Exeter, I looked out for the little English teacher. We usually went to wrestling practice together. I was always checking him over. Was he wearing the right clothes? Were there any telltale traces of my mom's makeup in the area of Elliot's eyes or lips?

That night when the night groomer got into bed with me, when I knew I wasn't dreaming her—Molly was just wondering what was on my mind—I almost told her about the snowshoer's cross-dressing. I was disappointed when the snowcat operator fell asleep. I'd wanted her to hug me, or give me a good-night kiss. Instead, I was left alone with my hard-on and my desire to touch her. Of course I didn't touch her, and soon I was asleep.

When I woke up with her arms around me, and I felt her breath on the back of my neck, I was dreaming I was with Molly. Then her hips snuggled closer to me. Even in the dimness of the predawn light, I knew the body next to mine was too small to be the trail groomer's. "Is this my Adam?" my mom whispered in my ear. "I have just my one and only—it sure feels like him."

"It sure feels like you, too," I told her.

"Of course it's me, sweetie," my mother said, clinging to me. "It's what we *do*." But for how much longer would we keep doing it? I wondered.

In the dim light, and with my back turned to her, I felt safe to speak. I knew she couldn't see my frightened eyes. I thought I could keep the fear out of my voice. "Do you know that Elliot wears your clothes?" I asked her.

"Do I *know*?" my mom cried, hugging me harder. "Oh, sweetie—of course I *know*! I'm always dressing him in my clothes—Elliot *loves* my clothes!" she cried. "It's what we *do*," Little Ray repeated.

"But is it safe—is the snowshoer *safe*?" I asked her.

"Oh, sweetie—don't be afraid," my mother said. The dawn was breaking as she turned me to her, holding my face in her hands. She could see my eyes. "Adam, we can't make being safe the guiding principle of our lives. We have to be who we are—we can only do what we do, sweetie."

"But if we love people, we want them to be *safe*. Isn't that the foremost thing?" I asked her.

"The foremost thing we want for the people we love isn't necessarily *their* foremost thing—is it, sweetie?" my mom asked me.

"I just want the snowshoer to be safe," I said. "I love him—I don't want anyone or anything to hurt him," I told her.

"Elliot wanted to be a little girl when he was a little boy," my mother told me. "Elliot *is* a woman, sweetie—she just wasn't born one."

"*He*," I corrected her. "Elliot is a man at an all-boys' school," I reminded her.

"*She*," Little Ray corrected me. "Elliot is a woman to me, sweetie. She's almost perfect for me, isn't she?" my mom asked me.

"Almost perfect," I could only repeat. I was once again seeing them on their wedding night—how they were when they were leaving for their honeymoon on the cliff, how my mom had told Elliot to keep hold of her. I was once more lying in the night groomer's arms—not yet beginning to understand how some people change, and some don't. Only now I realized I would forever be praying for this precarious and precious triangle to hold on. *Please stay on the cliff*, I would always be praying—to all three of them.

"Oh, don't cry, sweetie—don't be afraid," my mom repeated. She held me in her arms, the way she had when I was a child.

"Are you saying, 'Keep true to the dreams of thy youth'—is that what you're telling me?" I asked her.

"Oh, my—that's pretty! I like that," my mother told me. "Is that something you read, sweetie? Who wrote that?"

"Maybe Melville," I answered.

"Oh, him," Little Ray said, disappointed. A lifetime of hearing about *Moby-Dick* had predisposed her to dislike Melville, though she'd never read him. I was quoting what the author had pasted to his writing desk—Nana had told me about it. At the time, I didn't realize that Melville hadn't written it—I just liked the sound of it.

When the snowshoer took my grandmother and me to see the 1956 film adaptation of *Moby-Dick*—the John Huston version, with Gregory Peck as Captain Ahab—we all hated it. At least Ahab dies—he doesn't go home to his wife—but New Bedford isn't New Bedford, the great white whale looks like a bathtub toy, and all the poetry is lost.

"They lost the hyphen, too," Nora had observed. She'd seen the poster, not the movie. "That Dick is just one more white Dick in a sea of white Dicks," she said. "I'm not seeing it." Em just cringed at the thought of *a sea of white Dicks*.

After I'd seen the movie, when we were riding home in the snowshoer's VW Beetle, Nana said: "That film was not true to the dreams of Mr. Melville's youth." She didn't elaborate to Elliot and me on the admonition Melville had pasted to his writing desk. It turned out that Schiller had written it.

"Keep true to the dreams of thy youth"—ah, well, who wouldn't like the sound of that? But sometimes—for example, when you're born a boy and you want to be a girl—that's a tall order.

"Well, I like it—even if Moby Dick wrote it," my mother suddenly said. "And that's what my snowshoer is doing, Adam—she would have been a pretty girl. She's keeping true to the dreams of her youth." Little Ray took a deep breath before going on. "And that's what I was doing, sweetie—when I had you," my mom told me.

"When you *what?*" I said.

"When I wanted a baby—all mine, my one and only, no strings attached. I was keeping true to the dreams of my youth when I had you, sweetie," my mother told me.

"Who was he?" I asked her.

"He was just some kid, sweetie—he was younger than you; he wasn't shaving. He was just a boy who couldn't take his eyes off me. You know boys like that, don't you?" my mom asked me. "He was *small*," she whispered, kissing me. "He would have been a pretty girl. What he meant to me, Adam, was that you would be all mine. That's what 'no strings attached' *means*, sweetie," my mother said.

I was no longer writing in those clunky notebooks with the popping rings—they reminded me of meeting Rose. Mr. Barlow had found better notebooks for me in Harvard Square. They had hardcover bindings—like real books, but with blank pages—and the ones I liked best were the size of paperback novels. The pages were unlined.

This happened after my conversation with my mom in my attic bedroom, where she told me my father would have been a pretty girl. I'd been writing in one of my notebooks at the kitchen table of the Amen Hall apartment I shared with the snowshoer. I don't remember why I got up from the table— probably to get a glass of water, or to make myself a cup of tea. I do remember leaving the pages of my writing notebook open.

In the 1960s, I never saw those notebooks that had a hymnal ribbon. I love those notebooks—you never lose your place. At Mr. Barlow's kitchen table, I used the salt and pepper shakers to hold my notebook open. The little English teacher wasn't snooping; he just happened to see what I'd been writing.

It isn't surprising that I'd written down the two most indelible things my mother had said in her most recent, and most candid, conversation with me. The first was about Elliot Barlow as a woman; the second was about my very young father.

Nor is it surprising that the snowshoer thought I was contemplating two titles. I don't know why, but I'd written down the two things my mom said as if they were titles:

"Almost Perfect"
"No Strings Attached"

"I see you're having a title dilemma," the little English teacher told me, when I came back to the kitchen table. I saw what he was looking at. I'd not told him these stories. "I'm aware I don't know the context—I have no idea what you're thinking," Elliot said. "Both phrases are trite, but 'No Strings Attached' is more clichéd than 'Almost Perfect'—I think it's a worse cliché," the snowshoer said.

"I wasn't really thinking of them as titles—they're just a couple of things my mom said," I told him.

"Oh, of course, they sound just like your mom—they work fine as dialogue," the little English teacher assured me.

24.

MELANCHOLIC ENOUGH

That boy, the one who wasn't shaving, the boy who couldn't take his eyes off Little Ray—my mother told Molly he looked thirteen or fourteen. "The kid told Ray he was almost fifteen," Molly told me. Beginning with his age, Molly and I sensed there were likely some strings attached.

"He was no big deal!" my mom had insisted to Molly, but—whoever the kid was—he was a big deal to me.

Molly and I knew boys who couldn't keep their eyes off my mother—my wrestling teammates, Matthew Zimmermann among them. How my mom had described the kid in Aspen to Molly was consistent with what she'd said about him to me. "He was *small*," my mother had emphasized. "He would have been a pretty girl," she'd told Molly and me.

"She never told you about this kid before?" I asked Molly.

"Ray said she gave some of her clothes to a boy who was a little smaller than she was—she didn't say she slept with him," Molly told me. "Not at first."

"What clothes did she give him?" I asked the snowcat operator.

"Ray gave the kid a ski sweater—it was too small for her, but it was a little big on him," Molly said. "There was a ski hat, too—Ray said she never liked it, but she liked it on him."

"A ski hat with a pom-pom?" I asked Molly.

"Ray didn't say there was a pom-pom," Molly said.

"I'm not sure about it," I told her, truthfully.

"There are always strings attached, Kid," Molly said.

Had I seen my father as a ghost? Was he the short boy with the tall snow shovel? Had he been wearing my mom's ski sweater? Was that her hat, with the girlish pom-pom? And why did I think this ghost looked like it was still alive?

Yes, I put off telling my wife, Grace, about the ghosts. I know, I know—people who are guilty of lies of omission are usually guilty of more than one. But I did tell Grace about the snowshoer kiss. I told her the entire history

214

of that kiss. I wasn't trying to put her off. I'd been hearing about Grace for years—foremost from my mother, long before Molly jumped on the Grace bandwagon.

I heard that Grace did this, and that Grace did that, when Grace was still in high school. Thanks to my mom, Grace was reading my novels when she was seventeen—when I was thirty-one. It's a good thing I resisted my mother, who wanted me to meet Grace then. How could that have turned out well?

"Maybe later would be better, Ray," was all Molly said at the time, or words to that effect. Later the trail groomer joined forces with Little Ray. I didn't give in to my mother's nagging at me to meet Grace until Molly wanted me to meet her, too. When Molly and my mom joined forces, I gave in.

"I'm just saying you should *meet* Grace, sweetie," my mother usually began. This time, Molly was making pancakes in the Manchester kitchen; no doubt it was the ski season in Vermont, because it was dark outside when Molly was making breakfast, and my mom and Molly were wearing their long johns and their ski socks. "Grace is thirty-three, she's beautiful, she works in publishing—she's been reading your books since she was in *high school*, sweetie," my mother carried on.

"Grace is thirty-two, Ray," Molly corrected her.

"She's *almost* thirty-three, Molly," my mom said.

It was 1988, I think. Those two old ski jocks, who were spilling their coffee while they were trying to put on a second underlayer of clothes, were working at Bromley Mountain. Molly was a couple of years older than my mother, who was sixty-six.

"You wanted me to meet Grace when she was still in high school," I reminded my mom.

"It's just as well that didn't happen, Kid—I think now is a good time to meet her," Molly said.

"Grace was a darling little girl—I gave her ski lessons, you know," my mother reminded me.

"You gave me ski lessons, too, and look how I turned out—the serial bad-girlfriend guy," I said.

"I wouldn't go there if I were you, Kid," Molly told me. Too late.

"If Grace was a bleeder, sweetie, we would have heard about it," my mom assured me. "Manchester is a small town—a woman with continuous uterine bleeding would be a big deal here."

"Come on, Ray—no bleeding," Molly said.

"I know Sophie was a *writer*, sweetie—I'm not saying all she did was bleed!" my mother said. "But did Sophie ever publish anything?"

"I saw some short stories, in magazines, but there wasn't a collection—there was no book," I told my mom and Molly. "I don't think Sophie wrote a novel, not that I saw."

"Not a surefire page-turner, sweetie—a novel about *fibroids*!" my mother exclaimed.

"Cut it out, Ray," Molly told her.

"I'm pretty sure Grace doesn't have fibroids, sweetie," my mom reassured me. "Not that fibroids are the worst thing—except to the life of a washing machine, they're not life-threatening or anything."

"Just stop, Ray," Molly said.

"I'm stopping, I'm stopping!" my mother promised.

Her memory was remarkable, I was thinking. She'd first and last seen Sophie twenty-five years before—another early morning in the ski season, when Molly was making pancakes.

The washing machine was in the kitchen of the Manchester house, and Sophie had been loading it with our bloody bedsheets. My mom and Molly were in their early forties; I was twenty-two. I'd met Sophie in a creative writing class in college, but Sophie was a little older—twenty-four or twenty-five. The uterine bleeding had caused her to miss two or three years of school.

"Fibroids are benign muscle-tissue tumors in the uterine wall," Sophie was explaining to my mother and Molly. They hadn't asked her about the bleeding; Sophie was always explaining it, unasked. "Fibroids generally don't turn malignant or become dangerous, except for the sometimes severe bleeding they can cause—the bleeding can vary, from very little to *hemorrhagic*," Sophie further explained.

I had my arms full of bloody pillowcases and towels; Sophie pointed to the washer, and I stuffed them in. I was wearing a T-shirt and boxers; Sophie pointed to my white T-shirt, which I took off and put in the washer. I liked having a writer girlfriend. We talked about writing, and our wanting to be writers, all the time, truly more than we talked about her constant bleeding—but we were always doing laundry. Sophie hated the sight of blood.

That early morning in the Manchester kitchen, Sophie started the load of laundry; she sipped her coffee without ever pausing in her lecture to Molly and Little Ray, who were speechless. Of course I'd heard Sophie's fibroid prognostications before; I was always speechless. There's nothing you can or should say when a woman is telling you about her nonstop uterine bleeding.

"To understand how fibroids cause bleeding, you have to know what usually allows for uterine bleeding *not* to occur," Sophie was saying. This was the part of the ordeal when Sophie pressed her palms together, as if in prayer. I was checking out my boxer shorts, but there were no signs of blood—not that I could see—while Little Ray also held her hands tightly together. My mom was being a good sport, going along with Sophie's dramatization of uterine bleeding, but Molly was busy with the pancakes at the stove—Molly's hands were otherwise engaged. Molly wasn't praying.

"Imagine your uterus like your hands squeezed together," Sophie was saying. "The inside surfaces of your uterus are two walls, tightly opposed—the endometrial surfaces of your uterus would easily bleed, if the opposing walls weren't pressed together." Sophie wrung her hands. "The walls hold the blood in," she said, praying harder.

The way my mother was wringing her hands, it looked like a new off-season exercise. "Fibroids are irregular muscle masses; they *abut* the inner surfaces of the uterus, like marbles. Imagine marbles between your hands," Sophie said to Little Ray. "The walls of your uterus are pushed apart."

"Fucking *marbles*!" my mom cried.

"The blood sloughs off anytime, causing irregular or constant bleeding," Sophie continued calmly. She knew the story, but you can see why it wouldn't have worked as a novel. "Sometimes the bleeding doesn't amount to more than spotting. Sometimes the blood really flows," Sophie went on. Definitely not a novel, I hoped.

We were together a year; we read all of Thomas Mann together. Sophie thought Mann might have managed a novel about uterine bleeding. Fibroid sufferers meet at a women's clinic; they tell one another the stories of their ruined relationships. I suggested that Mann might have tried this as a novella, or a long short story.

"Maybe there are men who can only be with women who are fibroid sufferers," Sophie had speculated. Definitely not longer than a novella, I was hoping.

"During my actual period, the flow is much heavier than normal—there's severe cramping and pain," Sophie was telling Molly and my mother. "No one wants to have sex with me—not after the novelty wears off," Sophie said, looking at me. Molly and my mom looked at me, too. I was self-conscious and cold, standing around in my boxers. "I wouldn't want to have sex with me, either," Sophie said—more softly, to me. "I wouldn't stay with me as long as you have, Adam," she said. When she got to this part, it broke me up—every time—but we'd agreed not to cry in front of each other. Instead, we tried to imagine how Thomas Mann would have written it. Not an up-lifting novella.

Sophie stretched the waistband of my boxers, appearing to take a disin-terested look; she always let the waistband go with an audible snap. To Molly and Ray, this gesture might have seemed affectionate or cruel—perhaps both—but I knew Sophie. She was always looking for blood. "Aren't you cold, sweetie?" my mother asked me. "You should put some clothes on."

I tried to look like I was leaving the kitchen, but I took my time doing it. Sophie knew how to finish a story, and I knew exactly where she was in the fibroid saga—she was almost done with it. "Surgery is an option," Sophie was saying to my mom and Molly. I was edging toward the TV room with the giant futon—where Sophie and I had slept, where we'd had sex, where there'd been bleeding—but I knew I had to linger in the kitchen a little lon-ger. "I could have a fibroidectomy—or, one day, a complete hysterectomy," Sophie said, almost casually. She paused; she knew I was waiting to leave. "Don't worry, Adam," she said softly, letting me go. "I won't try the surgery till you've moved on. I won't make you go through the surgery part."

I love Thomas Mann. He was the perfect writer to discover in a year of bleeding. But twenty-five years later, I was alone with my mother and Molly in their Vermont kitchen. I was older than they'd been when Sophie and I broke up. I didn't want to hear my mom say, "Poor Sophie"—not again, not when those two old ski jocks were in their sixties, and I was in my forties.

I'd missed having a writer for a girlfriend, if not the bleeding. I'd been seeing another writer; there was something about it that made being a writer a little less lonely. I'd never gone out with a woman who worked in publish-ing, and Grace had been reading my novels since she was in high school. If you were a writer closing in on fifty—if your relationships had been a rocky road—wouldn't you have been interested in meeting Grace? Even if you were worried about the age difference. Even if Grace was your mother's idea.

"Okay," I said, looking at Molly, who was flipping pancakes. "Okay, okay," I told my mother, who was doing her wall sits in her long johns against the refrigerator, trying not to spill her coffee.

"Okay to *what*, sweetie?" my mom asked.

"Okay, I'll meet Grace. If that's what you want, I'll meet her," I said. I should have known this would make my mother suspicious.

"You're not seeing anyone, are you? You can't go out with Grace if you're seeing someone, sweetie," my mom told me.

"Ray, let Adam meet Grace—let *them* decide if they want to go out," Molly said.

"Are you seeing someone, sweetie?" my mother asked me.

"You know who I'm seeing. In my uncommitted way, I've been seeing her for a few years," I said.

"Oh, her—oh, God—that *other* writer, the one who's depressed all the time!" my mom exclaimed. "It's been more than a few years, sweetie. You're not *living* with her, are you?"

"I told you. We have an agreement. We don't live together, we don't have children," I said.

"She's probably too old to have children, sweetie. She's your age, isn't she? Are you sure she's not trying to have children?" my mother asked. She was spilling her coffee now, and there's no telling what her wall sits were doing to the stuff on the inside of the refrigerator door.

"Give it a rest, Ray," Molly said. "Wilson doesn't want children."

My mom had chugged the last of her coffee; she'd moved on from the wall sits to her single-leg lunges. *"Wilson!"* she cried. "What a name for a woman—no wonder she's depressed! It's a male given name. If Wilson was her last name—well, okay."

"Ray, you know Wilson's story—her parents named her after the president. Wilson won a Nobel Peace Prize," Molly said.

"The World War One guy—I *know,* Molly," my mother grunted, lunging. "But you don't name a *girl* Wilson! What was the president's *first* name? *Sue?*" She'd moved on from lunges; she was doing squats.

"Woodrow Wilson, the twenty-eighth president of the United States," Molly answered tiredly.

"Smarty-pants," my mom told her. *"Woodrow* would have been a better name for a girl." Her squats were so deep, she was bumping the floor with her little ass. "I'm not introducing you to Grace, sweetie, if you're still seeing Wilson. You can't hide things or keep secrets from Grace—you have to tell her *everything,*" my mother said.

"Ray, lay off the squats," Molly said sharply. Little Ray stopped; Molly didn't often speak sharply to her. "We didn't tell Adam we were more than friends, did we?" Molly asked her, more softly. "We didn't tell him *everything,* Ray."

"We were *going to* tell you, sweetie," my mom immediately said. "Smarty-pants," my mother told Molly, again.

There was no lasting acrimony, but what was lost in our conversation was my mom's advice. When I fell in love with Grace, I should have told her everything. I shouldn't have hidden things or kept secrets from her. I should have listened to my mother.

What I remember is trying to keep the peace between my mom and Molly. I quickly said, "Okay, okay—I'll stop seeing Wilson. I've been think-ing I should stop seeing her, anyway. We're not seeing that much of each other, as it is."

"You're always thinking you should stop seeing *someone*, sweetie," my mother pointed out.

"Let it go, Ray—let the Kid and Grace meet each other. Let them figure it out," Molly said.

I sensed a sea change coming. *Lucky me*, I thought.

I'd been lucky before. I competed as a wrestler for a relatively short time, and not very successfully, but wrestling did a lot for me. My small hands, my little fingers—the accumulated injuries—would keep me out of Vietnam. I was reclassified 4-F—"registrant unfit for military service." An untouchable draft deferment, before my student deferment expired. The wrestlers who knew me knew only that my hand and finger damage had saved me from the draft and Vietnam.

What my wrestler friends didn't know—what I didn't know, either, not for a while—was that my mother had her own hopes and plans for keeping me out of the draft. "Ray was angling to keep you out of the draft before we were in the Vietnam War, Kid," Molly told me.

Only then did I understand what my mom had meant when I mistakenly thought she must have overheard Molly and me talking about penis surgery. "It's a better surgery for a *boy* to have," was all Little Ray had said—meaning Caroline's meniscectomy. My mother's highest hopes for my wrestling were that I would have an old-fashioned, take-everything-out meniscectomy— a surefire 4-F draft deferment. In Little Ray's view, this surgery was wasted on a girl—girls couldn't be drafted.

When I told Nora, Em just nodded; I could see it was old news to them. "Did Molly tell you why they got a gun?" Nora asked me. I'd seen the gun, a twenty-gauge shotgun. Molly told me it was a good gun for varmints—she'd mentioned rabid raccoons, when I'd asked her what was around in terms of varmints. I saw it was a single-shot shotgun, and that they had a limited assortment of shells—buckshot and deer slugs. "The buckshot was for the varmints. The deer slugs were for your knee, kiddo," Nora told me. "If the wrestling injuries were insufficient, one shot would have worked—a twenty-gauge deer slug in the knee does as much damage as a meniscectomy." Em had covered her ears, as if to block out the sound of the shot; then she knelt at my feet, hugging my knees. I knew Nora wasn't kidding.

I knew Henrik had a 4-F deferment, too. (A lacrosse injury, when he was still in college, and the subsequent meniscectomy.) It was a shock to consider that my mother would have shot me to keep me out of Vietnam. When I asked Molly if what Nora had told me was true, Molly said, "You're her one and only, Kid, but she probably would have made me pull the trigger."

When I asked Nora if she would have shot Henrik in the knee if Henrik hadn't had the meniscectomy, Em went into a pantomime performance that resembled delivering her own child and killing it. "What Em is trying to say, kiddo, is that we might not have shot Henrik in his *knee*," Nora told me.

They'd met in a theater course in college. They had an onstage routine they'd been developing for a long time. Em wrote all their material, but she never spoke onstage—she only acted things out, in pantomime. Nora, with her deadpan delivery, interpreted what Em had mimed for the audience. They began with college audiences. Nora and Em were relatively late bloomers in finding their New York audience. Cabaret theater and burlesque shows weren't their best audience, but before the Gallows Lounge (a comedy club) launched them, Nora and Em had to start onstage somewhere. To me, their shtick onstage was pretty much the same as the way they were together—they'd always been dark. But over time, in the writing, Em made their dark shtick more entertaining. Over time, Em would speak to me, but very little—at first, only if Nora was with us. Once I asked Nora what would have happened if my mother and Molly had been unable to shoot me—if the wrestling injuries to my hands and fingers hadn't deferred me from the draft. Would *Nora* have shot me?

"No," Em said. She was shaking her head and biting her lower lip, but she was done talking.

"You have to explain what you mean, Em," Nora told her.

Em made me lie down on the floor on my back; then she directed Nora to lie on top of me, chest to chest but perpendicular to me. The way you'd pin someone, the wrestler in me was thinking, when Em pounced on my legs and bit me, hard, in one knee. I had to roll up the leg of my pants in order to examine her teeth marks—she didn't break the skin. Nora explained what Em meant. "The way we imagined we would do it, kiddo, is that I would hold you down and Em would shoot your knee." Once again, I knew Nora wasn't kidding.

My wrestling injuries at Exeter had been small ones. Some broken fingers, and a torn extensor tendon in the index finger of my right hand—my writing hand. I would keep tearing that same extensor tendon. My mom kept score; she wanted to know exactly how many times that tendon had been torn. "The index finger of your right hand is your *trigger* finger, sweetie," my mother reminded me. This went over my head. At the time, I thought my mom was worried about my *writing*.

At Exeter, I had two surgeries to repair the damage to flexor tendons in my palms—a surgery on each hand—but those surgeries were just the start of my trouble with flexor tendons. I had the smallest hands of anyone in my weight class. There's a lot of hand-fighting in wrestling; I lost most of the hand fights. When I broke a finger in a backward direction—if it was bent back against the back of my hand—the real damage was to the flexor tendon attached to that finger in the palm of the hand. The scar tissue builds up; one day, you can't make a fist or fully extend the affected fingers. My middle and pinky fingers, of both hands, were the ones most often broken in a backward direction; over time, those flexor tendons had the most surgeries.

My mother seemed unconcerned with what happened to my other fingers; she wasn't keeping score of all my flexor-tendon or extensor-tendon surgeries. Her obsession seemed to begin and end with what happened to the index finger of my right hand—my writing hand, as I thought of it. As I pointed out to my mom, the middle finger of my writing hand actually exerted more pressure on the pen, and my middle finger had really taken a beating—from *wrestling*, I'd pointed out to her, *not* from giving people the finger. "Your middle finger isn't your trigger finger, sweetie," was all she said. Even that went over my head. Nora said everything did, but all I thought about was being a writer. It hadn't occurred to me that I might become a soldier.

Wrestling at Exeter, I had the usual mouth injuries, requiring some stitches in my lips and tongue. In those days, mouth guards were uncomfortable, and I didn't wear one. My mom didn't keep score of the stitches in my lips and tongue. It never occurred to me that soldiers didn't need perfect lips and tongues, or that lip and tongue defects wouldn't qualify me for a 4-F deferment.

The snowshoer and Molly kept closer track of my cauliflower ears than my mother did. "Cauliflower ears look like dog turds, sweetie—I don't want my one and only to have dog turds for ears," my mom said. As a ski patroller, Molly had drained a few cauliflower ears—Molly knew how to do it. In the days before most recreational skiers wore helmets, there were occasional cauliflower ears from skiing. (Ears scraped on icy snow; ears abraded by contact with trees; unimaginable chairlift mishaps.)

"Ski hats do fuck-all to protect your ears, or your head," Molly told me. "I like to pack an ear with snow before I drain it," Molly said. "A cold ear doesn't feel the needle."

The snowshoer knew how to drain a cauliflower ear, too. Mr. Barlow was better at it than the one guy who knew how it was done in the Exeter training room. There was one nurse in the academy infirmary who knew how to do it without hurting you, the little English teacher told me, but she wasn't at the infirmary a lot. When the snowshoer drained my cauliflower ears, he used ice cubes in a white athletic sock instead of snow. The ear only hurt when the gauze, soaked in wet plaster, hardened—then the ear throbbed. The plaster cast on your ear was a funny-looking thing. Many wrestlers didn't bother to have their cauliflower ears drained, but I did. Most wrestlers liked the looks of their cauliflower ears, but Little Ray didn't. Not that my mom counted the number of times my ears were drained. "No one ever got a draft deferment for cauliflower ears, sweetie," she would eventually tell me, but this was after I got the 4-F deferment. "Soldiers can still kill, or be killed, with dog turds for ears," was the way my mom explained it.

When I was at Exeter, Elliot Barlow and wrestling were what I loved about the academy. I had my heart set on winning the New England Interscholastic Wrestling Championship. Two years in a row, I lost to the same guy in the championship tournament. I finished fourth in New England at 133 pounds in 1961. I appreciated what Coach Dearborn told me: "Better than halfway decent, Adam."

I had my heart set on wrestling in the Big Ten, too. Coach Dearborn had done it, and I wanted to try. I had no illusions that I would ever be good enough to start on a Big Ten team, but I'd met the wrestling coach at Wisconsin when I'd visited Madison. In those days, the wrestling room was in Camp Randall Stadium. So what if I would always be a backup in my weight class? I could see myself being happy in Madison, but Wisconsin didn't take me.

I went to Pittsburgh instead. Pitt had a tough wrestling room. There was no shame in being a backup there. I had more hand and finger injuries, but it wasn't because of the flexor- or extensor-tendon surgeries that I left Pittsburgh after only one year. Nor was it because of the competition, although a fourth-place finish in New England didn't amount to much in

Pennsylvania. The best guy in my weight class in the Pitt wrestling room was a fellow freshman. He would be an NCAA finalist the following year. It would have been better than halfway decent to have been his backup at 130 pounds.

I said I left Pitt because I was lonely. My only friends were my teammates—I met no one else. The classes were enormous and impersonal. I was used to Exeter's small classes and roundtable discussions. I complained that Pittsburgh was a big city. Almost anywhere—after Exeter, New Hampshire—would have struck me as a big city. The real reason I left Pittsburgh was that I was worried about Mr. Barlow. I was afraid that his dressing as a woman would get him in trouble.

I would never have predicted, upon my leaving Exeter, that I would miss home, but I did. I missed the snowshoer—I missed my mom and Molly, and Dottie and my grandmother. I must have been homesick, because I even missed the ghost of the fetus emeritus.

What was I writing? I wrote to Elliot Barlow more than anything else. I kept asking him if he was okay—meaning, Was he still a man? I was trying to write fiction, but I didn't finish anything. I wrote long fragments of larger things—everything was a work in progress. I'd had early indications that the short story wouldn't be the form for me. Even at Exeter, I had begun long stories—ones I never finished.

When the snowshoer wrote to me in Pittsburgh, he argued that my loneliness was of a different kind than homesickness. It went over my head when Mr. Barlow quoted Rilke to me. "Works of art are of an infinite loneliness," Rilke had written. I failed to see how this applied to me. Was the snowshoer saying that my trying to be a writer was why I was lonely? I was more worried about how he dressed.

Imagining the stories you want to write, and waiting to write them, is part of the writing process—like thinking about the characters you want to create, but not creating them. Yet when I did this, when I was just a kid at Exeter—when I thought about writing all the time, but I never finished anything I was writing—this amounted to little more than daydreaming. My trying to be a writer didn't help my performance as a student. When I read a novel I liked, I immediately read it again. If you're a student in a demanding school, you don't have time to read novels twice.

No wonder I didn't get into Wisconsin. I needed five years to graduate from a four-year school. I took Math III three times. I struggled with Spanish for two years, even with Uncle Martin's patient help. I struggled with

German for three years—despite Uncle Johan's robust encouragement, and Elliot Barlow's drilling me on strong and irregular verbs.

The snowshoer did his best to console me, concerning my additional year of high school. "Why be in a hurry to finish school, or a novel?" was the way he put it. The little English teacher introduced me to Graham Greene's writing—he was the first modern writer I liked. Before Greene, my heroes were all novelists from the nineteenth century. Living in the nineteenth century can expand your loneliness; as a writer, it's lonely living there.

It was still the wrestling season in Pittsburgh, and I was recovering from flexor-tendon surgery—the tendon attached to my right index finger, in the palm of my writing hand—when the snowshoer wrote me and told me to come home. He'd kept the same faculty apartment in Amen Hall. I'd imagined that my mom was sleeping in my bedroom, alone, whenever she was back in town. With his letter, Mr. Barlow had included the requisite forms for me to apply as a transfer student to the University of New Hampshire for the fall semester of 1962.

I could live with him in Exeter—"in your old room," the snowshoer wrote. I could commute to UNH, he proposed. Durham was an easy drive from Exeter. I could take his VW Beetle, or buy a used car. There were two fiction writers in the English Department at UNH, and there was a creative writing course—in those days, not common at the undergraduate level. The snowshoer didn't have to sell me on the Franklin Theatre in Durham. The art-house cinema was still in town. And if I wanted to wrestle, Coach Dearborn would welcome me back in the Exeter wrestling room. The coach had told the snowshoer it would be good to have another assistant coach in the room. I'd learned a lot about wrestling in one year at Pitt.

In Pittsburgh, I'd also had two more surgeries for a torn extensor tendon in the index finger of my right hand. My mother seemed especially interested in the third of these surgeries. "If it's a surgery involving your trigger finger, sweetie, please have the surgeon send the details of the procedure to me," she'd already instructed me. I assumed this was all about Molly making sense of the surgical results. This third surgery was of particular interest to Molly because the tendon not only had been torn, but had been detached. And then there was the flexor-tendon surgery in the palm, just below that right index finger. "That counts as a trigger-finger surgery—that makes *four*," my mom said.

I couldn't be bothered with this. I just turned over my surgical records to my mother and Molly. My hand and finger wrestling injuries were so

numerous, but they were minor; they were a nuisance, but they lacked gravi-
tas. Whereas my concern for the snowshoer, my fear about his dressing as a
woman—this preoccupied my thoughts, this was serious. And Mr. Barlow
had a plan to bring me home from Pittsburgh.

Ever my champion, Elliot Barlow was still helping me with my homework. He was trying to make my coming home to New Hampshire not feel
like a defeat. "Your mom and Molly will be happy to have you closer to
them," the snowshoer wrote. The clincher was that Elliot managed to make
me feel I could be a writer before I was one. The little English teacher gave
me confidence in my future as a writer, when all I'd written were unending
works in progress.

I was barely a beginner as a writer. I was too immature as an artist to understand how Rilke could connect "works of art" to "an infinite loneliness."
I didn't get it, not yet. But Elliot Barlow knew I'd read Graham Greene, if
not Rilke, and the snowshoer knew which passage from *The End of the Affair*
would resonate with me—a passage that gives confidence to all writers with
unending works in progress, a passage that resonates with me still.

"So much of a novelist's writing," Greene wrote, "takes place in the unconscious: in those depths the last word is written before the first word appears on paper. We remember the details of our story, we do not invent them."

"Buoyed up by that coffin," Ishmael tells us in the Epilogue to *Moby-
Dick*—when Queequeg's "coffin life-buoy" rises from the sea to save him.
Thus did the snowshoer offer me the academic equivalent of Queequeg's
coffin—a way to go home and work at being a writer. In those days, the
University of New Hampshire didn't have a wrestling team, but I didn't need
to compete to keep wrestling. If you're in a wrestling room, you can always
find a workout partner.

I'd not liked living in a dormitory in Pittsburgh. The faculty apartment
I shared with my mom and the snowshoer in Amen Hall was more private.
When I went back home to Exeter and commuted to college, I became more
of a writer. I also saw more movies with Elliot. It helped that I didn't make
many friends in Durham. As a commuter, how could I? I hadn't yet met
Sophie, the bleeder—the *writer*, I should say. But I latched on to the two
fiction writers in the UNH English Department. I took every course they
taught, following them around like their faithful dog. One of them told me
to apply for a junior year abroad. It occurred to me that he may have wanted
me to go away. "Americans need more melancholy," he said. I didn't realize,
at first, that he meant as *writers*. He seemed to be saying there was something

beneficial about melancholy—universally, for everyone. "Melancholy is good for the soul," he told me.

Naturally, I told Mr. Barlow about this. He agreed there was more melancholy in Europe. "I can see how melancholy would be good for a *writer's* soul," the snowshoer said, somewhat cautiously.

When I asked Nora what she thought about my studying in Europe for a year, she said, "I *told* you there's a foreignness inside you. That's just who you are. What you'll find in Europe is more of the melancholy that's inside you." I interpreted this to mean that Nora thought Europe would make me unhappier than I was.

Em spoke to me at greater length about Europe than she'd ever spoken to me before, and it was more than she would say to me again for years. Nora was with us, and Em didn't look at me when she spoke—she was looking at Nora, who seemed surprised. "In Europe, you'll meet some girl who's as sad as you, or sadder," Em said. "Then you'll be twice as sad together, until the sadness drives you apart," Em said. This sounded like a novel I would never finish—one I would keep beginning and stopping, again and again. I don't think Em needed to go to Europe to become more melancholic—Em was melancholic enough—but she and Nora went to Europe a lot.

Of course the little Barlows would have an opinion: I should go to Austria. When it came to what I should do to deepen my darkness as a writer, the Barlows were a writing team—they didn't hold back. But in this case, a rare one, Elliot reluctantly agreed with his parents. If I went to Vienna, the snowshoer said, I would certainly find sufficient melancholy there.

That was when I decided against a junior year abroad in Europe—I didn't want to meet a girl who was as sad as me, or sadder. I was afraid of being twice as sad together (with anyone) until the sadness drove us apart. Like Em, I was melancholic enough.

When I came home to New Hampshire from Pittsburgh, I was only twenty. I'd not yet had a girlfriend who was a keeper, though Maud turned out to be a keeper as a friend. Fantasizing was what I did for girlfriends. (Commuting to college would have its drawbacks.) I was living at home with my mom and the snowshoer, which meant I was living alone with Elliot Barlow for long periods of time. And hadn't I come home to watch over him, to keep an eye on what the little English teacher was wearing? Wasn't that situation melancholic enough?

I don't know if melancholy is good for the soul. Once you've seen ghosts, you've seen sufficient melancholy. If ghosts aren't melancholic, what are they?

What did my ghosts, if they were ghosts, want? I don't mean the infantile diaper man, as obvious in death as he'd been in life. I mean the static figures in those black-and-white photographs, their expressions frozen in time, their standpat characters not once revealed by action or dialogue—leaving me to fill in the blanks, to imagine the rest of their lives. What were those ghosts trying to teach me? What did they want me to learn from them? But didn't I come from a family of secrets? I would wait them out—my mother and the ghosts.

Now I was older than that boy or young man posing in front of the snow-bank. That fourteen-year-old was still leaning on his snow shovel—either a long shovel or a short boy. "He was just some kid, sweetie—he wasn't shaving," my mom had said. "He was *small*," Little Ray had whispered when she kissed me. "He would have been a pretty girl," she told me. She must have seen something of the small snow shoveler in the little snowshoer, I thought.

In black and white, his handsomeness, his shyness, his smallness alongside his tall snow shovel never varied—in black and white, he didn't change—but now I could see the feminine prettiness my mother had seen in him, an attractiveness she'd no doubt noticed in the snowshoer. Yet I still sensed in the short boy with the tall snow shovel a different kind of ghost—the kind who can hurt you—and I still thought there was something about him that didn't look dead. He may have been the boy who couldn't take his eyes off Little Ray, but whether or not he was the no-strings-attached kid my mom slept with in Aspen, he had the look of someone who was still alive.

He haunted me more than the other ghosts in black and white, the ones I knew were dead. No, I wasn't overlooking a certain similarity between the shyness of the snow shoveler's smile and the shy, childlike smile of the dark-skinned hotel maid—forever posing with her mop and pail in a hallway between rooms. When I'd asked my mother about the maid, Little Ray had merely said, "Oh, I didn't know she died—I think she was Italian."

The maid looked Mexican to me, but that was just a guess. She had the same dark hair and eyes as the short boy with the tall shovel, but the kid wasn't dark-skinned—he didn't look Mexican. The shy innocence of their smiles was the strongest bond between them, and they definitely didn't look like the 1880s or 1890s. I was pretty sure they came from the 1940s, where I'd come from.

Some secrets stay secrets for a long time. If my mom didn't know the hotel maid had died—not until I mentioned the maid among my ghosts—didn't that mean my mother had seen the shy maid when she was alive? Yet

Little Ray said next to nothing about her. "I think she was Italian." That didn't sound definitive. My mom didn't seem to care about the childlike hotel maid, dead or alive.

Why are people so interested in their ancestry? There's nothing you can do about what your ancestors did. When I would obsess to the snowshoer about who my father was—not only out loud, in spontaneous outbursts, but also in unfinished fragments of my juvenile writing—the good teacher would counsel me as best he could. "My dear Adam," he would say, "you can have no effect on what led up to your existence, can you? You can't change the past, my dear boy. What you can try to affect is the present and the future—not only your own but, *to some degree*, the present and future of those you love."

Mr. Barlow was right about the *to some degree* part. It began when I knew the little English teacher was drawn to wear my mother's clothes— henceforth I felt compelled to protect him, to keep him safe. Wasn't this within the realm of my trying to affect, *to some degree*, the present and future of someone I loved? I believed I was following Elliot's advice—at least I tried.

Today, I would echo my mom's heartfelt endorsement of the snowshoer's femininity. But, at the time, wouldn't that have put him in more danger of being found out? I not once neglected to tell him how nice he looked in Little Ray's clothes. I always praised how pretty he was in this or that outfit. But I stopped short of telling him that he *was* a woman. I didn't say he "just wasn't born one," as my mother had told me—only she'd used the *she* word for him.

I didn't go that far. Even when it was just the snowshoer and my mom and me, or when only Molly was with us, I thought it put Mr. Barlow at risk to use feminine pronouns for him. I would not refer to him, in the third person, as *she* or *her*. I even told my mother that she should stop using female pronouns for the snowshoer.

"What if you slip up?" I asked my mom. "What if you call him *her*, or you say he's a *she*, around someone else? Someone who doesn't know—someone who's not one of us," I said to her. "What if you call him *her*, or you say he's a *she*, around Abigail or Martha?"

"I didn't know you were such a nervous Nellie, sweetie," my mother said.

Poor Mr. Barlow. He was always mediating between my mom and me—he didn't like it when we quarreled. "Take it easy on Adam, Ray," the snowshoer said. "Fiction writers are worriers—they have heightened imaginations. They imagine worst-case scenarios."

I knew the trail groomer agreed with me. Molly knew my mother wasn't careful concerning what she said to whom—she just said it, whatever it was. I knew the night groomer had heard my mom use feminine pronouns for the snowshoer around the wrong people. "Listen to your one and only, Ray," the snowcat operator said. "The Kid's right—you could be more careful."

"You're not a fiction writer, Molly—you're just a nervous Nellie, too," my mother said.

"Pronouns are a habit, Ray," the little English teacher said, always mediating. "You don't need to have the writer gene to worry that you might repeat yourself—we all repeat ourselves."

This caused an uncomfortable silence. For an English teacher—a man of words—the mere mention of my having *the writer gene* was not the most carefully worded thing Elliot Barlow ever said. If I had the writer gene, if there was a writer gene, I certainly didn't get it from my mom—she didn't even read fiction. As Molly had said, I was the only fiction writer Little Ray ever read.

I'm guessing my mom and Molly and I couldn't help thinking about where my writer gene came from. I can't speak for my mother's thoughts, or the trail groomer's; they said nothing. As for me, I found it hard to discern the degree of imagination in the short snow shoveler with the long snow shovel. He looked younger than fourteen, and (frozen in black and white) even his smile was shyly enigmatic—as unreadable as his handsomeness was only slightly effeminate. The writer gene was not evident in the snowbank the young shoveler had created, although it was an artful snowbank—it was more than a haphazard pile of snow. It was not solely the effect of his ski hat with the pom-pom, but there definitely was—in his confident bearing, in his preoccupied demeanor—the air of an artist about the snow shoveler.

25.

THE "POLICE REPORT"

I was having a heightened-imagination moment—indulging a worst-case scenario, provoked by my unidentified writer gene—when I urged the snow-shoer to take a good look at himself in the mirror before he answered the door to our faculty apartment. When I was home, and Elliot was dolled up as a woman, of course I would answer the door. It was easy for me to tell the student that Mr. Barlow was on the phone or in the shower. The student could come back in twenty minutes, after the little English teacher had removed the makeup and was once more wearing men's clothes. Furthermore, I persuaded Elliot to attach a small notebook and a pen to our door in the dormitory hall. Students could leave notes for him if he happened not to be at home or he wasn't wearing the right clothes.

Unsurprisingly, there were smart-ass students who left funny notes for Mr. Barlow or (occasionally) for me. The important thing, or so I thought, was that we had a system in place—a way to keep the snowshoer safe when he was wearing my mother's clothes. It didn't occur to me that Elliot would ever dress as a woman when he went out, if only late at night or very early in the morning.

When I pulled an all-nighter—when I had a term paper due, or I was studying for an exam—the snowshoer would drive out to Portsmouth Avenue and pick up a pizza for me. There was a strip of fast-food joints, a bar or two, and gas stations galore. Portsmouth Avenue wasn't far from downtown Exeter or the academy campus, but it was far enough that you had to drive. Naturally, when I was pulling an all-nighter, Mr. Barlow went to the pizza place dressed as himself. And he always went for a walk, or took a run, in the early morning. After his walk or run, I would hear him in the shower—all this was before the dining-hall bells for breakfast, before the students were up and about in Amen Hall.

I didn't know that Elliot occasionally took an early-morning walk in downtown Exeter, dressed in Little Ray's clothes. And when the snowshoer pulled an all-nighter of his own—when he was grading blue books, or otherwise engaged, after I'd gone to bed—I only later learned that he sometimes drove out to the Portsmouth Avenue strip and picked up a pizza *as a woman*.

This was risky business for Mr. Barlow. I'm guessing it began when I was a student at the academy. I'm not sure if it continued when I was away in Pittsburgh, or if it went on later—when I was a college student in Durham, once again living with him in Exeter. In retrospect, it's obvious that Elliot's cross-dressing was meant to be; it was who she was.

Roland's, that pizza place on the Portsmouth Avenue strip, attracted an unsavory late-night clientele. Maybe it was open later than any other joint with a liquor license in Exeter. Late at night, it was more of a bar than an eatery, but you could call ahead and order a pizza—you could pick it up, if you dared.

Similarly sketchy, in terms of its clientele, was a downtown Exeter convenience store called Verne's, which was on Water Street—near the falls and the town's most frequented fish market. Verne's was open for business as early in the morning as Roland's stayed open late at night—accordingly, their respective clientele were not unsavory in the same way. Men, drinking alone or together, were the majority of the late-night lowlifes at Roland's. Teenage boys, actual or virtual delinquents—high school troublemakers (or dropouts), malingering before (and after) school—comprised the young thugs who hung out around Verne's. Smoking cigarettes on the sidewalk was the closest they could come to political protest.

It would later emerge that the snowshoer seriously outdid himself to look like a woman on certain late-night and early-morning expeditions, when he (as a she) drove out to Roland's to pick up a pizza or took a ten-minute walk to Verne's—under the pretense of picking up a pack of gum, or a take-out cup of tea to sip on his walk back to Amen Hall. I say the gum and the tea, or even the pizza, were pretenses, because I know now that Mr. Barlow made these intrepid sojourns as a woman to test his powers of transformation. But the way I learned what Elliot was up to was not quickly forthcoming.

When our wrestling matches were away, we had early-morning weigh-ins in our gym before we got on the team bus. The wrestlers who were worried about their weight went to the gym earlier to check what they weighed; if they were a little over, they put on their sweats and ran in the cage before weigh-ins. One early morning, Matthew Zimmermann was on his way to the gym to check his weight, when he saw my mother. She was walking on Court Street, coming from downtown. Zimmer waved to her, but she didn't wave back. "Either she didn't see me or she didn't recognize me—she just kept going," Zim said, when he told me of the sighting. We were talking on the team bus. Zimmermann was puzzled that my mom was in town in ski season, when we were wrestling away.

"It wasn't her," I told him. "She's not in Exeter."

"I would swear I saw her," Zimmer said. "Nobody looks like her."

He hadn't seen Little Ray, but I didn't think twice about it. I knew that Zim was gaga about my mother. I thought he'd been hallucinating and had imagined he saw her. I didn't doubt that Zimmer imagined her when he was beating off.

When I later told the snowshoer how Zim had fantasized that he'd seen Little Ray walking on Court Street at an ungodly hour of the morning, we both laughed.

"Zimmermann must be cutting too much weight," the little English teacher told me.

"Imagine Ray walking anywhere at that hour," I said. "*Skiing*, sure—she'd go skiing in the dark."

"Poor Zim," Elliot said, sighing. "I fear he is so infatuated with your mother that he sees her in his sleep." We laughed and laughed.

We also laughed at the "Police Report," which we read every week in our local newspaper, the *Exeter Town Crier*. The reported police business in the town of Exeter was generally not of a highly criminal nature, and the report itself was without attribution. Mr. Barlow and I could only speculate who might have written it: an exceedingly terse police officer or an unusually laconic journalist—in either case, a minimalist. There were wild animals causing trouble, and being captured, in town. "A raccoon, up to no good, was netted on Cass Street," said the "Police Report." There were pets in need of rescue, and "domestic disputes"—these were said to occur all over town. "A rowdy household on School Street merited an officer's visit," was one deadpan account.

There were often altercations, or similar incidents, in the parking lot at Roland's. "Young men, behaving like hoodlums," were more than once reported in the vicinity of Verne's—less than innocently whiling away their time in the out-of-school hours. Reports of "public indecency" were never sufficiently described—not, at least, to my satisfaction or the snowshoer's. Reports of "tense relations between town and gown" were downplayed or too vaguely stated; Elliot and I wanted to know more. Academy students were warned not to hang out at Verne's, where townie toughs picked on the prep-school kids.

And during that time when I was an Exeter student, someone was killing cats—not just killing them but hanging them, in perfectly made hangman's nooses. The cats were being executed. Not a breath of speculation in the "Police Report" in the *Exeter Town Crier* about who might be stringing up the cats—the unnamed reporter didn't venture to guess. Both the town and the academy were rife with rumors. On the Exeter campus, the townies were suspected. In town, the perpetrator was presumed to be one of the prep-school kids. Many of the cats were hanged on or near academy grounds; cats were popular pets among faculty families. Academy housing hadn't been conceived for cats or dogs, yet no one was slipping the perfectly made nooses around the necks of dogs.

"It must be a bird lover," Elliot speculated. "Probably a young person," he added.

"Another cat found hanging, this one on Spring Street," was the full extent of the coverage in the *Town Crier*.

"Whoever writes the 'Police Report' isn't a writer," Mr. Barlow told me repeatedly.

"A townswoman was charged with lewd behavior on the Swasey Parkway," was all the "Police Report" had to say.

"Lewd behavior *where* on the Swasey Parkway?" the snowshoer cried. "In a car, on one of the benches, in the grass?"

What *sort* of lewd behavior? I was dying to know.

"A cat in a noose on Tan Lane, the remains of another on Green Street," was all the "Police Report" deemed fit to tell us.

"Whoever is writing this isn't a cat—a cat would *care!*" Elliot said. He was more indignant about the writing than what was happening to the cats. Yet the little English teacher seemed scarcely interested in the most mysterious and most exhaustive "Police Report"—at least in my short memory of reading the *Exeter Town Crier*.

Late one weekend night, a married couple picked up a pizza at Roland's. As they were driving out of the parking lot, the wife saw what she thought was an assault in progress. When the couple got home, the wife called the police. The wife said she saw "a big man, who appeared to be making an unwelcome advance on a small woman, who was trying to fight him off." Before the police dispatched a squad car with two cops, the precinct called Roland's and asked Roland what he knew.

"Nothin'," Roland replied. This sounded like something the real Roland would say, but Roland took his baseball bat and went into the parking lot to investigate. Shortly before the squad car arrived, Roland found the big man—the alleged attacker. It appeared that the small woman had successfully fought him off, because the guy was lying facedown in the parking lot.

"It hurts to move," the big man whispered to Roland, who'd nudged him with the baseball bat.

"The guy looked dead, but he was moanin'," Roland told the *Town Crier*. When the two cops arrived, they rolled the big man onto his back. According to Roland, "There was gravel embedded in the guy's forehead."

The big man's two drinking buddies were still drinking in Roland's. The guy with the gravel embedded in his forehead had followed a "small, pretty woman" into the parking lot. Roland said he'd seen her before, but he didn't know her name. "She never calls and orders a pizza—she just shows up and waits," Roland said. "She drives a dark-colored VW Beetle—there's a lot of them around," he added, which (for Roland) was positively loquacious. Mr. Barlow and I had never known Roland to have this much to say.

And Roland wasn't through talking. The three drinking buddies were local Exeter men, all shipyard workers at the Portsmouth Naval Shipyard. The local Exeter men were said to be in their late twenties or early thirties. The big, gravel-pocked man who had a mix-up with the small, pretty woman was described by Roland as "havin' made unwelcome advances on women alone before."

The injured attacker was treated at Exeter Hospital for "two separated shoulders and two broken collarbones." He was released into police custody, but the police also released him—pending charges, "yet to be filed," by the mystery woman he'd attacked. The police were hopeful she would come forward and identify herself. "We only want to ask her some questions," a police spokesperson said.

Her injured attacker could not explain exactly how she'd gotten the best of him in the parking lot. "She was stronger than she looked," the shipyard worker told the police. "She got behind me, somehow."

The police spokesperson sounded unsympathetic about the attacker's injuries. It seemed the shipyard worker was attempting to kiss and fondle the woman—"when he found himself lying facedown in the parking lot, with the little woman cranking on his arms."

"Did you *read* this?" I asked the snowshoer. For the *Exeter Town Crier*, it was a virtual novella of a "Police Report."

"There's definitely more detail than usual, but it's both blandly written and inconclusive," the little English teacher said.

"I'm not talking about the *writing!*" I exclaimed. The snowshoer shrugged. "A 'small, pretty woman' who was 'stronger than she looked'—she also sounds like she knows how to *wrestle*," I told him. "*You* drive a dark-colored VW Beetle," I reminded him.

"How did the ever-eloquent Roland put it—'there's a lot of them around,' or words to that effect?" Mr. Barlow asked me. But I wasn't buying it; my suspicions were aroused. I must have sensed that this was something more than a cross-dressing compulsion. Something stronger was at work than Elliot's desire to wear a woman's clothes.

I began to believe my mother. Mr. Barlow *was* a woman—"she just wasn't born one," as my mom had told me.

Yet I didn't exactly confront the snowshoer—not entirely, not at first. What I said to him was: "It could have been you, Elliot. You look very pretty as a woman, and you're stronger than you look."

"And you thought *Zimmer* was fantasizing," the snowshoer said.

"You could easily get behind a bigger guy and take him down," I told him.

"Easily," he agreed, smiling. "But I'm not sure how I would manage to separate both his shoulders and break both his collarbones," Mr. Barlow said.

"I'm not sure how you would manage to do that, either," I admitted, "but I'll find out."

"Please tell me when you find out how one does that, Adam," the snow-shoer said, still smiling. "It definitely sounds like it could be a useful thing to know."

I definitely knew who would know, and I knew when and where to find him. Long before and after wrestling practice—even after the other coaches had showered and left the coaches' locker room, and well before the other coaches got there—Coach Dearborn could be found smoking on the locker-room bench. Mr. Dearborn lived and smoked in the coaches' locker room, as if he expected to die there. His wrestlers knew he was available to them there. In those days, no one minded the smoke. Coach Dearborn had been a middleweight at Illinois, but his weight-cutting days were over. Elliot and I had estimated that the revered coach weighed more than two hundred pounds.

One late afternoon, when I'd lingered after practice, I found Mr. Dearborn with just a towel around his waist in the coaches' locker room. He was alone, sitting on the bench, using an empty tennis-ball can as an ashtray. His big biceps and a formidable pair of trapezius muscles were the most noticeable—they hung in slabs. Although he smoked everywhere else, I never saw him with a cigarette in the wrestling room. He could still kick the ass of any wrestler at Exeter.

"What's up, Adam?" Coach Dearborn asked me. I had the "Police Report" from the *Town Crier*, which I put on the locker-room bench beside him. "I've seen it," he said, without looking at it. "I wondered if your mom was in town, and if someone made the mistake of hitting on her." We both laughed.

"Whoever she was, it sounds like she knew what to do," I told him. The butt of his cigarette looked small in his big hand. He used the butt end to light a fresh cigarette. When Mr. Dearborn dropped the butt in the tennis-ball can, there was a hiss—there was water in the can, which the coach swished around. I knew he was waiting for me to say more. "It sounds like she slipped behind him and took him down—a duck under, maybe, or some kind of slide-by," I suggested.

"I'll bet on a duck under—that way, all her weight would be riding him down. That would explain the embedded gravel in the big guy's forehead—he landed face-first," Coach Dearborn pointed out.

"Then what?" I asked him. He took a long drag on his cigarette, as if he needed to think about it, but it was pretty clear he'd already thought it through.

"A fight in a parking lot isn't the same as a wrestling match, Adam—you can pin a guy with a cross-face cradle, but a cross-face cradle doesn't end a fight. There's no ref in the parking lot—there's no one to stop the fight. You have to end it," the coach explained.

"You have to hurt the guy, you mean," I said.

"You've got all your weight on the back of his neck and his shoulder blades—that is, if you've hit the duck under right," Mr. Dearborn continued.

"It sounds like she hit it right," I pointed out.

"So you run an arm bar or a chicken wing past ninety degrees—you run the guy's elbow up to his ear, or to his temple. There's no ref to stop you," Coach Dearborn reminded me. "You run the arm bar or the chicken wing till you feel his shoulder pop—you'll hear his collarbone break, too. There's no crowd hollering in the parking lot—you'll definitely hear a collarbone break, if it's quiet. It makes a clicking sound," Mr. Dearborn added. "And popping the second shoulder, or busting the other collarbone, is even easier," he went on. "The guy's already hurting—he won't resist you. Most guys, especially the big guys, can't get to their feet if they can't support their weight with one or both arms. That guy at Roland's couldn't even get off his face," the coach concluded.

"I don't suppose you know a small, pretty woman who could have managed all that," I said to him. If the snowshoer even crossed Coach Dearborn's mind, the coach was poker-faced about it.

"She must be from out of town," was what the coach said, after another long drag on his cigarette.

"Roland said he'd seen her before," I reminded Mr. Dearborn. "If it happens again, I suppose we'll know she's from around here," I added.

"If that little woman is as small and pretty as the newspaper said, it'll happen again—if she's from around here," Coach Dearborn said. "I suppose you've noticed, Adam, there are more men who are assholes than there are small, pretty women—around here, anyway."

"Yes, I've noticed," I told him. As I was leaving the coaches' locker room, I saw him light another cigarette. I knew; Coach Dearborn knew, too. We wouldn't have long to wait for a follow-up episode—namely, the next time an asshole made the mistake of hitting on the wrong little woman.

From what I could visualize, given the subdued "Police Report," it began with two younger assholes the second time. Two of the town's troublemaking teenagers had followed what sounded a lot like the same small, pretty woman. She was walking away from Verne's when they saw her. In the early mornings, a French Canadian couple managed the convenience store. The husband said he'd seen the little lady before. "She's a real lady—her manners are very ladylike, and she wears the nicest-looking clothes," the husband added.

"She looks really nice for so early in the morning," the wife had observed.

"She likes tea, not coffee—she gets a hot tea to go," the husband remembered. I knew Mr. Barlow liked tea, not coffee.

About the two young hoodlums who'd followed her from Verne's, the French Canadian couple were less complimentary. Those two boys had been caught shoplifting once. Those two thugs had been known to harass any pretty girl around Verne's—many times, or so the French Canadian couple maintained. It appeared that the police had a history with those two. According to the "Police Report," their names were withheld because of their young age, but it was clear they'd gotten themselves in trouble before.

Keep in mind: Elliot Barlow was in his early thirties, but he'd always looked younger than he was. The two teenagers, who followed the snowshoer as far as the fish market before they made their clumsy moves, must have imagined the little lady was their age, or not much older. In the town of Exeter, these two miscreant yokels had never encountered a full-size woman—not to mention, a full-size man—who was only four feet nine.

"She was just real pretty," one of the yokels said later.

"We were just messin' around with her—we weren't tryin' to hurt her, or nothin'," the other yokel said.

"Yeah, we didn't know she was older—not till we got real close," the primary culprit reported. According to the *Town Crier*, he'd been the first of her two attackers.

"Those two boys were trying to kiss her, and she wanted no part of them," the fish deliveryman later said.

The two horny hoodlums had herded her into the fish-market parking lot. At that hour of the morning, the store wasn't open for business. The parking lot was virtually deserted—only the deliveryman was there, unloading his van.

"Come here, cutie," the first of the two teenagers said.

When he grabbed her, and tried to kiss her, the little woman did something to the boy's wrist. When the second teenager touched her, she did the same thing to him.

"I tried to come to her assistance"—not quite the full extent of the fish deliveryman's account. What he added was mystifying to me. "I thought there was something a little off about her," the fish deliveryman further said. This was noticeably not clear in the "Police Report," but the fish deliveryman's wrist was injured in the scuffle—if there was a scuffle; it didn't sound like much of one.

Inside the store, the fishmonger said he heard the "hullabaloo." By the time he got to the parking lot, the small woman in jeopardy had left—"she was nowhere to be seen," he said. "All I saw was three guys, holding their wrists," the fishmonger added.

The Exeter Hospital stated that the two teenagers were treated for "surprisingly similar wrist injuries" and released into police custody. The police summarily released them—pending yet-to-be-filed charges by the mystery woman the boys had attacked. The fish deliveryman, who was also not named, was released by the hospital and questioned by the police. The two teenagers had soft-tissue injuries—"tears in both the anterior and posterior radioulnar ligaments" for the first attacker, and "a single tear in the palmar radioulnar ligament" for the second. Somehow, in the scuffle that didn't sound like much of a scuffle, the fish deliveryman suffered "more extensive damage to the distal radioulnar joint"; in fact, he had "a distal radius fracture and more than one tear in the radioulnar ligament." All three were looking at "likely surgeries."

True to form, the "Police Report" did not speculate if this small, pretty woman was the *same* small, pretty woman who'd done different damage to the shipyard worker in the parking lot at Roland's. "We'd appreciate it if the woman or women attacked would contact us," was all the police spokesperson had to say.

"I don't suppose you know anything about this episode in the fish-market parking lot," I said to the snowshoer, when we'd both had time to read about the feisty woman—a martial-arts marvel—in the most recent *Town Crier*.

"She can't be from around here—it sounds like she knows some aikido-type techniques," Mr. Barlow said.

"Aikido-type techniques," I repeated. "What do you know about aikido?" I asked him.

"Nothing," the little English teacher said, smiling.

I went once more to the man I knew would know. This time, I didn't bother to bring a copy of the *Town Crier* with me. I already knew Coach Dearborn would have read the "Police Report." This time, he didn't ask me what was up. "Sit down, Adam," the coach told me. I sat next to him on the long bench in the coaches' locker room. Mr. Dearborn plunked his cigarette into the tennis-ball can, where it hissed. I was a little alarmed that he hadn't lit a fresh cigarette—he hadn't even taken a last drag—and he didn't bother to swish the water around in the tennis-ball can, which he put down on the bench between us. "You're right-handed, aren't you?" the coach asked me. When I nodded, he said, "Give me your left hand."

The pain was so sudden and sharp that I flinched and cried out. It happened so fast, I didn't see what the coach had done. When he felt me flinch, he stopped, but he still had hold of my wrist. Coach Dearborn knew how to control your hands—when he had your wrist, you weren't getting it back. "That was a rotational wristlock, Adam—it causes radioulnar rotation," he told me. Now he did something a little different. The pain was as sudden and sharp, but it came from somewhere else in the joint of my wrist. Once more, the coach stopped hurting me, but he still held my wrist. "That was a pronating wristlock, Adam—there are also supinating and hyperflexing wristlocks, but you get the idea, don't you?"

"I get it," I told him, and he let my wrist go. "Are they aikido techniques?" I asked him, rubbing my left wrist.

"I don't know much about aikido, but it strikes me as unrealistic," Mr. Dearborn said, lighting a cigarette. "Wristlocks in wrestling are submission holds—you make your opponent yield to the pain. Submission holds, like choke holds, are illegal now, but they used to be legal," Coach Dearborn told me.

"I don't suppose you would have shown Mr. Barlow any illegal holds—no choke holds or submission holds, no wristlocks," I said.

"Mr. Barlow is a good teacher, Adam," Mr. Dearborn said. "Good teachers are also good students—if you like to teach, you like to learn. Mr. Barlow has made himself a model student of the sport of wrestling, not just the moves and the holds but wrestling history—including the rules, and the changes in the rules."

"It sounds like you showed him some submission holds, maybe wristlocks," I ventured to say.

"I don't recall the context, but I'm pretty sure the subject of wristlocks would've come up," Mr. Dearborn said. He took a long drag on his cigarette. He could see I was still rubbing my left wrist. "There's ice in the training room, Adam—about twenty minutes before practice, put some ice on that wrist."

"What would you say if I told you Mr. Barlow sometimes dresses as a woman—what do you know about that?" I asked him.

"I've heard of it," Mr. Dearborn said neutrally. From the way he said it, I couldn't tell if he meant he'd heard of Mr. Barlow doing it, or he'd just heard of cross-dressing in general.

"I didn't think Mr. Barlow was doing it outside our faculty apartment— I don't really know if he *is* the small, pretty woman in those parking lots," I told Coach Dearborn.

"I think Mr. Barlow is one of the best guys at this school," Mr. Dearborn told me.

"I think so, too—I just worry about him," I said.

"Worrying about someone is fine—you just have to be selective in what you worry about, Adam." The coach could tell I was puzzling over what he meant. "Anyone can lose a fight, Adam—especially in a parking lot, where there are no rules. I lost twice," Mr. Dearborn told me, "and that was on the mat, where I knew the rules."

"I get it," I said. The coach sat smoking in his sweatpants and socks; he was wearing a T-shirt, but he still had to put on his wrestling shoes. The other coaches would soon be arriving in the locker room, the snowshoer among them. As before, I was leaving the coaches' locker room when I saw Mr. Dearborn light a fresh cigarette.

"You shouldn't smoke so much," I told him. I understood what he meant about selective worrying, but I was worried about him, too.

With his cigarette, which he held between the thumb and index finger of his right hand, Coach Dearborn pointed to his left wrist. "Ice, Adam," he said, smiling. "Twenty minutes should suffice."

When I once more mentioned the episode in the fish-market parking lot to the little English teacher, I tried to be as incisive concerning fights without rules as Coach Dearborn had been with me. "I don't care what you know about wristlocks, Elliot, or that your wrestling has enabled you to get the better of a drunk, a deliveryman, and a couple of teenagers—you were lucky," I told him. "Anyone can lose a fight, Elliot. Even Coach Dearborn lost—he lost twice—and that was on the mat, where he knew his opponent didn't have a knife or a gun. What if, next time, one of your attackers has a knife or a gun?"

"My dear Adam," the snowshoer said. "I'll be more careful next time—if there is a next time," he said. "I just wanted to see if I could be convincing as a woman."

"It sounds like you were pretty convincing," I told him. "I'm just not sure how the fish deliveryman got the worst of it—he was hurt worse than the boys. I thought the deliveryman was trying to help you, or is that just what he told the cops?"

"He tried to feel me up under my coat—under your mother's coat, I should say," Mr. Barlow explained. "I'm not sure how feeling me up constitutes coming to my assistance, as the fish deliveryman said."

"He said 'there was something a little off' about you. What did he mean by that?" I asked the snowshoer.

"I suppose he meant he couldn't find my boobs, though he was feeling all around for them," Elliot admitted.

"So you broke his wrist," I said.

"I thought he had it coming," the snowshoer said. "I feel bad that I had to hurt those boys, but I tried to hurt them a little less."

"I think they had it coming, too," I told him.

"I'll be more careful, Adam—maybe there doesn't need to be a next time," the little English teacher said.

"I thought we had a system in place—a way to keep you safe," I said. "You're easy to recognize, you know—as a man or as a woman. There's no adult as small as you, Elliot—no one I've seen, not around here," I told him.

"I'll be more careful—I promise," Mr. Barlow said. "I had to get your mom's coat dry-cleaned," he told me. "It smelled like fish!" We were both laughing when we heard the knock on the door to the dormitory hall; in the context of the moment, the knock made us jump.

"You look okay," I quickly told him.

The snowshoer sighed. "I know," he said, disheartened. It was only then I realized how much he hated looking like a man.

I opened the door and admitted Matthew Zimmermann, who was not a resident of Amen Hall. Zimmer looked a little disturbed about something, as usual. He had a note in his hand. "Here," he said, handing it to me. He'd taken it off the notebook on our door to the dormitory hall. "You must have a Holy Roller in the dorm—a genuine Bible-thumper," Zim said.

In rather elegant or old-fashioned handwriting, all the note said was "Deuteronomy 22:5."

"The Bible-thumpers are obnoxious with the shit they hold up at football games," Zimmer was saying. "They always sit in the end-zone seats, where the TV cameras can find them—John 3:16 is a big one with those end-zone Christians," Zim told us.

"Everyone has seen that one—I've looked it up," the snowshoer said. He gave a cursory look at the Deuteronomy note, which I'd handed to him. "John 3:16 is, 'For God so loved the world, that he gave his only begotten Son, that whosoever believeth in him should not perish, but have everlasting life'—you know, *that* one," Mr. Barlow said, handing the note back to me.

"What's the Deuteronomy say?" I asked the little English teacher.

"God knows—we'll have to look it up," Mr. Barlow said, smiling. "It'll be something worse," he told us. "The Gospel according to John is Jesus—Jesus says mostly nice things. But Deuteronomy is Moses—Moses is harsh. Moses is full of 'you shall not' this and 'you shall not' that. Moses lays down the law in an uptight, Old Testament way," the snowshoer said.

"I've been worrying about something," Zimmermann blurted out, in his 110-pound way.

"Oh, boy—there's lately been a lot of worrying going around, Zim," Mr. Barlow said.

"You should talk to Coach Dearborn," I told Zimmer. "The coach has a theory about selective worrying." This was meant, of course, for the snowshoer to hear, though I saw no reason not to share the selective-worrying theory with our starting 110-pounder.

"I've been thinking about something—it's just a crazy idea, but I thought I should say something about it," Zim told us. "That little woman who's been beating up those guys—what if it's your mom, Adam? What if it's your wife, Mr. Barlow? She could do it, you know," Zimmer told us. "And I swear I saw her—I *told* you!" Zim said to me.

"Adam told me. You didn't see her, Zim," Mr. Barlow said. "Ray hasn't been in town—it wasn't her you saw," the snowshoer said.

"The woman I saw was small enough to be her—she looked even *smaller!*" Zimmer exclaimed. "And there's no one as pretty as she is," he assured us.

It sounds like you were pretty convincing, I almost said again to the little English teacher, but I didn't.

"Stop worrying, Zim," Mr. Barlow said.

"And what do you guys make of the cat killer? The creepy feline hang-man!" Zimmer cried. The pitiless violence in the town of Exeter had seriously upset him.

"I'll bet a cat isn't doing it," I told our 110-pounder.

"I'll bet the small, pretty woman in the parking lot isn't the cat killer, Zim," the little English teacher said.

After Zimmermann left, the snowshoer and I had a hard time finding a Bible in our faculty apartment. "I know I have one, but I never read it—I just use it to look up things," Elliot kept saying. I kept looking at the almost ornate handwriting on the note—it was hard to believe an Exeter student had handwriting like that.

Mr. Barlow finally found a Bible. It was partially hidden behind an L.L.Bean catalog in the bathroom he shared with my mom; Little Ray got some of her long underwear, for skiing, from L.L.Bean. "The good old King James Version—just what I like to read when I'm taking a dump," the snowshoer said. We were both laughing when he put down the lid of the toilet seat and sat on it. He quickly found the passage in Deuteronomy. I could see his lips move as he read it to himself—our laughter dying. I could see in his expression what he'd meant when he said Moses wasn't as nice as Jesus.

"Read it," I said to him. Mr. Barlow was a good reader. I didn't doubt that he would find the voice to imitate how harsh Moses could be—in an uptight, Old Testament way.

"According to Moses, 'The woman shall not wear that which pertaineth unto a man, neither shall a man put on a woman's garment: for all that do so are abomination unto the LORD thy God.' Well, thank goodness, that couldn't be more clear!" the little English teacher declared. "Whoever Moses was, he was a much better writer than the tentative soul who is writing the 'Police Report.'"

"So you've been seen, you've been recognized—so somebody *knows*," I said to him.

The snowshoer shrugged. "Or someone has heard something," Elliot said, sighing. "My dear Adam, you have to stop worrying—you worry too much."

I held up the handwritten note. "This doesn't look like a kid wrote it," I told him.

"I'll tell you who *knows*," the snowshoer suddenly said. "The fish deliveryman definitely knows I don't have any boobs—he was groping all around for them! Does the note smell like fish?" Mr. Barlow asked me. I sniffed it—it didn't smell like fish.

"You've got to be more careful—you promised," I reminded him.

"I promise, my dear Adam," the little English teacher told me. "But it's not always clear what you need to be afraid of."

I would remember that, if not Deuteronomy 22:5—I would, in fact, make an effort to forget the judgmental Moses. But New Hampshire is Puritan territory. In a country of sexual intolerance, there's more than one Moses around.

26.

THE GETAWAY DRIVER

I was still a student at Exeter when Nora told me I had to see *The Wrong Car*. She and Em saw it somewhere—at a noir festival, Nora said. Nora didn't like gangster movies any better than I did, but she shared Susan Barlow's opinion that the getaway driver was *really* handsome—small, but handsome. "I think he looks a lot like our Elliot," Mrs. Barlow had said.

"Well, he's not *that* small, darling," Mr. Barlow had replied.

"He's *that* handsome," Susan Barlow had insisted.

"He's handsome, all right," Nora said to me, while Em did weird things with her eyes. Em was batting her eyelashes and pointing to my eyes; then she stood so close to me that I could feel her eyelashes flutter against my cheek. "This little actor, Paul Goode, is a dead ringer for *you*, kiddo," Nora told me. "He doesn't look a lot like the snowshoer."

Em's pantomime was pretty clear. "The getaway driver has my eyes?" I asked her. Em nodded, her hands on an imaginary steering wheel, driving purposely into an ambush.

"It's not only that your mother thinks this actor looks like you," I reported to the snowshoer. "Nora and Em think he looks like me."

Elliot sighed. "If my parents are extolling Paul Goode's *noirishness*, I'll bet he's awful," the little English teacher said, "but if the film is being shown at noir festivals, it'll show up around here." Mr. Barlow was betting it would come to Cambridge—to the Brattle Theatre, an art-house cinema he knew from his familiarity with Harvard Square—but *The Wrong Car* came to the Franklin in Durham in 1960, four years after its lackluster theatrical release. Virtually no one had seen the film, save Nora and Em and the little Barlows. As for Susan Barlow's prediction—that we were destined to see more of Paul Goode—it hadn't happened. Not yet.

Careerwise, it didn't bode well for Paul Goode that he was thirty when almost no one noticed him as the getaway driver in *The Wrong Car*. One winter night, my next-to-last year at Exeter, I drove to Durham, with the snowshoer riding shotgun beside me. In the backseat, my uncles were horsing around. In 1962, Elliot and I would see Truffaut's *Shoot the Piano Player*—a great noir film, melodramatic and funny (and not)—but Uncle Martin and Uncle Johan were already laughing in anticipation of how funny *The Wrong Car* was going to be. It wasn't. Not even Martin and Johan laughed. It was a bloodbath, a very repetitious one, but the getaway driver surprised us. No one thought Paul Goode looked much like the snowshoer. Yes, the actor was small and handsome, and although he was thirty, he looked twenty. Truly, he looked barely eighteen. For most of the film he wore an unflattering duckbill cap, a newsboy cap. His dark eyes were hard to see under that rounded flatcap, the brim at eyebrow level. The cap was a soiled herringbone pattern. Its eternal griminess suggested that the little driver slept under his getaway car.

What is noir about *The Wrong Car,* and about Paul Goode's taciturn but smiling performance, is that the getaway car never gets away—only the driver escapes, to drive again. The car is a death trap, if this little guy is driving it. The third or fourth doomed getaway car made Uncle Martin question us in the Franklin. "Is the getaway driver a *ghost?*" he whispered.

"An Angel of Death!" Uncle Johan loudly exclaimed, frightening the moviegoers seated around us.

An über-noir touch, late in the movie, is a bimbo along for the ride—a moll, we would call her. One of the gangsters has a girlfriend, but whose girlfriend is she? As the gangsters pile into the getaway car, there's no seat for the moll.

"Hey, what about me?" she asks.

"You gotta sit on someone's lap," one of the gangsters tells her.

"Not *his* lap," a different gangster says to her, pointing to the little driver. "He's gotta drive."

"No, thanks," the moll says, walking away. Before she goes, she takes a long look at the smiling driver.

"Who's the broad?" one of the gangsters asks, as the car pulls away—to all their deaths, except for the getaway driver.

"Just some broad," we hear a gangster say. This is a voice-over, during a long shot of the car driving into a hail of gunfire.

For the last not-a-getaway scene, the same broad shows up again. This time, there's a seat for her—the passenger seat, right next to the smiling little driver. The moll recognizes him, of course; she somewhat aggressively takes his flatcap off, just to be sure. It's the first time we can see how handsome he is—his dark-brown hair, his dark-brown eyes, the shy innocence of his boyish smile, which is beginning to betray his deadly sarcasm. I definitely had his eyes.

"It's *you* again!" the moll tells the driver. She gets out of the car, keeping his cap, which she puts on her head. "I ain't ridin' with *him*," she tells the three gangsters squeezed into the backseat of the death car. "You're dead meat, you know," the broad tells them, but this is über-noir in overkill—we *know*.

On the drive back from Durham, my uncles went on and on about the symbolism of the getaway driver; they were struggling to express what it means that he always gets away. The little driver is working for a rival mob, or he's a cop, or he's not real—these were among my uncles' bold interpretations.

"He's too pretty to be a *guy!*" Uncle Johan exclaimed.

"His eyes are your eyes," the snowshoer told me.

"What about his smile?" I asked Elliot.

"His smile is very noir," the little English teacher said.

"I like how the getaway driver hooks up with the broad at the end!" Uncle Martin called out from the backseat.

"It's like those two planned the whole thing!" Uncle Johan shouted.

I glanced at the snowshoer—only for a second, because I was driving—just long enough to see he was smiling. There was nothing noir about Mr. Barlow's smile.

At the end of *The Wrong Car*, the getaway driver is drinking a beer at a bar when the moll comes in. She's still wearing his flatcap.

"How'd it go, cutie pie?" she asks the little driver, cozying up to him on the nearest barstool.

"You know how it went," the driver tells her in his deadpan way. "Please take off that cap." The broad puts the duckbill cap on the empty barstool beside her.

"Better?" she asks him, snuggling closer.

"Such an improvement," the little driver tells her—giving her his shyly innocent, almost childlike smile. When you're over thirty and you smile like a kid, there is something noir about it.

I knew that smile. I knew who Paul Goode looked like, more than he did me or the snowshoer. But I was quiet; I just drove the car. My uncles and Elliot Barlow had not seen my ghosts. They'd not met the snow shoveler in that black-and-white photograph; they'd not seen the Aspen of my dreams, or of my nightmares.

"Paul Goode *doesn't* look like a very young George Raft, no matter what my father says," the little English teacher said.

"Not even if George Raft were *really* handsome," I pointed out.

"No matter what my mother says," Elliot added.

I couldn't tell them that I thought I'd seen Paul Goode, in documentary black and white, when he was only fourteen and he'd been shoveling snow—when he'd cleared the sidewalk in front of the Hotel Jerome. He was about the age he'd been when he might have met my mom, when he was just some kid who wasn't shaving—a no-strings-attached kid who couldn't take his eyes off Little Ray. How could I have told them that? I didn't know that for a fact, and they'd never seen the young snow shoveler—or so I thought.

In the Franklin, when the houselights came on—after the end credits for *The Wrong Car* had rolled—I'd told my uncles that Nora and Em thought I looked like the getaway driver.

"You're not an Angel of Death, Adam," Uncle Johan had assured me.

"Adam has the same eyes," Uncle Martin said.

"You look more like your mom, Adam," Uncle Johan said.

A good-looking woman had overheard us. She was my mom's age—she'd been in the row behind us, but she was making her way to the aisle alongside us. "Let me see your eyes, Adam," she said. When I looked at her, she asked me if I could smile. Under the circumstances, I suppose my smile was shy and childlike. I think I was more innocent than most eighteen-year-olds.

The attractive older woman spoke directly to my uncles, but she kept glancing at the snowshoer. "The kid has Paul Goode's eyes *and* his smile— he's going to get in a lot of trouble," the woman said. "And who are *you?*" she suddenly asked the snowshoer. Before Elliot could answer her, she said, "You and the kid are definitely *related*."

"I'm Adam's stepfather—we're not related," Mr. Barlow told her pleasantly.

The good-looking woman was now annoyed with all of us. "He looks like he could be your father, kid," she told me, pointing to the little English teacher. She was walking away from us, disappearing into the theater lobby—like a lost noir character from *The Wrong Car*. She was returning to the movie, I was imagining, when I felt Uncle Martin's hand on my shoulder.

"Johan's right—you look more like your mom, Adam," Uncle Martin said.

In the car, on our way home from Durham, the subject of physical resemblance took an abrupt turn.

"You know who the getaway driver really looks like, don't you?" Uncle Martin suddenly asked Uncle Johan.

"I was just thinking about him!" Uncle Johan exclaimed. "He looks like that little *mountaineer*—that Aspen local who was a ski guide at Camp Hale!" Johan declared.

"I'll never forget that kid," Uncle Martin said. "It was when the Eighty-seventh returned to Camp Hale, in February '44—the kid was turning eighteen. He couldn't wait to be a Tenth Mountain Division man."

"A very *little* man!" Uncle Johan yelled from the backseat. "He didn't look old enough to drive, but he sure could *ski*! Paulino—I remember him. He ended up in the Eighty-fifth, didn't he? The getaway driver looks like *Paulino*! He was Italian, wasn't he?" Johan asked Martin.

"Paulino is a Spanish name—Spanish or Portuguese," Martin corrected his brother. "In Colorado, I suspect, Paulino is probably a Mexican name."

"That kid didn't look Mexican," Uncle Johan pointed out.

"No, he didn't," Uncle Martin agreed, "but around Aspen, I'm guessing, Paulino would be a Mexican name."

No, the young snow shoveler didn't look Mexican, I was thinking, but how could I tell them that I might have seen the little mountaineer they were remembering, or that I might have mistaken the short boy with the tall shovel for a ghost? After all, in black and white, hadn't the small snow shoveler been in the company of ghosts?

"What was Paulino's last name?" I asked my uncles, but Uncle Martin was explaining to Johan that "Paulino" was the Spanish or Portuguese form of just plain "Paul." Was his name only a coincidence? I wondered, but Uncle Johan chose this moment to start talking to the snowshoer and me.

"We were just a couple of old volunteers, recruited by the National Ski Patrol to train the mountain troops—the young ones looked like kids to us," Johan told us from the backseat. "We already had kids of our own—Nora was eight, Henrik six."

"Paulino shipped with the Eighty-fifth, didn't he?" Uncle Martin asked his brother.

"I'm just wondering if you remember Paulino's last name," I interjected.

"The Eighty-fifth and the Eighty-seventh embarked together, from Hampton Roads in '45—bound for Naples," Uncle Johan told his brother, as I'd heard him say (rather wistfully) before. "Paulino shipped with them."

"What about Paulino's last name?" I asked again, to no avail.

"I was forty, Johan thirty-eight," Uncle Martin said, for no reason. I knew when their wartime thoughts veered off; I knew where their conversation was headed. My uncles started talking to each other as if Elliot and I weren't in the car.

"The Eighty-seventh's First Battalion had some casualties on the western slope of Mount Belvedere," Uncle Johan was saying.

"The Eighty-fifth's First Battalion attacked Mount Belvedere's sister peak, Mount Gorgolesco," Uncle Martin reminded his brother.

"There was action in the Po Valley and the Po River crossing," Uncle Johan said, as if he'd been there—he hadn't. But he'd trained young men who had died there—my mom told me.

"Some KIAs and DOWs, all right," Uncle Martin said.

"What?" I asked them, from the driver's seat.

"Killed in action," Uncle Martin explained.

"Died of wounds," Uncle Johan told me.

"I was just wondering if you knew Paulino's last name," I said.

"Johan thought he was *Italian*!" Uncle Martin exclaimed.

"He *wasn't* Mexican, Martin," Uncle Johan insisted.

In exasperation, I turned on the car radio, where Marty Robbins was singing "El Paso." My uncles instantly started singing along. They were a couple of old Tenth Mountain Division men, all right. Many of the ski troops they trained went to Italy, but my uncles had gone home—not to war. They were already married men, with children; they'd had the time of their lives at Camp Hale, playing hooky from their families, drinking beer with the boys. It was a wonder my uncles could remember anything from their Tenth Mountain Division days. Paulino's last name was too much to expect.

In exasperation, I turned off the car radio. Uncle Martin and Uncle Johan instantly stopped singing; they couldn't remember the words to the Marty Robbins song, although they'd just been singing it. That was when the snowshoer started to sing. I'd known him for four years, and I never knew he could sing, or what a pretty voice he had. My uncles and I were so impressed by Mr. Barlow, we didn't sing along—we just listened to him sing "El Paso."

I can't hear that song and not hear the snowshoer's voice, and not remember that night in the car, when I was driving and I'd just seen Paul Goode as the getaway driver.

A couple of old Tenth Mountain Division men thought Paul Goode looked like an Aspen local they'd encountered as a ski guide—"just some kid," as my mom remembered him, when he'd been three years younger than the mountaineer my uncles identified as Paulino. No, naturally, Uncle Martin and Uncle Johan didn't know—or they couldn't remember—Paulino's last name. I doubted that my mother knew or remembered the boy's first name. Little Ray only knew, or she thought she knew, there were no strings attached. You don't need to have the writer gene to imagine there are always strings attached.

I knew that Molly and my mom hadn't seen *The Wrong Car*—not in Manchester, Vermont. Paul Goode's career was languishing. He hadn't made another movie—not yet. My mother couldn't have seen the little actor on the big screen. I would manage to say to Molly that a possible name for my unknown father had surfaced—"maybe two names," was how I put it.

"How can he have two names?" Molly asked me. "I don't think Ray remembers his name—not even one name, Kid."

"If you find a moment, Molly, just ask her if she remembers a kid named Paulino—she might have called him Paul," I explained. I didn't say that he had become a movie star, because he hadn't—not yet.

Almost twenty thousand men served in the Tenth Mountain Division in Italy. Of the three infantry regiments that landed in Naples, almost twenty-five percent became casualties. Paulino *Somebody* may have been among them. I wondered if I'd seen Paulino among my Aspen ghosts. Or perhaps Paulino had become Paul Goode, because the innocent-looking snow shoveler didn't look dead.

Everyone said I looked like my mother, and I definitely did. Except for the eyes and the noir smile, I saw little of myself in the shy snow shoveler *or* in the getaway driver. Okay, the three of us were certifiably small, and I suppose we were somewhat handsome, but it's no big deal that we all had dark hair and dark eyes. In the area of inherited characteristics, these features aren't positively identifying. Your relative size, your conventional good looks, your hair and eyes—these things aren't the same as signatures, or as verifiable as fingerprints, are they? "You look like your mom, kiddo," Nora had always told me. "Whoever your dad was, you can't look a lot like him—you're already a dead ringer for Little Ray."

Upon seeing *The Wrong Car*, had Nora changed her mind? She'd said Paul Goode was a dead ringer for me. "I just mean he looks more like you than he looks like the snowshoer—you still look more like your mom, kiddo," Nora said. This echoed what Uncle Johan and Uncle Martin had told me, and Em was nodding in agreement, but I could tell Em had more to say.

Em held her right hand—her *writing* hand, like mine—in front of me.

I could see her fingers grouped together; Em wanted me to know she was holding an imaginary pen.

"You're still pissed off at me, aren't you?" Nora asked her. "I told you, I was *going to* tell him—I just *forgot!*"

Em was angrily writing with her imaginary pen on my chest. I could feel her bearing down harder when she was writing near my heart.

Of course I'd told them everything. If I'd learned anything, I'd learned not to keep secrets from Nora and Em. I'd already told them what Little Ray had said about the boy who couldn't take his eyes off her—he was just some kid who wasn't shaving. I'd already told them what those old Tenth Mountain Division men had said—how Paul Goode reminded my uncles of a little mountaineer they'd met at Camp Hale, an alleged Aspen local. Ghost or no ghost, I'd told them about my prior sightings of the young snow shoveler, too.

"I'm *sorry*, Em—I just *forgot!*" Nora was saying, while Em was acting out an excruciating giving-birth-while-trying-to-write scenario. "What Em is trying to tell you, kiddo, is that Paul Goode has the *writer* gene," Nora told me. "I forgot to tell you—he was the screenwriter for *The Wrong Car*, not just the getaway driver."

Even the little Barlows, that indefatigable writing team, had missed the screenwriting credit—"it's not a great gangster movie," was all John Barlow had said.

"But the guy who plays the driver of the getaway car is *really* noir—he's someone special," Susan Barlow had weighed in.

I suspected the snowshoer would be thrilled to know his parents had missed the screenwriting credit, but I was disheartened, because the writing of *The Wrong Car* was the worst thing about it. The writing, the snowshoer had said, was the most über-noir thing about it. If my writer gene came from Paul Goode, I was thinking, I would have to fight against the über-noir in myself.

Em and I did a lot of thinking about our writer genes; Em wanted to be a writer, too, and she had no idea where her writing came from. Nora thought we did too much thinking about this. "Why worry about it?" Nora had asked us. "There's nothing you can *do* about where your writing comes from!"

But Nora and Em and I agreed about the little English teacher's expeditions as a woman—it worried us. Nora and Em believed that the snowshoer would have a somewhat easier time living as a woman in a city like New York.

"Holy shit, *anywhere* but Exeter!" was the way Nora put it. As a girl who'd grown up in a faculty apartment in an all-boys' dorm, Nora knew how sexual minorities were treated at Exeter.

But Nora and Em and I knew why the snowshoer wasn't ready to move on from Exeter—he'd told us. Even in the early sixties, Elliot Barlow was advocating for the academy to become a coed school. Until Exeter let in girls, Mr. Barlow wasn't leaving; he wanted to be there for the boys who got picked on. "Once there are girls around as witnesses, boys will be kinder to other boys," the snowshoer said. He'd talked to his fellow teachers at several New England all-girls' schools; the teachers at those schools had told him how mean girls could be to girls. Having boys as witnesses would make the girls behave better, too. That was Elliot's argument for coeducation: kindness.

"Try being coed in the summer school—see if it works there," the little English teacher had been saying for years. In 1961, thirteen girls were admitted to the Exeter Summer School—they were day students, not boarders. The next summer, the first girl boarding students were admitted. A majority of the academy faculty supported the change; the summer school had provided convincing evidence of the academic desirability of coeducation and the feasibility of handling a boarding population of boys and girls.

In 1969, the board of trustees took up the matter. As Mr. Barlow had predicted, the principal argument against a coed Exeter was financial: women graduates would earn less than men; women would give less to the school. The snowshoer proposed polling recent Exeter alumni, who were now in college; Mr. Barlow already knew that the Exeter student body wanted a coed school. The only college students who opposed the idea were at Dartmouth. Nora said Dartmouth had a dick-oriented culture. Em's pantomime is best left to the imagination.

The Exeter board of trustees voted unanimously in favor of coeducation in 1970. The first girl day students were admitted to the regular session in September of that year; the girl boarders would come in 1971. In 1973, the snowshoer resigned from Phillips Exeter Academy, where he'd taught for twenty years. With Nora and Em's encouragement, Elliot Barlow would move to New York City.

When he'd been asked how the boys would treat the girls at Exeter, the little English teacher had said: "I can only hope they will treat the girls better than they have treated other boys." It would remain dismaying to Elliot, however, that there'd been no discussion among the trustees at Exeter concerning the possibility of inappropriate behavior by the faculty toward the female students at the school. Even in the early 1960s, when he was asked how the Exeter faculty would treat female students, the snowshoer had sighed. "As everyone knows," Mr. Barlow had said, "men generally behave very badly with women." (As the snowshoer had been finding out for himself, around town.)

Long before he left Exeter, the snowshoer made dinner for Nora and Em and me one night in our Amen Hall apartment kitchen. Elliot Barlow was the best cook I knew. Growing up in Europe must have had something to do with it. We'd just eaten his stuffed peppers in marinara sauce.

"Show me the Deuteronomy note," Nora said. I'd told her and Em what Moses had to say about cross-dressers. I'd been using the note as a bookmark in whatever novel I was reading—not the smartest way to forget the judgmental Moses.

"Oh, boy," Nora said, after I handed her the note. "I grew up with my mother's handwriting—she was always giving me Bible notes."

The snowshoer and I weren't surprised. We were pretty sure my mom must have used the *she* or the *her* word for Elliot around Abigail and Martha.

"We've all heard Ray use *she* or *her* for you," Nora told the snowshoer, with Em nodding her head off. It was clear that Nora and Em knew a lot more about men wanting to be women, and women wanting to be men, than Elliot and I did. When I'd told Nora and Em about the snowshoer's adventures as a woman in the town of Exeter, they weren't shocked. Like Coach Dearborn, Nora and Em knew there are innumerable men who are assholes. "Not only in New Hampshire," Nora had said.

Em's bodily movements, when she was pantomiming her thoughts about gender, were disturbingly similar to her enactments of childbirth and having sex; the graphic nature of her pantomime could be easily misunderstood, but Nora's deadpan interpretation was quickly forthcoming. "Em says there are almost as many women who are assholes," Nora reported; then she frowned. "No, there aren't, Em," Nora said. Em just shook her head.

Nora could remember a couple of the Bible notes her mother had written to her. There was a verse from one of the epistles of Paul to the Corinthians. "It was basically a list of wrongdoers who will not inherit the kingdom of God," Nora told us. "Thieves and drunkards were on the list, as were fornicators. Adulterers, homosexuals, and sodomites were definitely listed among the fornicators," Nora recalled. "And there was a scary one from Revelation about other abominable types, including murderers and the sexually immoral. We were all going to end up in something called 'the lake which burns with fire and brimstone, which is the second death'—that fucking part gave me nightmares," Nora said.

Em had left our kitchen table and was writhing around on the living-room floor. Em had been doing more pantomime workshops—"both taking them and teaching them," Nora had said. Em's tortured writhing around was her way of acting out what fire and brimstone in a burning lake can do to you. It was as meaningful an enactment of the second death in Revelation as I've ever seen. I knew Em wrote out many of her pantomime movements before she performed them; this was what Nora meant when she said Em choreographed herself.

Nora had seen Em's Revelation pantomime before, because Nora just kept talking at the kitchen table. "If you ever feel like letting my mother know you're on to her, I'll tell you the Bible note you should give to her. I gave her this one, and she stopped writing Bible notes to me," Nora told me and the snowshoer. "Check out Hebrews 13:2—it's a really weird one," Nora said. Elliot went into his bathroom and brought back the Bible that was forever obscured by the L.L.Bean catalog. This made Em stop dying the second death. Em came back to the kitchen table to listen to the little English teacher read Hebrews 13:2—all of us could appreciate how the very idea of it would drive Aunt Abigail bonkers.

The snowshoer solemnly read the verse twice. "'Be not forgetful to entertain strangers: for thereby some have entertained angels unawares.'" We were all at a loss for words. No one could imagine Aunt Abigail entertaining strangers, nor could we imagine Nora's mom believing that she might be missing out on entertaining angels.

In Em's impersonation of Aunt Abigail, Nora's mother appeared to be talking on the phone while giving birth. You would think Em had worked as a midwife, just to see how easily (and often) she imitated childbirth. "Your mother, Nora, is more *unawares* than most mothers," Nora told us Em had said, in Em's inimitable way.

The snowshoer could surprise us at times with a sudden seriousness. "Speaking strictly for me, as a man *or* as a woman," Mr. Barlow began, "I am not *unawares* when I have entertained angels." Nora and Em and I laughed. "You three have always been angels to me," the little English teacher said, bursting into tears.

Em, sitting beside Elliot, pushed her chair away from the kitchen table and opened her arms to him. The snowshoer sat in Em's lap. Em hugged him while he cried. Nora and I just held hands under the table. Nora didn't have the hand strength of Coach Dearborn, but she had a very strong grip for a girl. You remember the emotional moments—when you think you've done the right thing, or all that anyone can do.

What you forget are the more interior details—what may seem like minutiae at the time. Nora and Em knew everything—meaning they knew as much as I knew—but I hadn't told the snowshoer I was sure I'd seen the little getaway driver before. What would Elliot Barlow be inclined to believe about those black-and-white photographs—those ghosts, if they were ghosts, who were haunting me? Wouldn't the little English teacher tell me that my runaway imagination had run amuck? I was becoming more sensitive about hurting Elliot's feelings. He'd been better than a standby father to me; he'd loved me and advised me, as a good father (a real one) should. How did it make the snowshoer feel that I kept thinking about my mystery father, the one who'd done nothing for me?

It was another lie of omission. I hadn't told Mr. Barlow that Paul Goode looked like the smiling snow shoveler—that boy too young to shave, posing by the snowbank in front of the Hotel Jerome. But you don't see with hindsight in a first draft. You have to finish the first draft to see what you've missed.

It would soon be 1961. I would soon be on my way to Pittsburgh, and then, soon after, be on my way back. For a time, my focus was the snowshoer's safety—though loneliness (my own, included) would be my more abiding subject, as a writer.

Coach Dearborn promised me he would keep an eye on the "Police Report." Not only when I was away in Pittsburgh, but whenever I was out of town, the coach kept me informed. There was a lot of drunken driving and a shitload of domestic disputes and animal emergencies. The dangling cats continued for a while. The crafty hangman turned out to be a faculty brat— not quite old enough to be an academy student, but not exactly a townie. The cat killer was a young boy who loved birds, as Mr. Barlow had believed from the beginning.

But there were no further sightings of a small, pretty woman disabling the lustful men and boys of the town of Exeter. Either the artful snowshoer was not venturing out as a woman or the previously sighted little woman was venturing elsewhere.

I thought it sufficed that I'd given Molly a possible name for my unknown father, but I hadn't told Molly about Paul Goode—I hadn't even told her about the snow shoveler who looked like Paul Goode. I knew Molly didn't believe in ghosts—she simply didn't see them. I thought it sufficed that Molly might whisper the *Paulino* name, or just plain *Paul,* in my mom's ear—to see if Little Ray remembered the name of the kid she'd slept with in Aspen.

I was only beginning to discern the difference between those things I should have seen coming and those things I couldn't possibly have anticipated. Watching the snowshoer sob in Em's lap, I was no more ready to understand myself as a work in progress than I would have believed Paul Goode had a future as an actor—not to mention as a writer.

If you'd told me that the little getaway driver had a future, and that I was in it, I would have laughed. I would have sounded like an echo of what the moll says in the last not-a-getaway scene in *The Wrong Car*—that moment when the broad gets out of the car. "I ain't ridin' with *him*," she tells the three gangsters squeezed into the backseat of the death car. If you'd told me that Paul Goode would be a big deal in my future, I would have said I wasn't taking a ride with him.

27.

SEXUAL POLITICS, A FIRE, JEALOUSY

When did everything become political? In America, I didn't notice when or where the politics started—I just woke up one morning, and everything was political. In America, I wasn't paying attention when those things that divided us were just beginning.

I graduated from Exeter in 1961. That year, on the night of October 5, I was in Pittsburgh. It was a Thursday night, before the ski season, and my mother and Molly were in Exeter; the two ski jocks were staying with the snowshoer, but the three of them were having dinner with Nana in the Front Street house.

Since my graduation from the academy, my mom had stopped pretending that she lived with Elliot Barlow. Little Ray lived in Manchester, Vermont, with Molly—not only in the ski season—but Ray visited Mr. Barlow in Exeter frequently. In the winter months, the snowshoer often drove to Manchester, where he stayed with my mother and Molly. If my mom had married the little English teacher under publicly false pretenses, those two lovebirds were not pretending to love each other—they truly did love each other. As Molly had told me, "There's more than one way to love people, Kid."

"Since when are women a sexual minority, or are we just treated that way? For fuck's sake, we're half the population!" I had grown up hearing my mother say—to someone on the radio, or on TV, or even in the room—but for many years I'd not been paying attention to the context. I'd heard her say this without really understanding.

Then, one time—I was an academy student, we were at Nana's dining-room table, the snowshoer was there—Aunt Abigail said something, and the context was perfectly clear.

"Honestly, Ray, you sound like Nora, or like someone Nora's age," Aunt Abigail said.

"Or like Nora's friend Em—like what Em would say, if she ever said anything," Aunt Martha chimed in.

"I didn't learn that women were treated like sexual minorities from Nora and Em," my mom said. "I'm a *woman,* you know," Little Ray said. She was wearing a snug little sweater, and when she said the word *woman,* she stuck out her boobs and shook them at her easily shocked sisters.

This made everyone but Aunt Abigail and Aunt Martha laugh. Naturally, Uncle Martin and Uncle Johan laughed the loudest, but Molly was there—the ski patroller had a loud laugh—and even my grandmother laughed a little.

It was wrestling season; because I had a cauliflower ear, it hurt when I laughed. When I touched the little plaster cast, Mr. Barlow (who was also laughing) frowned at me and shook his head. My ear was pulsing, but I could hear just fine.

"I was treated like a sexual minority when I got knocked up and had my one and only," my mom was saying. "Unwed mothers are treated like shit, you know," she said, looking straight at my evil aunts.

"What I mean, sweetie," my mom said to me, in a much nicer voice, "is that I had some exposure to how sexual minorities get treated—when I was just an unmarried mom. I mean *before* I was with Molly, sweetie—I know you know what I mean."

I must have nodded—perhaps cautiously, given my throbbing ear. "Of course the Kid knows what you mean, Ray," Molly said, but my mother had worked herself up; she couldn't stop. She was talking to me, but I knew who her audience was: my seething aunts, who were glaring at her across the dining-room table.

"Molly and I are *actual* sexual minorities, sweetie—women like us get treated even worse than unwed mothers," my mom said.

"I know," I told her, but she was looking at the little English teacher. Elliot was sitting next to her, between her and Molly. From the way Mr. Barlow suddenly jumped in his seat, I could tell my mother must have touched him (just as suddenly) under the table.

"The smaller the sexual minority, the more vulnerable the group—they get picked on the worst, don't they?" my mom asked Elliot.

"That's right, Ray," the snowshoer said.

Like *homophobe, transgender* wasn't yet part of our national vocabulary, but I saw how my awful aunts were looking at Elliot Barlow. They were on to him as a cross-dresser; whenever this dinner party with a context happened, it was definitely after the message from Moses.

With her empty fork, not a magic wand, my grandmother appeared to be conducting an unseen, unheard chorus—her daughters' momentarily silent but eternally discordant voices. "Girls, girls," Nana softly chided them, as if their glaring at one another was as bad as raising a ruckus.

No one spoke, no one laughed—not even my uncles, who behaved like children when the topic of conversation was off-limits to them. Uncle Martin picked an olive out of his casserole and dropped it in Uncle Johan's beer. Uncle Johan found a green pea in his casserole and he put it in Uncle Martin's beer.

The sexual-minority subject had been near-constant background music in the years I was growing up. I was always hearing it, but I wasn't really listening. I didn't hear the politics in sexual politics—not at first. Then, one day, I did.

Whenever that dinner-party moment of belated enlightenment happened, and I don't remember exactly when it was, I was not in Exeter on the Thursday night of October 5, 1961, when the fire started. Naturally, my grandmother couldn't have invited my mom and Molly and Mr. Barlow to dinner without inviting my aunts and uncles, too. It was Aunt Abigail who inquired if Nana had burned the casserole. The snowshoer later told me that the casserole was no better or worse than usual; the dinner guests had been eating it, or pushing it around on their plates.

"Mine isn't burnt," Uncle Martin said.

"I ate mine—I didn't notice it was burnt," Uncle Johan said.

"Not that you would notice, Johan," Aunt Martha told him.

"Maybe the dessert is burning," Aunt Abigail said to Nana.

"That blueberry thing—the bottom is always burnt," Aunt Martha chimed in.

"There's nothin' burnin' here!" Dottie called from the kitchen.

"I do smell smoke," the little English teacher said.

"I smell smoke, too," Molly said.

My mother got up from the table and opened the door that faced downtown, in the direction of the academy. "There's more smoke outside—there's a fire somewhere," my mom said.

"The academy can't be burning—it could never burn!" Aunt Abigail cried indignantly, presuming an institution of such superior learning was divinely protected from anything as ordinary as a fire.

"The smoke isn't coming from the academy," my mother reported. "It's coming from the seminary."

The door to the outside was still open when the fire alarm blew from the Exeter Fire Station. It was about nine o'clock at night, Mr. Barlow later told me.

Dottie had cleared the dinner plates and the casserole; she was serving the blueberry thing. Now she clomped upstairs to the attic, guessing she could see the flames from the window there.

"It's the seminary for girls that's burnin'!" the diners could hear Dottie calling from upstairs.

"It's your old school, Rachel! Don't you want to see the fire?" Aunt Abigail cried, but my mom had closed the outside door; she'd sat back down at the table.

"The burnt part is better with vanilla ice cream on it," my mother reminded Mr. Barlow, indicating the blueberry thing.

"It's where you went to *school*, Rachel! Don't you care at all about it?" Aunt Martha asked her.

"We'll just be in the way at the fire," my mom answered. "I don't think about that old place, one way or another."

The final class had graduated from the Robinson Female Seminary in 1955. The lower floors of the towering old building had been boarded up to prevent further vandalism; this meant the vandals were targeting the windows of the upper floors. The floors themselves, only God knows why, were oiled annually—the wood was "super combustible," Elliot would tell me. The flames shot a hundred feet in the air. My uncles wanted to watch the fire from the attic window, but my aunts insisted on seeing the flames firsthand. There would be two thousand onlookers; the inferno raged for hours. It was almost two o'clock in the morning before it was under control.

"You're not even going to *see* it, Rachel?" Aunt Abigail asked my mother again.

"Nope," my mom said.

"Rachel cares more about her *sleeping arrangements* than her old school!" Aunt Martha chimed in.

"Rachel *never* cared about school—not about *any* school!" Aunt Abigail cried.

"Girls, girls," Nana murmured.

The Hampton and Stratham fire departments were called in, but there was no saving the seminary, where my mother never took to the subject of domestic science—cooking and so forth, what the seminary's founder, William Robinson, had once called "the practical duties of life." Not Little

Ray's duties. Molly and the snowshoer did the cooking and the household chores.

I can imagine the undue stomping in the hall, prior to my aunts and uncles making their dramatic exit to see the fire. "Be sure you close the door after yourselves, not to let more smoke in!" my mother called to them. But, as Elliot described to me, notwithstanding Uncle Martin and Uncle Johan's efforts to close the door, either Aunt Abigail or Aunt Martha reopened it and left it open.

"Rachel would rather eat the blueberry thing and pursue her *sleeping arrangements* than pay proper respect to her old school!" Aunt Abigail was shouting from the driveway.

"Rachel doesn't care a fig for *education!*" Aunt Martha shouted.

When Molly got up to close the door, she gave my aunts a piece of her mind. "You two are as stupid as skiing on bare ground!" the ski patroller called to them.

The way my mother was rubbing the neck of her beer bottle against the neck of Elliot's might have been misunderstood by anyone unfamiliar with their relationship—or so Molly told me later, when I called from Pittsburgh. The toast my mom proposed at Nana's dining-room table was repeated by all. "Here's to the Robinson Female Seminary," Little Ray said, her beer bottle suggestively rubbing the snowshoer's beer bottle. "Burn in peace!"

"Burn in peace!" even my grandmother repeated.

Dottie must have liked Molly's epithet for my awful aunts—*stupid as skiing on bare ground* was understandable in Maine.

In my imagination, I would denigrate and kill off no end of awful aunts in future novels and screenplays—a "fink of womanhood," I would label one such disapproving and frosty soul. She was known to put down couples who lived together as man and wife—either if they weren't married, or if (in this imperious aunt's unflagging judgment) they *shouldn't* be.

I pitied my fictional uncles, too. "As for Uncle Bob," I would write, "there were times when living with my aunt Muriel must have resembled a religious observance—the kind of demanding devotion that fasting requires, or perhaps a nocturnal trial (such as staying up all night, when going to bed would be both customary and more natural)." Poor Muriel. I would kill her off in a car crash:

"The car, which my aunt Muriel had been driving, was hit head-on by a drunk driver who had strayed into Muriel's lane," I wrote. I didn't give her a chance to survive "the carload of partying skiers."

As for my fictional mothers—oh, boy. Where to begin? When to stop? No, I didn't write about Little Ray; she was right not to see herself among my made-up moms. But I would write about my mother's circumstances, and mine.

Molly told me that my mom really hated this passage: "Even if my father's identity and his story were painful to my mother—even if their relationship had been so sordid that *any* revelation of it would shed a continuous, unfavorable light upon both my parents—wasn't my mother being selfish not to tell me anything about my father?"

"There was nothing *sordid*!" my mom said to Molly. "*I'm* not selfish, am I, sweetie?" my mother asked me.

And there was this passage—again, I thought, faithful to the situation between us but not intended as a portrait of her (Molly assured me that Little Ray had hated it): "One day, I always thought, she would tell me about it—when I was old enough to know the story. It was, apparently, the kind of story you had to be 'old enough' to hear."

My mom didn't use Molly as an interpreter to let me know how she felt about this passage: "I was aware that my mom was pretty, and I was increasingly conscious of how the other students at an all-boys' academy regarded her."

"You know how boys are, sweetie. I can't help it that I'm pretty, can I?" was all my mother said to me about it.

It's hard to know what I might have written about my mom and Matthew Zimmermann—I mean, if Zim had actually married an older woman who resembled Little Ray, or if there'd been anything of an actual nature between them.

They would see each other only three more times, following Zimmer's graduation from Exeter. Although Zim had a delayed growth spurt during his freshman year at Yale, the former 110-pounder was an undersize 123-pounder at the weigh-ins for the Freshman Eastern Intercollegiate Wrestling Association championships at West Point in 1962. Zim weighed in wearing his wrestling tights and his singlet; he had his socks on, too. I watched the bar when he stepped on the scale; it didn't budge. In those days, the lightest weight class in college wrestling was 123 pounds. The other wrestlers were naked for the weigh-ins, or wearing only their jocks. I was the Pitt 130-pounder at West Point. Only two of my freshman teammates had made the trip from Pittsburgh with me; the other Pitt freshmen were injured or academically ineligible. With only three Pittsburgh wrestlers in the tournament, we'd come to West Point without a coach.

"You're going to kill our guy at one-thirty—I can almost kill him," Matthew Zimmermann confided to me at the weigh-ins. I saw the Yale 130-pounder when we weighed in; we wouldn't meet in the tournament. "Look at me," Zim suddenly insisted, standing on his toes in his socks. "I've actually been growing, a little—I'll bet I'm as tall as your mother now."

"You're a little taller—she's only five-two," I reminded him.

"I'm almost five-*four*, and I'm still growing!" Zimmer cried. "Is your mom *here*? West Point is a long way from New Hampshire or Vermont—I was afraid it was too far for her to come, and I know it's the ski season," Zim said worriedly.

"She's here—she and Elliot Barlow made the trip, a long drive," I told him. Matthew Zimmermann looked like he might faint—not, I knew, from cutting too much weight.

"She's *here*—she came all this way!" Zimmer exclaimed, clutching his singlet at his heart. I was embarrassed for him, and although he'd grown taller, I was afraid he was going to get killed at 123 pounds. Zim said he was convinced he was going to get killed, too.

"How much do you weigh, Zim?" I asked him.

"Between one-fifteen and one-eighteen, as a rule. Once I got up to one-twenty, but I was constipated," Zimmer admitted.

They were weighing in the upper weight classes; I was getting cold, standing around in just a jock. I could see that one of my teammates, our Pitt 177-pounder, had to take off his jock to make weight. He'd been cutting down from 195. Some of Zim's fellow 123-pounders had cut down from 135 or 140. I was a 130-pounder, but I normally weighed 145 or 150. I could tell that Matthew Zimmermann had been spending a lot of time in the weight room, in addition to trying to eat his way *up* to 123 pounds.

The remoteness of the United States Military Academy at West Point on the Hudson makes a visitor feel isolated there. The river and the surrounding trees were dark gray in February; winter looked as constant as the soldiers guarding the entrance gate. The buildings were austere—beginning with the bad-smelling, overheated barracks, where the visiting teams slept. In the vast dining hall, the uniformed cadets seemed to size up the traveling wrestlers as if we were a military enemy. In the huge gym, with a wooden running track above—like an elongated version of the pit at Exeter—they were posting the brackets for the tournament weight classes on the walls. My two Pitt teammates and I were looking over the matchups, as were most of the other wrestlers.

Not Matthew Zimmermann; he had found my mother in the bleacher seats and was sitting next to her. "It doesn't matter who I draw in the preliminary round—I'm going to get killed," Zim told her. "It doesn't matter that I'm still growing—I'll never be big enough."

"I *love* how small you are, Zim—if you come to Vermont, I'll teach you how to ski. You don't have to be big to have fun skiing," my mom told him. "Just look at me!" Naturally, Zimmer needed no encouragement to look at my mother; he couldn't stop looking at her, though his pride in being taller than her was short-lived. It clearly confounded him to hear that my mom loved how small he was; it might have made Zim wish he would stop growing.

As the snowshoer later observed, the Freshman Eastern Intercollegiates was a tough tournament; the small shred of Matthew Zimmermann's confidence in himself as a wrestler was undermined by my mother's tempting offer to teach him to ski. Zimmer was pinned so quickly—in the opening period of his first match—I missed the move that led to the fall. I didn't even notice which college or university his opponent wrestled for. Zim didn't notice, either; he couldn't even remember how he'd been pinned.

"The guy had me in a three-quarter nelson, then he switched to a kind of front headlock, then he switched to something else," Zimmermann explained. He was wearing his warm-ups, and he'd curled up in the bleacher seats with his head in my mother's lap.

"The guy hurt Zim's neck," my mom told me. Zim made a painful effort to nod, slightly. "Don't move," my mother said, hugging him.

Mr. Barlow brought a bag of ice, wrapped in a towel, from the training room. Zimmer seemed content that his tournament was over—he was more than done for the day; he declared he was "definitely done with wrestling." Matthew Zimmermann lay enraptured in my mom's lap, where she secured the ice bag against his neck. I could imagine what Zim was imagining: this was how the après skiing would be, the two of them packed in ice, shivering. Elliot and I just looked at each other; we could see that Zim was already shivering, or he was quivering in anticipation of shivering.

"How are the hands—how are your fingers doing?" Elliot asked me, to change the subject. The snowshoer could see I'd taped my right index finger to my middle finger, to keep that index finger from flopping around. When you tear or detach an extensor tendon in a finger, you can't bend or extend that finger. And the snowshoer knew I'd been putting off the surgery in the palm of my right hand till the end of the wrestling season. The Freshman

Easterns was an end-of-the-season tournament for me and my fellow Pittsburgh freshmen.

Elliot also knew that my two teammates and I had come to West Point without a coach; he would be our coach for the two-day tournament. I was unseeded at 130 pounds, as was our Pitt 147-pounder; the seeding committee didn't think we were potential place winners. I didn't think we were, either. On the other hand, the Pitt 177-pounder was seeded first—he was a likely finalist. I'd looked over the brackets in my weight class. If I made it through the quarterfinals, I would see the number-two seed in the semifinals—he was a kid from Cornell.

I don't remember who I beat in my first two matches; in both cases, I got the first takedown and held on to a small lead. In the quarterfinals, I pinned a guy from Rensselaer Polytechnic Institute. I remember the school he wrestled for because Mr. Barlow was the only one who knew how to spell *Rensselaer*. My Pitt teammates were impressed by the snowshoer, but they were perplexed by Matthew Zimmermann; I'd introduced them to "my former teammate from boarding school," as I described Zim. When Zimmer wasn't at mat-side for my matches, he went back to the bleachers and my mother's lap.

"You know, that kid from Yale is hanging out with his mom in a kind of unnatural way," our Pitt 177-pounder pointed out to me.

"Actually, he is hanging out with *my* mom in an unnatural way," I explained.

"Is that a boarding-school thing?" our 177-pounder asked me.

"I don't think so," I told him. "I think Zimmermann just has an unnatural thing for my mother."

"It would be *more* unnatural if he had that kind of thing for his own mother," our top-seeded 177-pounder assured me.

The Pitt 147-pounder had heard everything we were saying, but he hadn't said a word. He won his first two bouts, but he lost in the quarterfinals, where he appeared to be permanently lost in his own thoughts.

I didn't wrestle badly in the semifinals, but the Cornell kid was better. It was a close match, but I gave up the first takedown and could never catch up. I don't remember if the Cornell kid won the weight class, or if he lost in the finals to a kid from Lehigh or Penn State. In a wrestling tournament, you're pretty much thinking only about yourself. By losing in the semis, I could still have placed as high as third or fourth, but I lost my first consolation match (the following morning) and was thereby eliminated from the tournament.

My opponent was an Army boy—a home-crowd favorite of those military academy cadets in gray, leaning over the mats from the wooden track above the gym. A consolation match can be a free-for-all. Both wrestlers have already lost once; there's the feeling that you have nothing to lose. My last match in a Pittsburgh uniform was a high-scoring one; as Coach Dearborn had forewarned me, a free-for-all wasn't the kind of match I would win.

The snowshoer was observant enough to notice how much better I'd become as a wrestler. He also observed that I didn't care if I lost my match against the kid from Army. I wanted to lie down with my head in my mother's lap; I wanted Zim to see me lying there, with no place to put his head. "I'll come see you in Vermont, you know," I told my mom. "You can't teach me to ski—not again; we've already tried that—but I'll come see you and Molly, anytime you like. You don't have to invite Zimmer to come see you, or are you starved for company?"

"Oh, don't be jealous, sweetie—you're my one and only!" my mother cried. "Zim is only invited if you come, too."

I didn't care if she taught Zimmer to ski, but I suppose I sounded a little jealous when I told my mom that I didn't want to see Zim with his head in her lap—not even if he broke his neck skiing into a tree.

Not to quarrel with Mr. Barlow's assessment, but I didn't think the Freshman Easterns was that tough a tournament. Back in Pittsburgh, I knew, there was an ineligible freshman who could have kicked the ass of every wrestler in the 130-pound weight class without breaking a sweat. But, to be fair, my jealousy—if that's what it was—had distracted me from the wrestling at West Point. I don't even know if our Pitt 177-pounder, who pinned his way into the finals, won or lost his weight class against a kid from Navy or Maryland.

My teammates and I would take a bus from West Point to the Port Authority in New York, and from there we were on a longer bus ride—back to Pittsburgh, where I had nothing but hand and finger surgeries to look forward to. Unlike Matthew Zimmermann, I was not done with wrestling, but I sensed I was done with the competition part. On our two bus rides, the Pitt 147-pounder never spoke; he remained lost in his own thoughts. As for our 177-pounder, whether he was a champion or not, he was as silent as a runner-up. Either he'd lost in the finals or he'd seen me spend the second day of our season-ending wrestling tournament with my head in my mom's lap. I'll bet our 177-pounder won his weight class, but I know he'd observed that I had a thing for my own mother. There's no question that my two teammates saw me hanging out with my mom in a kind of unnatural way.

In the locker room at West Point, after I'd lost my last match of the tournament, Elliot Barlow had kept on coaching me. "Don't get down on yourself for losing, Adam—you're not in New England anymore. And don't be embarrassed if your mom makes you feel jealous—she doesn't mean to, but sometimes she makes me feel jealous, too," the snowshoer said.

28.

STILL GROWING

I was still a college student at UNH, and still going out with Sophie. I took a break from the bleeder, the *writer*, by agreeing to meet Matthew Zimmermann in Vermont—"a ski weekend," Zim had called it, with my mother and Molly. I'd let Molly know I wasn't crazy about the idea, but the trail groomer assured me that my mom would be on her best behavior. After the weekend in West Point, Molly said, my mother knew better than to encourage Zim.

It wouldn't have worked if I'd brought Sophie to Vermont—not on the same weekend when Zimmer was coming. I couldn't imagine the bleeder sleeping between Zim and me, on that futon in the TV room. I hated the explaining of the bleeding. I was having a hard enough time just imagining Matthew Zimmermann and me on that futon.

You would have thought we were getting together for a weekend in the Alps. There were postcards from New Haven, detailing the formidable logistics Zimmer faced to get himself to Vermont. Zim was a New Yorker; his ski stuff was in the city. He wrote: "I'll have to take the train to Penn Station—it'll be a zoo. I'll pick up my parents' car, for the drive to Vermont. My parents are skiing in Gstaad, where they go every year. I try not to go to Gstaad—not when they're there. I try not to ski with them. Yet I wouldn't put it past them to have taken my ski stuff with them—I hope not!" This was on one postcard; there were other postcards, all in Zim's impeccable but small handwriting.

I hadn't known his parents went skiing in the Swiss Alps. At Exeter, other students had told me about his parents' penthouse apartment on Park Avenue, where Zim had grown up; I knew the Zimmermanns were a prosperous New York City family. Yet Zim never exhibited the snootiness I associated with the wellborn boys at Exeter. Zim wasn't a snob; he didn't condescend to anyone. But I was out of it—especially, if not only, at Exeter. I'd managed to miss what Zimmer later referred to as "the Jewish business"; he meant the anti-Semitic business, Mr. Barlow had to explain to me. Matthew Zimmermann wasn't Jewish, but the anti-Semites at Exeter thought he was because of his name. I was so out of it, I didn't think of Zim as Jewish or not Jewish. I didn't know or care.

"It may be a coincidence, but the majority of the Jewish Zimmermans I know spell the name with one *n*," Zim later told me. "My family's name has the double *n*—*Zimmermann* is the old German word for *carpenter*." What Zim didn't tell me, the snowshoer pointed out, was that being mistaken for a Jew made Matthew Zimmermann a fierce advocate for the Jews. At Exeter, Elliot said, Zim often pretended to be Jewish—just to expose the anti-Semites in the room. Some of the Exeter faculty thought Zimmer was a troublemaker, but Mr. Barlow defended Zim for his political activism. Given Matthew Zimmermann's history of exposing anti-Semitism, the snowshoer wondered if this was why Zim had expressed his misgivings to me about becoming a *Bonesman* at Yale. (Naturally, I imagined a weird and painful sexual practice I knew nothing about.)

"You've become a *what*?" I asked him.

"Skull and Bones—it's a secret society," Zim told me. "I shouldn't have joined—it's all wrong for me—but I'm the first Zimmermann in my family to be tapped."

"To be *what*?" I asked him. He explained that *tapped* meant being invited to join the fraternity. "But what's *secret* about this society, and what's *all wrong* about it?" I asked him.

"I can't tell you—it's a *secret*," Zimmer said. Zim was obdurately honest—the worst person to be burdened with keeping secrets. By telling me he was a Bonesman—this was in 1965—had Zim violated one of the rules of membership? He would say no more about "belonging to Bones," as he'd ominously put it, but his being a Bonesman clearly weighed on his conscience.

Mr. Barlow, who had a Harvard prejudice against Yale, was sympathetic to Zim's having a stricken conscience over his membership in this particular society. "Being a member of Bones is a big deal for Yalies," Elliot told me. "It's convenient that everything about the society is a secret, because the rest of us can't evaluate if the club is an empty vessel—a virtual crock of shit—or if it really *is* a big deal."

Skull and Bones was an honors society; students from distinguished and successful families seemed to be singled out for membership, but the students themselves must have demonstrated their own capabilities for success. "Zim was always an excellent student, and I don't doubt that the Zimmermanns are an illustrious family," the snowshoer said. Both Zim's father and his grandfather had gone to Yale, Zimmer had told me, but Mr. Barlow knew that Zim's father and grandfather had been big deals in the military, too. "The grandfather was an army general in World War One," Elliot informed me. "I think Zim's dad was an army colonel in World War Two."

It still troubles me that I never learned what bothered Zim about his "belonging to Bones." Were his fellow Bonesmen anti-Semites? What made them feel so entitled to their secrets? What made Matthew Zimmermann feel so burdened by the secrets he couldn't share?

"I trust that boy's moral barometer," the snowshoer always said about Zim. In reference to the Skull and Bones clubhouse, called the "tomb," the little English teacher said: "These tomb societies don't usually bring out the best in young men."

When Zimmer and I were at Exeter, the Republican senator from Connecticut was Prescott Bush—he'd been a Bonesman at Yale, where he was also a cheerleader, played varsity golf and baseball, and was president of the Yale Glee Club. In Skull and Bones lore, Prescott Bush and a few of his fellow Bonesmen dug up and removed the skull of Geronimo from the grave of the Native American warrior at Fort Sill, Oklahoma, in 1918.

The snowshoer and I knew that Geronimo's skull, hidden in the Bonesmen's clubhouse—a stolen trophy, squirreled away in the tomb—would not have quieted Matthew Zimmermann's moral barometer. "I'm sure those Yalies stole someone's skull," the snowshoer always said, "but I'll bet it wasn't Geronimo's. How would those Yalies know whose head they stole?"

In later years, it seemed small consolation that Zim never knew what became of Prescott Bush's son and grandson. It might have caused mortal damage to Matthew Zimmermann's moral barometer if he had known that a couple of Bonesmen, George H. W. Bush and George W. Bush, would both be presidents of the United States. Zim never knew that President George W. Bush won a second term by beating another Bonesman, Massachusetts senator John Kerry. I can't help wondering if Zim would have agreed with me—I thought John Kerry was a good Bonesman. We'll never know; what bothered Zimmer about being a Bonesman would remain a secret.

In the ski season of 1965, I was packing for the trip to Vermont, when I overheard the snowshoer accept a collect call from New York. "Yes, of course I can hear you, Zim—you're *shouting*!" I heard Elliot Barlow say. "You're in a *zoo*?" Mr. Barlow then asked. We were in the apartment in Amen Hall; my bedroom door was open.

"He must be in Penn Station—Zim thinks Penn Station is a zoo!" I called to Mr. Barlow from my bedroom.

"What's her name?" I heard the snowshoer ask Zim. "Buddy," Elliot then said. "She's your girlfriend?" Mr. Barlow immediately asked. When I finished packing and came out of my bedroom, the snowshoer was still on the phone. "Oh, here's Adam—do you want to talk to Adam?" Elliot asked Zim.

"Just tell him everything!" I heard Zim shouting, all the way from Penn Station.

"Zim has a girlfriend—he's bringing her to Vermont?" I asked Mr. Barlow, when he hung up the phone.

"Not exactly—it sounds more complicated than that," the snowshoer said.

"She's not his girlfriend?" I asked.

"Zim said he was bringing *a* girl—he didn't say she was *his*," Elliot explained.

"He's bringing a random girl to Vermont?" I asked.

"She's someone Zim ran into at Penn Station—maybe they were in elementary school together, an old friend," the snowshoer speculated.

"I heard you describing the size of the futon in the TV room," I told the little English teacher.

"I thought Zim should understand that the three of you would be sleeping together, but Zim assured me that Buddy is really small," Mr. Barlow said.

"How small?" I asked.

"According to Zim, Buddy is smaller than your mom but bigger than me," the snowshoer said. We agreed I should call my mother and Molly to let them know there would be a third person—just a small one—visiting for the weekend.

Naturally, Molly answered the phone; I had to tell her everything first. "If she's that small, she can wear Ray's clothes—if she needs ski stuff," the snowcat operator said.

"*Who* can wear my clothes?" I could hear my mom calling. I explained to Molly that Buddy wasn't a skier. Zimmer had told the snowshoer that Buddy would be hanging out with me.

"Buddy isn't Zim's girlfriend—she's just *a* girl," I told the trail groomer.

"I'm not surprised Buddy isn't a girlfriend—Zim has eyes only for your mother," Molly reminded me.

"Buddy sounds like a *boyfriend*!" I could hear my mom shouting.

Molly was surprised that Zimmer had his own ski stuff. I told her his parents regularly went skiing in Gstaad.

"If Zim has been skiing in the Swiss Alps, he probably already knows how to ski—at least a little," Molly said.

"I'm betting Zim is a beginning-to-intermediate skier—he's no better than that as a *wrestler!*" my mother was screaming.

"I should probably let you talk to your mom, Kid, before she loses her voice," the ski patroller told me.

"Who is Buddy? I wouldn't name a *boy* Buddy—not even a *dog!*" my mom was yelling. "Nobody would name a *girl* Buddy!" she screamed.

"Don't get started with the name business, Ray," Molly said, before handing her the phone.

"Where did Zim find a girl named Buddy who's as small as me?" my mom asked me.

"Buddy is smaller—it sounds like she's between you and the snowshoer," I said. I didn't say that Zim had found her in Penn Station. What Mr. Barlow had speculated was good enough for me: New Yorkers were always running into old acquaintances at Penn Station. Elliot guessed that Zim must have known Buddy in elementary school, his pre-Exeter years. In the back of my mind, however, I was bothered by something I was either remembering or imagining. (Fiction writers, even young ones, often can't or don't distinguish between the two.) I either remembered or imagined something Matthew Zimmermann had said to me, in a musingly sad way, when we were at Exeter. Zimmer told me he'd never been in school with girls.

Upon meeting her, Molly was the first to notice that Buddy was too young to have gone to elementary school with Zim. When Zim was pre-Exeter, Buddy would have been prekindergarten—"if Buddy was even born," Molly whispered in my ear.

"Isn't Buddy underage, sweetie? Maybe that's why she's so small," my mother whispered to me. I had to wait for Buddy to go to the bathroom before I could ask Zimmer if Buddy was underage.

"Of course she is!" Zim said miserably. "But Buddy doesn't think she's underage. And when I saw her in Penn Station, she was pretending to be a *boy!* She wasn't fooling anybody," Zimmer added crossly. When Buddy came out of the bathroom, Zim asked her: "Do you really believe you'll be safer with some guy who picks you up imagining you're a boy?" Buddy shrugged; she smiled as innocently as she knew how. It was disconcerting to see she was wearing Zim's clothes. One of his button-down shirts hung below Buddy's knees; she'd rolled up the cuffs of Zim's jeans to mid-calf, and she must have

cinched his belt in the last hole. Still, Buddy looked like what she was—
a pretty girl, maybe thirteen or fourteen, tops.

"I'm still growing," Buddy told all of us proudly.

"I took her home because her boy clothes were filthy, and she was getting
the once-over from every creepy guy in Penn Station," Zimmer told us. "I
thought my mom's clothes might fit her. My mom is small, but she's gotten
fat—Buddy won't wear fat women's clothes," Zim explained. "Buddy likes
the way she looks in my clothes better," Zimmer said despairingly.

Buddy smiled. She clearly enjoyed Zim's summation of his rescuing her
from Penn Station; Buddy even danced a little for us, her way of showing
Molly and my mom and me how good she thought she looked in Zim's boy
clothes.

"Maybe some of my clothes would fit you, Buddy," my mother said to her.
"Would you like to try on a few things?"

"Yes, please," Buddy said shyly. She became self-conscious and shy when
she looked at my mom and Molly, or when they looked at her. It made me
think that—on her own in Penn Station, where she wasn't fooling anybody
as a boy—maybe Buddy had met some women like Molly and Little Ray. Or
maybe I was just imagining, as usual.

What Molly and my mother and I were not imagining was that Matthew
Zimmermann, miraculously, was still growing. How was it possible that Zim
had inched a little taller than he'd been three years ago, at West Point? "I'm
almost five-six," Zimmer had said apologetically, when he arrived in Vermont. He was almost as tall as me. He'd been pumping iron, too; he'd given
up wrestling, but not the weight training. Zim would never be a big guy, but
he wasn't the skinny little boy we'd known.

"I can still see the smallness in you," my mom had told him, just to make
him feel better. "You'll always be small to me, Zim," she'd tried to reassure
him, "even if you're still growing."

When Buddy went off with my mother to try on a few things, Zimmer
had a meltdown in front of Molly and me. He took us into the TV room and
showed us Buddy's dirty pink backpack. Zim pulled an ornate glass ashtray
from the girl's backpack.

"Buddy stole this from my parents' apartment—she can't stop stealing
stuff," Zim said. "She'll try to steal your stuff, too," he told Molly. "I caught
her trying to pick my pocket in Penn Station. But I couldn't just *leave her*
there, could I?" he asked us.

"Is Buddy a runaway?" Molly asked him.

"She must be!" Zim cried. "But she won't tell me where she's running away from."

"I suppose she has no wallet, and no ID—she's too young to have a driver's license," Molly said.

"No wallet, no ID—just bills, balled up in a wad," Zimmer said. "What's a kid like Buddy do to get a hundred-dollar bill?" Zim asked Molly and me. "Buddy knows what a blow job is—she offered me one," he said. "She'll offer you one, too—just wait," Zim told me.

"You can't rescue everyone, Zim—some kids can't be saved, you know," Molly told him.

"No, Buddy!" we heard my mother say—loudly enough to hear her clearly, from behind the closed bedroom door. "Please stop it—just don't, Buddy," my mom told the girl. Zim hid his face in his hands. Molly gave him a hug, kissing the top of his head. From the way my mother spoke to Buddy, there was no mistaking that Little Ray had declined to accept what Buddy was offering her.

"I'm sorry—I shouldn't have brought her here. But Buddy doesn't know any better—I think it's all she knows how to do," Zimmer was saying, his voice muffled against Molly, who just held him in her arms. "I managed to get her out of Penn Station, but she wouldn't let me take her to the police. And won't the police bring her back to the people who taught her to do this?" Zim asked us. "I can't just take her back to Penn Station and *leave her* there, can I?" he kept asking us.

This was the way the weekend would go. When one of us was alone with Buddy, she would offer herself in overtly sexual ways; from our various encounters with her, we agreed that blow jobs weren't the extent of what Buddy had been taught to do.

I learned that no one had taught the child how to read. I was writing in one of my notebooks when she asked me to read to her. I read a small scene I was writing aloud to her; then I asked her if she would read aloud to me. The girl sat staring at the words in my notebook, shaking her head.

Molly discovered that Buddy was old enough to shave her legs and underarms, but she didn't know how. "Would you like me to show you how to do it?" Molly asked the girl.

"Yes, please," Buddy answered shyly. They went off to the bathroom together.

"Cut it out, Buddy," my mom and Zim and I heard Molly say, from the bathroom. "You're learning to shave yourself—that's all we're doing," the trail groomer told her.

Buddy showed us her legs and armpits, when she came out of the bathroom. "I only cut myself once—just a little one," she said. Buddy showed us the tiny cut, which she seemed proud of, too.

All night, on the futon in the TV room, Buddy tried to fool around with Zim or me. Zim woke me up saying, "Stop it, Buddy." Or I woke up Zimmer, saying something along those lines to Buddy.

Molly and my mother were friends with a Vermont state trooper named Mike; my mom had taught his kids how to ski. Molly tried to talk to Mike about Buddy's situation—at first, hypothetically. Mike knew Molly well enough to know she wasn't just conjecturing about a runaway girl. "If the minor is from out of state, I would need more information, Molly," he told her.

"I can vouch for the boy who brought her here, Mike—he has only good intentions," Molly said. "What we need to hear is a promise from the police—we need to know this child won't be returned to the swine who did this to her."

I don't doubt that Mike was a good guy, and an honest one; like Zim, the trooper had only good intentions. But you can't blame Mike for being truthful when he told Molly that he couldn't promise her what would happen to Buddy. "I would need more information, Molly," Mike could only repeat to her.

I don't believe Buddy overheard what Molly told Zim and my mom and me about her conversation with Mike, but Buddy must have known we were talking about her, and we kept asking the girl for more information—beginning with where she came from, and the circumstances that led to her running away. "No cops, please," Buddy said softly—to every question we asked. There were no answers to where she'd learned that sexual propositioning was the only thing that worked with adults. Was the weekend disheartening for the runaway child, because her constant propositioning didn't work with us?

Buddy slept like a dog; she would just plop down, on a couch, in a bed, on a rug, in someone's lap, and fall asleep. At night, she was restless and prowled around. She would get into bed with my mother and Molly; she would come back to the futon and insert herself between Zim and me. We would find her alone in the living room, where she had drifted away on the couch, the radio at a barely audible volume. Buddy seemed to like the local country station.

"Do you like country music, Buddy?" my mom asked her.

"No cops, please," the girl answered, like the radio in the living room, at the lowest possible volume. My mother and Molly thought Buddy should see a doctor; they meant their OB-GYN person. God knows what the girl had been exposed to. But maybe Buddy overheard the word *doctor.* "No doctors, please," she started saying to us, in her low-volume, country-music voice.

We were paralyzed; we couldn't, or we didn't, act. If Buddy hadn't taken her fate into her own hands—as (we presumed) the enterprising child had done before—I think we would have trusted Mike. I'm guessing we would have handed Buddy over to the Vermont State Police. But Buddy must have known we were deliberating about what to do with her. In an instinctual but aimless fashion, she went on stealing things, yet she made no attempt to hide any of it; we found more of my mother's clothes (and Zim's watch and Molly's makeup) in Buddy's pink backpack, or stuffed under the futon in the TV room.

"I'm giving you my clothes, Buddy," my mom told the girl. "If you want more clothes, I'll give them to you—you don't have to steal them."

"No cops, no doctors—please, Ray," Buddy begged her. On Saturday and Sunday morning, the girl ate her breakfast cereal out of the ornate ashtray she'd stolen from the Zimmermanns' Park Avenue apartment. Buddy ate so ravenously, she gave no indication that she recognized the ashtray, but on the second morning Zimmer pointed disparagingly at the girl's makeshift cereal bowl.

"That thing will never be of any *use*," Zim said. "It's too big for cigarettes, and it's the wrong shape for cereal. I think it was designed to serve caviar, but my mother smokes so much, she turns everything into an ashtray!"

"It could be Steuben Glass—you know, sweetie, Nana has some Steuben shit in the Front Street house," my mom said indifferently.

"It looks expensive," Molly said, watching Buddy eat out of it. We were all thinking that this was why the girl had stolen it.

"Who cares if it's Steuben shit?" Buddy asked, with her mouth full. "It's really heavy—you could kill someone with it," the girl told us. We were all thinking that this would have been a better reason for Buddy to steal it.

That same Sunday morning was when my mother brought up the name business. "I'm guessing no one named you *Buddy*—that sounds like a name you made up for yourself," my mom told the girl, who was scraping the sides of the Steuben Glass caviar server. It was shaped like an elongated turtle shell, a better bludgeon than a bowl.

"I never had a buddy, Ray," the girl said.

"It's the perfect name for you, Buddy—you made the right choice," my mother didn't hesitate to tell her, but none of us could see Buddy's face. The determined girl was bent over the glass bowl, licking it.

Buddy demonstrated no comparable interest in snowshoeing; she knew how to run away, but running for no reason didn't interest her. I went snowshoeing by myself on Sunday, when Molly and my mom took Zimmer skiing. As Little Ray foresaw, Zim was a beginning-to-intermediate skier; he'd had ski lessons, but my mother said she'd managed to make him ski a little better.

We'd all imagined that Buddy would run away while we were out. Molly was the one who said a girl like Buddy wouldn't have a hard time getting rides as a hitchhiker. We were troubled by how womanly Buddy looked in my mom's clothes. And Molly's observation was unquestionably correct: Buddy was too young to have a driver's license. Yet none of us had imagined that the girl might know how to drive.

She stole Zimmer's parents' car—naturally, she knew where Zim kept the keys. I'd wondered why Buddy asked me so many questions about the stick shift in the VW Beetle; Zim's parents' car had an automatic transmission.

Buddy only took the clothes my mother gave her. She swiped one tube of Molly's magenta or fuchsia lipstick, too. As for Zim's clothes, she took the things that she'd already worn. She stole nothing of mine, but she'd left an imprint of her lips on an otherwise clean page of my writing notebook. I recognized the magenta or fuchsia lipstick. I knew the ski patroller wouldn't have kissed my writing notebook; besides, the lips were too small to be Molly's. Everyone was relieved that Buddy had reclaimed the Steuben Glass billy club she'd stolen from the Zimmermanns' Park Avenue apartment. We all agreed that the *Steuben shit*, as my mom called it, was worthless as an ashtray; it had been a bad cereal bowl, too. If Buddy needed to kill someone with it, that was a different story—that was okay with us.

We knew what wouldn't have been okay with Mike, the state cop—namely, that we didn't report her. But if we'd told the trooper that Buddy had stolen a car, and she was driving without a license, the Vermont State Police would have gone after her; probably, they would have picked her up before she got out of the state. The girl was a minor. We didn't know if there would be criminal charges. We didn't know the odds of her being sent home. We definitely didn't have a good impression of the home Buddy had run away from.

"By the book, I'm guessing Zim is liable if Buddy hurts herself or someone else with the car—I mean, if you *don't* report the car as stolen, Zim," Molly said.

"I would prefer not to," Zim said automatically. The way he said it sounded so familiar, as if he were always saying this—or that someone was always saying it.

"By the book, we should call the cops," my mother said.

"I would prefer not to," Zimmer repeated. If I closed my eyes, I could remember hearing Zim say this in my sleep—when I'd thought we were both asleep. It was something he'd said, more softly, to Buddy—when he'd been trying not to wake me up. *I would prefer not to* was a more formal version of telling Buddy to stop it, or to cut it out. But why had I imagined that Matthew Zimmermann was always saying this, or that someone was?

It was like something you might read in a novel, something eternal. I knew I hadn't read it, but it sounded so resolute—someone must have written it. I decided I would ask Mr. Barlow about it; if anyone who was any good had written it, the little English teacher would know.

Meanwhile, we did what Zim wanted—nothing. We let Buddy go. I drove Zimmer back to New York City. After Zim did some haggling with the parking-garage attendant, I was permitted to leave the VW Beetle in the empty spot where the Zimmermanns normally parked their car. In his parents' Park Avenue apartment, Zimmer needed to assure Elmira, the family housekeeper, that I was not another of his rescue projects.

"Tell me you didn't get him where you got Buddy, Matthew," was Elmira's way of putting it. Zim promised her: I was from Exeter, not from Penn Station. Elmira seemed minimally relieved. She'd been Zim's nanny in his childhood years; she'd seen her share of Zimmer's Exeter friends, not always on their best behavior. "You don't look like you're homeless or a drug addict, Adam," Elmira said to me, when we were introduced. "Matthew will give you a tour of his father's bedroom and bathroom. Try not to pee on the Picasso," Elmira added.

I'd only heard or read about those married couples who slept in separate bedrooms; given her peregrinations between Mr. Barlow and Molly, my mother's sleeping arrangements were more original. In Zim's opinion, his parents were happy together, but they slept apart. "He says she snores, she says he farts," Zimmer confided to me. Zim refrained from having houseguests, or other overnight visitors, when his mom and dad were at home. He only invited his friends—or his rescue projects, like Buddy—when Colonel and Mrs. Zimmermann were skiing in Gstaad, or otherwise away.

Elmira was in charge of damage control. She'd ascertained that Buddy had swiped drugs from Colonel Zimmermann's medicine cabinet; Zim assured her that his dad would have taken the prescriptions he needed to Gstaad. "I'm just telling you, Matthew," Elmira said. She was a long-suffering housekeeper, I could tell—a martyr type, like Dottie. Also like Dottie, Elmira was the embodiment of common sense—an efficiency she generally found to be lacking in others.

There were no guest rooms in the Zimmermanns' palatial apartment. Elmira had her own bedroom and bathroom, adjacent to the kitchen. Zim had his own room; his mother's bedroom, he'd explained, was never to be used by guests. The modest and somewhat spartan bedroom where his father slept was the only one available for friends or desperadoes. Elmira had referred to Buddy as "the most recent, female desperado." From Elmira's surveillance, and her judgmental comments, I gathered that Zim was predisposed to bringing home lost wanderers—the strays and castoffs of humankind. "Buddy stole a pair of your dad's cuff links, Matthew—your dad didn't take them to Gstaad," Elmira added, for good measure. The Zimmermanns' faithful housekeeper came from the West Indies, via the Bronx. A rotund and motherly Black woman, she'd been a baby when her family emigrated from Anguilla to the United States; to my ear, Elmira's accent had more of the Bronx than the West Indies in it.

Matthew Zimmermann heard the intonations of the housekeeper's voice differently. To Zim, Elmira had perfectly parroted his mother's Silk Stocking District speech; to his ear, Elmira sounded like the Upper East Side. "Elmira has been more than a second mom to me—she's been my *main* mother," Zimmer told me. It was not necessary for him to explain that he loved Elmira, or for him to tell me that the housekeeper loved him; I could see this for myself.

"I've had no babies of my own—this one is my only baby," Elmira told me, giving Zim an impromptu hug. The three of us were crowded into the small bathroom adjoined to what would be my sleeping quarters for the night. The purpose of our being in the bathroom was to show me the Picasso I was not supposed to pee on.

"It's not really a Picasso," Zimmer said. I wouldn't have known, one way or the other. In a gilded frame, the small painting rested on the floor beside the toilet; leaning against the bathroom wall, it was small enough to fit under the roll of toilet paper. I know nothing about art, but the painting seemed mostly naturalistic to me—except the nude had three breasts. A friend of Zim's father had painted it; Zim's mother hated the painting. "My dad has tried to hang it on every wall of the apartment," Zimmer explained. "My mom always takes it down and puts it here."

"Two breasts should be enough," Elmira said.

"I promise not to pee on it," I told them.

"I had my fingers crossed that Buddy would steal it—I've got my reasons for calling it a Picasso," Elmira said. Zim just smiled, saying nothing. As for the car Buddy had stolen, neither my former teammate nor his former nanny seemed especially worried about it. And for good reason. As it happened, Buddy would park the car—illegally, and as close to Penn Station as she could leave it. The car was towed from West Thirty-fourth Street, near Seventh Avenue; Buddy had left the keys under the floor mat on the driver's side, where she knew Zim often left them.

The postcard Zimmer sent me later, from New Haven, described the "god-awful place" he had to go to retrieve the towed vehicle, but he didn't tell me what it cost. What I remember of my one night in his father's austere barracks of a bedroom has lasted longer. On the night table was an alarm clock and a gooseneck lamp, good for reading. There was a corner bookshelf—a narrow one, with not many books. From their titles, and my perusal of the flap copies, they seemed to be books about military history. Three photographs stood, as if at attention, on top of the small chest of drawers. General Zimmermann, I presumed—an army general in World War I. Colonel Zimmermann, Zim's father—an army colonel in World War II. And there was Zim, a toddler, not yet in uniform; the child was tightly holding what looked like one of the commanding officers' caps. I was aware of the weight of the expectations Zimmer grew up with. Had he always been still growing? Was he always trying to grow? Had Zim's dad always been worried that his only child wouldn't get big enough? What do they matter now—these domestic details?

In the morning, I would drive Zim back to Yale. New Haven was an easy stopover on my way north to New Hampshire. As for the cuff links Buddy had stolen, all Zim ever said was: "My dad has more cuff links than shirts with French cuffs." After my night in the military man's sleeping quarters, in

Colonel Zimmermann's barracks, I was more interested in discussing military matters.

It was the winter of my senior year at the University of New Hampshire and Zimmer's senior year at Yale. Zim knew I was 4-F. Zim knew I'd been saved by my trigger finger; he also knew I was going to the MFA program in creative writing at the University of Iowa, the Iowa Writers' Workshop. I hadn't bothered to ask where my friend and former teammate was headed. I should have known. Our correspondence about the war in Vietnam had been ongoing. Nora and Em were increasingly anti-war, as were my mom and Molly; in his own way, the snowshoer was always political. And Zimmer seemed to know from the beginning that the Vietnam War was not the kind of war we were good at.

On Christmas Eve, 1964, two American servicemen were killed in Saigon when Viet Cong terrorists bombed the U.S. billets. "Uh-oh," Zim's postcard from New Haven had begun. "Who the 'terrorists' are is a matter of opinion." In February 1965, just before Zimmer brought Buddy to Vermont, I'd asked him about Operation Flaming Dart—what the U.S. Air Force referred to as a *tactical air reprisal.*

"Tell me what *that* means," I'd written him.

"That means we're bombing the shit out of targets in North Vietnam," Zim wrote from New Haven.

In March of that year—not long after Buddy stole the Zimmermanns' car, and I drove Zim back to New York, and then back to Yale—the U.S. Air Force began Operation Rolling Thunder: "to interdict the flow of supplies to the south," I'd read in a newspaper.

"That means we're bombing the shit out of targets in North Vietnam," Zim wrote to me. That was the month when the first American combat troops landed in Vietnam. "Uh-oh"—this stood alone on one postcard from New Haven.

In April 1965, President Johnson authorized the use of U.S. ground troops—"for offensive operations in South Vietnam."

"That means 'search and destroy,' which is basically about the *destroy* part," Zim wrote.

In May, the U.S. Navy began Operation Market Time—"to detect and intercept surface traffic in South Vietnam coastal waters."

"They're just seizing and destroying enemy craft—what we're dealing with is guerrilla warfare," Zimmer wrote. He may have been still growing, but his handwriting was getting smaller. "Are we prepared to obliterate the whole country?" he wrote. "They can call it 'search and destroy' or 'seize and destroy,' but it amounts to just plain destroy—there's no good way to end this." I never understood the particulars of Zim's training at Fort Benning, Georgia, but Second Lieutenant Matthew Zimmermann would serve in Vietnam—Company A, 502nd Infantry, 101st Airborne Division.

From Fort Benning, there were no more postcards. As his criticism of the war grew more specific, and more obdurate, Zim's letters got longer. "Who doesn't question the war's 'morality'—don't you think I question that, too?" one of his letters from Fort Benning began. "But I feel one has to see something firsthand to be sure. I'm inclined to agree with Kennedy's assessment of the Vietnam problem—this was in '63. You may remember what JFK said: 'We can help them, we can give them equipment, we can send our men out there as advisers, but they have to win it, the people of Vietnam.' I think that point is, or was, valid, but it's clear the people of Vietnam aren't winning the war. We appear to be trying to win it for them," Zimmer wrote. I didn't know the details of Zim's Advanced Individual Training, or what went on in Officer Candidate School, but he couldn't have had more time to write than he'd had at Yale. And when he mentioned his "active duty," he didn't interrupt his ranting to tell me what or where it was.

Of course I quoted him to my mother and Molly, and whenever I got together with Nora and Em, they always wanted to know what Zim had to say about the war. Nora and Em hadn't seen Zimmer since his days as a 110-pounder at Exeter; they didn't believe me when I told them that Zim had grown, or that he was still growing.

"He can't be still growing," Nora said in her didactic way. Em agreed in her usual way—a violent, disembodied nodding of her head.

"There doesn't appear to be a government in Saigon that works without us," Zim wrote from Fort Benning. "Do the South Vietnamese people even like the military junta of Marshall Ky? Why would Hanoi and the Viet Cong negotiate for a peaceful settlement if they think they can win the war? There's every reason for the United States to keep enough ground forces in South Vietnam to persuade Hanoi and the Viet Cong that they could never achieve a military victory, but what do we accomplish by bombing the north?" Zimmer asked.

"I love that little boy—he must be driving everyone crazy at Fort Benning," Nora said, when I quoted Zim to her again. We were in the TV room at my mother's, where we'd slept on the futon. Em was doing something strange in the reclining chair in the TV room. It was a vintage Barcalounger, and no one liked it, but Molly said the chair was too big and heavy to throw out. Molly and my mom were in the kitchen, but they could hear us talking about Zimmer.

"Zim isn't the little boy he was—he's still growing!" my mother called. "But I can still see the smallness in him!" my mom added.

"Zim can't be still growing," Nora insisted to me quietly. "I just love him," she added. Em appeared to be humping the Barcalounger, or she was acting out how she would hump someone in a reclining chair. "Em says that Zim is the only boy she would ever fuck," Nora explained. "No, you *wouldn't* fuck him, Em. I don't love him *that* way!" Nora added crossly. Em was acting out ambivalence in the Barcalounger. Nora ignored her, but it seemed to me that Em was saying she reserved the right to remain undecided about fucking Zim.

"Supposing that we mean what we say—that we want South Vietnam to be free to govern itself—then we should be protecting South Vietnam from attack," Zimmer just went on, from wherever he was. "But it appears that we are attacking the whole country—from the air!" my former teammate, a born infantryman, wrote. "If we bomb the whole country to bits—allegedly, to protect it from communism—what kind of protection is that? I think that's a serious problem," Zim wrote, "but I would prefer to see the situation for myself."

My mom, of course, was opposed to Zim's seeing the war for himself. "If he were my one and only, I wouldn't let him go to Vietnam," my mother said.

"He's not your kid, Ray," Molly reminded her.

I stopped quoting Zim's letters to Nora and Em; their love for him got out of hand. Nora had threatened to sleep with Zim if Em slept with him. It was August 1967 when I saw Zimmer again. I don't remember the way he worded it—if he was on leave from Fort Benning, or from active duty somewhere else. What my mom would remember is that Zim said he would be in Vietnam before Christmas—this really upset her. Molly and I were more shocked to learn that Matthew Zimmermann was engaged.

"Is he bringing his *fiancée* to Vermont?" my mom asked. The way she said *fiancée*, Molly and I knew my mother would have been happier if Zim brought Buddy. I forget if he told me his fiancée's name. She was a New Yorker, like him; she worked at one of the women's magazines, Zimmer said. He drove to Vermont by himself. Maybe the fiancée didn't like the sound of the sleeping arrangements on the futon in the TV room; perhaps Zim didn't want to be reminded of our awkward threesome on the futon with Buddy.

"I would prefer not to," I imagined Zim said to his fiancée. I had learned from Mr. Barlow where this came from, and I'd since read the original dialogue. Knowing my attachment to *Moby-Dick*, the little English teacher had urged me to read more Melville. At his urging, I'd read "Benito Cereno" and "Billy Budd, Sailor"—not, however, "Bartleby, the Scrivener." The snowshoer didn't think I would like it, no matter how much I loved Melville. Elliot Barlow was right; I didn't care for the story, and I found Bartleby both irritating and enigmatic. There was no doubt, however, that Mr. Barlow was also right to identify Bartleby's repeated utterance as the source of Zim's uncharacteristic dialogue. Or was it characteristic? the snowshoer had asked. Zim was a little irritating, and he could be stubborn; a twenty-four-year-old who was still growing, Zimmer was certifiably enigmatic. Did *I would prefer not to* have imaginable use when Zim was speaking to his fellow Bonesmen? The snowshoer and I could imagine how Zim would say this when one or more of the Bonesmen had proposed a sexual impropriety, or had suggested something that was otherwise morally reprehensible to the former 110-pounder.

When Zim came to Vermont in the summer of 1967, he weighed what I did, about 150 pounds, and he was taller than I was. "I'm five-seven—I'm almost five-*eight*," he said. "And I'm still growing," Zimmer added, in an offhand manner—as if it were no big deal, or he'd become a little embarrassed about it. But how could he have grown three (almost four) inches since we were wrestling at West Point? It wasn't possible—not even, I thought, if Colonel Zimmermann had been willing it to happen.

Now Molly sounded like Nora when she said, "You can't be still growing, Zim." But he was.

Even my mom seemed suddenly subdued around him. It was without much conviction that she told him, "I can still see the smallness in you." I don't think Zim believed her; Molly and I certainly didn't.

"How about a hike—want to climb a mountain, just a small one?" Molly asked Zimmer. Molly and I had the feeling that my mother was just going to stare at him; it was a good idea to do something physical with him. In 1967, Molly was roughly forty-seven. Bromley isn't a big mountain, but—from the end of mud season till the first good snowfall—Molly hiked up Bromley, and walked down, four or five times a week. I had to work hard to keep up with her on a hike. That day, Zimmer set the pace; Molly and I had to make an effort to keep up with him. "You're in good shape, Zim," Molly told him. "I can tell you've been doing a lot of marching around."

"Second lieutenants are supposed to be platoon leaders—we're supposed to set an example," Zimmer said. My mom wasn't a runner or a hiker; she didn't even like to walk. The only way Little Ray would climb up Bromley was to skin up with her telemarks on. I was glad my mother hadn't hiked up Bromley with us. She would have found it even harder to still see the smallness in Zim.

At dinner, Molly mentioned the anti-war protests in April of that year; there'd been huge protests in New York City, Washington, DC, and San Francisco. The protests didn't concern Zimmer; he wasn't opposed to the protests, but they weren't a solution. "The problem is, the North Vietnamese and the Viet Cong are fighting the war on their own terms—their large units never engage our large units," Zim said. "Look what happened with Operation Buffalo, in one day—this was just last month," the future platoon leader told us. There were two companies of marines involved in an ambush from three directions. Zimmer talked so fast, I later had to look this up—Alpha and Bravo Companies, First Battalion, Ninth Marines. They first encountered sniper fire from the People's Army of Vietnam; the marines were then attacked with flamethrowers, artillery, mortar, and small-arms fire. There were so many details of a military kind, I lost track of whatever point Zim was making. He'd even memorized the number of casualties the two companies of marines had suffered, and the Vietnamese casualties. "We had eighty-four killed, a hundred and ninety wounded, nine missing in action—while the People's Army of Vietnam had fifty-five killed, not counting another eighty-eight believed to be dead but unaccounted for," Zimmer recited to us. My mother just stared at him, drinking her third beer; Molly mostly stared at my mom. I'd not seen Zim drink beer before, but I noticed he had a couple. When Zimmer got up from the table to go to the bathroom, my mother also got up from the table; she threw up in the kitchen sink.

"I'll do the dishes, Ray," Molly said to her. "Why don't you go to bed?" My mom slipped away to their bedroom—like a ghost, I would later think. "I don't believe it's the beer," Molly told me.

In Zim's case, he fell asleep so quickly and slept so soundly, I believe it was the beer—he wasn't normally a drinker. We'd helped Molly do the dishes. Zimmer was coherent in his questioning of our civilian and military leaders. He doubted those multidivisional operations that involved all branches of the military. "They're calling '67 the 'era of big battles'; they're targeting the 'Iron Triangle,' but I'm not buying the body counts," Zim told Molly and me. He pointed out the casualties (to both sides) attached to Operation Junction

City and Operation Cedar Falls. "Who cares that the casualties are ten to one in our favor? The Viet Cong and the North Vietnamese aren't keeping score—they're in this for the long haul; they're fighting the way they can win," Zimmer said. I would look up the numbers later; about 3,500 North Vietnamese and Viet Cong were killed, compared to a loss of 350 American lives. And Zim was right—we weren't winning the war.

When we got settled and were stretched out on the futon, I could tell that Zim was drifting away. "We didn't get to talk about your fiancée—you haven't told me anything," I said to him.

"I would prefer not to," Zimmer said. It was the coldness that was uncharacteristic.

"Okay, Bartleby," I said. We hadn't talked about Melville, either; there were so many things we never talked about.

I thought Zim had passed out—he was so still, so deathly quiet. "Please don't call me Bartleby—not you, Adam, of all people. Please don't," he begged me, his voice breaking.

"I'm sorry, Zim, I won't ever do it again—I never will," I assured him, but he was sound asleep; I felt the back of his hand fall against my shoulder, like a dead thing. I couldn't see him in the dark, but I vividly recalled the way my former teammate used to fall asleep on our wrestling team bus. We often sat beside each other; Zim preferred the window seat. But wrestling is a winter sport. The winters in New England are very cold; it was cold on the bus, next to the window. And Matthew Zimmermann always fell asleep with his face pressed against the window glass, which was as freezing cold as it was outdoors.

I asked him about it once. How could he sleep that way? "I love to sleep when my face is cold," Zim said.

I slept badly that August night in Vermont. I heard Molly's voice a couple of times; she sounded like she was arguing with my mother, but my mom said nothing I could hear. Later I heard a clunking sound; it came from the kitchen. Maybe my mom had thrown up again, and Molly was getting her something to drink from the fridge. I got up and went into the kitchen, where I saw my mother. She usually slept in a T-shirt or a tank top and a pair of athletic shorts—maybe sweatpants, in the winter—but she was wearing just a bra and panties. After she'd thrown up, she must have passed out in her underwear.

I could tell I'd startled her, because my mom froze for a second over what she was doing at the kitchen table. I could see I'd caught her loading the twenty-gauge. She quickly closed the lever-action, single-shot shotgun, but I saw the shell she'd slipped into the barrel—the gun was loaded. "I heard a varmint," my mother said softly. I knew she was hoping Molly hadn't heard her.

"Ray?" Molly called from the bedroom. My mom just looked at me, cradling the shotgun.

"What are you doing, Ray?" Molly asked, coming into the kitchen.

"Heard a varmint," my mother said; she was whispering.

"I shoot the varmints—give me the gun, Ray," the ski patroller said. My mom hesitated. "Zim isn't your kid—you can't shoot other people's children, Ray," Molly told her.

"If Zim's mother loved him, she would shoot him. And what's the matter with Elmira?" my mom asked me. "You said Elmira was Zim's *main* mother. Why doesn't Elmira shoot him, if she loves him?"

"You can't shoot other people's kids, Ray," the snowcat operator repeated. Molly took the twenty-gauge away from her and unloaded it. "You'd make a mess of a varmint if you shot one with a deer slug," Molly told my mother.

"One shot, just under the patella—you can have a good life with a bad knee, you can still get laid with a limp, and have children, and make friends," my mom told us. Little Ray didn't slip away to their bedroom this time; she was clearly pissed off, and left us in a huff.

I certainly agreed with Molly—as a rule, you shouldn't shoot other people's children. It wasn't lost on me that my mother and Molly seemed to think it was okay to shoot your own children, under certain circumstances, but this didn't seem to be a good time to take up the matter with either of them. Besides, Molly handed me the unloaded shotgun; she wanted me to hide it for her. "Your mom knows me too well, Kid—she knows where I would hide it," the trail groomer told me. "Just remember to tell me where it is after Zim has gone," she added.

The twenty-gauge was unloaded; it was safe to hide it under the futon in the TV room. The way Zimmer was sleeping, I'm not sure he would have woken up if my mother had shot him. Breakfasts in Manchester were not as early in August as they were in the ski season, when we woke up in the darkness. The coffee grinder was always my alarm clock in Vermont. On his back, with his right hand on his heart—as if he were pledging allegiance to the flag—Zim slept as peacefully through the grinding of the coffee beans as he had with his cheek against the frigid window of our wrestling-team bus. A streak of sunlight slanted across his forehead, giving him a godlike or angelic appearance. I was watching him when his eyes opened. Zim woke up to the smell of coffee brewing; at the time, I believed this was a better way to wake up than having a deer slug just under the patella.

My mother didn't speak at breakfast. When she allowed herself to look at Zimmer, her eyes would well with tears; then she immediately looked away. Zim seemed to understand and accept how my mom felt; when she let him, he held her hand. At breakfast, for the most part, Zimmer refrained from talking about the war, but he said one thing that upset my mother—it didn't matter that Zim was trying to reassure her, in his ill-advised and slightly irritating way.

"By the end of this year, I'll bet about fifteen thousand Americans will have died in Vietnam," Zimmer began, "but hundreds of thousands of Vietnamese will be killed." Those statistics would turn out to be fairly accurate, but statistics wouldn't win the Vietnam War or reassure my mother. This time, my mom didn't throw up in the kitchen sink; she just went to her bedroom and closed the door.

I hoped Zim wouldn't discover the twenty-gauge under the futon in the TV room while he packed up his things. Back in the kitchen, where Molly and I hugged him and said our goodbyes, I had a hard time speaking to him. "Take care of yourself, Zim," I barely managed to say.

"I'm supposed to be a second lieutenant—I'm the one who's supposed to take care of my platoon," Zimmer said, with some difficulty.

I could see it surprised him when Molly kissed him on the lips and crushed him in her arms. "Try to take care of yourself, too," the trail groomer told him.

"I'm not saying 'goodbye' to you, Zim—I'm going to hug you and kiss you like crazy when you come *back*!" my mother called to him, from her bedroom. The door was still closed.

"Okay!" Zimmer called to her. I could see he was a little shaken; he didn't know what else to say.

"No, it's *not* okay—it'll *never* be okay!" my mom was wailing. "You're just a boy, you're a little boy! You're still *growing*, Zim!" my mother screamed; then we could hear her sobbing.

To watch Matthew Zimmermann put his few things in the car was a lesson in inessential deliberation. It took him forever to drive away; Zim must have done a dozen single-leg lunges in the driveway before he finally got in the driver's seat. Molly and I were crying as we watched him out the kitchen window.

"You'll never guess where I hid the shotgun," I started to say to Molly, but she stopped me. The ski patroller grabbed my throat, in her big hands—choking me.

"Don't tell me where the twenty-gauge is, Kid," Molly told me. "If you tell me now, I might have enough time to load it and shoot him."

29.

THE GOOD SHEPHERD

Your first loss of a loved one, the first death of someone dear to you—when it happens, the pace of everything changes. In the past, there were times when nothing seemed to be happening. When you lose someone, you're aware of the earth's motion; the world is always moving, always ahead of you. For the rest of your life, you know there are other deaths coming—one after another, yours included.

Matthew Zimmermann turned twenty-five in October 1967. We were the same age when Zim went to Vietnam with the 101st Airborne Division, on December 13 of that year, but I turned twenty-six only five days later. In truth, Zimmer was almost a year younger than I was. As I read in one of the press reports, the news of Lieutenant Matthew Zimmermann's death was carried to his parents' Park Avenue home on a Sunday (February 18, 1968) by a special representative of the secretary of the army. Zim's father, Colonel Thomas Zimmermann, said only that his son was killed in action in Vietnam on February 17, 1968. A more explicit press report, quoting the official telegram of notification, stated that Zim died from "wounds received while on a combat mission when his unit came under hostile small-arms and rocket attack while searching for remains of a missing soldier of his unit." (As Nora later said, this sounded like an official telegram; a lot was left to the imagination.) Knowing Zim's ideas concerning what second lieutenants were supposed to do—a platoon leader was expected to set an example, and to take care of the platoon—I was not surprised to hear how Zim died, search-ing for the body of a missing soldier amid a rocket attack and small-arms fire.

When I called my mother in Manchester, I was a little surprised to hear what the trail groomer told me. "Your mom has shut herself in the bedroom—she's not talking about it," Molly said, not in her usual voice. I could tell she was trying to keep her voice down. "I should have shot him in the driveway, Kid—I had a pretty good angle, out the kitchen window," the ski patroller told me very softly. I knew Molly was trying to protect me from my mother, who not only must have been talking about it; knowing Little

Ray, she probably had a lot to say. "There was nothing obstructing Zim's knees when he was doing the lunges," Molly was saying, more softly, when I heard my mom calling. (My mother might have been in the bedroom, but the door had to be open.)

"Is that my one and only?" I heard my mom ask.

"Better hang up, Kid," Molly whispered to me.

"You should have let me shoot him! *Both* of you are to blame! Zim would be alive if you had let me shoot him!" my mother screamed. "He was just a *boy*—Zim was a little boy! He was still *growing*!" my mom was wailing, again, when Molly hung up the phone.

I read somewhere that daily burial rates at Arlington National Cemetery peaked at twenty-eight in 1967. Zim's burial was described to me in a letter from another Exeter wrestling teammate who was in the military: Zim was buried on a grassy knoll at Arlington, under the same kind of government-issued headstone as the good soldier beside him—Zim's grandfather, General Joseph Zimmermann.

"The big-deal, World War One Zimmermann," the snowshoer had called the general.

"Dear Team," the letter from my Exeter wrestling teammate in the military began, because he was writing to me and the rest of Zim's teammates. He explained to us that it was customary to wait several weeks or months for a funeral service at Arlington; however, in Zimmer's case, the scheduling was "expedited," our teammate told us. (There was the World War II Zimmermann, the colonel, to consider; Zim's grandfather wasn't the only big deal.) Our teammate mentioned the "military chaplain" and a "chapel service"—the "Caisson Platoon" was cited, but I never knew how Zim felt about horses. There'd been a "procession" and a "military band," even a "firing party" and a "rifle volley." I'm guessing it was at Zim's graveside, at Arlington, where a bugler played taps.

Of course they gave Zim a medal; it had been pinned to the flag, which was folded in a certain way (with the medal on top) and then presented to Zim's mother. Our teammate in the military took pains to tell us all this, and he told us there would probably be a "memorial service of some kind—at a later date, in New York."

I'd never met Colonel and Mrs. Zimmermann—only Elmira, the dutiful housekeeper. The memorial, I imagined, was for Zim's New York and New Haven friends—it was also, of course, for friends of the Zimmermann family. So I was more than a little surprised when I was invited, but not at all surprised that the invitation was mailed to me in care of Mr. Barlow at the little English teacher's Exeter address.

Before Zim left for Vietnam, he knew I'd already finished my two years at the Writers' Workshop in Iowa City. I was able to live off the small advance I'd been paid for my first novel—I was still writing the last third of it— because I was living rent-free. Between the snowshoer's faculty apartment in Amen Hall and the oh-so-familiar futon in the TV room of the house my mother shared with Molly, I always had a place to stay—I could, and did, write anywhere.

I could even write in Nora and Em's rat's-ass apartment in New York. If you were walking, it was equidistant from Columbus Circle and Carnegie Hall—in the northeast corner of Hell's Kitchen, near Ninth Avenue and West Fifty-fifth Street. I was welcome to sleep on Nora and Em's couch; I could write on their kitchen table. It was a walk-up apartment, over a bad restaurant that kept changing. It was a bad Greek place when I was finishing my first novel, but it would continue to evolve—it always got worse.

Longhand Man, Nora called me, because I wrote my first novel in notebooks. (Not just the first one.) I type too fast; it's better for me to write novels and screenplays by hand. Em wrote in longhand, too, but for a different reason. Em didn't like typewriters because they were noisy; typewriters were like talking. When Em wrote by hand, she could write quietly; writing, for Em, was like pantomime.

And before Matthew Zimmermann went to Vietnam, he also knew that the snowshoer's parents had offered me what they called a "research job." The little Barlows, a nonstop writing team, believed I would benefit from some exposure to the "adaptation process." *The Kiss in Düsseldorf*, the first of John and Susan Barlow's Nazi-era novels, was being adapted as a movie. The two Barlows were writing the screenplay; they were calling me their "literary assistant." As it would turn out, my "research job" wasn't quite as vague as it sounds. I was supposed to be of assistance to the writing team, and to the film's director. The snowshoer was cynical about my learning anything of *literary* value from his parents, but I was interested in the "adaptation process"; whatever one thought of their writing, the little Barlows were screenwriters, and their director had made some interesting films. The director wasn't an unknown.

So Zim knew, before he went to the war, that I would be living like a nomad for the foreseeable future. All writers are nomads, I would one day believe, but Zimmer knew more than I did; he would even instruct Elmira

to mail my invitation to his memorial in care of Elliot Barlow. Zim had told
Elmira to be sure the snowshoer was invited, too. (But not my mother. Zim
knew my mom wouldn't want to go. She'd told him she wasn't saying goodbye; Zimmer knew my mom only wanted to hug him and kiss him like crazy
if he came back alive.)

The little Barlows had a pied-à-terre in New York, and one in Vienna—
small but comfortable apartments, in both places. When Elmira mailed the
invitation to Zim's memorial to Elliot in Exeter, I happened to be working
with John and Susan in their Vienna apartment. The snowshoer called me
right away, telling me there was a printed invitation to the memorial service for Lieutenant Matthew Zimmermann at St. James' Episcopal Church
on Madison Avenue, between East Seventy-first and East Seventy-second
Streets—only a few blocks south, I knew, of the Zimmermanns' Park Avenue apartment. On the back of the formal invitation was a handwritten
message from Elmira; a "select few" were also invited to a "reception" at the
Zimmermanns' apartment, after the church service. Zim had given his *main*
mother, as he called Elmira, a short list. In the event of his death in Vietnam,
Zim wanted me at his memorial service, together with one of his wrestling
coaches at Exeter—"the small one," Elmira specified. Coach Dearborn had
made Mr. Barlow the lightweights' coach at Exeter; the snowshoer had been
Zim's principal workout partner there.

I really needed a break from the little Barlows and their Nazi storm
troopers—those two SA men who are seen kissing each other during Hitler's
two-and-a-half-hour speech in Düsseldorf in 1932. Those Sturmabteilung
guys, the two kissers, were John and Susan Barlow's main characters; one
of them murders the other. Soon the kissing killer is murdering more storm
troopers. I had some empathy for these fictional characters—even for the
murderer, but especially for his first victim. Their historical counterparts
were less sympathetic. Rudolf Hess and Ernst Röhm—they were actual SA
guys. As Uncle Johan had first informed me, Röhm was co-founder and a
leader of the Sturmabteilung. (It was Uncle Martin who'd told me Röhm was
wounded on the Western Front, where he'd lost a piece of his nasal bone.)
My principal "research job" for *The Kiss in Düsseldorf* was to view hours and
hours of archival footage, everything from newsreels to propaganda films.
The director wanted me to find early footage of Hess, Röhm, and Martin
Bormann from before they were Nazis. They were Freikorps guys originally,
as Uncle Martin had said. Right-wing nationalists, Uncle Johan called the
Freikorps. Uncle Martin said Hitler had Röhm killed because Röhm was a

homosexual, but Hitler had targeted other Freikorps guys for execution—including Röhm. (In a speech to the Reichstag, Hitler had implied that the Freikorps were enemies of the state.)

The director of *The Kiss in Düsseldorf* had been born in Philadelphia, but he thought of himself as an émigré; he said his parents were Russian Jews who were wise to get out of Russia and come to America from Europe. He knew a lot more about Nazis than I did. He wanted film of Hess, Röhm, and Bormann when they were young men—"even if they're so young that we don't recognize them," the director told me. He was a great guy; I really liked him. His idea was to intercut the archival footage of future Nazis with the fictional characters and their made-up story. He wanted me to find—on the youthful faces of these right-wing nationalists in the Freikorps—"some indication of their intrinsic intolerance, their xenophobic hatred of others." (The Freikorps were anti-communist, and they seemed to have some anti-Slavic racism going for them; the ones who later became Nazis took to the ideology of anti-Semitism and ethnic cleansing rather naturally.)

As for the elderly and crippled projectionist who screened the hours (and hours) of archival footage for me, he was the right age to have been a Nazi. The director and I were convinced that he had to have been a participant. The projectionist not only recognized Hess, Röhm, and Bormann when they were too young to look like the monsters they would become, but when they appeared onscreen, he stood and saluted them. During the lengthier screenings, the elderly projectionist was inclined to detach his prosthetic leg, which he bent at the knee before he placed it on an adjacent chair. As a result, when we were viewing the longer archival films, the projectionist stood and saluted Hess, Röhm, and Bormann on one leg.

The Freikorps guys weren't my only "research job" for the little Barlows. There was archival film of Hitler's speech to the Industry Club in Düsseldorf in 1932—these industrial magnates included many of Germany's wealthiest men. In their screenplay, the writing team was very clear concerning how they wanted the speech to be used. We see Hitler assuring the Industry Club that National Socialism would be good for business, but there is no sound; while we watch Hitler speak, we hear (as voice-over) the mundane conversation of the two SA men who are lovers.

Conversely, when the camera is showing us the kissing storm troopers—for two and a half hours, the SA lovers pay no attention to Hitler's speech—we are hearing Hitler's voice-over, the most confounding and ominous excerpts I could find. My German was (and is) terrible. I had an English translation of the Düsseldorf speech, and the infinite willingness of the one-legged projectionist, who showed me the two and a half hours—again and again. Occasionally, I called Uncle Johan for help—when I couldn't understand the German or the English translation. For example, when Hitler says, "But if a Weltanschauung cannot be applied to every sphere of a people's life, that fact in itself is sufficient proof of its weakness," I was lost.

"It's not a translation problem, Adam," Uncle Johan assured me. "It's Hitler's anti-democracy thing; it's a totalitarian argument. Hitler believed there was a conflict between the principle of democracy and the principle of authority—he was an authoritarian, he *hated* democracy!"

"You should be the Barlows' literary assistant," I told Uncle Johan, but he gave me a pep talk—as he used to do when I was a child. Uncle Johan made me feel guilty for not appreciating the opportunity the little Barlows had given me. I was learning about another kind of storytelling. My first novel, which I was still completing, was also a historical novel. I would be paid to adapt that novel as a screenplay; although the movie was never made, I would learn something from that process, too.

Uncle Johan was right about the little Barlows, and he was right about Hitler. As for "the principle of democracy," Hitler labeled it "the principle of destruction"; Hitler equated what he called "the principle of authority" with "the principle of achievement." In Düsseldorf, when Hitler said, "Internationalism and democracy are inseparable conceptions," he meant they were both bad ideas. (This appeared to go over well with the German industrialists.)

While the two Sturmabteilung guys are flirting with each other, but before their fatal kiss, I found a passage from Hitler's speech that the director chose to use as voice-over—when Hitler pontificates, "I am of the opinion that there is nothing which has been produced by the will of man which cannot in its turn be altered by another human will." The Industry Club of Düsseldorf must have loved that.

"Music to the ears of businessmen!" Uncle Johan shouted, reciting the chosen voice-over from the Düsseldorf speech—as Johan was wont to do—in German and in English.

The director also liked and used a shorter excerpt I showed him from Hitler's National Socialist sales pitch to the industrial magnates. When the storm troopers are kissing and groping each other, Hitler's voice-over is in German with English subtitles: "Life in practical activity is founded on the importance of personality." In the context of what is happening onscreen, and what will follow, I'm guessing the juxtaposition of Hitler's off-the-wall remark playing over the kissing SA men gave the director the lunatic dissonance he was looking for.

One of the kissers would kill the other one; the murderer would keep killing other storm troopers. One-liners from Hitler's Industry Club speech would work as voice-over for the first two murders. When the storm trooper shoots his lover, Hitler's voice-over—referring to "the superiority of the white race"—is the only sound. When the murderer strangles the next storm trooper, we hear Hitler's voice asserting "the right to organize the rest of the world."

This was arguably more effective in the film than it had been in the little Barlows' political thriller, but Elliot Barlow had disparaged his parents' writing—"overkill," he'd called it—and the snowshoer wouldn't like the movie of *The Kiss in Düsseldorf* much better.

"Mord, mehr Morde, noch mehr Morde!" Uncle Johan had once raved about the little Barlows' murder novels. ("Murder, more murders, still more murders!" my uncle had declared; he'd been praising the murder-writing team, of course.)

But Johan had made me feel guilty for failing to appreciate the opportunity the little Barlows had given me, and I felt more guilty for how relieved I was when the snowshoer called me to tell me about the invitation. John and Susan Barlow were generous to me; I knew they would let me go to New York for Zim's memorial. I'd given them the excerpts they wanted from Hitler's speech in Düsseldorf. I'd found the archival footage the director was looking for—or at least what we imagined was the "intrinsic intolerance" and the "xenophobic hatred of others" on the youthful faces of those right-wing nationalists in the Freikorps. The writing team and the director of *The Kiss in Düsseldorf* didn't need me anymore; yet I felt guilty for using Zim's death, and his memorial service, as an excuse to quit a job I was simply tired of.

"Cynical characters, bleak nonendings," Elliot Barlow had said of his parents' Nazi-era novels and their Cold War novels. Now I knew firsthand what the snowshoer meant; the über-noir of *The Kiss in Düsseldorf* was getting me down. When I left Vienna for New York, I also felt guilty that I was looking forward to the memorial service for Matthew Zimmermann—2LT US ARMY VIETNAM, as his headstone in Arlington had been marked. I felt guiltiest, of course, for my small hands—my multiple finger injuries, my many extensor- and flexor-tendon surgeries. My little hands had saved me from the war in Vietnam, where Zim had died.

The snowshoer said he was taking the train to New York. It took forever to take the train from Exeter to Boston, and then from Boston to New York, but the little English teacher didn't want to drive; he had student essays to read, and blue books to grade. "I can work on the train," he said. We would take the train together, back to Exeter from New York. I would have my writing notebook with me; I didn't care how long the train took. We would stay at the little Barlows' pied-à-terre in New York. The writing team's apartment was on East Sixty-fourth Street, between Lexington and Third Avenues, on the Upper East Side. We could walk to the church and the Zimmermanns' Park Avenue apartment from there; it sure beat staying at Nora and Em's.

We knew St. James' was an Episcopal church, but the snowshoer thought it had a Catholic-looking spire—a beautiful church with arches and a vaulted ceiling. On a sunny afternoon in late March, the stained-glass windows were brightly shining. The place was packed, but there wasn't much of a military presence. Of course there were soldiers in uniform around, but the soldiers weren't part of the service. No bugler played taps; the recessional hymn was a rousing one, about the resurrection to eternal life. The priest's readings from the Bible were strictly from the New Testament, beginning with one from Romans: "I consider that the sufferings of this present time are not worth comparing to the glory that is to be revealed to us." I stole a look at Elliot and saw that he took no comfort from this, nor did we feel more comforted by the priest's efforts to throw himself full-tilt into First Corinthians—that strained, overreaching passage about Christ, how he'd been raised from the dead.

As First Corinthians says: "For as by a man came death, by a man has come also the resurrection of the dead." I could see the little English teacher thinking: *What an awkward sentence!* Or so I imagined, while the priest ventured into even more abstract territory.

Since this service, I have stayed away from Second Corinthians. There are certain mystical generalizations that simply don't apply to young men killed in wars—such as, "we look not to the things that are seen but to the things that are unseen; for the things that are seen are transient, but the things that are unseen are eternal." The snowshoer and I just looked at each other; then we had to look away. We didn't want to think of Zim as *transient*.

There was a final prayer, of course, but I blocked most of it out—all I really remember is the sound all of us made when we knelt on the kneeling pads. "'Into thy hands, O merciful Savior, we commend thy servant Matthew Zimmermann,'" the priest read from The Book of Common Prayer, but I was determined not to listen; nothing in the memorial service had anything to do with Zim. Yet fragments of the final prayer remain—"'into the blessed rest of everlasting peace, and into the glorious company of the saints in light,'" the priest prayed on. Then the recessional hymn came crashing down upon us—more assurances of the resurrection of the dead—and Mr. Barlow and I were walking north on Madison Avenue, making our way to the reception at the Zimmermanns' Park Avenue apartment.

"'I am the good shepherd,'" Elliot Barlow was reciting, from the Gospel according to John. "'The good shepherd lays down his life for the sheep,'" the snowshoer recited. We both felt that the priest should have read this bit from the Gospel according to John. It at least sounded like the duties a good second lieutenant would risk his life to uphold. We both believed Zim had been a good shepherd.

It was a Sunday in New York—March 24, 1968. A week later, President Johnson announced that he would not seek reelection. Four days after LBJ's announcement that he wasn't going to run again, Martin Luther King Jr. was assassinated in Memphis. Only two months later, Bobby Kennedy would be shot to death in Los Angeles. But that Sunday in New York, the snowshoer and I already had the feeling that it was a little after midnight in America. Nora said the war in Vietnam wasn't the only thing that was going off the rails. At the end of August that year, there were tens of thousands of protesters in Chicago during the Democratic National Convention. Our fellow liberal Democrats wanted McCarthy, but Humphrey would be nominated. Many of the protesters were beaten by the police; Chicago looked like a police state. After the convention, Nora went around reciting a headline from *The Washington Post*—McCarthy was refusing to support Humphrey, or something like that. *Don't bother to read the article*, Em pantomimed. Nixon would win the election; there would be four more years of our guys in combat, seven more years of the war in Vietnam.

That Sunday in New York, in March 1968, I was twenty-six. I was young and naïve enough to say to Mr. Barlow that I hoped our country would never again be as divided as it was right then; what I meant, of course, was that we couldn't possibly be more divided as a country than we already were. I would be wrong. Elliot Barlow, as always, was kind to me—he never put me down.

"I hope so, too, Adam," the snowshoer said. "But we'll just have to wait and see."

Then we arrived at the Zimmermanns' apartment building, where the doorman showed us to the elevator and Elmira let us in. "Adam, you know where the colonel's bedroom is—please put your coats there," the housekeeper told me brusquely when I kissed her cheek; she'd been crying and was trying not to cry again. "And you must be Matthew's wrestling coach—the little one," Elmira said to the snowshoer.

"I'm Elliot Barlow," Mr. Barlow said. At Exeter, I was used to the unspoken understanding that the snowshoer was my stepfather, although he was the only father I'd known, and a good one; I never let the *stepfather* label pass without clarification.

"Officially, Mr. Barlow is my stepfather," I told Elmira. The housekeeper was leading us down a hallway to the colonel's barracks, as if she didn't trust me to remember the whereabouts of his solitary sleeping quarters. "But I never met my biological father," I was saying, as I was in the habit of doing whenever the word *stepfather* came up. "I know that Mr. Barlow is the best father I could have had," I told Zim's faithful family housekeeper.

In retrospect, this wasn't the smartest or the most stabilizing thing I could have said to Elmira, who'd been more than a second mom to Zim—she'd been his *main* mother. Elmira, who'd been holding herself together, broke down in the colonel's bedroom. She suddenly grabbed that photo of Zim, when he was a toddler, not yet in uniform—when Zim was tightly holding one of the officers' caps, either his grandfather's or his father's.

"Matthew was my only baby—I had no babies of my own!" Elmira cried, showing the photo of Zim as a child to Mr. Barlow. I felt responsible for her unraveling. My calling Elliot Barlow the best father I could have had—what bad timing. This made Elmira sense that her character was of a kindred nature to the snowshoer's. She wasn't wrong—she was just overwrought. "He knows how I feel!" Elmira said, sobbing; she seized the little snowshoer in her arms, hugging him to her big chest. I was afraid she would drop the photo of Zim, which I took from her trembling hand.

I'd been surprised to see Elmira snatch the photo from the colonel's night table. Someone had moved the photo from the top of the small chest of drawers, where it once stood at attention alongside the photographs of General Zimmermann and Colonel Zimmermann. The colonel must have moved Zim's picture closer to him. I returned Zim's photo to the exact spot on the night table where I'd seen the housekeeper grab it—the edge of the night table closest to the colonel's bed. The photo faced the colonel's pillow. His young son's face, in the light of the alarm clock, must have been the last face the colonel saw before he fell asleep; his young son's face, under the arching gooseneck lamp, must have been the first face the colonel saw when he woke up.

The way Elmira went on hugging Mr. Barlow, I was worried that he couldn't breathe. Then I realized the two of them were talking about the Picasso that wasn't a real Picasso. "I've heard about it," Elliot was saying. "Naturally, I would love to see it," the snowshoer said. But Elmira wasn't ready to let the little English teacher go.

"It wouldn't matter to me, if you peed on it—I keep wishing someone would *steal* it," the housekeeper told Mr. Barlow. "But as long as the painting is here, everyone is supposed to make an effort not to pee on it," Elmira was saying, when we all heard someone call her name.

"Coming!" the housekeeper called. Before someone had summoned her, we'd heard no voices, not even the murmur of quiet conversation. It was either a small reception or a silent one, or both, Mr. Barlow and I were thinking—when Elmira left us in the colonel's bathroom with the painting of the three-breasted nude.

"Two breasts should be enough," we heard Elmira mutter to herself in the hall.

The snowshoer was appalled by the painting. "This is the kind of thing only a novel can make credible," the little English teacher told me. He asked me to remind him why the Zimmermanns slept in separate bedrooms.

"She snores, he farts," I reminded him.

"The three breasts would do it for me," the snowshoer said.

The living room and dining room of the penthouse apartment were one big room, designed for entertaining. The dining-room table, piled with food, had attracted only the younger people; there were only three. Yalies, I presumed—probable Bonesmen, I knew Elliot was thinking. At opposite ends of a long sofa, two women in mourning sat as still as stones. The older one—small but fat, to use Zimmer's words—was surely Zim's mother, her face hidden in a black veil. People approached her and bowed to her, saying nothing. Occasionally, someone touched her hand. The other woman on the sofa, the younger one, was Zim's fiancée. His engagement had been mentioned in his obituary in *The New York Times;* it was there I'd learned her name. Francine DeCourcey—of New York and Paris, the newspaper had said without further explanation. "She's *French!*" my mother had cried on the phone to me, before handing the phone to Molly and shutting herself in the bedroom.

"What is *that* about?" I'd asked Molly.

"Don't ask me, Kid," the snowcat operator had said.

Small and thin, Francine DeCourcey sat on her far end of the sofa. No one came near her; perhaps no one dared.

A group of women around Zim's mother's age huddled together, discreetly whispering, or not speaking at all. A group of men in uniform had also formed, and they were talking in subdued tones. Whatever their subject was, they seemed to be in agreement about it, and whatever it was, they seemed angry about it. For this occasion, would Colonel Zimmermann be in uniform, or was it the protocol for retired military men to wear civilian clothes? The snowshoer and I didn't know. The soldiers in uniform were older men. We did not see any younger ones. Were there no young men from Lieutenant Matthew Zimmermann's platoon? And we didn't see someone who might have been Colonel Zimmermann among the military men.

What were they talking about? Mr. Barlow and I were wondering. We'd seen some scruffy-looking people gathered outside the apartment building—not near the front entrance, where they would have attracted the doorman's attention, but near an alley alongside the building. Anti-war protesters, the snowshoer and I had first imagined. But at the family home of a fallen soldier? We thought not.

Mr. Barlow was brave enough to bow to Mrs. Zimmermann, and to touch her unmoving hand. I did the same. But Elliot was hesitant to approach the fiancée. It was a very long sofa, and the motionless Francine DeCourcey seemed far, far away. She looked shattered; she looked as if she might continue breaking apart if you so much as spoke to her. Especially if you lied to her, I was imagining—if I told her, for example, that Zim had never stopped talking about her. Francine DeCourcey looked so sad, I was thinking of lying to her—just to say something. I'm guessing she noticed me because I must have been wringing my hands.

"Are you Adam?" she suddenly asked me; she patted the sofa cushion beside her. "Come sit here," Francine said. She had a French name, but she didn't have a French accent. "Give me your hands," she told me, when I was sitting next to her. I knew she wasn't interested in a palm reading. Zim had probably told her about my damaged hands, my 4-F trigger finger. She knew my hands had been my ticket out of Vietnam. Her fingers traced the ropey scar tissue from the flexor-tendon surgeries in my palms. "If Matthew had your hands . . ." Francine started to say, her voice just stopping. She'd seen the snowshoer hovering between the two mourners on the long sofa. "Is that Matthew's little wrestling coach?" Francine whispered to me.

"Yes, his name is Elliot," I whispered, beckoning Mr. Barlow to join us. I refrained from repeating the stepfather-but-not-a-stepfather saga.

When the snowshoer was sitting between us on the sofa, Francine

DeCourcey put one hand on his chin, turning him to face her, as if Mr. Barlow were a beloved but disobedient child. "When I first met Matthew, he was almost as small as you," she said.

"He was almost as small as me when I met him—I know," Mr. Barlow told her.

"I *know*!" Francine DeCourcey cried. "But why did he keep growing? If he'd stayed as small as you, they wouldn't have taken him, would they?"

"They wouldn't take me for Korea—I know," the little English teacher told her.

"You *see*? It's just so *unfair*! I could have *loved* him, if he'd just stopped growing," Francine said to the snowshoer. "I could have *loved* him, if he'd had your hands," she told me, reaching across Elliot's lap, again taking hold of my damaged hands. I imagined then that Francine DeCourcey had the highest aspirations for her love of Matthew Zimmermann. I thought of the photo of Zim as a child, now on the colonel's night table. I added Francine's aspirations for her love of Zim to the weight of the expectations Zimmer had grown up with. It amounted to a crushing weight.

Though I failed to recognize him at first, it was the former Yale 130-pounder who rescued the snowshoer and me from the end of the long sofa, where Zim's fiancée had no intention of letting us escape. "Weren't you the Pitt one-thirty at West Point?" the Yalie asked me. "Zimmer said you were going to kill me—Zim could almost kill me, so I believed him," the former wrestler said. I'd first seen him at the weigh-ins; he'd been stripped to his jock at West Point. Of course I hadn't recognized him here in a coat and tie. When he extended his hand to me, and I shook it, he pulled me to my feet. He quickly performed the same rescue procedure on Mr. Barlow. "And *you* must be Zimmer's wrestling coach, from Exeter—the workout partner who killed him in practice every day, Zim told me," the Yale wrestler said. "These two guys haven't met the other guys, Francine," the Yale 130-pounder said to Zim's bereaved fiancée. It was apparent that they knew each other; the cold dislike that passed between them seemed permanent and mutual.

The former Yale wrestler wouldn't have made weight at 130 pounds, but, like me, he hadn't really grown very much since that tournament at Army where we didn't wrestle each other. Zimmer was the one who'd kept growing. The snowshoer, of course, had somehow stopped growing—years ago. The Yale 130-pounder introduced us to the two other young Yale men who were standing around. "This guy was Bartleby's teammate at Exeter, and the smaller one was Bartleby's coach and workout partner," the former 130-pounder said.

"Bartleby," Elliot Barlow repeated. The snowshoer and I knew the Bonesmen had nicknames. We'd not known what Zim's nickname was; we didn't know if a Bonesman's nickname was supposed to be a secret. I just remembered that Zimmer had asked me not to call him Bartleby; it was clearly not a name he liked.

"Zimmer asked me not to call him Bartleby," I told the three Bonesmen.

"Was Bartleby your nickname for Zim?" Mr. Barlow asked them.

"Zim, Zimmer—you wrestlers have your own nicknames," one of the Bonesmen snidely said to the Yale 130-pounder. I empathized with my fellow wrestler, who seemed to be caught in the middle of a conflict of nicknames. Did the Bonesmen know Zim had hated being called Bartleby?

"I think Zim would have *preferred not to* be called Bartleby," the Yale 130-pounder told the snowshoer and me. I believe he meant this sincerely; he may have been apologizing, also sincerely. The former Yale wrestler definitely wasn't trying to be funny, but the other two Bonesmen laughed. The two who laughed definitely thought it was funny that Matthew Zimmermann would have *preferred not to* be called Bartleby.

"Fuck you two, and your secrets," the little English teacher suddenly told the two Bonesmen who'd laughed. The Yale 130-pounder was definitely feeling caught in the middle of something now.

What the snowshoer had suddenly shown me was an instinct he'd almost managed to hide in his faculty apartment in an all-boys' dormitory. Elliot Barlow had an interior mischief, an instinct for confrontation—not only a need to express himself as who he was, but to do so purposely, even at some real or imagined risk to himself. It was insufficient for Mr. Barlow to dress himself as a woman in the privacy of his apartment, or to venture out (as a woman) into downtown Exeter in the late-at-night or early-morning hours. This simply did not say, not strongly enough, who he was. It was necessary for the woman inside him to show herself to people who were predisposed to desire her—the very people who would hate her, and try to hurt her, for being who and what she was.

In the case of the two Bonesmen who thought it was funny that Zim hated being called Bartleby, or even that Zim regretted belonging to Bones, it was clear that the snowshoer had willfully provoked them. The little English teacher had known he was picking a fight. It was also clear that the Yale 130-pounder wanted no part of a matchup with me or Mr. Barlow; the former wrestler had been forewarned. Zim had told the Yale wrestler that I could kill him—and the 130-pounder also knew that Mr. Barlow had regularly killed Zim in practice.

But the other two Bonesmen weren't wrestlers; I could see they were sizing up the snowshoer as someone too small to be taken seriously—a big mistake. The former Yale wrestler could also see what his two pals were thinking. "Just don't," he told them.

The Bonesman who hadn't spoken, the one who'd only laughed, spoke to me—not to Elliot Barlow. "You should tell your little squirt of a wrestling coach to go fuck himself," the heretofore-nonspeaking Bonesman said.

"I would prefer not to," the snowshoer said, in the respectful but willfully irritating way the original Bartleby had spoken. I saw that the little English teacher had staggered his stance, his right foot ahead of his left, his weight on the balls of his feet, which he kept moving, and his knees were bent. Mr. Barlow, I knew, was one single-leg lunge away from a high crotch or an inside trip or a freight-train double.

"Oh, shit," I heard the Yale 130-pounder say.

That was when Elmira interrupted the standoff. I hadn't seen the housekeeper, or where she'd come from, but she was suddenly standing beside the snowshoer and me. Her arms were folded on her big bosom as she stared down the Bonesmen; Elmira's contempt for the Yalies was as evident as the dislike they'd earned from Francine DeCourcey. "Adam, if you and Mr. Barlow can lend me a hand—in the kitchen—there's something we need to carry outdoors," the housekeeper told us.

"Outdoors," Elliot Barlow repeated. Like a good wrestler, his feet never stopped moving, and his eyes were steadfast in their focus—staring at the sternum of the Bonesman who was of the opinion that the snowshoer should go fuck himself.

"It's windy outdoors," Elmira added, hooking arms with the little English teacher, and with me. "Let's go get your coats." She steered us along the hall to the colonel's quarters, where I was glad to see again that photo the colonel had moved closer to him—the one of Zim as a toddler in an officer's cap. It spoke well of the colonel that he wanted his dear son nearer to him, where the colonel could keep an eye on him—where the colonel slept, where the colonel dreamed.

"Where *is* the colonel?" I asked Elmira, when the snowshoer and I were putting on our coats.

"You'll see," the housekeeper said, sighing. She led us along the hall—

this time, to the kitchen. It was closed off from the dining room by two tall swinging doors, the way kitchens designed for servants often are. Two ovens, two refrigerators, two sinks—countertops, everywhere you looked. A service elevator opened into the kitchen. "The colonel has already taken the soup pot and the ladle—the rest is for us to take down," Elmira said, sighing again.

"Down," the snowshoer repeated, staring at the service elevator. There were sandwiches piled on a platter on one of the countertops—the same sandwiches we'd seen on the dining-room table. There were paper plates and paper bowls and paper napkins and plastic spoons on a second platter.

A third platter was empty. The housekeeper told us it was necessary—to prevent the paper and plastic stuff from blowing away in the wind. "I'll carry the empty platter," Elmira told us, picking it up. She'd already put on a wool jacket. I took the platter of sandwiches; Elliot was in charge of the paper and plastic stuff.

"Oh, boy—a picnic," the snowshoer said.

"You'll see—it's not exactly a picnic," Elmira told him, as we got into the service elevator. On the ground floor of the apartment building, the elevator opened into an area where the garbage and trash were separated and collected.

In the alley beside the building, where the refuse was picked up and taken away, Mr. Barlow and I recognized the scruffy-looking bunch of wanderers we'd noticed before; they were not, as we'd first imagined, anti-war protesters. They were the homeless people, the drug addicts, the strays and castoffs of humankind—just a few of the poor souls Zim had tried to help.

"There are only seven of them—I thought there would be more," Elmira said; she sounded disappointed. "They came to mourn Matthew, not for a handout," the housekeeper wanted us to know. "But Mrs. Zimmermann wouldn't let them in—they were not invited—and the colonel couldn't leave them unfed or unattended." Elmira sounded neutral about this. It wasn't clear what the housekeeper would have done, if left to her own devices. Would Elmira have let in the strays and the castoffs, or would she have left them unfed and unattended?

Mr. Barlow was offering the paper bowls and the paper plates; no one wanted a napkin, but the seven lost souls all took a plastic spoon. A dignified-looking older gentleman clenched the spoon in his teeth, like the stem of a pipe. He'd once been well dressed but was now disheveled. His gray flannel trousers had lost their crease; his tweed jacket, one with leather elbow patches, sagged off his shoulders. His button-down, pinstriped shirt was soiled and untucked; he'd not changed his clothes for days, even weeks, but an aura of dignity remained as attached to him as the full beard on his face. The gentleman purposely moved to the rear of the line that had formed for the soup. He may have been setting an example of good manners for the others, or the way he kept drinking from the flask in the side pocket of the tweed jacket had diminished his appetite. His sips from the flask required an unusual kind of coordination and dexterity; he would part his lips just enough to admit entrance to the short neck of the flask, while he kept his teeth tightly closed on the plastic spoon.

Colonel Zimmermann gripped the handles of the soup pot with a pair of pot holders. Elmira was ladling out the soup. She'd given the empty platter to the snowshoer, and had shown him how to use it to protect the paper and plastic stuff from the wind. "You must be Matthew's little wrestling coach!" the colonel had hailed Mr. Barlow. "Was it Korea, where they wouldn't take you?" he asked.

"Yes, sir—I was too small," Elliot answered him.

"Good for you!" the colonel said. "And you must be Adam, the wrestler who's going to be a writer," he said to me. "Does that trigger finger give you any trouble when you're writing?" he asked.

"No, sir—no trouble," I told him.

"Attaboy!" the colonel said. Whether or not he'd dressed according to military protocol for a retired colonel, I had no idea, but Zim's father was appropriately dressed for a memorial service; he wore a black business suit and a black necktie with a white dress shirt. A star-shaped medal of considerable distinction hung around the colonel's neck; the medal's weight prevented his necktie from flapping in the March wind. A cluster of other medals and military insignia decorated one breast of his suit jacket, giving him a lopsided appearance. The brightly colored ribbons, the glitter of gold and silver, marked Colonel Zimmermann as a man of undoubted bravery and distinguished service. He was so fit-looking, small but strong, the colonel seemed of indeterminate age. I'm guessing he would have been in his sixties, possibly in his early seventies—definitely closer to Uncle Martin's or Uncle Johan's ages than to my mother's. (Zim had only said of his parents that they were older.) In any case, the colonel was at work without a coat—with only his medals to keep him warm, or perhaps the steaming soup pot also warmed him.

"Fernando," the colonel suddenly said, not sharply but firmly. "Stop that."

"Stop what, sir?" a young man in the soup line asked, politely and with seeming innocence. At a glance, he was a good-looking guy with a bad tattoo.

"You know what," Colonel Zimmermann told him good-naturedly. The others in line gave Fernando their universally disapproving appraisals; they knew what he'd been doing. I'd seen nothing; I'd begun by offering sandwiches at the front of the soup line. A middle-aged woman took too many sandwiches; she had trouble balancing her soup bowl and her paper plate.

"You can come back for seconds, Mary—you don't need to take every sandwich in sight," Elmira said to her.

"Ya nevah know, Elmira—there are opportunities that don't come again," Mary informed the housekeeper with biblical authority. Mary promptly ate all of one sandwich, but she yielded her position to the boy in line behind her. Then it was the boy's turn to take as many sandwiches off my platter as he could hold.

"For God's sake, Felix," was all Elmira said.

"Attaboy, Felix," the colonel encouraged him. Felix was a nice-looking kid, except for a birthmark or a burn scar on his forehead; the boy's floppy bangs only partially concealed this blemish. Felix was too young a kid to be safely on his own. I imagined he must be a runaway, as Buddy had been.

Elmira had made no mention of Buddy. I'd immediately looked for Buddy, of course, but did not find her in the soup line. There was one young woman, certainly an underage girl, who at first reminded me of Buddy, with the same air of outer calm but inner mayhem about her. She was in line in front of Fernando. When I offered her the sandwiches, she was too shy to look at me; she took only one sandwich.

"Take more, Lucy—ya nevah take enough of nothin'," Fernando said to her, but Lucy shook her head. When she smiled at me, her lips parted only slightly. I had the impression that Lucy might have been missing some teeth, because she wouldn't open her mouth to take a bite of her sandwich while I was standing in front of her.

I moved on to Fernando, who helped himself to three or four sandwiches. "I'm takin' more for Lucy—she's gonna want more; she always does," Fernando told me. "Ya don't know the difference between what ya want and what ya don't—ya nevah do," he said to Lucy, who was vigorously chewing. She'd almost finished her one sandwich, but I still hadn't seen her open her mouth. I moved on.

Next in line, a young Black couple hadn't stopped whispering to each other. They clung together fearfully—as if they were being hunted, or they'd been betrayed—but I knew their story. Zim had written me about them. Not long before Zimmer left for Vietnam, the young man had been sent home from the war. Elmira had discovered that, in his absence, there was no one looking after his younger sister. The girl had managed to "get herself pregnant"—the unlikely way the housekeeper had described the pregnancy to Zim.

The way Zim had described the situation to the colonel was that "a kid was expecting a kid," and there would be no one to look after the young mother or her child if Colonel Zimmermann didn't "pull some strings" and bring the older brother back from combat. While it was highly unlikely that the younger sister had managed to *get herself pregnant*, the colonel did *pull some strings;* the older brother was brought home and relieved of further military obligations. The young man was endeavoring to look after his pregnant sister, as best he could. Elmira would help them, Zim had written me. What was not helping the young pair was their whispering to each other, because the whispering concerned the identity of the baby's father. The brother wanted to know who'd knocked up his baby sister. The sister, wisely, wouldn't say who it was.

Elmira (and the colonel, of course) had told the brother to let it go. It wouldn't help him, or his sister, if he knew who the baby's father was. "It'll only make more trouble," the housekeeper had told the brother. His sister didn't need to be told.

Their parents had abandoned them, Zim wrote me. The brother was Talib and his sister was Ayla.

"The only thing that matters, Talib, is that *you* aren't that baby's father, and we all know you aren't," Elmira had told him.

"Nothin' *that* bad happened, Talib—that's all you need to know," Ayla had said. But Talib was obsessed. *Who did it?* he kept asking. Talib whispered names. He named his high school friends—as if they were the only ones who could have done it, knowing Talib was away. "Are you kiddin', Talib?" Ayla whispered back to him.

Thanking me, Talib took two egg salad sandwiches; with one of the sandwiches, he pointed to his pregnant sister. "She's got mornin' sickness—just thinkin' about eggs makes her puke," Talib told me.

"Just you pointin' at me with those eggs makes me think about pukin', Talib," Ayla told him.

"I don't think there are any eggs in the soup," I said to her, trying to move on—not wanting to hold the platter of egg salad sandwiches in front of her.

"Thank you—I'll wait and see what's in the soup," Ayla said.

"I don't know why they call it *mornin' sickness*—the pukin' part isn't limited to the mornin'," Talib was saying.

"Not everyone needs to know everythin' about somethin', Talib," Ayla whispered to him.

"Not everyone, Ayla, manages to get herself pregnant—not even the Virgin Mary acted entirely alone," Talib whispered back to her. I moved on. Anyone seeing them would have thought they were an attractive young couple. A tall, slender young man with his hair cut short and wearing military fatigues—in Talib's case, the fatigues were his working clothes, not a costume—and a pretty young woman who was noticeably pregnant.

"If you're going to keep doing that, Fernando, you'll have to move away from Lucy," Colonel Zimmermann said. I saw that Fernando was dry-humping Lucy from behind. I just offered the sandwiches to the older gentleman, who seemed indifferent to eating or the humping.

"I'm sorry, Colonel," Fernando said; he sounded sincere, but his bad tattoo told another story. It was a sailor's tattoo—a tall ship's mast ran up one side of his neck, reaching to his temple. But the ship's mast was only the background of what was also a true-love tattoo. On Fernando's cheek was a heart, pierced by a dagger. The pommel of the dagger was a dark knob under Fernando's eye, the hilt stood parallel to his nose, and the blade crossed his chin, the tip touching his throat. The true love's name, written in small capitals on the bleeding heart, was not LUCY—she was someone Fernando had fooled around with, before Lucy. As tattoo artists know, a true-love tattoo lasts longer than many true loves.

"You're not doing anything to *encourage* Fernando, are you, Lucy?" Colonel Zimmermann asked the girl. With her lips tightly closed, she shook her head, but I could see that Lucy's denial was met with disbelief by the others in the soup line—not to mention by Elmira.

"You *are* encouraging Fernando, Lucy—I've seen you be encouraging to him," the housekeeper said.

"Lucy, go stand beside Adam—he's got the sandwiches," Colonel Zimmermann told her. The girl complied with downcast eyes—not looking at me, or at the sandwiches. The older gentleman was looking at me—not at the sandwiches.

"Not especially hungry today, Professor?" Colonel Zimmermann asked the dignified-looking gentleman.

"Not especially hungry *every* day, Colonel," the professor answered. I'd noticed that his flask was empty. He kept uncapping it and lifting it to his lips, where he tilted it, but there was nothing left in the flask—only fumes, I imagined. "And *you*—your name is Adam, and you're going to be a *writer?*" the professor asked me. The snowshoer would tell me later that I'd failed to understand the Em-like pantomime the colonel was performing with the soup pot; his gyrations and contorted facial expressions were intended to forewarn me not to speak of *publishing* my writing to the alcoholic professor. But I misinterpreted Colonel Zimmermann—I thought he'd burned himself with some spilled soup. I explained to the older, academic-looking gentleman that I'd received an advance for my first novel, which I was still writing. The novel would be published by Random House when I finished it, I said.

"Random House—not exactly a small-press publication!" the professor exclaimed, stumbling out of the soup line. "And they've paid you an *advance!*" he cried, the plastic spoon snapping in his clenched teeth and the paper bowl and paper plate falling from his outstretched hands, like the hands of a supplicant, or of someone praying. "Random House!" the professor repeated. That was when Lucy licked my face. I was too surprised to react right away, and I still had both hands on the sandwich platter. Lucy began by licking my cheek, then my ear, then the side of my neck.

"Stop licking him, Lucy—you don't even *know* him!" the colonel said. This time, he spoke sharply.

"You *see?* That's what she does—she don't know what she means, she don't know she's bein' *encouragin'*," Fernando said.

"You can't lick men and *not* encourage them, Lucy," Colonel Zimmermann advised her, more gently.

"It's disgusting, Lucy," Elmira added.

"She don't mean nothin' by it," Fernando tried to assure us. Lucy smiled. Nothing was meant by her smile, I was thinking, but her lips were parted. I could see the gaps where her teeth had been.

"He's publishing a first novel," the professor was saying to himself; he was shuffling away from us, leaving the alley. Lucy's licking was of no more concern to him than the humping.

"It's a historical novel—I don't think anyone will read it. It was just a small advance!" I called after the old academic, but he'd already reached the sidewalk.

"The professor has written some books, but I don't believe he's been *published*," the colonel confided to me quietly. It would have been best, I imagined, if the professor had walked into the traffic on Park Avenue, where he could have been instantly killed by a car, but he turned south on the sidewalk, where he was lost from our sight.

A strained silence and a loss of concentration seemed to unhinge the soup line. We could all hear what Talib whispered to Ayla, and what she whispered (more loudly) back to him.

"It wasn't Reggie, was it?" Talib had whispered.

"What must you *think* of me?" Ayla whispered, harshly. "I would sooner have sex with a *dog* than with *Reggie!*"

"Let it go, Talib, let it go," Colonel Zimmermann said, so softly he was almost whispering.

"There's lots more soup," Elmira said. Mary, Felix, Fernando, and Talib had the most soup. Even Ayla had a little, her morning sickness notwithstanding. Mr. Barlow and I were disinclined to return to the gathering in the Zimmermanns' upstairs apartment; we felt more at home in the alley with the castoffs Zim had helped.

Talib was the first to pay his respects to Zim, specifically; he spoke directly to Colonel Zimmermann as we were leaving the alley. "I know I speak for all of us—Colonel, sir—when I say how sorry we were to hear about your Matthew."

"Thank you, Talib," the colonel said. He would not let anyone carry the soup pot for him; he would not let Elmira persuade him to take the service elevator, either.

"They don't like us to carry food through the lobby, Colonel—not even you," Elmira reminded him.

"Then we'll forgive them for not liking us when we do it," the colonel told her.

We were a strange assortment of vagabonds—we looked decidedly out of place on Park Avenue. Not a single taxi, whizzing by, slowed down to take an inquiring look at us. Not even Colonel Zimmermann—elegantly dressed in funereal attire, and with half a chest of medals—caught the cabbies' eyes. To the taxi drivers, the colonel was just a crazy old man carrying a soup pot.

"Colonel Zimmermann, sir," Mr. Barlow began; he was struggling with the two platters, trying to shield the paper bowls and paper plates and paper napkins from the wind. A telltale trail of fallen plastic spoons marked the snowshoer's path along the Park Avenue sidewalk. "Sir," Elliot Barlow said a second time, as a paper plate was blown away in the wind, "your Matthew was a good shepherd."

"Good soldiers are good shepherds, Mr. Barlow—thank you for noticing!" the colonel warmly said.

"For God's sake—give me all that, Mr. Barlow," Elmira said. She took the two platters with the paper and plastic stuff, hugging them to her capacious chest—the soup ladle held fast in her fist, like a mace. "Adam, give those sandwiches to Talib—he's a good soldier; he can carry them," the house-keeper told me. Talib took the platter of egg salad sandwiches from me—he was clearly used to taking orders from Elmira—then the good soldier who'd been saved from combat spoke to Colonel Zimmermann.

"I doubt, Colonel, that I am dressed appropriately for the party upstairs," Talib told the retired commanding officer.

"You are most appropriately dressed, Talib—someone in fatigues should be there," the colonel said to the dutiful soldier.

Ayla was keeping her distance from the egg salad sandwiches, or she was worried about her close proximity to the eggs in the elevator that would take her to the thirteenth floor. Yet the colonel also considered that the pregnant younger sister may have doubted the appropriateness of how she was dressed for the party upstairs. "And *you*, Ayla—you and your baby—look wonder-ful. There is no one at the party upstairs who looks as wonderful as you do," Colonel Zimmermann told her. The hooded sweatshirt Ayla was wearing was probably Talib's, I thought, but everyone could still see the sizable bump in the skinny young woman's belly.

The doorman held the door open for the colonel and Elmira; he looked relieved that only Talib and Ayla followed those first two into the lobby. The snowshoer and I were left on the Park Avenue sidewalk with Fernando and Lucy, and with Mary and Felix—a couple of unlikely couples.

Mary was old enough to be Felix's mother, but she wasn't. "Where ya goin'?" Mary asked the boy, in a less-than-motherly way.

"I got nowhere to go," Felix told her matter-of-factly.

"I'm goin' to a nowhere I know somethin' about—if you wanna come," Mary said to him. The boy hesitated a long time; I thought the snowshoer was going to take him down and rub his face on the sidewalk. But Mary just started walking away; Felix quickly followed her.

That left the no-less-indecisive Fernando and Lucy. The bright sunlight was cruel to Fernando's facial tattoo. The bleeding heart, stabbed on Fernan-do's cheek, bled more profusely in the sun; the name of Fernando's onetime true love, MYRTLE, was easier to read on the pierced heart. Lucy looked at him, then looked away. She was an underage girl with missing teeth. Whatever else Lucy was missing wasn't clear, but it seemed evident she had not thought through the repercussions that could come from her licking men. "I'm goin'," Fernando said, looking at Lucy, but she wouldn't look at him. "You comin', or what?" Fernando asked her, but Lucy shrugged; she kept looking away from him. Fernando was half a block away, and walking faster, when Lucy called to him. Lucy's voice and her thoughts were clearer than the snowshoer and I were expecting.

"I *do* know the difference between what I want and what I don't, Fernando! Sometimes, I *do* know what I mean—sometimes, I *do* know when I'm bein' *encouragin'* !" Lucy called to him, but he just kept walking. "I know why Myrtle left you!" Lucy screamed after him. Fernando appeared to trip, or he staggered for a second, but he kept walking. "Because Myrtle found out about *Buddy*!" Lucy screamed. We watched Fernando veer west, across Park Avenue; speaking strictly for myself, I was hoping he would be struck and flattened by something. "Buddy left him, too—everybody with half a brain leaves Fernando, eventually," Lucy said to the snowshoer and me.

"Did you know Buddy?" I asked the girl.

"I wasn't around when Buddy was around—I just heard about her," Lucy told me. "Buddy isn't around anymore, or nobody's seen her around here," the girl said.

A taxi whizzed by, the windows open, the radio blaring—or Simon and Garfunkel, unseen, were somehow singing "Scarborough Fair" in the cab's backseat.

"What about you guys—where are you goin'?" Lucy asked us. I thought she was being a little encouraging. We walked together, east to Lexington Avenue, and along Lexington to East Sixty-fourth Street, to the little Barlows' pied-à-terre. Lucy had a look at the writing team's apartment, while Mr. Barlow and I packed up our things and changed our clothes. I had my writing notebooks with me, and all the other stuff I'd brought from Vienna.

I hadn't noticed that the snowshoer was wearing a bra until we were walking against the wind on Lexington Avenue. The wind whipped the little English teacher's necktie over his shoulder and pressed his white dress shirt flat against his chest, where I got a glimpse of the bra—only briefly, before the snowshoer clutched his overcoat closer to his chest. The cups of the bra were too small for my mother. Was Mr. Barlow buying his own bras now? I wondered. A training bra, I presumed. At least it was white, I was thinking—a black bra would have been more noticeable under a white dress shirt.

"Lose the bra, Elliot," I said to him when we were changing our clothes for the train.

"I thought you'd never notice," the snowshoer said.

"I noticed it, too!" Lucy called to us from the living room.

I felt I had failed to be the snowshoer's good shepherd. At Zim's memorial, of all occasions, I had failed to watch out for Mr. Barlow. I'd let the little English teacher pick a fight with a couple of Bonesmen in a *bra*. What a bad soldier I would have been, I was thinking, as the three of us took a taxi to Penn Station.

"Don't worry—I'm not goin' all the way to New Hampshire, but I'll take a ride to Penn Station," Lucy had told us.

Our taxi driver was a hippie with a dirty-blond beard and a ponytail tied with a red ribbon. His cab was adorned with peace symbols, and he had a GET OUT OF VIETNAM bumper sticker. All the way to Seventh Avenue, "Where Have All the Flowers Gone?" was playing on the radio—the old Pete Seeger song, but it was the Peter, Paul and Mary version.

I was also thinking I had failed Francine DeCourcey, Zim's fiancée. I believed I could have comforted her more—I should have tried harder to reach her in her grief. The song just repeated itself. Peter, Paul and Mary just kept singing. Lucy sang along with them. They were asking where the flowers, the young girls, and the soldiers had gone.

Where has the snowshoer gone—where is he going? I was worrying. Peter, Paul and Mary just sang. Our hippie cab driver was singing, too. The young girls in the song would never learn—that was the message.

I just looked at the little English teacher; he was always the smallest person, always stuck in the middle of every backseat. Mr. Barlow was between me and Lucy; he was even smaller than the underage girl beside him. Of course Elliot noticed how I was looking at him. I'm sure it was a desperate look.

"I'm sorry—please don't worry about me, Adam," the snowshoer whispered.

It was late afternoon or early evening, and it was a Sunday—Penn Station, as Zim used to say, was a zoo. Yet Lucy knew where to go; the wayward girl led us through the labyrinth. If Buddy had been around, we would never have found her in the swarms of arriving and departing passengers. If there were other runaways—other strays and castoffs of humankind, adrift in Penn Station—the snowshoer and I didn't see them. We followed Lucy; the girl knew her way around. "Outward-bound, Boston—right?" was all the girl asked us, before leading us to our track. We were waiting for the gate or entranceway to our platform to open; until then, I'd not noticed a police presence in Penn Station. But when we stopped moving—we were just standing with Lucy, and with our fellow travelers to Boston—Mr. Barlow and I began to notice all the cops.

When Lucy covered her mouth with her hand, before she spoke, Elliot and I just assumed she didn't want us to see her missing teeth. (Fernando wasn't the one who'd knocked out the girl's teeth, Elmira had told us; Lucy's father had done it.) "Don't talk to me—you don't even want to look like you know me, or anythin'," Lucy said into her hand, to the snowshoer and me.

The cops were usually in pairs; Mr. Barlow and I now noticed that two of them were looking at us, or they were checking out someone in our near vicinity. "Don't look at the cops when they're lookin' at you," we heard Lucy say, but we couldn't see her, and her voice sounded farther away. The two cops were threading their way through the crowd in our direction, but Elliot and I stopped watching them.

"Do you know that girl?" one of the cops asked the snowshoer and me, when they were suddenly standing in front of us.

"What girl?" I asked, looking all around. As expected, Lucy was nowhere to be seen; she'd slipped away.

"The officer must mean the girl who showed us to our departure platform," the little English teacher told me patiently—as if he were used to speaking to an inattentive child. "We asked a girl if she knew where the track to Boston was, and she brought us here," the snowshoer said to the policemen.

"Oh, *that* girl," I said, with steadfast indifference.

"Come on, let's go," the second cop said to his partner—the one who'd asked us if we knew Lucy. It was clear they weren't going to find the girl, nor would they try very hard to look for her.

"Never mind—thanks," the first cop curtly said to us. Then they moved on; we didn't watch where the cops went next, as if Lucy were still instructing us not to look at them.

Five years later, Mr. Barlow would be living in New York City. One day, I would try living there, too. But that Sunday in 1968, we were both beginners in Penn Station. On the station platform, we didn't know which train car we belonged in; one of the conductors had to show us where to board.

Then there was the awkwardness of all my luggage, from Austria—the giant duffel bag with my winter clothes, and the two heavy backpacks with my writing notebooks. When the well-built young man in the business suit spoke to me, the snowshoer and I were laughing. Mr. Barlow had been teasing me about the Canadian stickers I'd plastered both backpacks and my duffel bag with. If you were an American in Europe at that time, you knew you would be better treated by the Europeans if they thought you were Canadian. The Vietnam War was increasingly unpopular in Europe, if not yet as unpopular in the United States. "I hope you're an *actual* Canadian," the fit-looking young businessman said to me. The snowshoer and I were struggling to lift my giant duffel bag onboard the train. "Or are you just another fucking draft dodger?" the business guy asked me.

The bully patriotism was somewhat new then, or it seemed more surprising. I was taken aback by how well dressed the guy was, more than by his aggressiveness. The snowshoer, standing on the station platform, just bent both knees and shoved the duffel bag up to me; the bag drove me backward on the landing between the coupled cars of the train. Mr. Barlow's small bag and one of my heavy backpacks were already aboard.

"I'm talking to *you*, pal," the business guy said, pointing at me.

"He's not your pal—he's *my* pal," the little English teacher told him politely but firmly.

Where the snowshoer was standing on the station platform, he blocked me from getting off the train—he also blocked the businessman from climbing onboard. "Get out of the way, you flaming fag," the fit young man said, pushing Elliot out of his way. I just stood there, on the landing between the coupled cars. *Not everyone is cut out to be the good shepherd Lieutenant Matthew Zimmermann was,* I was thinking.

The snowshoer's hands were bigger than mine. Considering how small Mr. Barlow was, his hands always looked large to me. Suddenly his hands were locked at the businessman's waist, the knuckle of one thumb pressed into the guy's navel. The businessman was clawing at Mr. Barlow's locked hands, but there were no loose fingers to peel apart. When Elliot locked his hands, he knew how to tuck his thumbs and fingers away; there was nothing to grab. The snowshoer's locked hands were a double knot.

I just waited for the back-heel trip; Mr. Barlow had a good one. I knew it was coming. The business guy had no idea what was coming. His left cheek was what made a slapping sound against the pavement of the station platform. The little snowshoer had to step over the guy to board the train; Mr. Barlow brought the second of my two backpacks aboard with him.

We took a long time stowing my bags. When the train began to move, we had just sat down. The business guy was still on the station platform, but I was relieved to see he was sitting up of his own accord. The two people attending to him were not holding him up, and the businessman had a reasonably alert expression on his face. The way the guy just talked and talked made me wish I could have heard his account of what happened to him.

"'There was this midget fairy—he managed to get behind me, somehow,'" I said to the snowshoer, as if that were the whole story.

"'There were *four* of them—two of them held me, while the other two picked up the station platform and hit me in the face with it,'" Mr. Barlow began his version of the story.

"'Four *huge* guys—all of them were communists,'" I told the little English teacher, who began to laugh.

We were both laughing when the train pulled out of Penn Station, but I didn't really feel like laughing. I felt afraid. I knew I wasn't cut out to be a good shepherd. I was wishing I'd told Zim about Mr. Barlow. Matthew Zimmermann had been a hero. Maybe Zim would have known how to save the snowshoer.

ACT III

RULES FOR GHOSTS

30.

THE WOMAN WITH THE BABY CARRIAGE

There are certain scenes from films you wish you never saw: in your mind, you keep replaying these scenes—or I do. Like those songs that get into your head, the ones you hate but you can't stop singing.

Like most screenwriters, I keep rewriting my movies that were never made. I won't presume to speak for other screenwriters, but I also keep rewriting certain scenes I didn't write in the first place—even scenes from films I wish I never saw.

Am I the only one who does this? What if you wanted to be a fiction writer? What if you wrote novels, but you wanted to write screenplays, too? What if you suspected that your father had written the screenplay for a film you hated, and what if your father was in that same movie?

There are certain scenes in *The Wrong Car* that are in my head, like those songs I can't stop singing. In my head, I'm in black and white, in 1956— I would have been too young to drive.

INT. GETAWAY CAR, PARKED. DAY.

The car is parked, but the motor is running. The
GETAWAY DRIVER is Paul Goode (thirty); his handsomeness
is not evident in the duckbill cap, a newsboy cap.
A GUN MOLL sticks her pretty head into the open
passenger-seat window.

                GUN MOLL
  Hey, what about me?

The GANGSTER in the passenger seat looks her over.

              THIS GANGSTER
  You gotta sit on someone's lap.

The THREE GANGSTERS in the backseat give her a look.

> ONE OF THE THREE
> (points to the driver)
> Not *his* lap. He's gotta drive.

The gun moll takes a long look at the little driver.

> GUN MOLL
> (walking away)
> No, thanks.

> ANOTHER GANGSTER
> Who's the broad?

EXT. GETAWAY CAR, MOVING. DAY.

At a city intersection, the driver stops for a WOMAN WITH A BABY CARRIAGE in the pedestrian crosswalk.

> ONE OF THE GANGSTERS (V.O.)
> Just some broad.

INT. GETAWAY CAR, STOPPED. DAY.

In a hail of gunfire, the gangster in the passenger seat and the three thugs in the backseat are shot.

EXT. GETAWAY CAR, STOPPED. DAY.

The woman with the baby carriage has paused in the crosswalk while the ongoing gunfire riddles the getaway car; all four tires are shot, the car appears to slump, and gas and oil (and maybe blood) leak into the street.

CLOSER ON: the little driver sits unharmed and relaxed
at the steering wheel, as if waiting for the light to
change.

PULL BACK: the woman pulls a sawed-off shotgun out of
the baby carriage; she approaches the getaway car as
Paul Goode gets out of the driver's-side door. He tips
his duckbill cap to the woman, leaving the car door
open for her. She shoots the slumped-over bodies of the
dead passengers, just to make sure. Paul Goode nods to
camera as he exits frame, as if the camera were one of
the marksmen who ambushed the getaway car. Loose bills
float through the blown-out windows of the car. Camera
stays on the woman, transferring the satchels of money
to the baby carriage, where she also stows the shotgun.

I don't remember the name of the actress who played the woman with
the baby carriage. I never saw her in another film, but she haunted me—not
exactly like a ghost. I used to see her in line at my book signings, but she
never showed up at the front of the line. I never got to sign her book. At my
book signings, the woman wasn't with a baby carriage. She really got to me,
but she hadn't once bothered to introduce herself. I sensed her dislike of the
getaway driver. Maybe she disliked Paul Goode as a person, not only as an
actor and a screenwriter.

Before I found out whether Paul Goode was my father or not, I didn't
like him. I especially don't like him, as an actor or as a screenwriter, in
this scene in the bar. This happens later in *The Wrong Car*, when we first
find out that the getaway driver and the gun moll are a couple. I hate this
scene.

INT. CITY BAR. NIGHT.

The getaway driver (no duckbill cap) is having a beer;
he is evaluating himself in the mirror behind the
bar when the moll comes in, cozying up to him on an
adjacent barstool. She's wearing his newsboy cap, or
one just like it.

GUN MOLL
How'd it go, cutie pie?

GETAWAY DRIVER
(deadpan)
You know how it went.
(a pause)
Please take off that cap.

The moll puts the duckbill cap on the empty barstool
beside her. She snuggles closer to the little driver.

GUN MOLL
Better?

GETAWAY DRIVER
Such an improvement.

CLOSER ON: Paul Goode's shy, childlike smile.

FREEZE TO A STILL. FADE TO BLACK.

The woman with the baby carriage, that haunting woman from *The Wrong Car*, didn't show up only at my book signings, but showing up was all she did—just appearing seemed to be her thing. I know. I've learned I should be careful not to generalize about ghosts.

Some evenings, when I was visiting my grandmother, either Nana or Dottie would persuade me to spend the night. I would have a sleepover in my attic bedroom of the Front Street house.

"It'll make your grandmother happy, if you stay over," Dottie would tell me.

"Just for old times' sake, dear," Nana would say.

Well, it was one thing to have a sleepover and see my grandfather's ghost. I'd learned that you couldn't predict exactly how (or in what state of mind) the diaper man might appear. It was another thing, entirely, when the woman with the baby carriage just showed up. Was she a fictional character? If so, in certain ways, she was not in character. She never tried to shoot me;

she didn't *do* anything. She never showed up with the baby carriage, or with the shotgun—at least not in the Front Street house. If she was that woman from *The Wrong Car,* she didn't act like her—or like a ghost.

Besides, what would the ghost of the actress who played that character want with me? Why would she show up in the Front Street house? Was it a kind of casting call? The woman with the baby carriage was always a walk-on. If she was auditioning, she didn't appear to want a speaking part. She never spoke.

I would wake up with a feeling that someone was there—a feeling I was familiar with, in the attic bedroom of the Front Street house. The woman with the baby carriage, as I would always think of her—even without the carriage, and always without a baby—would be sitting at the foot of my bed. She was looking at me, but with no expectations. Maybe she just wanted me to know she could have shot me, if she wanted to, but she didn't appear to want anything.

"Oh, it's you," I said, the second or third time I woke up and saw her sitting there. But I could not compete with her insouciance. The woman with the baby carriage was more indifferent to me than I could ever pretend to be to her. In this respect, she was consistently in character. You couldn't match her at being noir. When I woke up and saw her, she couldn't be bothered to disappear. The woman with the baby carriage just got up from the bed and walked away.

I wrote her into my screenplays; even as a walk-on, she seemed too important for a minor character. I was influenced by *Jules et Jim,* not the devastating love triangle but the third-person, voice-over narration. There was nothing New Wave about my first-person, voice-over character—as close to *Jules et Jim* as I dared.

I started to write a screenplay about taking my mom to see *The Wrong Car,* but I never finished it. I won't say that nothing came of it, because I learned something about writing screenplays. You are basically describing a movie you've already seen, but you're the only one who's seen it. When you write about your life as a screenplay, it's as if you're watching someone else's life; it's not your life, and you're not living it. You're *only seeing* what the characters do, your character included. And screenplays are written in the present tense—as if nothing has already happened, as if everything is unfolding in the present. I'm only saying this is how it started—how I began to see my life as an unmade movie. The way it began was almost natural.

INT. NEW YORK CITY CINEMA, 1971. NIGHT.

Sam Cooke's "You Send Me" PLAYS OVER. Nora and Em (both
thirty-six), sitting next to Elliot Barlow (forty-two),
are looking along their row of seats to see how Little
Ray (forty-nine) is reacting—as is Adam (thirty), who
is barely interested in the movie but eager to detect
any reaction from his mother. Little Ray sits between
him and Molly (fifty-one), who is also interested in
Ray's reaction to the film.

> ADAM (V.O.)
> Paul Goode didn't come out with a new movie
> for seventeen years, but *The Wrong Car* was
> revived at a noir festival in New York in the
> early seventies. Nora and Em and I had always
> wanted my mom to see Paul Goode onscreen—to see
> if Little Ray thought I looked like the little
> actor, or if she thought Paul Goode looked like
> someone she'd met in Aspen in 1941. Naturally,
> Molly and the snowshoer thought we should leave
> well enough alone.

Ray stares blankly at the screen while everyone watches
her.

"You Send Me" CONTINUES OVER.

ONSCREEN, CLOSE-UP: in black and white, a doorknob
turns—first one way, then the other—but the door
doesn't open.

PULL BACK: beside the door is a hat rack with four or
five duckbill caps, all the same, hanging from the
hooks.

A WIDER ANGLE: the gun moll and the getaway driver
are undressing on a bed, dropping their clothes on the

bed or flinging them onto the floor of a small studio apartment. There's a radio on the bedside table. In her bra and panties, kneeling on the bed, the moll manages to take off her bra and turn off the radio—no more Sam Cooke. The getaway driver is wearing only his boxer shorts, which the moll swiftly yanks down; for half a second, we see his little bare ass.

CLOSER ON: the door to the apartment, as the driver's boxers are flung onto the floor. The door opens, and the woman with the baby carriage pushes the carriage ahead of her as she comes inside, the door key clenched in her teeth.

On the bed, the moll tries to cover herself, as does the little driver. The woman wheels the baby carriage up to the bed, staring down at them.

> GETAWAY DRIVER
>
> You coulda knocked, ya know.

> WOMAN WITH THE CARRIAGE
>
> You coulda put a note on the door—sayin' you was busy, or somethin'. You gave me a key, ya know.

> GUN MOLL
> (to the driver)
>
> You're *married*? You have a *baby*?

> WOMAN WITH THE CARRIAGE
> (to the driver)
>
> It's your turn with the baby, little fella.
> (as she leaves)
> I'm drivin' next time, ya know.

When the getaway driver gets out of bed, we very briefly see his bare ass again; the moll, still in

her panties, is hurrying to put on her bra. The driver
shoves the baby carriage out of his way. Camera follows
the carriage; it collides with the closed apartment
door, where we see the little driver's hand enter frame
and snatch his boxers off the floor. There's loose
money—scattered bills float around.

> GETAWAY DRIVER (O.C.)
>> (to the moll)
> I told ya, I'm *not* married.

A WIDER ANGLE: the getaway driver finds a pack of
cigarettes by the radio; he lights one and sits on the
bed. The gun moll goes to the baby carriage; she wants
to be sure the baby is okay. When she reaches into
the carriage, all she finds is the sawed-off shotgun,
which she cradles in her arms the way she might hold a
baby, smiling to the driver—a smile of eternal love and
forgiveness. He's not married; there's no baby.

On the bed, the cocky little driver takes a drag on his
cigarette, blowing the smoke in the moll's direction.

> GETAWAY DRIVER
>> (smiling)
> Be careful with that baby.

FADE TO BLACK. END CREDITS ROLL.

REVERSE ANGLE: on the audience, as "You Send Me" PLAYS
OVER. The OTHER MOVIEGOERS—a crowd of New Yorkers—make
Molly and Ray look out of place. Nora and Em and Adam—
Mr. Barlow and Molly, too—are trying to read Ray's
reaction to the film.

> ADAM (V.O.)
> My mother was the kind of moviegoer who was
> always comparing the appearance of people she

knew to movie stars. She thought I was going
to grow up to look like Alan Ladd—I don't. My
mom thought Toni Sailer, the Austrian skier,
looked like Farley Granger in *Strangers on a
Train*—he doesn't. But Paul Goode didn't start
out as a movie star. Paul Goode didn't inspire
much of a reaction from Little Ray, not at
first.

> NORA
> (to Ray)
> You don't think Adam looks like Paul Goode?
> (as Em gestures)
> Maybe a *little*?

> LITTLE RAY
> Paul Goode looks like a guy who never grew up.
> (hugs Adam)
> My baby looks like *me*!
> (as Em nods)
> If this movie is supposed to be noir, I don't
> like noir. What does noir *mean*, anyway?

EXT. NEW YORK CITY CINEMA, 1971. NIGHT.

Moving from Nora to Em, from Molly to Ray, and from
Adam to the snowshoer, as they exit the theater.

> MR. BARLOW
> *The Wrong Car* is a dark comedy—it's noir in the
> sense of *camp*. It's *campy*.

Em is pantomiming *camp* and *campy*—both a heartbreaking
drama and a slapstick comedy. PASSERSBY think Em is
crazy.

                    NORA
            (translates for Em)
        Em says it's funny and sad—it's tragic and
        comic all at once.

Em now appears to be gesturing obscenely. She opens the
palm of one hand as if she were holding an imaginary
beer can; she makes the fist of her other hand wriggle
upward, through her open palm.

                    NORA
        Sweet Jesus, Em!
                (translating)
        She says *camp* is an *inside* joke.

Adam glances at Molly, who smiles—Molly imitates Em's
obscene gesture.

                    ADAM
            (to his mom)
        Is there *anyone* Paul Goode reminds you of?

                    LITTLE RAY
        Sweetie, I don't see a lot of men—not their
        naked butts, anyway.
                (to Mr. Barlow)
        Well, there's your butt—*you* have a cute butt,
        Elliot, I must say.

Em and Molly are nodding and laughing. Elliot is shy.

                    NORA
            (to Adam)
        You're not in a crowd that's into naked male
        butts, kiddo.
                (to Elliot, hugging him)
        Sorry! I know *you're* into them!

Everyone laughs, the snowshoer included. They have
paused in front of the movie poster for *The Wrong Car*,
which Nora suddenly sees. Nora pushes Adam against the
larger-than-life poster, a black-and-white still from
the movie—that moment when Paul Goode is smoking in
bed, smiling at the gun moll.

>   NORA
>   Come on, Ray—look at Paul Goode's *smile*. You
>   don't see a resemblance?
>   (to Adam)
>   Come on, kiddo—*try* to smile.

We can see Paul Goode's shy, childlike smile alongside
Adam's half-hearted effort.

>   MOLLY
>   You can smile better than that, Kid.

Little Ray has her hands in the front pockets of her
jeans; she jock-walks in circles, her shoulders hunched.

>   LITTLE RAY
>   (scowling)
>   Baloney!

This makes Adam truly smile; his smile and Paul Goode's
look alike. From her gestures, Em is still unsure
of the resemblance. Molly and the snowshoer look
uncertain, too.

Adam puts his arm around his mom. Ray is still scowling—
in her hands-in-pockets, shoulders-hunched stance.

>   LITTLE RAY
>   (softly)
>   You look like me, sweetie.

> ADAM
> (kisses her)
> I know I do.

> NORA
> (to Little Ray)
> It doesn't matter who Paul Goode looks like, or
> who he doesn't look like. It's been too long
> since he's been in a movie—Paul Goode isn't
> going anywhere.

It looks like Em is doing *Hamlet,* Act III, Scene I.
"To be, or not to be"—that tortured proposition,
pantomimed.

> NORA
> Em thinks Paul Goode is going to be a big star.
> (Em has a fit)
> Sorry—a *little* star.

On the ignored movie poster in black and white, Paul
Goode is still smoking in bed and smiling.

> ADAM (V.O.)
> I would learn to listen to Em.

In 1973, when Mr. Barlow resigned from Phillips Exeter Academy and
moved to New York City, he was forty-four. I was thirty-one, a published
novelist—I was writing my second novel—but with Elliot Barlow's resignation from the academy, it was high time for me to get out of town. The
snowshoer said I'd prolonged my adolescence by sharing the faculty apartment in Amen Hall with him into my thirties. It's unclear what I would
have been prolonging if I'd moved in with Nana and Dottie. Those two
old ladies would have welcomed me, and what a wonderful workplace for a
writer it would have been—all those unused rooms I could have written in.
But the prospect of my sleeping, full-time, in the attic bedroom of the Front
Street house was forbidding. No one should sleep with ghosts every night,
not even writers.

Yet my most convincing reason for leaving the town of Exeter was an actual (not a ghostly) encounter. One late night, I drove out to Roland's to pick up a pizza for me and Mr. Barlow—thus sparing the snowshoer the possible temptation of going to Roland's *as a woman*. It was late at night, even by Roland's standards, but I'd called ahead and ordered the pizza. It was a quiet night; there were no drunken thugs lurking in the darkened parking lot, waiting to accost me as I carried the pizza to my car. There was only the woman with the baby carriage. The woman was walking toward me, out of the darkness—as if she and her baby were picking up a late-night pizza, too. I refused to be intimidated by her brazenness as a ghost. I should have known this woman wasn't a ghost.

"So now you're going public—you've got balls, I'll give you that," I said to her, but she wasn't the woman from *The Wrong Car*—she was the wrong woman, an actual woman with an actual baby. Scant light from Roland's reached the parking lot, but the woman I'd frightened pushed the baby carriage into what weak light there was. Her moonfaced baby was wide awake and staring up at me, with the noirish indifference some babies have, but the woman was clearly afraid. "Oh, I'm so sorry—I mistook you for someone else," I said to her.

She was just a young mother—maybe a single mother, I considered, because she'd had no one to leave the baby with when she went out for the pizza. A responsible young mother, I decided, because she'd not left the baby in her car—not in the parking lot at Roland's, not this late at night. And the poor woman had the misfortune to run into me. I looked like any writer and former wrestler at that time of night; I'd scared her as badly as any of the lowlifes who hung out at Roland's might have. Not to mention what an awful thing I said to her: I'd told her she had balls for going public. What might such an awful thing have meant to a young mother with a baby, late at night?

"And then you told her you mistook her for someone else?" Mr. Barlow asked me, when we were eating our pizza—after I'd related the saga to him. "It's a good thing we're both leaving Exeter, finally," the snowshoer said. "She wasn't anyone we know, was she?"

In the harsh light of this embarrassing encounter with the young mother who was not the haunting woman with the baby carriage from *The Wrong Car*, I was relieved I'd taken a teaching job at one of those fly-by-night colleges created by an increasing resistance to the draft. The pushback to the draft was borne of the anti-war movement. New colleges were created, and they didn't have the highest academic standards. Previously, if you wanted to take advantage of a student deferment from the draft, but you were no great shakes as a student, you could be hard put to find a college that would admit you. The Military Selective Service Act of 1967 expanded the ages of conscription from eighteen to thirty-five. It still granted student deferments, but your deferment ended upon your completion of a four-year degree—or your twenty-fourth birthday, whichever came first.

These colleges were fly-by-night financial opportunities for their enterprising founders, and for those of us who taught in them for a time; yet these institutions, of less-than-higher learning, were also borne of a moral condemnation of the Vietnam War and the draft. What I would discover about teaching in such a college is that there were moral dilemmas for a teacher, too. There were students who simply didn't or couldn't do the work; there were students who rarely came to class, and students who plagiarized. Plagiarism was punishable by dismissal, but if you expelled a male student from college, you could be sending him to Vietnam, posing a moral dilemma. And if you didn't expel him, could you justify expelling a female student for cheating, just because she was safe from the war? The politics of the war made you consider the male and female students differently. Certainly that was a moral dilemma, too.

I was reminded of my mother's wedding—that moment when the electrocuted body of the diaper man was covered by a sheet on the outdoor dinner table. With the body between us, the little Barlows were telling me that their feeling for noir was very American. America would always be a frontier country, they told me; noir was the tone that captured the frontier best, the little Barlows said. And I'd imagined that the diaper man himself, from his infancy to his electrocution, had been a noir frontiersman.

I took the job at the not-very-good college only because it was in southern Vermont, a little more than an hour's drive to Manchester, where my mother and Molly lived. I could see more of my mom and Molly without living in the same town with them. But in 1973, when I would go visit them, my mom always asked me, "How's it going at the draft-dodger college?"

"I wish you wouldn't call it that," I always answered.

"That's what everyone calls it, sweetie," my mother would say.

Yet when the snowshoer and I knew we would (and should) be leaving Exeter, I had to go somewhere, didn't I? Of course I could have gone to New

York City. With Nora and Em living there, and with Mr. Barlow moving there, I was tempted. But I would have needed much more of a full-time job to afford to live in New York City; I wouldn't have had as much time to write as I did at the draft-dodger college.

I'd written a screenplay, an adaptation of my first novel, but the movie was never made. I was bitter about it, at first; yet, in the process, I'd learned how to write a screenplay. For the rest of my writing life, I knew I would be writing novels and screenplays—often, concurrently. As for New York City, I knew I would be spending a lot of time there—even if I was just a visitor. I could always stay with the snowshoer, or with Nora and Em, I was thinking.

Looking back, 1973 was a political time; it was the year of the *Roe v. Wade* U.S. Supreme Court decision about abortion. And for me, 1973 was the year I began to realize that every year was a political time. Where was I, when Nixon, in his first campaign for president, appealed to those socially conservative Americans he later called the "silent majority"—those Americans who disliked the hippie counterculture and the anti-war demonstrators? Or when Nixon was promising "peace with honor" in Vietnam—where was I then? Not paying attention, according to Nora, who later pointed out that I managed to miss the first four or five times Em declared she was going back to Canada.

But how was I supposed to know that Em was from Canada, in the first place? Em didn't say where she was from. Em didn't talk. Em's declarations— namely, that she was returning to Canada—weren't spoken. I just missed (or misunderstood) Nora's translation of Em's pantomime on the Canadian subject. I'd seen Em do her seagull imitations before, but I didn't know what she meant. You had to watch her closely; Em's seagull thing didn't only mean she was considering going back to Canada.

I think 1973 was a watershed year for me as a writer as well: I was writing more than I had before. I was more of an introvert than ever, because I was consciously trying to live my life in such a way that I could write all the time. Yet, at the same time, 1973 was the year I began to notice more of the world—not to mention the behavior of other people in it. I still don't know how (or why) this happened. Nora, naturally, had an opinion, and she didn't hesitate to tell me.

"If you're looking for a title to your story, it's called 'Getting Out of Exeter'—it took you long enough, kiddo," my cousin told me.

BEGINNING A MONTAGE OF MOVIE POSTERS FROM 1973.

The poster for *The Exorcist*, the eerie light from the window shining on the ominous silhouette of Max von Sydow standing under the lamppost.

> ADAM (V.O.)
> Looking back, 1973 was a good year for noir.
> There was creepy noir.

The poster for *The Sting*, the lighthearted color illustration of the Paul Newman and Robert Redford characters—they're just fooling around.

> ADAM (V.O.)
> There was caper noir.

The poster for *High Plains Drifter*, directed by and starring Clint Eastwood; his gun is drawn.

> ADAM (V.O.)
> There was gunfighter noir.

The poster for *Bat Pussy*, XXX, ADULTS ONLY! The illustration of Bat Pussy (a.k.a. Dora Dildo) sitting on an exercise ball, in short shorts and knee-high boots, is not at all as pornographic (or as parodic) as the film.

> ADAM (V.O.)
> There was porno noir.

END OF MONTAGE.

INT. GALLOWS LOUNGE, GREENWICH VILLAGE, 1973. NIGHT.

A hangman's noose dangles above the bar, where a sign says: COME HANG YOURSELF. CUSTOMERS at the bar, and

at tables facing the small stage, are mostly a Village
crowd.

> ADAM (V.O.)
> The Gallows Lounge did stand-up noir; only dark
> comedy was welcome there. It was in an area of
> Seventh Avenue and Greenwich, where some jazz
> joints were. There was nothing iconic about the
> Gallows Lounge—it wasn't the Village Vanguard—
> but the comedy club was a step up from the
> cabaret and burlesque shows where Nora and Em
> got their start onstage. In 1973, Mr. Barlow
> had just moved to New York. He'd been married
> to my mom for seventeen years, and he'd taught
> at Exeter for twenty. Don't blame the snowshoer
> for trying to have some fun.

At a table close to the stage, Adam (thirty-two) sits
next to PRUE (twenty-eight), a Bardot type—a sex kitten
in a condom-tight dress. He smiles at her; she sticks
her tongue out at him, not alluringly. Embarrassed for
her, Adam looks away.

> ADAM (V.O.)
> In '73, I was dating one of the performers at
> the Gallows Lounge—*Prue, the Tongue Kisser,*
> her act was called. She'd started out in strip
> clubs, where a comedy act of that name had been
> badly misunderstood.

PULL BACK: at the same table, Elliot Barlow (forty-
four) sits next to a VERY PRETTY, MUCH YOUNGER
BOYFRIEND (twenty-four). Mr. Barlow doesn't respond to
his boyfriend's amorous gropings.

> ADAM (V.O.)
> The snowshoer was going out with the youngest
> performer at the Gallows Lounge. His act was

called *Eric's All-Gay Band,* but Eric was all
alone onstage—he was the entire band. Eric
sang beautifully. They were popular songs,
but Eric sang them in a gay way. The songs
were very sad, but the Gallows Lounge was
a comedy club, and Eric's act wasn't funny.
Only the homophobes laughed—the assholes who
made Eric cry.

In T-shirts, Nora and Em (both thirty-eight) come
onstage—hands in the pockets of their jeans, shoulders
hunched forward, a jock-walk imitation of Little Ray.
APPLAUSE.

> ADAM (V.O.)
> To be fair to Prue, the name of Em and Nora's
> act had been badly misunderstood in strip
> clubs, too. They called it *Two Dykes, One Who
> Talks.* Nora and Em were really late bloomers
> when they found their first audience at the
> Gallows Lounge on Seventh Avenue and Greenwich—
> where *Two Dykes, One Who Talks* took off.

> NORA
>   (to audience)
> If you don't know me, I'm Nora. This is Em—my
> ladylove, the love of my life. We're a couple,
> but Em doesn't talk. She won't say a word.
>   (Em shakes her head)
> Em is a *pantomimist.*
>   (Em nods)
> Em *acts out;* I translate.
>   (to Em)
> As for *acting out,* Em, where were you last
> night? You got home so late, I was asleep. You
> hit your head on my knee, getting into bed.

Em looks contrite and fearful.

                    NORA
    Did you go out with Simone? She sucked the
    sleeve of your blouse at that French place on
    Spring Street.

Em contorts herself, both shaking and nodding her head
while appearing to beat and strangle herself.

                    NORA
               (deadpan)
    I see. You didn't go to the dinner party with
    Simone—the slut just happened to be there.
               (pause)
    Did she suck the sleeve of your blouse again?
    You were wearing short sleeves, Em—don't lie!

Em violently shakes her head; she makes an X mark with
her index fingers.

                    NORA
    What did Simone do?

Em does a very weird thing with one of her pinky
fingers; she instantly looks ashamed.

                    NORA
    The slut hooked pinky fingers with you under
    the table?

Em pokes Nora's upper arm with her index and middle
finger in a V shape.

                    NORA
               (deadpan)
    You stabbed her arm with your salad fork. Did
    you draw blood?

Em nods vigorously.

                    NORA
Don't lie!
          (Em looks contrite)
What did you talk about?
          (Em looks hurt)
Sorry, not you. What did the *other people* at
the table talk about?
          (Em freezes)
Not a *literary* conversation, I imagine—given
that slut Simone.
          (Em shakes her head)
So Simone fondled your pinky while people
talked about *what*?

Em lifts her upper lip, exposing her gums; her index
fingers point straight down, like fangs. She flaps her
elbows, like wings; Em swoops, headfirst, at Nora's
crotch. Nora has to fend her off.

                    NORA
Bat Pussy, the porn film!
          (Em hides her eyes)
Not *our* kind of porn?
          (Em shakes her head)
You mean, *hetero* porn?
          (Em equivocates)
What's worse than hetero porn?

Em flops one arm, lifts her T-shirt, shows her navel.

                    NORA
          (deadpan)
A parody. The guy can't get it up. The man and
the woman are old and unattractive. They're
both drunk. They're amateurs. It's gross.
          (Em keeps nodding)
Just tell me the terrible premise of *Bat Pussy,*
please.

Em jerks and twitches, as if her vagina were suffering repeated electric shocks.

> NORA
>
> Okay, I get it! But *why* does Bat Pussy's twat twitch?

More unseemly sexual gyrations from Em.

> NORA
>
> Her twat twitches to alert her when and where a porn movie is being filmed?
>> (Em nods)
>
> Does Bat Pussy want to stop the porn film or join in?
>> (Em equivocates)
>
> Both . . . Is this a parody, or simply the worst porn film ever made?
>> (Em equivocates)
>
> Both . . .
>> (to audience)
>
> A typical New York dinner party. Everyone is talking about a movie they haven't seen, or a book they haven't read, but—whatever it is— everyone knows they are superior to it. Is there anyone here who's actually seen *Bat Pussy*?
>> (no hands)
>
> But how many of you have heard about *Bat Pussy*?
>> (nine or ten hands)
>
> I heard there's no penetration in *Bat Pussy*.
>> (one or two hands)
>
> A porn film with no penetration?
>> (erupts, to Em)
>
> But you were playing *pinkies* under the table with that slut Simone!
>> (Em is ashamed)
>
> You should have poked her *eyes* out with your fucking salad fork!

Em violently demonstrates stabbing an imaginary Simone;
one hand holds her own breast while Em stabs with her
other hand.

                    NORA
          (to audience)
     Em says she should have stabbed Simone in her
     nipples.
          (deadpan, to Em)
     So you noticed her nipples.

Em looks contrite again. She pouts; she extends her
bent pinky finger to Nora, as if it hurts, as if in
sacrifice. Nora kisses Em's injured pinky. Em jumps
into Nora's arms, wrapping her legs around Nora's
torso. In this embrace, Nora carries her offstage—Em
wiggling her pinky to the STANDING OVATION from the
audience.

Adam stands and applauds, too, but he watches Prue, who
is furtively retreating backstage. Poor Prue is not
a picture of confidence. Poor Mr. Barlow is trying to
applaud Nora and Em's performance, but Eric pulls the
snowshoer into his lap as Mr. Barlow tries to stand.
Elliot fights him off.

As the applause dies down, the sound FADES AWAY. The
only sound is Adam's voice-over.

                    ADAM (V.O.)
     I felt for Prue; she hated following Nora and
     Em. *Two Dykes, One Who Talks* was a hard act
     to follow, though the show's success was a
     surprise to me. I'd grown up with Nora and
     Em's love for each other, and their nonstop
     fooling around. What they did onstage was their
     usual business to me. And the snowshoer had his

hands full just trying to contain the public
inappropriateness of his boyfriend. Eric was a
most enthusiastic boyfriend. Like his act, Eric
was an all-gay band all by himself. Nora and Em
and I loved Eric, but—most of all—we wanted Mr.
Barlow to be happy.

The audience takes Prue's fragile appearance onstage as
a signal to bolt for the bar and the washrooms. NO SOUND.

> ADAM (V.O.)
> Only the first-timers at the Gallows didn't
> take a break or a pee when Prue came onstage.
> Stand-up noir was not Prue's friend. She was a
> small-town girl; in high school, Prue believed
> she had invented kissing with her tongue. Prue
> hadn't heard of French kissing; she didn't know
> the French had thought of it first, or that
> other kids in her high school were already
> doing it and knew what it was called.

We can't hear Prue's monologue onstage; she's showing
us her tongue, rarely appealingly, more often
grotesquely.

> ADAM (V.O.)
> When Prue French-kissed you, she gagged you;
> she bit her boyfriends' tongues, she made them
> bleed.

FACES in the audience: people talking to one another,
not listening to Prue; the few who are listening look
appalled.

> ADAM (V.O.)
> *Prue, the Tongue Kisser* was an all-noir act—all
> darkness, no comedy.

A SOBBING WOMAN, A GRIMACING MAN; they shut their eyes, they cover their ears with their hands.

> ADAM (V.O.)
> Prue was in college before she saw her first film with subtitles.

INT. MOVIE THEATER, A COLLEGE-TOWN AUDIENCE, 1964. DAY.

Prue (nineteen) watches the screen, open-mouthed, in shock. HER BOYFRIEND whispers in her ear; she closes her mouth, puts her fingers to her lips. We hear off-camera kissing sounds.

> ADAM (V.O.)
> She saw French kissing done right. Her date said he hoped he could French-kiss her—the first time she heard what it was called. Prue knew she could never go home, where everyone knew her as "the tongue kisser"; Prue hadn't realized they were not being complimentary.

INT. BACKSTAGE, GALLOWS LOUNGE, 1973. NIGHT.

In a dressing room, Nora and Em console Prue on another performance of unrelenting misery. Prue is changing out of her tight dress, into jeans and a T-shirt, but she still has the Bardot, sex-kitten look. The guitar, from the stage, has a country sound. Adam looks on sympathetically.

> ADAM (V.O.)
> Nora and Em and I were very fond of Prue, but stand-up noir was not for her. It was time for Prue to stop talking about her history

as a tongue kisser. It didn't help that we
always left the Gallows Lounge when Damaged
Don was onstage, singing "It Never Gets Better
with Gwen," or an equally awful song. Prue
and Damaged Don were the one-note acts at the
Gallows. Don sang every song he wrote in the
same tuneless drone. Country noir is the worst
country there is. Nora and Em and I loved Don,
but his songwriting and singing sucked. How he
got a major music label and radio airtime is a
wonder.

INT. GALLOWS LOUNGE, GREENWICH VILLAGE, 1973. NIGHT.

Damaged Don is performing onstage as Nora, Em, Prue, and
Adam make their way to the exit. The snowshoer, forever
fighting off Eric's ardor, is loyally staying for Eric's
act—hence for Damaged Don's, which comes first.

> DAMAGED DON
> (sings)
> You don't want to wake up with Maureen. She
> smells like a farm and her sheets ain't too
> clean! It's bad news to wake up with Maureen.
> (repeats with audience)
> It's bad news to wake up with Maureen.

ONSTAGE, CLOSE-UP: on Don starting a new stanza.

> DAMAGED DON
> (sings)
> Don't dream about diddlin' Babette. She's a
> case of the clap you won't ever forget! It's
> bad news to diddle Babette.
> (repeats with audience)
> It's bad news to diddle Babette.

EXT. SEVENTH AVE. S., WEST VILLAGE, 1973. NIGHT.

Adam with Prue, Nora with Em, walk arm in arm together.
Only Em isn't singing along with Don (O.C.)—Em won't
sing.

>   DAMAGED DON (O.C.)
>   (with Adam, Prue, Nora)
>   Your worst nightmare is knowin' Louise. She'll
>   drink all your money and give your dog fleas!
>   It's bad news just knowin' Louise.
>   (repeats with audience)
>   It's bad news just knowin' Louise.

INT. GALLOWS LOUNGE, GREENWICH VILLAGE, 1973. NIGHT.

Damaged Don has the Gallows enthralled. Mr. Barlow
won't let his young boyfriend kiss him in public.

>   DAMAGED DON
>   (more morosely)
>   Don't think it gets better with Gwen. She'll
>   run over the kids and fuck your best friend!
>   It's bad news the day you meet Gwen.
>   (repeats with audience)
>   It's bad news the day you meet Gwen.

EXT. CHRISTOPHER ST., WEST VILLAGE, 1973. NIGHT.

Nora and Em and Adam and Prue have turned off Seventh
Ave. onto Christopher St., where the traffic is coming
toward them.

They're past one watering hole, Kettle of Fish, and
close to the Stonewall Inn, when a bus comes to a stop
near the Waverly Place Station. Nora and Adam and Prue

are singing the last verse with Don (O.C.), but Em
breaks away from the group to take a closer look at the
stopped bus.

                    DAMAGED DON (O.C.)
        Just try livin' alone—you'll be happy, my
        friend, 'cause it never gets better with Gwen.
        No, it never gets better with Gwen.
                (repeats with audience)
        No, it never gets better with Gwen.

ANOTHER ANGLE: Em looks at her singing friends; she's
pointing at the king-size movie poster on the side of
the bus. Em is in an agitated pantomime mode, pointing
to the poster, and to herself, making the fingers
of her other hand "talk" like someone yapping away.
As Nora and Adam and Prue approach the bus, Nora is
translating for Em.

                    NORA
        Em says, "I told you so."

CLOSE ON: the movie poster for *The Kindergarten Man*,
starring Paul Goode. It's a creepy poster. A little
boy, an apparent kindergartner, is standing at a child-
high urinal. The boy looks anxiously over his shoulder
at Paul Goode, who is lying on the floor of the
washroom—under cover of the toilet stalls. Paul Goode
is holding a handgun against his chest, a silencer
on the barrel. The index finger of his other hand is
held to his lips, cautioning the kindergartner not to
speak or give him away. The gunman and the little boy
are both dressed like kindergartners—shorts, sneakers,
T-shirts with goofy cartoon characters.

                    ADAM (V.O.)
        We thought we knew what noir was; we thought we
        understood how dark comedy worked. Not Prue—she

didn't have a clue. She'd never seen *The Wrong
Car*. But Nora and Em and I knew that Paul Goode
hadn't gone away. The little noir man was back,
and he looked more noir than ever.

PULL BACK: a longer shot of the four friends, standing
on Christopher St. near Waverly Place Station, as the
bus with the movie poster for *The Kindergarten Man*
pulls away.

                    NORA
Shit.

                    ADAM (V.O.)
I wanted to tell the snowshoer—Paul Goode
wasn't washed up—but Mr. Barlow was busy with
Eric's All-Gay Band.

31.

WHERE HAVE THE BANANAS GONE?

My grandmother was ninety-one in 1973. She said there'd been more phone calls for me at the Front Street house since Mr. Barlow had moved to New York. "The calls are mostly from Jasmine, dear," Nana told me. Jasmine had learned to hang up whenever Dottie answered the phone. Dottie had done her best to discourage Jasmine from phoning my grandmother's house.

One time, when Jasmine had called and asked for me, Dottie was blunt about it. "Any self-respectin' woman would just get over it—shit is shit," Dottie told her.

"It didn't happen to you," Jasmine replied in her imperious fashion.

"I should be phonin' you, Jasmine—I was the one who cleaned up your shit," Dottie reminded her. There'd been another time, Nana told me, when Jasmine phoned the Front Street house and Dottie had labeled her a "walkin' shitstorm." I should have known better than to tease Dottie about it.

"I think, Dottie, it's safe to assume that Jasmine is still *walkin'*—she's only fifty-two," I told Nana's veteran housekeeper.

"I think, Adam, it's safer to assume that Jasmine is still *shittin'*—for as long as the old bag is still *livin'*," Dottie added.

It would not have been hard for Jasmine to find the phone number for Rachel Brewster in Manchester, Vermont—my mom and Molly didn't have an unlisted number. But my mother usually wasn't the one who answered the phone. When Jasmine called my mom and asked for me, Jasmine didn't know she was talking to Molly; Jasmine didn't know Molly. "Adam isn't here," the trail groomer told Jasmine.

"I know you're Adam's mother," Jasmine began. "I am an older woman who has slept with your son—I'm probably your age," Jasmine told the snow-cat operator.

Molly was as blunt about it as Dottie. "If you're the bed-shitter, you're a year older than Adam's mom—if you're the bed-shitter, go fuck yourself with a two-by-four," Molly told her.

"Is that Jasmine? Poor Jasmine!" my mother was calling, from another room, but Molly had hung up on the bed-shitter. Once, when Jasmine called, I happened to be staying with my mom and Molly. I was helping Molly with a risotto; my mother answered the phone. "Who shall I say is calling?" Molly and I heard her say. "Is this *the* Jasmine?" my mom then asked. Molly and I just looked at each other; I kept stirring the risotto. "It's poor Jasmine!" my mother told me, not bothering to cover the mouthpiece of the phone. I just shook my head; my mom got the message. "Adam can't come to the phone right now," my mother told her. Molly and I could hear Jasmine's rising voice—it reached us at the stove. "Well, I'm certainly not going to tell him all *that!*" we heard my mom say.

"Tell her she must have a vagina as big as a ballroom!" the ski patroller shouted from the stove. "The risotto is *ready*, Ray!" Molly called to my mom, who was getting an earful from Jasmine. Among the many things Jasmine was saying, she must have said the wrong thing—or one of those things you should never say to someone's mother. The trail groomer and I would not hear my mom use the word *poor* when she spoke of Jasmine again.

"Well, that's not what I hear," Molly and I heard my mother say to Jasmine. "I hear you've got a vagina as big as a *ballroom*," my mom told her, hanging up the phone.

It couldn't have been easy for Jasmine to find Nora's number; Nora had changed her name, and she had an unlisted number. Nora thought "Winter" was a better stage name than "Vinter"—maybe not in Norway, but Nora had never seemed especially Norwegian. *Two Dykes, One Who Talks* wasn't an act associated with last names; the two of them were called Nora and Em, not by their last names, but Nora Winter was known to be their spokesperson. Nora was the one who did the interviews—obviously, no one interviewed Em. At the start of the 1970s, I didn't know Em's last name, and I was one of the few who knew she'd been an Emily. Yet somehow Jasmine found Nora's unlisted phone number in New York.

When Em answered a phone call, all she did was breathe into the mouthpiece until Nora came to the phone. The first time Jasmine called for me, she must have thought I was the one not speaking to her; Jasmine must have imagined she'd finally found me. She'd asked for Adam and heard Em's breathing. "It's *you*, isn't it? You penis breath!" Jasmine shouted. This was not a welcome image to Em, who began to growl into the phone.

Nora, who was sitting on the toilet seat, could hear Em growling from the bathroom, where the door was closed. "I've *told* you not to answer the phone—just let the fucker ring, Em!" Nora was yelling, but Em was engrossed in Jasmine's litany of the younger, bigger penises she was regularly enjoying in my absence. Nora told me later that Jasmine had used the *springy* word to describe one of the eager penises in her exciting new life; the image of a *springy* penis had particularly repelled Em.

Unlike Nora, Em had experimented with having a boyfriend—this was in high school, before she met Nora. Unlike Nora, not everything about having a boyfriend was repulsive to Em—just the penis part. According to Em, everything had been okay: the cuddling, the kissing, the fooling around. Then the penis came into the picture. In Em's pantomime, she made the approach of the penis look like a one-eyed eel. In her penis pantomime, Em did a full-body slither. She closed her eyes and opened her mouth, in the shape of the letter O—Em's mouth looked like a single, sightless eye.

When Nora came out of the bathroom and interrupted Jasmine's call, Em had taken one of the cushions off the couch and was stomping on it—the phone held fast to her sweaty ear. The couch cushion must have represented the *springy* penis Jasmine had conjured, and Em was clearly killing it. "Who is it?" Nora asked Em, taking the phone from her. Em's pantomime—how Granddaddy's ghost had scared the shit out of Jasmine—would not have been difficult for Nora to interpret. "Everyone knows you shit in bed," Nora said to Jasmine; I know exactly how Nora would have said this, as if she were bored by bed-shitters. "Everyone knows your pussy is a subway station," Nora also said tiredly, hanging up the phone.

The next time I saw Nora and Em, and Nora told me about Jasmine's phone call, Em had perfected her pantomime of Jasmine's pussy as a subway station. It had potential as a skit for *Two Dykes, One Who Talks*, I thought—together with Em's pantomime of how Jasmine had shit in bed—but Nora told me that, even at the Gallows Lounge, they had to be careful how they put down straight women. There'd been some anti-lesbian backlash from the Gallows' audience, and the comedy club had dropped *Eric's All-Gay Band*—meaning Eric. But Eric wasn't funny, I pointed out—only the homophobes had laughed. The comedy club wasn't necessarily being anti-gay because they dropped Eric's act, or so I thought.

What did I know? I had no firsthand experience with the kind of sexual hatred Nora and Em (or Molly and my mother) were exposed to; I had no idea what the audience at the Gallows Lounge really thought about Mr. Barlow's getting groped in Eric's lap, but I certainly could tell that the snowshoer wasn't comfortable about it.

"It was the seventies, for Christ's sake—everyone was angry, everyone hated someone or something," Nora would say one day. "We thought the war in Vietnam was dividing us, but there was more divisiveness among us than we knew," Nora said.

The Gallows would drop *Prue, the Tongue Kisser*—so would I, but for different reasons. Prue wasn't funny enough for the Gallows, and I could never be reassuring enough for Prue. Mr. Barlow would stop seeing Eric, who was too young and too demonstrably affectionate for the snowshoer, who was clearly not at ease in Eric's lap at the Gallows Lounge; the snowshoer still had to be careful, even in New York. Even Eric managed to restrain his affection for Mr. Barlow *as a woman*. Eric hadn't become an all-gay band because he wanted to be with a woman.

I hadn't known that Mr. Barlow had been copyediting his parents' novels, which no doubt fueled his disdain for their actual writing; Elliot saw firsthand how badly they wrote. The little Barlows' U.S. publisher had given Elliot the training to be a copy editor—he'd taken a course at one of the publishing institutes, and he'd done some freelance jobs with supervision. I wasn't surprised to learn that the little English teacher had taken to copyediting, or that he'd proven his worth as a copy editor to the little Barlows' U.S. publisher, who'd connected him to other publishers in New York. When the snowshoer moved to New York City, he already had a job and some close contacts in publishing.

The long-termism of Mr. Barlow's decision-making was impressive. For how long had he planned to become a woman? Certainly Elliot Barlow was suited for copyediting, but had he been prescient enough to consider that that profession might work well with his transitioning to female? Yes, people in publishing are usually liberal or progressive—they're more tolerant than most—but I mean in addition to that. Copy editors aren't the most public people in publishing; they don't even take their authors to lunch. I published three novels with the same publisher before I met my copy editor. Copy editors work behind the scenes; for all you see of them, they might as well be working at home.

Or was Mr. Barlow prescient enough to imagine he would one day be able to support himself as a freelance copy editor, one who actually worked at home? When the snowshoer moved to New York, of course he could have found a job teaching English and coaching wrestling at any of several schools in the city. I'm sure he had outstanding recommendations from Exeter, but it wouldn't have worked out for him. How could Mr. Barlow be a schoolteacher and a coach when he became a woman? Surely someone would object—if not the kids, their parents or another teacher. Someone would say it was inappropriate for Elliot to use a women's washroom at the school; the women, especially the schoolgirls, wouldn't feel safe in the same washroom the little English teacher used. Of course I couldn't imagine women or girls being unsafe with Elliot Barlow.

"Imagine Elliot as a woman, all four feet nine of her, being safe in a men's washroom with a bunch of boys or men," Molly said.

"Or in a men's locker room with a bunch of wrestlers, sweetie," my mother said.

As Nora had said, in the seventies everyone was angry. But what the snowshoer wanted to do would never be safe or easy, not even as a copy editor.

The snowshoer was living in his parents' pied-à-terre on East Sixty-fourth Street. The little Barlows were rarely in New York; Elliot was welcome to move into their bigger bedroom, but he chose to stay in his childhood room. His women's clothes filled his closet—they were my mom's clothes, the snowshoer first told his parents. Some of them were. My mother cared little about clothes; she knew what Elliot liked to wear, and she loved giving him her clothes. But it made me sad that the snowshoer still had a hidden life, even after getting away from Exeter—a life he hid from his own parents. "From *her* own parents, sweetie," my mom kept correcting me. She knew him so much better than I did, I would one day realize—knew *her* so much better, I should say. I loved them all—I completely sympathized with Molly and my mother, with Nora and Em, and with Mr. Barlow. Yet I would always be an outsider to their sexual differences; I would always be just an observer, and a slow learner, as Nora knew. Some writers are.

I'm not saying Nora was wrong to be disappointed in the seventies. Nothing that seemed progressive was progressive enough—basically, that was Nora's point. The sexual revolution or the women's movement, feminism or gay liberation—whatever you called it, whatever you wanted, it didn't go far enough. Sexual discrimination and sexual violence were still around; sexual intolerance didn't go away. I get that. I'm not saying the seventies were great, but I was paying closer attention in the eighties; I hated them more. Of course, whenever I said how I hated that decade, Nora corrected me. She said it was Ronald Reagan we hated, but Em had hated him first. In the 1980s, Nora and Em's onstage shtick was often about Reagan and AIDS. *Two Dykes, One Who Talks* also went on the warpath against Jerry Falwell and the Moral Majority, and those two angry women went after Cardinal John

Joseph O'Connor. I could see it was complicated for Em to pantomime the Roman Catholic Archdiocese's position against safe-sex education in New York City public schools, condom distribution, and the cardinal's condemnation of homosexuality—not to mention the unchanging Catholic opposition to abortion. I get that, too.

In the 1970s, I was becoming a fiction writer, what Nora called a horse with blinders on—but the process requires a kind of tunnel vision. I prefer to say I was indulging in what John Updike called "a fiction writer's childish willingness to immerse himself in make-believe." I would write three more novels in the seventies; the fourth one, my first bestseller, would make me self-supporting as a writer. I didn't need to teach English or creative writing to make a living. My first reader, Elliot Barlow, would become my copy editor.

In that decade, I would also write two more screenplays that wouldn't be made as movies, but I would keep writing screenplays—as I've said, often concurrently with whatever novel I was writing. Sometimes I would start a story as a screenplay—it was a way to visualize the story, to see if I wanted to try writing the story as a novel.

Take my mother's story: I've tried to begin it as a screenplay, but the story doesn't add up. Real life is so sloppy—it's full of coincidences. Things just happen, random things that have no connection to one another. In good fiction, isn't everything connected to everything else? In my mom's story, I thought I understood her secrecy; there are things you don't tell your parents, things you should keep from your children. Of course the ghosts were confusing. Where did the ghosts fit in the story? And when your kid grows up, do you still have to keep the secrets from your kid—even the sexual secrets?

Nora traditionally took my mom's side. Ray's relationship with Molly spoke for itself, Nora always said. Little Ray was a lesbian, Nora would keep reminding Em and me. When my mother decided to get pregnant, of course she would have chosen the smallest penis around. "Why wouldn't she?" Nora was always asking Em and me; Nora thought we were *too harsh* on my mother. "You should just get over it, kiddo—you, too, Em—because Little Ray was probably on the lookout for a smallish penis," Nora told us. Then Em would do her "Returning to the Womb in Protest" pantomime.

If I'd shown Nora and Em the early pages of my Aspen screenplay, I would have had to relive the ceaseless speculation on the subject of whether or not my mother and Mr. Barlow did it. More to the point, since my mom lived with Molly, had Little Ray and the snowshoer *ever* done it? "Speaking of smallish penises," Nora always said, when this subject came up. It was Nora's opinion that all guys had to do it, all the time—even someone as small as the snowshoer.

Em felt differently, and rather strongly, about Elliot Barlow. Em adored the little English teacher; she was always hugging him, or spontaneously picking him up, or just holding him in her lap. "Honestly, Em—the way you handle the snowshoer, it's as if you think he doesn't actually have a penis!" Nora told her.

What Em told us took a while. Even for Nora, Em's pantomime wasn't easy to understand. I would see Em do Jerry Falwell onstage at the Gallows. Granted, the Christian Right didn't have a lot of fans at the Gallows, but the audience got Em *as Jerry Falwell* ahead of Nora's interpretation—even a conservative Christian could have understood Em's pantomime of Falwell's "AIDS is the wrath of God upon homosexuals." It was harder for Nora and me to understand what Em was trying to tell us about Mr. Barlow. Em was undertaking a sexual odyssey, which she wasn't enjoying—that much was clear.

"The snowshoer didn't do it with Ray—not once, not ever, not even blow jobs?" Nora was guessing.

I could see by Em's reaction that Nora had perceived only the tip of the iceberg. Em nodded, but briefly, barely interrupting her pantomime of sexual propositions and rejections. A vaginal activity was suggested, then spurned; an anal alternative was offered but declined, three times. *Wait a minute!* I was thinking. We all knew Elliot had two boyfriends after *Eric's All-Gay Band*—he'd had three boyfriends, counting Eric.

"Are you saying the snowshoer doesn't do it?" I asked Em.

Before Em could respond, Nora asked her, "You mean, he doesn't do it with *women*, right?" Em shook her head; she hadn't hesitated. Em pointed her index finger at me, like a gun—her thumb straight up, like a cocked hammer. But she didn't shoot; Em did nothing to imply pulling the trigger.

In Mr. Barlow's new life in New York, he'd broken up with three boyfriends rather quickly. Or had they broken up with him? We'd only heard Elliot's reasons for finding Eric unsuitable. We never knew what was wrong with Charlie or Dave, but those three guys might have broken up with the snowshoer if he didn't have sex with them.

"You're saying the snowshoer never does it—not with women or with men," I said to Em, who was nodding her head off. She lowered the imaginary gun; she wrapped her arms around herself, looking sad and lonely. What

Em wanted us to know was that Mr. Barlow wouldn't do it—he simply didn't pull the trigger.

"Bullshit!" Nora said. I knew what Nora thought of guys: they couldn't leave their dicks alone; guys had to pull the trigger. Em shrugged; she didn't expect Nora to agree with her. Moreover, Nora was angry that I'd understood what Em meant—I hadn't needed Nora to translate Em's pantomime for me.

Yet now I couldn't understand what Em was saying; she went off on a tangent, pointing to herself and Nora, as if this new pantomime were old business between them. Em was performing a kind of shorthand pantomime—Nora understood her immediately. "Well, that's entirely different—I get that, Em, but you're not a guy, for Christ's sake!" Nora told her.

Em just shrugged; she hadn't expected Nora to agree with her about this, either. Nora had to explain it to me. When Nora and Em were first together, Em told Nora that she hadn't been doing it with anyone. If Em hadn't met Nora, Em said she would have continued not doing it with anyone—not even with another woman. This was what Nora thought was "entirely different" from the idea of the snowshoer not doing it, because Em wasn't a guy.

It was all just weird to me, and I didn't really think about it, not then—nor did I have a strong opinion about it. At the time, in the 1970s, it didn't seem vital to know if Elliot Barlow actually did or didn't do it—with anybody. At the time, I just knew I couldn't stop imagining doing it with Em.

I'd noticed that Charlie, the snowshoer's second boyfriend, was not physically affectionate to the snowshoer in public. Even in the privacy of Mr. Barlow's apartment, Charlie was restrained in his physical displays of affection; Charlie would rub Elliot's shoulders when Elliot was standing over the stove, cooking. I would ascribe Charlie's reticence to his being older—Charlie was Mr. Barlow's age, and a fellow English teacher. As for Dave, the third fleeting boyfriend, he was a little older than Elliot. Dave didn't touch Mr. Barlow, not that I saw. "Dr. Dave," Nora always called him. Dave didn't specify what kind of doctor he was.

Once, when Nora asked him, Dave seemed purposely evasive about it. "In order for me to see you, your doctor would need to refer you to me," Dave answered her.

"Why didn't Dave just say he was a specialist, or what kind of specialist he was?" Nora asked Em and me. Em was doing a doctor pantomime, pretending a banana was a stethoscope. She pulled up her sweater and listened to her navel with the banana; then she pulled her sweater up higher and listened to her breast, or to her bra. "What the fuck are you listening *for*?"

Nora asked her. Em shrugged; now she was listening to her armpit with the banana. "She's Dr. Dave—she doesn't know what her specialty is," Nora explained.

Naturally, this became one of their routines at the Gallows. It was very popular. People in the audience would request the act; they would shout out for "The Specialist." Nora always got a laugh when she asked the people who made the request if they had a banana. This led some fans to put bananas on the stage, but having bananas onstage could be confusing. Em had more than one routine with a banana.

One night at the Gallows, I was there with the snowshoer and Dr. Dave. I'd warned Nora that Dave was going to be there. Mr. Barlow had already seen Nora and Em do "The Specialist"; he'd loved it, but he still hadn't told Nora or Em or me what Dave's specialty was. The night Dr. Dave came to the Gallows, no one was shouting for "The Specialist," but there were already a bunch of bananas onstage. Nora and Em were waiting for the applause to die down.

"What are the bananas for?" I heard Dave ask Elliot.

"You'll see," the snowshoer said.

Nora knew how to quiet the crowd. She took a banana from the bunch and handed it to Em. "I hear you're seeing a specialist," Nora began. Dr. Dave laughed as hard as anyone at the show; the snowshoer sat smiling beside him, the two of them not touching. It didn't really matter, not then, but nobody told Nora and Em and me what Dave's specialty was.

As an act, "The Specialist" kept evolving. I liked the most gynocentric version. "I hear you're seeing an OB-GYN *extra*," Nora begins. Em appears to be taking her pulse with the banana. "Extra *what*, Em?" Nora asks her.

This was what the seventies were like for us. We were at liberty—we had liberty, we took liberties. We felt free to say and write whatever we imagined. We felt free to live the lives we chose. We didn't see the pushback coming. We failed to imagine both the passive and aggressive forms the pushback would take.

"What are the bananas for? Long time passing," I remember Nora used to sing.

"Where have the bananas gone? Long time ago," the snowshoer sang back to her. I admired how Mr. Barlow stayed friends with his former boyfriends; Elliot was always happy to see them when they were with new boyfriends, and the snowshoer's old boyfriends always seemed happy to see him.

I asked Nora and Em if lesbians were like that—if they stayed friends with their former girlfriends. Boy, was that the wrong thing to ask. Em shrugged; then she did a sexy little dance. "What do you mean—*you don't know?*" Nora asked her. "If you left me, and I saw you with another girlfriend, I would tear off her tits and dance on her dead pudenda!" Nora told Em, who started to cry. Em kept doing her little dance, but she went on crying. "If I left Em, and she saw me with another girlfriend, Em would just cry," Nora told me, but I saw how Em was dancing. It was not exactly a dance on anyone's pudenda; it was more tender and more complicated than that.

Just for fun, I asked my mom and Molly about it. "I would never leave Molly, sweetie," my mother immediately said. "If I ever did, and Molly saw me with another woman, Molly would tie the woman to the snowcat and drag her up and down the mountain—until her tits fell off or froze, or her twat fell out, or something," my mom said.

Nora would have been comforted by this kindred theme, I thought, but I couldn't look at the snowcat operator, who immediately said, "That is *not* what I would do, Kid—and, by the way, I would never leave your mom," Molly told me.

"But you would do *something* to the other woman, if I was with her—wouldn't you?" my mother asked Molly.

"I would make her look at you, Ray, while I strangled her—so that you would be the last person she saw, as she was dying," the snowcat operator said.

"You see, sweetie? That's what I *meant*," my mom said.

My mother and Molly came to New York to see the snowshoer; they liked coming to New York for visits, more than they had ever liked Exeter. In the little Barlows' pied-à-terre on East Sixty-fourth, my mom slept most of the night with Mr. Barlow in his childhood bedroom. When I was visiting at the same time, I slept on the couch in what Elliot called *the study*. At night, I could hear my mother's bare feet, padding back and forth between Mr. Barlow in his little bedroom and the bigger bedroom, where she slept with Molly. Nothing had changed: my mom and the snowshoer were still married; they always would be. They still couldn't keep their hands off each other; they were still hugging or wrestling or giving each other piggyback rides, or they were curling up on couches or in chairs together. There had never been an edge, and there was no discernible edge now, to the way Molly called them *the lovebirds*.

At one time or another, I remember when my mother and Molly met Eric, Charlie, and Dr. Dave. "This is Ray, my wife. I've told you about Ray—she's never around in the ski season," the snowshoer often said. My mom already knew who Elliot's boyfriends (or his former boyfriends) were, or she'd paid attention to what Mr. Barlow had told her about them.

"You're as pretty as my husband said you were," my mother told Eric when she met him, giving the much younger man a hug. And we were all at Pete's Tavern, that old place in Gramercy Park, when we ran into Charlie, who was rubbing someone else's shoulders at the bar. "I've heard all about you, Charlie, and I'm jealous," my mom told the other English teacher in Mr. Barlow's life. "No one ever rubs my shoulders when I'm cooking," Little Ray said to Charlie.

"You don't ever cook, Ray—Elliot and I do all the cooking," Molly reminded her, but my mother was laughing. She was just having fun; everyone was laughing.

Once, when we ran into Dave, he was with a woman. Was she a patient or a date? Did Dr. Dave have a girlfriend? No one knew; no one seemed to care. "This must be your mom—she looks just like you, only she's prettier," Dave said to me.

"This is my wife, Ray—this is Dave," the snowshoer said, beaming.

"I'm so glad to meet you. It must not be the ski season," Dave told my mother.

"I never dated a *doctor*," Ray began, taking hold of the doctor's hands. She had a strong grip, from all the ski-poling. "There's stuff about me I could only say to a *specialist*," Little Ray whispered to Dr. Dave. He was charmed by her.

All of them made me feel welcome and at home with them, all the time, although I was the outsider among them—the straight guy with a questionable history of unfriendly former girlfriends.

Once in a while, I ran into Rose on the academy campus. I didn't ask her about her muscle spasms. Our friendship wouldn't recover from her headfirst, self-exposing descent of the attic stairs.

"There are worse things than limping," Rose told me.

It was Maud who warned me my grandmother was "losing her marbles." Maud ran into Nana in downtown Exeter, where Nana said she'd parked her car but couldn't find it. Maud knew we didn't let my grandmother drive—not after she'd driven into the garage and kept on driving, through the back wall. Maud knew Dottie drove Nana everywhere.

My grandmother mistook Maud for poor Rose. "Your limp is much better, dear—if I didn't know you had a limp, I would scarcely have noticed it," Nana told Maud.

"I'm Maud, Mrs. Brewster. I broke my arm, I had a cast for a while," Maud said to her. "Rose had a wicked limp, but her limp is all gone now."

"How are your muscle spasms, dear?" my grandmother asked her. Then Dottie showed up. "What on earth are you doing here, Dottie?" Nana asked her housekeeper.

"I was lookin' for you!" Dottie told her.

"As for exposing yourself on the stairs, dear," my grandmother was saying earnestly to Maud, "the best thing you can do is not think about it." Maud knew what and how much I'd seen of Rose, as poor Rose was descending the attic stairs. Maud had told me she couldn't stop thinking about it. Maud believed Rose's sex life was ruined by her unthinkable exposure.

"This is the one with the busted arm, Mrs. Brewster—not the one with her *whatsis* in the air, all the way down them attic stairs," Dottie tried to tell my grandmother.

Dottie had also warned me Nana was "slippin'," as she put it. "She makes tea all day and night, but she don't hear the kettle singin'," Dottie said.

"So she's losing her hearing?" I asked Dottie.

"She's losin' more than her hearin', Adam. When she takes the kettle off the burner, she leaves them flames burnin'—she's gonna burn the house down, if she don't piss herself to death first," Dottie said.

"She's incontinent?" I asked Dottie.

"I don't know about that, Adam, but she's just standin' there pissin', when she don't know she's pissin'—them diapers don't work, you know, if you don't remember to use 'em, and she won't let me put 'em on her," Dottie said. "As for them two aunts of yours, them two will hasten her death," Dottie added.

When my grandmother was napping, Aunt Abigail and Aunt Martha were "showin'" the Front Street house to Realtors. "Them two aunts of yours don't trouble themselves to introduce visitors to the hired help, but I'd know a Realtor in the dark, Adam—them Realtors smell the same as them morticians," Dottie assured me.

I already knew from Nora that her mother and Aunt Martha were impatient to inherit the Front Street house—they intended to renovate the house for resale while they waited, if Nana didn't die in a timely fashion, Nora had said. Uncle Martin had already retired, and Uncle Johan would be retiring soon. Those two old downhillers were looking for property up north, in ski country; my conniving aunts were scheming with Realtors on ways to make a killing on the Front Street house. My beer-drinking uncles were innocent of my aunts' conspiracies to cheat my mom out of her share of the inheritance, but Nora and I knew Nana was deteriorating; Nana would soon require assisted living, beyond Dottie's care.

The facility for old folks of means in the Exeter area was not in a safe location for the elderly who wandered off, or had otherwise lost their marbles. On the riverbank at a bend of the Squamscott River, the assisted-living facility overlooked the mudflats (at low tide) or the water (when the tide was in). River Bend, as the old folks' home was unimaginatively called, was bordered by water or mud, and by the town golf course. The location was equally ill advised for a golf course; errant golf balls would be lost in the river, or the golfers would sink to their knees in the mudflats in a doomed effort to retrieve their badly hit balls. The addled patients at River Bend would wander into the water or get stuck in the mud; if the patients who'd lost their marbles roamed the other way, they risked being bonked by golf balls.

The dumb but oft-repeated joke among the Exeter townsfolk who could never afford River Bend was that many of the patients had already gone around the bend, or they soon would be going around it. When the tide was out, it was possible to wade across the Squamscott River, where one of the addled River Bend patients was once found wandering among the black Angus beef cattle, talking to them while they grazed. This had happened when I was at the academy, but it was still the talk of the town. Even my grandmother had heard of it, and somehow remembered it.

"Don't send me to River Bend, please—not till I've gone completely around the bend," Nana had said. She was still saying it—even in her sleep, Dottie had confided to me. Even when Nana was napping, and the Realtors were assessing the Front Street house—looking for renovations (at my grandmother's expense) that would jack up the asking price—my grandmother kept saying, "Don't send me to River Bend, please."

As children, both Nora and I remembered my mother telling us that Nana had an unfounded fear of cows—maybe not so *unfounded*, Nora and I now thought. Even in her sleep, Mildred Brewster was imagining herself doomed to converse with cattle. I'm guessing Nana never knew why the renovations she would pay for were necessary.

It was still the 1970s; the real shit hadn't started. As Nora was always saying, there was shit in the offing. Nora usually meant this politically. The shit in the offing part of *Two Dykes, One Who Talks* was called "The News in English." Onstage, of course, this political satire of the news began with Em's pantomime; Em wrote all their material. The English translation was all

Nora. Naturally, there were differences of opinion between them regarding the fidelity of Nora's translation.

Em's spontaneous pantomimes were always ad-libbed. Yet Em got cross when Nora went off-script while they were performing. My empathy was with Em—she was the writer. Em didn't like it when Nora ad-libbed her monologue.

As written, "The News in English" was prescient about Ronald Reagan's rise to power. Nora and I missed it. "Why would a former sports announcer, actor, and president of the Screen Actors Guild not seek a third term as governor of California?" Em wrote. It was 1975, and this was a difficult question to put into pantomime. Nora gave the audience at the Gallows a faithful English translation. "I wish Ronald Reagan would be governor of California forever—we'll all be safer if that cowboy stays in California," Em had written. Nora faithfully translated this bit, but she went off-script for a moment—Nora always had to add her two cents' worth.

"For Christ's sake, Em, you don't need to worry about Ronald Reagan—he's a second-rate actor; he isn't going anywhere," Nora said. This got a laugh at the Gallows, but I didn't laugh, and Em was furious. I understood the impromptu pantomime Em was doing; I knew her pantomime was off-script, too.

Nora had been wrong about second-rate actors before. "Paul Goode isn't going anywhere," she'd said. Em knew that everyone at the Gallows had surely seen *The Kindergarten Man*. Em's pantomime of the anxious kindergartner at the urinal required no translation. We remembered Paul Goode lying under the toilet stalls, holding a handgun against his chest; Em didn't need to act out that part.

What needed a new pantomime, at least new to me, was Em's enactment of how manipulable American voters were. It was clear what Em was imitating when she squatted onstage, but Nora took some poetic license with her English translation.

"It doesn't take a first-rate actor to manipulate American voters"—that's my best guess at what Em's pantomime was saying.

It was Nora's way of saying things that would get Em in trouble, not only this time. "Even a second-rate actor is good enough to dupe the dumber-than-dogshit American people," was the unfortunate way Nora interpreted Em's pantomime.

No one laughed; even at the Gallows, there were murmurs of disapproval. The management of the Gallows would complain to Nora about it.

"You can't translate everything the Canadian acts out," Nora was told. The dopes in charge blamed Em for it. Whenever Nora said something too anti-American, the management at the Gallows Lounge—speaking of *dumber than dogshit*—held the nonspeaking Canadian accountable. To anyone who ever saw Nora and Em onstage, the most inflammatory things Nora said were all in the way Nora said them.

You can't call the American people *dumber than dogshit*—no one can. As Nora would say, the American people are the most sacred cows in American politics. No American politician can get away with saying anything derogatory about the American people, but Nora just let it fly—Nora wasn't running for political office.

Em was the one who saw Ronald Reagan coming; she was the one who was worried about him. Em also saw how the audience at the Gallows reacted to what Nora said about the American people, and she was worried about that. She knew that the audience at the Gallows generally loved *Two Dykes, One Who Talks*, but not this time. Em was the one who saw the hatred coming.

Nora just let it fly. "What are the bananas for? Long time passing," Nora kept singing. At first it was funny, but the way Nora sang it, it sounded like a dirge.

"Where have the bananas gone? Long time ago," the snowshoer sang, in his beautiful but elegiac voice—in *her* beautiful but elegiac voice, I would soon (I would finally) learn to say. Like Ronald Reagan and the hatred, the elegies were coming, too.

32.

A TURN IN THE ROAD

The residents of River Bend preferred the rooms with the river views. At low tide, their rooms overlooked mostly mudflats, but the residents preferred the mud to the golf course. Not my grandmother. "I rather like the mud, but I would prefer not to see the cows or even think about them," Nana said. The long view, across the river or the mudflats, was of the black Angus farm. At such a distance from River Bend, it was pointed out to Mildred Brewster, the cattle would appear to be the size of small dogs. "I do not care what the cows *appear to be*—I know what they are," my grandmother pointed out. "I would prefer not to see or think about cows, not even small ones." There was Bartleby's *I would prefer not to*, again—Nana remembered her Melville. She also remembered moments of her early childhood, unknown to us. Her life as a young woman had remained intact—most of all, her *reading* as a young woman.

"Her short-term memory is shot to shit," Dottie pointed out. "She don't know the difference between yesterday and fifty years ago." This was true. My grandmother's understanding of chronological order was shot to shit, too. *Moby-Dick* was clearer to her, and more real, than the births of her children or her children's children. Nana knew who Dottie was, but she always seemed surprised when Dottie showed up—as if Dottie belonged somewhere else, or Dottie herself were somehow out of chronological order.

Near the end, even before she left the Front Street house for River Bend, my grandmother didn't recognize Abigail and Martha—not until they spoke to her. "Oh, it's *you*—you should have said something," Nana told my aunts, as soon as she heard their harping voices.

Once, when Dottie was still taking care of her, my grandmother asked Dottie why she couldn't smell the diaper man. "Did you just change Principal Brewster's diaper, Dottie?" Nana asked.

"Wrong time, Mrs. Brewster—the diaper man is dead," Dottie answered her.

"Oh, it's *that* time—well, it's all downhill from here," my grandmother said.

It would have made my mother cry if Nana ever failed to remember her, but Rescue Ship Rachel didn't need to worry. Little Ray had been named for "the devious-cruising Rachel." Mildred Brewster, who could recite the rest of that last sentence of *Moby-Dick,* would always recognize her dearest Rachel.

Once, when my mom visited her aged mother at River Bend, she made sure she was recognized; she stomped into my grandmother's room, doing her single-leg lunges. "Stop, Rachel—you'll shake the chandelier!" Nana cried, but they weren't in the dining room. There were no chandeliers at River Bend, where my grandmother chose a room overlooking the golf course.

"Well-to-do men with clubs," Nana said, whenever she looked out her window and saw the golfers. "Are they all Republicans?" my grandmother asked me once, pointing to the golfers. They were a long way from the window; I could make out only the brighter colors of the golfers' clothes.

"I don't know if they're Republicans, Nana," I said.

"I know I'm not being fair—maybe the golfers just dress like Republicans," my grandmother said, sighing. She had great disdain for golf as exercise. The nurses at River Bend reported that Nana sometimes shouted at the golfers. "If you're doing this for exercise, just keep *walking*—don't keep *stopping!*" my grandmother yelled at them. It upset her more to see women playing golf—the women were definitely dressed like Republicans. "If women are Republicans, they've been brainwashed—the men have brainwashed them," Nana said. The nurses at River Bend reported that my grandmother was always saying this. There were residents at River Bend who refused to sit with Nana in the dining hall; probably they were Republicans.

Near the end, this made Nora like my grandmother—at least a little more than Nora used to like her. Nora actually said it was a good thing Nana never knew that Aunt Abigail and Aunt Martha had predeceased her.

"No woman wants to outlive her children, Adam—not even them two children," Dottie would tell me later. "I knew I shoulda gone back to Maine, when them two moved your grandmother to the bend in the river." Yet my aunts had persuaded Dottie to stay in the Front Street house. Aunt Abigail and Aunt Martha hadn't chosen a Realtor; my aunts were still renovating. Someone had to keep the old house clean, my aunts decided, and Dottie knew the Front Street house.

"Have you seen the ghost, Dottie?" Aunt Abigail asked my grandmother's faithful housekeeper.

"The Realtors have heard about a ghost in the house," Aunt Martha chimed in.

"I don't do spirits—I don't see 'em or clean 'em," Dottie answered. "There's people I know who sure as shit saw *somethin'*, but if I can't see it, I'm not messin' with it," Dottie told them.

"What on earth does *that* mean, Dottie?" Aunt Abigail asked her.

"I can keep the attic clean, but I'm not recommendin' that you mess with it," Dottie answered her. "I was wastin' my breath, Adam—I shoulda known that them two aunts of yours weren't listenin'," Dottie would tell me later. Fortunately, my grandmother would never know that *them two* had died—or how they'd died. Among the marbles Mildred Brewster had lost, she'd lost the marble for time. For Nana, losing the time marble was a blessing.

When had Abigail and Martha last visited my grandmother at River Bend? Why, it was *just the other day*, Nana would have answered, although Dottie had moved back to Maine, and my aunts had been dead for four or five years. The Front Street house kept changing hands; in four or five years, that house had seen as many new owners. The Realtor would keep lowering the asking price, following the repeated renovations to the attic.

It didn't matter what the Realtor renovated. The problem in the attic didn't stay in the attic. Granddaddy's ghost knew how to keep quiet. Principal Brewster had always known how to bide his time. Not even my aunts could boss the diaper man around, though those two would try. After Aunt Abigail and Aunt Martha managed to move my grandmother to River Bend, those two harassers went after the ghost in the attic.

Realtors hear everything. A ghost in the Front Street house was big news in the town. Even Rose, who no longer limped, said someone had told *her* there was a ghost in my grandmother's attic. "Yeah, I've already heard about it," Rose had replied, but my aunts were dead set on doing something about the ghost of the enfant terrible. Ghosts were bad for the real estate business, my aunts were told; in an old New England house with a history, a ghost will bring down the asking price. Aunt Abigail and Aunt Martha wouldn't hear of it. My aunts were determined to give this ghost a talking-to.

"Daddy will listen to *us*," Aunt Abigail told my mother.

"This is all your fault, Rachel—Daddy stopped talking because of *you*," Aunt Martha added, rubbing it in.

"Daddy stopped *listening* before he stopped talking—Daddy went batshit crazy before I was born!" my mom told her sisters.

"Them two aunts of yours were *born* batshit crazy, Adam," Dottie would tell me later. Dottie didn't encourage my aunts' plan; wisely, Dottie wanted nothing to do with it. In Dottie's opinion, the idea of those two sleeping in my attic bedroom was just asking for trouble. Ghost or no ghost, this sure as shit constituted "messin' with it," as Dottie had said.

"You didn't say anything about Jasmine?" I'd asked Dottie.

"Not to them two," Dottie said. "Them two have made their beds, haven't they?" Dottie asked me.

"You didn't tell them what happened to Jasmine?" I would ask my mother later.

"I don't tell tales out of school about you, sweetie—you're my one and only," my mom reminded me.

After the fact, even Nora would ask me the same thing—in her fashion. "I don't suppose you said something to my mom or Martha, regarding Jasmine's encounter with Granddaddy's ghost—or whatever you want to call it. Did you, kiddo?"

I was looking at Em while I shook my head. "I thought you might have already told them," I lied to Nora, speaking as slowly as possible. Em was shaking her head emphatically. *You would be crazier than batshit to try to tell those two anything*, Em was saying.

"Who would try to stop those two from sleeping in that attic?" Nora asked me. "Not me, kiddo," my cousin answered herself. Em was pantomiming something inexplicable. "Em says those two wouldn't have listened to me, anyway," Nora said.

All Dottie did was leave a light on in the kitchen. Dottie's bedroom, in the back of the Front Street house, was above the kitchen. My aunts left another light on, in the upstairs hall; it shed some light on the attic stairs and dimly lit the attic bedroom, enough for my aunts to find their way to the bathroom. Abigail and Martha were in their late sixties; maybe they needed to get up at night.

"Them two didn't get up *that* night," Dottie would tell me later. As always, when anyone was sleeping in the attic, Dottie left her bedroom door open—"just a crack," Dottie said, "just enough to hear somethin', if somethin' happens." According to Dottie, "There was nowhere near as much yellin' as the racket Jasmine made, and no shittin' whatsoever—them two were scared shitless before they could shit," as Dottie put it.

"Not Little Ray!" my aunts screamed; they were in chorus, but Dottie heard them scream only once. By the time Dottie clomped upstairs, Aunt Abigail and Aunt Martha had stopped breathing. They were hugging each other in my bed, their eyes wide open and staring. I knew where they would have been staring—at a spot on the floor, at the foot of my bed, under the skylight. It was the spot where the principal emeritus chose to appear—in my experience, when the tyrannical infant was in no mood to listen. What else could have frightened those two to death? It had to be Granddaddy's ghost, in his enfant-terrible phase.

"It sure as shit looks like somethin' scared 'em to death," was all Dottie would say to the police about it.

Not surprisingly, Dottie wasn't quoted in the *Exeter Town Crier*. "Two Sisters Pass Away Together" was the headline in the "Police Report." There was mention of their dying "in the house where they were born"—even more comforting, "in their sleep"—which made my aunts' deaths sound enviable.

"Them two didn't die when they were *sleepin'*!" Dottie exclaimed, when she read the "Police Report."

Mr. Barlow, as usual, disparaged the *writing*. "The words *scared* or *frightened* are avoided—the piece seems willfully unclear," the little English teacher observed.

"The cause of death was not immediately apparent," the *Exeter Town Crier* stated.

"As *apparent* as a turd in your beer!" Dottie had shouted. She had no doubt—those two had sure as shit seen *somethin'*.

The way the "Police Report" ended caused a little criticism. Of the two Mrs. Vinters, the elder Brewster sisters, it was written: "They had no known illnesses."

"That's like saying the *house* killed them—or like saying there's a ghost, without saying it," the snowshoer said. Mr. Barlow still subscribed to the *Exeter Town Crier*, even in New York. The snowshoer showed the "Police Report" to Em and Nora; for Nora, the piece amounted to an obit for her mother and Aunt Martha.

Em immediately did a couple of death scenes; she acted out two deaths from unknown (or at least unrecognizable) illnesses. "It's bullshit that those two had *no known illnesses*—they had sexual intolerance up the wazoo!" Nora was raving. "They had incurable hatred of sexual differences!" Nora shouted. This somewhat explained why I didn't understand the cause of death in the death scenes Em was pantomiming.

Realtors must know how to read between the lines of an obituary. All but one of the agents lost interest in selling the Front Street house. The one who remained lowballed the asking price. My mother couldn't have cared less; she wanted to be rid of the house, and she didn't care if she didn't make a killing. In fact, my mom had already removed herself from the inheritance.

When my grandmother's marbles were still intact, she'd granted power of attorney to Little Ray to act on her behalf. (It would have killed my aunts to know that Nana had done this.) Nana and my mom had long ago agreed that my grandmother's estate would go, in equal parts, to Nora, Henrik, and me. Aunt Abigail and Aunt Martha had been cut out of the picture some years before they saw the thing that appeared in my attic bedroom, under the nighttime skylight.

Fiction writers like what we call *truthful exaggeration*. When we write about something that really happened—or it almost happened, could have happened—we just enhance what happened. Essentially, the story remains real, but we make it better than it truly was, or we make it more awful—depending on our inclination.

I wrote, of a fictional grandmother, that she had died one day short of her hundredth birthday; I suggested she'd died "deliberately," knowing the hullabaloo over her centenary would doubtless have killed her. This almost happened to Mildred Brewster, who would have wanted no part of her hundredth birthday. Once—this was at River Bend, when I was reading to her from her beloved *Moby-Dick*—my grandmother said, "I should have gone down with the *Pequod*, Adam."

"Why, Nana?" I asked her.

"Because I've lived long enough, my dear boy," my grandmother answered. "Who wouldn't prefer to die at sea? Doesn't that beat being surrounded by golfers?"

This was during a period of conflict between the golfers and those River Bend residents whose rooms overlooked the golf course. A golfer had "relieved himself," as Nana put it, within sight of several River Bend residents who were looking out their windows; my grandmother was among the offended gawkers.

As I understood it, a golfer had to go; he'd unzipped himself and had taken a whiz in a grassy area between the putting green and the marshland along the river. There was only one green within sight of the River Bend residents. I don't play golf; I can't recall which hole it was. The flag that marked the green had been stolen from the cup; after the peeing incident, the golfers claimed, one of the River Bend residents threw the flag in the Squamscott River. The flag was not replaced, but juvenile hostilities persisted between the golfers and the residents. One morning, when many of the residents were looking out their windows, a golfer gave them the finger.

"It was a woman, Adam—she did *that*," my grandmother said, giving me the finger. A lady golfer had flipped her the bird, one of the brainwashed Republican women. Among the River Bend residents, Nana knew there was talk of retaliation.

The townies, the local people of Exeter, who weren't well-to-do or part of the academy community, called the River Bend residents River *Benders*; the near-death residents, of course, were called River *Enders*.

The act of reprisal against the golfers was expected by both River Benders and Enders—not by the golfers. "It appears that *one of us* pooped on the putting green," my grandmother told me, in hushed tones—as if she were speaking of a sacred act. A River Bender—maybe a River Ender, with nothing to lose—had retaliated by taking a big dump on the putting green, very close to the cup missing its flag.

The groundskeeper for the golf course was the one who discovered the giant mound on the green. It was suspicious that my grandmother and *all* the residents with views of the putting green had waited at their windows for the groundskeeper's arrival. "The residents definitely knew the poop was on the green before the groundskeeper got to it," a young nurse confided to me; she was more candid than the older nurses at River Bend, but she didn't go so far as to say the residents had foreknowledge of the outrageous act of defecation. Whatever person did the defecating became "an overnight legend at River Bend," or so the young nurse earnestly told me. Yet the defecator would remain an unnamed hero.

If Nana knew who did it, she took her knowledge of the daring dumper to her grave. (To Mildred Brewster's thinking, even defecating was better exercise than golf.)

When Dottie's postcards came, Nana didn't know who Dottie was—not to mention what Dottie was saying. "How are you, Mrs. Brewster? I'm still kicking," Dottie always wrote, before signing her name in the surprisingly legible handwriting of her grocery lists.

"Who is Dottie? Exactly what is she kicking?" my grandmother would ask me, or one of the nurses. When we reminded her who Dottie was, and how "still kicking" was just Dottie's way of saying she was *alive*, Nana was indignant about the misunderstanding. "Well, why doesn't Dottie *sound* like Dottie—why doesn't she *say* it the way Dottie would have said it? It's not 'kicking,' it's *kickin*'!" my grandmother exclaimed. It was Dottie's *voice* she still remembered, and mine.

In the end, Nana didn't remember me when she saw me. Even if I had visited her as recently as a week before, or only a day before, she would stare at me, not knowing who I was. "It's me, Nana—it's Adam," I would have to tell her each time. She always recognized my voice.

"Oh, Adam—you've gotten so *old*, dear," she would say.

Moby-Dick has a first-person narrator. It was Ishmael's voice my grandmother remembered. It didn't matter where Nana started reading, or where she stopped. She didn't remember where she'd stopped, or where she'd started the day before; she knew the story. She remembered all of *Moby-Dick*. Nana knew everything Ishmael said, and exactly how Ishmael was supposed to say it.

The young nurse at River Bend knew only that my grandmother's old eyes got tired from her constant reading, especially in the winter months, when there were no golfers and Nana read and reread her *Moby-Dick* day and night. For Nana, the winter was one day long; it had happened overnight and would newly arrive, again, every tomorrow, but her old eyes knew how long winters were in New Hampshire. "Oh, look, it snowed last night— enough to discourage the cowardly golfers," my grandmother would say every winter morning.

The young nurse, Emmanuelle, was from one of New Hampshire's French Canadian families; she spoke no French, only English. In the early going in *Moby-Dick*, Nana needed to correct Emmanuelle's pronunciation. "It's *Queequeg*," my grandmother told the intrepid Emmanuelle. "Keep your eye on the cannibal, dear—Queequeg is important. He's not just any harpooner; Queequeg isn't a Christian," Nana forewarned the young nurse, who (fearlessly) began reading *Moby-Dick* at the beginning.

I happened to encounter Emmanuelle when she was discouraged and in tears—this was following her mispronunciations in Chapter 32, the "Cetology" chapter.

"No one needs to know the names of 'the leviathanic brotherhood'—my grandmother won't know if you skip chapters like that," I told the young nurse. I forewarned her not to read Chapter 92, the "Ambergris" chapter— knowing that whale vomit, and everything to do with "the inglorious bowels of a sick whale," was distracting and not what was important.

It was not just Queequeg's name that caused trouble for young Emmanuelle; the stalwart girl had been chastised by my grandmother for mispronouncing "Tashtego" and "Daggoo," and Nana never failed to remind Emmanuelle that Queequeg is a savage (not a Christian) for a very good reason. "And there's his coffin," Nana revealed to the young nurse. "Please don't forget about Queequeg's coffin!"

Poor Emmanuelle; the nurse had read no farther than the end of Chapter 40, the "Midnight, Forecastle" chapter. It was commendable how the young nurse had devoted herself to reading all of *Moby-Dick,* but she would not get to Queequeg's coffin before Chapter 110. I didn't want to tell Emmanuelle that my grandmother might have spoiled the story by spilling the beans about the coffin too soon. When I was visiting Nana, I took over the reading from Emmanuelle—not necessarily where the dutiful nurse had stopped reading. Nana never remembered where you stopped reading, and wherever you started *Moby-Dick,* Mildred Brewster knew exactly where she was in the story. What my grandmother didn't know was where she was in her own story.

I often began reading to Nana from Pip's prayer. Pip is the Black cabin boy on the *Pequod.* At the end of the "Midnight, Forecastle" chapter, Pip has overheard the sailors swearing their allegiance to Ahab—"that anaconda of an old man," Pip calls Captain Ahab. Pip is afraid. "Oh, thou big white God aloft there somewhere in yon darkness," Pip prays, "have mercy on this small black boy down here; preserve him from all men that have no bowels to feel fear!"

"Poor Pip," my grandmother always said, sighing. We both knew what would happen to him; in a sense, the cabin boy would drown twice. Lost overboard, alone on the sea, and then rescued, Pip goes mad. "The sea had jeeringly kept his finite body up, but drowned the infinite of his soul. Not drowned entirely, though." Pip would live, to drown again—the last time, with the rest of the *Pequod*'s crew.

Or I would begin with "The Blacksmith," the gloomy Chapter 112, because Nana said she knew nothing as comforting on the subject of death as the line she loved in that dark chapter. "Death is only a launching into the region of the strange Untried." Melancholy comforted my grandmother.

Nana liked the door to her room at River Bend left open. The doors to the residents' rooms were closed at night—"for fire reasons," Emmanuelle had told me—but during the day, my grandmother insisted that her door remain open. Some of the residents who'd lost their marbles would wander in when I was reading, but they never stayed to listen. *Moby-Dick* wasn't written for passersby.

"Just keep reading, dear—perhaps 'The Shark Massacre' would be an appropriate chapter," Nana would tell me, when one of the marbleless trespassers entered her room, picking up photographs and putting them down, and otherwise aimlessly snooping around.

I would, as directed, turn to that passage in Chapter 66, where the sharks are snapping "at each other's disembowelments"—especially that bit where "those entrails seemed swallowed over and over again by the same mouth, to be oppositely voided by the gaping wound." These images were sufficiently unpleasant to make most of the trespassing residents leave my grandmother's room—even though they'd lost their marbles, or perhaps because they'd lost them. Only occasionally did I need to read to the end of the chapter, where poor Queequeg almost loses his hand to a dead shark on deck. In his semi-literate way, the savage speculates on what kind of irresponsible god could have created the shark. "Queequeg no care what god made him shark," the cannibal says, "wedder Fejee god or Nantucket god; but de god wat made shark must be one dam Ingin." Queequeg's irreverent, sacrilegious dialogue did the trick. Even the most marbleless of the intruders were offended; the trespassers quickly left Nana's room, not wanting to hear more of *Moby-Dick*.

"If you would close your door, Mrs. Brewster, the other residents would not wander into your room," one of the older nurses was always telling my grandmother.

"Fiddlesticks!" Nana always replied.

Nurse Fiddlesticks, as I now think of the well-meaning but wrongheaded nurse, couldn't understand how my grandmother might have enjoyed the intrusions by the River Bend residents who wandered into her room—the more marbles they'd lost, the better. Nana was not once disdainful of her fellow River Benders for being lost or addled; what Mildred Brewster disdained was the trespassers' lack of interest in reading. Yet, contradictorily, Nana did everything she could to discourage the intruders from staying to listen.

Emmanuelle had told me that my grandmother once made her read "The Whiteness of the Whale"—not only all of Chapter 42 but the terrible footnotes in small type. "It was the whiteness of the whale that above all things appalled me"; if only Ishmael had stopped there, but "the thought of whiteness" gives Ishmael no peace. There are footnotes concerning "the intolerable hideousness" of the polar bear and "the mild deadliness" of the white shark; an even longer footnote describes Ishmael's sighting of a white albatross, a "mystic thing." Then came "the Albino man" passage; the chapter's willful, "all-pervading whiteness" was enough to make a nonreader out of anyone. I loved *Moby-Dick,* and I knew that Emmanuelle wanted to love it—the young nurse was sincerely trying her hardest to love it—but both of us hated "the incantation of this whiteness," which Ishmael kept reciting in "The Whiteness of the Whale," which was *not* about the whale's whiteness.

"I hate that chapter," Emmanuelle told me, near tears.

"I hate it, too," I said to the young nurse, who didn't like it when my grandmother asked her to skip ahead in her reading of *Moby-Dick*. In my estimation, Emmanuelle was a principled young woman; she wanted to read the entire novel, in order. On one occasion, when a female resident at River Bend wandered into Nana's room, my grandmother had resorted to a trick she liked to play with Chapter 81. Just reading the title ("The Pequod meets the Virgin") or speaking suggestively about the chapter would compel a female trespasser to leave the room. Em once imagined *Moby-Dick* was a pornographic novel. God knows what a female River Bender might have imagined about "The Pequod meets the Virgin"—that chapter could sound pornographic to the uninitiated reader, or to a nonreader. (Although I could imagine the male River Benders and Enders might have been intrigued.)

I knew Nora's feelings about Nana's reading *Moby-Dick* to me. I'd been trying to explain to Nora and Em how Nana and I had reversed our roles— how I was reading *Moby-Dick* to Nana; how a young nurse at River Bend seemed committed to reading the whole novel to her. I told Nora and Em that Emmanuelle was intent on finishing her reading of the novel before Nana died. This hadn't sounded maniacally obsessive to me—not until I heard myself say it out loud to Nora and Em, when I made Emmanuelle sound like as much of a lunatic as Ishmael on the subject of whiteness. I saw that Em was writhing all around; she appeared to be depicting a series of tragic mistakes and subsequent agonies, what Em imagined might transpire in "The Pequod meets the Virgin." Em knew how to make a tragic story worse.

"Are you sure Emmanuelle is a nurse, kiddo?" Nora asked me. "How does a nurse have time to read *Moby-Dick* to one of the patients? Do you know how old Emmanuelle is? She sounds like a kid who doesn't have enough to do," Nora told me. Em's saga of unending errors and resultant grief was ongoing.

"Is that what Em's saying?" I asked Nora.

"That's what *I'm* saying, kiddo—you don't want to know what's bugging Em," Nora said.

I'd first thought Em was acting out what happens in "The Pequod meets the Virgin," which Em had interpreted as a succession of grotesque and humiliating wedding nights—a *Nibelungenlied* of lost virginity, leading to several deaths. It occurred to me, only then, that I might have misunderstood Emmanuelle when we were first introduced. She was young, she was shy, she mumbled; maybe Emmanuelle told me she was a nursing student, not a nurse.

Nora was inexactly reading my mind and Em's when she said, apropos of nothing, "If you didn't know what *Moby-Dick* was about, and you had no clue the *Pequod* was a ship, a chapter called 'The Pequod meets the Virgin' might make you think the *Pequod* is a nickname for a guy with a big dick, a bad idea for virgins." Then Em went off on a possible tangent—maybe related to her epic of the repercussions ensuing from lost virginity, maybe not. "Em says most dicks are a bad idea for virgins," Nora added.

"Is that *all* Em is saying?" I asked Nora. Em was violently shaking her head.

Em had more on her mind than what happens in "The Pequod meets the Virgin." In Chapter 81, the eponymous *Virgin* is a German ship—the *Jungfrau,* sailing out of Bremen. The *Jungfrau* encounters the *Pequod* at sea, but the captain and crew of the German ship are a bunch of amateurs; the *Jungfrau* is a ship of virgins, when it comes to knowing about whaling. Of course this wasn't what Em was worked up about. I was beginning to get the feeling that the loss of anyone's virginity, real or imagined, wasn't what Em was worked up about in the first place.

"It's about *me,* isn't it? What is Em saying about me?" I asked Nora. Em had crumpled; she was exhausted and she looked angry. Em wasn't only angry at me; she was angry at Nora, for being less than forthright in translating her.

"Em says you must be fucking Emmanuelle, or you soon will be, kiddo," Nora said.

"I'm not fucking her!" I cried, but Nora had touched a nerve—yes, I'd thought about fucking Emmanuelle.

"You soon will be," Nora repeated. "Em says you have to grow up. You have to stop fucking these women you feel sorry for, just because you know they will fuck you—and don't fuck young women, like Emmanuelle. Em thinks Nana will die before Emmanuelle finishes reading *Moby-Dick*—then Emmanuelle will want to read it to you, kiddo. Em says you're going to be taking turns reading *Moby-Dick* aloud to each other, and you know what that will lead to," Nora said.

"I have no intentions of reading *Moby-Dick* with Emmanuelle, or doing what that will lead to," I said, not as indignantly as I tried to sound. My indignation was muted, because (of course) I'd imagined Emmanuelle reading *Moby-Dick* to me, and our taking turns reading to each other, and what that would lead to.

It used to disturb me that Em knew so much about me. I didn't know as much as I'd wanted to know about Em, beginning with why she'd stopped speaking, but Em was not inclined to pantomime what I could only guess was a dark and twisted tale, and Nora wouldn't tell me Em's story.

The snowshoer knew only bits and pieces: what my mom had overheard or reconstructed from Abigail and Martha's gossip. Em had a Canadian father and an American mother; their marriage became unglued when they were outed, or they outed each other. How Em's speech was affected by her parents' divorce, or their coming out as gay and lesbian, Mr. Barlow didn't know; my mother hadn't overheard that part. "As for Emmanuelle, I've not met her—I've only heard about her. You should talk to your mom and Molly about Emmanuelle—they've met her," Elliot said, in *her* most offhand manner. *She* was still Mr. Barlow to me, but she'd had enough of living as a man.

The snowshoer was in her forties before she came out as a transgender woman; she'd been taking estrogen for three or four years. Dr. Dave's specialty was endocrinology. Dave had been prescribing and overseeing Mr. Barlow's hormone therapy from the start. Back then, most endocrinologists weren't prescribing spironolactone as a testosterone blocker. Nora and Em had confided to me what Elliot told them. After the snowshoer had been taking the estrogen, she started to feel desire more like women do—not the gross way men do, Em had vividly acted out for me.

"I wasn't *wanting it* all the time—what a relief that was," Elliot herself would tell me, later. There'd been a distinct disgust in the way Mr. Barlow spoke of *wanting it.*

You could look at this two ways, Nora and I decided. Either Elliot's admission of *wanting it,* as a man, meant that Em was wrong: the snowshoer had certainly been *doing it.* Why wouldn't she? Or Em was right: Elliot's self-disgust for *wanting it* all the time, her hatred of male lust, meant that the snowshoer had not once acted on *wanting it*—she'd never actually done it. "You should ask your mom and Molly if Elliot ever did it, kiddo," Nora said, but I knew it would be easier to ask those two about Emmanuelle.

In truth, I chickened out of asking my mother if she and Elliot ever did it—just as I'd chickened out of asking Elliot. And it simply felt wrong (it felt like prying) to ask my mother if the snowshoer had actually done it with men. My reasoning for not asking Mr. Barlow if her desire for men had ever been consummated was more convoluted. If Em was right, would Elliot Barlow be embarrassed that she'd never had sex with anyone? In truth, I was the one who was embarrassed; I was ashamed to ask the snowshoer if she'd actually done it, if she'd ever pulled the trigger. What business was this of mine? What did I know about a boy who'd always wanted to be a girl?

"Don't ask Elliot if she ever did it, kiddo. Ask your mom and Molly about that," Nora kept telling me. "If you want to ask Elliot something, ask her what she goes through—just being a woman. Ask Elliot how it's going, how she's treated as a woman. You have no idea, kiddo," Nora said, with Em nodding her head off.

I thought I saw how the estrogen was working. In just two or three years, Mr. Barlow had become more womanly; she'd put on weight, in a womanly way, and weighed as much as my mom now. The snowshoer had hips, she had boobs—little ones, but she was shapely, and she filled out my mother's clothes. Elliot could wear Em's clothes, too. Did the estrogen make her skin softer? Maybe the orchiectomy had helped.

On the days when the snowshoer saw the electrologist, she stayed overnight with Em and Nora; her face was so swollen and sore-looking after the hair removal that Elliot didn't want to be seen in public. Elliot was lucky that she didn't have a heavy beard; the process of applying an electric current to the face with a needle-shaped electrode, one hair at a time, was more painful for those transgender women who had heavy beards. "It takes a few years," was all the snowshoer said to me about the electrolysis, but Em or Nora had held her when she cried.

Elliot was lucky that her parents loved her, unquestioningly; the little Barlows were supportive when Elliot told them she was going through the transitioning. The writing team knew a surgeon in Zürich, a pioneer in facial-feminization surgery. At four feet nine, with small and delicate bones, Mr. Barlow did not have much in the way of masculine features; her jaw didn't jut and she did not have a prominent brow ridge. She wasn't seeking corrective surgery of a cosmetic kind. Elliot Barlow wasn't looking for beautification. An Adam's apple reduction was all she wanted, and the little Barlows found an Adam's apple wizard in German-speaking Switzerland— someone they could speak to and understand.

Nora and Em and I got tired of hearing how *lucky* the snowshoer was; even the snowshoer kept saying how lucky she was. There was a small scar under Elliot's chin where the Swiss surgeon had pulled apart the skin in the front of her neck—exposing her larynx. "The surgeon just scraped off some cartilage," Mr. Barlow said dismissively. Even the surgeon had told her she was lucky. Elliot was more feminine than many women, even when she still had an Adam's apple; Elliot was already prettier than most women, and she would keep getting prettier (even over fifty). As a woman, Elliot was luckiest of all for her smallness, the Swiss surgeon said. Were we supposed to believe that the snowshoer's smallness was no longer a burden?

"Bullshit," Nora said. "You're lucky if you can take your gender for granted." Em was acting out the throes of puberty; it looked like Em was having her first period, and not knowing what it was, again and again. I had to look away. "Is Elliot *lucky* that she feels like a thirteen-year-old girl, thanks to a shitload of estrogen?" Nora asked.

The snowshoer hadn't grown up as a girl; she wasn't *lucky* to be finding out what dickheads most men were when she was an attractive woman in her forties. Her smallness notwithstanding, Mr. Barlow had been a confident man. No matter how passable she was as a woman, her confidence was diminished. Elliot had the orchiectomy in Zürich—a different surgeon. "Don't tell me Elliot is *lucky* to lose her confidence—no woman wants to think her confidence came from her balls!" Nora said.

Nora had grown up hearing bad testosterone jokes. She'd been told she had more testosterone than most women—more than most men, Nora had heard. And one night at the Gallows, when Nora and Em were onstage, some dickhead in the audience had hollered at Nora that she should get her sex chromosomes checked. "Come up here, hamster-penis—I'll check your sex chromosomes for you!" Nora had shouted from the stage, reprising the *hamster-penis* from Jasmine's repertoire.

In certain circumstances, the snowshoer's smallness was still a burden. As a gay man, Mr. Barlow hadn't been out for very long. Whether Elliot actually did it or not, the gay men he dated didn't feel deceived by him. As a transgender woman, the snowshoer kept meeting heterosexual men who felt they'd been misled by her, but Elliot did nothing to mislead the men who were attracted to her. She did not flirt; she was conservative (to the degree of appearing overly proper) in the way she dressed. And why shouldn't Mr. Barlow try to look as pretty and as much like a woman as she could? When a man was interested in her in that way—when he asked her out on a date, before anything romantic or physical happened—the snowshoer never hesitated to talk about the *trans* part of her being a transgender woman. Over time, the little English teacher learned it was safer for her to initiate the transgender revelation publicly.

She had to tell the men what was different about her, didn't she? Before there was any awkward touching—certainly before Elliot reciprocated a man's advances—she had to tell the guy she had a penis, or there were questions and answers to that effect. Don't tell me the snowshoer was lucky. And how did the straight guys respond to her telling them the truth? All Mr. Barlow would say to me was: "Once in a while, you meet a really nice guy—I've met a couple of guys who were very nice about it."

Nora and Em—later, Molly and my mom—told me about the other guys, the majority of them. They called Elliot a tranny or a fag, or both; it didn't matter if the transgender subject came up in a private conversation or in public. Some of the men shoved her or hit her—this had happened even publicly. The men seemed to think it was okay to hit her or rough her up because she wasn't a *real* woman. Molly told me that Mr. Barlow knew how to take a punch and just walk away. "You know what happens when the guys keep hitting her, more than once—you know, you're a wrestler, Kid," was how Molly put it.

"Elliot *isn't* lucky to be small, sweetie. She's four-nine, she weighs one-fifteen—one-twenty, tops. She's *my* size, sweetie. No mouse-dick would try to beat her up if Elliot was a big girl, more like Molly," my mom said.

So far, as in downtown Exeter, the snowshoer *had been* lucky—she'd won the fights she got into. "I've had a couple of shiners, and a split lip or two"—this was the extent of what Elliot would say to me. The homo-hating men who'd tried to beat her up didn't know she was a wrestler. She had a good duck under, an arm drag, a slide-by, and a very quick single leg; so far, Mr. Barlow's arm bars must have been working. Or the snowshoer hadn't met a homophobic wrestler, or a homophobic boxer yet. I could see the scar from the stitches in one of Elliot's eyebrows, where one of the homo-haters had landed a punch, or he'd caught her with a head butt or an elbow. Nora told me there'd been a scuffle when Mr. Barlow had broken a rib.

My mom said a homo-hater had tried to break Elliot's arm; the snowshoer had slipped behind him and done her usual damage, but not before the guy had hyperextended her elbow.

I missed all this—I'd left the Northeast. I was back in Iowa, this time teaching at the Writers' Workshop. The war in Vietnam was over; the draft-dodger college in Vermont would go belly-up. I wasn't a household name as a novelist, but I'd published enough to get a good teaching job. I wasn't getting to Vermont and seeing as much of my mother and Molly as I used to; I wasn't getting to New York and seeing as much of Nora and Em and the snowshoer as I wanted to. And of course I knew why Elliot wasn't telling me about her travails as a transgender woman—the dangers of her interactions with straight men, in particular. The snowshoer knew I loved her, and how much I worried about her. It was almost the 1980s. Why did I ever imagine that decade would be better?

When I was visiting Vermont, and had a moment alone with Molly, I felt like an idiot asking her if my mom and the snowshoer had ever done it. (In the light of Elliot's risking her life to be a woman, this must have struck Molly as a trivial question.) "I don't know the details, Kid—I just know they love each other, and we both know they like to fool around," the trail groomer told me.

We both knew Mr. Barlow liked gay men, too. (Hadn't Elliot become a teacher at Exeter to protect those boys who were picked on? Hadn't she stayed until the school became coed, when she believed those boys would be safer?) It had to hurt the snowshoer when she became a transgender woman, and a few of her gay men friends wanted nothing to do with her.

Under the circumstances, it seemed truly extraneous for me to ask Molly if she thought the snowshoer actually did it with men, but I asked her anyway. "How would I know, Kid? Your mom's going to ask you if you're sleeping with Emmanuelle—that's all I know," the snowcat operator said. Under the circumstances, Molly was being kind. Even in my limited experience, I knew no one had ever behaved as badly as heterosexual men (except maybe Jasmine), and I wasn't trying to be a transgender woman.

"You could probably go to jail for sleeping with Emmanuelle—*Moby-Dick* is not an excuse, sweetie. You're not sleeping with her, are you?" was the way my mother asked me.

"I don't think Emmanuelle is *that* young, Ray—I don't think it's illegal to sleep with her," Molly said.

"You know what I mean, Molly," my mother said.

"I'm not sleeping with Emmanuelle," I told them. I admitted that I might have misunderstood Emmanuelle. "You've met Emmanuelle, you know she mumbles—not when she reads, but she doesn't speak clearly," I told them. "She may have said she was a nursing student, not a nurse—I may have misheard her," I explained.

"Emmanuelle is a high school student, sweetie," my mother informed me. This was embarrassing—to be almost thirty-eight and not have known that Emmanuelle was a high school kid. I was thinking she probably didn't have a real job, just a volunteer position. Emmanuelle must have been doing what they call community service—something that would look good on her college application, I imagined.

Actually, it was the court-ordered kind of community service. Emmanuelle wasn't exactly volunteering to be of use at River Bend; her service to River Bend was a substitute for other judicial remedies. "Emmanuelle was charged with indecent exposure, Kid—her community service is instead of paying a fine," Molly told me.

"Or instead of going to jail, sweetie," my mother said.

"She's a kid, Ray—they weren't going to send her to jail for mooning," Molly said. You know you know nothing when this is how you learn that a girl reading *Moby-Dick* to your grandmother has been charged with mooning.

I'd read the "Police Report" citing "an outrage to public decency on the Swasey Parkway."

"Another one!" the snowshoer had declared. To the little English teacher's vexation—as always, with the writing—the various indecencies and obscenities performed on or near the Swasey Parkway were not described. There'd been no mention of *mooning,* not in the *Exeter Town Crier.* Naturally, given the age of the young mooner, Emmanuelle's name had been withheld.

"She also flashed her titties, Molly—she flashed *and* mooned," my mom said. In the "Police Report," the unnamed Emmanuelle neither flashed nor mooned; readers were left to imagine exactly *how* a young female had exposed herself from a passing car on the Swasey Parkway.

"Exposed herself to *whom?*" the snowshoer had asked. To people who were outraged, Elliot and I could only guess. Older people, we'd assumed. It was a nice day. People were probably out for a stroll, or they were sitting on the benches in that grassy area along the Squamscott River. Along came a carload of high school girls; one of the girls stuck her bare ass out the passenger-side window. The couple who reported the indecent exposure said the car came by a second time; this time, the same girl flashed her tits out the window. "Was doing it *twice* what offended them?" the little English teacher had asked.

"Your mom asked Emmanuelle to tell us exactly what she did, Kid," Molly explained.

"Poor Emmanuelle," I said. "I would make the couple who reported her do the community service," I added.

"You shouldn't be seeing a high school girl, sweetie—not *this* high school girl, anyway," my mother said. Didn't my mom want me to meet the venerated Grace when she was still in high school—when Grace was only seventeen, and I was already thirty-one?

"Maybe later would be better, Ray," Molly had said at the time.

As a woman, it was a burden for Elliot Barlow that sex markers for U.S. passport holders became mandatory in 1977. The denoted symbols, an M or an F, made international travel difficult for transgender people. Mr. Barlow was an M, but she looked like an F. Binding her breasts was a bad idea; she'd been strip-searched. It was better for the snowshoer to wear a loose-fitting flannel shirt, no bra, baggy jeans. When she was just starting out as a woman, sometimes the snowshoer would lay off the electrolysis (or she would stop shaving) before she flew to Europe, or before she flew back.

Nora called the U.S. State Department "a bunch of sexual fascists." She said the International Civil Aviation Organization had "a bug up its ass about androgyny." Allegedly, there were more unisex-looking international travelers around; apparently, your photograph (your outward appearance) didn't adequately determine your sex. A panel of passport experts cited unisex attire and hairstyles, but I'd been living in Iowa City; gender-confusing fashion was rare in Iowa—not too many androgynous-looking people there. In my world, Nora and my mom were the most androgynous-looking people I knew, and Nora looked more masculine than androgynous. My mother was a very pretty woman; Little Ray looked masculine only when she walked, or slouched around, and I'd always thought her masculine way of moving was a jock thing, not an androgynous thing.

Nora had a bug up her ass about the U.S. State Department and the restrictive sex markers imposed on U.S. passports. She said the M and F symbols were "heterosexual presumptions and impositions."

Nora had a point. Not until 1992 did the State Department permit transgender people to change the sex markers on their passports, and only if they'd completed what was then called "sexual reassignment" surgery. (Not until 2010 would the surgical requirement be lifted, and only because Hillary Clinton requested it; she was then secretary of state.)

In the 1970s, *Two Dykes, One Who Talks* had a hard time getting the Gallows Lounge to let them do their thing about the State Department onstage. Not even the Gallows would permit Em's pantomime of the State Department's presuming to define her sex by a cursory and crude examination of Em's genitals—while Nora tells the audience that the State Department has no business messing with our privates. "The country is getting more uptight, or uptighter—even at the Gallows," Nora had told me.

This was what Molly and my mom and I were talking about in their Vermont kitchen when the phone rang. Molly was stir-frying; I knew she wasn't going to answer the phone. We'd also been talking about Mr. Barlow's unfamiliarity with being harassed as a woman. Something came up about androgynous-looking people. I'm sure I didn't say that Nora and my mom were the most androgynous-looking people I knew, but my mother said, almost neutrally, "Some people, sweetie, say *Molly* is androgynous-looking."

"I don't think so," I quickly said; I was hoping this didn't entirely give away that I had always been unequivocally attracted to Molly, as a woman.

"Me, neither!" my mom cried, giving Molly a squeeze at the stove.

"Are you going to answer the phone, Ray?" the ski patroller asked her, still stir-frying.

"I can get it," I said. But Little Ray, in her androgynous way, was always quicker.

"Whatcha want? It's dinnertime," Molly and I heard my mother say. It was funny to be in my late thirties, and only now understand why Molly usually answered the phone. I smiled at Molly, who just kept stirring. "Yes, this is her daughter," we heard my mom say.

"Uh-oh, Kid," Molly said; with her free hand, she gave my shoulder a squeeze.

"Just a minute," we heard my mother say. "Please talk to my son, Adam— he's her grandson," my mom said, putting down the phone. Little Ray went into the TV room, where she lay down on the futon; Molly and I could hear her sobbing. My grandmother had been my mother's advocate—for a while, her only advocate. Molly turned off the flame under the wok; she went into the TV room to lie down with my mom.

When the phone rang, we'd also been talking about moving my grandmother from River Bend to Manchester, where my mom could have seen her every day. But my grandmother had lost track of actual time; if you saw her every day or once a month, Mildred Brewster wouldn't have noticed the difference. "We're *going to* move her to Manchester, eventually," my mother had kept saying.

Could you see cows or golfers out the windows of the old folks' home in Manchester? I'd asked Molly.

"There are Republicans *in* the old folks' home in Manchester, Kid," the trail groomer had told me.

"There are Republicans everywhere, Molly," my mom had said.

"This is Adam Brewster—my grandmother is Mildred Brewster," I said into the phone, while my mother cried. Since my grandmother had arrived at River Bend, the voyage of the *Pequod* marked the passing of the only time Nana knew. She knew it was a long voyage; she knew how it ended; she knew only Ishmael would escape.

My grandmother had "passed away" in her sleep, or she'd fallen asleep when she was reading and had died in her sleep. This was what one of the older nurses at River Bend told me on the phone. "Her door was open, of course," the older nurse said, with a lingering disapproval, "and when Emmanuelle checked on her, your grandmother had passed away with that big book." I could still detect the disapproval, as if *Moby-Dick* had done it. I wanted to know *which scene*.

"Is Emmanuelle okay?" I asked the nurse.

"Stop thinking about Emmanuelle, sweetie!" my mother called from the futon in the TV room, between sobs. On the phone, I heard the nurse sigh; her sigh should have prepared me for her misunderstanding my question.

"As far as we know, Emmanuelle has been behaving herself," the older nurse said stiffly. I listened to the disapproving nurse a little longer; there were "the usual arrangements" to be made. My mom was crying more softly; I could hear Molly's voice, but not what the snowcat operator was saying. I spoke as quietly as I could into the phone.

"Please tell Emmanuelle I'm sorry she was the one who found her," I said. Had she found Nana's thumb between the pages?

"Forget Emmanuelle—she's a *stripper*, sweetie!" my mother screamed from the TV room.

"Emmanuelle was upset, so we sent her home—she'll get over it," the disapproving nurse abruptly told me.

"Emmanuelle is just a kid, Ray," I heard Molly say.

"A kid who *strips*, Molly—a kid who shows off her tushy and her titties!" my mom said. I didn't want to think about Emmanuelle's tushy or her titties, but of course I could imagine them. I was thinking I had no more relatives in the town of Exeter—none living, counting Granddaddy's ghost. I couldn't imagine my grandmother as a ghost. If Nana had wanted to see more of the diaper man, she wouldn't have hired Dottie. I thought being a ghost would have struck Mildred Brewster as undignified; the suddenness of all the appearing and the disappearing was beneath her, like bad manners.

I'd hung up the phone—I was at loose ends in the kitchen. I wished I knew *where* in *Moby-Dick* my grandmother was when she died. It didn't matter where Emmanuelle had stopped reading to her; Emmanuelle was way behind, just plodding ahead. But what had Nana been reading to herself, at the end? The rice was still steaming; the stove timer said the rice had two minutes to go. The stir-fry needed stirring. "Leave my wok alone, Kid," Molly said. She'd come out of the TV room, with my mother clinging to her—the way I'd seen Em cling to Nora.

"I was wondering when we were going to eat," I said. In truth, it was Emmanuelle I was wondering about: the kind of complications I might encounter, trying to track her down—just to ask her if she knew *which part* of the *Pequod*'s voyage had been the final part for Mildred Brewster. Had there been a bookmark or a dog-eared page?

"You know, sweetie, there's another thing about that kid, Emmanuelle— I was doing some single-leg lunges with her, and some wall sits, and some *squats*," my mom said.

"Don't, Ray," Molly said. The flame under the wok made a popping sound—simultaneously with my mother saying *squats*.

"Emmanuelle is a fairly athletic kid, sweetie—she's got pretty good balance, she nailed the squats," my mom said.

Maybe the "Sunset" chapter—Nana loved that one, I was thinking. "(*The cabin; by the stern windows; Ahab sitting alone, and gazing out.*)" I didn't want to imagine Emmanuelle nailing the squats, anything but her squatting. "I leave a white and turbid wake; pale waters, paler cheeks, where'er I sail," Ahab is musing to himself.

"You don't *know* Emmanuelle is the green-dumper, Ray—I don't think she's got anything against those golfers," Molly said.

I didn't want to imagine Emmanuelle taking a shit on the putting green; I really must have known I shouldn't be imagining Emmanuelle at all. My mother was pointing out how the River Bend residents wobbled; they even wobbled when they walked—not that all of them could walk, my mom told us. "Imagine the River Benders *squatting*—they'd fall over!" Little Ray was saying. I didn't want to imagine the River Benders I'd met *squatting*, my grandmother included.

"I don't think dumping is all that athletic a thing, Ray," Molly told my mom, but I was trying to tune them out. Should I make contact with Emmanuelle, her athleticism notwithstanding? Could I spend the rest of my life not knowing where the voyage of the *Pequod* ended for my grandmother? Did I believe her reading *Moby-Dick* to me had made me a writer? My childhood attachment to Exeter had ended; not even my uncles were around to remind me of it.

Uncle Martin and Uncle Johan were both in their seventies when their voyage on the *Pequod* ended. Nora said they were living like boys again. They'd moved up north, to be near the skiing; they'd traded their cars for a truck, like a couple of Carroll County old-timers. They'd bought a house near North Conway, and Uncle Martin and Uncle Johan went everywhere and did everything together. "With one truck," as Nora put it, "they had to." My uncles never got tired of each other's company; they just loved fooling around together. Everywhere they drove, they would sing along with the song on the radio.

I last saw Uncle Martin and Uncle Johan when they came to New York to see Nora and Em onstage at the Gallows. It was the first and only time my uncles saw *Two Dykes, One Who Talks*; it was understood (but unspoken) that they wouldn't have enjoyed themselves as much if my aunts had been alive and with them. My uncles had laughed and laughed; they'd loved the show. They'd loved seeing the snowshoer, too; Uncle Martin and Uncle Johan kept telling the snowshoer how pretty she was as a woman.

My uncles also loved Damaged Don, who'd written and was singing a new song. That night at the Gallows, we were told it was the *premiere* of "No Lucky Star," but, predictably, it was the same old song, and Damaged Don sang it in the same, near-death drone.

> I met Fuzzy Ouilette
> in a bar.
> He'd lost his last job,
> his wife just left him,
> his dog had been killed
> by a car!
>
> Poor Fuzzy had
> no lucky star.
> No, Fuzzy had
> no lucky star.
>
> Don't upset yourself
> thinkin' of Hal.
> He got struck by lightning,
> his balls caught on fire,
> there was no one to say,
> "Sorry, pal!"

You better not
dwell on poor Hal.
No, don't ever
dwell on poor Hal.

I last saw Bill Brown
in L.A.
His bike blew a tire,
his dick got run over,
he could never go out
and get laid!

The poor guy would
never get laid.
No, poor Bill would
never get laid.

The dumb fucks had
no lucky star.
No, dumb fucks have
no lucky star.

That night at the Gallows, you would have thought that was the funniest song my uncles had ever heard. When we walked them back to their hotel, they sang "No Lucky Star" the whole way.

When we were saying good night, Uncle Johan expressed concern for me—that I wasn't with someone. That was when Uncle Martin told me, "You can find anyone you're looking for in New York, Adam." Even an old Austrian zither-meister, I was thinking.

Of course I was remembering my mother's wedding—how Uncle Johan had cried, "Wagner's *Lohengrin* on a zither!"

Uncle Martin and Uncle Johan were killed on the Kancamagus Highway when their truck went off the road. Kancamagus, which means "Fearless One" in Algonquian, was the last sagamore of one of the Pennacook tribes. "The Kanc," as the locals call New Hampshire Route 112, winds through the White Mountain National Forest; in a series of turns, the road crosses the Kancamagus Pass. Uncle Johan, who was driving, drove straight off one of the turns. Nora always wished she didn't know the last song her father and Uncle Johan had been singing along with, on the truck's radio. I always thought that "No Lucky Star" would be a hard song to have in your head for the rest of your life.

Damaged Don had complained; he'd had to clean up the lyrics before "No Lucky Star" could be heard on the airwaves. Poor Hal, who'd been struck by lightning, had his *hair* catch on fire—not his balls. Poor Bill had his *head* run over, not his dick. And, somewhat diminishing the scale of Bill's bad luck, it was not the case that "he could never go out and get laid"; instead, it was only the last day he would get *paid*. As for the final stanza, the dumb *fucks* were changed to dumb *guys*. Censorship never made anything better, as Nora knew.

"Less bad ain't better," Damaged Don said.

But "No Lucky Star," or what was left of it, went out on the airwaves. In northern New Hampshire, there was a country radio station—my uncles' favorite—that played it all the time. Uncle Martin had told Nora that he and Johan always sang along when "No Lucky Star" was on the radio, but my uncles would insert the original lyrics, which they knew by heart.

Before the turn, Uncle Johan had overtaken a car of fall foliage gawkers; the leaf peepers later reported that the brake lights of my uncles' truck not once flickered on in the upcoming curve. My uncles knew the Kancamagus; Nora said they drove it all the time. But there were no skid marks on the road where Uncle Johan had missed the turn. A logging truck was coming toward them, through the pass; the logger later said that both men appeared to be singing, but their eyes were fixedly on the road. They were not speeding, the logger said, but their steadfast determination compelled the logger to keep watching their truck in his mirror.

The logger said Uncle Johan seemed to speed up as he drove off the Kancamagus; as Nora and I preferred to imagine, those two Norwegians never stopped singing. The logger stopped his truck, put on his hazard lights, and made his way to the wreck. Nora and I would imagine a cluster of trees, an outcropping of rocks. The leaf peepers had stopped their car, too; one of them followed the logger through the trees or over the rocks. They could hear the truck's radio—it was still playing.

"The dumb guys had no lucky star," Damaged Don was singing. "No, dumb guys have no lucky star."

"Those two weren't dumb—they knew how to have a good time, and they knew when to call it quits," was the way Nora saw it.

It looked like an accident to the leaf peepers. Uncle Johan may not have been speeding, one of the foliage seekers reported, but he appeared to be driving too fast for the curve; maybe he misjudged the particular turn.

The logging truck driver saw it more the way Nora saw it. "Those guys looked like they knew what they were doing," the logger said.

We'll never know, but Uncle Martin and Uncle Johan weren't cut out to be River Benders. Those two Norwegians were telemarking men; they liked to go telemarking through the trees. Their bend in the river was a turn in the road.

33.

JUST SMALL ENOUGH

When I was teaching at the Iowa Writers' Workshop in the seventies, my students thought *Century Review* was the zenith of literary journals. It was first called *New Century Review*, and one of my students published a short story in it; this one short story seems to have marked her zenith as a fiction writer. I don't believe she ever published other fiction. That literary journal had a similarly short life span, lasting only a decade. I don't mean to sound irreverent about *New Century Review*, or just plain *Century Review*; some very good writers were published in it, my former student among them.

I was never published in that literary journal. I didn't write poetry or essays or short stories; the fiction I submitted to *Century Review* was excerpted from novels in progress, which I'd edited to read like short stories. Or that was what I hoped. One of my rejections said, "This reads like an excerpt from something longer, or like something that should be longer." This was indisputably true, but the rejection pissed me off.

Though that literary journal is long gone, I remain most grateful it existed. It was where I first read Emily MacPherson's fiction. I was aware that Em had scripted Nora's monologues for *Two Dykes, One Who Talks*; I knew that Em composed many of her pantomimes in writing. It hurt my feelings that I hadn't known Em wrote fiction. I hadn't even known her full name— just that she'd been an Emily, who was shortened to an Em.

I read almost to the end of Emily MacPherson's first short story before I knew Em was the author. The histrionics of Em's pantomime performances were absent from her third-person omniscient voice. A teenage girl is fitfully dreaming; she is sexually attracted to one of her girlfriends, but she doesn't dare to make the first move, not knowing if her girlfriend is similarly attracted to her. She wakes from her erotic dream to discover her mother in her bedroom—her mom is sitting at the foot of her bed, sobbing.

"I'm an awful mother, I'm a worse wife, and if you have my genes, you're doomed!" the poor girl's mother tells her.

The next night is even better. This time, the teenage daughter is dreaming about her cloddish boyfriend. It's okay when he touches her boobs, but she knows he wants her to touch him *down there*, and the poor girl wants no part of his penis. Upon my second reading, I saw this scene as an obvious precursor to Em's penis pantomime—her depiction of an approaching penis as a one-eyed eel. Not upon my first reading, when the narrative detachment and restraint of Emily MacPherson's fiction did not connect me to Em as an unbridled pantomimist—Em's full-body slither, her mouth in the shape of the letter O, a sightless eye.

The second night, the poor girl wakes from her penis dream to find her father stripped to his boxer shorts, on all fours in her bedroom, where he is whipping himself with his belt—loud *smacks*, his back and shoulders reddened in the faint light.

"I'm a terrible father, an unconscionable husband, but your mother is worse!" the poor girl's dad assures her, between lashes. "If we've made you like us, I'm so sorry!" her father wails, still whipping himself. The self-flagellation continues while the father confesses his homosexuality; he denounces his wife as a repeatedly unfaithful lesbian. The daughter silently listens and observes. The teenage girl is justly angry that her own coming out has been dimmed by the self-centered coming out of her parents. (Only then did I realize that Emily MacPherson was Em.)

The clear-headed teenage girl also makes an astounding aesthetic judgment. Her oafish father should castigate himself either verbally or physically—not both, not at the same time.

"Either act it out or put it in words, Daddy—not the two together," the daughter tells her deplorable dad, who has barely managed to draw blood with his belt. If I hadn't already figured it out, her artistic doctrine gave Emily MacPherson away; she'd put in writing a pantomimic aesthetic. Pantomime is the art of conveying a story by bodily movements *only*. Clearly this was what Em was doing—*either* pantomiming *or* writing, "not the two together."

"A Family Comes Out" was the title of the first Emily MacPherson story I read. I asked my Iowa students to read it in our fiction workshop; some students, veteran readers of *Century Review*, had already done so. They duly noted Em's sardonic humor. The better writers cited the unusual focus of the story's physical details: how the bodily movements of the characters capture their haplessness, their sexual tension, their conflicted feelings of desire and regret. I did not point out the pantomimic rendering of the characters' inner lives: how their bodies betray their sexual turmoil. Only three of my fiction workshop students were New Yorkers, and only one of them had been to (or even heard of) the Gallows Lounge—a kid who'd been an undergrad at NYU, and he'd never seen *Two Dykes, One Who Talks* onstage at the Gallows. I didn't tell my Iowa students that Emily MacPherson had a parallel creative life as a pantomimist, or that Em (as a fiction writer) had virtually pantomimed the way her characters moved.

Emily MacPherson's second short story in *Century Review* was written in a different narrative voice—there was a deadpan first-person narrator, the lesbian daughter, now a college girl, whose homosexual parents are divorcing. "A Couple of Latecomers Get Divorced" was the title, prompting a couple of my fiction workshop students to say they thought the two stories might be back-to-back chapters in a novel Emily MacPherson was writing; the different narrative voices notwithstanding, these were clearly the same characters from "A Family Comes Out."

It hurt my feelings more to imagine that Em might have been writing a novel. It was bad enough that I hadn't known she wrote fiction—*short* fiction, I'd assumed, upon reading only one of the short stories. Maybe Em hadn't shown me her short stories because she knew they weren't my thing— or so I'd rationalized. I had shown Em my novels, in manuscript; she was a close reader and gave me good notes. (Naturally, Nora was among my first readers, but Nora wasn't a writer and never gave me notes; she just told me her thoughts.) Yet, surely, if Em was writing a novel, she would have shown me some pages, wouldn't she? If only a first chapter, I was thinking. Did "A Family Comes Out" or "A Couple of Latecomers Get Divorced" work as a first chapter? I wondered.

In the second story, the lesbian daughter decides to stop talking. She's not crazy; it's a wise and rational choice. The last person she speaks to is the psychiatrist at her college. The shrink defends the student's decision to the college community—the student's written work is faultless; she should be permitted not to speak. Her not talking is therapy for her breakdown, caused by her parents' clumsy coming out and their self-indulgent divorce.

The students in my fiction workshop at Iowa praised the parents' tell-all dialogue; the stuff they tell the daughter about their divorce totally justifies the daughter's decision to stop speaking. "For the things I've done with other men, I should be castrated. Or maybe just a vasectomy," the father tells his silent daughter.

"For the things I've done with other women—women you know, in some cases, mothers of your friends—with one of your contemporaries, I'm ashamed to say, I regret most of all that you'll do these degrading things yourself. I've done this to you—I've made you like me!" the mother cries. "But your father has done worse things," the mom quickly adds. "Women like you and me are unredeemable, but homosexual men do much worse things," the lesbian mother assures her lesbian daughter.

Maybe Em hadn't shown me her fiction because it was too autobiographical, I was thinking. Possibly, even Nora didn't know that Em was writing fiction. Em herself had disparaged autobiographical fiction in a famously censored "The News in English" pantomime at the Gallows; someone had dimmed the stage lights to prevent the audience from seeing what Em was acting out. In the darkness, Nora had told the audience: "Em is saying that writing about your own pathetic life, and calling it fiction, is *masturbatory*."

In the 1970s, autobiographical fiction wasn't revered; the memoir hadn't replaced the imagination, Mr. Barlow might have said. In my fiction workshop at Iowa, the students liked fables and myths and allegories. Social realism was okay, but fabulism was better, or there had to be a fabulist element enhancing or exaggerating the realism. My students had loved what they imagined were the fantastical extremes in Emily MacPherson's stories.

I didn't undermine my students' enthusiasm for Em's fiction. I didn't tell them what I suspected about Emily MacPherson's short stories—that they were diary entries from Em's family life. As a young woman, she'd simply had a more fantastical life than my fiction workshop students could imagine. Em wasn't prescient only about Ronald Reagan; she didn't just intuit how manipulable the dumber-than-dogshit American people were. When Em stopped talking, she also stopped typing. In longhand, Em wrote quietly—like pantomiming. I knew Em thought about her writer genes; she said she had no idea where her writing came from. But Em knew where the hatred came from. I thought her writer genes had something to do with her seeing the hatred—not everyone sees it coming.

I wanted to write Em and commend her; she'd made constructive use of the hatred her parents had passed down to her. My young and talented fiction writers in Iowa were excited that Emily MacPherson had created a pair of homophobic homosexuals—parents who hated themselves, and expected their lesbian daughter to hate herself accordingly. Yet the daughter wasn't just angry at her parents; she was determined to be proud of herself. In the eyes of my fiction workshop students, Emily MacPherson was writing fabulist fiction with a social conscience. The esteem my students felt for Em's two stories was unreserved, but I didn't know how Em felt about her fiction. Her stories were confident and poised; they reflected a restrained but focused anger. Emily MacPherson was the fictional lesbian daughter, the girl I'd met at my mother's wedding, where the submissive demeanor of the dollish Em was belied by the reputation of her unruly and clamorous orgasms. This insightful fiction writer was the same young woman who'd mistaken *Moby-Dick* for porn.

On matters of morality and writing, I always trusted and consulted the snowshoer. As my mom foresaw, Mr. Barlow was like a father to me—he'd been a good one. Since her transitioning, Elliot had become a second mother to me—not only when she was wearing Little Ray's clothes. I'd always shown the snowshoer my novels and screenplays—usually, my first drafts. I should have guessed that Emily MacPherson was showing her fiction to Mr. Barlow from the beginning; she'd heard from me that the little English teacher was a good reader. Em was always more at ease around Elliot than she was around other men; like Little Ray, maybe Em knew from the start that the snowshoer was meant to be a woman.

Em wasn't writing novels—"not yet," the snowshoer assured me. Em spent months writing and rewriting one short story. Many of the situations, and some of the characters, were the same—from story to story—but Em intended each story to stand by itself. "Em thinks her writing is smaller than yours—she thinks she's not ready to write a novel," Mr. Barlow explained. "She knows you write bigger than she does," Elliot said.

I knew the snowshoer was obsessed with her own smallness. "I'm just not big enough—I don't even weigh as much as the lightest weight class!" she was always saying. I knew Em had issues with feeling undersize next to Nora, and Em was small enough that Elliot could wear her clothes. I hadn't known what Em thought of my writing, or that she felt inferior for her own, smaller output as a writer. I don't think good fiction is a matter of size, but perhaps I failed to appreciate how the *just not big enough* thing was a big deal to Em. I certainly failed to appreciate what a big deal it was to Mr. Barlow.

When I wrote Em, from Iowa, I told her how much my students had loved her stories. I told her the things I admired about her pantomimes in prose. Of course I didn't say she'd hurt my feelings by not telling me she wrote fiction. I just said, sincerely, how happy I was that someone I knew and loved was also a fiction writer. I wasn't, as Nora would later accuse me, "trying to start something with Em." We were two writers who liked each other, and Em and I had discovered that we liked each other's writing. Why wouldn't we write each other? But Nora knew my having a relationship with Em, in writing, would be very intimate. At first, I thought Em's letters to me seemed so intimate only because Em didn't talk. I was overlooking that Em wasn't part of a community of writers; when I wrote to her, I became her only writer friend.

Em's friends were people she met when she was with Nora. "If you don't talk, you don't make friends when you're alone," Em wrote me. She knew her output as a fiction writer was small and restrained; Em knew she held herself back. She was embarrassed by her reliance on autobiographical material, although she'd "exaggerated like crazy," she wrote me. "I just don't dare to make up everything, like you do." Em was very self-deprecating about her fiction, and her letters to me were an outpouring of soul-searching. She still spoke to me only occasionally and very little—short utterances of one or two words, always when Nora was around—but in Em's letters I was reminded of the intensity of her pantomimes, and of the time she bit me. In my mind's eye, I can still see Em's teeth marks on my knee—indicating where she would have shot me, to keep me out of Vietnam.

My first letter from Em began with her telling me that she'd seen *The Kindergarten Man* a few times—after seeing it first in 1973, with Nora and me. "And I'm not counting when I saw it in Vermont, with Molly and your mother," Em wrote. She was right to discount that screening; Nora and Em and I weren't watching the movie. It was like the time in 1971, when we took Molly and my mom to see *The Wrong Car* in New York; all of us watched my mother watching Paul Goode, even Molly. We'd been disappointed by my mother's notable lack of a response to the little actor onscreen. Em's gestures were hard to read; she'd seemed ambivalent about my resemblance to Paul Goode. From Em's gestures, she wasn't convinced that my smile was the getaway driver's smile. Molly and the snowshoer had seemed uncertain, too.

But, in her first letter to me, Em pointed out that we rarely get to see the little getaway driver move in *The Wrong Car*. All Paul Goode does is drive, or drink a beer, or light a cigarette and take a drag. As for physical activity, we get to see the little getaway driver and the gun moll undressing on a bed; we have glimpses of the bare-assed little driver getting out of the bed and going back to the bed. "That's about it, for seeing Paul Goode move," Em wrote me.

Leave it to Em, a pantomimist, to analyze the movement of a getaway driver in a gangster movie. In *The Wrong Car*, Paul Goode moved so little, Em said she couldn't learn much about him. Em wrote that she didn't think my mom was pretending not to recognize Paul Goode as "that boy she'd seduced in Aspen." Em wrote that she believed my mother really didn't recognize Paul Goode as that kid who wasn't shaving, the fourteen-year-old snow shoveler who couldn't take his eyes off her—that boy (Little Ray had said) who would have been a pretty girl.

Paul Goode was forty-six when he made *The Kindergarten Man*; he is uncannily credible as a young man in his twenties (even credible, at moments, as a teenager). As a screenwriter, Paul Goode is less credible—the story of *The Kindergarten Man* is implausible. Two men, or a man and a woman, have been targeting kindergarten classrooms with children from wealthy families. The hostage-takers—twice there were two men, two other times there was a man with a woman—do their homework. Simultaneous to their taking over a kindergarten classroom, and holding the children for ransom, the most well-to-do parents have already been notified of the terms; the frightened parents come to the kindergarten and pay the ransom before the police know the children and their teacher have been taken hostage. Somehow—this is never explained—the two men, or the man and the woman, always get away. And this isn't the implausible part.

The police get a tip concerning the next kindergarten to be targeted. Someone has spotted a suspicious-looking couple—actually, two suspicious-looking couples. The same man has been seen scouting a kindergarten in an affluent suburb of Chicago; he is with either a woman or an effeminate-looking man. The implausible part is the plan the police come up with. They want to plant an undercover cop in the kindergarten. The police pay a visit to the kindergarten teacher in her classroom after school; the last few kids have been picked up by their parents when three cops come into the classroom, looking like cops.

The kindergarten teacher is played by Clara Swift—her first film role. It would later emerge that Paul Goode had picked her for the part. "I saw how you were looking at her—I felt the same way about her!" Em wrote me. I was thirty-two, Em was Nora's age, thirty-eight. We'd had the hots for women onscreen, but we'd not fallen in love with someone in a movie before; it seemed we both fell in love with Clara Swift, *and* we had the hots for her. "This must have been more awkward for you," Em wrote, "because you surely knew that Clara Swift looked like your mother—or didn't you?"

Well, no, I certainly didn't think Clara Swift looked like my mom—not then, not at first. Em had written that Clara Swift, who was twenty-six when she played the teacher in *The Kindergarten Man*, looked like Little Ray must have looked at that age—or at a younger age.

My mother was thirty-four when Em met her for the first time, at that lightning-struck wedding on Front Street. Clara Swift looked younger onscreen than she was; in *The Kindergarten Man*, she looked like a college girl and could have been nineteen or twenty. This begged the question: Did Paul Goode pick Clara Swift for the part because she reminded him of the pretty slalom skier who was not yet nineteen when he met her at the Hotel Jerome?

By the time Nora and Em and I were watching *The Kindergarten Man* (again) in Bennington, Vermont, with Molly and my mother—it was their first time—we knew that if Paul Goode was my father, he'd been only as old as I was at my mom's wedding. Paul Goode would have been fourteen, almost fifteen, when they met—if they ever met—at the Jerome. Molly never said that Clara Swift, who was twenty-six but passed for a nineteen-year-old, "looked like" Little Ray, but my mother was in her late twenties or early thirties when she and Molly met. All Molly would say was: "I've just seen pictures of Ray when she was younger, Kid—when, I suppose, she might have looked a little like Clara Swift."

"More than a *little*," Nora had argued, with Em nodding her head off. We were all more than a little distracted by Clara Swift—not just by her looks, but also by her impressive performance. The teacher steals the movie, at least until Paul Goode's first appearance.

I have to give Paul Goode credit for the three plainclothesmen in the kindergarten classroom—a noir stooge show. The detective in charge (Nora called him the "head dick") is an unamused, melancholic man given to mournful sighs. The two plainclothes cops assisting the head dick are Laurel and Hardy look-alikes, transporting Nora and me back to our favorite childhood comedians. Not Em; she couldn't watch Laurel and Hardy, because she thought Stan Laurel looked abused. The skinny, nervous-looking cop is a fidgeter; his sudden, impatient movements keep causing his gun to fall out of his shoulder holster. The fat, hearty-looking cop is too big and exuberant for a kindergarten classroom. The teacher opens fire first; she tells the detectives they're idiots to come to her classroom looking like cops.

"But we *are* cops!" the fat one says cheerfully. Unwisely, he attempts to sit in one of the kindergartners' undersize chairs—the kind that's connected to a tiny desk.

"If my kindergarten is under surveillance by that couple who take children hostage, surely *they* now know the cops are here," the teacher tells them.

"That couple has moved on—it's the *parents* of the kids in your class who are under the surveillance of that couple now," the head dick says. He sighs, seeing that the fat cop is stuck in the child-size chair, his knees wedged under the attached desk.

"Jeez, Ralph—those chairs are for little kids," the fidgety cop says, bumping into a globe of the world the size of a beach ball, knocking it off its stand. The skinny cop bends over, lunging to grab the falling globe as his gun falls out of his shoulder holster. The thud the dropped gun makes on the classroom floor causes the teacher to cover her ears with both hands; the three detectives cringe in anticipation of the stray gunshot.

"Mind your weapon, William," the head dick says, sighing.

Ralph, the fat cop, abruptly stands, but he's not getting away from the kindergartner's assembled desk and chair that easily. His heavy thighs are trapped under the desk; the attached chair, rising with Ralph as he stands, bends the big detective forward. Somehow, Ralph appears to be unsteadily standing in a seated position.

"You can't possibly . . ." the teacher has started to say to him when Ralph suddenly grunts and straightens up, the chair and desk splintering apart. The splintering sound seems to surprise William, the skinny cop, who has managed to holster his gun and return the world to its precarious stand. Or, maybe, it is Ralph's impromptu grunt—in the act of destroying the kindergartner's chair and desk—that startles William, who lurches off-balance into the blackboard. "I will not have a cop with a weapon in my classroom, not with the kids," the teacher is saying, as William, struggling to regain his balance, clings to the little shelf under the blackboard, breaking it. An explosion of chalk dust erupts from the blackboard area of the kindergarten classroom, caused by William's making face-first contact with the blackboard and his falling among the blackboard erasers, which were knocked off the broken shelf. Ralph, squatting to survey the irreparable damage done to the desk and chair, splits the seat of his pants. William, flailing on his back in a cloud of chalk dust, reacts to the unfamiliar ripping sound by drawing his gun, the barrel pointing every which way, as the teacher takes cover behind her desk.

"We have the perfect kindergarten man—he has infiltrated schools before; he fits right in," the head dick is telling the teacher. She has stepped away from her desk, bravely into the line of fire, now that William has once more holstered his gun.

"You've got to be kidding," the teacher tells the head dick. "You've got a cop who can pass for a kindergartner? Don't tell me the little guy will be armed."

"Our kindergarten man is not as small as a kindergartner, but he's small enough," the head dick tells the teacher. "Where *is* he, anyway?" the head dick asks his underlings.

"He's checking out the boys' room—he's attaching the fixtures for his weapons inside one of the toilet stalls, or something like that," William says in a voice like a duck in pain; he is pinching his nose, now bleeding profusely.

"That's our little kindergarten man—no detail is too small for him!" Ralph declares admiringly.

"And he's a master of disguises," William says, in his pained-duck way, still bleeding.

"Disguises," the teacher repeats, rolling her eyes in disbelief. It's as clear to us as it is to her that the three cops in the classroom couldn't disguise themselves if they tried. "Weapons in the boys' room? Are you crazy? *What* weapons?" the teacher asks the head dick.

There's someone standing on crutches in the classroom's open doorway; at first glance, he could be a boy, a young teenager, but he's a small man wearing a kindergartner's clothes. His shorts, his sneakers, his T-shirt with a goofy cartoon character—these surely contribute to his preternaturally youthful appearance. Maybe his hairless legs have been shaved, but the extreme smoothness of his face makes him look like he hasn't started shaving. "I have a handgun with the requisite ammunition, and a silencer—that's it for weapons," the little kindergarten man tells the teacher. "My crutches come apart, they disassemble very quickly—everything I need is concealed in the crutches," he explains to her. His voice is more adult-sounding and commanding than he looks, and he moves effortlessly toward her on the crutches. When he is standing in front of her, he hands her the crutches. They would have been face-to-face, but Paul Goode is noticeably shorter than Clara Swift, who is in no way a big woman. The kindergarten man's eyes are level with the teacher's collarbones when he says: "Every morning, when I'm standing at my chair and desk, I'll hand you my crutches. Only you should touch them—you don't let the kids touch them, of course."

"Of course," the teacher repeats, as if spellbound by him. We, the audience, and Clara Swift are astonished by the kindergarten man's lithe and athletic agility; freed of his crutches, which he clearly doesn't need, the little jock shows off his grace and precision of movement. First of all, in the movie theater—in Bennington, Vermont—the single-leg lunges and the squats got my mother's attention, and Molly's, but there was something else revealing in the kindergarten man's movements. For a man in his mid-forties, Paul Goode still knew how to move like a kid. The kindergarten man moves like a teenage boy. He lunges and squats his way around the kindergarten classroom, familiarizing himself with the layout of the space—an activities area, where the artwork is done, and the cozy spot for quiet time, where the kids can nap—but he comes quickly back to the little chairs and their adjoining desks.

There's a backstory the kindergarten man needs to tell the teacher; there's a reason for everything, not only the crutches. It'll be the teacher's job to tell the parents of her kindergarten kids—it's important that the parents know the story of the new kid in class. How, when he was in kindergarten, he was almost asphyxiated in a restaurant fire that killed his parents; how the lack of oxygen and excess of carbon dioxide caused the kindergarten man's brain damage. "The smoke inhalation affected my speech and the use of my legs. I kept growing, a little—my growth was affected, too—but my mental development was halted or interrupted," the kindergarten man tells the teacher.

"Is that even possible?" she asks him. "It doesn't sound very likely— there's not enough medical language," the teacher tells him.

"No medical language. There are two doctors among your kindergartners' parents—layman language is safer," he tells her.

"There are *three* doctors among my kids' parents," the teacher corrects him.

"Only two live at home—the third doctor has asked for a divorce; his wife kicked him out," the kindergarten man informs her. He was in a *kind of coma* after the restaurant fire—for twenty years, we're supposed to believe! An older sister has been looking after him. When he comes out of the *kind of coma,* the sister sends him back to kindergarten, where she believes his mental development stopped. His *condition,* he explains to the teacher, will require him to raise his hand and ask to go to the boys' room—a lot. One of the kindergartners (another boy, of course) will have to go with him.

"I survived the restaurant fire in a men's room, where my dad took me. He broke a faucet in a sink, so the water ran and ran. He told me to stay in the men's room—then he went to help my mom. I never saw them again. I can't be alone in a public washroom," the kindergarten man tells the teacher— leaving us to imagine the flooded men's room in the burning restaurant, the water starting to steam, the smoke becoming difficult to distinguish from the steam, the little boy all alone but *staying,* as his father had instructed him.

It unfolds that the couple in question, the hostage-takers, are a man and a woman; this time, the woman isn't pretending to be an effeminate-looking man. "It would be better if you stepped outside the classroom," the woman quietly tells the teacher. "There's been an accident," she more quietly says. "The father of one of your kindergartners, the doctor who's getting divorced—something's happened to him," she whispers.

The kindergarten man has prepared the teacher for this tactic; the hostage-takers always try to separate the teacher and the kindergartners. Not this time. "I stay with the kids, no matter what—just say what you have to say," the teacher tells the woman, who takes a handgun out of her purse. She doesn't point it at anyone, but she holds the gun in such a way that everyone can see it. Everyone can see the handgun the man is holding, too; he stands in the open doorway to the classroom, holding the gun against his chest, as if he were pledging allegiance to the flag.

"Listen to me, kids," the woman with the gun says to the quiet kindergartners. "No one will be hurt if you listen to me and do what I say. We are waiting for a few of your parents to come here—they have something to give us."

When the kindergarten man raises his hand, the teacher sounds exasperated with him. "Do you *have* to, really?" the teacher asks him.

"I really *have* to," he answers her, in a preternaturally high voice. "And I can't go alone," the little kindergarten man reminds her. Every boy in the class has raised his hand, volunteering to be the kid who accompanies the kindergarten man to the boys' room.

"Tommy, please go with him," the teacher tells a wide-eyed boy, whose belief in extraterrestrials and supernatural beings makes him a smart choice— a perfect witness to the kindergarten man's miraculous transformation.

"You come back in five minutes, both of you," the woman with the gun tells Tommy and the new boy on crutches.

"He sometimes takes longer," Tommy tells the woman, who points to the gunman in the doorway.

"Five minutes is all you get, crip, or he'll come get you," the woman with the gun tells the kindergarten man.

A little girl has raised her hand. "What is it, Henrietta?" the teacher asks her.

"*Crip* is not a very nice word," Henrietta says. The kindergarten man appears to stiffen on his crutches, but he keeps going—past the man with the gun, through the doorway, out of the classroom. Tommy, on the lookout for supernormal occurrences, follows closely behind.

"Listen, kids," says the woman with the gun, "wherever you are—even in kindergarten—there's always a goody-goody giving you shit about the language that you use."

"Five minutes, *crip*," says the gunman, without bothering to look at the two on their way to the boys' room.

"The *shit* word isn't very nice, either," says Henrietta indignantly.

"That's enough, Henrietta," the teacher tells the little girl, who is staring at the woman with the gun, who stares back at her.

In the boys' room, a supernatural being emerges before Tommy's enrapt eyes. Tommy has unzipped his fly but stands sideways to the urinal, his attention seized by the no-longer-disabled kindergarten man, who holds his crutches overhead, executing single-leg lunges and squats—back and forth along the row of child-high urinals. "He can walk—it's a miracle!" the kindergarten man keeps repeating softly. Tommy has to notice how the new boy's voice has changed; he has a lower voice, like a man's.

"Are you a grown-up now?" Tommy asks him.

"He can walk—it's a miracle!" the kindergarten man softly says again. "Let me hear you say that, Tommy. 'He can walk—it's a miracle!' Can you say that quietly—almost like you're whispering?"

"He can walk—it's a miracle!" Tommy whispers.

"Just a little louder, Tommy," the kindergarten man tells him; he lunges and squats his way inside one of the toilet stalls, closing the door.

"He can walk—it's a miracle!" Tommy is repeating, as instructed—a little louder. He keeps on saying this as he turns to face a urinal, finally peeing.

"That's good, Tommy—just keep saying that," the kindergarten man encourages the boy. Over his shoulder, Tommy can see a crutch tip—it briefly appears above the toilet stall, followed by the armpit pad of the other crutch. The mechanical sounds of the crutches being dismantled make Tommy keep turning his head, to look over his shoulder at the closed door to the toilet stall. One time, when Tommy looks anxiously over his shoulder, the boy sees Paul Goode lying on the floor, peering at him from under the door to the stall. The kindergarten man holds a handgun against his chest, a silencer on the barrel. The index finger of Paul Goode's other hand is held to his lips. A still of this shot becomes the creepy poster for *The Kindergarten Man*. Tommy has not stopped saying what he's been told to say; his marching orders are perfectly clear to him, and he flushes the urinal, washes his hands, and leaves the boys' room with newfound purpose.

There is an overhead shot of the closed toilet stall. The disassembled crutches are hung on hooks on the inside of the stall door. Attached to the side walls of the stall are other "fixtures" of a more complicated kind. What look like stirrups hold the kindergarten man's small feet; what resembles a child's car seat is mounted on the opposing wall, but the seat can swivel. Almost level with the toilet seat, the little kindergarten man is suspended—just above the gap under the stall door. If you look under the door for him, he'll see you first. If you go into an adjacent stall and stand on the toilet seat, to look over the wall to find him, he's got you covered.

Meanwhile, back in the classroom, the gunman is looking at his watch when Tommy walks past him in the doorway; Tommy is babbling incoherently, or he is speaking too quietly (or too insanely) for anyone to understand him.

"What?" Henrietta shrieks.

"Please speak up, Tommy," the teacher tells him.

"It's been five minutes," the gunman says.

"Where's the crip, dickhead?" the gun-toting woman asks Tommy.

"He can walk—it's a miracle!" Tommy tells her, loudly and clearly enough for everyone to hear him. "He can walk—it's a miracle!" the boy can't stop reciting.

"The *dickhead* word . . ." Henrietta has only started to say, but the gun-toting woman cuts the goody-goody off.

"Go get the crip," she sharply says to the gunman, who's not in the doorway—he's already on his way to the boys' room.

"He can walk—it's a miracle!" Henrietta is now screaming; other children are echoing Tommy's incessant refrain.

"Tell them to shut up," the woman with the gun tells the teacher.

"I think I won't—I don't want them to hear the shots," the teacher says.

"There's gonna be just one shot, if there's any shooting, and I want to hear it," the gun-toting woman says. "Tell the kids to shut up."

The teacher taps her desk with a ruler, and the kindergartners stop chanting; only Tommy mumbles, "It's a miracle," before he can stop. "I think we should sing it, like a song," the teacher tells the kids. "Like *this*," she says, before she starts singing. It is Clara Swift's scene; they still show the film clip.

We know from the astonished faces of the kindergartners that the kids have never heard their teacher sing before. In the audience, we aren't expecting Clara Swift to sing beautifully; every time I see and hear this scene, the purity of her voice is a shock.

"You try singing 'He can walk—it's a miracle!' beautifully. It's impossible," Em wrote me. (Naturally, it was impossible for me to imagine how Em would sound if she sang at all.)

In the boys' room, the gunman is disconcerted by the chorus of children's voices singing the miracle song back in the classroom. He is also perturbed by the toilet stall with the locked door. From a circumspect distance, he has peered under the stall door, but there's nothing to see—no crutch tips, no small feet in sneakers. The gunman steps up to the closed door, giving it a hard slap. "I know you're in there, crip—time's up," the gunman says. He tucks his gun under his belt and the waistband of his trousers.

As a writer, I'm distracted by what Henrietta would say about *my* language. The first time I saw *The Kindergarten Man*, it occurred to me that Paul Goode (as a writer) thinks the woman with the gun is right about Henrietta—there's always a goody-goody giving you shit about the language that you use. Every writer knows this is true.

In the boys' room, with its kindergartner-size urinals, the gunman looks huge; he also appears to be very fit. When he hooks his fingers over the top of the toilet-stall door, he does an effortless pull-up. This is such a snap for him, he looks like he could do twenty more. One quick pull-up and his head is above the stall door, where he gawks down. The kindergarten man has an easy shot, from point-blank range. The silencer does its job. There is an audible *pop*, but it doesn't sound like a gunshot—more like a disappointing champagne cork, muffled in a towel. The gunman falls faceup on the floor. His dead, unseeing eyes are bigger than the bullet hole between them. The bullet hole has only begun to bleed when the kindergarten man comes out of the toilet stall, being careful not to step in the spreading pool of blood from the back of the dead gunman's skull. "Time's up," Paul Goode tells him, quietly.

From the classroom's open doorway, we are looking at the frightened teacher, who is looking back at us—at camera. The woman with the gun stands in profile to us and the doorway; she is facing the children with her pistol pointed at (almost touching) the teacher's temple. "If I pull the trigger, the kids' faces are gonna be spattered with your blood—from the exit wound," the gun-toting woman tells the teacher.

There is another angle, on the kids' faces, when Henrietta shouts: "Stop! Stop singing!" Seeing that the teacher is afraid has made the children afraid, too; they stop singing.

Cut back to the angle from the doorway, on the teacher looking at camera, and on the woman with the gun—her face is still in profile to us, when something changes in the teacher's eyes. The teacher sees something, and the woman with the gun turns to face us—to look where the teacher is looking. In the silent classroom, the *pop* and the hole between the gun-toting woman's eyes are instantaneous; because the woman with the gun has turned her head, her body is spun sideways by the force of the bullet, her gun slips from her slack fingers, and her knees splay apart as she falls. She lies facedown, her hair and the back of her head already sodden with blood, which is now pooling around her face on the floor.

From the doorway, it takes the kindergarten man two single-leg lunges to enter the foreground of the frame and the classroom, where he squats beside the body of the dead woman. "It's been five minutes—I'm back," he tells her. For good measure, the kindergarten man speaks in the preternaturally high voice we last heard when he said he had to go to the boys' room.

There's a quick close-up of the much-abused globe on the teacher's desk; it is spattered with blood from the exit wound. The kindergarten man's voice-over is lower—he speaks in his more resonant, more grown-up voice. We hear the adult kindergarten man say: "It's been a tough day for the world—for this world, anyway." (Deadpan noir doesn't worry about overkill.)

When the camera pulls back, we see that Paul Goode is saying this to the shaken teacher, who has been spattered with a little blood; after all, she was standing at the periphery of the exit wound. With a white handkerchief, Paul Goode removes a spot of blood from the teacher's cheek. The two bloodstains on her white blouse, on one shoulder and one breast, are not removable with the handkerchief, which Paul Goode puts in his pocket. Where to put his gun is more awkward. The long barrel of the silencer makes the gun appear bigger than it is—too big for the kindergarten man to put in the pocket of his shorts, and to stick it under the waistband of his shorts would look ridiculous or dangerous. To take the gun and the silencer apart might make the children anxious. "Give that thing to me," the teacher tells him, putting the weapon on her desk, beside the bloodied world.

When Tommy starts babbling, the kindergarten man is eye-level with the teacher's breasts. "He can walk—it's a miracle!" Tommy mindlessly repeats.

"Actually, Tommy, I could always walk—it's not a miracle," the kindergarten man tells the boy. "There was no restaurant fire, I'm not disabled—I'm not a kid, I'm a *cop*," Paul Goode tells the kids.

"He's not a kid, he's a *cop*!" Henrietta shouts. It's sometimes hard to tell with Henrietta; there's a sameness to the sound of her voice in ecstasy and in protest. Yet the way the children follow Henrietta's lead leaves no room for doubt. The chorus of the kids' voices is ecstatic, even triumphant. The kindergartners are thrilled that Paul Goode is a cop. Only Tommy isn't lending his jubilant voice to the chorus; Tommy wanted the transformation he witnessed and believed in the boys' room to exist. When Tommy's lips begin to move, the unspoken words he is mouthing to himself are not in sync with the words the other kindergartners are so joyfully saying.

As for the actual kindergarten man, he is trying to make himself heard over the din of the children's chorus. Paul Goode is standing unnaturally close to Clara Swift, his face almost touching her breasts; she tilts her head down to him, her ear now near his mouth. "I'm wondering if you would go out with me, if I'm not too small for you—I hear that all the time, that I'm just not big enough," the little kindergarten man tells the teacher.

When she turns her head, still bending over him, her lips are almost touching his ear. "You're not too small for me—you're just small enough," the teacher tells him, quietly but clearly.

A close shot of Tommy, his lips stubbornly out of sync with the "He's a *cop!*" crap. As the kids' chanting fades out, the purity of Clara Swift's singing fades in—until Tommy's lips are perfectly in sync with her voice, singing Tommy's song. The first time you see *The Kindergarten Man,* you think that's the end of the movie—it could be. It *should* be.

But there's a quick cut to Clara Swift in the shower, beautifully singing her unlikely one line. She is startled to see something, or someone, through the glass door; she stops singing, momentarily covering her breasts. Then she laughs. "You keep *doing* that—you just *appear!*" she says, to camera. The shower door opens, and the naked kindergarten man steps under the shower with her.

"I don't like to interrupt you when you're singing Tommy's song," Paul Goode tells her. She has started to shampoo his hair, the lather getting on his face and on her breasts; he closes his eyes.

"Well, you *did* interrupt me—I don't mind," she says.

"You know what I like," he tells her shyly.

"What you like," she says, as if she has no idea what he means—she's teasing him.

"Go on—say it," the kindergarten man tells her. She has rinsed the lather out of his hair. When he opens his eyes and looks up at her, she pulls his face to her breasts and he closes his eyes again. "You're not too small for me—you're just small enough," she tells him earnestly, for what sounds like the hundredth time.

Fade to black. The kindergartners' voices, singing Tommy's song, play over the end credits. Both Em and I thought it was a cheesy ending—overkill noir with a schmaltzy sex scene, tacked on to reach the romance audience. The shower scene seemed to belong in a different film. One critic called the shower scene "almost European," but what did that mean?

Our critical opinion of Paul Goode, as an actor or a screenwriter, was not on our minds that night in Bennington, Vermont, when Nora and Em and I saw *The Kindergarten Man* with Molly and my mother. All we wanted to know was the same old thing: Did Little Ray think Paul Goode was my father? Was he the boy who couldn't take his eyes off her, just some kid who wasn't shaving? "He was *small*," she'd whispered to me once. "He would have been a pretty girl. What he meant to me, Adam, was that you would be all mine. That's what 'no strings attached' *means*, sweetie," my mother had said.

That night in Bennington was the first time Molly and my mom had seen *The Kindergarten Man*. After the movie, Molly was the first one to say anything. As usual, Molly was the driver—she and Ray were up front, I was with Nora and Em in the backseat. "Those looked like your single-leg lunges and your squats to me, Ray—like the little guy had paid pretty close attention," Molly said. "How come you didn't show him the wall sits, too?" Molly asked my mother.

"He was more interested in the sex, Molly—not that the sex took a lot of time. We spent more time on the lunges and the squats than the sex, but we didn't do any wall sits," my mom told Molly. "Like I told you, he was just some kid—we only did it once—but everyone said he was a good little skier, and I wanted to see what kind of balance he had. He could really hold the lunges, he really stuck the squats—you can't tell what kind of athlete some-one is from wall sits," my mother went on and on to Molly.

"No, you can't—that's true, Ray," Molly said. We drove some distance with no one saying anything. "I hate this road at night, deer everywhere," Molly told us.

"Just to be clear, Ray—you're saying Paul Goode is the guy, right?" Nora asked her.

"Dear Nora, when I see him pretending to be a kid—when he's hanging out with other kids, and moving like he's a kid—he sure *moves* like the kid I remember," my mom answered. "But, like I said, we spent more time doing the lunges and the squats than we spent fucking. He was a kid, it was his first time, and you know me—I'm not going to spend more time than necessary with a penis, not even a small one," my mother told Nora.

"I think that's clear, Ray—I think you've covered it," Molly said.

"Holy shit—your dad is a movie star, kiddo," Nora told me. Em was sitting between us in the backseat; she was holding my hand, but she gave Nora a punch in the upper arm with the fist of her other hand. "*And* a screenwriter—okay, okay," Nora told Em.

From the matter-of-fact way my mom had reacted to recognizing the kid who got her pregnant with me, I believed that the sex had truly been no big deal to her. Knowing the kind of concentration my mother put into her single-leg lunges and her squats, I didn't doubt that her having sex with Paul Goode must have been anticlimactic for her, if not for him. But, from the backseat of the dark car, I couldn't see my mom's face—only the back of her head and her hunched shoulders, as she repeatedly hit her forehead with the heel of her hand.

"What's wrong, Ray—what's the matter?" Nora and Em and I heard Molly ask her.

"He stole what I said—he took what I told him, and just gave it to the kindergarten teacher!" my mother said. She was really angry, almost in tears about it. "He was very insecure about being younger than me, and smaller than me—the kid kept asking me if he was big enough!" my mom cried. "I *told* him he wasn't too small for me, I *said* he was just small enough, because I'd been *hoping* he had a small penis!" my mother cried. "Of course, he would never have understood that I *chose* him because I hoped he would be small."

"It seems as if he understood you eventually, Ray," Molly said softly.

"But that was *my* line, those were *my* words—what I told him," my mother protested, her voice breaking. "Is that what you writers do, sweetie—you *steal* stuff that real people say?" my mom asked me. I could feel Em nodding her head against my shoulder; she was squeezing my hand harder.

"That's definitely what Em does, Ray," Nora told her.

"I do it sometimes," I said to my mother.

"Well, if you ask me, I think that's *immoral*," my mom said. I didn't know what to say. Em couldn't squeeze my hand harder. "And what about those little urinals?" my mother asked. "I don't think they had pint-size urinals for boys in kindergarten—the little urinals didn't show up till elementary school." Now no one knew what to say. Em's hand was limp in mine. "In kindergarten—if you ask me, sweetie—you little boys just peed in the toilet," my mom said.

If you ask me, we don't know what's anticlimactic, and what isn't, until we get to the end of it.

34.

OUR MARINE

In her first letter to me, only one thing Em wrote wasn't exactly true—when she said, "I just don't dare to make up everything, like you do." I don't make up everything, but when I use things that actually happened, I always change something; I try to make what happens not exactly true. Maybe that's what Em meant.

I'm making a very small point. In other respects, I wouldn't quarrel with a word Em wrote in that letter. She's a real writer. "Nothing has changed because you know who your father is, except you know where your writer gene comes from," Em wrote; she also echoed what Molly had told me privately.

"We should keep this business about who your father is to ourselves, Kid," was the way Molly put it.

To my knowledge, only Nora had looked into the legal side of it. Was it, or is it, a crime in Colorado for an eighteen-year-old woman to have sex with a fourteen-year-old boy? What mattered, Molly told me, was my mother's job. Little Ray taught beginners how to ski; most of them were children. "Fourteen and younger, Kid," was the way Molly put it. It was hard to miss her point. "I'm not saying what you writers do is *immoral*—stealing stuff that real people say, or do, seems fair to me," the trail groomer told me. "But there's people who would say what your mom did is definitely immoral—to have you in such a way that you would be all hers. If you see what I mean, Kid," Molly said. "Legal or illegal, fourteen is underage."

On the evidence of Paul Goode in *The Kindergarten Man*, I was not "all hers." Was it a lie of omission—to keep what Molly called "this business" to ourselves? It was what Nora always said: everything was about sex and secrets. Everyone who knew Paul Goode was my father loved my mother; we were committed to protecting her.

The snowshoer, even as a woman, was too much of a gentleman of the old school to brag about my mom's escapade to the little Barlows, who were congratulating themselves for being the first to recognize the noir genius of Paul Goode. Goode was forty-seven when *The Kindergarten Man* made him a movie star and a Hollywood celebrity—a little long in the tooth to be discovered. At my mom's wedding, it had been Susan Barlow who said, "I know we're going to be seeing more of him."

But Elliot Barlow, as a man and as a woman, knew how to be discreet. Little Ray was very much more and somewhat less than a wife to the snowshoer, who would never tell tales out of school about her.

Uncle Martin and Uncle Johan, those old volunteers, were right about that Aspen local who was a ski guide at Camp Hale. Paul Goode was the little mountaineer they remembered—a Tenth Mountain Division man. My uncles were right about the exploits of the Eighty-fifth Mountain Infantry Division in Italy. Paul Goode would see his first combat in the battles for Mount Belvedere and Mount Gorgolesco; the little kindergarten man would be part of the Po Valley breakout and the Po River crossing, too. The Eighty-fifth would be in Verona in April 1945, a month before the Germans surrendered. Paul Goode would set sail from Naples to New York in August of that year, returning home to Aspen from New York. He was nineteen, a very young veteran of World War II. Everyone who remembered him as a kid said he'd been a darling boy. His mother was thirty-six—she'd been very young when she had him, only seventeen.

My uncles were also right about the little guy's name. Paul Goode was born Paulino Juárez. Uncle Martin and Uncle Johan said Paulino didn't look Mexican, but his mom was Mexican. Paulina Juárez named her son after herself. In interviews, when he was asked about his father, Paul Goode always said, "The Hotel Jerome has been a good father to me. The Jerome is my father."

"You have to admit it, kiddo—your dad is pretty clear in interviews," Nora said.

Paul Goode grew up at the Hotel Jerome, because his mother was a single mom and she worked there; she was a cleaning woman, a hotel maid. Although no one would speak of the boy's father, Paul Goode's mother had spoken only once but most succinctly about him. He'd been a guest at the Jerome. "He was a very nice, older gentleman—I'm sorry, but I don't remember his name," Paulina Juárez said; that was all she ever said about him.

"It strikes me that everyone behaved very well"—this was what Paul Goode said in interviews. The nice, older gentleman didn't take advantage of the seventeen-year-old girl. The Hotel Jerome didn't disclose the identity of the older gentleman, but no one accused the hotel of protecting their client at the expense of their innocent young maid. "Over the years, to my

mother and to me, the Hotel Jerome has been a model of good behavior,"
Paul Goode always said. The little kindergarten man wasn't kidding when he
called the Jerome "a good father." Growing up, he had the run of the hotel.
The Jerome cherished Paulina. The hotel did everything it could to accommodate the needs of the young, unwed mother; the Jerome was no less warm
and welcoming to her illegitimate child. "The Jerome did more for my mom
than maternity leave—let's leave it at that," Paul Goode tried to say, but his
interviewers pressed him for more details. Had the hotel helped Paulina pay
for childcare? "More than helped" was Paul Goode's only comment. Later, if
the boy got out of school when his mom was working, he came to the Jerome.
"The hotel was my home, the other maids were all mothers to me—I had a
very happy childhood," Paul Goode said.

Wouldn't the circumstances of a child born out of wedlock to a hotel
maid have sparked some expression of reproof? Weren't at least one or two of
the hotel maids reproving of Paulina Juárez? Wouldn't you think that one or
more of them might have manifested some measure of reproval toward little
Paulino? These were questions journalists asked Paul Goode. How could his
young mother's situation, and the circumstances of his birth, have led to a
happy childhood? "Baloney!" my mom said, when Molly or I asked her about
this line of questioning from Paul Goode's interviewers. "He seemed like a
very happy kid to me," Little Ray maintained.

The snowshoer had said the writing was the most über-noir thing about
The Wrong Car, and of course I knew how much Mr. Barlow disparaged her
parents' potboilers and their adoration of overkill noir. My writer gene must
have been on my mind when I wrote the little English teacher, expressing
my disbelief in Paul Goode's happy childhood. "I couldn't write a credible
novel about people behaving in such an exemplary fashion," I wrote the
snowshoer. "How is it possible that everyone at the Hotel Jerome behaved
admirably to a knocked-up maid and her kid?"

"Don't be so cynical," Elliot Barlow wrote me back. She believed my
mother, who sacralized the Hotel Jerome—in the same way my mom had the
hotel's founder, Jerome B. Wheeler. To listen to Ray, you wouldn't know the
sainted Mr. Wheeler had lost the hotel to back taxes in 1909. You might get
the idea that the ghost of Jerome B. Wheeler ran the Hotel Jerome.

I know my mother believed the Hotel Jerome was sacred, to the degree
that she thought the staff and management were incapable of any wrongdo-
ing, but even my mom knew the staff and management couldn't control (or
be blamed for) the behavior of the hotel guests.

"What about the Aspen locals—how did the townsfolk behave?" I wrote back to Mr. Barlow. If you were one of the people who loved her, and she loved you, the snowshoer liked being called Mr. Barlow, but not everyone was welcome to call her Mr. Barlow—not now. As a woman, notwithstanding her transitioning, she saw no reason to change her name; Elliot worked fine as a female name. She and I had recently been back in Exeter—sadly, for the occasion of Coach Dearborn's memorial service. I wanted to go, and I knew the snowshoer wanted to be there, but I didn't want her to go back to the academy alone. I wasn't worried about how my wrestling teammates would treat her when they encountered Elliot Barlow as a woman; I wasn't worried about those wrestlers from before or after my time at the academy, who would have known Coach Dearborn's littlest wrestler and assistant coach. I'm not sure who I was worried about, exactly—I was worried *inexactly*. I didn't know who could be abusive to Mr. Barlow as a woman: the faculty members who might not have known her when she was a man, those wrestlers who hadn't been at Exeter when Elliot was a regular in that wrestling room? Both Mr. Barlow and I had been asked to speak at Coach Dearborn's memorial service. I struggled not to imagine Coach Dearborn's ghost, still smoking in the coaches' locker room. I preferred to remember him doing single-leg lunges with my mom at her wedding. I also struggled not to think of him carrying Granddaddy's body from the croquet court. "I'll speak just ahead of you, so I can introduce you," I said to the snowshoer. Naturally, I wanted to make it easier for Elliot—to let me say something about her transitioning from male to female, before all those good old boys got a look at her. Coeducation was still pretty new at Exeter; the snowshoer had resigned fairly recently.

"If you don't mind, Adam, I'll introduce myself—I'll speak just ahead of you, so I can tell all these wrestlers to read your novels," the little English teacher told me.

Of course I worried about how *that* would go over; in such an obdurately all-boys' atmosphere, at a revered wrestling coach's memorial service, Mr. Barlow's introducing herself as a woman seemed like asking for trouble. Actually, I thought it went over pretty well—I somehow managed to remain calm during the lingering silence. "My name is Elliot Barlow," Mr. Barlow began. "Some of you may remember me when I was a man."

She was over forty-five, but she was a knockout as a woman—pretty and small. Most of the mourners in Phillips Church didn't recognize Elliot Barlow, but many of them recognized Little Ray. My mother was in her fifties, but she was also pretty and small. "I used to be Mr. Barlow, when I taught

English and coached wrestling here, but you can still call me Elliot—I think Elliot works for a man or a woman," the pretty snowshoer said. "I talked to Coach Dearborn about it, and he gave me his approval. Coach Dearborn's approval was always good enough for me," the little English teacher said, her voice suddenly sounding strained.

There were two loud wolf whistles. My mom, who was crying, started laughing—ending the sepulchral silence. "Thank you, Martin—thank you, Johan," Elliot Barlow told my uncles, who were also laughing. Those two old Norwegians didn't have many years left—before the curve they saw coming, before that turn in the road. The pretty snowshoer's confidence in herself came back; she seemed uplifted by my uncles' crude appraisal of her womanliness. Thereby enlivened as a woman, the little English teacher exhorted the mostly male congregation in Phillips Church to read my novels. "Adam Brewster isn't *just* a wrestler," Elliot Barlow told them. Even the wrestlers laughed. Thus I was warmly introduced.

Later, at a cocktail party at the Exeter Inn, almost everyone was nice to the snowshoer; my teammates, also Matthew Zimmermann's teammates, were friendly to Mr. Barlow, who used to be Zim's principal workout partner. Of course, they were Exeter men; Exeter would expect them to be reserved. Maybe their homophobia was reserved.

When we were on our way back to New York together, Elliot and I talked about the physical standoffishness of some of our fellow wrestlers. "The guys hugged me more when I was a guy," the snowshoer said; she sounded a little melancholic about it. The standoffishness was strictly physical—not necessarily cold or unfriendly, we kept saying. Yet we both knew that wrestlers were not inclined to physical standoffishness with one another. "Maybe some of the guys were just being respectful of me as a woman," Mr. Barlow said. I tried to agree with her; I could see she was feeling a little let down, an almost physical disappointment.

My mom had made up for any lack of physical contact Elliot may have been missing. Whenever those familiar-looking faculty wives were approaching us, my mother was all over Elliot; my mom rode piggyback on Elliot, her arms around Elliot's chest, her legs locked at Elliot's waist. It was not lost on Molly that the rehearsal dinner for my mom's wedding had been at this same Exeter Inn, where an emotionally shattered waitress was brought to her knees by the aria of Em's orgasm ecstasies—and was later struck in her lower abdomen by a chocolate cupcake with cranberry frosting, a sidearm shot from Henrik's lacrosse stick. It seemed suitable to Molly that my mom would mount the snowshoer in public at the Exeter Inn, of all places. "Ray wants everyone to know they're still married," Molly told me.

"If my mom starts humping the snowshoer, maybe we should jump in and break it up," I said to the ski patroller.

"You're the wrestler, Kid—I'll let you jump in and break it up," the trail groomer said.

The faculty wives who approached us were warm to Elliot as a woman, but some of those ladies were less warm to Little Ray. A few of the faculty wives had read my novels, or at least one of my novels; there was only one wife who told me she was disappointed that I hadn't written more about "Exeter people." As for the younger Exeter people, there were some current students who spoke to me about my writing, but the ones who'd actually read my novels were relatively new girls at the school. If there were fiction readers among my former wrestling teammates—all of us were in our thirties—not one of them told me that he'd read my novels. Three or four of the guys mentioned that their mothers or their wives had read something I'd written.

Business as usual, I thought, when I noticed a long-armed guy who'd been keeping his distance. You know how it is when you know you know someone, but you don't remember who he is. With wrestlers, you remember the guys around your own weight class. The snowshoer didn't remember the sullen fellow's name, but she knew more than I did.

"He was never a happy-go-lucky guy, and he wasn't a starter—he was a backup heavyweight, a small heavyweight, but he was too big to make one-seventy-seven," Mr. Barlow reminded me. I remembered the guy then; he was still a small heavyweight—he'd kept himself lean and mean. When I was at Exeter, there was no weight class between 177 pounds and heavyweight—a sizable gap. If the lower weight class was too light for you, and you just weren't big enough to compete as a heavyweight, you were out of luck—in a no-man's-land. It was understandable that the snowshoer felt empathy for the guy. Elliot herself was in a similar kind of limbo—she'd always been too small for the lightest weight class. "Perhaps he was in the military—maybe he fit in there better than here," the snowshoer whispered to me. The backup heavyweight had a haircut that would have fit in better in the military than it did at Exeter, a buzz cut of the sort he might have had in boot camp. I decided to speak to him—if only to see if I could engage him in conversation. That turned out to be a bad idea.

"I know you were a heavyweight, but I'm sorry I don't know your name," I said to him, holding out my hand. He didn't shake it.

"I hope you haven't written anything about Lieutenant Matthew Zimmermann. I hope you never do write about the lieutenant, unless you get everything right," the backup heavyweight said, not telling me his name.

Well, what would you have thought? Was I crazy to imagine this angry soldier might have been in Vietnam? From what he said, I imagined the guy could have been a soldier in Zimmer's unit. I thought the unfriendly fellow was being protective of Zim, as a comrade in arms had a right to be, but the angry soldier hadn't known Zim in the war—he'd barely known Zim at Exeter. "I didn't hang out with the *lightweights*," he told me. I realized what he meant about my getting everything "right," if I ever wrote about Lieutenant Matthew Zimmermann. It was the Vietnam War I was supposed to get "right," or I shouldn't write about it at all.

I tried to tell the guy how Zim and I had talked about the policy of the war, how Zim had loathed the secretary of defense, Robert McNamara, how Zimmer thought of McNamara as the architect of the military tactics and the political strategy of a war that went awry—a war that had been "misbegotten from the get-go," I'd heard Zim say.

But the backup heavyweight was a hawk; there was no getting through to him. American involvement in the war in Vietnam had ended. Nixon had become the first president to resign from office. The fall of Saigon had already happened, but the small heavyweight with the long arms insisted that the Vietnam War had been a "just war"; it was a "war against communist aggression," he kept saying. We could have won it, he declared; "we should have obliterated the communists," he said. He kept glancing at Elliot Barlow, and then looking away from her—as if he purposely meant not to see her. My mother had her arms around the snowshoer, but she kept smiling at me and the heavyweight without a name. I was afraid she'd overheard the *Zimmermann* or *Zimmer* words; I didn't want my mom to join our conversation thinking we were reminiscing about her beloved Zim. "And your mom still has the big girlfriend, I see," the small heavyweight said, glancing quickly at Molly, then quickly away. "I'm a New Yorker, I've seen some shows at the Gallows—*Two Twats*, or whatever those *lickers* call themselves," the tall, lean guy went on. "I've seen what your dyke cousin calls 'The News in English,' I know her leftist politics," the asshole said. At the time, I was taken aback by his right-wing rhetoric and his homophobic, sexist slurs, but Ronald Reagan was coming. The Christian Right was coming. Was the certitude of the undersize heavyweight a harbinger of Jerry Falwell's Moral Majority? They were coming, too.

At a loss for words, I inquired of the heavyweight without a name if he'd perhaps known Zim at Yale. "Did you go to Yale?" I suddenly asked the guy, which made no sense at all—even to me. I just had to say something.

"I was in the Marine Corps," he answered me coldly. He made it sound as if his being a marine precluded a college education, or made the matter of where he'd gone to university superfluous. *"Yalies!"* he suddenly said, with scorn—the way he'd said *lightweights*.

At that cocktail party, I don't doubt there were some former Exeter wrestlers who'd gone to Yale, but they weren't the only ones who turned their heads when they heard the word *Yalies*. Suddenly my mother was beside us. She took hold of the heavyweight's wrist with one hand; she had taken hold of my wrist with her other hand, the way a wrestler would take control of your hands. The heavyweight had flinched, recoiling from her touch. My mom wasn't used to anyone resisting her hands-on approach to conversation; when she was eager to talk to you, she stood close to you and held your wrists. The tall, lean guy tried to free his wrist from her grip, but my mom wouldn't let him go. Her winter life, all the ski-poling, had given her a good grip—her hands were small but strong, like the snowshoer's. "Were you two talking about *Zim*—didn't I hear that dear boy's name? I know I heard the word *Yalies*," my mom said in her breathless way. I saw she was standing on her toes. Little Ray was making an effort to bring her smiling, uplifted face closer to the small heavyweight's scowling visage. It was the long-armed guy's turn to be struck speechless.

"He didn't really know Zim, not at Yale, not even at Exeter—they weren't in the war together," I tried to tell my mother.

"That awful war—poor Zim!" my mom cried. "You should have let me shoot him, sweetie—Zim would be alive if you'd let me shoot him, you know," she told me. "Molly says she could have shot him out the kitchen window, when Zim was doing lunges in the driveway, but I wouldn't have taken a chance with a deer slug in the twenty-gauge at that range—I would have shot him when he was asleep, just under the patella," my mom was saying, when the appalled way the unnamed heavyweight was looking at her finally registered. "Just his *knee*—I wouldn't have *killed* him, I could have *saved* him!" my mother cried. She let go of my wrist, taking hold of the heavyweight's other wrist with her free hand. "Zim would be alive today—he would have been here, with us, if I'd shot him!" my mom insisted. "You can have a good life with a bad knee—you can still get laid with a limp, you know, and have children, and make friends," she told the seemingly paralyzed heavyweight, as she'd told Molly and me. I knew she was about to burst into tears—what usually happened when she talked or just thought about Zim. Then Molly was there, with her big hands on my mother's shoulders.

"Let it go, Ray," the night groomer said softly. "I wouldn't fuck up that shot from the kitchen window—I use that twenty-gauge more than you do," Molly reminded her.

This was true; Molly was the deer hunter in their family, she shot a deer every hunting season. She had a friend on the ski patrol who butchered it for her; Molly gave the patroller as many steaks or chops as he wanted, keeping the rest for herself and Ray. My mom had gone deer hunting with Uncle Martin and Uncle Johan. She was a good deerstalker, my uncles told her, and she clearly liked walking around in the woods with a gun; those two Norwegians loved her company, but they never understood why she missed every shot. Molly and I and the snowshoer knew why.

My mother purposely missed the deer, but she made a point of telling us how she always hit what she was aiming at. Both Molly and my mom liked that twenty-gauge—a lever-action, single-shot shotgun. Most deer hunters wouldn't have chosen it; they would have wanted a rifle or a twelve-gauge, and more than one shot. But Molly swore by it. "My first shot is buckshot—that'll knock a deer down," the trail groomer had told me. "That little twenty-gauge is a cinch to reload. My second shot is a deer slug, the kill shot," Molly said. Molly also liked how easy a gun it was for my mom to handle. "No safety is safer than having a safety," the ski patroller liked to say about that single-shot twenty-gauge. "You have to cock it to shoot it—if it's not cocked, it won't fire. It's a hard gun to shoot yourself with, accidentally," Molly always said.

In the context of that cocktail party at the Exeter Inn, Lieutenant Matthew Zimmermann's proposed salvation from a hero's death in the Vietnam War must have been confounding to the adamant marine. Two lesbians—two *dykes*, two *lickers*—had told him they were prepared to shoot Matthew Zimmermann to save him from Vietnam. I decided to keep talking, before the undersize heavyweight thought of something to say. I quickly told the outraged but nonspeaking marine that my mother or Molly would have shot *me*, if I hadn't been 4-F. I showed the small heavyweight my palms; the scars from the flexor-tendon surgeries were very visible. "Wrestling injuries to my fingers and hands—extensor tendons, too," I was explaining to him, when my mom suddenly let go of the guy's wrists. In her excitement to show him her hands, she almost hit him in the face.

"Look at my hands!" Little Ray cried. "Adam has my little hands, so I didn't have to shoot him!" Molly was already hugging her when my mother started to sob. "You should have let me shoot Zim—both of you are to blame," my mom blubbered to Molly and me.

"We know, Ray," the night groomer was consoling her, when the snow-shoer just showed up—Elliot Barlow suddenly took hold of the small heavy-weight's wrists. In the Exeter wrestling room, Mr. Barlow had been the hand-control man. With all the chin-ups and the ski-poling, the little English teacher had more hand strength than most middleweights.

"You're a natural one-ninety-pounder, you know," the pretty snowshoer told the undersize heavyweight. "I always wondered if you found your proper weight class in college—if you wrestled in college." (In the marine's most likely wrestling years, after he'd been a backup heavyweight at Exeter, there was a weight class for 191 pounds—later, for 190 pounds—in college.)

"I didn't wrestle after Exeter," the natural 190-pounder told the beautiful Elliot Barlow. "I was in the Marine Corps," he repeated—this time, more proudly.

"Oh, you poor thing—I'm so sorry!" my mother wailed. She came toward him to give him a hug; the marine made an effort to turn away from her, but she hugged him from behind, locking her little hands around his waist, her face pressed against his broad back. "Are you okay now, are you all right?" my mom asked our marine.

The backup heavyweight could hear that her concern for him was genuine—he had to feel that her hug was heartfelt. "Yes, ma'am," the marine answered her—both politely and stoically. Wrestlers know who has the hand control, and who doesn't. Mr. Barlow had the tall guy's wrists locked up; my mother had him in a bear hug from behind. Our marine would have had to start a fight to break free of them. He didn't. I could see his hatred for all of us, but I also saw his restraint. In his mind, he was held fast by two queers, and I knew he didn't like Molly or me any better. I watched him restrain himself.

"We're glad you're okay—we're happy you're all right," I said to him, sincerely.

"We're an anti-war family—we're happy when a soldier comes safely home," the pretty snowshoer said.

"I didn't come *home*, I never *liked* home—the *Marine Corps* was my home," the soldier said bitterly, but without anger. He was doing all he could to hold back his anger. My mom didn't realize how angry the marine was; she just hugged him harder.

"As Ishmael says, 'a whale-ship was my Yale College and my Harvard.' I'm guessing the Marine Corps was *your* whale-ship," the little English teacher told the proud marine, who somehow managed to look more appalled. It was apparent that the heavyweight hadn't read Herman Melville; from the stricken look on his face, the marine must have imagined a "whale-ship" was a sexual expression peculiar to gay men, or to lesbian or transgender women. Molly tried to allay our marine's fears.

"It's good to have something you're proud of—I'm guessing the Marine Corps was good for you," the snowcat operator said.

"Yes, ma'am," the 190-pounder replied—with gratitude, and looking slightly relieved.

"The 'whale-ship' is from *Moby-Dick*—it's the last line of Chapter Twenty-four, 'The Advocate' chapter," Mr. Barlow gently explained to our marine. "I just meant that the Marine Corps must have been of special importance to you," the pretty snowshoer said. "Maybe more of a learning experience than any college could have been?"

"Yes . . . *ma'am*," the marine managed to say. He was struggling to be nice, to the degree that it was painful to look at him.

When we were on our way back to New York together, Elliot and I speculated on what sexual horrors a *whale-ship* might have conjured up for our restrained but homophobic marine. I liked the little English teacher's theory the best of all our speculations.

"Our guy is a right-wing homophobe who goes to the Gallows expressly to see performers he despises, and to look with loathing at most of the audience, who are enjoying the shows," Mr. Barlow began. At first, I didn't see where the snowshoer was going with this. I thought I understood the homo-hating guys Elliot was thinking of—those sexually intolerant types who haunted gay bars or lesbian hangouts, just to make trouble—but those guys were usually in groups. When they laughed at the drag queens, they laughed like a gang. Our angry marine was a loner. The Marine Corps may have been his home, but he wasn't a man who made many friends.

Mr. Barlow agreed. Our marine was a solitary type, and he tried to hold his hatred back. In his heart, our marine was a gay basher, but he wouldn't have gone out with a bunch of guys for the express purpose of abusing gays or lesbians. "Our marine might have thought the 'Whale Ship' was a more clandestine club than the Gallows," the snowshoer said. "Not the kind of gay bar or lesbian hangout that advertises itself, or a place like the Gallows, which is known to be politically subversive. Our marine was imagining much worse for the Whale Ship—a secret society, an openly perverse place," the little English teacher told me.

"Like *what*? What happens at the Whale Ship?" I asked Elliot. I was a little frustrated with her. I thought what she was saying was full of generalizations; she'd said nothing specific.

"At the Whale Ship, you have to show your penis or your vagina just to get in the door. And you better have a *good* one, or you won't get in!" the pretty snowshoer cried. We laughed and laughed. It was just a joke, I thought. At the Whale Ship, the price of admission was an aesthetic exam—you had to pass a weird kind of perfection test, just to be admitted. Our marine, little Mr. Barlow speculated, may have imagined that the Whale Ship wouldn't admit him, because the undersize heavyweight wasn't *perfect* enough.

As Em pointed out in her first letter to me, there was "something improbable" about the Whale Ship—"even as an imaginary sex club," Em wrote.

Em and I were on the same page regarding the pretty snowshoer's speculations. Elliot Barlow wasn't joking about what went on at the Whale Ship. The little English teacher used to worry that she just wasn't big enough. Bigness really mattered to Mr. Barlow, when he'd been a man. "Something still matters to the snowshoer," Em wrote me. I knew what Em meant, and she'd said it as exactly as I could have. Even as a woman, the pretty snowshoer believed she just wasn't *something* enough. Passing a *something* test at the Whale Ship was not what our marine might have imagined; an imaginary test was Elliot Barlow's obsession, which Em and I knew was no joke.

35.

AT THE WHALE SHIP

At that interminable cocktail party at the Exeter Inn, both the compassionate Mr. Barlow and our constrained marine were spared further tests of their tolerance or their toughness. The exuberant singing of Uncle Johan heralded his and Uncle Martin's arrival. "Bier, Bier—das Bier ist hier!" Johan sang. Each of my uncles' big hands held two freshly opened beer bottles. The four of us—Molly and my mom, and the snowshoer and I—took a bottle each, which left my uncles with two beers apiece. The retired Norwegians, who'd made the trip to Exeter from up north, did their best to force a beer on our retreating marine, but I'd already noticed that the natural 190-pounder didn't drink. Besides, in accepting their beers, Mr. Barlow had relinquished her highly esteemed hand control and my mother had given up her strong grip on the bear hug. The tall, lean heavyweight had seized the moment to slip away.

I was glad to see him go; both his hatred and his effort to contain it had been hard to bear. And what if the conversation had turned to military matters—to the long-armed guy's life in the Marine Corps, to my uncles' being recruited by the National Ski Patrol to train the troops in the Tenth Mountain Division? What if that conversation had led my uncles to remember Paulino, the little mountaineer? I'll never know if my uncles knew Paul Goode was my father. Not just Molly, but also Nora and Em, had cautioned me about that. "Your dad was definitely underage, kiddo—my dad and Uncle Johan would just say your dad was lucky," Nora told me, with Em nodding her head off.

I regret I didn't spend more time with Uncle Martin and Uncle Johan at that cocktail party at the Exeter Inn. I didn't know it was the next-to-last time I would see them. They were so much fun, especially after my aunts were gone, and my uncles loved Little Ray. Uncle Martin and Uncle Johan had much affection for Molly, and for the snowshoer—not only when Mr. Barlow had been a man, but also when she was a woman.

The last time I saw those two Norwegians was when they came to New

423

York to see Nora and Em onstage at the Gallows, the first and only time they saw *Two Dykes, One Who Talks*—when they also saw and heard the premier performance of Damaged Don's "No Lucky Star," the original lyrics, the uncensored version. Not then, at the Gallows in New York, or only shortly before then—that next-to-last time, when I saw Uncle Martin and Uncle Johan in Exeter—did I detect in my uncles their desire to call it quits, to drive off the road. Not even the people you love in your own family tell you everything, and there are always the things you miss.

"Those two men never misjudged a turn," my mother said, when Uncle Johan drove off the Kancamagus.

"I thought that's what you said about their *skiing,* Ray—I thought that's what you meant," Molly said.

"That's what I'm saying about their *driving,* Molly—that's what I mean," my mom said.

As for Uncle Johan and her dad misjudging a turn on the Kanc, Nora saw it the way my mom saw it—"they knew when to call it quits," Nora always said.

In 1977, the same year Uncle Johan accelerated as he drove off the Kancamagus, Clara Swift, who played the teacher in *The Kindergarten Man*, gave birth to Paul Goode's child. To be sure, they'd been an item since they made that first film (of their many films) together—when Paul Goode was forty-six, and Clara Swift was twenty years younger. But the age difference between them wasn't what got the goat of the Hollywood press and the scandalmongers in the media. What ticked off the tabloids was how pregnant Clara Swift was when they got married—she was already showing.

THE BRIDE WORE WHITE—A WHITE MATERNITY DRESS! was one headline. FLAUNTING IT! was another one. And, of course, there was HAVE YOU NO SHAME?

Nora was six when I was born. "I remember what your mom looked like when she was pregnant, kiddo—your dad definitely married a woman who reminded him of your mom," Nora told me. Well, okay. In 1977, there was so much gossipy media about Paul Goode and his much younger, pregnant bride, even my uncles must have made the little *mountaineer* connection. Nora said her dad and Uncle Johan surely would have seen the resemblance to Little Ray in the pregnant Clara Swift.

Em and I kept it to ourselves. Clara Swift was no less attractive to us when she was hugely pregnant than she was when we first saw her in *The Kindergarten Man*. What also appealed to Em and me about Clara Swift was that she refused to be interviewed; she would not talk to journalists, period. "You would have to be a journalist not to like that about her," Em wrote me.

As for the former Paulino Juárez, he continued to do interviews, in which he remained calm—he kept his cool, even with the worst questions—and he always seemed to care about being clear. He was refreshingly candid about his less-than-successful efforts to find work in the movie business after the war. As a veteran of the Tenth Mountain Division, he could always get a job in Aspen—from the first, at the Hotel Jerome, later both at the hotel and on the ski mountain. With the help of the G.I. Bill, he'd enrolled in the film program at USC, but things didn't take off for him in Hollywood until he met Lex Barker and Lana Turner at the Hotel Jerome.

Not surprisingly, my mother remained mute on the subject of the advice and assistance Lex and Lana gave my father. At the time, Lex was done making Tarzan movies for RKO Radio Pictures, but he still must have known people at RKO, and Lana would have been under Louis B. Mayer's wing at MGM. According to Paul Goode, he couldn't remember if it was Lex or Lana who advised him to change his name. Paulino Juárez was only half-Mexican, and no one ever said he looked Mexican, but either Lex or Lana told him that his name begged the question. The choice of "Paul" was easy. It was Lex, not Lana, who came up with the "Goode"—with the *e* on the end. Lana had worried about "Goode"; it looked British, not American, to her. Lex said British was better for an actor.

In his interviews, when Paul Goode talked about his stage name, he always credited Lex Barker with the "Goode," and with telling him about the Latin origins and various meanings of "Paul." " 'Paul' means 'small'—also 'humble,' 'scarce,' and 'rare,' but mainly 'small'—like me," Paul Goode had said. He also liked to tell the story of what Lana Turner had told him.

"You're small and dark, small and handsome, and small and strong. But you're mainly small," Lana had said.

Yet even with help from Lex Barker and Lana Turner, it took a long time for Paul Goode's career in Hollywood to take off. "I had a lot of time to write, because my life as an actor was slow to start," Paul Goode liked to say. *The Wrong Car* (1956) was his first speaking part; he was already thirty, and the role of the getaway driver didn't make him a star. He didn't count what he called the "uncredited" characters he'd played in earlier films, those roles where he was unnamed but typecast as small—Small Man on Escalator, Small Man with Large Woman, Small Man Attacked by Big Dog.

Paulina Juárez, who, from all reports, loved being a maid at the Hotel

Jerome, would not live to see her one and only Paulino become a movie star. One winter night in Aspen, in 1957, after almost no one had noticed Paul Goode in *The Wrong Car*, his mother slipped on the ice and fell. She hit her head on the stone stairs leading to the back door of her duplex apartment, dying of hypothermia after lying unconscious in the freezing cold. Her neighbor found her in the morning, when there were no vital signs. Paulina Juárez was only forty-eight when she left her thirty-one-year-old son behind. "My mom loved her job—when she came home from work at the Jerome, she couldn't stop being a cleaning woman," Paul Goode would later say in interviews. "She never went to bed at night before taking out the garbage." When the more aggressive interviewers asked him to comment on the alcohol—cited as a factor in his mother's hypothermia—Paul Goode kept his cool. He answered, without any edginess, "My mom liked to have a nightcap or two before her bedtime—I never saw any harm in it."

Naturally, I remembered asking my mother about the shy, childlike hotel maid—the Mexican-looking woman among my ghosts. "Oh, I didn't know she died—I think she was Italian," Little Ray had said, although she later admitted she knew the boy she slept with had a mom who worked as a maid at the Jerome. "I just didn't know which maid she was, sweetie," my mother said.

"Whatever you think of your dad's writing, you shouldn't blame him for the noir—he came by his darkness naturally," the little English teacher told me.

Em echoed this theme in her first letter to me. What we both called overkill noir or über-noir in my father's writing wasn't overkill or über to Paul Goode. The noir was just the way things were for the little kindergarten man and his creator. And Paul Goode had gotten better as a writer—"the way writers do, by writing," Em wrote me. After *The Wrong Car*, when the acting jobs didn't exactly pour in, Paulino Juárez came home to Aspen, where he wrote and wrote. He lived in the duplex apartment he'd grown up in with his mother; he worked at the Hotel Jerome, and on the ski mountain. The rest of the time, he did a lot of writing. When *The Kindergarten Man* made him famous when he was forty-seven, Paul Goode had written a lot of unmade movies—"a lot of *unread* screenplays, I'll bet," Em wrote me.

Okay, "he came by his darkness naturally," as the snowshoer said—whatever I think of my dad's writing, I'll give him that.

As for Em's writer genes, not knowing if she had any, she did what an imaginative fiction writer would do—she made up some simply awful writer genes for herself. In her inchworm way of crafting a short story, Em imagined her self-hating lesbian mother as an autobiographical novelist with no imagination at all. The writer mom's first novel incorporated the sobbing mother's confession to her teenage daughter—the part about the lesbian daughter who is "doomed" to have her mom's genes, as Em had written in "A Family Comes Out." Worse, Em's fictional autobiographical novelist describes in soporific detail her sexual relationships with women her daughter knows—not only with several mothers of her daughter's friends, but also with one of her daughter's contemporaries. While Em herself had written about this, albeit briefly, in "A Couple of Latecomers Get Divorced," there is nothing spare in the prose style of the writer mom, whose autobiographical logorrhea is fueled by her self-righteousness. If gay women, such as herself and her "doomed" daughter, do "degrading things" and are "unredeemable"—well, in the writer mom's opinion, "homosexual men do much worse things." Sparing no detail, the lesbian mother's first novel describes the horrible things her "homo husband" has done with other gay men.

In Em's third-person omniscient voice, all this happens in one short story—in which Em seems to be barely involved. Even the title sounds detached and academic. "The Problem with Autobiographical Novels" doesn't sound like fiction, which it is. Em's awful mother, who (by her own admission) was a worse wife, wasn't a writer. Not yet. I read Em's short story in manuscript. "The Problem with Autobiographical Novels" would be published in *Ploughshares*. Em's awful mom—with whom, of course, Em wasn't speaking—read Em's short story there. So did Em's much-worse dad.

In "A Family Comes Out," the gay dad ineffectually beats himself with his belt in his daughter's bedroom, while confessing his homosexuality and denouncing his wife's lesbian affairs. In "A Couple of Latecomers Get Divorced," the gay father tells his nonspeaking daughter that he should be castrated for the things he's done with other men. He changes his mind rather quickly about castration—"maybe just a vasectomy," the chickenshit dad decides.

Em had already written a new short story when the one about the writer mom was published in *Ploughshares*. In the new one, "Why I Hate Memoirs," the copycat father reads the writer mom's confessional first novel and decides he can do better. The gay dad writes a more immoderate and unwholesome memoir, which is described in the deadpan, first-person narrative voice of the nonspeaking lesbian daughter. The homo-hating gay father's self-hatred causes him to outconfess the lesbian mother, while at the same time he contends that his wife's incessant need to do it with other women was more damaging to their daughter than his prurient interests in other men.

Em had written me that her actual gay dad's religion, the Church of Scot-land, was "kind of Calvinist, definitely Reformed, and of course Protestant." In her new short story—"just to be funny," Em wrote me—she made the homo-hating gay father a self-described "Presbyterian atheist" who converts to Catholicism. In the 1970s, there was a first wave of ex-gay Christians preaching conversion therapy. Em gave the gay father in her story a crackpot conversion therapy all his own; her fictional memoirist father believes he can cure himself of his homosexual desires by adhering to Catholic teaching. But we know this guy—he hedges his bets. First he is going to be castrated, then he says he'll have "just a vasectomy"; of course he doesn't do either. The real reason the coward converts to Catholicism is that he likes the possibility of forgiveness provided by the Catholic Church. "You confess, you're forgiven—that's how Roman Catholicism works," the self-serving memoirist tells his nonspeaking daughter. She doesn't say a word—she just tells the story.

This one, "Why I Hate Memoirs," was published in *Antaeus*. By the end of the seventies, Em and I were in the habit of writing letters to each other, and we always showed each other our new writing before it was published.

This wasn't (I hoped) what Nora meant when she said to me I was "try-ing to start something with Em." I truly believed Em and I were innocent or unaware of starting anything—just as Em, I know, never thought that her actual parents would actually become two terrible writers. Em was writing fiction. Em never intended to give her awful parents the idea of becoming writers. Who could read "The Problem with Autobiographical Novels" and ever want to write one?

"Someone with zero imagination, like my mother," Em would later write to me, when she was beating herself up about it. And who could read "Why I Hate Memoirs" and even want to read one—not to mention write one? "Just wait—my dad will actually become a Catholic, too," Em would write me. She wasn't kidding.

You couldn't write more literary (or more obscure) short fiction than Em was writing, or so I'd thought. Boy, had she managed to reach the wrong audience. Like me—but in her small, well-crafted way—Em was imagining worst-case scenarios. Sure, her stories were based on the worst things that had happened to her, but Em had purposely made them unimaginably worse; she'd exaggerated her own family's dysfunctional behavior to the worst ex-tremes she could imagine, short of suicide or murder.

"I'm not sure suicide or murder would have been worse," Nora later said.

The syndrome of so-called ex-gay Christians undergoing conversion therapy struck Nora as good material for her and Em to take onstage at the Gallows. Em, understandably, was feeling a little snakebit from her experience of giving her parents the idea that they could be writers. Em had thought she was being funny; she'd tried to take the self-hatred that sometimes goes with being gay or lesbian to comic extremes, but her own parents didn't get the joke.

Even Elliot Barlow had cautioned Nora not to make fun of gay and lesbian self-doubt or self-loathing in *Two Dykes, One Who Talks*. "The Gallows isn't ready for political comedy or satire on that subject," the snowshoer said. "I'm all for putting down ex-gay Christians in conversion therapy, or satirizing ex-gay converts to Roman Catholicism, but I'll bet the Gallows won't go for it—it'll look like Catholic-bashing to the Gallows," the little English teacher told Nora and Em.

Nora, naturally, was in favor of full-scale Catholic-bashing, but Em knew what it was like to be completely misunderstood by an audience. We were all in Nora and Em's rat's-ass apartment in Hell's Kitchen, over the bad restaurant that kept changing. It had once been a bad Greek place, and although the Greeks were gone, Nora still said the bad smell was probably octopus. Mr. Barlow and Nora and I were watching Em, who appeared to be performing hari-kari in slow motion on the couch. "For Christ's sake, Em—you look like you're trying to change a tampon with bread tongs," Nora told her, but Em kept trying.

The snowshoer took a stab at what Em was pantomiming. "If Catholics and other Christians are sacred cows, even at the Gallows, it won't be funny if we make fun of mothers and fathers—it'll look like mother-and-father-bashing," Elliot guessed. Em nodded, stopping her suicide in progress on the couch. Mr. Barlow believed the end of the 1970s and the start of the 1980s was the beginning of hard times for political comedy and satire.

"We're at the Whale Ship now," the snowshoer inexplicably said, while we were enduring the smell that was probably octopus. We'd complained to the little English teacher about her idea of the Whale Ship. She never said what *happened* at the Whale Ship, once you and your perfect penis or your perfect vagina were admitted, once you were let in the door. "What could possibly be as big a deal as getting into the Whale Ship—what could ever happen inside the place that means as much as getting in?" Mr. Barlow asked us. "It's getting harder to tell jokes about hatred," the little English teacher told us, but she could see she'd lost us.

To begin with, Nora and Em didn't go to the memorial service for Coach Dearborn—they'd not met "our marine," as Elliot Barlow and I called him. And what Elliot meant about jokes and hatred went over my head, too. I was as lost as Nora and Em by what the snowshoer had said. In the years ahead, there were hard times coming for comedy of any kind. For Em and me as writers, for Nora and Em onstage at the Gallows, it was going to get harder to be funny—about anything. Just imagine trying to call yourselves *Two Dykes, One Who Talks* today. You can't tell jokes about hatred today. I can tell you when today's hatred was just beginning—at the end of the 1970s and the start of the 1980s, the pushback was already there.

Did an imaginary sex club like the Whale Ship represent the sexual unknown? Would sexual differences and sexual minorities eventually be accepted? Would sexual intolerance become outdated, or just go away? If you remember, sexual hatred used to be different. Sexual hatred was always there, and it was already changing or beginning to change, but it wasn't like it is today. I remember our marine. I would never say I miss him, or his hatred, but his hatred was restrained—at first, he tried to hold it back. He wouldn't hold it back today. Guys like our marine are at the Whale Ship now, intent on doing damage. I know that's what the snowshoer would say. Whatever went on at the Whale Ship, guys like our marine got in. Guys like our marine are worse now, but their hatred was always there.

36.

BOOK SIGNINGS

A book signing is a public event; you don't know who might show up. My favorite publicist, Mary Marinelli, was returning to work after what she called a "record-setting short maternity leave." Mary only meant she'd come back to work too soon. "I'm breastfeeding—pumping my breasts is a messy business, and not the best use of my time on an author's book tour," she said. She was a marvelous publicist, and I'm confident that Mary was also a marvel as a breastfeeding and breast-pumping mom. I don't remember how many children Mary had, but she was on maternity leave a lot—always for a record-setting short time. My impression of Mary is that she never stopped breastfeeding, although I didn't see her breastfeed anyone, and I never met Mr. Marinelli or any of their kids. I was, however, a witness to what a marvel Mary was at finding opportune moments to pump her breasts, considering the multiple obstacles that an author's book tour presented.

Mary was a compact person, small and well-proportioned, notwithstanding the size of her breasts. What was also overlarge about Mary was her shoulder bag. The other things in the shoulder bag, besides copies of my novel, had a breastfeeding and breast-pumping connection. There was more than one kind of breast pump in the big bag. There were ice packs to keep the mother's milk cold. Mary had a low opinion of nursing moms who let their breast milk spoil.

Backstage, in the greenroom at the 92nd Street Y in New York, Mary Marinelli had taken charge of the audience Q and A in what was then a new way—at least to me. I was going to give a reading from my novel, followed by the Q and A; then there would be a book signing. But Mary had insisted that the audience be given notecards, where they could write their questions; then the cards were collected and brought to the greenroom before I went onstage.

"This eliminates the idiots who have no questions—they just want to tell you what they think," Mary now said. She was reading through the questions on the notecards and sorting them. "This also identifies the dolts who always ask, 'Where do you get your ideas?' They get their own pile, too—the never-to-be-answered pile," Mary said. Before I went onstage, Mary told me, I would get to pick the questions I liked, and I could put them in the order I wanted to answer them. "I'm weeding out the whack jobs," Mary Marinelli said.

The idea of weeding out the whack jobs interested Em; she and Nora were just hanging out in the greenroom with me before I went onstage. Em was reading through the questions on the notecards with Mary. I'd had to explain to Mary that Em was a pantomimist who actually didn't talk. Mary had seen Nora and Em onstage at the Gallows; she'd wrongly assumed that Em's nonspeaking role was just part of the act. Mary Marinelli had listened closely to what I told her about Em's conscientious objection to speaking.

"Since you're a full-time pantomimist—I mean, someone who has chosen a nonspeaking life—I'm wondering if you were a breastfed baby, or not," Mary asked Em. It was hard to tell if this was a first-time breastfeeding question for Em, who took a moment to compose the requisite pantomime.

We all knew that Mary had been to the washroom several times. "Excuse me—I have to milk myself," Mary had made a point of announcing each time, and she was forthcoming in telling us how the milking went when she came back from the washroom. "My left boob is outperforming the right one," she would tell us with a heartfelt sigh. I couldn't help sneaking a look at her underperforming right boob, and we could all imagine for ourselves—even in the greenroom—Mary's misgivings about the electric breast pump. "One day they'll make them more portable—the ones they make now are too big and bulky," she complained. Mary was candid in confiding her fear of the electric pump to us. "I'm afraid I won't be able to shut it off—it'll just drain me to death," Mary informed us.

The drained-to-death theme appeared to influence Em's answer to the breastfeeding question. Until Em got to the gagging part, it was difficult to discern if she was the one doing the breastfeeding or the one who was being breastfed.

"If I had to guess, I would say that breastfeeding was a conflicted experience for Em," Mary ventured to say. More like an entirely negative experience, I was thinking.

"Em says it's a toss-up whether she or her mother would have been more grossed out by breastfeeding," Nora told us. Em nodded; she went back to reading the notecards.

"I see," Mary said; she was always saying this.

One of the young men on the staff at the Y brought more notecards to us in the greenroom. He'd been opposed to the notecards; he was bitter about the very idea of written questions. His name was Fred. He had a bug up his ass about spontaneity at public events. Fred had told Mary that the Q and A was more of a "spontaneous thing" if you just handed a microphone to anyone in the audience who wanted to ask a question.

"I'm not looking for spontaneity in the audience," Mary told him. "Show me spontaneous, and I'll show you the whack jobs."

Young Fred was an indignant type. "As a rule, there isn't a surfeit of whack jobs in our audiences—this is the Upper East Side," Fred reminded Mary.

"We should have hooked up Fred to the electric breast pump—you know where," Nora would say, with Em pantomiming, *The bigger and bulkier, the better.*

All Mary Marinelli said, at the time, was: "It takes just one whack job, Fred, to ruin the night—I'm not looking for a surfeit." Behind his back, Nora gave Fred the finger—Nora's spontaneous thing.

"Here are more questions, and there's no time to gather more notecards— when you do the Q and A *in writing*, not everyone in the audience gets to ask his or her question," Fred said in his pissy way.

"Not everyone in the audience *should* get to ask his or her question, Fred—hence the weeding," Mary told him.

"Well, I'm sure you'll show us the whack job—when you find one," Fred said, in a pique.

"Oh, fuck off, Fred," Nora said. This enlivening dialogue no doubt distracted me from what Em was trying to say, in her original way. Em was often sudden in her movements—jumping to her feet and dancing around, with no apparent purpose. I'd noticed that Em was calling our attention to the notecards. I hadn't understood why Em was showing us her ballroom-dance repertoire. As usual, Nora understood what Em was trying to tell us before I got it. "We should look for a question from *Jasmine?*" Nora asked Em, who nodded her head off. Nora explained to Mary. "About five years ago, Adam's mother told Jasmine that Adam said Jasmine had a vagina as big as a ballroom."

"I see," Mary Marinelli said.

"About the same time, *you* told Jasmine that her pussy was a subway station," I reminded Nora. Em just kept nodding.

"Jasmine had a bed-shitting episode when she was having sex with

Adam—I don't think she'll ever get over it," Nora further explained to Mary. Em vigorously shook her head while rereading the notecards; Em clearly didn't think that Jasmine was likely to get over the bed-shitting episode.

"Just tell me what Jasmine might ask, please," Mary said to Nora.

"Bed-shitters are usually spontaneous, Fred," Nora began. "Here's a whack job for you—a question Jasmine might ask Adam: 'Am I the only woman who has been befouled by you—beshitted, in your bed?' Now *there's* a question! I'll bet Em and Mary might have noticed that one," Nora said.

"That one would have caught my eye," Mary Marinelli said.

"Or Jasmine might ask: 'What sort of grown man lives with his grand-mother and his grandmother's maid and his grandfather's ghost?' I think that's actually a worse question, kiddo," Nora told me, with Em nodding.

"Definitely worse," Mary said.

"I don't live with my grandmother or her maid or my grandfather's ghost anymore," I felt it was necessary to tell Mary.

I hadn't heard about Dottie. We had been in the habit of keeping in touch with postcards. I had sent her a few unanswered postcards; someone in Dottie's family would eventually write me back, but not for a year. There was a lighthouse on the postcard, as on other postcards from Maine. "Dottie is dead—don't write her here no more," the postcard said.

"Do you like older women, Fred?" Nora asked. "Jasmine is older than Adam's mother. How old is Jasmine now?" Nora asked me.

"Jasmine is only one year older than my mom—Jasmine would be fifty-seven now," I said.

"I see—too old for Fred, I think," Mary said. Em was back to the ball-room dancing. She merely meant to remind Fred that Jasmine's vagina was as big as a ballroom. I was relieved that Em would spare us (even Fred) her pantomime of Jasmine's pussy as a subway station; Em was crawling around the greenroom on all fours, seizing hold of our ankles. Fred was the touchiest about having his ankles seized. Em's narrative moved on; she was on her feet, shadowboxing, or perhaps she was shadow-wrestling.

"If we get through the reading and the Q and A without a deeply em-barrassing disturbance, we need a plan about how to deal with Jasmine at the book signing," Mary Marinelli was saying, not realizing that Em was pantomiming a plan.

"Em and I will pull Jasmine out of the signing line," Nora started to explain. "Em can grab hold of Jasmine's ankles, not letting her get away. I'll beat the shit out of Jasmine—I'll break her arms, or just one of her arms,"

Nora was saying. "Then we can drag the old subway pussy out to the side-walk, and dump her there," Nora said. Em just nodded.

"Maybe not that plan," Mary Marinelli said. "You must have some secu-rity personnel on hand, don't you?" Mary asked Fred.

"We don't usually need security personnel at a fiction reading or a book signing," Fred said in his pissy way.

"I see," Mary said again, before she shut herself in the washroom once more. Fred was reflected in the greenroom mirror; he was bent over the telephone on the makeup counter.

"I *know* he's just a fiction writer, but I think security personnel at the book signing is merited," Fred was saying into the phone.

I was looking over the questions on the notecards Mary had selected, but I was tempted to look at just one of the notecards in the pile of discarded questions. Although Fred was trying to conceal his telephone conversation, his pissiness was audible to us. When Mary came out of the washroom, she caught me sneaking a look at the topmost notecard among the whack jobs.

"Don't read those questions, Adam—there are questions you'll never get out of your head," Mary told me. I instantly regretted reading the one question I took from the discards. It wasn't a question I would have answered onstage; it definitely belonged among the whack jobs. When I went onstage, the question was resounding in my head. I saw Mary take a second look at the question I'd read before we left the greenroom. "Like that one," Mary said to me.

"Like you, I'm a fiction writer. Are you depressed all the time, too?" That was the question. To distract myself from thinking about it, I read over the questions that were about my mother. Mary wanted me to pick the best question about my mother and answer that one. We left all the questions concerning "Where do you get your ideas?" in the greenroom, where we'd heard Fred yelling on the phone as we were leaving.

"I *know* the potential troublemaker is just a woman, but it's not my job to be the security personnel, is it?" Fred was screaming at someone.

"When it comes to Jasmine, Fred, you better let Em and me deal with the subway-station pussy—we're the best security personnel you can get," Nora was telling Fred. I didn't need to see Em to know she would be nodding her head.

"I don't suppose your cousin Nora would harm Jasmine physically, would she?" Mary asked me.

"Not very much," I answered, or I said something along those lines.

"I see," Mary Marinelli said, leaving me in the wings. I've since grown to love that moment in the wings. You can find a strangely solitary peace in the sides of a theater stage, where you're out of view of the audience. At least for me, in those few minutes before I've gone onstage, time stops. I've had lifelong reflections backstage—soon gone, of course, but I've had those moments nevertheless. Not that time—my first time at the 92nd Street Y. Jasmine's unlikely but possible presence unnerved me; I wanted Nora to harm Jasmine, physically.

All the mother questions were unsettling. "The mother in your most recent novel is a radical feminist who is assassinated by a misogynist. Is she your mother? If not, what does your mother think of the mother in your novel?" Of the ten or twelve mother questions, this one didn't have the most dulcet tone, but it was the most clear.

It was also disquieting that I could have answered the question by telling the audience what my mom had already said about the novel, but I didn't want to—especially not with Nora in the audience. "I know this mother isn't me, sweetie, but what does Nora think about it?" my mom had asked me.

"Nora is okay about it—Nora knows it's *fiction*," I told my mother.

"You know Nora would never choose to have a child, Nora would never be a mother, but someone might really kill Nora, sweetie," my mom told me.

"I know—that may be why I wrote the novel," I told my mother. But that wasn't the audience's business, I decided; I wouldn't answer any of the mother questions onstage.

Everything went all right, considering. When I was reading, I could easily locate Nora and Em in the audience; they were sitting in the front row, next to Mary Marinelli and her breast-pumping paraphernalia.

I had fun with the Q and A. When there are written questions, you can think of an imaginary notecard—you can make up a question. No one will know, I thought. But back in the greenroom, where I was given a brief reprieve before the book signing, Mary not only knew the question I made up to ask myself; she chided me for ducking the mother questions. "It wouldn't have killed you to answer *one* mother question—you can't write a novel about such an inflammatory mother, and not expect readers to be curious about *your* mother, Adam," Mary told me, before going to the washroom to milk herself.

Fred had refrained from comment, but he was at his pissiest when he informed us that Nora and Em were "staking out" the area of the lobby where the book signing was—"in case the bed-shitter shows up."

I was relieved to learn that, in Nora and Em's estimation, Jasmine was nowhere in sight. I'd been imagining that Nora and Em had thrown Jasmine into the traffic on Lexington Avenue. At the book signing, I was further reassured by Em's pantomimic gestures from the back of the signing line; it was easy to see, from the way Em was prancing around, that there was no sign of the subway-station pussy in the signing line. And Nora interrupted her stakeout of the lobby area to have a word with me at the signing table. "The bed-shitter isn't coming tonight, kiddo," Nora assured me.

Mary Marinelli was bossing around my readers in the signing line. "He's not signing T-shirts, or bras, or anything like that," I could hear her saying. People who wanted their books "personalized" were instructed to write out their names. "Don't expect him to know how to spell your name," I heard Mary say.

All the mother questioners seemed to be in the signing line. "What about your mom?" one asked me point-blank. She looked like a mom—a rather clingy one.

A young woman, who looked too independent and relaxed to be a mother, had written something on the same piece of paper where she'd spelled her name. "Matilda, like the stupid song," she wrote. "You didn't an-swer my question about your mother. I have issues with my mother," Matilda also wrote.

I gave the mother questioners off-the-cuff answers. No one seemed sat-isfied with my answers, including Mary Marinelli. "I talk about my mom only when she's in the audience, and she's not here tonight"—that was one of my unsatisfying answers. "My mother knows she's not the mother in my novels"—that was another one that got a lackluster reception, especially from Mary.

"Before we go to Boston, you have to come up with a credible answer to the mother question—it's not going away," Mary told me.

"Okay," I said. I was distracted by someone who kept moving to the back of the line. I know this about book signings: it doesn't bode well when some-one wants to be last in line. She was a tall young woman—attractive, in a forlorn way. Even at a distance, she struck me as a woman who would never be entirely present; wherever she was, she wouldn't be wholly there. I would look up from the signing table and see her at the end of the line, a head taller than anyone else. The next time I looked up, maybe four or five people were in line behind her, but not for long. When I looked again, she'd moved backward—reclaiming her hopeless but chosen place at the end of the line.

"Who wants to be last in line?" I asked Mary Marinelli.

"I'm keeping my eye on her—she's the one to watch out for, probably the writer who's depressed all the time," Mary said. I hadn't been married; I didn't have children. Maybe you need those experiences to understand that a person who pumps her breasts with religious fervor could be the smartest person you know.

Of course that's who the tall young woman was—a depressed fiction writer, like me. I was thirty-seven. As the signing line got shorter, I had a closer look at the tall young woman. She was taller than I thought, and not as young as she looked at a distance.

"She's your age, if you ask me—not to mention the depressed part," Mary said. Nora had circled back to the signing table, now that the end of the line was near.

"Em and I don't like the looks of the tall one, kiddo," Nora told me. I could see that Em had slipped into the hindmost spot in the signing line—purposely, to annoy the tall woman. Mary let Nora know that the tall woman was a depressed fiction writer, but Nora said Em had guessed the writer part. "Em knew something was wrong with her," was the way Nora put it.

"No visible injuries, no casts or anything—she's too thin to get stuck in a shower," Nora pointed out. "She's so tall, she could hurt herself washing her hair—her legs are so long, the penis-bending possibilities are innumerable, kiddo," Nora told me. As the end of the signing line came closer, I watched Em and the other fiction writer trading places for the hindmost position. Em was as persistent as a terrier. The tall woman didn't have a chance; she wasn't going to outlast the pantomimist, physically. We could see her trying to talk to Em; we knew that wouldn't work. Em would be last in line. Em stood so closely behind the depressed writer, Em's forehead was almost touching the slight indentation between the taller woman's shoulder blades. The woman was wearing a sheer white blouse. The fabric was so sheer, you could see her old-fashioned bra through her blouse. I didn't want to think about the depressed writer's breasts, but I found myself imagining she must have been wearing her mother's bra.

Mary Marinelli hadn't read my mind; her dedication as a nursing mom gave her empathy for other women's breasts. "The poor thing—that old lady's bra is all wrong for her," Mary said to Nora.

Nora was forty-three; she didn't wear bras. "Everything will always be all wrong for her—she's a *writer*," Nora said.

"The poor thing," Mary repeated. I'm guessing the *poor thing* part was the only part of their conversation the tall woman and Em would have overheard, but Em and I had heard before what Nora thought of writers—not to mention the way Nora said the *writer* word. Em and I didn't doubt that everything would always be all wrong for writers. As for the *poor thing* part, Em adamantly agreed. When Em nodded, her head bumped the long back of the tall woman with the small breasts and the sad bra. The depressed writer had painstakingly drawn an ornate-looking picture frame around her name, which she'd written on an otherwise blank notecard. (She had not included her name with the question I regretted reading on the notecard from the discard pile.) Her name was Wilson; there was what looked like a wedding ring on the ring finger of her left hand.

"Mrs. Wilson?" I asked her, just to be sure—before I inscribed her name on the title page of my novel.

"I'm not married. I thought, if I wore the ring, guys would stop hitting on me, but that was a bad idea—now only married men hit on me," the tall woman said.

"I see—so what's your first name?" Mary asked her, just to speed things up.

"Wilson is my first name—I'm one of the last girls to be named for that old president, I hope," Wilson said. "I'm the fiction writer who asked you if you're depressed all the time, like me," she confessed.

"Yes, all the time," I answered. I was signing her copy of my novel when Nora kicked my leg, under my chair. I'd been dotting the *i* in *Wilson* when Nora kicked me, and the dot ended up over the *W*.

"Maybe we could get together, just to talk about it," Wilson suggested. Perhaps I was attracted to her because she had no guile concerning how to come on to someone. "You have my number," Wilson added meekly, as she was leaving. Not only had I been slow to respond; I hadn't noticed that what I'd mistaken for an ornate frame around her name on the notecard was actually a phone number. And now Nora was giving me an overly familiar shoulder massage; Nora never massaged me. Em, who'd come around to my side of the signing table, suddenly sat in my lap.

"Imagine being a woman named Wilson! At least she's leaving," Mary observed.

In a faraway part of the lobby, we could see that Wilson was about to cross paths with Fred. We knew what Fred had been up to. Fred was obsessed with Jasmine. He'd been outside, looking for a bed-shitter on Lexington

Avenue and Ninety-second Street. "She's gone—the bed-shitter is gone, or she never came!" Fred called to us, unmindful of Wilson, who was walking the other way.

Poor Wilson, I thought, putting the notecard with her name and number in my pocket. Pity was always my undoing. Nora had stopped massaging me, and Em got out of my lap, now that Wilson was gone. In addition to her constant depression, Wilson had wandered away on Lexington Avenue, knowing a bed-shitter was on the loose in the Upper East Side. If she'd known Jasmine was fifty-seven, Wilson might have been even more depressed.

All I was thinking was that I missed being with another fiction writer, and (at the same time) I didn't. I'd not seen Sophie for more than a decade. We both loved Thomas Mann, but our mutual admiration for the writer wasn't enough to keep us together; not even *Death in Venice* could overcome our disheartening conversation and disturbing sex. To be fair, there was the bleeding—the blood itself wasn't as bad as Sophie's need to dramatize the constancy of her uterine bleeding. We were together only a year, when we were in our early twenties. We were just kids. The bloody sheets and towels in the washing machine were disheartening and disturbing, too. Yet it was because of Sophie, and what I missed about being with another fiction writer, that I put the notecard with Wilson's name and number in my pocket.

Now I know why Nora suspected I was "trying to start something with Em" when I wasn't. (Nora knew Em was innocent of "trying to start" anything.) But when Em and I started writing each other, there was a newfound intimacy between us; as writers, Em and I were discontented in the same way. Discontent is one thing writers have in common. I was never a threat to the intimacy Nora and Em had as a couple. Nora knew that, too—she wasn't jealous, not exactly. Yet Nora felt excluded from how alone Em felt, as a writer. When you write fiction, you go it alone. Quite correctly, Nora felt excluded from the aloneness Em and I had in common, too. And when Em and I started writing each other, this also made me miss being with another fiction writer. It wasn't just meeting Wilson, or that I missed being with Sophie.

It didn't help that Sophie would show up at my reading and book signing in Boston. Mary Marinelli spotted "something funny" about Sophie's handwritten question for the Q and A. It was a good question, the kind of question a fellow fiction writer would ask. Sophie had read all my novels. She'd noticed that I'd written two novels in the third-person omniscient voice, and there were a couple of novels with a first-person narrator. Her question was a writer's question, about narrative point of view. Mary knew I would like Sophie's question, but "something funny" caught Mary's eye about Sophie's handwritten notecard. Mary handed me the card.

Under her name, Sophie had written, "Still bleeding, after all these years."

"Sophie has nonstop uterine bleeding—she has fibroids. And she's a fiction writer," I explained to Mary.

"I see," Mary said.

I would spend a lot of time answering Sophie's question in the Q and A. I made an effort to put the endless mother questions to rest, knowing I never would. I talked about my repeated interest in a mother's influence; I said the part of a mother that remains a mystery to her children is the part that interests me *as a writer*. I could tell I didn't go far enough. The audience was polite about it, but they didn't really buy it. Mary simply told me I could do better.

I was happy to see Sophie in the signing line. We gave each other a hug, but I could sense that neither of us wanted to be together. I was relieved about that. Yet even Sophie, who was completely pleasant, had something to say about my mom and the various mothers in my fiction. "I think you can say more about that, Adam—I've met your mom, you know," was how Sophie said it, however pleasantly.

When I got back from Boston, I already knew I would call Wilson. The snowshoer and I were still sharing the little Barlows' pied-à-terre. It was too small for us, especially when the little Barlows visited—if they were in town, I stayed with Nora and Em. And now that I'd written my first bestseller, Nora and Em were wondering why I didn't get my own apartment in New York. Of course my mother kept telling me what was for sale in Manchester, Vermont. "You should live here, sweetie," my mom had said.

But there was no one place I wanted to live, and I would always be undecided about living in New York. At the time, Elliot Barlow and I liked living together—"again," as we would say. I still imagined I could keep the little English teacher safe.

"There are writers who are regionalists, and then there are the homeless ones," I'd heard the snowshoer say. The pretty Mr. Barlow had pegged me as a homeless type, but Em and I had written each other about Elliot's two categories of writers. Em and I thought we were in a third category—the undecided ones.

Naturally, when I got back from Boston, a letter from Em was waiting for me, telling me what a bad idea Wilson was. I knew Em understood why

I thought about being with another fiction writer; Em thought about it, too. Yet Wilson was all wrong for me, Em wrote. Em knew I hadn't read Wilson's writing, but Em had read a couple of things. "Wilson could be depressed all the time because she knows she can't write," Em wrote me.

This was followed by a long part about the way I'd looked at Wilson's breasts. "You still look at my breasts, you know," Em pointed out. She reminded me how we had danced together at my mom's wedding; I was a very tentative dancer, Em wrote, but I was not at all tentative about staring at her breasts. Em had lifted my chin and pointed to her eyes, indicating where I should look. I'd been fourteen, at my mom's wedding; my eyes had roamed back to Em's breasts. Em had kept lifting my face to her eyes. I was relieved to learn, later in Em's long letter, that I didn't *stare* at Em's breasts—"not as much, or in the same way"—anymore. My mom's wedding had been more than twenty years ago. Not even Nora had complained about the way I still looked at Em's breasts—"not for ten or twelve years, or so," Em wrote.

My boy-girl etiquette had been lacking. I knew better than to stare at a woman's breasts, but both Em and Nora had noticed the way I was looking at Wilson. (Mary Marinelli must have noticed, too.) Why would Wilson wear such a see-through blouse with such a sorrowful, older woman's bra? Why would a preternaturally tall woman with noticeably small breasts want you to see exactly how small her breasts were? Wasn't Wilson *pathetic*? I was thinking, even as I checked to be sure I hadn't lost or misplaced the notecard with her phone number. I knew I was attracted to Wilson in the way I was attracted to *pathos*, as a writer.

Both the past and the future are a couple of things not to like about book signings.

37.

THINGS TO DO WITH A PENIS

I was thirty-nine in late January 1981, when Ronald Reagan became the fortieth president of the United States. The most loving and best-loved people in my life were two lesbian couples and the trans woman who was my stepfather. I was still seeing Wilson, who was still depressed and very tall, but she hadn't hurt herself washing her hair and she never bent my penis. Wilson and I weren't living together; I was still living with the snowshoer in the little Barlows' apartment on East Sixty-fourth Street. The next year, Em would pantomime Reagan's proposed constitutional amendment on school prayer. President Reagan, a born-again Christian, was an advocate for reinstating prayer in public schools.

Reagan tried again in 1984, when he asked Congress, "Why can't freedom to acknowledge God be enjoyed again by children in every schoolroom across this land?" In 1985, Reagan complained about the Supreme Court ruling banning a "moment of silence" in public schools—Em had trouble pantomiming a "moment of silence." In 1987, Reagan repeated his request for Congress to end what the president called "the expulsion of God from America's classrooms."

Em's expelling-of-God pantomime made the management of the Gallows Lounge draw the line on the issue of school prayer. Nora was more riled up about abortion. In 1986, President Reagan addressed a joint session of Congress in his State of the Union address. "We are a nation of idealists," he said, "yet today there is a wound in our national conscience. America will never be whole as long as the right to life granted by our Creator is denied to the unborn. For the rest of my time, I shall do what I can to see that this wound is one day healed."

Nora observed that Reagan sounded so righteous on behalf of prayer in schools and the unborn, yet he kept quiet about the AIDS crisis. In the United States, AIDS began in 1981—the same year Reagan took office. By the time Reagan made his first extensive comments on the epidemic—six years into his presidency, in 1987—more than thirty-six thousand Americans had been diagnosed with AIDS, and more than twenty thousand had died. It was Nora's opinion that, in Reagan's silence, Pat Buchanan was just one of the goons who spoke for him. Buchanan was Reagan's White House communications director for a couple of years. It was Buchanan who said that AIDS was "nature's revenge on gay men."

"More God-loves-AIDS business—Reagan is in bed with the Christian Right," Em wrote me. "Nora says we'll see how that goes over at the Gallows."

At the Gallows, it was okay to put down Baptist minister Jerry Falwell's Moral Majority. "AIDS is the wrath of a just God against homosexuals," Falwell said. "AIDS is not just God's punishment for homosexuals. It is God's punishment for the society that tolerates homosexuals."

Em was having her own issues with God's wrath against homosexuals. Her father, the Catholic convert, had written to Pope John Paul II, asking him to baptize him. Em's father was "renouncing" those things that John Paul II also found profane and sinful—such as contraception, abortion, remarriage after a divorce, and homosexual acts. Em had been copied on her dad's plea to the Polish pope, who did not write back. Em didn't blame John Paul II for not writing back. Em didn't believe that her self-hating, homophobic dad deserved to be baptized by the pope.

In her short stories, Em would exaggerate how many times her homo-hating father wrote John Paul II—she mostly made up what the fictional dad tells the Polish pope. "My being gay, and my having a lesbian wife—not to mention our having a lesbian daughter—made me think of those three big vehicles that injured you when you were a younger man," the repentant gay father writes to John Paul II. In 1940, the future pope was hit by a tram, fracturing his skull; that same year, he was hit by a truck in a quarry, leaving him with one shoulder higher than the other and a lifelong stoop. Four years later, he was hospitalized with a concussion and another shoulder injury, having been hit by a German truck. To anyone reading Em's short stories, the future pope's injuries sound a lot worse than the plight of the gay father with the lesbian wife and daughter, but Em doesn't stop there.

In Em's short stories, the fictional father's last letter to Pope John Paul II likens the "outbreak" of homosexuality in his family to a "disease." As for the "ongoing and unspeakable sin"—namely, the lives led by his lesbian daughter and her lesbian mom—the demented dad likens his pain to the pope's survival of two assassination attempts. In 1981, in St. Peter's Square, John Paul II was shot in the abdomen by a Turkish gunman—a member of a militant fascist group. A year later, in Portugal, a Spanish priest tried to stab the pope with a knife.

Emily MacPherson's first collection of short stories would be published in April 1987, right after Reagan said: "After all, when it comes to preventing AIDS, don't medicine and morality teach the same lessons?"

"It sounds like Reagan is saying that people with AIDS deserve it," Nora said.

I liked the title Em originally gave to her collection of short stories—*Letters to the Pope*. All the stories were about the family that comes out together; the last stories were the ones about the renunciations of the gay father, the Catholic convert who begs John Paul II to baptize him. This was Emily MacPherson's first book, and her publishers knew they could push her around; they rejected *Letters to the Pope* as a title, and insisted on something less inflammatory. The book would be called *The Coming Out Stories*—not a bad title, and the stories themselves were no less inflammatory; Em's publishers didn't censor her stories, just her title. For a collection of literary short stories by a first-time author, the book did pretty well.

Em did a book signing of *The Coming Out Stories* for the regulars at the Gallows Lounge. Naturally, these fans hadn't known that the silent panto-mimist was also a fiction writer. And, like Mary Marinelli, most of the *Two Dykes, One Who Talks* fans hadn't known that Nora's nonspeaking partner actually didn't speak in real life. When Em was signing her book at the Gallows, Nora and I had to explain this to them.

In the Reagan years, Nora and I would see a lot more of Em's seagull thing—her arms spread like a seagull's motionless wings. We knew this some-times meant that Em was thinking about drifting back to Canada; yet her seagull thing was also Em's way of pantomiming Ronald Reagan's laissez-faire approach to the AIDS epidemic.

"Reagan isn't laissez-faire or do-nothing about communism, but he seems content to let an epidemic run its course through the gay community," the snowshoer had said.

The pretty English teacher was always reminding us of what Reagan said in his first inaugural—that "government is not the solution to our problem; government is the problem." A seagull's seemingly directionless drifting was Em's way of imitating Ronald Reagan as the Pontius Pilate of the AIDS ep-idemic. That went over all right at the Gallows. Reagan wasn't as beloved in New York as he was in the rest of the country. There were the occasional angry walkouts when the onstage subject of *Two Dykes, One Who Talks* was the dearth of attention Reagan gave to AIDS. Nora just shrugged; she said the walkouts were from out of town.

There were only a few times when Em tried to pantomime excerpts from her short stories onstage at the Gallows. The lunatic dad's letter to the pope did not go over well, not even in New York. There were more than a few walkouts when Em acted out the part about the three big vehicles hitting the pope, and someone threw a beer bottle at Nora when Nora merely mentioned the first of the two attempts to assassinate John Paul II.

"Okay, no more popes," Nora agreed, when the craven management of the Gallows Lounge had complained that the *Canadian* was making fun of the pope.

Now that Em and I were writing each other, I understood Em's connection to Canada a little better. Em didn't think of herself as coming from Canada, yet she was always imagining going back. She'd been born in Canada, and she had a Canadian father, but Em's memories of Toronto were a nonlinear narrative; her early childhood hadn't gone in a straight line, according to plan. She distinctly remembered various girls in the all-girls' school where she'd worn a uniform, but she only dimly remembered herself as one of the uniformed girls. In Em's mind, it was always Christmastime in Toronto, and all the Christmas trees in Canada were blue.

Em couldn't remember how old she was when her parents were in the process of separating, or how long it took before they were divorced. Em soon moved to the United States with her mother, who was American. Em had a more reliable memory of some small towns in Massachusetts than she had of Toronto. She'd gone to a couple of private elementary schools, then to a boarding school in the western part of the state. During and after the divorce, Em had visited her father only once a year—over the Christmas holiday. It wasn't only in her mind that it was always Christmastime in Toronto, but it was entirely in Em's mind that all the Christmas trees were blue. The blueness of Christmas began for Em when her parents separated. It started with the self-hatred of Em's mother and father, and their expressed hatred of each other. This was when Em began to think that not speaking might be her best option. In Em's mind, this was why all the Christmas trees in Canada were blue. I knew the blue trees weren't real, but I understood what they signified for Em; the blue Christmas trees were psychologically true.

When Em's mother read *The Coming Out Stories*, she wrote to Em in care of the publishing house. Em had been careful not to let her parents know her home address. Em's mom had always known how to be hurtful. "I hope you're not still kidding yourself about going back to Canada. As long as your father lives there, you know you'll never go back to him, but it's just like you to hold on to things that aren't true," Em's mother wrote her.

Em's father wrote her, too. He wasn't interested in her fiction; he cared only about the truth, her dad told her. Yet he had been inspired by Em's fictional letters to the pope. Her dad began writing to John Joseph O'Connor in 1984, when O'Connor became the archbishop of New York. He'd been consecrated to the episcopate in 1979 by Pope John Paul II. He would become John *Cardinal* O'Connor in 1985; he was created cardinal by John Paul himself. "Dear Cardinal O'Connor . . ." later, and more urgently, "Your Eminence . . ." the multiple letters from Em's dad would begin. He was thinking the archbishop of New York was his best bet for a big-deal baptism, or a better bet than the pope. Of course Cardinal O'Connor didn't write back.

"I confess I have acted out my homosexual inclinations, but I am no longer guilty of homosexual behavior, Your Eminence," Em's father wrote to John Cardinal O'Connor. Her dad had plagiarized Em's letters to the pope from *The Coming Out Stories*; he made an all-out effort to persuade Cardinal O'Connor to baptize him in St. Patrick's Cathedral, where he hoped his homosexual daughter could be converted to the church. Em's father also claimed he was "inspired by" Cardinal O'Connor's opposition to any New York City or New York State legislation that would guarantee the civil rights of homosexuals. "If you baptize me in St. Patrick's, Your Eminence, this could inspire my wayward daughter to give up her lesbian lifestyle," Em's dad wrote to the cardinal.

That was the kicker. Of course Em was angry that her homophobic father had plagiarized her in his letters to Cardinal O'Connor, but what really pissed her off was the stupid idea that she would walk out on Nora if the cardinal baptized her hateful dad. "Dear Cardinal O'Connor, I doubt that my dad has given up his homosexual behavior—he just thinks you'll believe him, and he's counting on the Catholic Church to forgive him for it," Em's letter to the cardinal began. "I have no plans to give up my lesbian lifestyle, but if you baptize my homophobic father, I will burn down St. Patrick's Cathedral, or something."

Nora and I weren't making much headway in our efforts to discourage Em from sending her letter to the cardinal. "You can't threaten to burn down St. Patrick's, Em—not even at the Gallows," Nora said, but Em just stared at the nearest wall, as if she knew she could run through it.

"Show your letter to the snowshoer before you send it," I told Em. I was hoping the little English teacher could talk her out of it. Elliot Barlow was a good teacher.

"Cardinal O'Connor is as homophobic as your dad, Em—the cardinal is just much smarter and better organized about it," the snowshoer said. "Your threatening to burn down the cathedral, or 'something,' gives O'Connor a weapon he can use. The cardinal would love to be able to say there's a homosexual conspiracy against the Catholic Church—he would love to portray St. Patrick's as a victim of homosexuals," Mr. Barlow told Em. She didn't send the letter. That was a bullet dodged, but there would be other bullets. There's more than one bend in the road.

Eric, the stand-alone singer in *Eric's All-Gay Band*, had AIDS; he was dying. PCP was the big killer—a pneumonia, pneumocystis carinii. In Eric's case, this pneumonia was the first presentation of AIDS—a young and otherwise healthy-looking guy with a cough (or shortness of breath) and a fever. It was the X-ray that didn't look great—in the parlance of radiologists and doctors, a "whiteout." Yet there was no suspicion of the disease. There was the phase of not getting better on antibiotics, and then, finally, there was a biopsy, which showed the cause to be PCP, this insidious pneumonia. They usually put you on Bactrim; that's what Eric was taking. Eric was the first AIDS patient I saw waste away.

"It should be *me*, Adam," the snowshoer said. She was trying to prepare me for seeing Eric. "I've had a life—Eric is just beginning his." Eric was placed in hospice care in his parents' Chelsea brownstone; he had his own nurse. Eric had chosen not to go on a breathing machine; this allowed him to be cared for at home. As the little English teacher would explain to me, intubating at home is problematic; it's easier to hook a person up to a ventilator in a hospital. Eric wasn't intubated, not at home.

I remember Eric's parents—how they lovingly fed him. I could see the cheesy patches of candida in Eric's mouth, and his white-coated tongue.

Eric had been a beautiful young man; now his face was disfigured with Kaposi's sarcoma lesions. A violet-colored lesion dangled from one of Eric's eyebrows, where it resembled a fleshy, misplaced earlobe; another purplish lesion drooped from Eric's nose. The latter was so strikingly prominent that Eric later chose to hide it behind a bandanna. Mr. Barlow would tell me that Eric referred to himself as "the turkey"—because of the Kaposi's sarcoma lesions.

We saw Eric age, in just a few months—his hair thinned, his skin turned leaden, he was often covered with a cool-to-the-touch film of sweat, and his fevers went on forever. The candida went down his throat, into the esophagus; Eric had difficulty swallowing, and his lips were crusted white and fissured. The lymph nodes in his neck bulged. He could scarcely breathe, but Eric refused to go on a ventilator, or to a hospital. He wanted to be with his mom and dad.

Eric was twenty years younger than Elliot Barlow, who was in her fifties when the soloist who was *Eric's All-Gay Band* passed away.

Around that time, I remember I ran into Prue, the Tongue Kisser. I was in my forties. Prue was only four years younger than me. She brought her husband to the Gallows; she wanted him to see where she'd once had an all-noir act. "We're staying in a hotel, and we're traveling with our own babysitter," the former tongue kisser wanted me to know. Nora and Em had taken their bows and left the stage; they'd just wrapped up "The News in English." AIDS was the new all-noir act in town. Prue's husband was staring at everything, with his mouth open. He'd been appalled by *Two Dykes, One Who Talks*. Now Damaged Don was doing a dirge onstage.

The AIDS years were hard years for a comedy club, even for dark comedy. The management of the Gallows Lounge had considered taking down the hangman's noose above the bar, or at least removing the sign with the graveyard humor—the one encouraging the club's patrons to come hang themselves. The way Prue's husband kept staring at the hangman's noose made the COME HANG YOURSELF sign seem inadvisable. Perhaps Prue's husband only felt like hanging himself because of Damaged Don. "He's supposed to be *funny*," I heard Prue saying to her suicidal-looking husband, but I knew Damaged Don. It had never been Don's intention to be funny—his comedy was strictly the unintentional kind. In the AIDS years, Damaged Don wasn't funny at all.

Charlie was dying—he was the one who rubbed the snowshoer's shoulders when the snowshoer was cooking, the boyfriend who was Mr. Barlow's age. Elliot didn't know Charlie was married—not until Charlie's wife called with the news that Charlie was dying. Her name was Sue. Charlie was "slipping away," Sue had said on the phone; Charlie was "asking for Elliot," Sue told the snowshoer.

"They live somewhere like Yonkers or New Rochelle—one of those places north of the Bronx," the pretty Mr. Barlow told me. She would never sound like a New Yorker. It turned out to be Bronxville. The snowshoer and I drove up there together.

When she saw us, Sue thought I was Elliot—she wasn't expecting

Mr. Barlow to be a woman. "I didn't know Charlie was seeing another woman," Sue said.

"I was a man when Charlie was seeing me, and we never had sex—we didn't do it," Mr. Barlow told her. This was confounding to Charlie's wife, but the AIDS crisis had clarified certain things for those of us who knew and loved the snowshoer. We needed to know the facts. Had Elliot Barlow actually done it? Did Mr. Barlow ever do it? Or had Em been right from the beginning?

"Are you saying the snowshoer doesn't do it?" I'd asked Em. She'd pointed her index finger at me, like a gun—her thumb straight up, like a cocked hammer. But she didn't shoot. Em had lowered the imaginary gun; she'd wrapped her arms around herself, looking sad and lonely. Em had wanted us to know that Mr. Barlow never did it—he simply didn't pull the trigger.

When the AIDS business began, even my mother was forthcoming about what Elliot did and didn't do. "There's no penetrating, sweetie—there's just rubbing. It's very sweet, but that's all the snowshoer does—just rubbing," my mom told me. "I think there's something Greek about it," she added.

"I think it's only Greek when men do it that way with other men, Ray," Molly told my mother.

"Women do it that way, too, Molly," my mom said. "That's all some women do with other women, under certain circumstances—just rubbing!"

"I know, Ray—that's when there's nothing *Greek* about it," the night groomer said.

"Smarty-pants! When it comes to just rubbing, Molly, you don't know everything!" my mother told her.

"I don't want to know everything, Ray," Molly tried to tell her.

"I don't want to know any more—I think the rubbing is clear enough," I told them.

Naturally, Nora wouldn't let it go. "There was a whole lot of rubbing going on in the girls' dorms at Northfield," Nora said. "Rubbing was never enough for me," Nora always added, while Em covered her ears with her hands and violently shook her head.

The Gallows had pulled the plug on the *Two Dykes'* skit about things to do with a penis, but Nora and I knew Em's pantomime by heart. Em demonstrated that she knew all about just rubbing; she would put a penis between her boobs or between her thighs, but nowhere else. This got a pretty good laugh at the Gallows, but Nora's punch line was why the comedy club had pulled the plug. "Not me," Nora said onstage, in her deadpan way. "The only thing I would do with a penis is cut it off."

People shouldn't have to tell their parents exactly how they have sex. It's nobody's business what works for you. Understandably, the little Barlows were worried about their one and only Elliot. Was their gay son, who was now their transgender daughter, in danger of dying of AIDS? The poor snowshoer. The little Barlows weren't alone in their wanting to know. We were all badgering Elliot Barlow about it.

"What the snowshoer does is called intercrural, or between the legs—'legs' in Latin is 'crura'—but it's also called femoral intercourse," Em wrote me. "Same idea as mammary intercourse—between the boobs, you know." Even I knew that, but Em had done her homework on the subject—as had Mr. Barlow.

The little English teacher knew those boys who'd been teased (or worse) at Exeter; those all-boys' schools were familiar with just rubbing. The poor snowshoer was embarrassed that rubbing was all she did, but in our fear for Elliot Barlow, we made her spell it out for us. We needed to know, for a fact, that the snowshoer was safe from AIDS. That was why we made such a big deal about the rubbing; under the circumstances, it was a relief to know it was just rubbing. Of course we knew the snowshoer wasn't safe from other things. And we all knew another thing about Elliot Barlow. I know my mother and Molly knew it; I know Nora and Em knew it, too. We knew the snowshoer wasn't afraid of dying. In the AIDS years, when we were afraid for Mr. Barlow, we were afraid that she felt guilty because she *wasn't* dying.

That day in Bronxville with Charlie and Sue, I could see that the snowshoer had a whole lot of guilt going on. Sue had been frank on the phone when she told Mr. Barlow that Charlie was dying—Charlie had been asking for Elliot, we knew. The snowshoer and I were inside the Bronxville home when Sue told us that Charlie had developed a rash from the Bactrim. That was when we knew Charlie was being treated for the PCP. From the way Sue kept looking at the pretty Mr. Barlow, it was clear Sue was wondering about Elliot.

Sue seemed to be delaying the inevitable moment of showing us the dying Charlie. She wanted us to see the photos of their children, who were staying with her sister. That day in Bronxville was not the time and place to explain Elliot Barlow's transitioning, or to tell Sue about Mr. Barlow's preference for just rubbing. Sue wanted to forewarn us that Charlie's breathing was harsh and aspirate. Since Charlie was in hospice care at home, we knew he wasn't likely to be on a ventilator. Sue also said something about how hard it was for Charlie to eat. "He has trouble swallowing," she told us.

"From the candida—he can't eat?" Elliot asked her.

"Yes, it's esophageal candidiasis," Sue said, the terminology sounding terribly familiar to her. "And he has a Hickman catheter," Sue explained. Mr. Barlow knew that if there was a Hickman, there would be a nurse.

"If they have you on a Hickman for hyperalimentation feeding, you're probably starving," the little English teacher had told me.

"Peter is Charlie's nurse," Sue was saying; she sighed. "One of our neighbors said it was 'kind of funny' that Charlie had a gay nurse named Peter, because Charlie's *peter* was what started the trouble. I don't think that's the least bit funny—do you?" Sue asked us, but she was looking solely at the pretty Mr. Barlow.

"No, that's not funny," the snowshoer said. "I'm guessing that one of Peter's jobs is to take care of the catheter—you have to keep flushing out the catheter, or it will clot off," Elliot Barlow told her.

"Yes, I know," Sue said.

It was an exertion for Charlie to breathe. We knew that his hands and feet would be cold; the circulation to Charlie's extremities was closing down, trying to shunt blood to his brain. Charlie barely moved in his hospital bed. Maybe it hurt him to move his head. It seemed strange that his head and the rest of his shrunken body lay still, but Charlie's bare chest was heaving. The Hickman catheter dangled from the right side of Charlie's chest, where it had been inserted under his clavicle; it tunneled under the skin a few inches above the nipple, and entered the subclavian vein below the collarbone.

"Is that you, Elliot?" Charlie asked. The snowshoer saw Charlie try to move his head, and stepped closer to the bed. "Elliot Barlow—are you here?" Charlie asked; his voice was weak and labored. His lungs made a thick gurgling. The oxygen must have been for only occasional (and superficial) relief. Morphine would come next, Mr. Barlow knew. It seemed impossible that poor Charlie didn't recognize Elliot Barlow as a woman.

"Yes, it's me—Elliot—and Adam is with me, Charlie," the snowshoer said. I could tell by the way Elliot touched Charlie's hand, and then withdrew her hand, that Charlie's hand was cold. I could see Charlie's face—that greasy-looking seborrheic dermatitis was in his scalp, on his eyebrows, and flaking off the sides of his nose.

"Adam, too!" Charlie gasped. "Elliot and Adam! Are you all right, Elliot—are you still not doing it?" Charlie asked me.

"The other one is Elliot—she's a woman," Sue pointed out.

"Are you a woman now, Elliot?" Charlie asked her.

"Yes, I am, Charlie—the transitioning is a slow process," the snowshoer said.

"But you're all right, aren't you, Elliot?" Charlie asked her.

"Yes, I am, Charlie," Elliot Barlow told him, but I hated how ashamed she sounded—she felt awful to be *all right*.

There was a tray of medications and other stuff on the bedside table. I would remember the heparin solution—it was for flushing out the Hickman catheter. I saw the white, cheesy curds of the candida crusting the corners of Charlie's mouth.

Of course I couldn't blame Charlie for not recognizing Elliot Barlow as a woman. Charlie thought I was Elliot—poor Charlie didn't recognize me, either. "The great horror"—as I would say to the snowshoer, when we were driving back to New York—was that I didn't recognize Charlie, but how do you recognize a grown man who weighs less than ninety pounds?

Charlie's hair was translucent and thin. His eyes were sunken in their sockets, his temples deeply dented, his cheeks caved in. Charlie's nostrils were pinched tightly together, as if he could already detect the stench of his own cadaver, and his taut skin, which had once been so ruddy, was an ashen color. *Hippocratic facies* was the term for that near-death face—that tightly fitted mask of death, which so many of Mr. Barlow's friends who died of AIDS would one day wear. It was skin stretched over a skull; the skin seemed so hard and tense, it looked like it was going to split.

Elliot and I were disconcerted that Sue had left the room, after twice mentioning that the oxygen wasn't working anymore. "I'm not the one to oversee this process," Sue had told us as she was leaving. "I'll go get Peter." The snowshoer and I mistakenly thought Sue meant she wasn't the one to supervise the oxygen, but Sue meant the *dying* process. Charlie had been so still when he was alive, Mr. Barlow and I had failed to notice that he had stopped breathing.

At first, we thought Charlie had fallen asleep, but he'd pushed the oxygen mask away from his mouth and nose—his face frozen in a grimace. Charlie must have known that the oxygen wasn't working. I think he knew it would never work again, because his cheeks were wet with tears. Elliot and I were not alone with Charlie for long. We didn't expect to see Sue again. There was no reason for Sue to say goodbye to us. I was surprised how Peter, the gay nurse, behaved, but Mr. Barlow wasn't taken aback by it.

"Oh, you're still here," Peter said, when he saw me, but the nurse did a double take when he got a look at the pretty Mr. Barlow. "No one told me you were also married—that's too bad," Peter said unpleasantly to me. Peter had looked twice at Elliot Barlow, but he'd quickly looked away from her.

"I'm not married. Charlie had been asking for Elliot—*she's* Elliot," I told the indignant nurse, with a nod to the pretty Mr. Barlow. But Peter made a point of not looking at her.

"Charlie had been asking for a *man*—Charlie wasn't asking for *her*," the nurse told me, in a huff. I was feeling like an outlier, or a complete know-nothing, again. I wasn't at all prepared for such unmasked hatred from a gay man for another sexual minority—in Mr. Barlow's case, a more minor one. I'd had no experience with the hatred of some homosexual men for trans women; it looked and sounded the same as homophobic hatred to me, but I knew nothing about hatred of the transphobic kind.

"We should go, Adam—we'll have some traffic, going back to the city," the snowshoer said. She appeared unperturbed by Peter's hatred, or she was used to it to the degree that she didn't react to it—hatred made Mr. Barlow speak slowly.

The nurse, we noticed, didn't like being ignored. Peter was roughly washing the crusted candida from the area of Charlie's slack mouth. "If you don't mind, I want to clean him up before the kids come see him," Peter told me, with the utmost prissiness. The nurse had been deliberate in his disregard for Elliot Barlow as a woman, but he wasn't expecting to be overlooked by her.

I wanted the transphobic nurse to hate me more than he hated the pretty Mr. Barlow, but Elliot Barlow had been my wrestling coach—she knew exactly what I was doing. "It didn't seem that the oxygen was working. Wasn't the oxygen your job?" I asked the nurse, but Mr. Barlow answered me before Peter could overcome his surprise.

"The oxygen was working only a little, Adam," the snowshoer said. "The problem with PCP is that it's diffuse. It affects both lungs, and it affects your ability to get oxygen into your blood vessels—hence into your body. That's why Charlie's hands were so cold," the little English teacher told me. She'd been speaking to me, only to me; she'd not once looked at the nurse. I knew exactly what she was doing.

"It's a dry cough—or there's no cough, Adam," the snowshoer went on. "When we hear it, we make too much of the cough. It's the shortness of breath that gets worse—Charlie just ran out of breath," Elliot told me.

Peter was at last looking at the pretty Mr. Barlow. I took a closer look at the Hickman catheter dangling from Charlie's unmoving chest, not because I liked looking at it. "If you want to clean up Charlie before the kids come see him, Peter, you ought to get rid of this thing," I told him. That was when the snowshoer stepped seamlessly between us. Mr. Barlow had turned her back to me, but she spoke to me—only to me—with her pretty face uplifted to Peter.

"It's not necessarily a nurse's job to remove the Hickman, Adam—an undertaker will pull it out," the snowshoer said, with her face still looking up at the nurse, who was repulsed by how close she was standing. The little English teacher was almost touching him. "Look at the cuff, Adam—it's like a Velcro collar around the tube, just inside the point where it enters the skin. Charlie's cells, his skin and body cells, have grown into that Velcro mesh. That's what keeps the catheter in place, so it doesn't fall out or get tugged loose. All the undertaker has to do is give it a good *yank*—it'll come right out," the pretty Mr. Barlow said. She'd taken hold of the nurse's hands when she said the *yank* word, but Peter had recoiled from her, and she let go of his hands—as quickly as she'd first touched him, as if sensing his revulsion.

"If a man wanted a woman, he would want a *real* one—he wouldn't want *you*," the hateful nurse suddenly said to her. "As for a man who wanted a man, what would he want with you?" Peter asked Elliot Barlow. I put my hands on her waist—just to move her out of the way, so I could get to the guy—but that slight contact was all Elliot needed to take control of my hands. The snowshoer was in her fifties, but her hand control was as good as ever. I knew the pretty Mr. Barlow would have heard the nurse's kind of hatred before; maybe this was why it was so hard for me to take.

When we were back in the car, Elliot and I didn't really talk about the gay nurse's repugnance at the very idea of a trans woman. All the snowshoer would say was what I'd heard her say before—about how much she loved gay men. "Most of my friends are gay men—I *love* gay men. Of course there are a few gay men who hate trans women, but there are more straight men who hate us," the snowshoer said. I was the one who was hung up on the moment, and on this gay nurse in particular.

On the way back to New York, we didn't talk about Charlie and Sue's neighbor—the one who thought it was funny that Charlie's gay nurse was named Peter. That wasn't the only *peter* joke in the 1980s. There were a lot of AIDS jokes going around. I don't remember when it was that I heard about the 1986 rededication of the Statue of Liberty, but it was after the fact. Either what happened at the centennial celebration wasn't in the news or I just missed it. Yet I was living in New York at the time, and the Statue of Liberty is in New York Harbor. How could what Bob Hope said not have been in the news? How could I have missed who laughed at Hope's wisecrack? It was the hundredth anniversary of Lady Liberty in New York Harbor. Bob Hope, the wisecracking comedian, was entertaining the audience. President Reagan and his wife, Nancy, were seated beside French president Mitterrand and his wife, Danielle. It was Em who brought this AIDS joke to my attention. Em wrote me that Bob Hope had been accustomed to entertaining the troops. Maybe Hope had forgotten that he wasn't speaking to soldiers, Em wrote. Hope had joked that the Statue of Liberty had AIDS, but that nobody knew if she got it from the mouth of the Hudson or the Staten Island Ferry—pronounced *Fairy*, I would guess, having grown up subjected to Bob Hope and Bing Crosby. Maybe Hope had forgotten that the statue came from France. The Mitterrands were shocked by what Hope had said, but the Reagans were laughing. In some news stories, Nancy Reagan was only smiling—she wasn't laughing. By all accounts, President Reagan was laughing. In one report, Em had read, Reagan was "roaring" with laughter—in another, he was "howling."

Bob Hope's smart-assed remark about AIDS might not have gone over well even at the Gallows, where bad taste was generally well received. But when Dr. Dave (Elliot's endocrinologist) got sick, Nora and Em stopped doing "The Specialist" at the Gallows—not even the OB-GYN *extra* version. The bananas would pile up onstage, or Em would do one of her other pantomime routines with a banana. When someone in the audience would shout out for "The Specialist," Em closed her eyes and looked like she was praying. "Dr. Dave is sick—out of respect for him, we're not doing that one," Nora would say. Later, Nora would give the audience more information about it. "Dr. Dave is HIV-positive—we won't be doing 'The Specialist' again," Nora told the audience. No one laughed, not even at the Gallows. And it was a comedy club, for Christ's sake. People went to the Gallows to laugh.

"What are the bananas for? Long time passing," Nora used to sing, in the 1970s. Not anymore.

"Where have the bananas gone? Long time ago," the snowshoer sang back to her. It wasn't funny anymore. No more bananas.

Dr. Dave had a transgender patient, Diane, who was dying at St. Vincent's when Dave, at his own request, was sent there to die as well. As if that weren't confusing enough, after Diane died, Dave spoke of her as if he were still treating her.

The estrogen Diane had been taking caused side effects in her liver. Dr. Dave told the snowshoer and me that estrogen can cause a kind of hepatitis; the bile stagnates and builds. The itching that occurred with this condition was driving Diane crazy, Dave told us. Diane had to stop taking her hormones; then her beard grew back. It seemed unfair to Dr. Dave that Diane, who'd worked so hard to feminize herself, was not only dying of AIDS, but was dying as a man. "It doesn't help that the nurses shave her," Dave said to the snowshoer and me. Dr. Dave only meant that Diane was spared *seeing* her beard, but she could feel it.

In the end, when Dave was dying at St. Vincent's, he looked like he was starving. By then, the snowshoer and I knew what the Hickman catheter in Dave's skeletal birdcage of a chest was for. They'd had him on a breathing machine, Mr. Barlow told me, but Dave was off it—"for now," Elliot said. Dave would have been in his late fifties—he was only a little older than Elliot Barlow.

"You know doctors—they like experimenting," Dave's most candid nurse told Mr. Barlow and me. They'd been experimenting on Dr. Dave with sublingual morphine, versus morphine elixir, Dave's candid nurse had informed us. "At this point, the suction is very important—to help clear secretions," she said. I had no idea what she was talking about, and the snowshoer never explained the suction or the secretions to me, but we liked Dr. Dave's most candid nurse; she clearly knew what lay in store for Dave.

The snowshoer sensed that all of Dave's nurses were wary of his parents—"not wary enough," the candid nurse would later tell us. Dr. Dave's parents had instructed his nurses not to allow other visitors to see Dave— not when his parents were with him. When the snowshoer and I were seeing Dave, the nurses warned Dave's parents that we were there. The parents waited in their limousine until we were gone. "They have a Russian chauffeur—she's a woman driver," Dave's candid nurse told Elliot and me.

"Why don't your parents want to meet us, or your other friends?" the snowshoer had asked Dr. Dave.

Apparently, Dave's parents didn't want to meet anyone who might have given their son AIDS in the first place. As the little English teacher put it, Dave's parents thought of us as "among the perpetrators." We never saw them, but we'd seen their woman driver—she looked more like a Russian shot-putter than a chauffeur. Sometimes, while she was waiting, she got out of the limo to stretch; the Russian driver did her stretching on the hood of the car, which looked cleaner than anything in that area of Seventh Avenue.

Dave died at St. Vincent's. He'd told the snowshoer that his parents had wanted him to die at home, in their apartment—not at St. Vincent's, where so many people were dying of AIDS. But Dr. Dave wanted to die where other AIDS patients were dying, including some of his endocrinology patients.

I thought Dave's parents were crazy. "No, they're not crazy—they're just parents," Mr. Barlow had said.

When you write fiction from so-called real life, there are those details you feel free to change, because you know you can make them better—or worse, if making things worse is your thing. "As a writer, Adam, making things as bad as they can be is your predilection," the little English teacher told me.

"You're a worst-case-scenario guy, as a writer," Em wrote me.

"It takes one to know one," I wrote her back. As a writer, Em had moved on from *The Coming Out Stories*. Her mom and dad were still writing to her, and Em's father kept writing to Cardinal John Joseph O'Connor. Her dad had continued to copy Em on his letters to the cardinal, but Em didn't write back to her parents, and she had stopped writing fiction about them.

When you write fiction from so-called real life, there are also those details you sense are unchangeable—because you know you can't make them any better, or any worse, than they already are.

After Dr. Dave died, the snowshoer was visiting another friend who was dying at St. Vincent's. The candid nurse we knew recognized the pretty Mr. Barlow. The nurse said the hospital's security personnel had to be vigilant in their efforts not to admit Dave's parents to St. Vincent's. The snowshoer said it was understandable why St. Vincent's had to keep Dave's parents out of the hospital, after Dr. Dave died.

Dave's parents tried to sneak into St. Vincent's, where they looked for AIDS patients who were dying alone. The parents sat with the dying patients, until someone asked them to leave. After a while, they'd stopped coming, but the Russian chauffeur still parked the limo and sat in it, waiting for someone; the woman driver still stretched on the hood, as if she thought Dr. Dave were still alive in St. Vincent's. Maybe the Russian driver was crazy, I was thinking, but the snowshoer said the limo driver must know something. "Maybe the driver knows the parents have killed themselves, or she knows they soon will," Elliot Barlow said.

"What do you think my mom would do, if I had AIDS?" I asked Mr. Barlow.

"Your mom wouldn't wait for you to die, Adam—she would shoot you first," the snowshoer said. I thought this was true. My mom would have shot me if I had AIDS; she wouldn't have watched me die with one or more of those AIDS-associated, opportunistic illnesses. She would have shot me first, and then shot herself. Little Ray was not inclined to prolong things, except for dramatic effect.

As for shooting someone else, I didn't doubt that my mother could have done it. At the end of the 1980s, Little Ray would express her surprise that only one person had shot Ronald Reagan. "And it was a *guy*," my mom said, in her wide-eyed, disbelieving way. What my mother *meant*, Molly said, might have gotten Little Ray fired as a ski instructor—even in Vermont, where President Reagan wasn't as popular as he was in the rest of the country. What my mother *meant* was something Molly and I tried to discourage Little Ray from saying. "But it's true," my mom always said. "A mother who lost her son to AIDS could be forgiven for shooting Ronald Reagan, sweetie."

38.

PLAGUE SONG

There were a lot more guns in my mom and Molly's Manchester house after Uncle Martin and Uncle Johan went off the road. Those two Norwegians left all their guns to their children, but the guns ended up with Molly and my mom—originally, "for safekeeping." Or that's what Henrik had said.

Henrik wanted the entire arsenal for himself, but he sensed there might be "compromising complications" for him—a member of the U.S. House of Representatives, transporting firearms from New England to a southern state, "across state lines." Henrik had a plan—"one gun at a time," he said. He'd persuaded Nora to drive a carload of lethal weapons from New Hampshire to Vermont.

"I drove a shitload of guns across state lines—Henrik wasn't worried about *compromising complications* for me," Nora complained. I liked Em's pantomime about the political radical and stand-up comedian who was arrested for gunrunning, but Nora didn't think it was funny.

It was dismaying to me that Molly and my mother were happy to stash Henrik's guns in their Manchester house. Molly once swore by her single-shot shotgun—her little twenty-gauge was the only gun my mom and Molly owned. "It's a hard gun to shoot yourself with, accidentally," Molly always said. (I liked the sound of that.) "No safety is safer than having a safety," the ski patroller liked to say.

"We're just keeping the guns for Henrik, sweetie—we're not going to start a war, or anything," my mother told me.

"I'm going to make a little more trouble for the deer, Kid—that's the only trouble I'm making," Molly assured me. In the stash of firearms, the trail groomer had seen a couple of deer rifles she wanted to try, and a twelve-gauge or two.

Henrik had been in the habit of coming to Manchester once a year to ski at Stratton, but he always spent one day skiing with my mom at Bromley. "Ray would ski with anyone, kiddo," was how Nora put it. Henrik stayed in an inn in Manchester, not with Molly and my mother. (Henrik had always been wary of Molly.) Before the guns were in the picture, Henrik had flown to Boston or to Hartford, where he'd rented a car. It was a long drive to Manchester, Vermont, from down south. But now that the guns were with Molly and my mom, Henrik drove.

"One gun at a time—really?" I asked the night groomer and my mother. My uncles had so many guns, I calculated that Molly and my mom would die long before Henrik could drive those guns to Dixie, one at a time. Molly admitted that Henrik had been taking more than one gun at a time down south. Henrik had ski bags and boot bags. Henrik stuck a rifle or a shotgun in the ski bags—maybe one of each, my mother had observed—and he usually slipped a handgun in one of his boot bags. Even so, the arsenal of weapons was not visibly depleted. The closet in the TV room, where the pillows for the futon were stored, was full of rifles. "They're not loaded, I hope," I said, every time I slept on the futon—imagining myself shot by a falling rifle, in my sleep. The shotguns, I was told, now took up most of Molly's side of their bedroom closet. I didn't ask where the handguns were hidden, but I was careful how I opened drawers.

There were so many guns, not even Henrik could keep track of them. Henrik had told my mom and Molly that they could give some guns away—if they wanted to, if they had any friends or loved ones who wanted any. "You can't give away a gun in Manchester, Kid—they sell any kind of gun you could want in a gas station in town," Molly told me. I knew the gas station; I'd seen all the guns.

My mother tried to give guns to the snowshoer and me, and to Nora and Em. My mom was convinced we needed guns to be safe in New York. On the contrary, Mr. Barlow argued—for two people living in a small apartment, it would be unsafe to have a gun.

"Elliot is so quiet, even when she is moving around—I would mistake her for an intruder and shoot her," I said.

"You should each have your own gun, sweetie," my mom said.

"So we can shoot each other?" I asked her.

"Adam gets up to pee at night—I would surely shoot him if I had a gun, Ray," the snowshoer said.

Nora had said that a handgun (or two) was the only kind of weapon you would want to have in a New York City apartment. "In New York, I'll bet you could be arrested just for carrying a rifle or a shotgun from your parking garage to your apartment," Nora pointed out. Growing up with all those guns, it was a wonder Nora and Henrik hadn't shot each other. Now that half the guns belonged to Nora, she was surprisingly picky about choosing the gun (or guns) she wanted. Nora was uncharacteristically judicious; she wanted Em to learn to shoot before Nora took any guns to their rat's-ass apartment above the perennially bad restaurant in Hell's Kitchen.

When Nora and Em visited my mom and Molly in Manchester, Molly took Em shooting in a quarry outside of town. There were safe things you could shoot at in the quarry; everyone went there for target practice, Molly said. This was a safer bet than turning Em loose with a handgun on Ninth Avenue on the West Side of Midtown Manhattan, Nora said. Molly told us that Em had "taken to" shooting at things in the quarry.

Whenever we went to see my mother and Molly, Elliot and I refused to take a gun back to New York with us. "You should take *two*," my mom always told us. She was already mad at us for taking our cross-country skis to the city. We'd never wanted the skis in the first place; in Vermont, Elliot and I preferred snowshoeing. But sometimes when it snowed in New York City, they closed Park Avenue to traffic. It was magical to ski at night on Park Avenue in the falling snow, but my mother was mad that we wouldn't ski with her in Vermont.

"You don't even like cross-country skiing, Ray—you're a downhill girl," the snowshoer said.

"I would ski on Mars or the moon, if I could ski with my honeys," my mom said. She was hurt by it. Maybe that was why she snuck the gun into Mr. Barlow's backpack. On an earlier weekend, she'd tried to slip the same .357 Magnum into my suitcase, but I was wise to my mother's not taking no for an answer, and I knew that it was one of the handguns Nora had her eye on—a six-shooter Em had been blazing away with, out at the quarry. It was nowhere near Valentine's Day, but my mom had included a Valentine's card with the gun she snuck into the snowshoer's backpack. There was a big heart on the card, where Little Ray had written: "To keep my darling snowshoer safe, and to protect my sweetie!"

To my surprise, Elliot Barlow said she thought it was "a pretty little gun," and she liked "the feel of it." I pointed out that we could bring the gun back to Vermont the next time we went there for a weekend, or maybe Nora and Em would want it. Em had liked shooting the .357 Magnum. It had a short barrel, but it wasn't a little gun—not from a shooter's perspective.

"That sucker packs a wallop," was all Molly said about it.

I wasn't that surprised the snowshoer wanted to keep the gun, but I thought she was funny about it. "I don't want to know where it is, but I also don't want it to surprise me if I just happen on it," she told me. When the little Barlows were around, I was instructed to "take pains" to keep the gun hidden from them, too.

"Your parents don't like guns?" I asked the snowshoer.

"My parents love guns, but they're thriller writers—they're drawn to disasters," the little English teacher told me.

We should have hidden our cross-country skis from the little Barlows. They were hurt to see the skis in the front-hall closet of their Upper East Side apartment. Like my mother, the writing team was angry that we went skiing on Park Avenue when we wouldn't ski with them—in the Alps.

The pains I took to hide the gun were not very creative. I wrapped it in a pair of underpants I didn't like, in the bottom of my underwear-and-socks drawer. I put the bullets in a pair of athletic socks; they were big bullets for such a small-looking gun. Of course I concealed the socks with the ammo under other pairs. This was not a novel idea. It was what my mom did with the bullets she'd snuck into the snowshoer's backpack—she put them in a pair of socks.

All this had happened when Eric and Charlie and Dr. Dave were dying and when God knows what Dave's parents were up to, or their Russian driver. Nora and Em ended up taking two guns from Henrik's stash. Contradicting herself, Nora slipped a double-barreled, twelve-gauge shotgun into a ski bag, carrying it over her shoulder from her parking garage to her apartment. Em had chosen her own handgun—one she'd used at the quarry. "Em wanted the Colt," Nora said to Mr. Barlow and me. Em's gun was a .357 Magnum—"a different kind than you have," Nora told us. Em's pantomime was startling to the snowshoer and me; Em seemed to be saying that her penis was bigger than both of our penises, together. "She means her *barrel*—the barrel of Em's gun is twice as long as your barrel," Nora explained.

The snowshoer and I had been waiting for the next time it snowed all night in New York City. And when it did, Elliot Barlow and I had a plan. We were New Englanders—we knew what to wear for snow. We wore our winter hiking boots to the Gallows Lounge. We wore our snowshoeing clothes, the layers and layers. We had extra gloves and ski hats in our backpacks—rain gear, if the snow turned to sleet, extra socks and warmer clothes, if it turned cold. I'd put a second pair of hiking boots in my backpack. "Overkill, Adam—you'll regret carrying the extra weight," the snowshoer had said, but we were proud of ourselves. New Yorkers were lost souls in a snowstorm; New Englanders were prepared. We'd planned a late-night hike home from the Gallows—from the West Village to East Sixty-fourth Street. We knew some New Yorkers who would think this was a long way to trek through the snow, but we were snowshoers—the walk from the West Village was just a warm-up for us. When we got to East Sixty-fourth Street, we would put on our ski boots and grab our ski poles and our cross-country skis. Still later that night, we thought they would be closing Park Avenue to traffic; from the forecast of the snowstorm, it sounded like a skiing-on-Park-Avenue night to the snowshoer and me.

We were not prepared to have Damaged Don with us. Nora used to say that having Don with you was "like going to a brothel with a child." I never knew what Nora meant, but we knew we were supposed to protect Damaged Don. What eluded us was what to protect him from, and exactly how. Don was well-meaning, good-hearted, and kind, but he had no talent as a singer-songwriter, and he was a sad sack onstage—Don was a doom-and-gloom guy. You could see it in the faces in the audience at the Gallows—those poor people who were hearing Damaged Don sing for the first time, the ones who hadn't run to the washrooms. You could not prepare yourself for the overwhelming sadness, or the way Don droned. "In a comedy club, you need some sorrow relief," Nora used to say—in Don's defense—but she'd stopped saying it. "Maybe not *that* sorrowful," Nora later said.

Don was always getting evicted from his apartment; it didn't matter where he moved. The last time he was homeless, he'd crashed on Nora and Em's couch. Nora nearly suffocated him with a sofa cushion—Don had been singing in his sleep. "The same old song," was all Nora said, but it could have been fragments from a song Don was writing. The way Don sang, even in his sleep, his new songs sounded like the same old song. It was always Don's neighbors who got him evicted; Don was up all night writing and singing when he wasn't singing in his sleep. Now that Nora and Em were heavily armed, it was out of the question that Damaged Don could stay with them. In the dead of night, Don's plaintive yowls might have been mistaken for the confessions of Em's father to the unresponsive Cardinal O'Connor. In the dead of night, it wouldn't have been safe for Em's homo-hating dad or for Cardinal O'Connor—to be wandering around, lamenting, in Nora and Em's apartment. Nora and Em despised conversion therapy; they would have blasted away at either one of the Catholics. Damaged Don was an all-night moaner. In the dead of night, it wouldn't have been safe for Don to sing at Nora and Em's.

That snowy night in New York, the snowshoer and I knew we were stuck with the Damaged Man—Don had nowhere to go after he'd performed. There were dressing rooms backstage at the Gallows, but it was a challenge to dress Don for the snowstorm. He'd brought his few clothes to the Gallows. The clothes, the songs he was writing, his guitar—that's all he owned. "Doesn't it snow in Montana—where are your winter clothes?" Mr. Barlow asked Don.

"I hate the snow—I left my winter clothes in Great Falls," Damaged Don said. It sounded like a line from one of his songs, dismal and lacking foresight. We had winter wear in our backpacks, but most of Elliot Barlow's stuff was too small for Don. For a first layer, we crammed Don into the snowshoer's turtleneck, though this seemed to compromise the singer-songwriter's circulation. Don complained that he couldn't straighten his toes in the snowshoer's socks, but my second pair of hiking boots would have been too big for Don—if we hadn't doubled up on the socks. We doubled up on the ski hats, too, though Don said he couldn't feel his ears—whatever that meant. Don definitely couldn't hear.

The snowshoer and I had enough room in our backpacks for Don's meager assortment of clothes. Don didn't have a suitcase, not even a backpack, and he wouldn't leave his guitar at the Gallows—not even overnight. There was a case for the guitar, with backpack straps, but it would be cumbersome to carry in the snow. The songs Don was writing went in the guitar case.

"You can lock it in a dressing room, Don—no one at the Gallows is going to steal your guitar or your writing," the snowshoer told him.

"What?" Don shouted. It was pointless to shout back at him. "My writin' and my guitar go with me, every night—even if it's the night I'm dyin'," Damaged Don shouted. Definitely, the same old song. Of course the Damaged Man was shouting, or he couldn't have heard himself. Dressed for the snowstorm, with his guitar and his writing on his back, Don looked like a doomed clown. We tried to make the two ski hats look less clownish and not crush his ears, but Don's hearing was completely impaired and he looked no less doomed.

Like the New Englanders we were, the snowshoer and I felt superior to the New York taxi drivers in the snow. Many of the cabs didn't have proper snow tires, and a lot of the cabbies didn't know how to drive in the snow. The subways and the buses were a mess from everyone's wet shoes and boots. But we must have been crazy to imagine Damaged Don could make it even a third of the way up Seventh Avenue in the snow. Don didn't run; he didn't walk anywhere, not even when it wasn't snowing. It didn't matter that the snow was just starting to accumulate when we left the Gallows Lounge. There were only a couple of inches on the sidewalk, but the Damaged Man was slipping and sliding from the get-go. We'd trekked up Seventh Avenue only as far as West Eleventh Street and Greenwich Avenue—we were still in the West Village. Don was already winded, having inhaled the snow as he sang.

"You can't prepare for everything, Adam," the snowshoer said, as we were leaving the Gallows and Don had already started to sing.

Don will die before we're halfway home, I was thinking. "You don't want to wake up with Maureen," Don was singing when we began trekking. *We will all be killed, if Damaged Don starts singing on a bus or in a subway*, I thought. "Your worst nightmare is knowin' Louise," Don was singing, when he started to cough.

Then something else we couldn't have prepared for happened. We'd stopped on Seventh Avenue, just to give the Damaged Man a breather. We were standing outside that last stop of a hospital, St. Vincent's, when the snowshoer started to sob. Don probably thought it was his song. Don didn't know where he was; he'd never been in St. Vincent's. Don didn't know that Mr. Barlow felt guilty for not going inside. If someone the snowshoer knew wasn't dying at St. Vincent's, Mr. Barlow worried there was someone inside she hadn't known was sick. Once or twice, in St. Vincent's, the snowshoer had spotted someone she hadn't known was gay.

Damaged Don wasn't gay. Don was no homophobe; he was a sweet man— he often didn't know who was gay or straight. Don didn't care what you were; he probably had a few gay friends he didn't know had died. While the snowshoer sobbed, Don just kept singing. He was singing lines from "It Never Gets Better with Gwen"—a song was all Don knew how to do, even in the snow. "She'll run over your kids and fuck your best friend!" Don sang, while the snow kept coming down and Don kept coughing. I sometimes wonder if we would all still be standing there—if time would have stopped—if Damaged Don had just kept singing, but the Damaged Man suddenly stopped. "No, it never gets better with Gwen," he'd been repeating, in his customary moan—made worse by his respiratory distress. Between the nonstop singing and the coughing, Don had inhaled and swallowed a lot of snow, and we'd been walking only for a few minutes.

The broad-shouldered Russian woman wore a mannish black suit with a white dress shirt and a black scarf, instead of a necktie. For the winter storm, she'd donned a black overcoat with a fur collar, but the chauffeur's cap didn't cover her ears. She appeared impervious to the snow and the cold; the stiff brim of the soldierly cap gave her a military resolve. She stood like a sentinel on guard, on the corner of Seventh Avenue and West Eleventh Street. Her blonde ponytail notwithstanding, she struck me as a Nora type. Despite her masculine attire and military bearing she wouldn't usually be mistaken for a man. Even in the overcoat, the prow of her bosom preceded her—as surely as a ship's bow above water. It was unusual to see the sturdy chauffeur standing closer to the hospital buildings than where she'd parked the limo. We'd heard that Dave's parents had stopped visiting other AIDS patients; we knew the Russian driver wasn't waiting for Dave's parents anymore. Yet the way the imposing woman stood sentinel, she looked like she was keeping watch for someone. Her commanding presence made the snowshoer stop sobbing. The big Russian woman had seized Damaged Don's attention, too.

Don was always seeing prostitutes who weren't prostitutes. The Damaged Man would try to save them from themselves, which was always misunderstood. Surely the Russian limo driver was too respectfully dressed for a streetwalker, I was thinking; this wasn't my part of town, but I'd not noticed any streetwalkers outside St. Vincent's before. "She's not a streetwalker, Don," Mr. Barlow told the Damaged Man, but Don was as good as deaf in the two ski hats. Don resumed singing; he'd already made up his mind about the big woman on the corner of Seventh Avenue and West Eleventh Street.

"She's one of those militant hookers I've been hearing about—she's into tyin' you up and causin' you pain," Don interrupted his song to confide to Elliot Barlow and me, in a raspy voice. "She shouldn't be standin' out in the snow—that's just so sad!" Don struggled to say, between coughs. He was shivering, his teeth were chattering, he could barely talk, but he couldn't stop singing.

The limo driver had heard Don's song and his cough, and she recognized the little English teacher and me—even in our snowshoeing clothes. "Well, look at *you two*—you look like a couple Russians tonight," she told us. The way she'd said *Russians* didn't sound entirely complimentary. "The poor choirboy shouldn't be out in this weather," the Russian chauffeur said. "Don't bring this poor boy here to die—he'll be better off dying at home," she told us.

We knew this had been Dave's parents' theme, but Mr. Barlow and I just looked at each other. We knew it was beyond us; we had no hope of sorting out the misunderstandings between Dave's parents' driver and the Damaged Man. Don thought she was a militant hooker, into bondage and whips, or worse—this sounded like a Damaged Don song. The limo driver thought Don was a dying AIDS patient, who should go back home to die, instead of dying at St. Vincent's—all because of Don's cough and the lamentation of the song she'd heard him singing. "You were singing, weren't you?" the chauffeur asked Don, but he hadn't heard her—not with the two ski hats.

"I should go home, to Montana—I should just go back to Great Falls," Don told us, as if he'd suddenly decided to go home to die, although he'd not heard what the driver said.

The snowshoer took off Don's two hats. "Going back to Great Falls is one option, Don, but not tonight—tonight you should stay with Adam and me," Elliot Barlow said. There was more confusion caused because the snowshoer had first met the driver when the little English teacher had been dating Dave. "That was when I was a man," the pretty Mr. Barlow had to explain. That Dave's parents' driver wasn't a prostitute had to be explained to Don; that Damaged Don was a singer-songwriter, who was not dying of AIDS, had to be explained to the Russian chauffeur.

Her name was Zasha, she told us. "Like Sasha, it's short for Alexander or Alexandra—it means 'defender of the people.' Not an easy name to live up to," Zasha said. The big woman was of indeterminate age. She seemed younger than Dr. Dave had been when he died, but Zasha spoke of him as if she'd known him as a child. She was paid a generous retainer by Dave's parents; Zasha had her own bedroom and bathroom in their apartment. "I'm not only their driver—I'm more like the family servant," Zasha wanted us to know. When we asked her how Dave's parents were doing, and why the family servant was hanging around St. Vincent's in the dead of night, Zasha told us how she was trying to live up to her name. "The people who leave St. Vincent's late at night really need a ride," was the way she put it. Like a genuine defender of the people, it didn't matter to Zasha if her passengers could pay her or not. "Some riders overpay me—the ones with nothing pay nothing," Zasha said, shrugging her big shoulders.

The Damaged Man, hatless and shaking with cold, had clearly heard what the Russian woman said, but from Don's awed or stricken expression, he might have imagined that only the most militant prostitutes referred to their clients as riders—the snowshoer and I hoped not. We were getting Don a ride with Zasha; that's all we knew.

I was overthinking how Zasha or Sasha could be a kind of nickname for both Alexander and Alexandra; I should have left the subject of Russian names alone.

"It's a gender-neutral name, Adam," the little English teacher told me.

"I'm not gender-neutral—I'm a girl," Zasha told us; she wanted us to know there was no funny business about her. She'd accepted the pretty Mr. Barlow as a woman, but the snowshoer should have left the subject of Russian literature alone.

"Take Gogol's barbed satire, or Chekhov's portrayals of upper-class sadness," Mr. Barlow began.

"I'm not really Russian," Zasha said. "My parents came from Russia, but I was born and grew up in Brooklyn. I've never been in Russia," she wanted us to know, but I knew there was no stopping the snowshoer now.

"Take Tolstoy—think of poor Pierre in *War and Peace*," Elliot Barlow persevered. "Pierre tries to liberate his serfs; he only manages to make their lives worse."

"It wasn't that bad in Brighton Beach, but some of my Jewish friends had a hard time everywhere else, and there was a Ukrainian girl in my grade in school—her name was Bogdana, which means 'gift from God.' Talk about a hard name to live up to—poor Bogdana wasn't God's gift to anybody," Zasha wanted us to know.

"Think of Dostoyevsky's approach to human suffering—the moral problems imposed by politics and religion," the little English teacher lectured to us. For some reason, Elliot Barlow wanted Zasha to know there was little joy in Russian literature. It would later emerge that the snowshoer saw Zasha as a somber character in a Russian novel—"grave but brave," Mr. Barlow called her. The snowshoer saw Zasha as a noble servant, loyally performing her duties to a couple of doomed aristocrats. Dr. Dave's parents were suicidal, Zasha told us.

"They're going to kill themselves—they just need to work up to it, but they'll get there," Zasha said. "There's a gas stove—I'm always sniffing around for gas—but it's easier to take pills," Dave's family servant told us. "They never leave the apartment. I do all their shopping. Their pharmacy delivers. Their only kid died in a *plague*—I would kill myself, in their situation," Zasha said. Either Damaged Don reacted strangely to the word *plague*, or he dropped to his knees in the snow for no reason. "Speaking of human suffering, we should put this poor guy in the car—the car is running and the heat is on," the limo driver told us. "I'm an American—I've never read a Russian novel," Zasha wanted the snowshoer to know.

"Start with Turgenev," the little English teacher told her. The Damaged Man stopped singing when we lifted him off his knees.

"I'm writin' a plague song," Don said to Zasha. Elliot and I had heard about Don's plague song. He'd been writing it since the start of the AIDS epidemic; it was still the 1980s, and AIDS had a ways to go. We didn't know what was holding up Don's plague song, but we weren't eager for Don to finish writing it; we were hoping we would never have to hear it.

"I hope you'll sing one of your songs to me," Zasha said to Don, as we followed the limo driver to the car. The snowshoer had put just one of the ski hats back on the Damaged Man. Don didn't have a lot of walking to do; he wouldn't need two ski hats. The keys to the little Barlows' apartment—not to mention the little English teacher's written instructions regarding which key opened which door—were in Don's guitar case. If you wanted anything to be safe in Don's hands, you had to put it with his guitar and his songwriting. Naturally, we'd taken Zasha aside just to be sure she understood where she was taking Don. Zasha looked like a contemporary character in a New York novel, I was thinking; there was nothing recognizably Russian, or of the nineteenth century, about her. Of course I said nothing, not wanting to provoke the pretty Mr. Barlow's passion for the gloom in Russian literature.

"I met Fuzzy Ouilette in a bar," Don began to sing, as he and Dave's faithful family servant got in the limo. "He'd lost his last job, his wife just left him, his dog had been killed by a car!" Don sang.

"Sounds like Coney Island!" Zasha exclaimed.

"Poor Fuzzy had no lucky star," the Damaged Man kept singing. "No, Fuzzy had no lucky star."

It was hard to reconcile the high hopes Mr. Barlow and I had for a snowy night in New York with everything else that was happening. "Do you think Don will be safer in Great Falls?" I asked the snowshoer, as we were trekking uptown through the snow on Seventh Avenue. Given our ski hats, and the way the snow was coming down, I thought the little English teacher hadn't heard me.

We were almost at West Fifty-seventh Street—we were passing Carnegie Hall—when Elliot answered my question. I could tell she'd been thinking about it. "Don is a danger to himself in New York, but someone might shoot him in Montana," the snowshoer said. That was all she said, the whole way. We were a couple of New Englanders, trekking in new snow; we weren't out for a stroll and a conversation. Mr. Barlow had insisted that we not cross Park Avenue "too soon"; she wanted to put off finding out if it was a ski night, or it wasn't. I think the snowshoer didn't want to be disappointed until the last possible minute. We walked all the way to Central Park South before turning east. It was beautiful walking alongside the park in the falling snow; keeping the park on our left, we headed north on Fifth Avenue. We could have been trekking north on Park Avenue, I was thinking; we could have seen for ourselves if there were skiers on the avenue, or not. Mr. Barlow was just stalling, I knew.

We were on Park Avenue for only one block; then we turned east once more, on East Sixty-fourth. They'd not yet closed Park Avenue to traffic, whether they were going to or not. "We're not real New Yorkers, and we never will be—we not only don't know the rules for when there's skiing on Park Avenue, we don't even know who to ask," the snowshoer said. Our not being real New Yorkers was a theme with her. She was a trans woman. What I was afraid of, for her, was that she would be an outsider anywhere—while she blamed herself for not knowing there were Russians in Brighton Beach, Brooklyn.

There were a multitude of doormen on Park Avenue, I was thinking; a long-standing doorman must know what rules applied to closing Park Avenue to traffic when it snowed. That snowy night, we weren't on Park Avenue long enough to ask a doorman—we didn't actually see a doorman standing out in the storm. What we did see was a skier carrying his skis and poles on one shoulder; he was coming toward us on East Sixty-fourth, between Lexington and Third, the little Barlows' block. Unfortunately, the skier wasn't a real New Yorker—he was from Minnesota, as much in the dark as we were.

"Maybe they only close Park Avenue if it's snowing on a Sunday night," the skier said. None of us could remember if the last time we'd skied on Park Avenue had been a Sunday. That it was late at night, and there was more than enough snow to ski on—these were not hopeful signs. We sensed we weren't going skiing.

"We're too out of it to live in New York," the snowshoer was saying when we got to the apartment, which was unlocked. Damaged Don had let himself in, and he'd turned on all the lights, but Don hadn't relocked the door. Two out of three wasn't bad for the Damaged Man, I was thinking—three out of four, if you counted Don's daring to ride with a militant prostitute. "Maybe we should go to Great Falls with Don—maybe we wouldn't be so out of it in Montana," the snowshoer was saying, but Don's singing in the shower discouraged us.

"Don't give Ronald Reagan eight years," Don sang. "He talks tough to commies, he kills all the gay boys, but that does fuck-all for our fears! Please don't give the Gipper eight years. No, don't give the Gipper eight years."

It was Don's plague song, clearly. Notwithstanding the importance of the plague, there was no discernible difference in Don's cadence or tone—his plague song was as doleful and morbid as any Damaged Don song. In the shower, the Damaged Man sang like a drowning man, yet Elliot and I were relieved to hear him keep repeating the same verse. It seemed there was only one verse to Don's plague song, so far. But later that night, when Don was singing in his sleep, the snowshoer and I were awakened by a different verse. It sounded like a last verse to us, but how would you know with Don? How could we have slept through the middle of a plague song? We could only hope the Damaged Man hadn't written the middle; we hoped his plague song would forever be in progress. In his sleep, Don still sang like a drowning man.

It's time to head back to
Great Falls.
I'm lackin' the talent,
I can't stand the sadness,
I don't have big enough balls!

It's time to head back to
Great Falls.
I'm just goin' back to
Great Falls.

They would give the Gipper eight years. There were only two verses to Don's plague song, which we'd heard Don sing in the little Barlows' apartment. "Goin' Back to Great Falls," the Damaged Man would call his last song. When we first heard it on the radio, the censors had bleeped out the *balls* and the *fuck-all*. "Less bad ain't better," as Don used to say. There was no bleeping out Ronald Reagan, who would be reelected in a landslide—naturally, the right-wing radio stations wouldn't play "Goin' Back to Great Falls," not at all.

Don would be killed in Montana. He'd been playing with a band in Bozeman, but the band was based in Missoula; the details weren't clear, not at all. They were a couple of college towns; Don had been playing with college kids. That was all Nora knew about the band. Someone shot Damaged Don in a parking lot, after he'd been singing "Goin' Back to Great Falls." This was after Reagan's reelection, when the gay boys Don had been singing about were still getting killed.

After Don was killed, there were sympathetic DJs who played "Goin' Back to Great Falls" as a protest song. There was a resurgence of the Damaged Man on the airwaves—of "It Never Gets Better with Gwen" and "No Lucky Star," and the rest.

For as long as Ronald Reagan was in office, Nora closed out every performance of *Two Dykes, One Who Talks* with a Damaged Don song. "I can't sing, but neither could Don," Nora always said, bringing tears to the eyes of the veteran patrons of the Gallows Lounge—even before she started singing. Em would just hug her, crying, while Nora sang.

In the Reagan years, when Em and I wrote each other about our writing, we always asked how the plague song was going.

39

WENGEN

While Ronald Reagan was preaching the doctrine of American exceptionalism, the snowshoer and I went to Switzerland. My mother and Molly met us in Wengen. The little Barlows were still skiing, albeit more cautiously—they were in their seventies, almost in their eighties. Wengen was their idea; they were always looking for new places to ski, in Austria or Switzerland, and they invited us to join them. My mom and Molly loved skiing in Europe; Elliot and I felt the same way about winter hiking and snowshoeing. Wengen, in the Bernese Alps, was new to all of us—not even the little Barlows had been there before.

Elliot Barlow and I were at home with being first-timers in Wengen. We still felt like newcomers in New York. Whereas Nora tried to insert herself among the activists at ACT UP (the AIDS Coalition to Unleash Power), Mr. Barlow and I weren't cut out to be activists—no more than we were to be real New Yorkers. The snowshoer said she was "too small" and she spoke "too quietly" to be an activist. "I'm just an advocate of activists," Elliot Barlow said; she always put herself down.

Some ACT UP members questioned Nora's participation in the group, especially at the demonstrations. "We're not a comedy club—we're not in this for the laughs," one of the ACT UP guys told Nora. The way Nora affected a crowd, including people who agreed with her, was a problem. For the most part, Em would keep her distance from the ACT UP demonstrations. What could a pantomimist do at a demonstration? Em was increasingly concerned about Nora's effect on crowds, even at the Gallows.

To many ACT UP members, Nora would find it necessary to repeat herself. "I'm not always funny, you know—I'm not *just* funny," Nora kept saying. In 1987, ACT UP was only getting started. I was just out of it; I didn't notice the earliest ACT UP demonstrations, but Nora did. Nora was cut out to be a shit-disturber; for a New Hampshire girl, Nora seemed like a real New Yorker. I'll always be a New Hampshire boy.

Nora was pissed that President Reagan was still badgering Congress to bring back God to America's classrooms; the gay boys were dying in droves, but the president cared more about a moment of silence in public schools than he did about AIDS. In 1987, it was Reagan's silence about AIDS that led ACT UP to join forces with those guys who thought up the SILENCE=DEATH poster—an all-black poster with a pink triangle, right side up. SILENCE=DEATH was in white caps, under the triangle. That poster became the image for ACT UP; there would be T-shirts later. Nora tried to persuade the Gallows to let their bartenders wear SILENCE=DEATH T-shirts, but the dickless management said the comedy club wasn't into single-issue politics. The Gallows Lounge would allow Nora and Em to wear the T-shirts, but Em didn't like the way Nora looked in a T-shirt— not in public. A T-shirt made Nora's boobs appear to be protesting something all by themselves. In the SILENCE=DEATH T-shirt, the pink triangle was at a weird angle above Nora's boobs, pointed at her throat. There would be more poster art from the people who created SILENCE=DEATH. You may remember their AIDSGATE poster—Reagan with a green face and the pink eyes of a laboratory rat. If that poster was a T-shirt, I never saw Nora wear it.

In 1988, Nora would be one of the ACT UP women who protested a misleading article published in *Cosmopolitan* magazine, where a doctor purported that penis-to-vagina transmission of HIV was virtually impossible. The doctor turned out to be a psychiatrist; he wouldn't take back what he'd said. More than a hundred women protested in front of the Hearst building. "Say no to *Cosmo!*" they were saying. Some women held signs: YES, THE COSMO GIRL can GET AIDS! Nora was disappointed there were no arrests, but she got to be on television. Em would write she was relieved that Nora wore more than a T-shirt on TV.

"It's January, Em—everyone is wearing more than a T-shirt," I wrote her back. Em continued to keep her distance from ACT UP, but Nora was proud to be part of it, and Mr. Barlow's business as a copy editor was branching out. Not only did publishers of crime fiction and thrillers want her to work for them, but other publishers were interested in her, too. The snowshoer would soon be the freelance copy editor she wanted to be. Nora was the only born shit-disturber among us. Em was afraid Nora would get arrested. We both imagined Nora might fight back, if she ever got arrested.

Time stops in ski resorts; you lose track of it when you're there. In Wengen, in the late 1980s, you wouldn't know there was an AIDS pandemic or that people were getting arrested. Elliot and I never learned our way around

Wengen; we were lost or confused the whole time. To begin with, it wasn't just Wengen; snowshoers were increasingly unwelcome at ski resorts everywhere. Mr. Barlow and I got the hairy eyeball from skiers when we were carrying our snowshoes around the village. My mom and the little Barlows were not so secretly heartened to see ski resorts shunning snowshoers. "You and Elliot should just rent some skis and ski with us, sweetie," my mother not so sweetly said.

An old stationmaster in Wengen told Elliot Barlow to take the train to Interlaken; he thought there were trails for snowshoeing near one of the lakes. A younger stationmaster in Wengen contradicted his colleague. The snowshoer was advised to take the Wengernalpbahn to Kleine Scheidegg; the Wengernalp train was a rack-and-pinion railway. From Kleine Scheidegg, you could transfer to the train to Jungfraujoch. The best snowshoeing was "oben," a ski patroller told Elliot—"above" meant Kleine Scheidegg, where you could snowshoe above the tree line, or you could take a second train to Jungfraujoch, the highest station. We could see the Jungfrau from our hotel in Wengen. "Obenan," another ski patroller said to the snowshoer—"at the top." There were electric locomotives on the slowly moving cog railway trains. You could climb up the mountain alongside the train track, one of the ski patrollers suggested, halfheartedly.

The snowshoer had looked closely at the cogwheel railroad; the sides of the railway bed looked a little narrow for snowshoeing, she thought. What if a train was passing? What if there were tunnels or bridges? Someone climbing up the railway bed would be better off in hiking boots, the snowshoer said. I knew this was her way of telling me not to snowshoe alongside the train track.

"The ski patrollers don't want snowshoers on the piste, not on the lower slopes," the little English teacher told me, although not one of the patrollers had actually said this.

I'd brought the novel I was writing to Wengen and I was finishing a difficult chapter. I thought I would write in the mornings in my hotel room, imagining I would meet up with Mr. Barlow for some snowshoeing in the afternoons. The cog railway complicated our plans to meet up in the middle of the day.

"You have to take two trains to get to Jungfraujoch, and it'll be much colder up there," the snowshoer said. I knew what she wanted—more working out, less time on a train. She would take the train from Wengen to Kleine Scheidegg, just one train. It took only about thirty minutes to get there—the snowshoeing there would be "gut genug," Elliot had decided. My German was rudimentary, but I knew the words for "good enough."

The skiers made their own plans; where they were skiing, they would take ski lifts, not trains. I knew how my mom and Molly skied; they were in their sixties, but they still skied hard. Those two would start out skiing with the little Barlows—just a couple of warm-up runs. Then my mother and Molly would go off by themselves; they would find more challenging terrain, leaving the little Barlows to ski alone. John and Susan Barlow had told us they liked to ski on the gentler slopes. There was a train station and a gondola lift station in the village of Wengen; the stations were an easy walk from our hotel. At night, we would all meet for dinner in the hotel restaurant. But I wasn't paying attention to the lay of the land.

Our first full day in Wengen, everyone else made their plans and went off without me. I wrote all morning in my hotel room and finished the difficult chapter. I could go snowshoeing the next day, I was thinking. I put on my hiking boots and walked the wrong way—to the gondola lift station, not the train station. Then I had trouble understanding the stationmaster; either my German was awful or his Swiss German was hard for me, or both. I was hiking "oben"—if nothing else, the *above* word was understood. I would not walk *on* the train track but *beside* it. There were *two* stations between Wengen and the Kleine Scheidegg station. The stationmaster seemed to doubt I would get as far as Kleine Scheidegg—it was already the early afternoon. I think it was clear that I intended to take the train back to Wengen, but the reason why was beyond my bad German. At one or another station above Wengen, I would take the train down. You're not doing your knees a favor by hiking or snowshoeing down a mountain, but I couldn't explain this in German.

It was my first day hiking at altitude—I took it easy. What would be the harm of skiing with my mother? I was thinking. My determination not to ski was waning. Weren't the necessary rebellions of childhood and adolescence behind us? I'd asked the snowshoer. We could make my mom and the little Barlows so happy, if we skied with them. And the way ski resorts were treating snowshoers, it would be less of a hassle to go skiing. "I know, I know—and, in spite of ourselves, we do know how to ski," Elliot Barlow had said, sighing.

"It's your parents' *genre* you don't like, not their skiing—not anymore," I reminded the pretty Mr. Barlow. She really did love her parents—just not their *writing*—but it wasn't my intention to make her feel guilty for not skiing. It was something the snowshoer and I kept talking about. We'd made our point about the kind of exercise we preferred, but it wouldn't kill us to ski occasionally—would it?

The passing trains had blown the powdery snow off the railway bed. In the deeper snow, a footpath emerged and disappeared; for short stretches, the snow on the path was trodden down by hikers. There was a bridge, a narrow crossing, where I hoped I wouldn't meet a train. I don't remember a tunnel; I would have been afraid to enter a tunnel. Off one side of the cog railroad was a mountainside—a snow-covered forest, with glacial peaks above the timberline. Off the other side of the train line, I caught glimpses of skiers; occasionally, I could hear the skiers' voices, but I couldn't see them. They were ghost skiers. The railroad ran parallel to the piste. *This hike is pointless—I could be skiing,* I was thinking. Yet the climb felt good. It was an unseasonably warm day; the sun was hot. I was peeling off layers of clothes as I climbed, stuffing the clothes in my backpack. A train passed, without alarm or incident—I had plenty of room to get out of the way.

The stationmaster at the Allmend station greeted me cordially. As expected, but in a friendly fashion, he told me to "aufpassen" (to "watch out") for the Zug. (A *Zug* is a train.) I had a small map with me. The stationmaster was a helpful fellow; he volunteered to show me where my climb would get steeper. The next station was almost as high as Kleine Scheidegg, the stationmaster was explaining. *"Lawine!"* the stationmaster suddenly exclaimed, interrupting himself. In ski resorts in Austria and Switzerland, I'd learned the *avalanche* word. The stationmaster saw it before I did. A cap of icy snow broke free of the glacier above the forest; the snow made a whooshing sound, descending through the trees. We saw whole trees swept down the mountainside in the rush of snow. We were in no danger at the Allmend station. We watched the avalanche pass below us, at a right angle to the railway line. We couldn't see if the avalanche had enough momentum to cross the train tracks, or where it might have come in contact with a passing train—closer to Wengen than to the Allmend station, we could only guess. The stationmaster ran to his radio, inside the station. When he reappeared, he was pointing down the track toward Wengen; he spoke so quickly, I could understand only the *Zug* word. The avalanche had hit a train—I understood that much. I started jogging down the mountain; the railway bed was flattest between the two lines of track. My knees would feel it, but the altitude didn't affect me as much going down. I felt pretty sure that no one I knew would be on the train. Elliot Barlow was snowshoeing at Kleine Scheidegg; she wouldn't be taking a train back to Wengen till the end of the afternoon.

I was a late arrival at the scene of the accident. The avalanche had knocked three passenger cars off the train track. When I got there, most of the passengers had been evacuated from the derailed cars; there were more rescuers around than victims. The half-buried cars had fallen on their sides, where they slid down the railroad embankment, stopping on the ski slope. Skiers on the piste were the first rescuers on hand. The toppled train cars were visible from Wengen. Some villagers had hiked up the ski slope to help the skiers trapped inside the partially buried cars. There was a lot of bleeding, from facial cuts—from the flying skis. I saw blood in the snow, and lacerations on the faces of skiers who'd been cut by the sharp edges of the skis inside the derailed cars. I climbed up one of the cars lying on its side, just to be certain there was no one inside. Most of the train windows that were pressed against the snow of the ski slope were unbroken. I could see more broken windows on the sides of the train cars facing the sky. I was wondering if the first rescuers needed to break the windows to get inside; perhaps the train doors could be opened only from inside.

I heard the hysterical child, but I couldn't understand what he was saying. Not surprisingly, he was screaming in German. They were the last family to be rescued from the passenger cars that had been tipped over and half-buried, but the boy seemed to be saying there were more people in need of rescuing—more children, from what I could understand of the kid's German. The boy kept repeating the same things. A short, declarative sentence was easy to understand. "Man muss ihnen *helfen*!" the boy cried and cried; he was six or seven. His parents could not console him; the father had an ugly gash on the bridge of his nose, from a flying ski. "Someone should *help* them!" the boy had declared.

A rescuer was climbing out of a train car—the middle car, the one the kid kept pointing to. "Niemand . . . niemand . . ." the rescuer was repeating. "Nobody . . . nobody . . ."

The other sentences the kid kept screaming were longer or garbled together, or both. I could make out the *Fenster* word, meaning *window*, and something about "ihre kleinen Gesichter" ("their little faces"), which made me imagine children's faces.

The poor parents, I was thinking; they had to carry their skis and poles, and the child's skis and poles. And the father with the gashed and bleeding nose had to drag his hysterical son away from the wrecked train. They could have put on their skis and skied to the village, but the boy was too upset to ski. I watched the family slipping and sliding their way down the ski slope toward Wengen. The poor kid would have nightmares all night, I was imagining.

A medical emergency helicopter had landed on the piste. A pregnant woman on a stretcher was carried from the toppled train cars to the helicopter. She was being airlifted to a hospital near Interlaken. This was only a precaution, one of the rescuers explained to me; while the woman showed no signs of miscarrying, she'd been shaken up in the avalanche and she was frightened. When I got back to my hotel room, the news of the avalanche in Wengen was already on TV. It wasn't difficult to understand that no one was killed and there were no serious injuries. I even understood the human-interest part of the story: the pregnant woman and her unborn child were going to be okay. The news on television had been easier to understand than the hysterical boy.

My mom and Molly had a good day skiing. When they skied back to Wengen at the end of the day, they went right by the half-buried, derailed cars, wondering what had happened to the train. The snowshoer had heard about the avalanche; her train back to Wengen from Kleine Scheidegg was delayed. The derailed cars would be lying in the snow overnight, but someone had to move the locomotive and check the cogs between the rails.

My mother and Molly and I were sitting at our table in the hotel restaurant; we'd been wondering where Elliot and the little Barlows were when Elliot came to our table. She was alone, and she wouldn't sit down. Her parents had not returned to the hotel from skiing. "At their age, they usually stop skiing before the end of the day—I should have gone skiing with them," the little snowshoer said. She was agitated, and my mom tried to reassure her that everything was all right. The little Barlows were very social; they loved talking to strangers. They'd probably met some skiers their own age; they were just having a beer or a glass of wine, my mother was saying, when the family with the hysterical child came into the hotel restaurant. The mother and father were discussing the bandage on his nose, but they stopped talking when they saw me; they recognized me from the scene of the accident, politely greeting me in their reserved way. The boy also recognized me. The kid had calmed down, but he kept staring at me—as if he had more to say. "Germans," the snowshoer quietly said. Her German was so good, she could identify accents from incidental conversation. The German family was seated at an adjacent table, where a dinner roll captured the boy's attention; for the moment, he stopped staring at me.

I kept my voice down when I was telling Molly and my mom the drama of the German family at the site where the avalanche hit the train, both because I didn't want the German family to know I was talking about them and to entice Elliot Barlow to sit down with us at our table. The snowshoer was interested in the story; she finally sat down. "Man muss ihnen *helfen!*" I was whispering—telling them what the hysterical German kid kept repeating.

"Someone should *help* them!" Elliot had whispered back, translating for my mother and Molly.

"The boy thought there were people left behind on the train?" Molly asked me; she also whispered.

"The boy said something about 'their little faces'—it sounded like 'ihre kleinen Gesichter,' if I heard him right," I told the snowshoer, who was looking straight at the boy.

"Did he mean children's faces, sweetie?" my mom whispered to me.

That was when the German boy stopped playing around with the dinner roll. The kid was looking in our direction when he suddenly stared at the pretty Mr. Barlow, as if transfixed by her little face. This time, the kid was not hysterical; he was calm but trembling when he stood (without the dinner roll) beside his family's table, pointing to the snowshoer. "Ihre kleinen Gesichter waren wie *ihr* Gesicht!" the German boy said.

"Their little faces were like *her* face!" the little English teacher translated for us. "He means like *my* face," Elliot added, though what the boy meant was perfectly clear.

"Ich habe ihre kleinen Gesichter am Fenster gesehen," the boy was babbling to Mr. Barlow.

"I saw their little faces in the window," the little English teacher translated for us.

"Unter dem Zug!" the child cried assertively—as if no one had been listening to him. From the shocked expressions on his parents' faces, they hadn't. Elliot Barlow was taken aback.

"Under the train!" the little English teacher translated for us. She was standing again; she approached the boy at the German family's table. I heard the *Kinder* word (the word for *children*) in what the snowshoer asked the kid.

"Nein!" the boy said immediately, before he began to babble. He said more about the "Gesichter"—exactly what about the faces was hard for me to understand.

"They were not children's faces—the small faces were the faces of two old people, a man and a woman who were under the train," the snowshoer said to us. We could see she was crying. The German boy's mother and father were talking to her, but I couldn't understand what they were saying, or what Elliot Barlow said back to them; only the *Eltern* word, the word for *parents*, was clear.

The snowshoer was still crying when she explained everything to my mom and Molly and me. The German boy's mother and father hadn't understood what their hysterical son was saying. The little faces the child saw were outside the train, not inside it. The victims who'd been left behind weren't in the derailed train—they were under it. "I think your son saw my parents," the little English teacher had told the German boy's mother and father. It was what the snowshoer had said about the little Barlows before: they were thriller writers, drawn to disasters.

Elliot and I left Molly and my mom, and the German family, in the hotel restaurant. The two policemen met us in the lobby, after we'd put on our snowshoeing clothes. As Mr. Barlow had requested, the cops came with two extra flashlights for us. It seemed we waited forever for the two policemen to arrive. By the time the cops came to the hotel, Elliot and I had a pretty good grasp of the little Barlows' story; between us, we'd worked out the plot of what we imagined had befallen the writing team. The little English teacher and I were, respectively, a veteran reader of fiction and a dedicated fiction writer. Elliot imagined that his parents had decided to call it a day in the middle of the afternoon. They had been skiing back to Wengen; they were near the base of the mountain, a little above the gondola lift station, when they must have seen the start of the avalanche, when the mass of descending snow was still above the tree line. From the little Barlows' perspective—on the ski slope, with the railroad embankment between them and the avalanche—maybe it seemed safe to take a closer look. "Are you thinking they would have sidestepped up the embankment on their skis?" I asked Elliot.

"Not them. They would never let me sidestep—even as a child, I had to herringbone uphill," the snowshoer said. We imagined the little Barlows skiing off-piste, herringboning up the embankment, to get a better view of the avalanche on the other side of the cog railroad tracks—the thriller writers, drawn to disasters. "And then the train came, blocking their view of how much momentum the avalanche had maintained, coming through the trees," the snowshoer said. Elliot and I imagined we'd visualized everything, except for seeing their little faces pressed against the window of the train that crushed them—dragging the little Barlows down the embankment, back to the ski slope. It was hard to visualize that part.

My mother had wanted Molly to go with us. "You two should take Molly with you—she's an old ski patroller; she's seen her share of accidents," my mom had said.

It wasn't that the snowshoer didn't want Molly to come with us, but Elliot didn't like my mother to be left alone—my mom would worry more, alone, the little English teacher thought. "This isn't a rescue, Ray—I'm not hopeful of saving them. I think this is a done deal," the snowshoer said.

"I've seen some done deals, Elliot—the done deals are the worst ones," the night groomer tried to tell her. At first, Elliot wouldn't listen, but I kept begging her to take Molly with us.

By the time the two policemen got to the lobby, my mom and Molly—not to mention the German family—had finished their dinner and were waiting in the lobby with us. The ski patroller had already changed into her ski clothes. "I asked the police to bring only two extra flashlights," Elliot told Molly, who just patted her backpack. The snowcat operator was used to carrying her own flashlight. "I guess the ski patroller is coming with us, Adam," the snowshoer said. My mother didn't stop hugging the pretty Mr. Barlow until the cops came. The cop who did the talking told us to call him Werner. The silent policeman didn't tell us his name.

It was cold; the hard-packed snow on the piste was dry and made a squeaky sound under our boots. We couldn't keep up with the ski patroller; even in her sixties, Molly got to the derailed cars first. She knew the little Barlows were under the middle car; she'd climbed the car and lowered herself inside before we arrived at the wreck. On our trudge uphill, the snowshoer reiterated to the policemen the plot of his parents' death. The logic of the doomed thriller writers, when it came to avalanches, was clearly contrary to common sense, the little English teacher was telling the cops as we climbed. Werner, who'd seen the movie of *The Kiss in Düsseldorf*, deferred to the snowshoer. The little Barlows were experienced skiers; they should have been wary of avalanches, not drawn to take a closer look. Yet Elliot's parents were also experienced thriller writers; I thought I heard Elliot say to Werner that her parents were done in by their disaster genes, which I took to mean their writer genes (or words to that effect).

"Was denkst du?" I heard Werner ask his silent partner. ("What do you think?" he'd asked the nonspeaking cop.)

"Möglich," the one-word policeman replied. ("Possible," the minimalist cop had answered.)

We saw only the ski patroller's head and shoulders in the open door of the middle car. From the look on Molly's face, she'd found what she was looking for; the snowshoer had imagined everything truly. "You shouldn't see them, Elliot," Molly told her.

"I should have been skiing with them, Molly—I have to see them," the snowshoer said. The little Barlows had been afraid that AIDS would be the death of their gay son—later, of their trans daughter. During the AIDS pandemic, we were so afraid of the death of loved ones we imagined were vulnerable; there was a kind of forgetting or relaxing about all the other things that could kill us.

It wasn't that seeing their little faces pressed against the window of the train was worse than anything Elliot had imagined, although it was. And when we were all inside the train car, with our flashlights on their frozen faces, no one said (in English or in German) that the little Barlows hadn't *suffered*, for they surely had—if only for a few seconds. They'd died quickly; it wasn't that.

What would stay with the snowshoer was reflected in their little faces in those few terrible seconds: the thriller writers' recognition of the enormity of their miscalculation—how the writing team had failed to imagine a force of nature as capable of catastrophic damage as criminal or political intrigue. I saw only their fear of pain, or their actual but quickly passing pain, in the little Barlows' faces. I saw how their little noses were flattened against the window, and how their skin was whitened by the cold—as if their freezing blood had turned them the whitish gray of ice. But the little English teacher would read more into her parents' expressions than I could see. What the snowshoer saw had eluded me; she'd seen "a kind of crazy rapture, or at least relief," in their frozen faces, the snowshoer would later say. I saw no such *rapture* in the little Barlows' shocked expressions, but the little English teacher would later tell me what I'd missed. She'd seen (or had imagined) "the intense joy, or at least relief," parents feel when they know their children will outlive them. In the case of Elliot's parents, their *rapture* came from knowing that their only child would not predecease them or die with them. "For once, they were happy that I wasn't skiing with them," the snowshoer would say.

That frigid night, in the derailed car, we didn't talk much more than the policeman I'll call Möglich, because the one-word cop never divulged his name and "möglich" was all he'd said so far. In the freezing-cold car, our breathing fogged up the window where the snowshoer knelt and cried. The two policemen were patient with the pretty Mr. Barlow, who took her time saying goodbye to her parents. Their little faces were disappearing in the foggy window, which their loving daughter wiped clear with her ski glove.

"We should tell Ray—she'll be worrying more, as the time goes by," the ski patroller finally said.

"We'll tell her together, Molly," the snowshoer said. I watched them go down the mountain; even holding hands, those two knew how to walk on snow.

"You should go skiing with your mom, Kid," Molly had told me, before she and Elliot left me at the avalanche site with the two policemen. The cops wanted to double-check their EINTRITT VERBOTEN business, the KEEP OUT signs and the battery-powered lights in the area of the accident the police had cordoned off.

In my bad German, I tried to tell Werner and Möglich my thoughts. If the pretty Mr. Barlow had been skiing with her parents, she might have prevented them from climbing the embankment to get a better look at the avalanche. On the other hand, childhood was the truest teacher. As a child, the snowshoer had been taught to herringbone uphill; she might have herringboned up the embankment after them, or she would have led the way.

Werner didn't express his opinion. "Was denkst du?" Werner asked Möglich, as we were starting down the mountain—as if there was any doubt about what Möglich thought.

I imagined it was a fait accompli what Möglich would say. On matters of mayhem, whether they were man-made or elements of nature, the one-word policeman was a man of experience. "Möglich," Möglich said, after a thoughtful pause—pretending he had to think about it. Of course, everything was *possible*. Wasn't that usually the safest thing to say? And more than beauty is in the eye of the beholder, I was thinking, when I looked back—up the nighttime mountain—at the wrecked train, lying in the snow.

In the garish brightness of the battery-operated lights, the derailed train cars had a sepulchral glow. In the enveloping dark, there was no evidence of a railroad or the railway embankment—only the ascending ski slope, rising into a vast darkness. To someone seeing the avalanche site from this perspective, and for the first time, the derailed cars looked like a train that fell from heaven. The derailed train looked like a tomb, a holy shrine—not only because the little Barlows lay dead and buried under it. That frigid night, the wrecked train struck me as a sepulcher to all souls lost or killed in transit—as one day we all would be, I thought.

"Okay, I'll ski with her—I'll ask her to ski with me, I promise!" I shouted down the mountain, to those two contrasting figures. The seeming giantess, who was Molly, had her arm wrapped around the shoulders of the apparent child, who was the pretty Mr. Barlow. I could hear their voices, but they didn't hear me; those two were talking up a storm. For the moment, I'd forgotten I was going down the piste with the Swiss policemen.

"Sagen Sie das bitte noch einmal," Werner politely said. ("Please say that again.") I saw that the ski patroller and the snowshoer were almost back to the village; the lights of Wengen shone brightly below us. We were close enough to town that I thought I could make out the lights of our hotel— we would be there, in just a few minutes. In my bad German, there wasn't enough time for me to tell the Swiss policemen the story of what it meant for me to ski with my mother.

"Meine Mutter . . ." I began, in German. I told them how she'd taught me to ski, but how much I hated skiing, and then I stopped skiing with her. Now I believed I *should* ski with her, I said, but God knows what a mess I made of this (in German) or if the Swiss cops could understand me.

By now I knew that Werner wouldn't tell me his opinion, if he ever expressed one. "Was denkst du?" Werner asked Möglich again. By now I knew this was their routine, and I was tired of it. From the mother-and-son story I'd described—no matter how briefly, or how badly—the *possible* word simply didn't apply.

If Möglich replied with the *möglich* word, that would just be *bullshit*, I was thinking, but the taciturn policeman surprised me. Möglich spoke in English; he'd heard enough of my bad German to doubt my capabilities at speaking or understanding his language. "With our mothers, we are always alone," Möglich told me. I realize that this sounds like a translation. In German, what Möglich meant might have been clearer. But what he said was clear enough, and it still sounds true to me.

"There were two women with you, the big one and the small one who spoke German—which one was your mother?" Werner asked me. Taking his cue from Möglich, Werner was also speaking English.

Before I could answer Werner, Möglich interrupted us. The formerly one-word cop had become quite talkative. "There are *three* women with him, counting the one back at the hotel," Möglich pointed out to his partner. We were in Wengen, in the village; we were almost back at the hotel. Before I could tell them who my mom was, Werner wanted to know what Möglich thought.

"Was denkst du?" Werner asked Möglich.

This time, there was no hesitation. Möglich didn't need or pretend to think about it. "You're a lucky man—those three women love you," the Swiss policeman said. "But the one back at the hotel loves you the most—you should ski with that one," Möglich said.

"Ja, you should ski with her," Werner said, taking his cue from Möglich yet again. Thus it was decided: I would learn to ski, once more. You are never over your childhood, not until you are under the train—unter dem Zug.

40.

THE NIGHT OF THE SANTAS

There'd been another marine in the making in the Exeter wrestling room when I was wrestling there. Sam was our starter at 121 pounds, the year before I graduated. Everyone liked him. Sam was practically a marine before he came to Exeter; he'd been born on the Marine Corps base in Quantico. He went from Exeter to the U.S. Naval Academy and he did two tours of duty in Vietnam. We had our differences over the war, but we'd been good friends at Exeter and we remained good friends. A decorated hero, Sam was awarded the Silver Star, for valor in combat, and a Purple Heart—the one you get if you're wounded. He had a Bronze Star Medal, too; I forget what that one is for.

Sam and I weren't workout partners when we were teammates in the Exeter wrestling room; we were the wrong size to wrestle each other. Sam was a little guy. Elliot Barlow had been Sam's principal workout partner at Exeter. The Marine Corps would promote Sam to brigadier general in 1989, and to major general and lieutenant general in 1992. Sam would be promoted to general in 1995, the same year he became commandant of the Marine Corps. In my opinion, and in Mr. Barlow's, Sam was always very determined—both a positive guy and a fair-minded one. Sam was a far cry from the backup heavyweight without a name, the one we called *our* marine.

The natural 190-pounder was a prick of misery in comparison to "the general," as the snowshoer and I called Sam. "The good marine," we also called Sam, to distinguish him from the undersize heavyweight who was "the bad marine"—our other name for *our* marine, whose actual name was one that no one could remember in the monosyllabic utterances of life in boarding schools.

"Too many syllables to keep in mind. A New York mercantile family—originally, an English name," the little English teacher told me. She'd found a photo of the saturnine boy who was too big to make weight at 177 pounds, but too small to be a starting heavyweight. Elliot Barlow had her own collection of Exeter yearbooks, from every year she'd been a teacher and a coach at the academy. She found the unsmiling Emory Trowbridge in the back row, in the photo of the JV wrestling team. Gloom appeared to be Emory's constant companion. Was a perpetual pessimism characteristic of the Trowbridge family, perhaps inherent in all Trowbridges, or was Emory's gloominess entirely his own?

"Our marine hasn't changed much, has he?" the pretty Mr. Barlow asked me, when we looked at the small heavyweight in the JV wrestling team photo. Emory Trowbridge's hatred had been restrained even then, even as a teenager. No wonder no one could remember him. Emory Trowbridge hadn't done anything; maybe, as a teenager, he'd also refrained from saying what he thought. The snowshoer and I knew that our marine had overcome his youthful reticence to express himself. We could only guess that being in the Marine Corps had given him more confidence; maybe the experience had shaped, or had hardened, his political views. He'd told us (bitterly, but without anger) the Marine Corps was his home. Yet in his sullen standoffishness, even in the JV wrestling team photo, our backup heavyweight didn't look like a team player. To Elliot and me, our marine had behaved like a born loner.

"Tell me how a loner is likely to fare in the Marine Corps. We should ask the general about our marine," the snowshoer had said. But we let it go, or we were too busy—or we didn't want to bother Sam. The general, we knew, was busier than we were, and we weren't imagining we would see our marine again.

Mr. Barlow was busier as a copy editor than she'd ever been; she was also the sole trustee of her late parents' estate, not only their real estate but the little Barlows' literary holdings. It was in the realm of the little English teacher's expertise to choose a biographer for the departed writing team, but Elliot was over her head as a landlord. For now, she'd been advised, it was more profitable for her to rent the little Barlows' ski chalet in St. Anton and their pied-à-terre in Vienna than it would be to sell them. On the other hand, the snowshoer said, she was told she should sell the apartment on East Sixty-fourth Street, but she didn't. Notwithstanding her conviction that she would never be a real New Yorker, the pretty Mr. Barlow said she was too busy to think about moving somewhere else.

My mother and Molly wanted the snowshoer to move to Manchester, but Nora and Em (and Elliot herself) had made fun of me for moving to

Manchester. "I guess you're really serious about writing all the time, kiddo, because I don't know what else you're going to do in Vermont," Nora said.

Em wrote me that my moving to Vermont amounted to my "consenting to an arranged marriage"; Em was kidding, but not entirely. Everyone knew I'd agreed to meet Grace, and that Grace was my mom's idea. I still hadn't met Grace, but my meeting her was as much in the offing as my going skiing with my mother. And everyone knew I'd stopped seeing Wilson, which had also been my mom's idea—not that anyone really liked Wilson. "Not even Wilson liked Wilson, but you know your mother is setting you up to fall in love with Grace—and you know I love your mom," Em wrote me.

The snowshoer, ever a good stepfather, teased me a little. "I said you should ski with your mother, not move in with her. You're almost fifty, Adam, a little old to live with your mom," the snowshoer said. She was just teasing me; Elliot knew I was looking for a place of my own in Vermont. I was staying with my mother and Molly until something turned up. There were some brand-new houses for sale in Manchester—large, empty houses that had been built on spec. I'd thought about renting one of the spec houses that hadn't been sold, but the Realtor forewarned me they would still be showing the house to prospective buyers, and it was an unfurnished house. I had no furniture, befitting a vagabond.

"Molly and I will get you what you need for furniture, sweetie. When you buy some land and build your own house, the furniture that we get for you can go in your own house," my mother said. That was when I realized my mom was imagining my moving to Vermont for the long haul; she'd already been looking at land for sale. Molly was no pantomimist. Em would have been clearer, but the look Molly gave me was clear enough: my mom didn't tell Molly everything she was up to. "I saw an uphill piece of land, off Dorset Hill Road. If you cut down some trees, sweetie, you could see the top of Bromley from there," my mom said. I wondered how *uphill* she meant, and why seeing the top of Bromley Mountain would necessarily be of interest to me. "So you can see how hard the wind is blowing, sweetie. Then you'll know how to dress, for skiing," my mother told me. As for the *uphill* part about the land for sale: "You should have all-wheel drive if you're going to live anywhere in Vermont, sweetie."

Molly tried to say I should wait and see if I was going to like skiing—that is, before I bought a piece of land with a view of Bromley Mountain. "As I recall, Ray, Adam didn't much care for skiing the last time he tried it," the ski patroller said.

"Don't be a know-it-all, Molly," my mom said. She had the highest expectations for my moving to Vermont, a little like her expectations for my meeting Grace.

"Ray, let Adam meet Grace—let *them* decide if they want to go out," the trail groomer had told my mother, who was buying me ski clothes before it started to snow. "Your mom is not one to doubt herself, Kid," Molly reminded me.

"It's kind of bad timing, sweetie—that you're leaving New York and moving here, when Grace lives in New York. If you know what I mean," my mother said, which was simultaneously clear and mystifying. Given all the ballyhoo about Grace, I certainly remembered she worked in publishing; I knew she'd started as an editorial assistant, one of the few who'd been promoted and was actually working as an editor and a publisher. Of course I remembered that Grace had grown up in Manchester, and she'd learned to ski at Bromley. I knew her family lived in town; I'd been told she was good about coming home to see her parents. It was the *bad timing* part of my moving to Manchester that was mystifying to me. Molly had to explain my mom's logic.

My mother had first imagined my meeting Grace when I lived in New York. Then I would have loved living in New York, with Grace, Molly explained. My mom had to rethink how the rest of my life (with Grace) would go, now that I'd moved to Manchester before I met Grace. I asked Molly if my mother had imagined where our children would go to school—that is, if I was a writer in Vermont and Grace kept her publishing job in New York. The trail groomer laughed. "Your mom hasn't imagined herself as a grandmother, Kid—she's got all she can handle, managing your life and mine," Molly said. The ski patroller and I knew how managerial my mother could be.

In 1989, my mom was sixty-seven; Molly, who would only say she was "a year or two older," was almost seventy. The night groomer said her birthday was "nobody's business"—she refused to celebrate it. But my mother knew exactly how old Molly was. Little Ray also knew the ski business.

"Ski patrollers don't last as long as ski instructors, sweetie," my mom said, in her matter-of-fact way. I didn't realize, at first, what kind of longevity my mother had in mind. Sensing my concern for Molly's mortality, my mom explained. Trail groomers were typically men; at Bromley, grooming was mostly a night job. As a night groomer, Molly usually had an eight-hour shift—from when the ski lifts closed at 4 p.m. till midnight. When one of the groomers got sick, Molly would take an occasional night shift, but she'd switched to ski patrol when my mom got tired of waiting up to have a beer with her after midnight. As a patroller, Molly had started out as a strong skier who'd worked hard on her emergency first aid. Molly was a quick thinker who worked well with others; she'd been "the best toboggan handler on a black-diamond run on an icy day when there's an injured adult skier on the trail," my mother said, in her breathless way. In my mom's opinion, Molly was still one of the better toboggan handlers. Some of the older patrollers were "embarrassing," my mom said. "They shouldn't be skiing in public with their patrol coats on, sweetie—let them put the Band-Aid on a crying kid in the first-aid room, or let them calm down the distraught mother," my mother said. She didn't want Molly to end up in the first-aid room with the crying kids and the distraught moms, or even end up being the patroller who was dispatched to look for the lost kid—instead of being the go-to toboggan handler the old night groomer (for now) still was. "That's why I'm recommending Molly as a ski instructor, sweetie—ski instructors get better with age, especially at teaching beginners. Molly can be most effective with adult beginners, like those male jocks from other sports—they're the ones who get hurt or they kill someone else, the first time they go skiing," my mom told me. "It starts happening with ski patrollers around seventy, or a little older—that's when they start losing it, sweetie."

"There's a right way and a wrong way to put an oxygen tank together, Kid—I still do it the right way, but your mom thinks my days as a patroller are numbered," Molly said. I knew there wasn't a lot of crossover among the personnel on ski patrol and in the ski school, but Molly was beloved at Bromley; she could do, or she'd already done, everything on the mountain. She'd filled in as a lift operator—when somebody had to, or nobody else would do it. "Not too tough a job, Kid—there's a reason the lifties get minimum wage," I remember her telling me. At Bromley, the *lifties* were often older locals—men with nothing better to do, waiting for their Social Security checks to come in, Molly told me. "One day, Kid, most of our lifties will be Southern Hemisphere skiers, college kids on their summer break—you just tell them what their job is, and nobody will have to fill in for them," Molly said.

I had no doubt that the former ski patroller would be a formidable ski instructor. Molly would definitely get the attention of what my mother called the *adult beginners*; I had a hard time imagining *those male jocks from other sports* ignoring Molly. "And if you still don't like skiing with me, sweetie, we both know someone who can probably improve your skiing," my mom said. That was when I realized there was an objective to my skiing with my mother—namely, if she couldn't *improve* my skiing, maybe Molly could.

"What's wrong with being a full-time fiction writer, kiddo, is you spend more time with the characters you make up than you do with the people you already know and you should have figured out," Nora told me. I knew Em was being careful not to nod or shake her head; the issue of being a full-time fiction writer was a tricky one for Emily MacPherson.

Em knew the Gallows Lounge wasn't the only comedy club that was looking over its shoulder. At the end of 1989, we didn't realize that political correctness was coming; we just knew there was a whole lot of second-guessing going on. The second-guessers who ran the Gallows were like squirrels on the ground, too far from the nearest tree. What used to be funny wasn't funny anymore—that was all the second-guessers knew.

Nora was fifty-four. "All I know is, I'm getting angrier—not funnier," Nora said. Em nodded, just once; she was so fast, I almost missed it.

It was December 8, 1989—a Friday night in New York. I remember the usual guys in the Santa suits at the Gallows; at that time of year, there were always some motley Santas in the audience. "Working Santas, for the most part," the snowshoer said optimistically.

"I've seen other kinds of Santas out there," Nora observed ominously. The Santas in the Christmastime audience had always creeped out Em. Among the fake beards, and what looked like real ones, there were some scary Santas at the Gallows.

"I've seen Santas you wouldn't hire—you wouldn't let your kids near some of these Santas' laps," Nora said.

There'd been a mass shooting in Montreal two days before, and Nora was all worked up about it. Fourteen women had been murdered at an engineering school affiliated with the University of Montreal. The women had been separated from the men; they'd been singled out, purposely targeted. The killer had had a semiautomatic rifle and a hunting knife; he'd shot and killed thirteen women, and had stabbed another woman to death, before turning the gun on himself. Obviously, the École Polytechnique massacre was an anti-feminist attack; the gender of the victims and the killer's remarks during the attack had made this clear. The killer had said he was "fighting feminism"; it bothered him that the women students were "going to be engineers." In the media, there were denials of the anti-feminism motive—regardless of what the killer said. "You're all a bunch of feminists.

I hate feminists," the killer had told the women students, before he started shooting. It was a bad choice of material for *Two Dykes, One Who Talks*. The École Polytechnique massacre would go over like a lead balloon in Nora and Em's "The News in English."

Em did her best backstage; she tried to discourage Nora from mentioning the massacre. Em's backstage pantomime convinced me, but not Nora. Em's humming of "O Little Town of Bethlehem" was the completely wrong accompaniment to her pantomime of misogynist violence against women—this was Em's point. It was Christmastime in New York, for Christ's sake; there were a bunch of Santas in the house. And what Nora wanted to vent about wasn't the least bit funny. But Nora didn't buy it. When Nora was politically engaged, she was onstage to inflame, not to entertain.

Talk about bad timing—you never saw so many malcontent Santas. "The News in English" had never been such a downer. Yes, it's easy to say now that it was prescient of Nora to say there would be more misogynist violence against women. There were already advocates for so-called men's rights who claimed that feminism was responsible for *provoking* violence against women, Nora was saying; Nora said this would lead to *condoning* violence against women. Poor Em, I was thinking. There were not a lot of ways for Em to pantomime being paralyzed by fear.

Even the snowshoer seemed distracted, her attention wandering. The pretty Mr. Barlow kept turning around in her chair. She was wary of one of the Santas, a tall one with long arms. He was standing at the back of the lounge, at the farthest distance from the Gallows stage. He looked too lean to be a convincing Santa, although he'd brought a bag of gifts—a long sack, slung over his shoulder. The gift bag wasn't exactly brimming or overstuffed with presents. Like the standing Santa himself, his bag looked a little lean on contents. This Santa looked like a marauder—like he was stealing stuff, giving nothing away.

"Not a very kid-friendly Santa—not one of your 'working Santas,' I guess," I whispered to the snowshoer.

"Not a working Santa," the snowshoer whispered back. She kept turning to look at him.

"Some guy in Montreal kills fourteen women in an engineering school, because he doesn't want women to be engineers. Don't tell me he wasn't hunting women—he killed only women!" Nora was shouting. It was hard to watch Em—her gyrations signifying someone trying not to get shot, but she got shot every time. It made some Santas cringe to watch Em die. Other

Santas, and not only Santas, were walking out. "The next thing you know, guys will be killing us because we won't put out for them," Nora was saying. I saw that a Santa sitting near us had fallen asleep, or he had died—his chin on his chest, his beard askew, the pom-pom on his stocking cap unmoving. Em had stopped moving, too. This was not her pantomime for paralyzed by fear; Em just wasn't moving. *How is Em supposed to pantomime being killed for not putting out?* I was wondering. I'd seen people in the audience walk out on "The News in English" before. Pissing people off just meant you were pushing the limits of what was funny—that was what a comedy club was for. But on the night of the Santas, the walkouts weren't angry; they were bored. I'd not seen *Two Dykes, One Who Talks* lose an audience at the Gallows before.

I knew Nora had been putting herself down a lot lately. She'd agreed with the ACT UP members who questioned her participation in the group, especially at the demonstrations. Nora loved ACT UP, but now she saw her presence as a distraction or a disruption. What Nora loved about ACT UP was the specificity of the group's cause and purpose. Nora was always hard on herself, but now she put down her kind of "protest comedy," as she called it. She was "too broad, too all over the place," she said. Nora wasn't a nihilist or an anarchist, but in the world outside the Gallows Lounge, Nora was perceived as nothing but a rabble-rouser, and she knew it. On the night of the Santas, Nora also knew she wasn't funny—not even at the Gallows. If you were no more than a rabble-rouser, you were just plain boring at the Gallows.

I knew it was not Nora's best subject for comedy: those men who feel entitled to have women put out for them. Nora had known boys like that, at Exeter. On weekends or on holidays, when she'd come home to the academy campus—both when she was in boarding school at Northfield and when she was a college student at Mount Holyoke—Nora had been hit on by those cocksure boys who presumed she would be grateful for the attention (for *any* attention). Nora was never pretty; to many men, she was too big, or too masculine. Yet there were certain younger boys who were attracted to her. I suppose they saw an undeniable voluptuousness in the way Nora was too heavy, and you know the kind of arrogant young men I mean—the ones who knew they were good-looking, and that Nora wasn't.

I understood what Nora looked like to good-looking young men who'd been successful with less-than-attractive women. She looked like she would be *a wild ride*, as one of my wrestling teammates told me, not knowing Nora was my cousin.

The presumption that she would be easy got to Nora. "Are you kidding me?" she would ask the pretty boys who hit on her at Exeter. Or, if Nora was not in the mood to be nice: "Keep your pecker in your pants, pretty boy, or you could lose it."

Those good-looking boys weren't used to being rejected. Nora was well acquainted with the *dyke* word—it was invariably what those arrogant young men called Nora when she turned them down. Instead of paying attention to *Two Dykes, One Who Talks*, I was thinking about where the *dyke* word came from in my cousin Nora's life. I was proud of Nora for standing up for herself, and for the good use she'd made of the *dyke* word. Wouldn't Nora have the last laugh on those hateful boys? I was hoping.

I would later feel terrible for daydreaming at what would be Nora and Em's last performance onstage at the Gallows. On the night of the Santas, when I wasn't daydreaming, I was whispering with Elliot Barlow. Em would one day write me and ask me what we'd been whispering about. Surely Nora had noticed us whispering, if Em had. Both Mr. Barlow and I would feel terrible about our whispering, but we should have done something about the Santa standing in the back of the lounge—not just whisper about him. A kind of evil magic, like a spell, seemed to emanate from the tall Santa with the long arms and the skinny sack; there was something strangely witchlike about him. "Maybe he's a witch in a Santa suit—that's a broomstick in the gift bag," I whispered to the snowshoer.

"Not a witch. You don't recognize him, do you?" the pretty Mr. Barlow whispered. Then, of course, I did—the unfocused vacancy of his multiple hatreds came back to me.

"Our marine . . ." I'd only started to whisper, but the snowshoer outwhispered me.

"Not a marine. I spoke to Sam—I was going to tell you. The general says our backup heavyweight was never in the Marine Corps. Emory Trowbridge didn't serve in any other branch of the armed forces, either," the snowshoer said. That was a sizable deceit to process in one continuous whisper, and just then the sleeping Santa sitting near us fell sideways into the lap of the woman seated next to him. This got a laugh, a small one, but it was more of a laugh than Nora had been getting. The woman grabbed hold of the sleeping Santa's head, shoving him away from her, but his beard, wig, and stocking cap ended up in her hands. They were both indignant about their sudden contact.

"What? Why'd you do that?" the startled Santa asked the woman next to him, as if she'd assaulted him. This got a somewhat larger laugh, but the woman holding Santa's beard, wig, and stocking cap, was clearly at a loss for words. Not Nora.

"If you're going to go down on someone, you should take your Santa stuff off first," Nora said to the Santa who'd been asleep. This got the biggest laugh Nora would get that night; it caused enough of a disruption for those people who'd been dying to leave to make a break for the exit or the washrooms, or at least bolt for the bar. In the chaos, or in her own harsh judgment of her less-than-riveting performance, Nora didn't try to bring the audience back; she knew she'd lost them. Besides, Em was giving her the X sign—when Em's index fingers were crossed, that was as clear to Nora as the *no* word.

That was when I heard the snowshoer say, "Shit—not a broomstick!" She didn't whisper. I should never have looked away from our marine, who was not a marine. When I looked again at the back of the lounge now, the small heavyweight had removed the rifle from the long sack slung over his shoulder—not a gift bag, I was thinking, when I saw the tall Santa take aim, sighting down the barrel.

We would later read that there was nothing special about the inexpensive gun—a bolt-action .30-06 Springfield with a magazine that held four rounds. We would learn that it was Emory Trowbridge's intention to shoot Em first; he'd written in a notebook that he wanted Nora to know Em was dead before he shot Nora. After that, if he had time, he would shoot Mr. Barlow. The fourth bullet was for Emory Trowbridge himself. Not knowing his diary entries, I saw Trowbridge take aim at Em—that was all I knew.

In the dispersing crowd, most of the remaining audience were waiting for the next act, whether they were sitting or standing. From the stage, Nora and Em had the clearest view of the Santa with the long arms and the rifle. They had no reason to recognize Emory Trowbridge; they'd not been at Coach Dearborn's memorial service. I saw that Em had found a new way to panto-mime being paralyzed by fear—Em knew where the gun was pointing. Nora knew, too—Nora never hesitated. Nora couldn't have looked paralyzed by fear if she tried. It looked almost like a dance move—the way Nora threw her hips into Em, knocking Em to her knees. (How those two loved to dance!) Then Nora stood in front of Em, completely blocking her from the shooter. Notwithstanding the backup heavyweight's plans, he began by killing Nora; his first shot hit her in her heart.

There was only one shot, but pandemonium broke out and I lost sight of the stage. I knew Nora was down; I assumed Em was down on the stage with

her. I'd seen the snowshoer drop to all fours before the first shot was fired.
I knew she wasn't taking cover. Mr. Barlow could move fast on all fours. I
watched her make her way through the ankles in the crowd, navigating the
legs of chairs and tables. I quickly lost sight of her, but I'd seen where she was
headed—toward the shooter. I could have tracked the little English teacher's
progress through the panicked audience, the drinks spilled on tables, the
toppled chairs—the suddenly falling people who tripped over the snowshoer,
not expecting someone so small to be scampering on all fours—but I didn't
dare take my eyes off Emory Trowbridge. He was watching me, too, but I had
nowhere to hide; there were people cowering under the nearby tables, where
there was no room for me.

The long-armed Santa was scanning the stage—he could see me, but I
knew he was looking for Em. *Stay down, stay with Nora*, I was wishing for Em.
I knew the snowshoer would come in low, level with the tall Santa's ankles,
but there was a wide-open space where the shooter was standing—there was
no one near him. It was too big an area for Elliot Barlow to be exposed, I
was worrying. Why didn't Emory Trowbridge just shoot me—what was he
waiting for? I was wondering. I'd watched him eject the shell from the first
bullet. I'd seen him slide the bolt back and forward; I knew his second shot
was in the chamber.

That night at the Gallows, I held my arms straight up, above my head; I
waved my hands at Emory Trowbridge. I wanted the backup heavyweight to
look at me, only at me. If he was looking at me, maybe he wouldn't see the
snowshoer coming—that was all I was hoping for. Trowbridge held the rifle
butt tight to his shoulder, but he wasn't sighting down the barrel. His inde-
cision made no sense to me. He'd obviously planned this, but he'd stopped
shooting. He definitely saw me; he was looking at me, with such loathing,
when he suddenly turned his attention to the stage. We both did. People
screamed when they saw Em standing onstage, not the same kind of scream
as the caterwaul caused by the first gunshot. Em was covered with blood.
It was Nora's blood, I knew. The shooter surely knew whose blood it was.
Trowbridge had wanted to shoot Em first; he'd taken aim at Em, before Nora
put herself in harm's way. Yet now, when Em just stood onstage, as still as a
statue, the backup heavyweight hesitated. Did Trowbridge hesitate because
Em was beseeching him to shoot her?

Em was a pro at pantomime; nothing could have been clearer. She was
done with doing paralyzed by fear; she held out her arms to the shooter,

palms up, the pose of a supplicant. *Shoot me*, the pantomimist was begging Emory Trowbridge. *You killed the love of my life—please kill me, too.* That's what Em was saying. I started doing jumping jacks, like crazy. "Fuck you, Trowbridge!" I called to him. I just knew it would have killed me if he shot Em. "You were never in the Marine Corps—you never did anything!" I reminded him. But the way he looked back and forth, between Em and me, I knew I was no match for the pantomimist; she was better at beseeching, hands down.

People later said it was the sudden commotion at the back of the lounge that *unnerved* the shooter. I don't know; people later said a lot of things. The shooter looked unnerved to me before the pretty Mr. Barlow was anywhere near him. People said the small, older woman on all fours would have unnerved anyone, but I saw how the shooter had hesitated; his hatreds had confounded him. Nothing in his life had gone according to plan. Yes, Elliot was fast on all fours, but I doubt she was *moving sideways like a crab* (as people later said) when she suddenly scuttled out from under a table. I'm not saying the shooter wasn't taken aback by the snowshoer, but the small heavyweight had been unable to make up his mind about shooting Em or me. For a split second, he was then confronted by a third choice. Mr. Barlow (as a woman) had cupped his heels in her small, strong hands.

"I don't know why he didn't shoot me in the back of my head," the snowshoer later said. "I'd heard only one shot—I knew two of you were still alive, not which two," the little English teacher would tell Em and me. But Emory Trowbridge had hesitated too long. Trowbridge was a man of so many hatreds, he couldn't choose among them. In the sudden commotion at the back of the lounge, all Trowbridge seemed to know for certain was about the bullet he'd been saving for himself. From Em's and my perspective—begging, as we were, for the tall Santa to shoot us—we were caught off guard when the shooter shot himself. We hadn't known there was a reason or a purpose for the tall Santa to have such long arms, not until we saw him put the end of the rifle barrel in his mouth—so seamlessly, without a hitch, we knew he'd practiced this part before.

By today's standards, the Gallows Lounge shooting wasn't much of a shooting—only two shots were fired. I saw just enough to know that Em and the snowshoer were safe. The tall Santa's stocking cap was blown off—also his white wig, which was spattered with blood. Of course there was more of a mess, but I saw little of it. Long after the fact, there would be a magazine article about the other Santas in the lounge that night—how they *felt* about being Santa, if their *feelings* for Christmas had changed—but I didn't care how the other Santas were affected by the homicidal and suicidal Santa. Onstage, where I went to hold Em in my arms, I could see how Em would forever be affected—*please kill me, too,* her eyes, her hands, her whole body was still pleading.

41.

STARTING SOMETHING

From the stage, Em and I saw how the snowshoer had persevered; her small, strong hands still had hold of the killer's heels. The force of the second shot had blown Trowbridge backward; his head wound left a smear of blood on the wall of the lounge, where he slid sideways as he fell, dragging the little English teacher after him. The pretty Mr. Barlow's hand strength has been accounted for; when she was dragged across the floor at the back of the lounge, she'd not given up her grip on the shooter. One newspaper report was syndicated to two hundred (or more) other papers—Elliot Barlow was called "the only hero." She was sixty, she was four feet nine, yet she was the only one who confronted the Gallows Lounge killer—she went after him, on all fours. Eventually, when Emory Trowbridge's diaries revealed that Elliot Barlow had been an intended victim, Mr. Barlow would be outed. In one entry, the brave trans woman would be called *not an actual woman but a former wrestler*, and Trowbridge wrote worse things about her in other entries. While some journalists didn't hesitate to call the Gallows Lounge shooting *a hate crime*—in more than one instance, *a singling out of sexual minorities*—other journalists categorized the killing as *part of a widespread societal misogyny*. There would be some nonsense about *a commando-minded murder-suicide*—in which the killer targets a specific group, usually in a public space—but the biggest bullshit would be perpetrated by the Trowbridge family psychiatrist. The psychiatrist said that Emory's *primary motivation* was suicide—specifically, *a homicide-suicide strategy* that entailed killing himself after killing others. The psychiatrist concluded that this was a sign of *a serious personality disorder*. It's impossible to know what Nora would have said about this assessment, or how Em might have pantomimed the disorder.

There was no actual suicide letter—only the diary entries in Trowbridge's notebooks. Criminal-justice officials decided that a public inquiry or extensive public discussion of the Gallows Lounge shooting would cause pain to the families and could lead to more violence against sexual minorities. Speaking as Nora's most immediate family, Henrik had not expressed any pain; he was "estranged" from his cousin, the Republican congressman wanted everyone to know. Henrik had mentioned Nora's "left-wing political radicalism" as the cause of his estrangement.

Emory Trowbridge's father wanted everyone to know he was "estranged" from his son. "His mother is entirely to blame—Emory was a mama's boy," was all the divorced dad had to say.

Emory's mom said she had worried that Emory would "hurt himself." She believed Emory suffered from "attachment disorder—due to his being abandoned by his bad dad," the mom said.

Notwithstanding the father's estrangement and Emory's sense of abandonment, Emory Trowbridge had been provided for by his parents; he'd been completely supported by his divorced mom and dad since the backup heavyweight's time at Exeter. He spent four years at the academy, but Trowbridge didn't graduate; he'd made so few friends among his fellow students, and was so unmemorable to his teachers, no one noticed the absence of his unsmiling face at commencement. He'd always been borderline antisocial, but in the spring term of his senior year, he'd stopped going to classes and he wouldn't speak when spoken to; he was sent home for nonperformance and psychiatric evaluation. His teachers, the dean, the school psychiatrist, the faculty who had dorm duty in Emory Trowbridge's dormitory—they knew that Emory left school before graduation. The rest of us never noticed his absence. How would we know that the backup heavyweight had just pretended to apply to college, or that his only job had been befriending cows?

Trowbridge had tried to enlist in the army, but he was rejected. Like me, he was reclassified 4-F. He'd not tried to enroll in another branch of the armed services. More surprising to the snowshoer and me was that Trowbridge had lived (for almost thirty years) in a trailer on a piece of land his parents purchased from a dairy farmer in Stratham—on the outskirts of Exeter. The dairy farmer said Trowbridge had been a good neighbor, on the grounds that he was considerate of the cows. Emory's thoughtfulness on behalf of the cows was demonstrated when he constructed a firing range on his property. Not wanting to disturb the cows, Trowbridge had asked the dairy farmer first about where the gravel pit should go, and in which direction he should shoot.

For twenty-eight years, Emory Trowbridge was considerate and kind only to cows. In exchange for his parents' continuing support, Trowbridge agreed to come to New York on a regular basis to see the family psychiatrist. Over the years, in his frequent visits to the city, Trowbridge developed his obsessive dislike of the Gallows—his hatred of *Two Dykes, One Who Talks*, in particular. For how long, and how intently, had he been stalking Nora and Em? The press coverage of the Gallows Lounge shooting was unclear. As for what Trowbridge wrote in his diaries, there was no narrative progression; the entries were undated. What stood out were his diatribes against women and *queers*; Trowbridge believed that women and *sexual weirdos* were receiving *preferential treatment*. My mother and Molly were mentioned, *among the dykes*, and Elliot Barlow was referred to (interchangeably) as *the lightweight in women's clothes* and *the cross-dresser*. The media cited the last-minute nature of Trowbridge's written plans for the Gallows Lounge shooting. More forethought went into his memorizing the names of the cows, and his detailed observations of the milking process. And there was the small heavyweight's careful account of his target practice in the gravel pit; according to the dairy farmer, the shooting was a regular occurrence. The dairy farmer insisted that his cows were not disturbed by the gunfire.

But why had Emory Trowbridge wanted to live in a trailer on the outskirts of Exeter for almost thirty years? Mr. Barlow, who was more observant than most, never recognized the natural 190-pounder among the spectators at the home wrestling matches, yet for more than a decade, Trowbridge didn't miss a match. The backups in a wrestling lineup are often unnoticed, and Trowbridge was more unrecognizable than most. No one saw him when he was watching all those wrestling matches; no one knew when he stopped attending, or why he stopped.

Trowbridge's hatred of Mr. Barlow began before the little English teacher's transition to a woman. Elliot Barlow had been among the first on the faculty to advocate for coeducation at Exeter. The backup heavyweight with the long arms stopped attending the home wrestling matches after girls were admitted to the academy. Trowbridge wrote in a notebook that he couldn't concentrate on the wrestling—"not with all the girls around." Yet this unwelcome distraction, purportedly caused by coeducation at Exeter, didn't stop Trowbridge from attending the girls' soccer or field-hockey games in the fall; the girls' basketball games, or their swimming and diving, in the winter; the girls' softball games, or their track meets, in the spring. Wrestling was a winter sport, but Trowbridge became a steadfast spectator in all three seasons of athletics at Exeter; his hatred of seeing *all the girls* at his old school somehow compelled him to scrutinize them. Emory Trowbridge wrote derogatory things in his diaries about the girls he watched playing sports. Had Trowbridge been stalking the girl students at the academy, in the obsessive way he'd watched Nora and Em at the Gallows? What was written about Emory Trowbridge was largely speculative; his motives remained murky. Yet, in the media coverage of the Gallows Lounge shooting, there was more about Trowbridge than there was about Nora.

The New York Times was not Nora's friend. The paper condemned the Gallows Lounge shooting and duly noted the "exceptional valor" of Elliot Barlow, but there was more than a whiff of reproach in the way the writer for the *Times* characterized Nora and Em's "incendiary antics"—their "purposeful vulgarity."

Elsewhere in New York, there was some love expressed for the Gallows; there was notably more love for *Two Dykes, One Who Talks*. Nora had been interviewed in *Rolling Stone*, where the Two Dykes were praised for their "political prescience."

The Village Voice pointed out the noticeable lack of a security presence on that Friday night at the Gallows Lounge. When the shooting started, the bouncer went out on the sidewalk—ostensibly, to inform the security guard of the trouble inside. One of the bartenders had already called the cops. It was unexplained why the security guard stayed on the sidewalk. To prevent people from entering the club until the police arrived or the shooting stopped? That Friday night, a spokesperson for the Gallows couldn't confirm if the guard had been armed. All the idiot management would say was that sometimes the security guard had a gun, sometimes not. "We know," the writer for the *Voice* would write. Of the New York media covering popular culture, the *Voice* and *Rolling Stone* had been alone in paying tribute to Damaged Don when he was gunned down in a parking lot in Montana for singing "Goin' Back to Great Falls" to a Reaganite.

"Don's only friends are my friends," I remember Nora saying, with Em nodding her head off. "Just wait. When someone shoots me, the *Voice* and *Rolling Stone* will be my only friends, too," Nora said, with Em shaking her head and punching her. It was just talk—just Nora being Nora—but I remember that Em was in tears.

After the Gallows Lounge shooting, what was scary to me was that Em didn't cry at all. Of course we expected that Em, being Em, wouldn't speak, but Em didn't emote, and we knew she was an emoter. Em didn't show a single emotion—no acting out, not one gesture. Em was expressionless; she barely breathed. The snowshoer and I never left her alone, except when she went to the bathroom.

It was a weekend in December, in the ski season. The Gallows Lounge shooting had happened on a Friday night; my mother and Molly couldn't come to New York till the following Monday, but Molly gave me an earful on the phone. "Get Em, and all her stuff, out of the apartment she shared with Nora—leave the guns, Kid. Your mom and I will take the guns, and Nora's things, back to Vermont," Molly told me. I explained to Molly that I'd already moved most of my clothes from the snowshoer's apartment to Vermont, and everyone agreed that Em should move in with Mr. Barlow. I'd left only some socks and underpants in a chest of drawers—in the smaller of the snowshoer's two bedrooms. I told Molly that I'd wrapped the .357 Magnum in a pair of underpants I didn't like; the bullets were in a pair of socks. "We'll take that gun and the bullets back to Vermont, too—even your ugly underpants, Kid. That'll be Em's chest of drawers now," Molly said. I got the picture. Em would sleep with Elliot, or with me; we wouldn't let her sleep alone, just go to the bathroom by herself.

That was when my mother got on the phone; she must have been listening to Molly's part of our conversation. Little Ray wanted to remind me what happened when she'd asked Nora to be a bridesmaid. "I better not leave Em alone," Nora had said. "She gets a little strange in a crowd when she's not with me."

"Don't leave Em alone, sweetie—especially not in a crowd," my mom told me.

"He knows, Ray!" I could hear Molly calling from somewhere in the Vermont house, where two handguns and a twelve-gauge shotgun were destined to be returned to the arsenal.

On the weekend of the Gallows Lounge shooting, the snowshoer and I were not expecting to expose Em to a crowd. We'd already declined to be interviewed about the shooting. Mr. Barlow would forever be identified as *the only hero*; as Nora's cousin, I was usually referred to as *the novelist* or *the bestselling author*. Naturally, we would protect Em from interviewers. As Em would one day act out for me, pantomimists are always misquoted.

For two nights, when Em would lie down in bed with me or Mr. Barlow, she lay back on the pillow, as straight and unmoving as a cadaver in a coffin. All day Saturday, Elliot and I were transporting Em's belongings from her Hell's Kitchen apartment to the snowshoer's pied-à-terre on East Sixty-fourth Street. Em went with us; she seemed to understand that we were moving her out. She packed her own clothes; she carried things to and from the car. Em had more books than clothes; there were more pages of her writing in progress than I'd expected. She wanted all the photos—the photos of Nora, too—

but Em wouldn't touch or look at Nora's clothes. No one mentioned Nora's double-barreled twelve-gauge or Em's long-barreled .357 Magnum. Em never touched or looked at the guns. The little English teacher told her that Molly and Ray would take care of everything we left behind. Em didn't nod or shake her head; watching her closely, we noticed she was biting her lower lip. That Saturday night, when we'd moved Em's clothes into the smaller bedroom of Mr. Barlow's apartment, I told Em that this bedroom would be all hers once I went back to Vermont. When Em crossed her index fingers, giving me the X sign, I thought she meant she didn't want me to go. I was relieved to see a reaction from her, any reaction at all. I was also moved to tears by the thought that Em might miss me, but when I tried to hug her, she pushed me away. Em stomped off to Elliot's little living room. There was a worktable; it served as a desk, where we'd told Em to put her writing materials. I'd written on that worktable; I liked writing there.

Nora had called me Longhand Man, but Em wrote in longhand, too. I watched Em leaf through the pages of her writing on the worktable. I was wrong about the meaning of the X sign Em gave me; I'd wrongly assumed her writing in progress was strictly fiction. When Em came back to the bedroom that would be all hers, the pages she gave me were from a long letter she had begun writing me before the shooting. Em had been giving me the X sign for my mom's matchmaking activities in Vermont; Em was crossing her fingers to the Grace idea, and where it came from.

"Grace looks like a young Clara Swift, and I know how Clara Swift affects you—she gets to me that way, too, you know," Em wrote me. By *a young Clara Swift*, Em meant that Grace was now in her early thirties—about the same age Clara Swift was in '77, when she gave birth to Paul Goode's child. (That kid was almost a teenager now, and Clara Swift was in her forties—if not the hottie Em and I once imagined she was, still very much a hottie.) Em was hell-bent on making more comparisons between Grace and *a young Clara Swift*, some of which were (I thought) more literary than actual. I could imagine that I might be smitten with Grace because I was already smitten with a movie star, and Grace looked like her. But it struck me as far-fetched that women in their thirties—especially, women who marry much older men—want to get pregnant and have a baby almost immediately. Clara Swift was thirty-one when she had Paul Goode's baby; Paul Goode would be in his sixties when that kid was a teenager. If I met and married Grace, and we had a baby, bang-bang, I would be a virtual geezer (in my sixties) when our kid was a teenager. "You know your mom has an agenda. Trust me, at her age, Grace will have her own agenda," Em wrote me. This much of her long letter to me was all about *the arranged marriage* and subsequent fatherhood I would be facing, upon my moving to Vermont. Em had further decided that she wanted the snowshoer to read this much of her letter.

The rest of her letter, Em made clear, was for my eyes only. All I said to Em, loudly enough for Elliot to hear, was: "You also wrote me that my *mom* must have looked like Clara Swift."

"When Ray was younger—yes, she did," the snowshoer said. *How many women can look like Clara Swift?* I was wondering. *Not my mother, not at any age,* I was thinking. "Ray is your mom, Adam—you're not supposed to see her as an attractive woman, in the way other men do," the little English teacher told me, with Em nodding her head off. Elliot Barlow had always been able to read my mind, I was thinking, when the snowshoer suddenly sighed. Mr. Barlow had finished reading as much of Em's letter to me as Em had wanted Elliot to read. Poor Elliot—she knew all about my mother's penchant for agendas. Little Ray had married the snowshoer, thereby giving me a stepfather who would get me through Exeter, and through much more. Hadn't *that* arranged marriage also worked for the snowshoer—not to mention for my mom and Molly? "Ray is a good mother—she's just doing what she believes would be best for Adam," the snowshoer discreetly said, handing the selected pages of Em's letter back to Em.

The way Em began to dance with me brought me back to the first time I had danced with her, at my mom's wedding—when Em tried to make me look at her eyes, not at her breasts. The way Em tilted my head, so that I was staring at her breasts, and then she lifted my face to her eyes, made her pantomime of our wedding dance completely clear. "I remember the dancing," I told Em, but she kept making her point: I'd been too young to know better; I was only fourteen. I didn't know you weren't supposed to stare at a girl's boobs when you were dancing with her. The snowshoer and I understood Em's pantomime; it was unnecessary for Em to count out fourteen on her fingers, but she did. We thought we saw where Em was going with her pantomime—namely, it was okay for a mother to be proactive in arranging her kid's future when the kid is only fourteen. But I was going to be forty-eight in a little more than a week. My mom shouldn't be arranging my marriage, or my procreative future—not now. That's where Elliot and I believed Em's pantomime was headed.

We were surprised when Em enacted full-on childbirth; we weren't sure whose birth it was, but Mr. Barlow figured it out. "Yes, we know—Grace was born the year Ray and I got married, which makes Grace fifteen years younger than Adam," the snowshoer said, but Em didn't stop giving birth for long. There was more finger-counting, to indicate the passage of time; then Em was back at it, giving birth again. Elliot and I had watched Em give birth before; in her pantomimes, childbirth was often symbolic. Not this time. You wouldn't want to watch anyone you love go through this childbirth; it would be hard to watch a total stranger give birth in such an agonizing way. It was instantly clear to the snowshoer and me that we were witnessing Em's pantomime of Grace giving birth to my baby—not a good idea, in Em's opinion. I was hoping it would be easier to read the rest of Em's letter, but I should have known there was a reason why this part of her letter was for my eyes only.

At a glance, I could see the new part had been hastily written—with more urgency, it became apparent. Em had written the new part after the Gallows Lounge shooting. What she wrote was an awakening—the writing-out of a childbirth of the symbolic kind. "Nora was half right when she accused you of trying to start something with me—you may not have been trying to, but you've already started something," Em wrote. Trowbridge had wanted to shoot Em first; he'd taken aim at her first. But when Em was covered with Nora's blood, standing onstage, as still as a statue, I didn't know Em had seen me looking at her. I just saw how Em was begging Trowbridge to shoot her—*please kill me, too*, her eyes, her hands, her whole body had been pleading. I just knew it would have killed me, if he shot Em—this was how I'd been looking at her; that was the look Em had seen.

"I saw how you were looking at me. You can't look at me like this—you can't love me that way! How could it ever work?" Em wrote. "I saw you doing those jumping jacks, I heard you calling 'Fuck you!' to him—you were trying to get him to shoot you instead of me. Are you crazy? Maybe you should let your mother marry you off to a skier who works in publishing, but you won't stay married to anybody if you keep looking at me like this. You're still the boy I danced with at your mom's wedding. When are you going to grow up? You can't love me that way," Em wrote. There was no *Love, Em*.

While I'd been reading, I could hear Em taking a bath. When I'd finished the new pages, I could tell that she had gone to bed. She was starting out the night in the snowshoer's bedroom, not with me—that was clear. I certainly understood what was private about the new pages of Em's letter, but I showed the pages to Elliot Barlow. "Am I crazy, or is Em crazy?" I asked Mr. Barlow, handing her the pages. My good stepfather had always been my first reader;

now the little English teacher was my copy editor, too. Here I was, in my late forties, still seeking her advice. According to Em, I still wasn't a grown-up.

I saw Elliot frown when she was reading the pages; she sighed when she gave them back to me. "This is between you and Em. Of course you're crazy—you're both crazy," the snowshoer said. The little English teacher revealed she had more to say when she began to pace, as if a classroom of students sat in front of her, and behind her was a blackboard where she'd already written something of importance—something she was poised to say. "I didn't see you, Adam, or your jumping jacks—I was on all fours, you'll recall; I wasn't looking in the direction of the stage. But I certainly heard you taunting Trowbridge. 'You were never in the Marine Corps—you never did anything!' I heard you tell him. You certainly sounded like you wanted him to shoot you, Adam," Mr. Barlow said.

"I just knew it would have killed me if he shot Em," I told the little English teacher.

"The way you looked at her must have made this clear to Em," the snowshoer said.

"If she were only halfway interested, I would ask Em to marry me!" I blurted out.

"I believe Em knows this, Adam—I think this is the problem," Mr. Barlow said.

"I don't know how I look when I'm looking at Em—I can't see myself when I'm seeing her," I said to the snowshoer.

"I've seen you when you're imagining, Adam—mostly, when you're writing," the little English teacher told me. "I know how you look when you look at Em—like you're writing the end of the story. You're imagining that you and Em are a couple, that you're already together—this is how you look at her," the snowshoer said.

I understood why Em had told me I couldn't look at her like this. How would it ever work, for me to love her that way? *I must be crazy*, I was thinking. I'd seen Em's penis pantomime; I knew how she felt about penises. I felt so out of it. *I might as well marry a skier who works in publishing*, I thought. And Em had just lost the love of her life. How could I look at Em like this? How could I even dream of loving her that way? I went to bed feeling so ashamed. You have to be careful what you show or act out to a pantomimist. You better not pantomime those things you can't take back.

42.

A NORMAL LIFE

On the second night, Em went back and forth between my bed and Mr. Barlow's. Em would lie back on the pillow and not move, but she couldn't sleep, and she was too restless to stay in bed. I knew better than to try to hug her; I didn't even touch her hand. I kept my back turned to her and pretended I was sleeping. Once, when I actually was asleep, I felt her arm around me and her breath on my shoulder, or I just dreamed this—for old times' sake, or because I couldn't forget how Em had hugged me, the way she would bump me with her head when she locked her hands around me from behind.

Em was getting dressed when I woke up. I looked away; I didn't see what she was wearing. When I went into the kitchen, Elliot Barlow asked me if Em was going to church. It was Sunday morning, but we both knew Em never went to church. "Em is dressed like she's going to church, or to a funeral," the snowshoer said.

Nora had been blunt about her death; she wanted no "remembrance bullshit," as she put it. "When I die, let there be nothing—I want you to do fuck-all about my dying," Nora had told us. Considering the unlikelihood of Em going to church, Mr. Barlow and I remembered a more recent conversation. Nora had been railing against John Cardinal O'Connor and the Roman Catholic Archdiocese's opposition to safe-sex education in the city's public schools. We'd heard Nora on this subject too many times; Mr. Barlow and I were barely listening. We knew O'Connor had campaigned against LGBT nondiscrimination laws, and how he'd described homosexual behavior as *sinful*—even Em's gay but homo-hating dad knew that. And of course Cardinal O'Connor was opposed to condom distribution. Who hadn't heard about that?

Then Nora said something we hadn't heard before. Her fractured relationship with ACT UP notwithstanding, Nora knew about the planned Stop the Church protest at St. Patrick's Cathedral. Nora had friends who were ACT UP members, and knew of the disagreements among them. The Stop the Church protest was aimed at Cardinal O'Connor, not at the worshipers attending Mass. The protesters had planned to gather outside St. Patrick's during a Mass, but a bunch of activists wanted to demonstrate inside the cathedral. Nora had said it was a "piss-poor idea" to protest inside the church. "Some dork will do something stupid—it won't take much to offend the worshipers," Nora had railed, with Em nodding her head off.

There'd been a compromise within ACT UP. (Nora didn't usually have a high regard for compromises.) One talking point had been not to disrupt the Mass. The people intent on protesting inside the cathedral agreed to dress conservatively, to blend in with the congregation. The plan was to stage a die-in during the homily, the least-sacred part of the service. How the die-in might turn out didn't sound promising to Nora. How does a die-in not disrupt a Mass?

Nora said "some fink" would tip off St. Patrick's. She swore there would be plainclothes cops inside the cathedral for the 10:15 A.M. Mass. "The cops know how to dress for church—the cops can blend in with the congregation, too!" Nora had railed. She said "some fink political leaders" would attend the Mass to show their support for Cardinal O'Connor. "I'll bet the fink mayor will be there!" Nora had cried. She meant Mayor Koch. His name rhymed with *crotch*, but Nora called him Mayor Cock—or, sometimes, Ed the Cock. Naturally, the Gallows Lounge had not allowed Nora and Em to make fun of Mayor Ed Koch onstage—not in the way Nora intended. Em had been relieved; she didn't think it was fair to make fun of the mayor's head. "Ed's head looks like a penis—he's a cockhead!" Nora had argued with Em.

"In the LGBT community, there are better reasons to be disappointed in Mayor Koch," the snowshoer had said, with Em nodding her head off. This time, Em was on the side of the fink management at the Gallows. Em had thought it would be an inappropriate use of her penis pantomime; it would be cruel to mock Mayor Cock because his head looked like a penis. "You can't blame Ed for his head," Mr. Barlow had said, but Nora was a no-holds-barred girl.

That was why Elliot and I remembered there was a Stop the Church protest planned on the Sunday after the Gallows Lounge shooting—because Nora had been opposed to the protesters entering the cathedral and interrupting the Mass, and Nora wasn't known for being the voice of caution and respect. "There's no stopping the Catholic Church. You shouldn't try to stop them; all you can do is try to control the damage they do," Nora had said. She'd said this calmly; she had stopped railing. It seemed Em also remembered what was happening at St. Patrick's. Em not only knew that Nora had planned to go; Em had made Nora promise not to enter the cathedral.

Exactly how had Em dressed to go to church? I asked Elliot Barlow. Elliot was still wearing her flannel pajamas; she'd made herself a cup of tea and was making some coffee for Em and me. I was no more dressed to go to church than the snowshoer—socks, sweatpants, a T-shirt—and I was wondering why it was taking Em an eternity to do her makeup. She'd indicated to Elliot that she would be in the bathroom, tracing her eyebrow with an index finger, and touching her lips, to pantomime putting on her makeup. "Em was wearing black tights, that black skirt your mother gave her, a black turtleneck—for God's sake, if Em had a black veil, I'm sure she would have worn it!" the snowshoer was saying.

"Em couldn't have put on her makeup in a veil," I pointed out to Mr. Barlow.

"Shit—I'll bet she's given us the slip!" the snowshoer suddenly cried, spilling her tea. Sure enough: Em had slipped away. We rushed around, putting on our running clothes. "There's no dress code for a Mass—it's not like a wedding *or* a funeral!" I could hear the little English teacher yelling.

That Sunday morning, December 10, 1989—two days after the Gallows Lounge shooting—it was below freezing, in the twenties, in New York City. Elliot Barlow and I had checked the coat closet; we knew Em was wearing her black ski parka with the hood. With or without makeup, she would be looking a little severe. We hoped she wouldn't go inside the church; we were sure there would be trouble at the Mass. What would Em do if the police stopped her, if a cop asked her any questions? We knew Em wouldn't speak, not even to the police.

The snowshoer and I ran south on Park Avenue to East Fifty-second Street, where we ran west to Fifth Avenue. We assumed the protesters would be everywhere we looked on Fifth; we expected they would be all along East Fiftieth, at least as far as Rockefeller Center, perhaps lying down and blocking traffic on East Fifty-first Street, from Madison Avenue to Sixth. There *had been* demonstrators lying down on Fifth Avenue, Mr. Barlow and I were told, but we'd missed it. You had to be really out of it to be late to the Stop the Church protest.

Inside St. Patrick's, the Mass had long since started—maybe an hour and a half before we got there, one of the protesters said. The organist had played loudly at times, a demonstrator told us; there'd been shouting from inside the church. The cops had arrested more than a hundred protesters, one of the hangers-on had said. We heard that half the demonstrators who'd been taken away had been seized inside St. Patrick's. The snowshoer and I were alarmed to hear that the cops had carried protesters out of the cathedral on stretchers.

"Were the protesters injured?" Elliot asked one of the demonstrators, who was just hanging around.

"I don't think so," the guy told us. "If you don't go of your own accord, the cops tie you to a stretcher and you go that way."

I don't understand how anything works, I was thinking. Once more, Em had been right: I might as well marry a skier who works in publishing; I might as well be living in Vermont and skiing with my mother. I was of no use to anyone in New York. I couldn't even get to a demonstration on time. The remaining protesters were barely protesting; there were so many cops around, you couldn't get close to the cathedral. By the time the snowshoer and I arrived, it seemed there were almost as many bystanders as demonstrators; maybe the bystanders had come to gawk at the protesters. Mr. Barlow and I were just bystanders. From what we'd been told, the more demonstrative of the demonstrators were already under arrest. At 9 A.M., someone said, there'd been about four hundred police officers lining Fifth Avenue. We'd not been there to watch the loaded paddy wagons drive away. I saw only one police van—it was parked near one of the police barricades, in front of the church.

"The twin spires of St. Patrick's, a Gothic Revival cathedral, look all the more medieval today—under the circumstances," the snowshoer enigmatically said.

"Under what circumstances?" I asked the little English teacher.

"In the Middle Ages, there was widespread religious persecution of non-Christians by the Catholic Church—that's why St. Patrick's is looking more medieval today," Mr. Barlow proclaimed in her schoolteacher's voice; the rise and fall of her voice had a classroom intonation, as if she hadn't been speaking only to me. The little English teacher knew how to attract and hold an audience. In the overall disarray of the deteriorating demonstration, sundry protesters were drawn to the snowshoer's voice; Elliot was now accusing Cardinal O'Connor, the archbishop of New York, of religious persecution. We had no hope of finding Em among the disparate elements in the protest, which was petering out. We feared that she might be one of the demonstrators who'd been arrested. It would be just like Em to be among the persecuted.

We'd tried to talk to the cops, behind their barricades—to ask them how we could find Em. "We have a friend who doesn't speak," the snowshoer had said to the policemen. "What will happen to her, if she was arrested? Is there a precinct where we might find her? Is there a number we can call?" Elliot had kept asking the cops. They told us to stay back, on our side of the barricades. Our worrying about Em was hypothetical to the cops. They were fixated on the actual—on what was happening then and there. The cops cared about what they could see; their focus was on the waning demonstration in front of them.

I was praying Elliot Barlow wouldn't recite the part of the First Amendment that the Roman Catholic Church ignores, but she went ahead anyway: "'Congress shall make no law respecting an establishment of religion, or prohibiting the free exercise thereof.'" Those cops who'd told us to stay back were watching the little English teacher now. They couldn't hear what the pretty Mr. Barlow had been saying, but they saw she'd found a few followers; they could see she'd attracted a motley group within the lingering mob.

Some lost-looking souls were carrying condom signs; they hovered around Mr. Barlow. I didn't see Nora's favorite condom poster, the one of Cardinal O'Connor's smiling face alongside a condom twice the size of his head. KNOW YOUR SCUMBAGS, the poster said. In smaller letters, under the condom: THIS ONE PREVENTS AIDS. Nora had loved that poster, but the condom protesters who were hanging around Elliot Barlow carried tamer signs. CONDOMS NOT PRAYERS, one protest sign said. TAKE ONE AND SAVE YOUR LIFE, said another condom sign; rows of condoms were attached to this sign. God knows how long those condoms had been outside in the cold.

The snowshoer was blaming Pope Pius XII for what sounded to me like a 1951 papal encyclical, an "Address to Midwives on the Nature of Their Profession." *The poor midwives*, I was thinking, when I saw the cops cross the barricades; the cops who'd been watching Elliot were coming our way. I knew the snowshoer was hurrying; she saw the cops closing in. "But just you wait and see what Cardinal O'Connor and his craven supporters say about *us*! We'll be condemned for infringing on their freedom to worship!" Mr. Barlow cried. I could see she'd lost half her listeners even before the police broke through and dispersed the few followers still surrounding the snowshoer. A woman with a reproductive-freedom sign was the last one who went away. When the cops closed in, the little English teacher took hold of my hands; she was delighted. "*Finally*—I was thinking the cops would never come!" Mr. Barlow whispered to me. This was when I understood she was trying to get arrested; it struck me as a rather roundabout way to find out if Em had been arrested, and where the police were holding her. Elliot Barlow would be right, of course—concerning what Cardinal O'Connor *and his craven supporters* would say about the Stop the Church protesters.

As for the die-in: some protesters had thrown themselves on the floor of the central aisle of the cathedral to symbolize the victims of AIDS; some had chained themselves to the pews. A guy had blown a whistle and shouted, "You're killing us!"

That same year, the American Catholic Bishops had explicitly condemned the use of condoms to stop the spread of the AIDS virus. Cardinal O'Connor had advocated abstinence instead of condoms—"good morality is good medicine" was one way he put it. During the disrupted service in St. Patrick's, Cardinal O'Connor had told his parishioners: "Never respond to hatred with hatred." Nora would have pointed out that the cardinal hated homosexual acts, a woman's access to abortion, safe-sex education, and condoms. Over the protesters' shouts in St. Patrick's, the cardinal had led his parishioners in prayer; he had handed out a written homily, to replace his regular sermon.

Mayor Koch was sitting in a front-row pew at the interrupted Mass. The fink mayor would criticize the demonstrators. "If you don't like the church, go out and find one you like—or start your own," Ed the Cock would say. His time as a mayor was running out; Ed Koch would become a movie critic. What Nora would have said is anybody's guess.

The New York mayor-elect, David Dinkins, and the New York governor, Mario Cuomo, said they "deplored" the Stop the Church protest. Finks for the cardinal, Nora would have called them.

In the media, much would be made of the demonstrators' disruption of the Mass—their disrespect of a religious service. To desecrate the Eucharist was wrong; host desecration was a sacrilege. Some guy had crushed a Communion wafer in his hand; he'd dropped or thrown it on the floor of the cathedral. "Certainly sacrilegious," Mr. Barlow would say, "but if the rites of the Roman Catholic Church are sacred, isn't the First Amendment sacrosanct?"

When the cops closed in on us, the little English teacher wasn't talking politics—not to the police. There were demonstrators dressed as clowns, and guys wearing homemade miters—mock versions of the high hats (those tall headdresses) worn by Catholic bishops. A very handsome Jesus was walking around; he had a crown of thorns and the right beard, but we could see the cops were tired of the carnival atmosphere. The two cops who came up to us now were the ones we'd tried to talk to before. This time, they had handcuffs, or they'd always had them, only now they were carrying the cuffs where we could see them.

"Hello, again—we're the ones who have a friend who doesn't speak," the snowshoer said, holding out her wrists to be cuffed.

"We know," the older, clean-shaven cop replied, not cuffing her; he was pleasant, even smiling a little.

"We just want you to come with us—we need to know more about your friend who doesn't speak," the younger policeman told us. He had a mustache that overran his upper lip; I couldn't tell if he was smiling or not.

"You don't have to handcuff us—we'll go peacefully, wherever you take us. We hope you'll arrest us and take us where you're holding our friend— she just doesn't *speak*; she's not trying to make trouble," Mr. Barlow was babbling.

"We won't handcuff you—we aren't arresting you," the older, clean-shaven cop said tiredly.

"We just want you to come with us—we need to know more about your friend who doesn't speak," the younger policeman with the mustache repeated. The two cops held their hands close to us—both to indicate where they wanted us to go, and to guide us through the crowd, to the police side of the barricades—but they barely touched us, or they touched us only incidentally. There were no strong-arm tactics.

We would later learn there were 4,500 protesters at the Stop the Church protest. The police arrested only 111 demonstrators, from inside and outside the cathedral. Those arrested faced minor charges; they were released without trial, that same night, and sentenced to community service. A small number of protesters were later tried for refusing their community service; no one would serve any jail time.

In the case of Elliot Barlow and myself, our two cops treated us well. We went with them along Fifth Avenue to Fiftieth Street, where the demonstration had started. We were making our way west on Fiftieth—we were almost to the Avenue of the Americas—when the snowshoer asked our police escorts if they were taking us to Radio City Music Hall. She wasn't kidding, but our good-natured cops both laughed; they thought the pretty Mr. Barlow had been joking. "I just imagined you might be holding the other prisoners in the music hall," the little English teacher told them seriously.

"You're not prisoners, you're not under arrest—we're just trying to get to the bottom of your friend's business with the cardinal," the older, clean-shaven cop said.

"Let's start with her name, including how you spell *MacPherson*—then we'll get to her business with the box," the younger one with the mustache told us. We'd not mentioned Em's name to the policemen, I was certain. Elliot spelled out both *Emily* and *MacPherson* for the cops. I was watching the older policeman, who was nodding his head. He was looking at something written on a small scrap of paper. He already knew how to spell Em's name; the cops were just making sure we were talking about the same person.

"*What* box?" I asked them. The snowshoer and I had just moved Em and her stuff out of Hell's Kitchen. Em had a number of cardboard boxes, of the kind that paper comes in; they were boxes of writing paper, or for her manuscript pages, we'd assumed.

The snowshoer had stopped spelling; she was now babbling about the Gallows Lounge shooting. She wanted the cops to understand who Emily MacPherson was—Em was the silent partner of the performer who'd been shot and killed onstage. Nora had planned to go to the Stop the Church protest, the snowshoer was saying.

"We *know*," the older policeman interrupted her. "But Emily MacPherson shouldn't have brought a *box* to St. Patrick's—not during a demonstration."

"You can't try to give a *box* to Cardinal O'Connor when there's a protest going on, and she wouldn't say what was *in* the box!" the younger cop cried.

"She doesn't *speak*!" the snowshoer exclaimed.

"We know," the clean-shaven cop told us, shaking his head.

"*That* box—the copies of her crazy father's letters to Cardinal O'Connor," I said to the snowshoer.

"I know," the snowshoer softly said. Em was not an old hand at protests or demonstrations; this much was clear.

The policemen apologized for frisking us against the squad car parked at the intersection of West Fiftieth Street and Sixth Avenue—not that Mr. Barlow and I knew what the protocol was, or if there was any protocol. We knew barely enough to know that the policeman driving the patrol car was probably not an important pooh-bah on the police force; he was just the cop who drove the patrol car, taking us to the police station. The younger, mustached cop came with us; he sat up front in the passenger seat. The older cop called to us from the sidewalk, before the patrol car pulled away.

"One thing about your friend—she won't have to do any community service, because she doesn't speak!" he called.

The younger policeman with the mustache was shaking his head as the patrol car pulled away. "Your friend can't bring *anything* in a *box* for Cardinal

O'Connor—not to St. Patrick's, not even when there *isn't* a demonstration!" he told us.

"Got it," the snowshoer said. We wouldn't remember which precinct we were driven to; we were trying too hard to remember what had happened with Em's homo-hating dad, who was dying of AIDS in Canada. He was in hospice care in Toronto; he'd asked Em to come see him. Nora hadn't let Em go to Toronto alone—they'd gone together. Em had not written me about her visit with her dying dad, not a word. All Elliot and I knew about Em's trip to Toronto, we knew from Nora.

The hospice was "quite a wonderful place, under the circumstances," Nora had said; she meant "with all the dying going on," as she told Mr. Barlow and me. She'd been impressed by how thoroughly the nurses explained the pain control for Em's father. "The morphine shit escaped me," Nora said.

"Sublingual morphine versus morphine elixir versus fentanyl patch?" Elliot had asked her.

"I don't know," Nora said; she'd paid closer attention to the awfulness of Em's dad.

The dying father had called Em and Nora "a couple of lesbos"; yet he'd begged Em to "personally deliver" his unanswered letters to Cardinal O'Connor. All that mattered to Em's dad was his hope of being baptized by the cardinal and receiving Communion from him. To Nora, all this was undermined by the parting shot the dying dad took at his daughter. "You're just another licker, like your mother!" Em's father told her.

Yet the homophobe was leaving what he had to Em—his money, and a house in midtown Toronto. Nora and Em had met with a Realtor and a lawyer in Toronto. The house was on Shaftesbury Avenue, in the Summerhill neighborhood—just north of the Canadian Pacific railway tracks. Em showed Nora the exterior of the house, but she declined the Realtor's invitation to take them inside. Em remembered liking the sound of the train at night, but she didn't like most of her memories. Following her parents' separation and divorce, her father had divided the house into two apartments; he'd lived in one half of the house and had rented out the other. Of course Em could have taken the money and sold the house; she would have paid some taxes, but she could have walked away. No one believed Em would ever move to Canada, as she repeatedly threatened to do. Yet Em had refused to sell the house in Toronto. She'd been born in Canada to a Canadian father; she was both a Canadian and an American citizen. Em wanted to have a place to go if she ever left the United States.

When they'd been in Toronto, Em had also shown Nora the Bishop Strachan School, where Em had gone when she'd been little, although Em remembered it only dimly. On that late afternoon Em and Nora had watched the day students heading home from school. The older girls were walking away from the school by themselves, perhaps going to the subway, but the little girls were met by a parent or a nanny. The little girls in their school uniforms were the ones who fascinated Em; she was always trying to imagine herself as one of them, but Nora (of course) had preferred looking at the older girls—the ones who looked the hottest in their short skirts. Em had burst into tears, Nora told the little English teacher and me. "All because Em saw how I was looking at a couple of hot girls!" Nora said, laughing. I'd seen how Nora looked at a hot girl. I knew how sensitive Em was to the way I'd looked at her.

Not only would Em not have to do any community service, but she wouldn't even be counted among the 111 demonstrators who'd been arrested. The charges against her were dropped. The plainclothes cops in the cathedral made sure that Em got nowhere near Cardinal O'Connor with the box she was carrying. And, upon further investigation, there'd been nothing threatening to the cardinal in the box. At the precinct or the police station, wherever we were, an older policewoman had been put in charge of *overseeing* Em—as the kindly policewoman explained to Mr. Barlow and me. We went with her to collect Em's personal effects before we were led to where they were holding Em. We saw the box of letters to Cardinal O'Connor among Em's more recognizable things. "Bless her heart—we know she wasn't one of the protesters who got out of hand at the church, and we understand she's been through a bad time lately," the policewoman wanted us to know; the police knew about the Gallows Lounge shooting, and who Emily MacPherson was. Em had answered the questions the police had asked her, in writing. "She doesn't have to tell us any more, but she won't stop writing," the policewoman said. This made perfect sense to the snowshoer and me: Em was a writer; writing was one thing she had confidence in. We were relieved to learn Em hadn't been trying to pantomime her life story in a police station.

Mr. Barlow and I saw the handwritten note Em had Scotch-taped to the box she'd brought to St. Patrick's to give to the cardinal. We were familiar with Em's exquisite longhand. "Your Eminence, please read my father's letters to you; he is dying. Thank you, Emily MacPherson," Em had written.

We went along a hall to the room where they were keeping Em. There were some chairs around a table, where Em sat writing, the pages piled near her and across the table from her, where a young policeman sat reading them. "Bless her heart," the older policewoman murmured to us again, when she let us into the room. In our labyrinthine journey through the station, the kindly policewoman advised us what to do with the dying dad's letters to the cardinal. "Personally, I would just get rid of them, but if you want to take the trouble, you should call and speak to someone at the Roman Catholic Archdiocese of New York, or you should just go there and speak to someone—even if it's only a secretary," the policewoman had said. "Ask someone at the archdiocese what you should do with these letters, but if you bring the letters to the archdiocese, don't bring them in a *box*! Just tie some string around the stack of pages and carry them that way," the older policewoman kindly suggested.

"Got it!" the snowshoer had exclaimed enthusiastically; she'd not meant to startle our *overseeing* policewoman.

Em was excited to see us; she looked less than happy to see the box, but Em pantomimed her eagerness for Elliot and me to read what she'd written. "She's been on a roll," the young policeman, Em's appointed reader, said to his elder colleague. "You two are in it—I'd recognize you anywhere," he told the snowshoer and me. As he was leaving the room, he patted the pretty Mr. Barlow on her shoulder. "Good job, ma'am," the young cop said to the snowshoer, *the only hero* of the Gallows Lounge shooting.

Em was as pantomimic as her former self when we brought her back to the little Barlows' apartment. In spite of the undelivered copies of her father's confessions to Cardinal O'Connor, Em had been energized by her arrest at the Stop the Church protest, and the subsequent dropping of the charges against her; she'd been writing up a storm, and she couldn't wait for the little English teacher and me to read her handwritten pages. Nora had called me Longhand Man, but Em was a longtime longhand woman. While the snowshoer and I were impressed by Em's narrative, we were no less impressed by the literary prowess of her police readers. Em had chosen to write about herself in the third person. I'm sure the line of questioning by the police did not begin with the Gallows Lounge shooting, but that's where Em began her story.

"Emily MacPherson, a mute pantomimist and fiction writer, saw her partner shot and killed onstage at the Gallows Lounge; two days later, the nonspeaking pantomimist tried to deliver copies of her father's unanswered letters to Cardinal O'Connor in St. Patrick's Cathedral. The mute knew her dead partner had planned to go to the Stop the Church protest," Em narrated, as if she were writing stand-up shtick for Nora's deadpan delivery of *Two Dykes, One Who Talks*.

The snowshoer and I saw ourselves described as "the mute's two best friends." Not surprisingly, Mr. Barlow came off better than I did—as anyone would expect of *the only hero*. My efforts to entice the Gallows Lounge shooter to kill me instead of Em were described as "brave but stupid." Fair enough, I thought. And both Elliot and I liked what Em had written about her homophobic father: "The pantomimist pitied the police officers who had tried to read her dad's awful letters." No wonder the police found Em endearing.

We were surprised to read that Em's mom was also dying. The hateful mother had "some kind of cancer"; she'd written Em, expressly forbidding Em to come see her. "I have my women friends, and I don't want them to meet you—when I die, one of my friends will notify you," Em's mom wrote her.

"Can't wait!" Nora had written her back. Nora knew how to imitate Em's signature.

Not long afterward, one of the mother's women friends wrote Em. "Your mom is dead. There's nothing for you," the woman friend wrote. Naturally, Nora wrote her back—doing a good job with Em's signature. Em's handwriting was so perfectly legible, it was fairly easy to imitate; it almost didn't look like handwriting.

"Yahoo! And fuck you to death, too," Nora had written.

As always, the little English teacher was fixated on Em's *writing*. "I really like the third person—you impart your point of view, but the voice is mostly omniscient," Mr. Barlow said to Em, who nodded her head a little. I saw how Em's *writing* could be what would save her. I was aware of my dependence on writing, in this way.

"I don't see you writing something like an Op-Ed piece for *The New York Times*—about either surviving the Gallows Lounge shooting or being arrested at the Stop the Church protest," the snowshoer was saying to Em, who pantomimed vomiting to indicate her agreement.

I was remembering how the snowshoer had saved me; she meant so much more to me than my mother had first imagined. My mom married Mr. Barlow to help me get through Exeter, but Elliot Barlow had been better than the stepfather Little Ray had imagined. I believed that Mr. Barlow was the best actual father I could have had.

"I don't see you writing a memoir, Em, although a book about *Two Dykes, One Who Talks*—I don't mean only about the Gallows Lounge shooting—would certainly appeal to a publisher," the little English teacher was telling Em, who was elaborating on her vomit pantomime. Em wasn't a true memoirist; nonfiction wasn't for her. "You can be true to what's true about you and Nora, you can be truthful when you write about what really happened, but keep yourself in the third person, and you can take some other liberties—you can make up a Santa or two, or a bunch of Santas," the snowshoer was saying. "You can also make up what should have or could have happened, you can be truthful about the things you make up in a different way—you just have to keep it real when you make things up!" the English teacher was telling Em, who was nodding flat out again. I could see the pep talk working. I'd heard the *writing* pep talk before; Mr. Barlow had made me feel like a writer before I was one. I was remembering how the snowshoer had rescued me when I needed rescuing. I knew Elliot Barlow was good at rescue jobs. Now Em was the snowshoer's rescue job. "You want to be a full-time fiction writer, don't you? You understand this is a third-person omniscient novel—don't you?" the little English teacher was asking Em, who was nodding her head off now, like the Em I knew and loved.

They'll be fine without me—if I stay in New York, I'll just be in their way, I was thinking. Everything had taken a fatalistic turn. It didn't matter that Mr. Barlow wasn't a real New Yorker; for the time being, Elliot Barlow had a rescue job that would keep her in New York. I was just one of the rescue jobs that had made the snowshoer stay at Exeter; the little English teacher probably stayed longer than she wanted to, I was thinking.

There was no one for me like Em, I knew, but I understood this was crazy. What Molly had told me on my mother's wedding night wasn't true for everyone. "There's more than one way to love people, Kid," the trail groomer had told me. This was true for Molly and my mom and the snowshoer, I believed, but this wouldn't work for Em and me. Em loved women—maybe only one woman, I was thinking. It was pie in the sky for me to imagine Em would ever love me. I remembered the reenactment of the snowshoer kiss—how watching the way Em kissed Nora had numbed my tongue, how I'd wanted Em to kiss me like that. Had I forgotten that I showed Em the snowshoer kiss, and Em didn't kiss me back?

I would be forty-eight in a matter of days. I knew enough about skiing to know I would never be an expert skier. If I gave skiing with my mom a chance, I knew my mother could help me get a little better, but I was an intentionally intermediate skier. When you're an intermediate on purpose, you'll never get a whole lot better. "Bad habits die hard, kiddo," Nora once told me. Naturally, Nora didn't mean my skiing; Nora didn't give a rat's ass about skiing. But bad habits are bad habits. "Most guys would fuck anyone—wouldn't they, kiddo?" Nora had asked me. At the time she asked me, I definitely would have. You don't unlearn your bad habits overnight—that was Nora's meaning.

Yet here I was, not only moving to Vermont and going skiing with my mom; I was even imagining I might be happy, marrying a young and pretty publisher. I didn't doubt that Em was right about my mother's expectations for my meeting Grace. And what was I to make of Em's conviction that Grace would have her own agenda? How did Em know Grace was dying to get pregnant? It was with trepidation that I intruded on Em's euphoria; her writing was her only road ahead. I knew Molly and my mom would intrude on all of us tomorrow; there would be no candid conversation about *my* road ahead, not around my mother. I was feeling overwhelmed by how much I would miss Em and the snowshoer. If I told them how I really felt, I was afraid I would choke up—that was why I tried to sound lighthearted about it. You can say stupid things, or things you don't mean, when you're trying not to sound too serious.

"I know you guys are going to miss me," I suddenly said, apropos of nothing. Em looked uncertain, but she nodded—warily. "I know you two will look after each other," I just rambled on. "Don't worry about me—maybe marriage and fatherhood will work out, as unlikely as that seems," I said. I had no idea what I would say next. I was unprepared for how the thought of fatherhood affected me, but I was my mother's son, wasn't I? Look what Little Ray had done—to have her one and only, with no strings attached. Why wouldn't I want to be a father before it was too late? "I would like to be a father," I said, surprising them. The thought had surprised me, too.

"I think you would be a good father, Adam," the snowshoer said sincerely. Em was nodding her head like she meant it, not in her pro forma way.

"Why wouldn't I want to be a father? Maybe this is my chance to have a normal life," I just blurted out. I immediately saw how I'd hurt them. I didn't mean that Elliot and Em were abnormal, or not normal in any way, but I saw their faces and how they turned away. "I'm sorry, I didn't mean . . ." I started to say, but Mr. Barlow was quicker.

"We know what you didn't mean, Adam," the little English teacher told me. Em barely nodded, with her face still turned away.

The next day, Molly and my mom would be there—packing up Nora's stuff and all the guns. My mother and I would spend that night together, in the empty Hell's Kitchen apartment. My mom said she wanted to be with her one and only, and the sleeping arrangements were up in the air with Nora out of the picture. The bad smell from the restaurant below us would need to be explained. Naturally, my mother wasn't happy about blaming an octopus. Because the first bad restaurant had been Greek, Nora held an octopus accountable for the bad smell. "The poor thing—it's not the octopus's fault!" my mom proclaimed.

In my effort to change the subject from the bad smell, or the innocence of the octopus, I tried to have a serious conversation with my mother about my wanting to be a father before it was too late. I was being serious when I told my mom that, however belatedly, she must have inspired me, because I found myself wanting a one and only of my own.

"If you want to have a normal life, as I hear you do, you'll have your one and only with someone else—not exactly a one and only *of your own*, sweetie," my mom reminded me. "I know you didn't mean to hurt our feelings, sweetie, but every creature wants to have a normal life—even an octopus!" my mother added. I knew the snowshoer would have assured my mom that I never meant to hurt their feelings; yet my careless remark had hurt my mother's feelings, too.

I was reminded of my inappropriateness, more than a decade before, when I'd asked Molly and my mom to tell me *more exactly* how the snowshoer was *affected* by the orchiectomy; I'd inquired, furthermore, if they knew whether or not the little English teacher was considering a vaginoplasty. Instead of telling me that the surgical stuff was none of my business, or that I should at least have the courtesy to ask Elliot herself, Molly just shook her head. My mother sighed.

"Mr. Barlow is a better woman than some women I know who have vaginas, Kid," Molly told me.

"Mr. Barlow has more balls than some guys I know who have balls—if you know what I mean, sweetie," my mom said.

"He knows what you mean, Ray," the trail groomer told her.

Our one night together in the apartment above the restaurant, my mother decided for herself what the bad smell was. "It's a dead Greek, sweetie—a dead man smells worse than any octopus," my mom said. I guess blaming the Greeks was okay, but not their octopus. When it had been a bad Greek restaurant, maybe the cooks got into a fight in the kitchen; perhaps an errant sous-chef had been chopped to pieces with a cleaver. The dismembered sous-chef was somehow interred in one of the heating ducts, my mother decided. I was glad it would be my last night in that rat's-ass apartment in Hell's Kitchen.

In the morning, I hesitated to tell my mom about something I'd been putting off. "One should meet one's obligations before leaving town," I remembered the snowshoer saying, before she left Exeter. I'd dedicated one of my novels to someone I felt beholden to—Lieutenant Matthew Zimmermann. It had been my intention to autograph a couple of copies of this novel for Zim's parents and his adored Elmira. I thought it would be too impersonal to have my publisher send the books in the mail, so I planned to carry the inscribed and signed copies to the Zimmermanns' Park Avenue apartment building; if Colonel Zimmermann wasn't at home, I would leave the books with the doorman.

I remembered the outgoing colonel among Zim's homeless friends. He was a man who enjoyed the fraternity of others; I believed the colonel would like to see me again. But my teammate Sam—the general, and a real marine—told me Zim's dad had died. I could envision their white headstones at Arlington National Cemetery, though I didn't ever want to see Zim's actual headstone. General Joseph Zimmermann had been the first to die—"the big-deal, World War One Zim," the snowshoer called him. Zim and his dad were the next to arrive in Arlington. Under the circumstances, I thought it would be difficult or awkward for me to see Elmira again—maybe for both of us. I was embarrassed that I didn't remember Mrs. Zimmermann, Zim's mother, at all; I wouldn't have recognized her. Yet I imagined that my giving the books to the doorman was less impersonal than mailing them.

My mom said it would mean more to Elmira and Mrs. Zimmermann if I delivered my books to the doorman in person. "I'll go with you, sweetie—just in case anything happens," my mother reassured me. Her coming with me wasn't reassuring. What I worried might happen was a chance encounter with Elmira or Mrs. Zimmermann in the lobby—a possibility I mentioned to my mom, as casually as I could. "I'm not going to *say* I should have shot Zim, sweetie—although I should have shot him," my mother told me. Not exactly reassuring. We set forth from the snowshoer's; we'd already brought our bed linens from Hell's Kitchen to the Upper East Side. I should have known that the weather wouldn't deter my mother from walking with me. It was right around freezing, and the forecast was calling for a mix of snow and freezing rain—wimpy weather for an old Vermont skier, my mom would have told me. She was sixty-seven, but she insisted on carrying the two books in her ski backpack.

We went a roundabout way to Park Avenue. I wanted to show my mother St. James' Episcopal Church, the site of Zim's memorial service. It was on Madison, between East Seventy-first and East Seventy-second—a few blocks south and a block west of the Zimmermanns' apartment building—but my mom didn't want to go inside the church. "I don't want to see it, sweetie," was all she said. "That stupid, futile war!" she suddenly cried out, only a block later—we were still on Madison. Two young men wearing stylish top-coats turned to look at her; I tried to see my mother in their eyes. Her hiking boots exaggerated her mannish way of walking; even when Little Ray was barefoot, she still walked like a jock. In her stretchy ski pants, her tightly fitted parka, with her ski hat pulled low, barely above her eyebrows—well, on a Madison Avenue sidewalk, let's say my mom was more unisex than most. I saw our reflection in the plateglass window of a storefront for menswear; we looked more alike, and more like men, than the mannequins in the window. We looked more like two guys than those two fashion plates we'd passed on the sidewalk. "People here don't even know how to dress for the weather," my mother was saying. "I don't mean you, sweetie—you're not *from* here, and you don't *belong* here," she reminded me.

When we were walking on Park Avenue, my mom stared at the uniforms of the doormen we walked past. "You can't tell diddly-squat about men in uniform, sweetie—you don't know what their politics are, you don't know what they're thinking!" my mother told me. I didn't dare ask her how she knew what men who *weren't* in uniform were thinking. I scarcely trusted her to know the doormen were not military men, though they weren't wearing military uniforms. "Are we almost there, sweetie?" my mom asked me. We were close enough that I could point to the Zimmermanns' apartment building; we could discern their doorman's uniform. No doubt my mom had waited for the best time to tell me what she'd been thinking. "You were the wrong age to hear Em's orgasms, but you should try to stop thinking about it—it's just not *realistic* for you to think about Em in that way, sweetie," my mother told me.

There were no secrets between my mom and the snowshoer. I could imagine how Molly and my mother would have worried about my infatuation with Em. It was tempting to think how Em might have pantomimed her thoughts about it. Maybe Molly would revise what she'd told me on my mom's wedding night. *There's only one way to love Em, Kid—just forget about it*, I could imagine Molly telling me. I knew it wasn't *realistic* for me to think about Em in that way, but my mom had known we would run out of time to talk about it.

"How may I help you?" the Zimmermanns' doorman was asking us, because we'd stopped in front of their apartment building. He was an older man—not quite my mother's age, but close to it. I explained that I had two gifts—one for Mrs. Zimmermann, one for Elmira. I said I'd been in school with Matthew; I told him we were wrestling teammates. My mom had taken her ski backpack off; she showed the two books to the gentlemanly doorman. "I'm going to miss the colonel, but it's just so sad—what happened to young Matthew," the doorman said.

"I *loved* young Matthew—that darling boy!" my mother cried, hugging the doorman. He ushered us into the lobby of the building, where I doubted the residents ever hugged him. The name tag on the breast pocket of his uniform jacket identified him as MILOS. The epaulets on the shoulders of his jacket were a little silly; they made him look like the leader of a lost marching band, but he was an otherwise dignified-looking doorman with what I thought was an Eastern European accent. He was wearing one of those Russian winter hats with earflaps—nothing of a marching band about it. I was trying to remember a Milos or two I'd met in Vienna. One was Czech; Milos was a Slavic name, the diminutive of Miloslav, I think he told me. Maybe the other Milos in Vienna was Serbian, but I can't remember. I was distracted by my mother; she was showing off for Milos, doing her single-leg lunges in the lobby. Little Ray didn't look sixty-seven; Milos probably thought she was younger than he was.

"Do you ski, Milos?" my mom asked him. She let him know she knew how to say *MEE-losh*. Given all the time she'd spent in Austria since she met the snowshoer, Little Ray had met a Milos or two.

"No, I do not ski," Milos told her regretfully.

"Well, I could teach you," my mother said flirtatiously. I'd not anticipated that my mom and a Park Avenue doorman would charm each other. They read my dedication to Zim; they agreed my author photo could be better. I knew it was only a matter of time before they would be talking again about Lieutenant Matthew—they'd both loved him.

"I could have shot him—I *should* have!" my mother cried out, seizing Milos by his wrists in her strong hands.

"She means Matthew's knee—she would have shot him in the knee," I told Milos. Nobody knew diddly-squat about what Milos was thinking, or what his politics were.

"If I'd shot him in the knee, no Vietnam—that darling boy would still be with us!" my mom cried, bursting into tears.

"You would have gone to jail," I reminded her.

"I *should* have, sweetie—that darling boy was worth going to jail for," my mother told me. I could feel the weight of the passage of time. Enough time had passed for me to agree with her.

"Yes, you should have," I said to her softly; she'd made me cry, or just remembering Zim had done it.

"Yes, you should have shot him—I would have visited you in jail, just to thank you!" Milos told her; he was sobbing. This would be my last day as a New Yorker.

I could see what I was letting myself in for. I would be renting the spec house in Manchester, I would be buying the uphill land with a view of Bromley Mountain—not to mention I would be meeting Grace. I was considering that I would be crazy to put myself in my mother's hands. Going skiing with her would be just the beginning.

Out on Park Avenue, my mom wouldn't let up with her single-leg lunges. It was what happened when she didn't get enough exercise, but she was also excited; she'd just kissed the doorman, as we were leaving the lobby. It was not a snowshoer kiss, but my mother gave Milos a pretty good one. I could see that Milos liked it.

"First time I kissed a guy in a uniform—first and last time, sweetie!" my mom kept singing, over and over. Whatever happened, I would always love her, I knew.

Thus, with my secondhand knowledge of sexual politics, I moved to Vermont—to what Em feared was an arranged marriage to a much younger woman, who would soon be pregnant. And what would such a life be like? I was wondering. It would be like learning to ski for the first time, I was imagining; it would be a fresh start. It would be my chance to have a normal life, I thought.

43.

A BOHEMIAN LIFESTYLE

There is no explaining certain things, not only the ghosts. It's a mystery to me why I missed the ghosts—except for the diaper man. When I moved to Vermont, I couldn't remember the last time I'd seen a ghost. I would have welcomed that woman with the baby carriage—the one who made me think she could have shot me, if she wanted to. If she'd ever had her shotgun with her, when she appeared. But even she didn't show up anymore. She'd never been credible as a ghost. Even my verifiable ghosts had gone away; with their departure, the story of my life was diminished. Without the ghosts, my life had lost its plot. I missed them.

Speaking of plot, now that I knew who my father was, there wasn't much to keep his story going forward—the momentum was gone. What had been the main event of my life, so far, turned out to be an underage boy. "He was just some kid, sweetie—he wasn't shaving. He was just a boy who couldn't take his eyes off me," my mom had told me. "He was *small*," she'd whispered, kissing me. "He would have been a pretty girl."

Finding out that Paul Goode was my father felt like an anticlimax to me. And I wasn't supposed to talk about him? I couldn't tell anyone who my father was, because he'd been underage. "That sucks," as Nora was known to say.

"We should keep this business about who your father is to ourselves, Kid," Molly more succinctly put it. We didn't want my mother to go to jail—or lose her job, teaching underage kids to ski.

Em echoed what Molly told me. "Nothing has changed because you know who your father is, except you know where your writer gene comes from," Em wrote me. Although I missed her when I moved to Vermont, I never wanted to see Em pantomime where my writer gene came from. Yet the past is everlasting. I imagined I would always hear Em's orgasm, from a distance.

"You were the wrong age to hear Em's orgasms," my mom had recently reminded me, "but you should try to stop thinking about it—it's just not *realistic* for you to think about Em in that way, sweetie." I should have listened to my mother, but not on the subject of Em's orgasm. What was *not realistic*, for a fiction writer, was for me to imagine I could ever stop thinking about Em *in that way*. And to think I used to wonder what it would be like to hear Em's orgasm firsthand. It might make you deaf, or otherwise cause permanent damage.

I do not believe I should have listened to my mom about everything, although I take to heart her "every creature wants to have a normal life—even an octopus!" In the context of how I'd hurt the feelings of people I loved, my mother was right to criticize me.

Yet what I really should have listened to my mother about were the lies of omission. So what if she was a hypocrite? As Nora knew, my mom was an authority on the subject of lies of omission; on that subject, like skiing, my mother knew what she was talking about. "You can't hide things or keep secrets from Grace—you have to tell her *everything*," my mom had told me.

"We didn't tell Adam we were more than friends, did we?" Molly had asked her. "We didn't tell him *everything*, Ray."

"We were *going to* tell you, sweetie," my mom had responded. There was no lasting acrimony, but what was lost in our conversation was my mother's advice. And then there was the underage business; to protect my mom, Molly and I (not to mention Little Ray herself) were disinclined to tell Grace everything. We were all okay about keeping my family history a secret from Grace.

There would be no follow-through to all the talk about lies of omission. As of Christmas Day, 1989, I still hadn't met Grace; I was beginning to wonder if my mother had changed her mind about my meeting her. I hadn't even gone skiing with my mom, as if she'd changed her mind about skiing with me, too. "What are you waiting for, Ray?" Molly asked. "Are you waiting for the week between Christmas and New Year's, when so many assholes are on skis that Adam will surely be struck and killed by an asshole skiing out of control?"

"Smarty-pants, Molly," my mother said, not answering the question.

I didn't delay in renting the spec house off West Road in Manchester, nor did my mom and Molly delay in furnishing it. They went overboard; the spec house had three bedrooms, and all the beds were in place before I even moved in. I found out, only after the fact, that the snowshoer was helping to pay for it. The death of the little Barlows was a windfall for Elliot, who'd been very generous to my mother—sharing with her the writing team's royalties and the profits from their properties in Austria.

"What a breadwinner Mr. Barlow has turned out to be—I couldn't have asked for a better husband!" my mom was fond of declaring.

And I couldn't have asked for a better father, I would always think—while the furniture kept coming to the spec house. Every two or three days, a new piece would show up. There were two hutches, but I had only one dining room, and the second hutch was even bigger than the first one—a giant cupboard or dresser, with open shelves above. I had the deliverymen put the huge hutch in one of the bedrooms—a guest bedroom, I was calling it. I knew Molly had to restrain my mother from buying a fourth bed. "This furniture isn't just for the spec house, sweetie—you'll need more than three bedrooms one day," my mom assured me.

I knew, of course, she meant the house I would *one day* build on the uphill piece of land I'd just bought in East Dorset. It was uphill, all right. Molly and I had walked around up there, in the knee-deep snow. "The land is a deal, Kid—you can always resell it," Molly said. I'd made an offer on the land, which had been instantly accepted. My mother had already been talking to a local contractor; I'd seen the drawings. I asked Molly why my mom believed I would one day need more than three bedrooms. "You should ask your mom yourself, Kid, but I can tell you how she does the math," Molly said. "There's the master bedroom, for you and Grace, and adjacent to it would be the baby's room—for the baby you're going to have as fast as humanly possible. But the baby's room would become Grace's dressing room as soon as the baby is old enough to have a room of its own, and that'll leave you without a guest bedroom."

"So I need four bedrooms, just to have one bedroom left over for guests?" I asked Molly.

"You're opening a can of worms, Kid, but your mom thinks you need *five* bedrooms—she says your kind of extended family needs more than one guest bedroom," the trail groomer told me.

"Extended to whom?" I asked.

"To be fair, Kid, your mom didn't name names," Molly said.

As it turned out, I could actually make use of the two guest bedrooms I had in the spec house—Em and the snowshoer came to stay with me for Christmas. Given Em's proclivity for nighttime traveling to the accessible bedrooms, the surplus furniture presented a hazard. Even armed with a flashlight, Em stubbed her toe on a chair in the upstairs hall, she banged her knee on the giant hutch—a formidable obstacle in her guest bedroom—and she walked into a tall armoire in Elliot Barlow's guest bedroom, scraping her shoulder.

For Christmas Eve dinner, Mr. Barlow made her beloved stuffed peppers. Molly and my mother came to dinner. I had a much bigger dining-room table in the spec house than the one Molly and my mom had; that was when Molly saw I had a bigger oven, too. Molly decided she should roast the turkey for our Christmas Day dinner in my kitchen; the snowshoer applauded this idea, because we could take turns basting the turkey. And on Christmas Day, Em entertained us with a funny pantomime enacting her furniture injuries, showing us the damage she'd incurred in her bedroom wanders: her swollen big toe, her scraped shoulder, her bruised knee. It's true that we saw Em's bra, and part of one breast when she showed us her shoulder, and Em just dropped her jeans when she showed us her knee. I knew when my mom was only pretending to laugh; I could tell she was inwardly seething. When she got me alone—I was basting the turkey—my mother cautioned me along these lines. "An outsider to our family, such as Grace, might misunderstand the unusual houseguest behavior of someone like Em, sweetie," my mom said.

"What are you saying, exactly?" I asked my mother.

It discomfited me to hear her say that Grace came from a *conventional* family—even more so, to hear that Grace sought to have such a family for herself. Yet I was unprepared to hear what my mother had to say about Em. "It's weird enough, sweetie, that Em is unable or unwilling to speak, and her pantomiming doesn't work so well offstage. Em needed Nora to be understandable, sweetie. But what really wouldn't work for Grace is Em's nocturnal wanderings—I know Em isn't sleeping around, sweetie, but Grace might misunderstand what looks like bed-hopping. If you know what I mean," my mom said.

After Christmas Day dinner, when Molly and my mom had gone home—and Em had gone to bed, alone, or she was starting out that way—the snowshoer and I did the dishes. I asked Elliot Barlow what she made of my mom's micromanaging of my meeting Grace. "You know your mother, Adam—she just doesn't want Grace to think you're one of those older writers who has been living a bohemian lifestyle," Mr. Barlow said.

"But haven't we all been living a bohemian lifestyle?" I asked the little English teacher, who just laughed. I should have considered the trans woman I was doing the dishes with. The snowshoer knew all there was to know about Little Ray's propensity for micromanaging. We both loved her, but we knew it was impossible to change her. That Christmas night, when Em wandered into my bedroom and got in bed with me, she just hugged me for a long time before she fell asleep; when I woke up, Em had moved on. I would lie awake thinking a bohemian lifestyle was a desirable way to live, but now I was destined to try living a different way.

I hadn't even met Grace, but I'd started to wring my hands again. I had stopped for a long time, but now that I had resumed, everyone noticed.

"I used to wring my hands, too, sweetie, but I stopped—around the time I stopped competing as a skier," my mother told me, out of the blue; it was the first I'd heard of her wringing her hands. There was no end to my mom's secrets, as Nora was known to say.

I just looked at Molly, who was laughing. "News to me, too, Kid," the trail groomer told me.

The snowshoer said she'd not seen me wring my hands since that time in the Zimmermanns' Park Avenue apartment, after Zim's memorial service, when Zim's fiancée—Francine DeCourcey, *of New York and Paris*—noticed me wringing my hands. Zim had probably told her about my damaged hands, my 4-F trigger finger. She knew my hands had been my ticket out of Vietnam.

"Give me your hands," Francine said to me, after she made me sit beside her. "If Matthew had your hands . . ." she started to say, her voice just stopping. "I could have *loved* him, if he had your hands," she told me a little later, when she reached again for my hands, wishing they were Zim's.

I hadn't wrung my hands for more than twenty years, but Mr. Barlow and I didn't believe I'd stopped wringing them because of my brief contact with Francine DeCourcey. Em was more interested in why my hand-wringing started up again. Em had stopped writing to me. I missed her writing me, but the little English teacher told me that third person was the voice Em should be writing in. Right now, it was better for Em when her voice was omniscient—a far cry from Em's first-person shtick as a pantomimist, or her letter-writing voice. I knew I would just have to wait for Em to write me again, or perhaps I could persuade her to write me in the third person.

Even if she wasn't writing me about it, I knew what Em thought about my hand-wringing making a comeback. I knew Em hadn't changed her mind about my walking into an arranged marriage. Elliot Barlow and I were familiar with Em's pantomime signifying a pending disaster. In Em's mind, my meeting Grace signified everything that was pending for me. It was no wonder I was wringing my hands again, in Em's opinion. If Little Ray had wrung her hands and stopped, my hand-wringing—not to mention my stopping for more than twenty years—was genetic. Given Em's parents, and their effect on Em's refusal to speak, it was understandable to me that Em was obsessed with inherited characteristics. Yet the snowshoer said the bad dad's letters to Cardinal O'Connor seemed to help Em control her animosity toward His Eminence.

I remembered how the kindly policewoman had recommended getting rid of the letters, or putting the letters in the hands of someone at the arch-diocese and just walking away. To my surprise, and Mr. Barlow's, Em had followed the second part of the policewoman's advice. With the snowshoer's help, Em took the letters—not in a box, just tied with some string—to the Archdiocese of New York, leaving the stack of pages with a secretary, or with someone in charge. The little English teacher had done the talking. These were the letters of a dying man who hoped to be baptized by and receive Communion from Cardinal O'Connor, the snowshoer had explained to the secretary. Indicating Em as the dying dad's daughter, with Em nodding her head off, Elliot Barlow assured the secretary that Em didn't expect the car-dinal to grant her father's wish. Em knew the archbishop of New York was too busy to baptize her father. Em knew her dad was a crackpot. Em only wished that someone in the archdiocese would acknowledge receipt of the letters and send her a note.

I knew Em's dad had died; I didn't suppose a note from someone in the archdiocese had shown up before her father's death. This didn't matter to Em, the snowshoer said. The return address on the letters to Cardinal O'Connor was the one on Shaftesbury Avenue, the Toronto property Em had inherited from her father; Em had crossed out the Toronto address on every letter. Elliot Barlow gave her East Sixty-fourth Street address to the person in charge at the archdiocese. Em seemed content to know that she would hear from the archdiocese, eventually.

"So what makes you think Em *can* control her animosity toward Cardinal O'Connor?" I asked Elliot Barlow.

"You know those things Em sometimes writes on the grocery list," the snowshoer said.

"You mean those things she writes that aren't groceries," I said.

"Precisely. Those things," Mr. Barlow said.

There was no mistaking Em's handwriting, even on a grocery list. When Em and I were living with Elliot in the pied-à-terre on East Sixty-fourth Street, the grocery list was always a work in progress under a magnet on the fridge. If I saw the snowshoer had put granola on the list, I might add, "Not that shit with the dried blueberries."

Em might come along and write, "Or the stuff with the organic almonds that break your teeth." This was not what Mr. Barlow and I meant about those things Em wrote on the list.

There were those times when Em would come along and use the grocery list as a forum for what she had to say—whatever happened to be on her mind, as a nonspeaking person who had her own ideas, but who didn't feel like writing you at the moment. In Em's mind, a grocery list was a message board; everyone saw your grocery list. My mother and Molly put their grocery list on the fridge, too. When I moved into the spec house in Manchester, my mom brought me some magnets for my fridge.

The snowshoer and I laughed about the time Em added a treatise to our small grocery list at the pied-à-terre. A longtime longhand woman, Em's incisive comments on our shopping list were meticulously punctuated. After the tea bags and the coffee beans, and the pork tenderloin with a question mark, Em had posed a pro-choice manifesto.

"In 1980, the right-to-lifers took control of the Republican Party's platform committee. Pro-life people, who sacralize the fetus, are the same people who generally oppose any meaningful welfare for unwanted children and unmarried mothers," Em wrote.

"At first, I thought this was Em's response to my asking about the pork tenderloin," the snowshoer said.

"What did Em put on your grocery list about Cardinal O'Connor?" I asked Elliot. It's a good thing there were only tea bags on the list, I'd been told; there was enough room for what Em had to say.

"It's not okay that Cardinal O'Connor is on the wrong side of a woman's right to choose an abortion, but the cardinal is just a lackey representing the Catholic hierarchy," Em began. "You can't hold His Eminence accountable, when what you're up against is a doctrine," Em went on—she was now writing on the other side of the shopping list. "And you can't blame the good Catholics who go to Mass, because they believe in something—not even if His Eminence is a doctrinaire son of a bitch who is servile to the Catholic hierarchy!" Em wrote on Mr. Barlow's grocery list.

"You can see why the third-person omniscient voice is a *safer* voice for Em to be in," the snowshoer said.

I agreed with Elliot Barlow: Em's writing was what would save her—the more all-knowing and somewhat detached, the better. No more threatening to burn down St. Patrick's Cathedral, not even if Cardinal O'Connor was a doctrinaire son of a bitch. Mr. Barlow and I didn't doubt that His Eminence was just a lackey, but the snowshoer was keeping her focus on Em as a rescue job.

Before they went back to New York, I showed Elliot and Em the uphill piece of land I'd bought off Dorset Hill Road. The little English teacher and I put our snowshoes on so that we could circle the perimeter of the property, but Em just flailed around in the hip-deep snow. I'd shown both of them the drawings of the house a local contractor had made, but there wasn't even a driveway off the access road. Among the trees and in all the snow, it was anybody's guess where the five bedrooms might be. This didn't deter Em from tramping all around and making five snow angels where she thought the bedrooms ought to go. The snowshoer and I didn't discourage her, although Em's snow angels were so far apart that they covered two acres—a bigger house than the local contractor was proposing to build for me. Em didn't have the best outdoor winter wear; her clothes got wet in the snow, and she was shivering with cold when we drove her back to the spec house for a hot bath.

Em revived, and her teeth stopped chattering, by the time I took her and Elliot to dinner at Molly and my mother's house in Manchester, where Molly made a lamb chili. I could sense that the night groomer and my mom weren't seeing eye to eye about something.

"The problem with men . . ." my mother was saying; she paused, to make sure she had everyone's attention. "The problem with men is that most of them get married before they're ready," my mom said; she was looking at Molly, expecting an argument, but the ski patroller just stirred her chili.

The snowshoer was wary, saying nothing; Mr. Barlow must have been down this road with Little Ray before. Em was nodding her head off; maybe Em didn't need to know the context of this conversation, or Em believed most men did everything before they were ready.

My mother suddenly embraced Elliot Barlow; all five feet two of Little Ray just hugged all four feet nine of Mr. Barlow. The snowshoer's face was pressed against my mom's breasts. "You were so ready to be married, perhaps because you were always a woman," my mother told the little English teacher. "You are the perfect husband for me, and the readiest man I ever met!" my mom declared. We could see that Elliot Barlow found it hard to breathe against my mother's breasts.

"I'll bet I was the smallest, if not the readiest, Ray," the snowshoer managed to say. Everyone laughed, Em and Molly included.

"I've told you, Kid—you know what I'm going to say," the trail groomer said. "I'll bet you your mom and the snowshoer last the longest—I'm betting they go the distance." Everyone cheered—even Em let out a holler. But the way Molly kept looking at my mom, I knew something was amiss. The snowshoer sensed it, too.

"Is there a context we're not getting, a married man who's behaving badly—is this about the new Paul Goode business?" the little English teacher asked. She asked the question pensively, with a far-off look; I couldn't tell if she was asking Molly or my mother.

"That's all it should be about, the new Paul Goode business," Molly answered Elliot. "Let it be, Ray—this is a good place to stop, to just let it be," the trail groomer told my mom.

"Smarty-pants, Molly," my mother said.

The French media had been rife with rumors about Paul Goode and his French co-star in the Argonne Forest war movie, *Argonne*—a World War I film that had finished shooting in the northeast of France; the movie was now in postproduction. A salacious story was going around, a scandal in the making. Some journalists were cynical about the truth of the story; it could be a marketing ploy. But the French journalists were taking the story seriously; a room-service waiter in a French hotel had captured Paul Goode and Juliette Leblanc on videotape.

Em sashayed around in a sexy way whenever Juliette Leblanc was mentioned. In my mom and Molly's kitchen, Em put two tangerines in her bra to make her boobs bigger. We understood that Em was doing her Juliette Leblanc imitation; Juliette was an ooh-la-la, va-va-voom kind of girl. *Argonne* was a black-and-white film, in French with English subtitles—not up to Paul Goode's kind of commercial expectations. Maybe the marketing mavens had had a hand in videotaping Paul Goode and Juliette Leblanc having breakfast in bed in their hotel; even with Paul Goode in it, a black-and-white movie with subtitles needed all the publicity it could get. *Argonne* would be in theaters in early 1990. "A film like that won't be in Manchester for two or three years, if ever," Molly said. In France, there was more interest in when the surreptitious videotape would be shown than there was in the theatrical release of *Argonne*. Paul Goode had finished shooting another new film, with his wife.

Unless there was a mystery guest coming to dinner, we were all in agreement that my philandering father was the epitome of *the problem with men*—as my mom had put it. Paul Goode wasn't ready to settle down and keep his pecker in his pants. Everyone sympathized with the wronged wife, Clara Swift, at home with her and Paul Goode's son—while my dad had been dipping his wick with Juliette Leblanc in France. As for Paul Goode and Clara Swift's kid, we took a guess at how old the boy would be—when the incriminating videotape was being shown, everywhere and all the time, when *Argonne* was playing or had already played in most movie theaters, though not yet playing in Manchester. We guessed the boy would be thirteen, old enough to know what was going on, young enough to be devastated by it. Our sympathies, surely, were with Clara Swift and the kid; none of us could remember the boy's name. But did any of us truly care if Paul Goode could or couldn't keep his pecker in his pants? Was that what this was about, or was my mom imagining I might have a *genetic* pecker problem?

"Are you thinking I may have inherited Paul Goode's unreadiness to be married?" I point-blank asked my mother.

Em's pantomime was immediately clear; I didn't need Nora to know what Em was saying. Em didn't nod or shake her head; she just pointed to herself and shrugged. Her expression was inquiring but nonjudgmental. *This is what I can't help wondering,* Em was saying. She wasn't speaking for my mom, only for herself.

"Don't go there, Kid," the night groomer told me.

"I don't think of infidelity as an inheritable characteristic, Adam—I've not heard of anyone who had a genetic predisposition to it," the little English teacher said.

"I've told you, sweetie—I don't think about Paul Goode at all. He was a nice boy when I knew him, but he was just some kid—he didn't know what he was doing," my mother said.

"That's a good place to leave it, Ray—right there," Molly told her.

Yet I couldn't help wondering what Em had been wondering. Her pantomime wasn't accusing me; Em was just thinking what I was thinking. I was my mother's son, wasn't I? Why wouldn't I want a one and only? But if I was my father's son, wouldn't I have a pecker problem, too? Em was watching me; I knew she knew what I was thinking. I was watching Molly at the stove. Whatever the argument was between my mom and Molly, I was betting I would take the trail groomer's side. Molly was as trustworthy as the snowshoer. There was a lot of lamb chili, more than enough for the five of us; maybe there really was a mystery guest coming to dinner. My mother liked drama, and she was good at it. What if Grace was coming to dinner? What if my meeting Grace, that old business, was all this was about?

"I'm just thinking about you, sweetie—I'm only thinking about your readiness, or unreadiness, to be married," my mom said.

"He knows, Ray—he must be wondering where you're hiding Grace," Molly told her.

"You're not ready to be married if you still think about that girl Zim found in Penn Station—you know, that *Buddy*, sweetie," my mother went on.

"Not again, Ray—no more of this," the night groomer tried to tell her.

"Or if you still think about that *principled young woman*, I think you called her—the one who wanted to read all of the dick novel, in order. You know, that *Emmanuelle*. You don't still think about her—do you, sweetie?" my mom asked me.

Like many smart people, Grace was very observant. If Grace had been there, I'm sure she would have noticed that I didn't or couldn't look at Em, who not once—for the rest of the dinner party—looked at me. If Em and I had looked at each other, we both would have known I was still thinking about her. It was *Em* I was still thinking about—not that *Buddy*, or that *Emmanuelle*—but I would not meet Grace, not that night, not when Em was around. There was no mystery guest coming to dinner; Molly's lamb chili was all for us. I took an enormous amount of leftovers back to the spec house. I would be eating lamb chili for days. Elliot and Em were leaving for New York the next morning, but we were up late in the spec house—telling *Moby-Dick* stories, and trying to translate Em's pantomimes.

Em wasn't the only serious fiction writer I knew who hadn't read *Moby-Dick*, but she was the only one I knew who once imagined it was a pornographic novel—a *dick* novel, as my mom had just called it. Em blamed Nora for this misunderstanding, but we all remembered Nora's hyphen theory fondly. Mr. Barlow and I had trouble understanding what Em was acting out for us—a certain moment Em was waiting for, when she intended to read *Moby-Dick*. It was necessary for Em to tip over the coffee table in order for us to understand she was waiting for an *upheaval* of some kind.

It was harder to get what Em was telling us about the unfolding Paul Goode scandal. Elliot and I got the part of the pantomime about Clara Swift—namely, how her longstanding decision not to give interviews served her well in this instance. The gossip columnists knew Clara Swift was off-limits. But the snowshoer and I didn't get what Em was saying about Paul Goode himself; it wasn't about his writing or his acting—that much we understood. Em seemed to be saying we might like him, if we knew him, but the little English teacher and I couldn't get what we might like about my father, or exactly what we would like him for. Em just gave up and went to bed.

It was already late, but Elliot and I stayed up a little longer. When we couldn't get what Em was pantomiming, we felt like we'd let her down. We were also exasperated with her; although it felt like we were betraying her, we wished Em would *talk* to us. Her terrible parents were dead. Hadn't she stopped speaking because of them? When Em lost Nora, she lost more than a partner; she lost her only collaborator. The snowshoer and I felt guilty for thinking about Em this way, but we wished we knew what could make her *speak*.

In the predawn light, I could see Em better than I usually did when she made her nighttime bedroom visits. Em looked stressed out, but I knew she wouldn't talk to me, and it was too early in the morning for an impromptu pantomime. She gave me a hug, but she didn't go back to sleep; she moved on. I thought I heard her doing something in the kitchen; then I heard her come back upstairs. She was probably visiting the snowshoer. In the morning, I watched them drive away; seeing them leave, I imagined my bohemian life was leaving with them.

I would wonder, later, if I might have been happier living in Manchester Village or Manchester Center rather than on that uphill piece of land so far from town. I was brand new in town; I'd just moved into the spec house, but I already liked living in town. I could put on my hiking boots and walk everywhere; I loved putting on my backpack and walking to the Northshire Bookstore in Manchester Center. It's a terrific bookstore—in the same league with Prairie Lights, in Iowa City. The first time I went to the Northshire, they treated me like a local author; the staff had read my novels. At first, I didn't realize that my mother had prepared the Northshire booksellers for my moving to town. And before my mom knew I was moving to Manchester, she and Molly had been buying my novels at the Northshire. I suddenly saw Grace from a new perspective: my mother had been giving my novels to all her ski-school students. As one of the booksellers at the Northshire told me: "Your two moms have been giving your books to everyone who works at Bromley, for years."

Not only at the Northshire, but at other places in Manchester, they knew who I was; they'd been expecting me to show up. I was happy that everyone already knew my *two moms'* story. I should have known that Little Ray was a local celebrity, and that the night groomer was no one you could overlook. I saw Molly's perspective on my underage dad in a new light; the story of the local author with two moms who worked at Bromley was a better story.

I would wonder, later, if it might have worked out if I'd stayed in town and bought the spec house. After all, it was for sale. As for the land off Dorset

Hill Road in East Dorset, Molly said I could always sell it. I should have sold it. I should have bought the spec house with the excess furniture; I could have put books in the second hutch. But when something doesn't work out, you don't know what might have worked. I don't believe that my staying in town would have helped.

The lies of omission were insurmountable. Once you start to acquiesce, there's no stopping the acquiescence. Passive resistance didn't work with Little Ray, and I wasn't capable of winning a full-on fight with my mother. Of course I didn't need a five-bedroom house with a view of the top of Bromley Mountain—nor did Grace. The three bedrooms in the spec house in Manchester would have sufficed for what went wrong.

44.

MEN WHO SHOULD BE CASTRATED

It was still the week between Christmas and New Year's when my mom took me skiing. Young kids skied up to us. "Hi, Ray!" the kids said. She was, or she had been, their ski instructor; all the kids called her Ray.

"This is my son, Adam—he's the writer," my mother reminded the kids. *They must hate me*, I was thinking; they'd probably been forced to read my novels when they were too young. My mom didn't even like my novels, I'd always thought.

Everyone who worked at Bromley spoke to her. She was just "Ray" to all of them—the other ski instructors, the patrollers, the lift operators. "This is my son, Adam—the *writer*," my mom always said. My novels must have been a burden to all these ski instructors, patrollers, and lift operators, I was thinking, but that didn't matter. I hadn't known my mother was proud of me as a writer. At that moment, I would have followed her instructions—not only as a skier. I would have married the next ski instructor or patroller who skied up to us, or the next kid who was of age, if my mom had said, *This is her, sweetie—this is the one I've been telling you about.*

"This is our new Poma fixed-grip quad, sweetie," was what my mother actually said, when we were riding the Blue Ribbon Quad to the top together. We'd started out on the old two-seater, the double chairlift everyone called "Number One." That old chair had a center post, and it came up behind you pretty fast. If you weren't ready for it, that Number One chair could knock you down; or, if you weren't looking for it, the safety bar would come down and bonk you on the head. "You have to pay attention to that old Number One, sweetie," my mom instructed. That was the lesson; the rest of the day, we were on the Blue Ribbon Quad. It was a better, faster chairlift than the old Number One two-seater, and many of the trails on that east side of Bromley were black-diamond runs.

My mother made me warm up on the blue runs; we probably took Upper Twister to Yodeler to the base of the Blue Ribbon chair. I just followed her. At the end of the day, my mom took me down a couple of black diamonds—certainly Stargazer to Lower Stargazer, and once or twice down Havoc. "You're a better skier on blue runs, sweetie," my mother told me. That was the lesson; on the steeper runs, I was struggling to keep my skis parallel, stemming my turns. I could have more fun on the blue runs; there was no shame in being an intermediate skier, my mother wanted me to learn. "Grace is a better skier than you are, and she always will be—just get over it, sweetie," my mom told me.

Skiers are always talking about a last run, as if the last run they take is the one that's going to kill them. My last run that first day was with Molly. The old ski patroller was almost seventy; she was waiting for us at the top of the Blue Ribbon Quad, as if she'd been expecting us. "I'll take the kid from here, Ray," the trail groomer told my mother.

"My one and only is a blue-run boy, Molly," my mom cautioned her.

"The last run should be a good one, Kid," the ski patroller said. She took me down black diamonds, definitely. We took Corkscrew to Pabst Panic or Pabst Peril; I can't remember if there was a No Name Chute then. If the names of ski trails were better, I might remember them. The management of Bromley kept changing hands. Before he died, Fred Pabst, Jr., the beer guy, had named some trails for his family's brewery and his Blue Ribbon beer.

Molly didn't give me any tips about my skiing; the trail groomer wanted to warn me about hotshots. "If you're skiing with people who ski better than you do, don't let them push you into anything," the ski patroller said. "Here's the thing about hotshots, Kid—assholes are assholes, no matter how good they are at something." For the rest of my life, it would be easier to remember Molly's warning about hotshots than the names of ski trails.

There was a lot to like about my first day back on skis. I had upheld my status as an intermediate skier, and I had a good time. I couldn't remember when I had last gone skiing, but I probably had hated it. Skiing with my mom and Molly, I knew I would get a little better, but not a lot. I would always be a blue-run guy. I didn't have a problem with that. I was living in a ski town with a great bookstore; everybody I met already knew I was a writer, whether they'd read me or not. I was going to get a lot of writing done, I was thinking. I didn't have a problem with that.

Nora had surmised the Barretts were likely to be Irish. I was so out of it, I'd not paid any attention to Grace's last name. "I suppose the Barretts go back to the Norman invasion," the snowshoer had said, but Nora hadn't been worried about the Normans.

"We originally came from County Cork, but our branch of Barretts were from Norfolk County in East Anglia—we were from the East of England," Grace's father, Arthur Barrett, had told my mother.

"I was just wondering if Grace is Catholic, Ray," Nora said.

"Goodness! Not that I've noticed," my mom said.

It was Molly who found a way to ask Catherine, Grace's mother, about the Catholicism. According to Catherine, those Barretts from England had let their Catholicism lapse a long time ago. The English Barretts were Anglicans. Catherine's maiden name was Barnard; her family came from England, too. "Both the Barretts and the Barnards were Church of England people, same as Episcopalians here," Catherine told the trail groomer.

It had been Nora's opinion that lapsed Catholics were the best ones. My mother assured Nora that Grace had grown up going to the Episcopal church in Manchester. Grace and her parents had always skipped going to church on Sundays in the winter; they'd gone skiing instead. By the time Grace was in high school, the whole family had stopped going to church at all. "If you ask me, sweetie, Grace is a lapsed Episcopalian," my mom told me.

"There is no such thing as a lapsed Episcopalian, Ray—Episcopalians are lapsed to begin with," the little English teacher said.

"I just didn't want you to go down the nonstop-procreation road, kiddo," Nora told me. That bullet dodged, there was nothing holding me back from meeting Grace. Even Jasmine had stopped calling.

"Jasmine is old enough to have died, sweetie," my mother reminded me.

I would wonder, later, why the difference in our ages had not held Grace back from meeting me. She was nearly fifteen years younger than I was; she was born the year my mom married Mr. Barlow, the year I started at Exeter. Grace was seventeen, in high school, when she began reading my novels—when I was already thirty-one. As the little English teacher would tell me, I was forgetting how the novels I'd read at Exeter had affected me; those nineteenth-century novels had made me want to be a writer. What if there'd been a contemporary novelist who affected me that way? There wasn't, but I was overlooking how my novels led to Grace's passion for reading other novels; Grace would tell me her interest in publishing began with her reading my novels.

We were married on June 9, 1990, a Saturday—scarcely six months after we met. Grace said she knew I knocked her up on the Wednesday before our wedding night—June 6, D-Day. About a month before we were married, the contractor had broken ground for the house we were building on that uphill piece of land in East Dorset; Grace and I already called it "our house," long before the ground had thawed and they were able to start digging. We knew we would still be living in the spec house when our baby was born; our new house wouldn't be ready to move into until June 1991.

Grace was good at making plans; editors need to be organized. As soon as she knew she was pregnant, she was setting up the amniocentesis. From Manchester, we would have to drive to Dartmouth-Hitchcock in New Hampshire for the procedure. This would be in mid-October, when the leaf peepers were cluttering up the roads in Vermont and New Hampshire. It would be a long, slow drive to Dartmouth-Hitchcock in foliage season, Grace forewarned me. When this trip was still four months away, Grace was factoring in the autumn foliage; she was well organized.

Grace would be thirty-five when she became a mother—old enough to make the amnio worth doing, her doctor told her. I don't remember the leaf peepers or the foliage when Grace had the amnio. I couldn't keep track of the plans Grace made; Molly had teased Grace and me about our determination to know the sex of our baby before it was born. Molly knew my mom had her own ideas about knowing the sex, and about the amnio.

"There wasn't the amnesia option when I had you, sweetie—but I wouldn't have wanted to know what sex you were, beforehand," my mother told me.

"Amnio is short for *amniocentesis*, Ray—not *amnesia*," Molly said.

"I know, smarty-pants—I was trying to be funny about it!" my mom said. She knew all about the reasoning behind amnio, she assured us—the sampling of amniotic fluid, to screen for abnormalities in the fetus. Little Ray just didn't like the idea of the needle. "I don't want anyone sticking a needle in my uterus, sweetie," my mother said. I would remember that.

I didn't notice, at first, how Grace overplayed the planning part of our lives. As a full-time fiction writer, I was happy to have someone come into my life and take charge of things. Until I met Grace, I'd never had as much time to write. Everyone said we were well matched. I felt free to concentrate on the fictional details; I entrusted the details of our real life to Grace.

Did I disregard the early signs of differences between us? I suppose I did—I wanted it to work out. "We all wanted it to work out, Kid," Molly later said.

One day, Grace would tell me, the ultrasound picture, which she'd had framed, faded from sight; the image whitened, until there were no details. I could only imagine that the tiny penis on the fetus was the first detail to disappear. Notwithstanding what a tiny penis it was, its meaning had once been so clarifying for us. We were going to have a baby boy. At the time, one rift between Grace and me had been avoided—we hadn't been able to agree on a girl's name. From the Barrett side of her family, Grace was asking me about Deirdre, Elizabeth, or Beryl; from the Barnard side, Grace asked me about Mary, Kate, or Rebecca. For a girl's name, I really wanted Nora or Rachel. There was no one alive who called my mother Rachel anymore; my mom was Ray to everyone.

Rachel was not a rescue ship in this instance. Grace had the highest esteem for Melville and *Moby-Dick,* but a girl who'd tormented Grace in school had been a Rachel—not a nice one—and I could sense Grace's misgivings about Nora. I knew Nora could be a bully to younger, prettier women, but I didn't know the particulars of Grace's fleeting contact with Nora and Em. Grace had seen *Two Dykes, One Who Talks* onstage at the Gallows; she'd introduced herself to Nora and Em backstage, at my mom's prompting. A ski-school student of Ray's from Vermont, now a New Yorker—a Clara Swift look-alike, but a pretty girl in her own right; in my imagination, those two dykes might have given Grace more than a once-over; they might have looked her up and down, but I didn't know what (if anything) actually happened.

Grace was a fiction editor who became a publisher; she admired Emily MacPherson's writing. Backstage at the Gallows, Grace thought it was strange that Em wouldn't speak to her; Grace assumed that Em's not speaking was part of her pantomime act. My mother and Molly had to explain later: Em didn't talk. At first, Grace only said that Em's not speaking hurt her career as a fiction writer. Later, when Grace was pregnant, she said: "When our child is learning to talk, it will be confusing to be around a nonspeaking adult—Em's not talking will seem unfriendly, or just weird, to a child." I let it go, although I knew what Grace was thinking. Em's not talking seemed unfriendly, or just weird, to *Grace.* I not only could sense Grace's misgivings about Nora; Grace's misgivings about Em were there from the start.

It didn't matter to me or Grace whether we had a boy or a girl. We just knew the naming business would be easier with a boy; for a boy's name, we both wanted Matthew. I was remembering Matthew Zimmermann, whereas Grace's father, Arthur Barrett, had lost a beloved brother in a different war— another Matthew, another soldier. Yet our knowing we would have a boy gave rise to an awkward moment. For the second time, Grace asked me to confirm that Elliot Barlow truly was my stepfather; Grace wanted me to reassure her that the snowshoer wasn't my actual father.

Like the first time she'd asked me, Grace didn't seem curious to know more about my biological father. Grace seemed content with my mom's dismissive version. "He was just some kid" was good enough for Grace.

"I assume they were both kids—I suppose he was a skier, too," Grace said, shortly after we met. She wasn't fishing.

"He was a skier, too," I repeated.

"I was only wondering if Mr. Barlow might be your *actual* father," Grace had said that first time. She was definitely fishing.

"No, my dad was just some kid—they were both kids," I'd assured her, that first time. I let it go both times, although I knew what Grace was thinking. She'd been thinking *genetically*. Grace had met the snowshoer—as a man, and as a woman.

"Elliot Barlow is wonderful—I adore him!" Grace had exclaimed to me.

"You adore *her*," I'd quietly said. Even people who meant well slipped up with the pronouns. And it didn't help that those of us closest to the snowshoer still referred to her as Mr. Barlow. I don't know why—it's just one of those things families do.

Yet I did know what Grace was thinking, twice, and I let it go. If we were going to have a baby boy, Grace wanted to be sure that our Matthew wouldn't change his mind about being a boy. I'm not saying there's no forgiving Grace for having such thoughts, but I don't forgive myself for letting it go.

That week between Christmas and New Year's, the final days of the 1980s, I went skiing with my mother and Molly two more times. Both days, my mom never mentioned Grace, and my last run was reserved for the night groomer. My mother always led me down the mountain; I turned where she turned, if nowhere near as perfectly. Molly made me go first; she told me which trail or trails to take, but she wanted to see if I knew how to follow the fall line, or if I even knew where the fall line was. Molly skied behind me; she was so close to me, I could hear her edges and her every word.

On Havoc, a black diamond, there was some constructive criticism. "Your inside edges are your best friends, Kid," I could hear the trail groomer (and her edges) telling me. The next day, Molly told me to take Pushover, a blue run—the longest, slowest run down the east side of the mountain from the top of the Blue Ribbon Quad. I should have known the night groomer had more to tell me than there would be time to say on a black-diamond run. "I'll bet you think you don't have any plans for New Year's Eve," the old ski patroller started.

"I *don't* have any plans for New Year's Eve," I asserted. Behind me, there was only the sound of the patroller's precise edging. "*Do I, Molly?*" I asked her.

My bigger dining-room table was the reason we were having the party in the spec house, the trail groomer told me. "I'll do the cooking, Kid, but your mom wants the Barretts to see where you're living, and she wants to show Grace some of your furniture," Molly said. Grace and her parents were coming for dinner.

"I see," I said. It was easier, on Pushover, to stay on top of my inside edges, and Molly made efficient use of our longer, slower run down the mountain. There was more to explain about my mother's plans for New Year's Eve. I assumed Little Ray wanted to be sure the guest bedrooms and bathrooms were presentable. "My recent guests were pretty tidy," I told the night groomer.

"Your mom has a full-scale sweep in mind, Kid—no trace of a female visitor left lying around," the ski patroller said. The *sweep* word was patroller lingo. Was my mother on a hunt for traces of Em's bedroom visits—a pair of panties or a bra she'd left behind? What other vestiges of Em might my mom be imagining?

"Nora was the one who wasn't neat," I reminded Molly.

"I know, Kid," the trail groomer told me.

Come New Year's Eve, even my fridge was clean; it was practically empty, except for beer. I'd finally finished the leftover lamb chili. I'd not been grocery shopping since Em and the snowshoer went back to New York. Even with the skiers in town, I could always find a seat at the bar when I went out to dinner alone in Manchester—or I ate at my mother's with her and Molly.

I tried not to notice my mom's *sweep* of the upstairs of the spec house, before our company came for dinner. My mother gave Grace and her mom a house tour, but Arthur Barrett chose to have a beer in the kitchen with Molly and me. Arthur asked me a couple of leading questions; they were questions I'd been asked before, ostensibly about my writing, but Molly and I both knew that Mr. Barrett was asking as a dad whose daughter might be interested in a much older man. They were *fatherly* questions, the ski patroller and I decided.

"In your novels, things that are already bad escalate into worse things—don't they?" Arthur Barrett asked. "You take things to extremes, to political extremes, to violent extremes, to sexual extremes—don't you?" Grace's father asked. "Is this just because you have what my daughter calls a 'disaster-prone imagination,' or do you believe this is how we actually live—that we are who we truly are when we go to these extremes?"

"I just have a disaster-prone imagination," I assured him.

"You know, Arthur, I've known Adam since he was a teenager, and he's never *tried* to make disasters happen—not that I remember," Molly told him.

"I *asked* you not to ask him those questions, Daddy—*everyone* asks him those questions!" we could hear Grace yelling from the dining room. The likeness to Clara Swift was all the more confounding, because Grace was cheerful and open—not the wary woman in a crisis I was used to seeing onscreen. Her physical resemblance to Clara Swift was unnerving, chiefly because Grace wasn't a character of Paul Goode's doom-laden creation— Grace wasn't a steely but brittle woman, facing a calamity of a noir kind. I really liked her.

Before we'd sat down to dinner, Arthur Barrett announced: "On New Year's Eve, I like to be home and in my pajamas before the ball drops on TV." Grace ignored him, but Catherine Barrett promised her husband he would be home in time to put his pajamas on. It didn't bode well for a rollicking late night. Undaunted, Grace regaled us with the story of her onetime attempt to see the ball drop in Times Square.

"It was all because of a visiting author," Grace began, but she was discreet; if you were her author, you could count on her discretion. Grace never told us the author's name. He was European; she was publishing him in translation. It was his first time in New York, and he'd arrived ahead of schedule— on New Year's Eve day. He'd called her home number; he had no plans and sounded forlorn. Grace changed her New Year's Eve plans. On such short notice, the only place she could take him to dinner was the restaurant in his hotel—he was staying at the Plaza. He had insisted on staying there, though that hotel was usually too expensive for publishers. "It would not be where we would choose to put *most* of our authors," Grace explained discreetly. The only table Grace could get was a late seating.

"He *hit* on her, after dinner—he tried to take her to his hotel room!" Arthur Barrett blurted out. "Are all authors so badly behaved?" Grace's father asked me.

"Absolutely yes. Don't give the story away, Daddy," Grace scolded him. "This author also hit on our pregnant publicist, on my editorial assistant, and on several of the journalists who interviewed him," Grace explained. "In lieu of going to his hotel room, I asked him if he'd ever seen the ball drop in Times Square. It was only an hour till midnight. I knew there would be a mob, and we'd never get close enough to see the ball, but I imagined we would get closer than we did," Grace said. She'd walked with the European author along West Fifty-ninth Street, but when they turned down Seventh Avenue, they couldn't get below West Fifty-sixth before the crowd and the police blocked their way. When the ball dropped, they could barely hear "Auld Lange Syne"; they saw some fireworks from a distance, but that was all they could see.

"It's better to watch the ball drop on TV," Grace said.

"That writer is one of those men who should be castrated," Arthur Barrett told us, but he was looking at me.

"We'll get you home in time to put your pajamas on," Catherine Barrett repeated to him, like a prayer.

I told a story about trying to see the ball drop—a misadventure with Em and Nora, one frigid New Year's Eve in Hell's Kitchen. Em was determined to leave early—to get as close as we could to Forty-second Street or Forty-third. "You'll be cold, you'll have to pee, some yahoos will try to feel you up," Nora had warned her, but Em pantomimed that she would go crazy watching the ball drop on the TV in their rat's-ass apartment in Hell's Kitchen.

The crowd was already shoulder to shoulder on Seventh Avenue when the yahoos came out of the Forty-ninth Street subway—four guys, big and sloppy, noisy and rude. It was clear they knew Nora and Em were a couple; they were closing in on Em, and making remarks about Nora, from the beginning. In the crowd, inching ahead, we came to a standstill before Forty-eighth Street; we couldn't get away from the yahoos. They were the type of guys who would ignore me, or pretend I wasn't there, until the fight started.

"I wonder if the cute one has ever been with a guy," one of the yahoos said, looking at Em.

"What's your name, cute one?" another yahoo asked Em, who was cringing between Nora and me.

"You gotta put a bag over the other one's head—you can't come lookin' at her," the third yahoo said, looking at Nora.

"I would bite your face off through the bag—I would crush your nuts with my knees," Nora told him.

The fourth yahoo reached around me and put his hand on Em's ass. Em's pantomime was obvious to Nora and me, not so obvious if you didn't know Em. She was cold, she had to pee, she wanted to watch the ball drop on

TV—with her head in Nora's lap. Nora never wanted to be anywhere near Times Square on New Year's Eve in the first place, but I knew Nora would be disinclined to leave because of a bunch of yahoos.

The police were all around; Nora waved to one of the cops, who made his way to her through the crowd. The first yahoo who'd spoken came to his own conclusions about Em's pantomime. "I wonder if the cute one is retarded, or if she's a mute or somethin'," the yahoo said.

"There's somethin' wrong with her, all right, but she's still the cute one," the second yahoo said; he was the one who had asked Em her name.

"How can I help you girls?" the policeman asked Nora.

"These guys are harassing us—that one put his hand on her ass," Nora told the cop, pointing to Em and the yahoo who touched her.

"Where are you girls from?" the policeman asked Em, who just froze.

"She doesn't speak," I told him.

"She's *retarded,* or somethin'!" the first yahoo was shouting.

"We're from *here*—we live in the neighborhood," Nora said to the policeman.

"Are you with these girls?" the cop asked me.

"Yes," I said.

"You should take them home," the cop told me; he was picking his way through the crowd, back to his fellow policemen, when Nora called after him.

"You're not helping us! *We're* not the problem—*they're* the problem!" Nora called to him, pointing to the yahoos.

"Just go home!" the cop called back to Nora, not bothering to turn and look at her.

"Just go home!" the yahoos chanted, emboldened by the feeble police response.

We weren't going to get close enough to see the ball drop, anyway. "We should go," I said to Nora, with Em nodding her head off, but I knew Nora.

"Where are *you* from—are you from out of town, or somewhere worse?" Nora asked the yahoos.

I knew how Nora felt about the walkouts at the Gallows; she always said the walkouts were from out of town. I hadn't known there was somewhere worse to be from. Clearly, the yahoos were confused.

"What's worse than from out of town?" the stupidest yahoo asked Nora; he was also the biggest. He was the one who had suggested putting a bag over Nora's head.

"From New Jersey," Nora told him. I don't know how Nora knew where the yahoos were from, or if she was just winging it, but that's when things got out of hand. A fiercely patriotic passion for the Garden State was ignited in the yahoos. The biggest guy—"the bag yahoo," as Nora would later refer to him—was purposely standing too close to Nora. He was the right height for her to head-butt him, I was thinking, when the yahoo who'd put his hand on Em's ass reached around me again. This time, he groped Em under her parka; from the way Em flinched and yelped, he must have pinched one of her breasts. I knew what Nora was going to do, but I was the one standing closest to the groper. I took his hand and put him in one of Coach Dearborn's wristlocks. The boob-pincher was a screamer, which brought our policeman back to us; this time, two cops came with him.

I knew Nora would head-butt the biggest guy. She butted him in the lips and the nose. When the bag yahoo tried to shield his face with his hands, Nora grabbed him by the balls; she held on until the cops came. "Like I said, *they're* the problem," Nora told our policeman.

"Where are you boys from?" our cop asked the yahoos.

The two yahoos who could speak spoke in unison. "Jersey," the yahoos said.

"You should go back to Jersey," our policeman told them.

The boob-pincher was holding his arm in a funny way. "Yeah, but . . ." he started to say.

"Just go back to Jersey!" one of the other cops said sharply to him.

The bag yahoo was curled in a fetal position on the Seventh Avenue sidewalk; his mouth was bleeding, but he wasn't talking because of his balls. We went west on Forty-ninth Street, heading uptown on Eighth Avenue. "Just go back to Jersey!" Nora was singing to herself. We would be back in that rat's-ass apartment in Hell's Kitchen in time to watch the ball drop on TV. Em was curled up on the couch, with her head in Nora's lap; I had the other end of the couch to myself.

"You know I loved Nora, but she made a lot of people angry, sweetie," my mother said now. This led to mention of the Gallows Lounge shooting.

"I read that you tried to attract the shooter's attention. Did you really want him to shoot you?" Arthur Barrett asked me.

"Em was onstage, and she was an easy target—that's all I knew," I told Grace's father.

"My dear Elliot went after the shooter—she went right at him!" my mom declared.

"The snowshoer was *the only hero*—I just tried to distract the shooter," I said.

Grace was discreet in the way she changed the subject from the shooting. "Some of my authors would never move to Vermont—they're more interested in their public appearances as writers than they are in writing," Grace began. She wasn't singling out her authors who lived in New York; writers' festivals were proliferating everywhere. We both knew authors who spent more time talking about writing than doing it. Grace asked me about screenwriting; at the time, I'd written a couple of adaptations and an original screenplay, but none of my movie scripts had been made.

I asked Grace about her driving from New York to Vermont almost every weekend; she must like to drive, I ventured to say. She loved to drive, she told me, but she also liked listening to audiobooks in the car. She listened to novels other publishers were publishing, and to those classic novels she'd read and loved in school. Our talk about writing put Arthur Barrett to sleep during dinner, but he awoke with a start in time for dessert. Mr. Barrett's mind must have been back on Seventh Avenue, with the ya-hoos from New Jersey, because this was the earlier conversation he seemed to be addressing.

"Castration is the only answer—those men from New Jersey should be castrated," Arthur Barrett said. "Castration really works, you know," he assured us.

"We know it works, Daddy," Grace told him.

Thank goodness Catherine Barrett's refrain was ready when we needed it. "We'll get you home in time to put your pajamas on," Mrs. Barrett promised her husband, who was wolfing down his dessert.

Molly had sautéed some salmon steaks with tomatoes and black olives, and she'd baked an apple pie. There was no drinking to speak of. Catherine kept telling us she was the driver; she didn't drink at all. The rest of us weren't knocking back the beer. After his second helping of pie, Arthur was antsy to leave; his pajamas and the ball drop beckoned him home, although the Barretts lived close by and it was nowhere near midnight. When my mom and Molly went out, the night groomer never had more than two beers; Molly was always the driver. "I'll drive you home, Grace, when Ray and I go home—if you want to stay and watch the ball drop with us," the trail groomer told her.

The lead-up to the ball drop was already on TV, after the elder Barretts went home and Grace was helping us clean up in the kitchen. Grace and I rinsed the dishes and loaded the dishwasher, while my mother and Molly wiped down the dining-room table and put away the leftovers. That was when Grace made two observations about Em and me, as writers. "I know you and Emily MacPherson are friends, and your writing has certain similarities—you both write about dysfunctional families, and you both like semicolons," Grace said.

I told Grace how I hadn't known Emily MacPherson was writing fiction until my students and I started reading her at the Iowa Writers' Workshop. Em had never told me, I explained to Grace. "But you and Em must write to each other now, don't you? Writers who are friends write to each other, don't they?" Grace asked me. As an editor, Grace understood fiction, and she knew fiction writers.

"Em is writing a third-person omniscient novel right now," I started to say, but I already knew I couldn't bullshit Grace. I didn't try to convince Grace that writing a novel in the third person precluded Em from writing me in the first person. "Em needs to feel a sense of detachment from herself in order to write about the Gallows Lounge shooting. I think Em needs to live in the third person for a while—maybe writing letters is too personal right now. We seem to have stopped writing letters to each other, for now," I told Grace. My mom and Molly kept quiet.

"Em seems eccentric, even for a fiction writer," Grace said.

"Em is eccentric—isn't she, sweetie?" my mother called from the dining room. I looked at Molly, who was putting the leftover salmon and apple pie in the fridge. The old ski patroller just stared back at me, as if my inside edges were in need of attention.

"Em is eccentric," I repeated. I hated myself for saying this. I felt like I was betraying Em. I really missed writing her, and receiving her letters. She'd written me not that long ago, but I'd put off answering her, and now we were no longer writing to each other.

"You used to talk all the time about going to Aspen and the Hotel Jerome. If you're still interested in going there, you better do it before you have a wife and kid," Em had written to me. "You would have a lot of explaining to do, if you went there with a wife and kid, wouldn't you?" Em had asked me.

While the night groomer was finding the channel for the ball drop on the TV in the living room, my mom was doing her jock walk in the kitchen, where she was watching Grace and me at the sink. At that moment, we must have struck my mother as a model of domesticity—I was washing the pots and pans, Grace drying them. We were standing hip to hip at the sink, almost touching; the way we'd been talking about the writing business, anyone would have thought we knew each other. I stole a look at her in profile; she seemed flawless. It felt completely natural to be standing this close to her. Em was right: I would have a lot of explaining to do if I went to Aspen and the Hotel Jerome with a wife and kid. *That's a trip I should take alone*, I was thinking—as soon as there was a window of opportunity.

The relaxed way Grace spoke to me made me think we were already living together. "If you feel like having half a beer, I'll split one with you," Grace said. My hands were wet; hers were dry.

"Sure—the beer is in the fridge," I told her. That was why she saw the grocery list. I'd not written anything on the list since the snowshoer and Em had gone back to New York. I saw Grace pause at the door to the fridge; she was reading the grocery list. At a glance, I could see it was a longer list than I remembered writing—ever.

"This is an *eccentric* grocery list," Grace said. *Uh-oh*, I was thinking—my mom's sweep of the upstairs had not found every trace of Em. Only Em would write a grocery list as long as the one Grace began reading to us, just as Molly came back in the kitchen. Given Grace's familiarity with Emily MacPherson's writing, Grace knew who'd made such an unusual contribution to my grocery list—and Em wasn't writing to me in the third person. Of course I remembered the recent context of what Em was now saying on a shopping list; Grace read aloud Em's pantomime, the one Mr. Barlow and I had struggled to understand. Poor Em had given up and gone to bed. Maybe mime wasn't the best theatrical technique for conveying an interior monologue. What Em meant was perfectly clear on the grocery list, and Grace Barrett was a good reader; Grace was easy to understand.

"In his interviews, even now, Paul Goode comes across as more believable and sympathetic than he ever does in his writing or his acting," Em had written. "I wonder if you might like him, if you met him; I wonder if you might think he was a good guy in real life. Maybe, if you met him, he wouldn't be the disappointment he is to you—as a writer. Perhaps, if you knew him, he would come off better than the one-note sarcastic little shit you think he is—as an actor," Em wrote.

"I've never seen a grocery list with a semicolon," Grace said, "and her handwriting is almost too precise to be handwritten. Does Emily MacPherson write in longhand?" Grace asked me.

"Em writes in longhand," I told her.

"You write in longhand, too, sweetie," my mom said; she was trying to change the subject. But Grace Barrett was an editor; she knew the subject on the grocery list was Paul Goode, not writing in longhand.

"Your mother told me you write in longhand, but I never knew you didn't like Paul Goode!" Grace exclaimed, taking a beer from the fridge.

"I'm not crazy about his writing or his acting," I said, trying to keep it simple.

"The heck with his writing or his acting—Paul Goode was the first man I imagined losing my virginity to," Grace told us. She'd been sixteen when she saw *The Wrong Car* for the first time. Her driver's license was brand new when she drove to Bennington to see the movie; maybe there was a noir film festival at the college. Grace thought it was a funny story; she seemed disconcerted that we weren't laughing. I'd seen *The Wrong Car* in 1960—when Grace was a four-year-old. She'd still been in high school when she saw *The Kindergarten Man*, she told us—"when Paul Goode was a little younger than you are now," Grace said to me. Our silence made her tentative.

"I've told you, sweetie—I don't think about Paul Goode at all," my mom suddenly blurted out.

I just looked at Molly, expecting the old ski patroller to say (as I'd heard her say before), "That's a good place to leave it, Ray—right there." But this time, Molly didn't speak up.

We must have been waiting for my mother to say more of the same old Paul Goode business. How I wish she had—I wish she'd told Grace everything. Molly and I were just waiting for it all to come out, but it didn't. My mom managed to stop herself from saying more; someone else had to say it.

"Well, I'm embarrassed about it now, but *actually* losing my virginity was not that big a deal—not compared to how I imagined losing it to Paul Goode," Grace felt compelled to say, since the three of us looked so stricken. "You all look like you would rather go back to the castration conversation," Grace told us. At least we laughed; an air of gloom had lifted.

"I don't think about Paul Goode, but I generally don't think about *men*," Molly reminded us; I knew she was just being funny, so we would keep laughing.

"Smarty-pants, Molly," my mother said. I looked at Grace; she was over her embarrassment. She'd forgotten we were going to share a beer; she was already drinking it, out of the bottle. I felt like having a whole beer myself. That was when I should have told her, when all of us were laughing. It would never get easier to tell Grace the story, I knew, but I got sidetracked by where to begin.

You've just met a woman you really like, but you need to tell her that the first man she imagined losing her virginity to is your father. She is now only a few years older than your father was when she first saw him; Paul Goode was thirty when he made *The Wrong Car.* He was forty-six when he made *The Kindergarten Man*—he was only two years younger than you are now. And, just to put the age thing into perspective, you have to tell her that your dad was only fourteen when he lost his virginity to your mom. I knew this detail might not be the best beginning. At fourteen, Paul Goode was a far cry from the getaway driver Grace had imagined losing her virginity to; that fourteen-year-old was too young to be driving. But, while I was wondering where to begin, Grace had moved on.

"Well, I'm glad my virginity story is over—I was beginning to feel like that woman with the baby carriage and the shotgun in *The Wrong Car.* You know what happened to her, don't you?" Grace asked me.

It would not be a surprise to me to learn that the woman with the baby carriage wasn't a ghost. And if my mother had interjected, about Paul Goode, *He was just a boy who couldn't take his eyes off me*—well, that would have been okay with me. *He would have been a pretty girl,* I wished she'd said, again—she didn't. My mom wasn't saying a word.

Maybe I could begin the story with the ghosts, I was thinking—remembering how that woman with the baby carriage never did anything but show up. Yet all I said to Grace was: "No, I don't know what happened to the woman with the baby carriage."

"She threatened to commit suicide after a restraining order was issued against her—prohibiting her from approaching or contacting Paul Goode," Grace said. I learned that the woman with the baby carriage never had a romantic relationship with Paul Goode—they weren't even lovers in the film. The woman had stalked Paul Goode; she'd sought to have a relationship with him, she spied on every woman who ever knew him. "Career-wise, she might as well have committed suicide," Grace said. That was when I wished I was in Aspen, at the Hotel Jerome—waiting for the ball to drop, among the ghosts. I said nothing to Grace about the ghosts, or about my father. I just watched my mother, never knowing what she might do or say.

Little Ray glared at the grocery list on the fridge door before she took out two beers, giving one to me. The solemnness that had greeted Grace's virginity story gripped us again; there was nothing lighthearted about the suicide threat of that woman with the baby carriage. I knew the night groomer's good intentions when she decided to dispel our gloom with a little levity.

Molly's mischief lifted our New Year's Eve out of the doldrums, just before the ball drop in Times Square.

"We should tell you two virginity stories, Grace—Adam played a part in losing two virginities," the trail groomer told the woman I would marry in June. "Didn't you, Kid?" Molly asked me. I knew the lost virginities Molly meant—mine and Maud's—and my mom was shrieking with laughter. Grace knew this wasn't to be taken seriously.

"You lost your virginity twice?" Grace asked me; she was already laughing. I was grateful to the night groomer for making Grace feel happy. We watched the stupid ball drop on the TV in the living room, while my mother and Molly did most of the storytelling.

My first time, my penis bender with Caroline, prompted my mother to whisper to me twice, as she had at the time—"You shouldn't have sex with a girl on *crutches*" and "You don't have sex with someone who's just had *surgery*"—but the old ski patroller, with her emergency medical training, provided Grace with the more comprehensive details of my penis injury. It was not a *permanently* bent penis that needed a surgery, Molly assured Grace, as the ski patroller had once assured me.

My mom took over telling Grace about my *next time*, when it was Maud's turn to lose her virginity. I had to interrupt my mother when she got confused about the two Helens, as she'd been confused before; the Helen who was thrown out of school, the girl Maud wanted to lose her virginity to, *didn't die*. She wasn't the same Helen as the one who dies in *Jane Eyre*, I explained; she was just a girl Maud didn't get to sleep with. "You don't have sex with a girl who thinks she may like girls," my mom told me, again, before she gave Grace the details of Maud's contradictory behavior—the way Maud wrapped her long legs around me as she clubbed me with her cast.

"Maud was in a cast?" Grace asked; my mother had overlooked Maud's broken arm and the cast, but she'd not forgotten Maud's *Yes!-No!* cries. Molly mentioned the bloodstains she'd painted over on Maud's cast, while my mom was putting the antiseptic on my face and ears.

"The *Yes!-No!* cries went on and on—it was not the *next time* I hoped you would have, Kid, after your penis bender," the old ski patroller told me.

Grace would tell me later that she made up her mind about me that New Year's Eve. "The way your mother and Molly teased you, and the way you went along with it—that's what made me trust your good nature," Grace would say. "You were *all* so good-natured," she said.

I didn't doubt Molly's good nature, or—most of the time—my mom's. My good nature wasn't that reliable. Grace may have misjudged the way I was happy to take a teasing from Molly and my mother. With everyone having such a good time, it was possible for me to do what writers do—we're always imagining a future story; we're already writing it. That New Year's Eve, I drifted away. I was no more present at the loss of my virginity, or Maud's, than I was at the ball drop in Times Square. I was already in Aspen—alone, at the Hotel Jerome. I saw myself there; it was a movie I was already writing. I was not yet plotting when a window of opportunity might come—the plotting, and the window, came later.

Expecting a baby when she would be thirty-five, Grace was careful and deliberate about her pregnancy. She was mindful of the discrepancies among the airlines, concerning when it was still safe to fly. Many airlines let you fly up to nine months; that sounded unsafe to Grace. Some international flights only took you up to seven. Grace asked her obstetrician, who was also a skier. No skiing, no flying, no altitude—not after the seventh month, her doctor said. I knew when I would go to Aspen and the Hotel Jerome—when Grace was starting her eighth month, my window of opportunity. I wasn't thinking about meeting Paul Goode, or wondering if I might like him. I didn't want to tell him he had a son, or get to know him, but we all want to know where we come from. I wanted to see the Hotel Jerome; I wanted to know more about the ghosts.

In December 1990, a couple of weeks before Christmas, Grace was six months pregnant; she was still working in New York, and driving almost every weekend to Vermont. Grace had seen the new Paul Goode movie, *The Other Man*, in New York. I hadn't seen it. *The Other Man* wouldn't be playing in Manchester anytime soon, but this didn't prevent people in Vermont from talking about it. Paul Goode's wife, Clara Swift, plays his unfaithful wife in *The Other Man*. In light of my father's scandalous affair with Juliette Leblanc, his co-star in *Argonne*, this was the talk of the town. No matter, my thoughts were in Aspen, where I knew I would be going. February 1991 would be Grace's eighth month. It hadn't occurred to me that *The Other Man* might be playing in Aspen long before it came to Manchester, Vermont. I wasn't interested in seeing more of Paul Goode. I just wanted to see the Hotel Jerome, and know more about the ghosts.

When you see ghosts, they're just there—they just show up. I don't know why, but either you see ghosts or you don't. You can see ghosts better in a movie than you can in a book. If you've ever been in an accident, or seen one close up, you will relive it again and again. When you relive an accident, it's always happening in the present—as if for the first time. Screenplays are written in the present tense, as if what you see is happening for the first time. That's why what happened to me in Aspen is a movie; it's always happening, again and again, for the first time. I will always see it as a movie.

45

LOGE PEAK

Black-and-white photo: five rough-looking men in front
of a crudely built shack.

> ADAM (V.O.)
> I've seen some ghosts before I knew they were
> ghosts—like these guys, in an Aspen mining camp
> in the 1880s.

Black-and-white photo: a group portrait of two dozen
miners, two children, a couple of dogs.

> ADAM (V.O.)
> I've seen this bunch in my sleep, or in my
> dreams—an afternoon shift at the Smuggler Mine,
> 1880s.

Black-and-white photo: two men working underground, one
with a sledge.

> ADAM (V.O.)
> These Aspen miners setting black-powder charges
> were blown to bits in the 1880s, but their
> ghosts are unscathed.

Black-and-white photo: heavily armed white men pose by
the bullet-riddled body of a dead Ute; one of the white
men's dead companions is propped up in a more dignified
position than the splayed-out body of the Ute.

                    ADAM (V.O.)
These Aspen volunteers helped put down the Ute
uprising of 1887. The Utes got the worst of it,
all around.

Black-and-white photo: a posed headshot of a well-
dressed, bearded gentleman.

                    ADAM (V.O.)
Jerome B. Wheeler, mine owner, Aspen patron—
financier of the first Hotel Jerome, 1889.
Wheeler went bankrupt in 1901. He lost the
Jerome for back taxes in 1909; he died in
1918.

Black-and-white photo: two mounted animal heads on the
wall of the Jerome ballroom; the unseeing glass eyes
of the bear and elk look down on three hunters with
rifles. The men are posed by a bulky thing, covered by
a stained tarp.

                    ADAM (V.O.)
Hunters with a new head for the hotel ballroom,
1890s.

Black-and-white photo: the Hollywood couple Lana Turner
and Lex ("Tarzan") Barker, dining at the Jerome.

                    ADAM (V.O.)
Lana Turner and Lex Barker, guests at the
Jerome in the 1950s. I didn't see Lana, but I
would see Lex.

Black-and-white photo: the pressed-tin ceiling of the
Antler Bar in the Hotel Jerome, 1990s. The mounted
animal heads are a mule deer, a buffalo, an elk, a
Rocky Mountain bighorn sheep.

> ADAM (V.O.)
> I wonder if there are rules for ghosts.

Black-and-white photo: the mule deer heads and antlers beside the mirror above the fireplace in the lobby of the Hotel Jerome, 1990s.

> ADAM (V.O.)
> And if there are ghosts who don't follow the rules.

Color photo: the movie poster for the new Paul Goode and Clara Swift film, *The Other Man*. Paul Goode is looking over Clara Swift's bare shoulder while she clings to him on a dance floor.

> ADAM (V.O.)
> Hollywood stars Paul Goode and Clara Swift— frequent guests at the Jerome.

EXT. ASPEN SIDEWALK, ISIS THEATRE, E. HOPKINS. NIGHT.

We see the imposing red-brick building, the ISIS sign, the poster for *The Other Man*—now playing in Aspen.

> ADAM (V.O.)
> My first night in Aspen, I was alone. The movie theater was near the hotel.

INT. ISIS THEATRE, E. HOPKINS. CONTINUOUS.

ONSCREEN: as they enter their hotel room, we should recognize PAUL GOODE and CLARA SWIFT, who were pictured dancing on the movie poster for *The Other Man*. They're returning from a formal party—he's wearing a tuxedo, she a fancy dress.

                    ADAM (V.O.)
In the film, they're married, but there's been
trouble—like in their real life. Speaking
of *trouble*, I didn't realize who was sitting
across the aisle from me—not until the movie
was near the end.

Paul doesn't look at Clara as he takes off his tux
jacket and unties his tie. She lets her pashmina shawl
fall off her bare shoulders; the décolletage of her
dress is revealing.

                    CLARA SWIFT
You could touch me, you know.

He is indifferent to the suggestion.

                    PAUL GOODE
    I know.

CUT TO: THREE WOMEN JOCKS in their late thirties are
seated together in the movie theater; the one with
the wheelchair has the aisle seat, with one hand on
her wheelchair in the aisle. The light from the film
flickers on their faces as we hear the voices of the
actors onscreen.

                    CLARA (O.C.)
              (her voice breaking)
You don't even look at me!

                    PAUL (O.C.)
I know what you look like.

MONIKA, the woman with the wheelchair, has an Austrian
accent; she doesn't bother to whisper.

MONIKA

He's going to kill her with sarcasm. That's his
thing—deadly sarcasm.

NAN, the woman jock next to Monika, whispers to her.

NAN
(whispering)
Someone will ask you to stop, Monika.

MONIKA

No one fucks with me, Nan—no one kicks out a
cripple.

BETH, the third woman jock, is captivated by the film.

PULL BACK: on Adam, watching the women jocks from his
seat across the aisle.

ADAM (V.O.)
The wheelchair and the Austrian accent gave
her away. Monika Behr was only in her early
twenties when she crashed on the women's
downhill course at Cortina. A spinal injury,
paralysis of both lower limbs—she became a
paraplegic.

ONSCREEN: Clara Swift is half-undressed; she sits at a
makeup table looking in the mirror, wearing just her
bra and panties. Clara is removing her jewelry.

CLARA
It's as if my body disgusts you.

MONIKA (O.C.)
This is pure exposition. Paul Goode can't write
or act. Have you seen *The Kiss in Düsseldorf*?
Gay Nazis kissing, a gay storm trooper killing

other storm troopers—it's better than this
shit!

DOUG, THE USHER, a teenage boy, stands in the aisle
beside Monika's chair.

>   DOUG
>   (whispers)
>   Please stop talking, Monika . . .

>   MONIKA
>   Sit in my wheelchair, Doug—I'll suck you off.

Doug goes away, talking to himself.

>   DOUG
>   No, thank you . . .

ONSCREEN: Paul's white shirt is unbuttoned, but he
holds his cuffs out to his wife. Clara takes off his
cuff links for him.

>   CLARA
>   You act as if I'm still seeing him. I haven't
>   seen him in months!

>   PAUL
>   I can still see him. As you say, I'm the one
>   with the imagination.

With a sob, Clara throws herself on the bed. Paul
reluctantly sits beside her. He stops himself from
touching her.

>   MONIKA (O.C.)
>   A lethal dose of sarcasm!

Clara lies on the bed, weeping. Paul is looking at the doors. He rubs his wife's back, still not looking at her. She rolls over, opening her arms to him. Even as he sinks down on her, he is warily looking around the hotel room—not at her.

> CLARA
>
> Please look at me, at least *look*!

Paul does, albeit briefly and not warmly, as they embrace on the bed; then he looks over her shoulder and sees one of the mirrored doors to the wardrobe closet swing open. The mirror reflects the foot of the bed, where (impossibly) THE OTHER MAN sits, removing his shoes. He looks over his shoulder and smiles at Paul, who lies frozen. The other man is no stranger to Paul.

ANOTHER ANGLE: the other man is unbuttoning his shirt when the bathroom door swings open, into the bedroom. Clara emerges from the bathroom, naked. She goes to the other man, kissing him.

EARLIER ANGLE: Paul lies rigidly in Clara's arms. They are alone in the room (and on the bed) as Paul continues to stare in the direction of the other man, who has vanished.

> CLARA
>
> (pushing Paul away)
> What is wrong with you?

CUT BACK TO: Adam and the women jocks in the Aspen audience. Nan and Beth are entranced by the movie; Adam and Monika look less enthralled.

> ADAM
>
> (to Monika)
> This is more noir than noir.

Monika is sizing up the smaller, older Adam (forty-nine).

                        MONIKA
    I'll show you more noir than noir.

Adam is sizing up the bigger, younger Monika.

ONSCREEN: Clara has drawn herself into a fetal position under the covers while Paul sits at the foot of the bed, smoking.

Paul sees the other man zipping up his pants, putting his shirt back on, carrying his shoes to the hotel-room door. As he leaves, the other man holds his index finger to his lips, cautioning Paul not to wake up Clara.

MUSIC OVER the end credits to *The Other Man.*

In the Aspen audience: house lights come up. The women jocks are clearly skiers. The way they're looking over Adam is simultaneously suspicious and predatory.

Monika makes sure that Adam notices her arm strength, as she lifts herself from the aisle seat into her wheelchair.

As Adam and the three big skiers go up the aisle together, the OTHER MOVIEGOERS are familiar with these women jocks. Nan pushes Monika's wheelchair; both Nan and Beth tower over Adam.

EXT. ASPEN SIDEWALK, ISIS THEATRE, E. HOPKINS. NIGHT.

The exiting moviegoers pass the poster for *The Other Man.* From her wheelchair, Monika watches Adam, who's looking at Paul Goode and Clara Swift.

> MONIKA

It ruins it for me—that they're married in real
life.

> NAN

So what if he's married? He still screws
around. Paul Goode has been screwin' that
Frenchie.

> MONIKA

Juliette Leblanc—not just any Frenchie, Nan.

> BETH

Married guys screw around the most.

> MONIKA
> (to Adam)

How about you? I saw your wedding ring.

> NAN

He's an old guy, Monika.

> BETH

Old guys screw around the most!

Adam is walking with them, but he doesn't know where
to go.

> ADAM

I'm lost. I'm trying to get back to the Jerome.

> NAN

Stick with us—that's where we're goin'.

> ADAM

You're staying at the Jerome?

>   BETH
> We *live* here. We don't stay at the Jerome—we
> just *drink* there.

Adam is puzzled. Nan and Beth are Americans, but Monika
Behr is Austrian.

>   ADAM
>   (to Monika)
> You live in Aspen? I know you're Austrian. I
> saw you ski.

>   MONIKA
>   (bitterly)
> You saw me *fall*—if you know who I am, you saw
> me fall.

>   NAN
> Give him a break, Monika—he's an old guy.

>   MONIKA
> What is it with you and old guys, Nan? He's not
> that old.

Beth purposely bumps her hip into Adam.

>   BETH
> He's old *and* small *and* married.

The three downhillers laugh. Adam is wary of these
three women jocks.

>   MONIKA
> Back to Paul Goode. I'm serious. Actors have to
> be believable. Once you're married, you're not
> believable.

                    BETH

If you look like Paul Goode, you don't have
to act.

                    ADAM

His wife is the actor in the family.

                    MONIKA

She's one of those women who is terminally
unhappy.

                    ADAM

You can tell she's unhappy?

                    MONIKA

I basically just hate her.

                    NAN

Where is your wife? Is she too old to fly, or
somethin'?

                    ADAM

She's expecting—she's too *pregnant* to fly.

                    BETH

If she's pregnant, she's a lot younger than
you are.

                    ADAM

Yes, my wife is younger than I am—we're kind of
newlyweds.

Beth bumps Adam with her hip again.

                    BETH

Newlyweds screw around, too, huh?

                        NAN
        Or are you just into the skiin' in Aspen—are
        you one of those old guys who thinks he's a
        hotshot skier?

Because she's not walking, Monika hasn't taken her eyes
off Adam. The way she examines him would make anyone
uncomfortable.

                        MONIKA
                (her most serious)
        This guy is not a hotshot skier. I know hotshot
        skiers.

                        ADAM
                (his most candid)
        I'm no better than an intermediate skier. My
        mom is an expert skier. My mother has been
        a ski instructor her whole life—she's still
        teaching kids to ski.

                        NAN
        Your mom must suck as a ski instructor, if
        you're just an intermediate.

                        ADAM
        It's not her fault. As a kid, I hated skiing—I
        tried not to learn, or I learned badly on
        purpose.

Nan and Beth laugh. Monika, watching Adam, knows he's
being truthful.

                        MONIKA
        Exactly what do you *do*?

                        ADAM
        I'm a writer—I write novels and screenplays.

                    NAN
          (to Beth)
I don't read novels. Do you?

                    BETH
Nah.

                    MONIKA
Nobody reads novels.

                    ADAM
Well, I've published some novels, but no one
has made my screenplays into movies—not yet.
          (to Monika)
I was a researcher for the film of *The
Kiss in Düsseldorf*. I spent most of my time
finding archive excerpts we could use from
Hitler's speech to the Industry Club of
Düsseldorf—it's a long speech, and my German
isn't very good.

Monika says something in German to him. No subtitles.
It's clear that Adam doesn't understand her.

                    MONIKA
Your German is intermediate.

                    ADAM
          (no subtitles)
Es tut mir leid . . .

                    MONIKA
He says he's *sorry*.

                    BETH
He's old and small and married, *and* he's an
intermediate—at everything!

Adam is aware that many of the PASSERSBY on the
sidewalk recognize Monika Behr; she is a celebrity in
Aspen.

> NAN
>
> Where are you from, intermediate man?

> ADAM
>
> Vermont. There's a small ski area close by—a
> family mountain, compared to what's around
> here.

> NAN
>
> Small-time skiin' in Vermont . . . mostly blue
> runs.

> BETH
>
> You should've stayed in Vermont, blue-run man.

> MONIKA
>
> You left a pregnant wife at home. You grew up
> hating skiing. But you came all the way to
> Aspen, to ski on blue runs. You're like Paul
> Goode—you're not believable.

Monika notices that Adam is sensitive to being told
he's *like* Paul Goode.

> MONIKA
>
> You even *look* like Paul Goode.

> NAN
> (to Adam)
>
> What are you doin' alone in Aspen, if you're
> not into skiin'?

EXT. HOTEL JEROME, E. MAIN. NIGHT.

Looking across East Main Street at the three-story
brick building.

> ADAM (O.C.)
> My mother stayed at the Jerome—the way she talks
> about the hotel made me want to stay here.

> NAN (O.C.)
> You're really into your mother!

CLOSER ON: two adjacent entrances—the main entrance to
the Jerome, and the entrance to the hotel's J-Bar.

> ADAM (O.C.)
> My mom and I see ghosts. She seems to know that
> some ghosts I see come from the Jerome.

ANOTHER ANGLE: on the sidewalk, peering in the window
of the J-Bar, is the DEAD UTE we saw in the black-and-
white photo of the Ute uprising in 1887. TWO SKIERS
come out of the bar; the Ute is invisible to them.

INT. J-BAR, HOTEL JEROME. NIGHT.

The bar is busy, lots of SKIERS. The skiers don't see
the TWO MINERS we saw setting black-powder charges
in the black-and-white photo of an Aspen mine in the
1880s. The ghost miners stand unnoticed at the bar; the
miner with the sledge glowers at LEX BARKER AS TARZAN,
shivering in a loincloth.

> NAN (O.C.)
> You should stop listenin' to your mother! If
> you grow up in this town, you get sick of
> hearin' about the ghosts at the Jerome.

At a table in the J-Bar, giving the WOMEN SKIERS a once-over, are the heavily armed ASPEN VOLUNTEERS from the 1887 Ute uprising—their dead, propped-up companion isn't with them. The invisible Indian-fighters sit unnoticed among the skiers. Tarzan knows he's not welcome to join them.

> BETH (O.C.)
> (a bored recitation)
> The drowned ten-year-old, the sobbing silver miner, the hotel maid who died of pneumonia—she still shows up, to turn down the beds . . .

Camera follows a WAITER from the J-Bar, bringing drinks to the Jerome lobby. Tarzan tags along.

INT. LOBBY, HOTEL JEROME. NIGHT.

We see the stuffed animal heads and the big mirror over the fireplace, as the waiter from the J-Bar serves drinks to some OLDER, WELL-HEELED GUESTS, who prefer the elegant decorum of the lobby to the rowdier atmosphere of the bar.

> MONIKA (O.C.)
> (irked with Beth and Nan)
> I've told you two—you don't listen. *Those* ghosts, the ones you hear about, are just tourist attractions. There are other ghosts.

The DEAD COMPANION of the 1887 Aspen volunteers looks out of place in the lobby. He is seated, in a propped-up fashion, in an overstuffed chair by the fireplace. No one sees him; he appears to be still bleeding from his wounds, looking barely more alive than he was in the black-and-white photo. He has

difficulty drinking the last of his beer; he regards
the half-naked Lex Barker as a no-good Ute.

> ADAM (O.C.)
> Those aren't the ghosts I've seen. I came to
> the Jerome without my wife, because I didn't
> want to frighten her—she doesn't know about the
> ghosts.

Camera follows the waiter from the lobby, back to the
J-Bar.

> BETH (O.C.)
> It's better not to talk about ghosts around
> Monika.

> NAN (O.C.)
> Monika didn't see the ghosts when she was first
> stayin' here—when she was still skiin'.

> BETH (O.C.)
> Yeah . . . it was only after the crash at
> Cortina, when Monika came back to Aspen. She
> stayed at the Jerome until she got a place of
> her own—*that* was when she saw the ghosts.

INT. J-BAR, HOTEL JEROME. NIGHT.

Coincident with the waiter's return to the bar, Nan
and Beth wheel Monika into the J-Bar—the two of them
jabbering, with Monika seething in her wheelchair. Adam
just follows along.

> NAN
> Yeah but, Beth, Monika had decided she was
> movin' to Aspen—she'd already started the

process of becomin' an American resident—before
the crash at Cortina.

> BETH
>
> I *know*, Nan—I'm just *explaining* to intermediate
> man . . .

> ADAM
>
> Adam, like the Garden of Eden guy.

> MONIKA
> (explodes, to Beth and Nan)
>
> You two don't *listen*! How many times do I have
> to tell you? Stop *explaining* me! You two don't
> explain me—I'm the one who explains me!
> (to Adam)
> If you were seeing ghosts from here before you
> came here, you should have stayed at home . . .
> Garden of Eden guy.
> (to Beth and Nan)
> I keep telling you two—not every ghost is seen
> by everyone.
> (to Adam)
> That's the only safe generalization about
> ghosts I know.

ANOTHER ANGLE: on Monika, watching Adam, as he surveys
the patrons in the J-Bar. She sees that he sees the two
miners, unnoticed by the skiers at the bar. Monika nods
to the table where the Aspen volunteers sit unseen; she
sees that Adam sees them, too.

> BETH
> (cautiously)
>
> Sometimes you're the one who doesn't listen,
> Monika.

                    NAN
          (also being careful)
Yeah, Monika—you don't always listen to us, you
know. I keep tellin' you—if you don't believe
in ghosts, you don't see them.

                   MONIKA
          (ignores her pals)
It isn't that simple, Adam. Maybe the ghosts
are just biding their time; after all, they
have lots of time. Maybe the ghosts are in
control of when or if they want you to see
them.

Adam is startled: suddenly the Ute we saw looking in
the window is standing next to him. There is an abiding
hatred that passes between the stoic Ute and the
Indian-fighters who killed him; the uprising isn't over
for them.

                   MONIKA
          (she knows the history)
There was only a small Ute uprising in 1887—it
was quickly put down. There would be no keeping
the white men from the Ute hunting grounds.

Beth and Nan have managed to secure a table; they're
signaling to Monika, who understands why Adam is so
fixated on the ghosts.

                   MONIKA
Is this your first day in town?
          (as Adam nods)
Your first night at the Jerome!

This gets the attention of some nearby skiers; the
Ute gives Adam a closer look, as Adam wheels Monika to
their table.

> MONIKA
> (to Beth and Nan)
> First night—he'll get clean sheets!

Nan and Beth know this routine; they know where this is going.

> ADAM
> (clueless)
> Well, I've just checked in. I *hope* I'll get clean sheets.

> MONIKA
> When I die, I want to lie in the sheets at the Hotel Jerome—I won't care if the sheets are clean. The sheets at the Jerome are the best in the world; even the dirty sheets at this hotel are the best sheets there are.

Adam is having a hard time moving on from the ghosts. The change of subject, to the bedsheets at the Jerome, is an agreeable one to the three women downhillers—they're behaving like the best of friends again. The waiter knows what the women jocks drink; he brings them their beer. Adam indicates that he'll have what they're having.

INT. BAGGAGE CAROUSEL, ASPEN AIRPORT. NIGHT.

Paul Goode and his wife, Clara Swift, have arrived in Aspen. They appear to be arguing, in as contained a manner as possible—given that they are traveling with TOBY, their fourteen-year-old son. There is no sound, except Adam's voice-over. Toby, wearing headphones, is listening to his own music; he stands apart from his unhappy parents. TWO BODYGUARDS gather bags from the carousel; then they collect the skis. OTTO is the

scary-looking one; BILLY is handsome but distracted.
They're aware of the unstable dynamic in the family
they're safeguarding.

> ADAM (V.O.)
> I wasn't expecting to encounter Paul Goode in
> Aspen, although he was a hometown boy. Given his
> much-publicized affair with Juliette Leblanc,
> his French co-star in *Argonne*, I didn't think
> Paul Goode would take his family skiing; I
> thought the Hollywood couple would keep out of
> sight. I was a little uneasy at the prospect of
> seeing the son of Clara Swift and Paul Goode—the
> boy had just turned fourteen, close to the age
> Paul Goode was when he met my mother and became
> my father. Paul was fourteen, almost fifteen; my
> mom was eighteen, almost nineteen.

EXT. PICKUP AREA, ASPEN AIRPORT. NIGHT.

Paul Goode and Clara Swift keep their voices down, at
some distance from Toby, who's cruising the sidewalk
in his headphones, and from Otto and Billy—they're at
curbside, overseeing the loading of the van.

> CLARA
> It's not how *public* an affair it was that
> bothers me, Paul—the publicity isn't your
> fault. It's that you had an affair at all.

> PAUL
> I know. I'm sorry . . .

They seem the reverse of their roles in *The Other Man.*

> CLARA
> I want to forgive you—I'm *trying.*

> PAUL
>
> I know you're trying . . .

> CLARA
>
> I want Toby to forgive you, too.

> PAUL
>
> It's awful that Toby knows.

> CLARA
> (softly)
>
> Everyone knows . . .

> PAUL
> (softer)
>
> I know . . .

Camera follows Toby in his headphones, cruising closer to Otto and Billy—they're talking quietly to each other while the DRIVER loads the Hotel Jerome van.

> BILLY
>
> I mean the Frenchwoman from the war movie. Do you know other Frenchwomen?

> OTTO
>
> *That* Frenchwoman! Does Toby know?

> BILLY
>
> Otto, only *you* don't know.

> OTTO
>
> Jeez, Billy . . . the poor kid.

Toby is near to them now, nodding his head—as if to his music. The bodyguards assume Toby can't hear them.

                    BILLY
Toby's a good kid—he'll be fine.

                    OTTO
Toby's a *great* kid. And those two will be okay—
they love each other. Fuck that Frenchwoman!

                    TOBY
        (he's heard everything)
Yeah, fuck her . . .

                    BILLY
We thought you were listenin' to your music,
Toby.

                    TOBY
        (nods, toward his parents)
I'm just not listening to *them*.

Toby is very much a kid. It's uncomfortable to imagine
Toby—or his father, when he was close to Toby's age—
making anyone pregnant.

INT. J-BAR, HOTEL JEROME. NIGHT.

The women downhillers have been hitting the beer.
The talk at their table has devolved into two
conversations: Adam and Monika are talking about her
gym in Aspen; Nan and Beth are bored and looking for
guys.

                    MONIKA
I wanted to open a gym in Aspen before I moved
here. I was always going to call my gym The
Last Run. I was thinking of my life after
racing—not my fall.

> ADAM

Do the para-alpine skiers train in your gym?
They must love you.

> MONIKA

I love the para-athletes. They don't have to
love me back—it's enough they know I can make
them stronger. I'm just a gym rat now.

> BETH

I don't see one guy who makes me feel like it—
no one I'm considering.

> NAN

No one worth considerin'?

> ADAM

I'm more of a gym rat than I am a skier. I was
a wrestler in high school—nothing came of it,
but I still like going to a gym.

> BETH

No aerobic machines in The Last Run.

> NAN

You want to run or ride a bike, do it outdoors.
The Last Run is a gym for weight trainin'.

> MONIKA
> (ignores them; to Adam)

There's a kind of circuit training that's
aerobic. I know how to get you out of breath.

Adam sees a tall, elegantly dressed ghost at the bar—a
STATELY, BEARDED GENTLEMAN.

> ADAM

Jerome B. Wheeler was a Civil War hero in the

New York Cavalry and the former president of
Macy's.

Monika isn't impressed by this important ghost.

>   MONIKA
>   Jerome is such a big deal.
>   (as Adam nods)
>   He thinks he still owns the place.

Playing bartender, Jerome acts like he does own the
place; he fills a pitcher of draft beer from the bar.

>   BETH
>   The place is packed, but there's no one!

>   NAN
>   It's dead tonight, packed but dead.

The two miners at the bar react with disbelief to Nan's
remark, but Jerome B. Wheeler just smiles to the miners
as he refills their beer glasses. The miner with the
sledge gives Wheeler a salute with his hammer.

EXT. ENTRANCE, HOTEL JEROME, E. MAIN. NIGHT.

The van we saw at the airport pulls up. The JEROME
DOORMEN in their long coats and cowboy hats rush to
assist.

>   BETH (O.C.)
>   We could see who's in the lobby.

>   NAN (O.C.)
>   The la-di-da guests like the lobby.

Otto and Billy escort Paul Goode and Clara Swift into
the hotel; Toby sullenly follows them.

>   ADAM (O.C.)
>   Okay, let's see who's in the lobby.

INT. LOBBY, HOTEL JEROME. NIGHT.

Not as la-di-da-looking as the other guests, the Aspen
volunteer is still propped up in a chair by the fireplace,
as Jerome B. Wheeler refills his empty beer glass.

WIDER: to include Adam and the women downhillers in the
lobby.

>   MONIKA
>   (to Adam)
>   I don't know how that guy can still be
>   bleeding. I don't mean Jerome.

>   NAN
>   (to Adam)
>   Monika's goin' to ask you if she can sleep
>   over, just to feel your sheets.

>   MONIKA
>   You're explaining me again, Nan.

>   BETH
>   I've never *stayed* here, but I've slept here
>   with some guys. I never noticed the sheets.

It's an old joke, but the downhillers laugh.

ANOTHER ANGLE: as Paul Goode and his family pass
through, the two bodyguards look warily around, but the
Jerome lobby is a relatively fan-free place. The other

guests keep their distance. It's Paul Goode they stare
at. No one notices his wife. Clara Swift is lovely,
but she keeps herself plain. Adam looks quickly at his
father; as quickly, he looks away.

> BETH
> If I checked into a hotel with Paul Goode, I
> could come before I got to the room.

> NAN
> I could be comin' now.

Monika notices how Adam looks at Clara Swift.

> MONIKA
> See something you like, Adam?

> ADAM
> She's a great actor.

> MONIKA
> That's not how you looked at her.

It takes TWO PORTERS with two luggage carts to tote the
stuff for this entourage. Adam awkwardly blocks Clara
Swift's path.

> ADAM
> Excuse me, Ms. Swift—I just want to say how
> much I admire your work.

The bodyguards surround Adam, letting Clara pass. She's
not offended by Adam; she's embarrassed by Billy and
Otto's protectiveness.

> CLARA
> (to her bodyguards)
> He's okay—he's being nice.

She is so shy, so self-conscious—she can barely speak.
Toby, coming last, captures Adam's attention.

> ADAM (V.O.)
> The kid looked like a ghost I'd seen before.

Black-and-white photo: the same actor who plays Toby
at fourteen; he is standing with a snow shovel at the
entrance to the Jerome. The boy is wearing jeans and
cowboy boots.

> ADAM (V.O.)
> The sweater was too wide for his shoulders and
> the pom-pom on the ski hat was too girlish. A
> hotel guest, a woman, must have given her old
> hat and sweater to this boy. I once believed
> he was the ghost of the fourteen-year-old who
> became my father.

As Toby reluctantly follows his family through the
lobby, Monika sees how Adam is transfixed by the boy.

> ADAM (V.O.)
> But Paul Goode was alive. How could my father
> be a ghost if he was still alive?

> MONIKA
> That's their *kid,* you know—he's not a ghost.

> ADAM
> I know . . .

> MONIKA
> The way you were looking at him, you looked
> like you'd seen another ghost.

Standing confused and ungreeted in the lobby are the
THREE HUNTERS toting rifles; they're dragging a thing

covered by a stained tarp. The severed head of a big
animal, to be stuffed and mounted in the ballroom or on
another wall. The epitome of a gracious hotelkeeper,
Jerome B. Wheeler greets the hunters, leading them and
the unseen head out of the lobby.

> MONIKA

The hunters don't get it—taxidermy is a dying
art. There's no room for an animal head here.
> (as Adam nods)

About the *sheets* . . . no pressure.

> ADAM

I'm being faithful to my wife.

> MONIKA

I'm serious about the sheets at the Jerome—just
the sheets.

> BETH
> (eavesdropping)

She's not into you, intermediate man—Monika's
into the sheets.

> NAN
> (pulls Beth away)

Stop explainin' . . .

> MONIKA

If you change your mind, Adam, I know how to
get you out of breath.

> ADAM

I'm new at having to be faithful—I'm not tired
of it.

> MONIKA

I'm mainly into the sheets, and you're new to

this altitude—you would be out of breath when I
was just getting started.
            (with a nod of her head)
The elevator is that way.

Adam takes the handles of Monika's wheelchair and wheels
her out of the lobby. Beth and Nan stare after them.

                BETH
She did it again—there's a sort of cute guy,
and he goes off with the paraplegic. We were
losers as skiers, too, Nan.

                NAN
Beth, Monika can't *walk.* I'm just sick of
hearin' about the *sheets.*

                BETH
We're depressed and angry most of the time,
Nan. So what if we can *walk*? Monika gets laid
more than we do.

                NAN
            (depressed and angry)
And she gets off on the sheets.

INT. ELEVATOR, HOTEL JEROME. NIGHT.

Adam and Monika are riding the elevator. A forlorn
ghost rides with them, A COWBOY carrying his saddle;
the cowboy regards the wheelchair with disdain—not his
idea of a good ride. Adam has to lean over Monika to
hear what she says.

                MONIKA
Aspen never was an easy town for cowboys.
Miners, hunters, a few trappers—they're the

ones who made it here. Mules are more capable
than horses in the mountains.

INT. HALL, HOTEL JEROME. NIGHT.

The elevator lets Adam and Monika out on the third
floor. The cowboy stays on the elevator.

>   ADAM
> Doesn't the cowboy know there are only three
> floors?

>   MONIKA
> That cowboy just rides the elevator.

They pass a BLONDE HOTEL MAID, not a ghost, then
the barefoot Tarzan. Monika makes apelike grunts and
gestures, mocking Lex.

>   ADAM
> Maybe you've seen a ghost maid—she looks
> Mexican to me. My mother saw her here when the
> maid was still alive—my mom thought she was
> Italian.

>   MONIKA
> I know her—she's Mexican. She's Paul Goode's
> mother.

Black-and-white photo: a Mexican hotel maid with a shy,
childlike smile.

INT. BEDROOM, HOTEL JEROME. NIGHT.

Adam and Monika talk, but Adam's voice-over is all we
hear.

> ADAM (V.O.)
> Monika told me that Paul Goode was adored in
> Aspen and beloved by the Jerome. Either Lex
> Barker or Lana Turner told him to change his
> name from Paulino Juárez. Lex came up with with
> the Goode, with an e on the end.

Monika is feeling the sheets. Adam offers her a hotel
bathrobe; she wheels herself into the bathroom, leaving
Adam to undress for bed. He considers how he looks in
his undershorts before putting on a hotel bathrobe.

> ADAM (V.O.)
> I'd once thought that the Jerome's acceptance
> of their unmarried maid's pregnancy was an
> unlikely story—surely someone at the hotel must
> have made the unwed mother feel unwelcome.

Monika wheels into the bedroom in the bathrobe; she
turns on the radio, to a plaintive country song. When
Adam goes into the bathroom, Monika takes off the robe
and vaults onto the bed. She's naked except for her
panties, and she's soundlessly mouthing the words to
the song.

> ADAM (V.O.)
> But Monika convinced me I was wrong. In her
> Austrian way, she asserted that New Englanders
> were a bunch of Puritans—people out west
> weren't as sexually uptight, she said.

Monika experiments with how she wants to present
herself to Adam. She lies on her back, breasts up,
the top sheet and blanket covering her legs. She tries
lying on her stomach, showing her bare back and only
enough of her panties to indicate she's not entirely
naked.

                    ADAM (V.O.)
Monika hated Paul Goode's acting and his
writing, but she said he wasn't lying about his
happy childhood.

Adam enters the bedroom from the bathroom. Seeing
Monika's bare back, and enough of her panties to know
she's almost naked, he takes off his bathrobe and turns
off the country music.

                    MONIKA
               (on her stomach)
Don't look for a scar. If there'd been
shattered bone and fragments, there could have
been a surgery, but the damage was what they
call *clean*. No surgery, no scar.

She rolls over on her back—breasts up.

                    ADAM
     I see.

INT. J-BAR, HOTEL JEROME. NIGHT.

Country music masks how near-empty and quiet it is.
Even the Aspen volunteers are gone. At a table, the Ute
and Jerome B. Wheeler are talking, but we can't hear
them—only Adam and Monika's conversation.

                    MONIKA (O.C.)
Are you ready to feel the sheets?

                    ADAM (O.C.)
     I guess so . . .

ANOTHER ANGLE: at one end of the bar, Otto and Billy
are talking too quietly for us to overhear them. One of

the ghost miners has passed out on the middle of the
bar; the one with the sledge is still standing, but he
can barely keep his eyes open.

> MONIKA (O.C.)
> Are you just going to look at me all night, or
> do you always sleep with a light on?

> ADAM (O.C.)
> Oh . . . sorry.

> MONIKA (O.C.)
> (we hear a *click*)
> That's better.

At the opposite end of the bar from the bodyguards,
Beth and Nan are sloshed; we can hear their
conversation.

> BETH
> Not the scary-looking one—I said the other
> bodyguard is kind of cute.

> NAN
> You should never go anywhere alone, Beth—you
> could get in trouble.

> BETH
> Nan, we don't get in enough trouble.

The miner with the sledge falls asleep on his feet,
dropping his sledge with a RESOUNDING THUMP. Only
the Ute and Jerome B. Wheeler hear it. The courteous
Wheeler gives the miner a benign smile. The fallen
sledge wakes up the miner who dropped it—if not his
partner, passed out on the bar. The bodyguards are
leaving. Billy gives the women downhillers a glance;
Otto gives them a ghastly smile.

>   NAN
No bodyguards, Beth—they could be into rough
stuff. And those two guys look like they do
everythin' together.

>   BETH
I don't like rough stuff. I don't do two guys,
not together. Do you?

Nan gives Beth an incredulous look. Beth stares at her
beer.

INT. BEDROOM, HOTEL JEROME. NIGHT.

On Clara Swift's troubled face—she's asleep, dreaming.

INT. FIELD HOSPITAL, NORTHEASTERN FRANCE. DAY.

Black-and-white World War I movie: the French actress
JULIETTE LEBLANC is a nurse. As STRETCHER-BEARERS bring
in the WOUNDED SOLDIERS, Juliette is asking a MEDIC
about their wounds.

>   JULIETTE
>   (French, English subtitles)
The ones from the mortar?

>   MEDIC
Oui.

>   JULIETTE
>   (French, English subtitles)
What are his wounds?

                MEDIC
        (French, English subtitles)
   Neck, upper chest.

Juliette continues down the line of NEW ARRIVALS.

              JULIETTE
        (French, English subtitles)
   And this one?

                MEDIC
        (French, English subtitles)
   His hands, his face.

She stops at the next soldier—Paul Goode lies on the
stretcher, his expression glazed with pain, bloody from
his waist to his upper thighs. She looks at him as if
she's been waiting to meet him her whole life.

                MEDIC
        (French, English subtitles)
   This is the American.

Juliette leans over Paul.

              JULIETTE
        (in English)
   Hello, my dear.

               PAUL
        (French, English subtitles)
   I am American.

              JULIETTE
        (English)
   I know. Where are you wounded?

Paul can't or won't say. Her eyes drift to the bloody area.

> JULIETTE
> (English)
> May I look? Okay?

Juliette doesn't like what she sees; she quickly looks away, then into his eyes. Paul has never taken his eyes off her.

FREEZE TO A STILL. This shot is the black-and-white movie poster for *Argonne,* starring Paul Goode and Juliette Leblanc.

INT. BEDROOM, HOTEL JEROME. NIGHT.

Clara is still asleep; she hates this dream.

INT. HALL, FRENCH HOTEL—CLEARLY NOT WORLD WAR I. DAY.

Color: a ROOM-SERVICE WAITER wheels a breakfast cart down the hall, stopping by a door. From a basket that could hold bread, the waiter turns on a video camera, which he covers with a white napkin. Then he knocks on the door of the room.

> WAITER
> (French, no subtitles)
> Good morning! Breakfast!

INT. BEDROOM, FRENCH HOTEL. DAY.

Paul Goode lets the waiter in. We see the lens of the video camera under the napkin as the waiter takes

various items from the cart and sets a table for two.
Paul is wearing a towel around his waist; he looks like
he's just had a shower. The waiter asks him something
in French.

                    PAUL
          (French, no subtitles)
      I am American.

From the bed, Juliette answers the waiter in French—
no subtitles. The waiter turns the breakfast cart
so that the video camera is on her. She is sitting
up in bed with the covers pulled around her; she
must not be wearing any clothes. Paul pours a cup of
coffee and brings it to her. The waiter is through
setting the table; he's angling the breakfast cart
to catch them both on camera. As Juliette sips the
coffee, she lets one bare arm reach out; her hand
touches Paul's leg. Paul and Juliette see that the
waiter is still there in the room. They give him an
inquiring look.

ON FRENCH TV NEWS: IN FRENCH, ENGLISH SUBTITLES.

An unseen woman journalist babbles away, voice-over to
the footage of Paul and Juliette captured on videotape.

                 JOURNALIST (V.O.)
          (French, English subtitles)
      It seems that the American actor Paul Goode and
      the French actress Juliette Leblanc were more
      than co-stars in the Argonne Forest war movie,
      Argonne, when they were shooting the film in
      the northeast of France.

We see Paul admitting the waiter to the room—then the
jerky PAN to Juliette, still in bed.

>   JOURNALIST (V.O.)
>   (French, English subtitles)
> While they were registered in separate rooms,
> they appear to have enjoyed breakfast together.
> This poses no problem for Juliette—she is
> unmarried and has no boyfriend at the moment—
> but Paul Goode is very much married to the
> American actress Clara Swift.

File footage of Paul and Clara together in happier
times; there's also a shot of Clara with TOBY AS A BABY.

>   JOURNALIST (V.O.)
>   (French, English subtitles)
> Cynics say this was publicity for *Argonne*—the
> story came to light just before the film's
> release.

Paul and Juliette look inquiringly at the hidden video
camera as the breakfast cart retreats from them, the
door to the hotel room closing on our view.

INT. BEDROOM, HOTEL JEROME. NIGHT.

Clara is still dreaming; her dream just gets worse.

>   JOURNALIST (V.O.)
>   (French, English subtitles)
> Good movie marketing, maybe, but the publicity
> couldn't have been good for Paul Goode and his
> family.

INT. BEDROOM, FRENCH HOTEL. DAY.

Clara's dream: she's imagining what happened after
the waiter with the concealed camera left the room.

Juliette pulls Paul onto the bed with her. They repeat their lines from *Argonne,* but the lines are delivered playfully in this context.

> JULIETTE
> (in English)
> Hello, my dear.

> PAUL
> (French, no subtitles)
> I am American.

> JULIETTE
> (English)
> I know. Where are you wounded?

She is undoing Paul's towel; he lets her.

> JULIETTE
> (English)
> May I look? Okay?

INT. BEDROOM, HOTEL JEROME. DAY.

On Clara Swift's face, she's awake—she's just lying there. Tears run down her cheeks; she bites her pillow to keep herself quiet. When she rolls over, she sees Paul sleeping beside her. From her soft whisper, Clara sounds like she's rehearsing what she would like to say to Paul.

> CLARA
> I love you, Paul—I know you love me. And I believe you've been faithful to me, except for Juliette.
> (her tone changes)
> Your dirty Frenchwoman!

She makes a fist; she sticks the big knuckle of her
index finger into her mouth, stopping herself from
raising her voice. Clara turns away from Paul; she
stops biting her hand, and closes her eyes. Her face is
a face praying for sleep.

> MONIKA (O.C.)
> Are you happy you were faithful to your wife?
> Was it worth it?

INT. BEDROOM, HOTEL JEROME. MORNING.

On Adam's sleeping face as his eyes open. Monika isn't
in bed—she's in her wheelchair, wearing the bathrobe.

> ADAM
> Yes, I'm happy—it was worth it.

> MONIKA
> Would your wife be happy how we felt the
> sheets?

> ADAM
> (laughing)
> No, she wouldn't be happy—my wife would leave
> me, if she knew.

> MONIKA
> (smiling)
> Then why was it worth it, to be faithful to her—
> if she would leave you for feeling the sheets?

Monika wheels herself into the bathroom, closing the
door. Adam has no time to ponder what Monika said.
Standing beside the bed—smiling down at him with her
shy, childlike smile—is the ghost of PAULINA JUÁREZ,
the Mexican maid.

> ADAM (V.O.)
> One winter night in Aspen, when she was only
> forty-eight, Paulina slipped on the ice and
> cracked her head; she froze to death, lying
> unconscious in the cold.

> PAULINA
> (Spanish, no subtitles)
> ¿Cómo está tu madre?

Even this is beyond Adam's schoolboy Spanish. Paulina's
ghost is a young woman in her early thirties; she
smiles at Adam with a grandmother's uncritical love.

> PAULINA
> How is your mother?

> ADAM
> She's fine, thank you. Are you my grandmother?

> PAULINA
> (her hand on her heart)
> Sí . . . tu abuela.

> ADAM
> I'm pleased to meet you.

> PAULINA
> (slowly, teaching him)
> Mucho gusto en conocerle.

> ADAM
> (he tries to repeat)
> Mucho gusto . . .

That's all he can manage; they both laugh. Paulina
vanishes as Monika, fully dressed, wheels herself out
of the bathroom. She needs no help putting on her
winter wear.

> MONIKA

Talking to yourself is a sure sign you don't get off enough.

> ADAM

I'd like to work out at your gym, maybe later today. I thought I'd go skiing tomorrow.

> MONIKA

I can tell you where to ski, blue-run man. I'll see you later.

> ADAM

I haven't seen any recent ghosts—only the ones from the past.

She's impatient to leave—or just impatient with him, in general.

> MONIKA

The more recent ghosts seem like everyone else— they look alive. Until they don't.

> ADAM

Have you seen a ghost who *is* alive, a living person who's a ghost?

> MONIKA
> (as she leaves)

You really don't get off enough.

INT. BATHROOM, HOTEL JEROME. MORNING.

Après-shower, wearing only a towel, Paul Goode is putting sunscreen on his face. He's going skiing, a very fit sixty-five.

INT. BEDROOM, HOTEL JEROME. MORNING.

Après-shower, in her bra and panties, Clara Swift is
brushing her hair—a young and beautiful forty-five. An
interior monologue emerges. Clara holds her hairbrush
like a microphone. She is a new character—coy, ironic,
insincere. She's interviewing herself.

>   CLARA
>   Well, with a child at home, there aren't many
>   convenient opportunities to act in a film with
>   my husband. Naturally, I jumped at the chance
>   to do *The Other Man* with Paul.
>   (pause)
>   What's that? Oh!
>   (laughing)
>   No, I have no experience as an unfaithful wife—
>   only as a faithful one. But playing a character
>   unlike myself is fun.

In self-disgust, Clara goes back to brushing her hair,
glaring at herself in the makeup mirror. Clara's
interior monologue is now directed to her husband.
She's sincere.

>   CLARA
>   Aren't you lucky, Paul—that I'm on record for
>   never giving interviews? What could I say about
>   us, in an interview—what is there to say? I
>   should just *fuck* someone, Paul—the first guy
>   I see! Maybe then I can forgive you. I want to
>   forgive you, Paul. I love you, but God *damn* you!

Clara is the consummate actor, switching gears but
completely composed when Paul comes into their bedroom
from the bathroom. Clara holds up clothes to try on—a
skirt, a sweater. Paul is putting his long johns on,
and a turtleneck.

> PAUL

Toby is old enough to have his own room—at his age, he wouldn't have been happy with the sofa bed in the living room.

> CLARA

Toby wanted his own room to get away from us.

> PAUL

I know . . . Toby will be here soon—Billy is already in the living room. Toby and I can meet you for lunch.

> CLARA

No. You two have fun.

> PAUL

I'll leave Otto with you—he's a disaster on skis, anyway.

> CLARA

No, take both guys with you—especially Otto!

Although Clara appears composed, she seems brittle. She isn't happy with the way she looks in the mirror, but there's nothing wrong with her skirt and sweater. Paul gives her a worried look. He has his ski pants on, and a sweater over his turtleneck, when he opens the door to the living room of their suite, leaving Clara alone in their bedroom.

INT. LIVING ROOM, HOTEL JEROME. MORNING.

Billy is assessing how he looks in his ski clothes, in the mirror, when Paul enters.

>   PAUL
> Tell Otto to get his stuff on.

>   BILLY
> His ski stuff?

>   PAUL
> I'm afraid so.

INT. HALL, HOTEL JEROME. MORNING.

Otto is sitting guard outside Paul and Clara's suite;
he's too big for the chair. Billy surprises Otto when
he opens the suite door. The chair falls apart when
Otto stands; the bodyguards don't pay it any mind.

>   BILLY
> Get your stuff on.

>   OTTO
> My ski stuff?

>   BILLY
> I'm afraid so.

As Otto heads off in one direction, Billy sees Toby
coming from the other end of the hall. Toby, dressed to
ski, gives a passing glance at the destroyed chair.

>   TOBY
> Is Otto coming with us?

>   BILLY
> I'm afraid so.

INT. BEDROOM, HOTEL JEROME. MORNING.

Clara is fussing over her appearance in the mirror. She
tucks in her sweater, she untucks it; Clara takes off
her wedding ring, putting it in her purse. She leaves
the room, rubbing her ring finger.

EXT. ENTRANCE, HOTEL JEROME, E. MAIN. MORNING.

The guests' skis and poles are ready in a rack on the
sidewalk. Paul and Toby are talking, while Billy and a
COWBOY DOORMAN take their skis and poles to the ski van.

> TOBY
Mom didn't feel like skiing?

> PAUL
She'll ski with you tomorrow.

> TOBY
With us, you mean . . .

> PAUL
I have an interview tomorrow.

> TOBY
Another one . . .

> PAUL
It goes with the job.

The sidewalk is slick from melting snow. Otto can't get
the hang of walking in ski boots; he slips and falls on
the sidewalk. Paul looks away. Toby winces in empathy.
Billy knows it'll be a long day.

INT. J-BAR, HOTEL JEROME. MORNING.

SUPER: BREAKFAST AT THE JEROME, 1991

Country music PLAYS OVER—a melancholic song about sexual betrayal, a woman's lament. TWO CLEANING WOMEN are at work. We see an assortment of black-and-white and sepia photographs around the bar, miners and hunters and the earliest skiers; there are framed newspaper clippings from *The Aspen Times.*

EXT. POOL AND HOT TUBS, HOTEL JEROME. MORNING.

Steam rises from the hot tubs; a MAINTENANCE MAN vacuums the heated outdoor pool. The melancholic song CONTINUES OVER.

INT. ELEVATOR, HOTEL JEROME. MORNING.

Adam (in a sweatsuit, dressed for the gym) rides the elevator with the forlorn cowboy, forever carrying his saddle. The song is FADING OVER.

> ADAM (V.O.)
> There are things about writing fiction that
> are true of real life. There's always a
> *what-if* . . .

INT. HALL, HOTEL JEROME. MORNING.

Clara has decided to tuck in the sweater. She looks nice—more like a wife and mother than a movie star. Coming toward her is a PORTER pushing a luggage cart that contains a heavy armchair. Unseen by Clara (or the porter) is a ONE-LEGGED MINER, using a crutch,

hopping on his only leg. As they pass each other, the
ghost miner turns his head—to get a look at Clara, from
behind—tripping on his crutch, sprawling in the hall.
The lament FADES OUT.

> ADAM (V.O.)
> If I hadn't decided to go to Monika's gym, I'd
> have gone skiing.

INT. BREAKFAST ROOM, HOTEL JEROME. MORNING.

Adam arrives; a WAITRESS immediately sees him.

> ADAM (V.O.)
> I would have skipped breakfast at the Jerome,
> if I'd gone skiing.

> WAITRESS
> One for breakfast?

> ADAM
> Yes, please.

She shows him to a small table, pours his water.

> WAITRESS
> Coffee?

> ADAM
> Yes, please.

INT. ELEVATOR, HOTEL JEROME. MORNING.

Clara, unaware of the cowboy with his saddle, thinks
she's alone. She looks at her puckered lips in a
compact mirror; she's agitated, trying to calm herself,

when she closes the compact, returning it to her purse.
The cowboy can't take his eyes off her.

INT. BREAKFAST ROOM, HOTEL JEROME. MORNING.

Adam, reading the menu, drinking some water, doesn't
see Clara arrive in the dining room, but she recognizes
him—that nice man who admires her work. Perhaps it
calms her that he's not a total stranger, and he's
close to her own age.

Adam looks up from the menu; he sees Clara standing
next to him.

>   CLARA
>   Are you alone?

>   ADAM
>   Yes, I'm alone . . .

Star-struck and embarrassed, he awkwardly stands. It's
a table for two; clumsily, Adam offers Clara the empty
chair.

>   ADAM
>   Would you have breakfast with me?

>   CLARA
>   I don't want to eat with you—I want to have sex
>   with you, right now.

Adam looks at her as if she's a character in a movie,
not real.

>   CLARA
>   (near to breaking)
>   Please don't make me beg you.

EXT. LOGE PEAK CHAIR, ASPEN HIGHLANDS. DAY.

Paul and Toby are talking; Billy and Otto are behind them in the chairlift line for the two-seater chair.

>   PAUL
> Toby, I won't disappoint you again.

>   TOBY
> You won't disappoint Mom, you mean.

>   PAUL
> I mean both of you—never again.
>   (turns to Billy)
> If we get separated, don't worry!
>   (to Toby)
> You'll have to remind your mom tomorrow—there's no safety bar on this chair. She hates the wind.

>   TOBY
> I know . . . It's windy up there.

On Billy and Otto.

>   OTTO
> We always get . . . separated.

>   BILLY
> We'll try not to, this time.

Paul and Toby get on the chairlift. They don't see the mess Otto causes behind them—he drops a ski pole, two empty chairs go by, an IMPATIENT COUPLE takes the next chair. Billy and Otto get on the chairlift; as they ascend, Otto is reaching wildly above himself. Otto screams as he falls, dragging Billy off the chair. No center post to grab hold of.

                        OTTO
    There's no pull-down bar!

On Paul and Toby riding the ascending chairlift,
as the lift suddenly stops midair. Father and son
instinctively extend an arm, to prevent each other from
sliding forward in the chair.

                        PAUL
    You'll have to watch out for your mom if the
    lift stops near the top.

                        TOBY
    I'll stick to the blue runs. You don't have to
    tell me. I know how Mom is.

INT. BEDROOM, HOTEL JEROME. DAY.

Her hands shake as Clara self-consciously undresses.
Adam is embarrassed by the two bathrobes on his unmade
bed; he puts the robes on a chair. Clara's voice is
extremely fragile.

                        CLARA
    There were women with you last night. You're
    not with one of them?

                        ADAM
    I'm not here with anyone—I don't really know
    those women.

                        CLARA
    You don't really know me, either.

                        ADAM
    Perhaps we should talk.

> CLARA

No talking. No dialogue in this movie.

She's naked. She turns on the radio—more country music, too loud this time. Clara begins by undressing Adam, fiercely.

EXT. LOGE PEAK CHAIR, ASPEN HIGHLANDS. DAY.

On Otto and Billy riding the chairlift, near the top.

> BILLY

There's no safety bar on this chair.

> OTTO
> (petrified)

And no center post! I hate unloading worse than I hate getting on.

> BILLY
> (crossing himself)

I remember you unloadin'.

INT. BEDROOM, HOTEL JEROME. DAY.

The radio is still too loud. It's an awful country song, a male singer's stuporous drone. On the bed, Adam is fucking Clara; we see her face over his shoulder. Her mouth is open in a soundless scream—her pained eyes are open, too. She is hating this, wishing it was over. This is the worst thing she's ever done, onscreen or off.

> ADAM (V.O.)

Of course I should have stopped her, but no dialogue was allowed.

EXT. BLACK-DIAMOND RUN, ASPEN HIGHLANDS. DAY.

Paul and Toby are good skiers. They stop together; Paul
looks back, up the piste.

>   PAUL
> We've lost them—they'll stick to the blue runs.

>   TOBY
> We always lose them—Otto should stick to the
> green runs.

>   PAUL
> There are no green runs up here—that's what I
> like about it.

>   TOBY
>   (his first smile)
> Me, too.

EXT. BLUE RUN, ASPEN HIGHLANDS. DAY.

Billy is a halfway-decent intermediate skier. He
carves a couple of almost parallel turns, stopping
to wait for Otto, whose stem turns deteriorate into
blundering snowplows. Otto manages to stop by hugging
a tree off the side of the slope. TWO SKI PATROLLERS
blow by them. Their patrol jackets mark them—as
clearly as their hips and their long hair identify
them as women.

>   OTTO
>   (hugging tree)
> This is a *blue* run?

> BILLY

I keep tellin' you—this is a blue run, as easy
as it gets up here.

Billy skis off. Otto, watching him go, releases the
tree.

EXT. UNDER THE CHAIRLIFT, ASPEN HIGHLANDS. DAY.

The passing chairs are high above Beth and Nan, who we
recognize as the ski patrollers who blew by Billy and
Otto. The two women have stopped near a lift tower, on
a run that passes under the Loge Peak chair.

> NAN

They were the bodyguards!

> BETH

The cute one is an intermediate man.

> NAN

The scary one skis like I imagine him havin'
sex.

> BETH

Don't make me throw up, Nan.

Nearby, closer to the lift tower, ANOTHER PATROLLER
waves to them. We see the patroller's toboggan—SOME
SKIERS, just standing around, are blocking our view of
an injured skier.

INT. BEDROOM, HOTEL JEROME. DAY.

A new country song is on the radio, which is still too
loud—a female singer's woeful tale. The sex is over.

Clara is too distraught to be able to dress herself;
when Adam tries to help her, she recoils. She is
repulsed by him and ashamed of herself. All he can do
is offer her one of the Hotel Jerome bathrobes. Clara
puts on the robe, covering herself as she slips her
bare feet into her shoes and gathers up her clothes.
Adam turns the radio off, but the silence between them
is worse without the music. Clara leaves, carrying her
clothes and purse.

> ADAM (V.O.)
> Clara Swift hated what we did.

INT. HALL, HOTEL JEROME. DAY.

The armchair we saw on a luggage cart is by the door
to Paul and Clara's suite, replacing the chair Otto
broke. Paulina, the ghost maid, isn't smiling; Paul's
mother looks sadly upon her daughter-in-law as Clara
comes into view. In the Hotel Jerome bathrobe, Clara
could be mistaken for someone coming from the pool.
She struggles to find the key to her suite in her
purse. Her panties fall from her bundle of clothes
as she manages to let herself in. Paulina picks up
Clara's panties, hiding them in the apron of her maid's
uniform.

INT. BEDROOM, HOTEL JEROME. DAY.

Clara's open purse is on the bedside table, where the
radio plays a country song—an elegy. On the bed are
Clara's skirt and sweater, and her bra. On the floor—
by the open door to the bathroom, where we hear the
tub filling—are Clara's shoes and the bathrobe she was
wearing.

INT. BATHROOM, HOTEL JEROME. DAY.

The bubble bath in the tub conceals most of Clara;
disgusted with herself, she feels dirty. The elegy
PLAYS OVER.

INT. THE LAST RUN GYM. AFTERNOON.

The sound of flat cast-iron plates sliding on or off
barbells and dumbbells; the metallic bashing of weight
machines; the grunting of weight lifters.

CLOSE ON: a MUSCULAR YOUNG MAN bench-pressing a heavy
barbell; a woman's two hands grip the bar, helping him
finish his last rep.

PULL BACK: there's a ramp leading to an elevated
platform above the bench, where Monika in her
wheelchair is assisting the young weight lifter. He has
no legs.

On another bench, a REALLY RIPPED WOMAN in a tank top
with a bikini bottom is doing bicep curls. She knows
what she's doing; she needs no help.

On a slanted bench, a VERY FIT WOMAN is doing leg
curls. Wheeling by, Monika pauses to put her hand on
the woman's butt.

                    MONIKA
        Don't lift your butt, Jill.

On a leg-press machine, Adam is punishing himself. When
Monika wheels herself into frame, she puts her hand on
Adam's forehead—pressing his head against the headrest.

                    MONIKA
Stop jerking your head. I would lay off the leg
presses if you're going to ski tomorrow.

                    ADAM
          (as she wheels off)
I was just going to take a few runs on Aspen
Mountain—I can walk to it.

We stay on Monika; the *walk* word has negative
connotations.

                    MONIKA
The problem with Ajax is that everybody in town
can *walk* to it.

She stops at the lat machine, where a GUY WITH A
PROSTHETIC LEG is doing pull downs.

                    MONIKA
Keep your back straight, Freddy.

Adam enters frame.

                    ADAM
I hear Buttermilk is nice.

                    MONIKA
For beginners; if you like children.
Personally, I hate children.

                    ADAM
          (as Freddy laughs)
You mean as skiers.

                    MONIKA
I mean in general.

All the gym rats laugh—they're regulars; they know
Monika.

>   MONIKA
> You should ski at Aspen Highlands—you want the
> Loge Peak lift up there. You'll find some blue
> runs.

More laughs from the gym rats, as Monika wheels away.
No music in the gym—only the grunting of the lifters
and the clank of metal. No TVs; the walls are covered
with photos of Monika and her fellow competitors.
There are photos of a young Arnold Schwarzenegger as a
bodybuilder, and one of an older Arnold in a Tyrolean
hat—a fellow Austrian, and a fan of downhill racers, at
the Hahnenkamm in Kitzbühel.

>   ADAM (V.O.)
> One error of judgment can lead to another. And
> there was no dispelling Clara Swift's hatred of
> herself for having sex with me—unless I had sex
> with someone else.

Adam is using the chest-fly machine when Monika wheels
up to him.

>   MONIKA
> Keep your feet firmly on the floor.

>   ADAM
> About the sheets at the Jerome . . .

>   MONIKA
>   (as she wheels off)
> I'll check my schedule.

EXT. POOL AND HOT TUBS, HOTEL JEROME. NIGHTFALL.

Snow falls on the tired skiers in the hot tubs—Billy
among them—but only Otto and Toby are in the heated
pool. Toby clings to Otto's back; Otto's thrashing
breaststroke is slopping water out of the pool. Toby
hangs on, as happy as we've ever seen him—a boy
riding a small whale, an adored child playing with
his devoted bodyguard. Billy is explaining to a YOUNG
COUPLE in the hot tubs, while they watch the tsunami
in the pool.

> BILLY
>
> They've been doin' this since Toby was a
> little boy.

An OLDER WOMAN in a huff overhears him; she is standing
poolside, in a Hotel Jerome bathrobe, as the water
washes over the deck.

> OLDER WOMAN
> (leaving)
> He's not a little boy now!

INT. BEDROOM, HOTEL JEROME. AFTER DARK.

The blonde maid we saw earlier turns on the radio to
a country song; she is confronted with more than a
turndown service in Adam's room. She sees he's had
no maid service all day; on his unmade bed are the
sweatsuit he wore to breakfast and the shorts and
T-shirt he worked out in at the gym. The maid begins by
picking up the bathrobe on the chair.

ANOTHER ANGLE: Paulina watches the maid do her job.

INT. THE LAST RUN GYM. EVENING.

The country song CONTINUES OVER. Après-skiing, the gym
is busier—LOTS OF LIFTERS and a NEW TRAINER, a muscle-
bound man.

INT. WOMEN'S LOCKER ROOM, GYM. NIGHT.

Beth and Nan are undressing and talking; we hear only
the song.

INT. WOMEN'S SAUNA, GYM. NIGHT.

Monika—topless, a towel covering her lap—is talking
to the ripped woman we saw doing bicep curls (also
topless, with a towel). No sound but the country song.
Fist bumps all around, when Beth and Nan enter the
sauna—four strong women.

INT. BEDROOM, HOTEL JEROME. NIGHT.

A new country song PLAYS OVER, but it sounds like
the same radio station. Clara, casually dressed,
keeps looking at her wedding ring, to be sure it's
back on. She keeps looking at her husband, Paul, in
an anxious way. A world of unsaid things is readable
on her face; she seems as prone to shattering as
glass.

Paul is also casually dressed. He's aware of Clara's
attention to him; he's very attentive to her. Paul
tucks an errant label under the back of Clara's
sweater; he smoothes her hair.

INT. BEDROOM, HOTEL JEROME. NIGHT.

The blonde maid finishes her turndown service of Adam's
room. As maids do, she leaves the radio on when she
exits. Paulina appears, turning down the volume on the
country song. Paulina takes Clara's dropped panties
from the apron of her maid's uniform; it's not a happy
decision, but she doesn't hesitate to put the panties
under one of Adam's pillows. Paulina seems sad, as
she plumps up the two pillows and straightens the top
sheet.

INT. LITTLE ANNIE'S, E. HYMAN. NIGHT.

Paul and Clara are being overly considerate of each
other. Checkered tablecloths, a wagon-wheel chandelier,
not fancy.

> PAUL
> We had a good time skiing—no one recognized me.

> CLARA
> I want you two to have a good time.

> PAUL
> I understand why Toby didn't want to go out
> with us—the way people look at us . . .

OTHER ANGLES: the curiosity on VARIOUS FACES in the
local hangout.

> PAUL (O.C.)
> We can all have dinner together at the Jerome
> tomorrow night.

> CLARA (O.C.)
> They don't stare at us the same way.

INT. THE BAR, LITTLE ANNIE'S. NIGHT.

At the bar, Billy fails to impress the BARTENDER. Billy
can see Paul and Clara at their table.

> BILLY
> I drink nothin' but water when I'm workin'.
> A good bodyguard is not *omnipresent*. You keep
> your distance, but you're observin'; you can't
> miss somethin'.

Unimpressed, the bartender goes about his business.
Billy sees that Clara has left Paul alone at their
table; Billy has lost her.

INT. WOMEN'S ROOM, LITTLE ANNIE'S. NIGHT.

Clara is vomiting in a toilet.

INT. BEDROOM, HOTEL JEROME. NIGHT.

Toby is eating a hamburger while he changes channels
with the TV remote. The light from the screen flickers
on his face, as we hear what sounds like a basketball
game, a car chase, a comedy show, a shoot-out. Toby
suddenly stops changing channels.

On the TV: a series of stills from the black-and-
white movie *Argonne,* all of Paul Goode and Juliette
Leblanc. The voice-over is an American journalist for a
Hollywood gossip show.

> PAIGE (V.O.)
> I caught up with Juliette Leblanc at her L.A.
> hotel. Everyone is still talking about her and

Paul Goode, and I don't mean what happened *on
set* in *Argonne.*

On a patio, under an umbrella, PAIGE and Juliette are
talking.

> JULIETTE
> American women hate me because they live in a
> repressive society and I live in France!

> PAIGE
> American women hate you, honey, because you had
> an affair with Paul Goode and they didn't!

> JULIETTE
> (a characteristic shrug)
> That's what I mean.

> PAIGE
> Your affair has been so public—on TV, in all
> the newspapers.

> JULIETTE
> I didn't *do* it in public!

> PAIGE
> But it's such a scandal!

> JULIETTE
> (once again, the shrug)
> Scandals don't affect me.

> PAIGE
> Boy, are you ever not American!
> (Juliette shrugs)
> Did you shrug as a child?

Juliette just shrugs.

Back on Toby, changing the channel; he finds a hockey
game.

INT. HALL, HOTEL JEROME. NIGHT.

As quiet and gentle as a lullaby, a country song seems
to have put Otto to sleep in the armchair—a tired whale
guards the door.

INT. BEDROOM, HOTEL JEROME. NIGHT.

The softly playing song is ill-suited to Adam and
Monika's lovemaking. They are seriously out of sync.
She's trying to have a good time; he's intent on
punishing himself. She's acutely aware of his self-
hatred—as Adam was of Clara's. Adam's guilt is a
turnoff to Monika. She throws him off her—knocking
the clock radio off the night table, stopping the
music.

> MONIKA
> What is *wrong* with you? You're supposed to
> *enjoy* this, you asshole!

She throws a pillow at him, the one covering Clara's
panties. Monika holds them up—much too small to be
hers.

> MONIKA
> What the fuck?!

> ADAM
> (heartfelt)
> Yes, I'm an asshole.

Monika throws the panties at him.

INT. J-BAR, HOTEL JEROME. NIGHT.

Beth and Nan have a table, where they're checking out the guys. Some YOUNG MEN, who look barely old enough to drink, are too young for them. A Damaged Don song PLAYS OVER—an oldie, "It Never Gets Better with Gwen."

> NAN
> I want someone who's stayin' here—it's too depressin' to see where some guys are livin'.

> BETH
> Don't bring a guy back to our place!

> DAMAGED DON (V.O.)
> You don't want to wake up with Maureen. She smells like a farm and her sheets ain't too clean!

> NAN
> Is this Damaged Don? I hate him.

> BETH
> Somebody shot him.

> NAN
> He *sings* like somebody's shootin' him.

> BETH
> Jeez . . .

EXT. ASPEN SIDEWALK, S. MILL. AFTER DINNER, NIGHT.

The way Paul and Clara hold on to each other as they walk, they look like a couple falling in love for the first time. Billy follows them at a respectful distance. The cowboy boots in a storefront window

distract him, but he tears himself away. Damaged Don
CONTINUES OVER.

> DAMAGED DON (V.O.)
> Don't dream about diddlin' Babette. She's a
> case of the clap you won't ever forget!

INT. J-BAR, HOTEL JEROME. NIGHT.

Beth and Nan see Monika wheel herself into the J-Bar.

> NAN
> The sheets aren't workin' tonight.

An ANXIOUS WAITER brings Monika a beer.

> DAMAGED DON (V.O.)
> Your worst nightmare is knowin' Louise. She'll
> drink all your money and give your dog fleas!

> MONIKA
> (to the waiter)
> I hate Damaged Don—everyone does.

> WAITER
> (running off)
> I'll see what I can do.

> NAN
> Damaged Don is dead.

> MONIKA
> (furious)
> I know! I'm glad! I still hate him!

"It Never Gets Better with Gwen" abruptly stops.

                              BETH
      Jeez . . .

INT. BEDROOM, HOTEL JEROME. NIGHT.

Adam, in a Hotel Jerome bathrobe, restores his room
from the wreck Monika made of it. The clock radio still
doesn't work, even after he plugs it back in. Adam
doesn't know what to do with Clara's panties; he gently
places them on one of the pillows. On the opposite
side of the bed from Adam, Paulina appears; she is
determined to take the panties, putting them under her
apron.

They look sadly upon each other. Paulina's faint smile
registers her disapproval and her affection. Adam is
overwhelmed with shame.

                              ADAM
      I'm so sorry . . .

Paulina knows; she just nods.

INT. HALL, HOTEL JEROME. NIGHT.

Paul and Clara are listening at the door to Toby's
room, while Billy edges away from them.

                              CLARA
      I can't hear the TV—maybe he's asleep.

                              PAUL
      Toby likes to watch old movies with the sound
      off. I just want to see him and say good night.

>   CLARA
> Me, too. I just don't want to wake him up. I
> don't know what to do!

She breaks down, clinging to him. Paul hugs her back.
Billy is embarrassed for them.

>   BILLY
> I'm just goin' down the hall, to check on Otto.

>   PAUL
> You don't have to wait for us, Billy—we know
> the way.

>   CLARA
>   (as Billy leaves)
> Good night, Billy!

>   BILLY (O.C.)
> Good night!

Paul and Clara decide not to disturb their son; holding
tightly to each other, they follow after Billy.

INT. BEDROOM, HOTEL JEROME. NIGHT.

Toby is awake, watching TV with the sound off; the
light from the screen is on his face, streaked with
tears.

ONSCREEN: *The Kindergarten Man* (1973) is even worse
without sound. From the open doorway of the classroom,
we are looking at the FRIGHTENED TEACHER, Clara Swift.
The WOMAN WITH THE GUN is in profile to us; her lips
move when she speaks to Clara, with her gun pointed at
Clara's temple, but we hear Toby say her dialogue.

                    TOBY (O.C.)
       If I pull the trigger, the kids' faces are
       gonna be spattered with your blood—from the
       exit wound.

On the soundlessly SINGING CHILDREN in the kindergarten
classroom, when the HYSTERICAL HENRIETTA shouts
something to make them stop.

                    TOBY (O.C.)
       Stop! Stop singing!

From the doorway, something changes in the teacher's
eyes. The woman with the gun turns to face us—to see
what Clara sees. We don't hear the gunshot, but the
gun-toting woman falls facedown; blood pools around her
face on the floor.

It takes two single-leg lunges for the absurd
KINDERGARTEN MAN, Paul Goode, to enter the classroom,
holding the gun with the silencer. Paul is speaking to
the dead woman, but the TV sound is off. Toby must have
memorized the dialogue to the first film his parents
made together.

                    TOBY (O.C.)
       It's been five minutes—I'm back.

With a handkerchief, Paul removes a spatter of blood
from Clara's cheek, but the little kindergarten man
doesn't know what to do with his gun; the long barrel
of the silencer makes it awkward to stick under the
waistband of his shorts.

                    TOBY (O.C.)
            (as Clara's lips move)
       Give that thing to me.

Clara takes the gun from him—putting the weapon on her
desk, next to the blood-spattered globe of the world.

On the classroom of jubilant kindergartners; Henrietta
starts chanting, and Paul has more dialogue, but we
hear nothing, and the TV goes black.

On Toby in the semidarkness of his room. He's still
crying. He doesn't want to see any more. It's too
painful to watch his parents fall in love.

INT. BEDROOM, HOTEL JEROME. NIGHT.

Paul, in his undershorts, goes into the bathroom,
closing the door. Clara is already in bed, in her
nightgown; she is changing channels with the TV remote
when she sees the end of the movie Toby was watching.
We hear her inhale, but Clara has muted the sound on
the TV.

ONSCREEN: the little kindergarten man is trying to make
himself heard over the chorus of children's voices.
Paul is level with, and almost touching, Clara's
breasts. She tilts her head down to him, to be able to
hear him. As his lips move, we hear Clara's soft voice;
she speaks his lines, from the bed.

>   CLARA (O.C.)
>   I'm wondering if you would go out with me, if
>   I'm not too small for you—I hear that all the
>   time, that I'm just not big enough.

In the movie, Clara bends over him—her lips almost
touching Paul's ear. When her lips start to move, we
CUT BACK to Clara in bed; she speaks her lines in a
whisper.

> CLARA

You're not too small for me—you're just small
enough.

Clara is crying; she turns the TV off. When Paul comes
out of the bathroom and gets into bed, Clara has dried her
tears on her pillow. They lie in bed, hugging each other.

INT. J-BAR, HOTEL JEROME. NIGHT.

Monika, Nan, and Beth are knocking back the beer. The
object of their interest is a CUTE BOY at the bar.

> BETH

That kid isn't old enough to drink.

> NAN

So he's got a fake ID—I'm just wonderin' if
he's of legal age to do it. I don't want to go
to jail or somethin'.

> MONIKA

There's no fake ID for doing it.

> NAN

I just know he's stayin' here—he came from the
hotel; he has no outdoor clothes with him.

> BETH

That kid's still sleeping on the sofa bed in
his parents' suite.

Near the cute boy at the bar are the bodyguards.

> NAN
> (to Monika)

There's no keepin' Beth away from the
bodyguards.

                    BETH
              (to Monika)
Not the scary one—the other one is kind of
cute.

                    MONIKA
              (shocking them)
The scary one is more interesting.

Nan stands up from their table; she looks ready to make
her move.

                    NAN
       I'm done talkin' about it—that boy is up past
       his bedtime.

On the bodyguards, talking, as Nan sits down beside the
cute boy at the bar.

                    BILLY
       The one in the wheelchair is European—a
       downhill skier, Monika Behr.

                    OTTO
       Like a bear, the animal?

                    BILLY
       Sounds the same. Spelled different. She's
       famous for fallin'.

                    OTTO
       So she's, like, paralyzed, from the waist down?
       I don't suppose she can, you know, do it.

                    BILLY
       That's not what I hear.

On Nan and the cute boy, talking.

                    NAN
Because I could get in trouble, if you're not
old enough. Just tell me: Are you old enough to
be with me, or not?

                    CUTE BOY
              (candid but clueless)
I don't know. I've never been with anyone.

                    NAN
Really. And where are your parents?

                    CUTE BOY
In their room—they go to bed early.

                    NAN
You have your own room?
              (as he nods)
Really.

INT. BEDROOM, HOTEL JEROME. NIGHT.

Conscience-stricken, Adam lies awake in bed.

INT. BEDROOM, HOTEL JEROME. NIGHT.

Conscience-stricken, Clara lies awake. Paul sleeps
beside her.

INT. J-BAR, HOTEL JEROME. LATER THAT NIGHT.

With only A FEW PATRONS, the country music—a song with
driving dance rhythms—seems louder than before.

INT. BEDROOM, HOTEL JEROME. LATER THAT NIGHT.

The song with the dance rhythms CONTINUES OVER, as Nan has her hands full with the cute boy—an eager newcomer to sexual experience.

INT. BEDROOM, HOTEL JEROME. LATER THAT NIGHT.

The driving song CONTINUES OVER, as Beth and Billy are going at it with abandon.

INT. BEDROOM, HOTEL JEROME. LATER THAT NIGHT.

That country song is reaching a crescendo, as Otto looks like he's breaststroking the length of the pool again; this time, it's Monika who hangs on to the breaching whale. The only potential for damage or unhappiness here might be the bed.

EXT. POOL AND HOT TUBS, HOTEL JEROME. EARLY MORNING.

Tarzan looks wary in the hot tubs, as the maintenance man vacuums the pool. The ski trails on Aspen Mountain are visible in the background. The new snow is dazzling in the sun.

EXT. LOGE PEAK CHAIR, ASPEN HIGHLANDS. EARLY MORNING.

It's too early for the lifts to be running; the groomers are on the mountain and the PATROLLERS are busy with morning setup.

VARIOUS ANGLES: on trails served by the Loge Peak lift. A patroller is running a sled downhill. Nan is driving a snowmobile up the mountain—towing Beth, on skis, behind her. The two of them are laughing about something.

INT. BEDROOM, HOTEL JEROME. EARLY MORNING.

A DISMAYED MAID and the two porters we saw toting Otto's armchair on the luggage cart are dealing with the wreckage of Otto's bed. They've separated the mattress and box spring from the broken, collapsed frame.

INT. LIVING ROOM, HOTEL JEROME. MORNING.

Clara and Billy are dressed to ski; Paul is in a bathrobe. It's still emotional but brittle between Paul and Clara.

> CLARA
> > (to Paul)
> Your interview is . . . later?

> PAUL
> Much later. Hollywood reporters aren't early birds.

> BILLY
> > (to Clara)
> Toby's comin'—I knocked on his door.
> > (to Paul)
> Otto's in the gym, but he knows when your interview is.

> PAUL
> The gym here, in the Jerome?

                    BILLY
That downhill skier—her gym.

                    PAUL
The Last Run—it's the real deal.

                    BILLY
              (gives nothing away)
So I hear . . .

Clara answers the knock on the door, letting Toby in.

                    CLARA
          Here's Toby!

More standing around, more awkwardness.

                    PAUL
              (to Clara)
Have a wonderful day!

                    CLARA
              (to Paul)
Have a good interview!

Toby and Billy are embarrassed to be there.

EXT. LOGE PEAK CHAIR, ASPEN HIGHLANDS. MORNING.

Adam is in the lift line for the two-seater chair.

Not a long line; Adam gets on a chair alone. When it
gets busy on the two-seater chair, he'll probably pair
up with another single.

>   ADAM (V.O.)
>   The only reason I was at Highlands, and skiing
>   the Loge Peak lift, was that Monika told me
>   where to ski.

Minutes later: on Adam, riding the chairlift, near the
top. It's windy up there; aware the two-seater has no
safety bar, he holds on to a side post.

The chairlift goes up and over a high, narrow ridge—
exposed rock and snow, but not a very long fall from
the chair, if you were to fall exactly here. Then the
lift dips down, passing over a ravine—a deep gulch or
gully, where the chair is as high as thirty feet above
the bottom of a rocky gorge. In the wind, the depth of
the ravine is an unexpected drama—just before the lift
station at the top.

>   ADAM (V.O.)
>   I'd only recently gone back to skiing. I
>   was trying to correct the bad habits of my
>   childhood and adolescence, when I'd been
>   determined not to learn to ski.

Minutes later: on Adam, a halfway-decent skier, on
one of the blue runs under the Loge Peak lift. Adam
can keep his skis parallel if the fall line isn't too
steep; when he gets in trouble, he reverts to stem
turns.

>   ADAM (V.O.)
>   But the ideal time to learn how to ski is when
>   you're a kid. I'd blown the best chance I had
>   to learn how to ski—namely, the first time.

The lift line for the Loge Peak chair isn't a long one.
Billy gets on a chair alone—the chair after the two-
seater Clara and Toby take.

> ADAM (V.O.)
> Monika Behr and Paul Goode must have liked the
> old Loge Peak lift for some reason.

Minutes later: on Toby and Clara on the chair, near
the top.

It's extremely windy; Clara clings to a side post.

> ADAM (V.O.)
> But it was just bad luck that Clara Swift and I
> were riding the same chairlift on that day.

The exposed ridge comes closer; Toby knows the steep
precipice that comes after the high ridge.

> CLARA
> I hate this chair . . .

> TOBY
> Don't look down.
>   (she shuts her eyes)
> Don't close your eyes—it can make you dizzy.
> Just look at me.

> CLARA
>   (stares at him)
> You should ride with Billy. He's strong enough
> to hold you if you start to fall.

They're over the deep ravine.

> TOBY
> We're almost at the top—just get ready to
> unload.

> CLARA
> There's nothing to do to get ready—there's no

safety bar to raise! Next time, you ride with
Billy!

Clara turns in the chair—to look for Billy, behind
them.

> TOBY
> (too late)
> Don't look back!

> CLARA
> (sees the gulch)
> Oh, God. You ride with Billy!

> TOBY
> You're the one who's afraid—*you* should ride
> with Billy!

> CLARA
> No, you . . . Oh, God.

INT. PRIVATE LOUNGE, HOTEL JEROME. DAY.

The lounge is set up for a TV interview. The MAKEUP
GIRL attends to Paige, the movie journalist, while Paul
is getting hooked up to his microphone.

> PAIGE
> I bring greetings from your friend Juliette.
> Your *ex*-friend Juliette?

> PAUL
> Friend will do.

> PAIGE
> "Friend will do." I love that!

                    PAUL
Let's not go there.

                    PAIGE
I like that, too, but seriously, Paul, in *The Other Man*—a movie I *love*—you play a man who can't get over his wife's infidelity.

PULL BACK: Otto, arms folded, stands guard at the closed door. Paul knows where Paige is going—he doesn't respond. They're not on camera—the interview hasn't started—but Paige pushes ahead.

                    PAIGE
And your actual wife, Clara Swift, plays your unfaithful wife. That's kind of *ironic,* isn't it? That couldn't have been easy, Paul.

The door opens—a TIMID WAITER with a tray of bottled water and glasses. Otto takes the tray, waving the waiter away.

                    PAIGE
You kind of reversed your roles in *The Other Man.* Not easy, given the Juliette Leblanc business.

The CAMERAMAN is ready; Paige and Paul are in place for the interview to start.

                    PAUL
I'm not here to talk about *The Other Man.* I'm here to talk about the new film. And, as you know, I won't talk about Juliette Leblanc or my marriage—at all.

                    PAIGE
           (nonplussed)
Right . . .

(gushing, to camera)

Hi! I'm here in Aspen with Paul Goode—he's a hometown boy. Paul's new film, *Leaving Hong Kong,* releases next week—a movie I absolutely *love*! We're going to show you a clip. It's a kind of uncomfortable scene, actually. Don't let the kids watch!

(to Paul)

Wasn't it uncomfortable for you?

PAUL

Which scene is it?

PAIGE

(to camera)

Maybe we should just show it?

(to Paul)

That backseat scene!

Paul shrugs. We know the shrug, as does Paige.

PAIGE

Nice shrug, Paul . . .

(to camera)

Show it! Run the clip!

From *Leaving Hong Kong,* in a moving car—city streets, night. An AMERICAN IMMIGRATION LAWYER is in the front seat beside the CHINESE DRIVER. The lawyer is talking to Paul Goode and the BEAUTIFUL CHINESE WOMAN next to him in the backseat.

LAWYER

They're going to ask you for distinguishing features.

                         WOMAN
The bedroom wallpaper is roses, red and white
on a cream background. The bedroom curtains are
lavender.

                         PAUL
He doesn't mean the bedroom decor.

                         LAWYER
              (points to Paul)
I mean him, your alleged husband. Does he
have a scar or a birthmark? It should be in a
private place.

                         WOMAN
              (sincerely, to Paul)
Do you?

Paul feigns indifference.

                         LAWYER
Show her. They'll ask her.

Paul and the Chinese woman are displeased, but Paul
pulls down his pants, fumbling around in the backseat.
We see only the woman's reaction.

                         WOMAN
Oh . . .

                         PAUL
I was attacked by a dog.

                         LAWYER
You said it was a bicycle accident, when you
were a kid.

                        PAUL
                (pulls up his pants)
        I was a kid. I was attacked by a dog when I was
        riding my bike.

                        LAWYER
                (to the woman)
        What about you?

                        WOMAN
        What?

                        PAUL
        Is there a . . . *mark* in an area of your body
        only a husband would know?

                        WOMAN
        Oh . . .

        She unbuttons her blouse. When she pulls down her
        bra to show Paul one of her breasts, we see Paul's
        face, then the lawyer's, then the driver's eyes in the
        rearview mirror. As the lawyer speaks sharply to the
        driver in Chinese, the woman buttons up her blouse; she
        looks trustingly into Paul's eyes.

                        PAUL
        Nice tattoo.

                        WOMAN
        I was a kid . . .

                        LAWYER
                (to them both)
        And the sexual positions. They always ask the
        woman what position her husband likes. They'll
        ask the man what his wife likes, too.

PAUL

I like the usual, on top.

WOMAN

I like on top, too—not the usual.

LAWYER

That's good—say it just like that! It sounds
real. You know, like a long-standing domestic
dispute, like real married couples have.

Paul and the woman look at each other with new
interest.

LAWYER

No, no—don't look at each other that way!
You're supposed to be fucking *married*, for
Christ's sake—not falling in love!

It's too late. In the backseat, we see that Paul Goode
and the Chinese woman have fallen in love.

EXT. LOGE PEAK CHAIR, ASPEN HIGHLANDS. DAY.

The lift line is a little busy: couples ride together;
singles pair up. Clara, a distraught mom, gets her way.
Toby is paired with Billy; just ahead of them, Clara
is a single, about to merge with a newly forming line
of singles. Clara and Adam don't recognize each other
until they get on the same chair.

Toby and Billy get on the next chair.

BILLY

Your mom's ridin' with that guy who's stayin'
at the hotel.

                        TOBY
What guy?

                        BILLY
Some guy who spoke to her in the lobby—he's
just a fan.

On the panicked Clara, with Adam in the ascending
chair.

                        CLARA
              (barely audible)
No talking . . .

Adam just looks at her, ashamed.

                        CLARA
              (even quieter)
No looking at me . . .

As Adam looks away, up the mountain, Clara awkwardly
tries to look behind her while she hangs on to the side
post.

On Toby and Billy, in their chair.

                        TOBY
              (calls to his mom)
Don't look back!

On Adam extending his arm in front of Clara, to keep
her safely sitting back in the chair.

                        CLARA
              (a harsh whisper)
No touching . . .

Back on Billy and Toby.

>   BILLY
I thought your mom should ride with me, but you
know . . .

>   TOBY
We both said she should ride with you! I
know . . .

Toby has taken his gloves off to put sunscreen on his
face. Toby tucks the gloves under one thigh on the
chair.

>   BILLY
I'll hold your gloves.

>   TOBY
I got them.

>   BILLY
Toby, give me the gloves.

On Clara and Adam, not looking at each other.

On Toby and Billy—a fumbled exchange of the gloves.
Billy grabs one. Toby has caught the dropped glove
between his ski boots. Toby tries to lift his boots and
skis while he leans forward in the chair, reaching for
the glove. One of Toby's hands is holding on to the
side post, but he can't reach the glove with his free
hand—not without letting go of the side post.

>   BILLY
>   (raises his voice)
Toby, let the fuckin' glove go!

There's a bump as the chairlift goes up and over the
high ridge—Toby falls and Billy jumps after him.

                        BILLY
                  (calling)
            I'm comin', Toby!

On Adam and Clara, as Clara turns completely around in
the chair to look behind her. She sees Toby and Billy
floundering in the crusted, ungroomed snow on the
narrow ridge. Exposed rocks are all around them; it's
not instantly clear that they missed the rocks, where
they landed.

                        CLARA
                  (shrieking)
            Toby!

Adam reaches to grab her as she jumps, but she pushes
him away; she's still looking back, at the receding
ridge, but Adam knows where they are. The lift has
dipped down; they're over the gulch when Clara pushes
him away and jumps.

                        CLARA
            No touching . . .

From Adam's POV: Clara caroms off a tree, then a rock
or two, as she slides down the gully. The chair has
stopped; it sways in the wind. Clara's motionless body
is marked by the bright colors of her ski clothing;
the colors stand out against the snow and rocks at the
bottom of the ravine.

On the ridge: Billy and Toby have made their way to the
steep side of the gulch, but Billy won't let Toby go
down into the gorge. The tall trees are close together
and sharply slanted; there are bare rocks, jagged and
wind-swept, in the thawed and refrozen snow.

> BILLY
> The ski patrol can get her out of there, Toby.
> If we got down there, what could we do?

Toby dissolves in tears; Billy holds the boy in his arms.

CLOSE-UP: on Clara's lifeless face. Strands of her
hair, from under her ski hat, blow over her open eyes,
staring at the sky. Gentle hands enter frame, tucking
Clara's hair under her hat; careful fingers close her
eyelids.

WIDER: kneeling next to Clara is the ghost of a UTE
WARRIOR. He stands, looking up at the invasive and
absurd chairs high above him.

> ADAM (V.O.)
> I shouldn't generalize, but whoever or whatever
> ghosts are, they seem to know who you are and
> what you've done.

On Adam in the windblown chair, looking down at Clara
and the ghost. The chairlift starts to move again.

> ADAM (V.O.)
> The Ute I saw might have been looking at the
> chairlift, with understandable disapproval, but
> I thought he was looking at me.

In the gorge: on Clara's body and the Ute standing
protectively beside her, his eyes following the chairs
nearing the top. His buffalo robe, or maybe it's a
bearskin, is the natural color of the rocks or the bark
of the trees against the snow.

> ADAM (V.O.)
> This was once Indian territory. Aspen was
> originally named Ute City. But the Ute's

hunting grounds were long gone; the Ute knew
how it felt to be betrayed. Clara Swift had
also been betrayed.

INT. PRIVATE LOUNGE, HOTEL JEROME. DAY.

The Paige interview goes on.

> PAIGE
> That's a *marvelous* scene, but it had to be
> uncomfortable for you, Paul. Wasn't it?

> PAUL
> It's just a movie, Paige.

> PAIGE
> (to camera)
> "It's just a movie."
> (to Paul)
> I *love* that!

PULL BACK: Otto gapes at Paige in disbelief.

EXT. LOGE PEAK CHAIR, ASPEN HIGHLANDS. DAY.

The Loge Peak lift station, at the top. Nan and Beth,
with a third SKI PATROLLER, an old silverback, are
waiting for Adam to arrive and unload from his chair.

> ADAM (V.O.)
> Nan and Beth told me the ski patrol procedure
> for getting someone out of the gorge. Two
> strong guys take a toboggan down the gully to
> a snowmobile path at the bottom, where they
> traverse out.

There's unintelligible jargon on the patrollers' radios
the whole time they're talking with Adam, after he gets
off the chair. We don't hear their dialogue, only the
incomprehensible babble on the radios and Adam's voice-
over, as they talk.

> ADAM (V.O.)
> The old guy with the beard was Buck. He was
> waiting for a toboggan and two young guys to
> help him bring her out of the gulch.

LONG SHOT: looking down the steep walls of the ravine
to the bottom of the rocky gorge, where a bright speck
of color marks Clara's body.

> ADAM (V.O.)
> Buck said the ravine was basically an avalanche
> chute; there was no easy exit point. Not even
> locals liked to ski there—lots of rocks, tight
> trees, a bad fall line, and a long catwalk to
> get out.

Back up top: TWO PATROLLERS—young men on a snowmobile,
towing a rescue sled—have hooked up with Buck. They
go off together—Buck on skis, the young guys on the
snowmobile—leaving Adam with Nan and Beth.

> ADAM (V.O.)
> The only words I'd understood on the
> patrollers' radios were "Code Red"—I'd heard
> Molly rattle off the details. Trauma, head or
> neck, open femur, internals, cardiac. Given
> where Clara Swift had fallen, I got the feeling
> that everyone thought she was dead.

Nan and Beth are being nice to Adam, patting him on the
back, showing their concern. They start skiing down the

mountain, all together; the women downhillers are being
careful not to go too fast.

> ADAM (V.O.)
> If Monika had told her friends about me, they
> didn't hold it against me; they were kind to
> me, preparing me for the necessary business at
> the base.

On Billy and Toby with TWO PATROLLERS, a man and a
woman, all carrying their skis and poles, trudging out
of the ungroomed snow on the ridge. They make their
laborious way under the chairlift to the piste, where
they get into their skis.

> ADAM (V.O.)
> There would be questions about the accident at
> the base, Beth and Nan told me, but everyone
> understood what had happened. The son fell,
> the bodyguard jumped after him. The hysterical
> mom, looking back, saw only where they fell—not
> where she was, when she jumped.

On Adam, following Nan down a blue run to the base;
Beth follows behind them.

> ADAM (V.O.)
> Everyone understood that I was just a fan, a
> nobody to Clara Swift. I didn't really know
> her; we weren't skiing together. We were just
> two singles who, coincidentally, paired up on
> the chair.

On Billy and Toby, following the woman patroller to the
base; the other patroller, the man, follows them.

> ADAM (V.O.)
> The question everyone would ask was: Why wasn't
> the bodyguard on the chair with the mom? The

ski patrollers had seen the son ski; the boy
was an expert skier, like his dad. The mom was
the intermediate in the family; she should have
been on the chair with the bodyguard, everyone
would say. No one would blame me.

INT. PRIVATE LOUNGE, HOTEL JEROME. DAY.

The interminable Paige interview; we are looking at
Otto but hearing the interview off camera. Paul is in
the middle of a monologue. Otto is blocking the door,
which suddenly opens behind him. TWO COPS are there;
one of them whispers to Otto.

> PAUL (O.C.)
> Acting is a dangerous profession. Imagine not
> just inhabiting another person's body but
> believing that this character's emotions and
> motives are yours.

ANOTHER ANGLE: Paul has seen the cops; he watches Otto
approach, knowing something is wrong. Otto looks like
he's ready to burst into tears. Paul tries to keep
talking.

> PAUL
> The degree to which you succeed at becoming
> this other person is called talent, but your
> success is more a matter of risk. When I say,
> "Acting is a dangerous profession," I'm not
> talking about embarrassment or the fear of
> failure.

Paige, losing eye contact with Paul, looks where Paul
is looking. She sees Otto's bereaved face.

EXT. BASE, ASPEN HIGHLANDS. DAY.

An ambulance and police cars are there. The two young
patrollers carry Clara's covered body to the ambulance.
Buck is talking to the AMBULANCE TEAM while TWO
POLICEMEN keep the CURIOUS ONLOOKERS away. We hear only
Adam's voice-over.

> ADAM (V.O.)
> No one would listen to me.

Another squad car pulls up. Paul Goode and Otto have
a hurried POLICE ESCORT into the patrol room. Buck
goes with them, leaving the young guys to deal with
the rescue gear. When the Hotel Jerome van pulls up,
letting out the overeager Paige and her cameraman,
SEVERAL COPS surround them; the media jackals are
forced to get back in the van.

INT. PATROL ROOM, BASE, ASPEN HIGHLANDS. DAY.

A meeting room, a narrow table with chairs on both
sides. Paul sits between Adam and Toby, with his arm
around the shoulders of his sobbing son. Next to one
another, Adam's resemblance to Paul is no less striking
than Toby's resemblance to his father. Next to Toby,
Billy and Otto sit beside each other; Billy is as
inconsolable as Toby. Everyone talks, except Otto, but
we only hear Adam's voice-over.

> ADAM (V.O.)
> Billy blamed himself—he should have been on
> the chair with Clara, the bodyguard said. The
> son blamed himself, too; Toby said either
> he or Billy should have been riding with
> his mom.

On the other side of the table: TWO POLICE OFFICERS sit near Buck; next to the old silverback, Nan and Beth sit beside each other. Everyone has something to say, except Buck, but we only hear Adam's voice-over.

> ADAM (V.O.)
> I told them how I tried to grab her, but Clara pushed me away—she was so upset, I said.
> I told them it was my fault: I should have grabbed her; I could have tried harder. But they said there was nothing I could have done. Paul Goode said it was all his fault; everyone knew why his wife was so upset. No one would contradict him.

CLOSE-UP: a kind of sign language is going on with the ski patrollers. Nan and Beth give Buck an inquiring glance; the old silverback taps the side of his head with one index finger, the side of his neck with the other.

> ADAM (V.O.)
> Old Buck was a man of few words, and not a medical examiner, but he was clear about the cause of death—trauma, head and neck, from the look of it.

CLOSE-UP: on Adam, wringing his hands on the table; Paul notices the hand-wringing.

> ADAM (V.O.)
> Paul Goode never looked at me—only at my hands. I used to wring my hands, but I had stopped for more than twenty years. It might have been getting married that brought my hand-wringing back. Now I was doing it again. There is no explaining certain things, not only the ghosts.

INT. ELEVATOR, HOTEL JEROME. LATER THAT DAY.

Adam in his ski clothes rides the elevator with the
cowboy carrying his saddle. The cowboy looks like he
knows everything.

> ADAM (V.O.)
> If Clara Swift was going to be a ghost, I hoped
> that she wouldn't be one at the Jerome. Enough
> had befallen her in Aspen. My last night and
> the next morning, when I checked out, I saw
> only the ghosts I knew—the ones who seemed to
> know me, and all about me.

INT. BEDROOM, HOTEL JEROME. EVENING.

Paul Goode is packing Clara's clothes while Paulina
hovers near him; her heart is breaking. A country
lament is on the radio. When Paul starts packing
Clara's bras and panties, he is overcome. When he
covers his face with his hands, Paulina takes Clara's
panties from under her apron—properly placing them in
Clara's open suitcase. When Paul composes himself and
resumes packing, the dutiful maid has vanished.

INT. BEDROOM, HOTEL JEROME. EVENING.

The same lament plays on Toby's radio while he's
packing. Paulina now hovers near Toby. She is invisible
to him, as she was to Paul.

INT. J-BAR, HOTEL JEROME. NIGHT.

A quieter country song is background music. Adam is
alone at the bar.

PULL BACK: on Monika, Beth, and Nan—eating and drinking, but not talking, at their table. They are aware of Adam, by himself, at the bar. Monika wheels herself over to Adam, poking him in the back from her wheelchair.

> MONIKA
> They should replace that old chairlift—one day, they will. I'm sorry.

> ADAM
> I'm sorry, too.

Monika nods, wheeling away.

EXT. ASPEN SIDEWALK, S. GALENA. LATER THAT NIGHT.

The rock music is coming from a bar, as Otto and Billy walk by. The PUKING GUY comes out of the bar on all fours, his DRUNKEN GIRLFRIEND following him. She walks around him on the sidewalk, kicking him. Billy indicates to Otto that this place might be promising. They go inside.

> ADAM (V.O.)
> Autobiography just isn't good or bad enough to work as fiction.

INT. BEDROOM, HOTEL JEROME. DAWN.

Adam is asleep. Paulina, his grandmother's ghost, sits in the chair beside his bed, watching over him. She is crying.

> ADAM (V.O.)
> Unrevised, real life is just a mess.

EXT. ENTRANCE, HOTEL JEROME, E. MAIN. EARLY MORNING.

The LOCAL PRESS and a few CRAZED FANS are no match
for Otto and Billy, who shield Paul and Toby as they
exit the hotel and get into the Jerome van. Billy
sits up front, with the DRIVER—Otto is in the back.
A fan, a TALL HIPPIE GIRL wearing a ski sweater over
a turtleneck, stands at the window on the side of the
van where Paul is sitting. Lifting her sweater and the
turtleneck, she presses her bare breasts against the
glass; it must be cold.

> ADAM (V.O.)
> What happened to me in Aspen wouldn't work as a
> movie.

On the COWBOY DOORMEN at the Jerome, restraining the
hippie girl as the van drives away.

> ADAM (V.O.)
> What happened at the Jerome was just a mess.

INT. LOBBY, HOTEL JEROME. EARLY MORNING.

Adam follows a PORTER pushing a luggage cart through
the lobby. Under the mounted head and antlers of a mule
deer, Jerome B. Wheeler and Paulina are having coffee
together on a couch. Even knowing he's been badly
behaved, Paulina gives Adam a reassuring smile. When
Adam stops to smile back at Paulina, Jerome B. Wheeler
gives Adam a somewhat formal but dignified nod.

> ADAM (V.O.)
> I don't blame Aspen, or the Jerome, for what
> happened to me—I blame only myself.

INT. FRONT DESK, HOTEL JEROME. EARLY MORNING.

The porter with the luggage cart takes Adam's ski bag, boot bag, and duffel bag outside. Adam is checking out with the DESK CLERK.

> ADAM (V.O.)
> We've all been in uncertain situations—when we want to know what happens next.

EXT. ENTRANCE, HOTEL JEROME, E. MAIN. EARLY MORNING.

The local press and the crazed fans who showed up to see Paul Goode have since departed, except for the tall hippie girl. She seems disgruntled and is behaving strangely—scuffing her boots on the sidewalk, kicking a snowbank by the entrance to the hotel.

> ADAM (V.O.)
> It's only natural to want to know how it ends. Everyone wants to know the outcome.

It takes only one cowboy doorman to put Adam's stuff in the van. Both the doorman and the porter have gone back inside the hotel when Adam comes out on the sidewalk. HIS DRIVER holds the van door open for him, but Adam hesitates; he looks at the Jerome, as if capturing a last memory.

> ADAM (V.O.)
> Everyone hates this kind of ending—the uncertain ending.

The hippie girl has kicked a chunk of frozen snow free from the snowbank. She is kicking it in circles on the sidewalk. Adam looks at her only because she is behaving so strangely.

                    ADAM (V.O.)
It's not like writing a novel. It's easy to
know the future when I'm making up the story.

The hippie girl sees Adam looking at her. She seems
disinclined to show him her breasts; the crazy girl
gives him the finger instead.

FREEZE TO A STILL.

                    ADAM (V.O.)
At the time, I couldn't imagine what would ever
bring me back to Aspen and the Hotel Jerome.

FADE TO BLACK.

46.

"FOUND YOU!"

On the New Year's Eve when I met Grace, I assumed my mother took Em's grocery list with her when Molly drove her and Grace home. It made sense to me that Little Ray wouldn't want me to think about meeting my father, or to imagine I might like Paul Goode if I got to know him—"in real life," as Em had written. And since Em and I weren't writing to each other, a whole year would pass without our being alone together; there was nothing personal between us, not even another grocery list. When I went with Grace to New York, and we saw the snowshoer and Em for dinner, Em's pantomimes were restrained. Did Em sense that Grace disapproved of her not speaking? When Mr. Barlow brought Em to Manchester, they stayed with Grace and me in the spec house, but my mother and Molly were always around; Em's pantomimes were toned down then, too.

Whenever we had overnight guests in the spec house, Grace closed our bedroom door. I could still hear the pad of Em's bare feet in the upstairs hall—when she was visiting Elliot, or on her way back to her own bedroom. I'd given Em a brighter flashlight, and she'd learned where the obstacles were; there were no more collisions with the excess furniture. But sometimes— when Em woke up alone, and she felt frightened—she ran to a bed with a body in it. Then the pad of her bare feet resounded in the upstairs hall.

"Do you miss her getting into bed with you?" Grace asked me one night, when Em sounded like she was sprinting in the hall.

"No," I lied, but I was wondering how Grace knew what Em was up to. "There was never any fooling around," I added.

"I know," Grace told me; she gave me a hug and went back to sleep. I was awake, just wondering. Maybe Mr. Barlow had forewarned Grace of Em's nighttime wanders. Knowing my mom's fixation with Em's bedroom visits, Molly wouldn't have mentioned them.

That week between Christmas and New Year's, in the last days of 1990, Em and the snowshoer stayed with us in the spec house. It was near the end of Grace's sixth month. I was surprised to see the physical affection between

Em and Grace, the hugs and the hand-holding—Em was excited to feel the fetus move. I'd seen Em's childbirth pantomimes; they were not positive experiences. Yet Em was attentive to Grace's pregnancy. Em did the dishes and the kitchen cleanup; she was her old self in pantomiming how she wanted Grace to lie down and call her when the fetus was acting up, so that Em could feel the kicks.

I kept an eye on the grocery list on the fridge door, hoping Em would leave me a message. But Molly and my mother were with us every night; maybe my grocery list was too public for what Em had to say. It was only a week or two before this that I told Grace I would be going to Aspen and the Hotel Jerome in early February—a month before she was due. "I just want to see where I came from—I don't need to know more about what happened," I said.

"Okay—I'll tell Matthew to wait to be born until you come back," Grace said with a laugh; we were both laughing.

The going got tougher when I told my mom and Molly my reasons for taking a trip to see the Jerome when my wife would be eight months pregnant. "I just want to see where I came from," I said again, but this time I paused; I knew I couldn't tell them what I'd told Grace. "I just want to get the ghosts over with, without involving Grace," I told my mother and the night groomer. The *without involving Grace* part was true, but I wanted the ghosts to come back. The last thing I wanted was *to get the ghosts over with*.

"This is a funny time to go to the Jerome, sweetie—you should have gone there already; you should have long been back," my mother said.

"Just be careful, Kid—not only when you're skiing. I mean, in general," the old ski patroller said.

"When you come back, don't even think about going there again—you don't want to end up at the Jerome, sweetie," my mom told me. This was a new one for the night groomer and me; Molly and I just looked at Little Ray, but she ignored us.

The little English teacher and I were still writing to each other, and there were any number of times I could have told Elliot and Em about my upcoming trip to Aspen and the Jerome, but I didn't. I couldn't beat around the bush with Mr. Barlow; she knew me too well. The snowshoer would know there was more to my restlessness with married life than my missing the ghosts. And wouldn't Em have wondered about my going anywhere without my new wife? I suppose these were the reasons I didn't tell Em my plans to go, but someone told her.

It was the night before New Year's Eve. Mr. Barlow and Em would be driving back to New York in the morning. Em and I were doing the dishes after dinner. Grace was lying down on the couch in the living room; we could hear her telling stories about the elder Barretts, her parents. "My father has to put his pajamas on before the ball drops—you're lucky you're leaving," Grace was saying to the snowshoer. I knew another reason Grace was relieved that Elliot and Em were leaving. Grace was afraid her father might ask Em about the Gallows Lounge shooting. Grace knew that Em didn't like to be asked about it. I didn't like imagining how Em might pantomime it. I only knew what Elliot Barlow told me, about how Em's third-person novel was going. I wished Em would send me some pages; that was all I was thinking. From the kitchen, Em and I could hear Molly and my mother laughing.

"Oh, Arthur isn't so bad, Grace—you don't know what it's like to have a father in *diapers!*" we heard my mom say.

Em and I had loaded the dishwasher and had moved on to the pots and pans; I was washing, Em was drying, when I felt her hand slip in and out of a front pocket in my jeans. The folded piece of paper she put in my pocket made a crinkling sound when I touched my jeans with the knuckles of my wet hand. I was reaching for a dish towel to dry my hands when Em crossed her index fingers, giving me the X sign. I had to wait to read what she'd written till Em and Mr. Barlow went to their bedrooms, and Grace was in the bathroom. "I hear you're going to Aspen and the Jerome," Em wrote me. "I hope you don't have a lot of explaining to do when you come back. You have a very nice wife, you know. Grace is also a very good editor, but don't let her be your editor," Em had written.

There would be no way to be alone with Em, or to have a private conversation with the snowshoer, before they went back to New York the next morning. I thought about writing Em, but I wrote to Elliot Barlow. I assumed my mother must have said something about my going to Aspen and the Jerome, and the little English teacher had mentioned it to Em. "What does Em know about Grace as an editor—why is Em even thinking about Grace, editorially?" I asked Elliot.

"You and Em should be writing to each other—I'll guess that Em is waiting for you to write her first," Mr. Barlow wrote me back. This was four or five weeks before I went to Aspen; Grace was starting her seventh month. The snowshoer said Em and Grace had been writing each other for a year. On the New Year's Eve when I met Grace, it was *Grace* who took Em's grocery list with her when Molly drove my mom and her home. The snowshoer assured

me that Grace had not imposed herself on Em, as an editor; Grace was offering to be an early reader of Em's novel, not presuming she would be Em's
publisher. What Grace *did* presume, Mr. Barlow wrote, was that this would
be a more commercial and accessible work of fiction for Emily MacPherson.
Despite the third-person omniscient voice—as deadpan and detached as Em
could make it—the novel was based on Em and Nora's life together, onstage
and off, and on the Gallows Lounge shooting. Grace had advised Em against
Two Dykes, One Who Talks as a title. I'd known Grace for only one year, but I
knew how freely she gave advice. Was this why Em told me not to let Grace
be my editor? I asked Elliot.

Mr. Barlow repeated what Em had told me—Grace was *a very good editor.* Elliot and Em were worried that my having Grace as an editor could be
a strain on our marriage. "It might be too much Grace," was all the snowshoer said about it. I was surprised to learn Em had decided Grace would
be her publisher—not surprised to hear Em would stick with the snowshoer
as her editor and her copy editor. I'd known Grace for only one year, but I
knew there was such a thing as *too much Grace*—as the snowshoer put it.
"You should write Em—you should talk to Grace," the little English teacher
told me. In the month before I left for Aspen, I could have written Em. I
didn't; I was waiting for her to write me first.

When I asked Grace why she didn't tell me she and Em were writing each
other, Grace began by saying Em and I were childish—we were each just
stubborn about not being the one who wrote first. I had to hear all about the
fate of the Gallows Lounge. "The Gallows is going under—by the time Emily
MacPherson finishes this novel, the Gallows will be gone," Grace assured
me. I didn't understand why this mattered to Grace; she'd not been a regular
Gallows-goer. But after the shooting, the regulars were the ones who stopped
going. Grace said the Gallows had become a tourist attraction—naturally,
because of the shooting. When some of the regulars started to go back, they
stopped going again; it was uncool to be in a comedy club overrun by tourists.
Didn't Nora always say the walkouts at the Gallows were from out of town?

The out-of-towners didn't matter to Grace. From a publisher's perspective, it was good the Gallows was going under. Grace knew Em's novel was
less likely to raise legal questions if the comedy club was no longer in business, and the management of the Gallows had moved on. Wouldn't it be
great, Grace asked me, if Emily MacPherson's novel could make the point
that the Gallows Lounge shooting had killed the comedy club itself? I said I
doubted that the death of the Gallows Lounge was a point Em cared about.

I knew Em well enough to say that Nora's death would be the one that mattered, though *Two Dykes, One Who Talks* had been killed—not only as a title.

I half expected Grace to lecture me, to the effect that the demise of the Gallows was a watershed in cultural history—hence more important than the killing of one comedienne, or the last performance of a fringe comedy act. From Grace's perspective, I'd imagined, Em's title *Two Dykes, One Who Talks* was marketing suicide. The chain bookstores would not display such an inflammatory title; all the booksellers would find the title willfully provocative. Even relegated to the LGBT section of a bookstore, it was an offensive title—although it was written by a lesbian and was about two known lesbian performers. Knowing Nora, surely she knew she was being offensive in choosing that name for a comedy act, even if it was for fringe comedy.

Yet, whatever Grace thought, she said none of these things. Grace was merely dismissive. "You and Em are childish—you're just stubborn, you two. She misses you, you know—I know you miss her, too. But you won't even write each other!" was all Grace said. I would soon be on my way to Aspen without writing Em or hearing from her, and not once revisiting this conversation with Grace—nothing further about Em, not even about her writing, and nothing more about our missing each other (or one word about how Grace knew we did). After I came back from Aspen, the topic of conversation would change.

The news of Clara Swift's death got back east from Colorado before I did; as a minor celebrity in Manchester, I would be a topic of conversation in town. A bestselling author isn't famous in the same way a movie star is, but I was the guy on the chairlift with Clara Swift when she jumped. In the news, I would be identified as "the writer Adam Brewster."

It was not unlike when Nora was killed at the Gallows, where I was the guy doing jumping jacks in the audience, trying to draw the shooter's attention away from Em. It was the same thing, my being mentioned as a minor celebrity—only occasionally had I been called "Nora Winter's cousin Adam Brewster, the writer."

When Clara Swift jumped to her death from the Loge Peak chairlift, no one in the media mentioned I'd been ineffectual both times—no better than a bystander. No one asked why I hadn't just grabbed Clara Swift, holding her in the chair. My culpability wasn't an issue. It stayed the way it was at Aspen Highlands. The bodyguard made an effort to take the blame; both Billy and Toby tried to blame themselves—but Paul Goode wouldn't hear of it.

"It's my fault," my father said. "Everyone knows why Clara was distraught. It's all my fault that Clara was not herself," Paul Goode resolutely said.

Whatever you thought of Paul Goode's acting, he knew how to run lines; he got off book in a hurry. Yet what Em wrote on my grocery list was true: Paul Goode came across as more believable and sympathetic in his interviews than he ever did in his writing or his acting. From what little I saw of him in Aspen, I thought he might be a good guy—"in real life," as Em had written. I thought I might like him—if I actually had a chance to get to know him. *Fat chance of that happening now,* I was thinking.

The little English teacher wrote me; she reminded me how disheartened Dickens had been by the circumstances of his early childhood. "I thought life sloppier than I had expected to find it," Dickens wrote. I wasn't sure what sloppiness the snowshoer had in mind, or if she meant that my being on the same chairlift with Clara Swift was an example of life as sloppier than expected. The snowshoer was passionate about Dickens; she knew I loved and admired Dickens, too, but what Elliot Barlow meant was mysterious to me, one of her Whale Ship ideas.

Em wrote me. "What sounds like real life is the coincidence of your being on the same chairlift with her—shit like that happens in real life," Em wrote. "There should be a better reason for your ending up with her in that chair. You could just send me some pages of whatever it is you're writing," Em added.

"What happened in Aspen is a movie—I will always see it as a movie," I wrote Em back. It was true, but I was stalling; it was one way to say I had nothing in writing.

Grace recognized Em's handwriting on the postcard that came next. "Just send me some pages, if there's anything you want to show me," Em had written.

"I'm glad you two are writing each other again," Grace said, handing me the postcard. If we'd been living in New York, Grace would have kept working till the day she delivered, but the driving bothered her; in her eighth month, she was uncomfortable in the car. She stopped working in the middle of February. Matthew would be born the first week of March. Six weeks was standard for maternity leave in the 1990s. Grace would add her vacation allotment for the year to her time off for maternity; Grace said this was also standard. What would not feel standard or normal to me was how everything changed when I had a child.

I was a first-time father at forty-nine, old for a new dad. I had never been afraid in this way before. As new parents learn, loving a child means living with the fear of losing a child. When Matthew was born, my fear for him was passed on to my fictional characters, but you don't purge the dread of losing a child by writing about it. Writing as catharsis doesn't work; it's bad therapy and bad writing. Nothing purges the fear of losing a child; it's why night-mares are recurrent. You don't choose your nightmares; they choose you.

Everyone, even the elder Barretts, had teased Grace for having such an elaborately planned agenda; as Arthur Barrett had put it, "All these plans, just to have a child." But when Matthew was born, I was the one who had an agenda—to keep him safe, to guide his path, to be the best father an old dad could be. More: to be Matthew's rescuer, as the snowshoer had rescued me.

I didn't question Grace for her overmanaging; I tried to let it go. I was writing a new novel and an adapted screenplay of a previous novel, and also what I first called *Loge Peak*, my Aspen screenplay—not to purge my guilt or my shame, and not to redeem myself, but to visualize my most irredeemable behavior.

I kept my *Loge Peak* screenplay to myself; it got worse and worse. "Just send me some pages, if there's anything you want to show me," Em had written. She meant the movie of what happened in Aspen. I thought about it, but I didn't send those pages. I couldn't show *Loge Peak* to Em; I couldn't even show it to the snowshoer.

As a writer, I was impatient with Matthew's early childhood; I was wait-ing for him to find the words. For the first three months, he fussed, he cried, he burped, he cooed; he was startled by loud sounds. When you spoke to him, he paid close attention to your mouth and your eyes. Matthew recognized his mom's voice, her breast, a bottle. It was June, our last week in the spec house, when Mr. Barlow and Em came to stay with us, and to meet Matthew. Em made faces at him, the exaggerated facial expressions of a pantomimist. The first face Em made was one of wide-eyed, open-mouthed astonishment; then she lolled out her tongue and panted like a dog. Matthew imitated her—this made them both happy. When Em and the snowshoer went back to New York, Grace and I tried making faces at Matthew, but he made no response to us. We weren't doing it right. "Em isn't just babylike—Em *is* a baby," Grace said. I couldn't tell if there was an edge to this, if she was editing.

At six months, the babbling began; Matthew could say "Mama" and "Dada," but he had no idea what the words meant. Matthew made sounds to amuse himself; he liked to yell. When Elliot and Em came to see us again, their first time in our new house in East Dorset, Mr. Barlow brought Matthew two musical toys; there was a rattle and a ball with a bell inside. Matthew loved these toys.

"Boys are into cause and effect," the little English teacher told us. *For better or worse*, I would think—after Aspen.

Em held a makeup mirror parallel to her face. Matthew was excited to see himself in the mirror; he smiled, he blew raspberries (or made farting sounds), he reached to touch himself. "Matthew," Em said, pointing to the mirror. "Em," she said, pointing to herself.

Matthew learned the *Em* word, but not *Matthew*; he would learn his own name later. When Em and Mr. Barlow went back to New York, Grace and I experimented with the mirror; we did something wrong. "Em!" Matthew said, when he saw himself in the mirror.

"Em is infantile—the mirror just confuses Matthew," Grace said. There was definitely an editorial edge to this. *Em actually spoke*, I thought.

Between a year and eighteen months, Matthew knew his name and the names of familiar people and objects; he knew the word *no*, too, both what it meant when you said it to him and how to say it himself. He was interested in the TV; he liked listening to songs, and to simple stories that rhymed. He could name the pictures in his favorite books.

At eighteen months, when Em and the snowshoer visited us, Matthew was drinking from a cup. He would now notice if you did something that was meant to be funny, if you were purposely clowning around. Em made Matthew laugh by putting a pot holder on her head; when she put a salad bowl on her head, Matthew laughed and yelled, "No, no, no!"

Between two and three, the words were coming—now in sentences. "What Daddy doing?" Matthew would ask Grace, or one of the nannies, when I was writing. "More milk," he would tell us. "Read book," he said, holding out the book he wanted me to read. "Share toys," he said, sometimes for no reason—just because he was in a preschool play group, and he heard it there.

Grace was spending four nights a week in New York—three workdays in the office—before Matthew was five months old. She was reading and editing all the time, in Vermont and in New York. Grace had signed up our nannies when she was pregnant. My mother and Molly often stayed with Matthew and me when Grace was in New York—even in the ski season. My mom got up with Matthew at night; Molly did the cooking, so that I could have a longer writing day.

I became more interested in the books I read to Matthew after he was three. You can only read *Little Fur Family* or *Green Eggs and Ham* or *Brown Bear, Brown Bear, What Do You See?* so many times before you go crazy, but we both loved *The Ghost-Eye Tree*, and Matthew never got tired of *The Caboose Who Got Loose*. When Matthew was between three and four, we were loving *Winnie-the-Pooh*, one of the early chapter books I read to him.

Matthew liked Elliot Barlow's reading voice the best—we all did. Em would curl up on the couch beside Matthew when any of us read to him; it was as if Em were another child, listening to the story. Matthew seemed to accept that Em didn't read to him, and she rarely spoke; if Matthew asked her one of his two- or three-word questions, Em would answer him quietly, in as few words as possible. I'd noticed how Matthew was drawn to Em, in the hesitant way children are curious about other children. In due course, he liked sitting in Em's lap; he hugged her and she hugged him back. When you read to him on the couch, he looked around for Em—expecting her to curl up next to him. "Matthew isn't sure what Em *is*—she's like a strange pet," Grace said, certainly with an edge. I would never let her be my editor.

When I asked Grace how Em's novel was going, Grace was bitchy about it. "You know that Emily MacPherson writes very well; her novel will be very good," Grace told me abruptly. "But Em is so stubborn—you know how she is. There's no telling if she listens to me, or if she only listens to Mr. Barlow." I didn't like how Grace emphasized the *Mr.* Only those of us who knew and loved the snowshoer when she was a man were welcome to call her a mister, and we never said the word like we were rubbing it in.

When Matthew was four, he used contractions—*can't* and *won't* and *don't* and *didn't*. He asked a lot of how and why questions. "Do I have to?" he asked. "I don't want to," he stated. He knew the names for pennies, nickels, and dimes—but not what to call a quarter. He could recite the days of the week. Matthew knew that Friday was the day his mom came home from New York.

One weekend, Grace brought Elliot Barlow and Em back up with her. They would drive back to the city with her on Monday, too. Em brought a book she'd picked out for Matthew—*Madeline*, by Ludwig Bemelmans. "I told Em, in the car, I think it's a little young for Matthew—she should have given it to him a year ago," Grace said to me.

Matthew loved looking at the pictures in *Madeline*. Perhaps he loved the book because Em had given it to him. Matthew thought Em was special. "I remember *Madeline*—I loved that book," Molly told me when we were making dinner. I remembered my grandmother reading *Madeline* to me; I loved it, too. Molly was in her twenties when she'd read it the first time—to a niece, who had hated it. "She was my most insensitive niece—she deserved to have an agonizing experience with appendicitis," the night groomer said.

Elliot Barlow remembered what a big deal her parents had made of Ludwig Bemelmans because he was Austrian. Mr. Barlow was eleven or twelve when she'd been introduced to *Madeline*. "I think I was too old for it," the snowshoer said; she and my mom were setting the table in the dining room while Molly and I did the cooking.

"You were definitely too old for it—Matthew is already too old for *Madeline!*" Grace chimed in, all the way from the living room. In our East Dorset house, the kitchen and the dining room were one big room, and there was only a chimney with a two-sided fireplace between them. All the way from the kitchen, Molly and I could see the living-room couch, where Matthew sat by himself, looking at the pictures in *Madeline*.

"You should read it to him after dinner," I told the trail groomer. We were the cooks; someone else would take charge of the cleanup. As it turned out, my mom and Mr. Barlow did the dishes—after they finally stopped horsing around with their piggyback rides. Their constant piggybacking irked Grace; whenever Matthew saw them doing it, he wanted a piggyback ride. My mother was seventy-three—too old to be doing single-leg lunges with a four-year-old on her back, in Grace's opinion. Although Molly was a couple of years older than my mom, the night groomer was a workhorse; even Grace had to admit that Molly could carry Matthew on her back to the top of Bromley.

After dinner, Grace and Em had cleared the dining-room table, while the old ski patroller was giving Matthew a piggyback ride—all over the house, upstairs and downstairs. "*Reading* after dinner, *not* roughhousing!" Grace kept calling to them.

I knew what Nora would have said, if she'd been with us: *Grace sounds just like my mother and Aunt Martha.* I was watching Molly; she was trying to get Matthew to settle down on the couch in the living room. Matthew was more in the mood to roughhouse than to listen to a story about robotic-looking little girls in Paris. The ski patroller sat on the couch, waiting for Matthew to climb into her lap; Molly was leafing through the pages of *Madeline*.

"All of my pants are too tight," my mother was saying to the snowshoer in the kitchen. They were washing and drying the pots and pans, while my mom was showing Mr. Barlow her bare belly. She'd been complaining about her ski pants back in March, at the end of the ski season. She couldn't button the top button on a single pair of her ski pants. "If I don't work on my abs in the off-season, I'll have to get a bunch of new ski pants next year," I'd heard her say to Molly. Now it was May 1995; for the first time, she was wearing pants with elastic waistbands. "Like an old woman!" I'd heard her exclaim to the snowshoer. "I like my sweatpants with drawstrings better." They were both staring at her exposed abdomen. "Am I getting a pot?" she was asking Elliot. "Tell me the truth!"

"You don't have a pot, Ray—you look the same to me," the little English teacher told her. Molly and I had been telling her and telling her. Little Ray didn't have a pot.

"The name of the little girl in this story is Madeline," I heard the ski patroller say, in the living room. "Can you say her name?"

"Madeline," Matthew said, the same way Molly said it. I saw that Em had curled up next to them on the couch.

Grace was in the dining room, obsessively removing the melted wax from the candlesticks on the table. That was when Grace intervened in the reading. "Em should read *Madeline* to Matthew—she gave him the book," Grace said; she sounded insistent about it. *The pushy bitch!* I was thinking. At that moment, I hated her for putting Em on the spot.

I must have looked like I was going to say something, because I felt Mr. Barlow's strong grip on the back of my neck; her hand was wet from washing the pots and pans. She caught me in a collar tie, pulling my head down to her level, where she could whisper in my ear. "Let it go, Adam. Don't worry about Em—she's been practicing," the snowshoer whispered. I thought Matthew looked a little unsure about the prospect of Em as a reader, but the night groomer never hesitated. At Grace's directive, Em had sat bolt upright on the couch. Molly just picked up Matthew, passing him from her lap to Em's.

The lap-to-lap exchange was fun for Matthew, but when Molly handed *Madeline* to Em, Matthew looked worried. *The dear boy is more sensitive than his mother,* I was thinking, when Grace asserted herself again. "Em is going to read to you, Matthew," Grace said, in her most matter-of-fact manner.

"You don't have to," Matthew said to Em.

"But I *want* to read to you," Em assured him, as if speaking had suddenly become second nature to her. Em sounded as self-assured but offhand about her reading as she'd sounded when she talked me out of studying abroad for a year—when she convinced me I was melancholic enough, without adding to my melancholy by going abroad. "In Europe, you'll meet some girl who's as sad as you, or sadder. Then you'll be twice as sad together, until the sadness drives you apart," Em had said, as if she'd been talking her whole life.

From the kitchen, the banging of the pots and pans had ceased—the washing and drying done. On the hearthstone bordering the fireplace, my mom sat on a cushion, pulling the little English teacher into her lap; those two couldn't stop fooling around, but they managed to compose themselves and sit quietly, in readiness for the reading. I was too angry at Grace to look at her, but I stole a glance in her direction; it was sufficient to see she was staring at me, before I looked away. I was watching Matthew and Em when Em began to read. As a pantomimist, she could control the exertion she put into her pantomimes. I didn't know that, as a reader, Em knew how to modulate her voice—ramping up the cadence when there were rhymes to hit at the ends of lines.

As far as Matthew was concerned, the creepy house in Paris, which appeared to be run by nuns, might have been a Catholic boarding school for little girls who ate like automatons—they even brushed their teeth by rote and slept like dutiful soldiers in barracks.

Em's audience in the living room was riveted—Matthew, most of all. I'd not seen Em in such command since she'd been onstage at the Gallows, in a nonspeaking role.

In the ghostly nuns' command, the highly disciplined little girls, as a unit, bestowed their blessings or showered their disapproval on the do-gooders or criminals they saw in their city surroundings. Or—like the nuns, Matthew could only imagine—the little girls moped in unison, too. Em was animated and vocally transcendent in capturing the endearing but frightening militancy among the identically trained little girls.

Grace sighed, loudly enough to make Matthew look at her. Grace had stopped staring at me. She was looking at her hands, picking at her fingers—at the candle wax. The reading was not what she'd expected. Grace was hoping Em would fail. I saw that Grace had wanted Em to embarrass herself. Grace was fucking around with her fingers when she left the living room. The sound of running water, in the kitchen sink, made Em pause before she continued reading. She'd just read the part about Madeline's size—she was littler than the other little girls.

"*I'm* the littlest one!" Matthew cried, as if he'd just realized he was the smallest in our extended family.

"Don't interrupt, Matthew!" his mother called from the kitchen. Matthew looked remorseful; he'd meant no disrespect to Em, but had merely meant he identified with Madeline.

Once more, Mr. Barlow prevented me from saying something. I was sitting on the hearthstone beside my mom, but not on a cushion. In Little Ray's lap, Elliot was elevated; she had to reach out and down to grab my wrist. The snowshoer spoke to Matthew, not to me, but her strong hand had stopped me from speaking. "It's true—you're the littlest one here, Matthew—but when I was your age, I was smaller than you," the little English teacher told him.

"When I was a kid, I was smaller than you, too," Little Ray said to Matthew. The way my mother was sitting—with her T-shirt tucked into her sweatpants, in profile to me—I was surprised to see that she did have a very small potbelly.

"Let me tell you, Matthew—I'm sure you'll be bigger than me, when you grow up," I told my son. Em was nodding her head off—like the old, nonspeaking Em—which made Matthew laugh.

"You see what you started, Matthew—this is what happens when you interrupt someone!" Grace shouted, over the sound of the water she was running in the kitchen.

Fuck! I almost said, but Mr. Barlow had control of my wrist; she was just born quicker, Coach Dearborn would have said. I felt the snowshoer slip the wristlock on me with her other hand. "Not now, sweetie," my mom whispered. I saw Molly lean over Matthew; she was whispering to him on the couch, too quietly for anyone but Matthew and Em to hear.

Em would write and tell me what the old ski patroller had said. "You didn't do anything wrong, Kid," Molly whispered to Matthew. What my mother and Mr. Barlow and I could hear from the hearthstone was what Matthew whispered to Em, and what she whispered back.

"Read, please."

"Okay."

Em didn't wait to start reading—then we all heard Grace turn off the water in the kitchen. Undaunted, Em cited Madeline's bravery—her lack of fear of rodents, her adoration for winter, her disdain for the tiger in the zoo, her knack for upsetting the nun on night duty. The second syllable of that nun's name rhymed with *well*. "Miss *Vell*," Matthew called her, shortening her name.

Grace stood over me, where I sat on the hearthstone. "I don't feel well— I'm going to bed," she told me.

"I'm sorry you don't feel well, Grace, but don't interrupt," my mother said.

"Good night, Matthew," Grace said; she gave my mom a look before going upstairs. Little Ray had grown up with disapproving looks; she was impervious to being looked down on. My mother went on hugging the snowshoer in her lap; she knew perfectly well that Grace disapproved of all the lap-sitting and the hugging in my extended family. Em was in the habit of holding and hugging Elliot in her lap. "God knows what Matthew might make of Mr. Barlow—sitting in Em's lap *and* your mother's, while your mom also sits in Molly's lap!" Grace had said to me. Matthew gave no indication that he was disturbed by lap-sitting or hugging. How could someone as smart as Grace also be so unquestioning of conformity? I was thinking; I was done letting it go.

"Read, please," Matthew repeated to Em, who'd stopped again. Em ad-libbed what Miss Vell said when she turned on her light in the dark of night. The nun had had a premonition of Madeline's appendicitis.

Matthew was laughing at the bad French accent Em gave to Miss Vell. "Now what's *rrr-rong?*" Em had ad-libbed, rolling her *rrr*'s.

"Something is wrong with you and Grace, sweetie," my mom whispered to me.

"I know," I whispered back.

Mr. Barlow had released me from the wristlock. The snowshoer still held my wrist with one hand, but she'd relaxed her grip. It was the way you might take hold of a child you were walking across a street, I was thinking—remembering how Grace had objected to what she'd called my "hand-holding with Elliot Barlow." God knows what Matthew might have made of Mr. Barlow's and my hand-fighting. My resentment of Grace was rising.

Em's reading rolled along. Madeline kept crying. A doctor came; he knew the problem was her appendix.

As the ambulance drove Madeline and her appendix through nighttime Paris, my mind drifted ahead—to my coming separation and divorce from Grace, to our joint custody of Matthew. When the nun Matthew called Miss Vell and the little girls were visiting Madeline in the hospital, I was already imagining myself living with Em—somehow, somewhere. The snowshoer gently squeezed my wrist, reminding me to pay attention to the reading. My mom had untucked her T-shirt to dry the tears on my cheeks. I saw her bare belly again; even sitting down, she had such a small potbelly. It was crazy for my mother to be worried about her belly, I was thinking, while Em was reading the appendectomy part.

Em read to Matthew that the little girls were most surprised to see the scar on Madeline's tummy. (It comes as no surprise that the little girls will wake up Miss Vell one night, crying to have their own appendectomies.)

"You can't see the scar," Matthew pointed out to Em. In the book, there's a picture of Madeline showing her scar to the other little girls, but no picture of the scar itself.

"Molly, show Matthew your scar—Molly had an appendectomy," my mother said.

"Em had her appendix out, too—Em has a scar," the little English teacher told us. I'd seen Molly's scar; the old ski patroller had shown me, years ago, when we were talking about surgeries. But of course I got up from the hearth-stone to take a look at Em's scar. I didn't know she'd had an appendectomy.

"No, sweetie—you shouldn't see Em's scar," my mom whispered, but it was too late. Mr. Barlow had let go of my wrist, and Em was already showing Matthew her scar. That's how I saw it. On the right side of Em's abdomen was a small, faded scar—an incision of three or four inches. It wasn't the scar my mother thought I shouldn't see, but where it was—between Em's navel and her panties, closer to the panties. In 1995, Em was sixty, but the pantomiming had kept her fit. She had a flat stomach, even sitting down. I'd not seen a lot of Em's abdomen before; I was staring.

"If you'd looked at my scar that way, I would have slugged you, Kid," the trail groomer later told me. Em's bare belly became an enduring distraction. I lost track of the rest of Madeline. What would stay with me about Ludwig Bemelmans's story was the orderly determination of those little girls who liked straight lines. This resonated with so many different meanings; one meaning that would stay with me was unintended in Madeline. It was in straight lines, away from each other, that Grace and I would separate and divorce—the way those little girls had marched around and brushed their teeth and gone to bed.

When Em finished reading Madeline, I wasn't surprised that Matthew wanted her to put him to bed. I watched the two of them, holding hands as they went upstairs together. I was imagining the rest of my life, with the two of them in it—just the two of them.

"You shouldn't stare, sweetie—stop staring," my mom whispered, although only Molly and the snowshoer could have heard her. "It's a good thing you have five bedrooms—tonight you might want to be in a bed by yourself, sweetie," my mother told me; she'd stopped whispering. It didn't matter anymore that she was the one who'd wanted me to meet Grace; I knew my mom would be my and (most of all) Matthew's ally when the disso-lution of my marriage started. Obviously, the dissolution had already begun.

Mr. Barlow told me that Em had been practicing more than Madeline. Most nights, when the snowshoer went to bed, she fell asleep listening to

Em read aloud to herself. Elliot Barlow had heard Em reading her own novel, the one she was writing.

"What about *Moby-Dick?*" I asked Mr. Barlow. We'd both been there when Em tipped over the coffee table—her way of pantomiming that she was waiting for an *upheaval* of some kind, a certain moment when she intended to read *Moby-Dick,* now that she knew the novel wasn't about a penis.

"I've not heard her reading *Moby-Dick.* This is not that moment, Adam— this is not the *upheaval* Em is waiting for," the snowshoer said.

It was enough of an upheaval for me. Em was a long time putting Matthew to bed. "Matthew wanted to show me how he brushed his teeth, then he had to show me everything in his room, and he wanted to see my scar again," Em told us, when she finally came downstairs. I couldn't look at her, or she would have known I wanted to see her scar again, too. I thanked her for reading to Matthew, not looking at her. I knew what Em was going to say, because I knew how Grace would have pressured her. "I didn't want Matthew to think I was weird. All my life, I haven't cared that everyone thought I was weird. But I don't want Matthew to think so," Em said; she was looking right at me.

"I used to think you were pretty weird, but now I think you're just a little strange," my mother said to Em, hugging her. "We're all a little strange—you especially, sweetie. Straight people are the strangest!" my mom declared, deciding she should hug me, too.

When I went upstairs, the four adults I loved most remained in the living room. *They are all wound up; they'll talk till dawn,* I was thinking. I kissed everyone good night—Elliot and Em, Molly and my mother. I wasn't surprised that Grace was awake; she was seething. "Your family is so weird—I won't let them, or you, make Matthew weird," she started.

"We won't make Matthew weird," I said to her.

"First Em seduces you, then my son—you don't even know it's obvious that you're in love with her," Grace told me.

"I *am* in love with her, but nothing can come of it," I said.

"It's a good thing we have so many bedrooms, and you're used to sleeping in another one," Grace told me. "Em can come visit you, in her fashion."

"Do you want me to stay or go?" I asked.

"I heard Em, putting him to bed—I guess that's what you want it to be like," Grace told me.

"Matthew wanted Em to put him to bed," I told her.

"What is the scar she has? Matthew asked to see her scar—I know Em showed him," Grace said.

"Em had her appendix out, like Molly—like Madeline," I said.

"Fuck *Madeline!*" Grace screamed.

I went into Matthew's bedroom, to make sure he was asleep, before I went looking for the empty guest bedroom—the one Em or the snowshoer hadn't put their stuff in. I left the bedroom door open. I wanted Em to be able to find me when she came wandering. It was a moonlit night; I knew Em could see me in the moonlight. I was trying to stay awake until she came, but I was asleep when Em found me—in the predawn light, no thanks to the moon. I knew it was Em with my eyes closed, from the way she hugged me.

"Now what's *rrr-rong?*" Em whispered, rolling her *rrr*'s. "I know you're in trouble, Longhand Man. Whatever you do, I hope you know your biggest priority is the littlest one."

"I know," I whispered. At first, Grace and I had tried to make it work; we'd tried to stay together for Matthew's sake. Lately, I told Em, Grace and I had been strategizing about the best way to break up—meaning the best way for Matthew. "But there's no way to do it without hurting Matthew," I whispered to Em.

"When you're a child," Em whispered back, "you don't understand how the adults who love you and protect you can hurt you."

I didn't want to go down the childhood road with Em—not with her hugging me in the guest bedroom in the predawn light. I tried to change the subject, but there was nothing as important to me, or to Em, as protecting Matthew from the fallout of my deteriorating marriage. "What happened in Aspen is a movie," I'd written Em, but I hadn't shown her the movie; I'd not sent her my no-end-in-sight *Loge Peak* screenplay. I could tell Em knew I came back from Aspen with a lot of explaining to do, and I hadn't done any explaining. I didn't want to go down that road with Em, either.

I should have known Em knew what was on my mind, as long ago as when I danced with her at my mom's wedding, or when I gave her the snowshoer kiss—the best kiss I could manage at fourteen, the kiss Em ramped up when she gave it to Nora.

"When I was a kid," Em went on whispering, keeping our conversation on the childhood theme—or so I imagined—"I had a feeling, not as strong as a conviction, that I didn't want a penis or a baby's head in my vagina." (That was when I realized we weren't going down the childhood road.) "This didn't mean I couldn't love a child—I just didn't want to give birth to one," Em whispered. "And there were always other things I could imagine doing with a penis—just not in my vagina." (For Em, a formerly nonspeaking person, I understood this was a lot to say—it was unforgettable as pantomime.) "When I met Nora, she already had her convictions—stronger than my feelings. Nora knew she wanted nothing to do with penises or having children—not only in her vagina. I just went along with what Nora wanted," Em whispered.

I was reminded of the time the Gallows nixed the *Two Dykes'* skit about things to do with a penis. Em's pantomime was pretty clear about the rubbing; she would put a penis between her boobs or between her thighs, but nowhere else. This got a good laugh at the Gallows, but Nora's punch line was why the comedy club pulled the plug.

"Not me," Nora said onstage, in her deadpan way. "The only thing I would do with a penis is cut it off."

Em wrote the *Two Dykes'* dialogue, including Nora's monologues; knowing how frequently Nora went off-script, ad-libbing her lines, I wondered if what Em had written about a penis for the stage was true, or just for laughs. Did Em feel the same way she'd felt about penises when she was a kid? The morning light was stronger now; I could see Em clearly. "I'm just like Matthew," I whispered to her. "I want to see your scar again, too."

"Your interest in my scar, Adam, is *not* the same as Matthew's," Em whispered back. She took my hand and put it under her T-shirt, placing my palm against her bare abdomen. "That's my scar—you're a writer; you can imagine it," Em told me. She held my hand against her bare belly; if I closed my eyes, I saw her scar.

Em went back to her bedroom, or to visit the snowshoer, before we could fall asleep together. We knew Matthew would come looking for me when he woke up and didn't find me in bed with his mom. Matthew was used to finding me in one of the guest bedrooms in the morning. He thought I was playing a game with him—hiding in another bedroom. "Found you!" Matthew would say with such delight, you'd think it was the first time he'd discovered me, every time. It was the best time of my days and nights, when Matthew climbed into bed with me. I could imagine he was my one and only—no strings attached. I am my mother's son, as Nora and Molly always said. For Matthew and me, there were strings attached. The morning after the *Madeline* reading, when Matthew found his sleeping father, I was still seeing Em's scar.

The morning after the *Madeline* reading, Matthew couldn't be separated from those little girls in Paris; he carried the nuns and their charges with him everywhere he went. Em was Matthew's new favorite reader, but she was aware that Grace hated listening to her read. Grace's body became tense; her physical movement resembled the wariness of someone anticipating a muscle spasm with every step. Over the weekend, although we must have listened to Em's rendition of *Madeline* half a dozen times, Em kept suggesting other readers to Matthew.

"It makes Molly sad not to read to you—Molly loves *Madeline*, you know," Em would say to Matthew.

Even my mom was called upon to read. Little Ray wasn't much of a reader; I couldn't remember her reading to me. Yet my mother was the first reader who paused before saying the end of certain lines. She let Matthew speak the words that rhymed. Matthew had memorized the rhymes—the *vines* that rhymed with *lines*, the *scar* that rhymed with *far*. And my mom made sure to pause, to let Matthew say Miss Vell's "Now what's *rrr-rong?*"—the way Em always said it, *not* the nighttime nun's actual words.

For the rest of the weekend, all the *Madeline* readers paused before reading the part about Madeline's being littler than the other little girls—inviting Matthew to whisper in their ears.

This pause, and the whispering that Grace could still hear, made her so tense that she trembled in an unspoken rage. "*I'm* the littlest one!" Matthew would whisper in his readers' ears; then the reading would proceed. Even at four, Matthew knew better than to ask his mom to read *Madeline*; Em didn't suggest Grace as a reader.

I declined to be a *Madeline* reader when Em suggested to Matthew that I should have a chance to read to him. I could see Grace stiffen. I said that Matthew and I would soon be alone—when the weekend was over and Matthew's mom and our guests went back to New York. I told Matthew I was looking forward to reading *Madeline* many times during the coming week. That must have been when Grace decided to take the book with her when she went back to the city.

On Monday, when one of the nannies brought him home from preschool, Matthew couldn't find *Madeline*; we looked everywhere for it. When Matthew was searching upstairs, I looked for the book in the trash, but I couldn't find it. I called the Northshire Bookstore to see if they had a copy; they had a good children's section, but the book was on backorder. I was told that they would have it in a couple of days.

The prospect of a couple of days was no consolation to Matthew. "Maybe

Mommy took it," Matthew said, when I was putting him to bed. I tried to assure him that his mother wouldn't have taken the book—it was just lost, somehow, and a new copy was coming. Yet it had been apparent, even to a four-year-old, that his mother had it in for *Madeline*.

I raised that point with Grace when I called her Monday night in New York—after I knew Matthew was sound asleep.

"Maybe Em took it—she might have realized that *Madeline* is too young for Matthew," Grace told me.

I tried to say what Em had said to me. "Forget *Madeline*—Matthew is the littlest one, and our biggest priority," I said to Grace.

"I know that," Grace said, hanging up.

I sat on the floor of Matthew's bedroom and watched him sleeping, for about an hour. I went to bed in Grace's and my bedroom, now that I was alone again. This didn't diminish Matthew's greeting when he woke me up in the morning. "Found you!" the littlest one cried, climbing into bed with me. Matthew sounded so happy, as if our being apart was the only thing wrong with the universe—or *rrr-rong*, as Em had ad-libbed when she found her voice.

47.

WRITTEN IN THE SNOW

"You don't want to end up at the Jerome, sweetie," my mom had told me. Molly and I hadn't heard her say that before; we let it go. In Vermont, in mid-August, some nights already felt like the fall; a few of the maple trees changed color early. "Every year, the same dumb trees jump the gun," my mom said.

"The smart trees, Ray—they know what's coming," Molly told her.

"Smarty-pants, Molly," my mother said. Come late August 1995, she'd started talking to her potbelly. "I know I'm not still growing, but *you* are. Haven't you figured out you belong to someone else?" my mom would say to her stomach. She was definitely thicker in the middle than Molly and I could remember.

"Is your mother putting on weight?" Grace asked me. We were making an effort to be civil to each other, for Matthew's sake.

At the end of that summer, when Em and the snowshoer were visiting, Molly mentioned that my mom wasn't hiking up Bromley Mountain the way she used to. "The snowshoer is still the first one to the top, but Ray used to get there ahead of me," Molly said. "Something's going on, Kid, but she won't see a doctor—she just gives me the 'no one's messing around with my privates' business," the old patroller said.

By September, I'd moved my clothes to one of the guest bedrooms. Matthew accepted my move; he was used to my nomadic bedroom wandering. In our growing detachment from each other, Grace and I were better behaved—both around Matthew and with each other. A kind of coldness had replaced our lashing out. Grace's instincts as an editor had taken over; if you can't make something better, you should delete it, she said to her authors.

That September, my mother must have told me she was sorry a hundred times. If Molly was worried that something was going on with Little Ray, my mom's apologies made me worry more. There was a finality to the way she blamed herself for my marrying Grace. My mother had observed how Grace managed to improve the people and things around her. "I don't waste my time with people or things that aren't essentially good to begin with," Grace had told my mom. I knew this was Grace's standard spiel about herself as an editor, but maybe it sounded original to my mother.

"I didn't know she was one of those women who latch on to people they say they love, when they have every intention of trying to change them—I'm so sorry, sweetie," my mom said.

"Nothing is your fault," I told my mother. "It'll work out—Grace and I want what's best for Matthew." I knew Grace was a perfectionist; she wouldn't allow herself to make more of a mess of a bad situation. In our marriage, surely I'd behaved the worse, and I hadn't paid for it. I didn't know if I'd been lucky, or if there was another word for it.

I made a nonreligious confession to Elliot Barlow and Em. I sent them my never-ending *Loge Peak* screenplay—"too much voice-over" was all I said about it, in my covering letter. I didn't tell those two that I considered calling it *Breakfast at the Jerome*—the snowshoer and Em hated *Breakfast at Tiffany's*, and the cult celebrity of Truman Capote. Those two said Capote was a fake; they believed he'd ruined *Breakfast* as a title, for eternity.

"Overkill with the voice-over, but at least you didn't call it *Breakfast at the Jerome*—just don't," Mr. Barlow's letter began. When it was possible, the little English teacher would begin with the *writing*. Eventually, I knew, the snowshoer would circle back to the heart of the matter. "Everyone discovers it's easier to get married than it is to be married, Adam," Elliot wrote me. "Not everyone can separate and share a child in an exemplary way. Here's hoping a good writer and a good editor can get this part right—the breakup is what couples with kids get wrong."

Molly had said as much to me. I'd told Molly, but not my mom, how badly I'd behaved in Aspen. "At this point, Kid, it doesn't matter how bad a husband you've been, or if Grace was the wrong wife for you to begin with," Molly said. "It's the next part you two have to do right—Matthew is the only part that matters now, Kid."

That September of 1995, Matthew was still in preschool. Since Grace and I doubted we would be living together by the following fall, we didn't know where Matthew might start kindergarten. I kept thinking I should tell Grace everything—I knew I had to pay for it. But I'd withheld too much to imagine telling her all of it. How would telling her help us to stay focused on Matthew? I could always think of a logical basis for my lies of omission.

"It seems to me you are paying for it—you definitely will pay for it, even-

tually," Em told me. "Grace will end up knowing everything, you know—you might as well start somewhere," she added. "One day, Matthew will want to know who his grandfather is—if only for the medical history. You wanted to know who your father was, didn't you?" Em asked me. "You're a melodrama of your own making—you're not telling this story, you know. You're in it," Em told me.

That September, my mother found a tiny spot of blood in her panties. "I've been trying to tell you, smarty-pants, there's something going on—I'm not having my first period all over again, not in my seventies," she said to Molly, showing her the blood.

"It was like she knew it all along, Kid—it was never about her having a potbelly," Molly told me.

On examination, the gynecologist noticed a "fullness" to Little Ray's lower abdomen and pelvic areas. An exam revealed "bulkiness" and "nodulation" in the "adnexa and tubes," and one of her ovaries seemed to be "notably enlarged and irregular."

"What does all that mean?" I asked Molly, who'd been quoting the gynecological findings.

"Don't beat around the bush, smarty-pants—you know what they think it is," my mother told Molly.

"At Ray's age, a show of blood could be uterine cancer—it's usually treatable. That's not likely, but that would be better," Molly said.

"Better than what, Molly?" I asked.

"Tell him, smarty-pants! I've got eighteen months—two years, tops, sweetie," my mom said.

"They're thinking it's ovarian cancer, Kid—it's insidious, and slow to show symptoms. You probably don't have eighteen months, Ray—that would be a long time," the trail groomer told her.

A subsequent CT scan showed "a complex ovarian mass with both solid and cystic components, as well as widespread lymph node enlargement with nodulation and stranding throughout the pelvis." That didn't sound good; I refrained from asking the old ski patroller what all that meant. There was a blood test, too—the cancer antigen 125 blood test, Molly told me. It returned at 413—an abnormally high level, compatible with what was now an almost certain diagnosis of ovarian cancer.

CT scans of my mother's lungs, abdomen, and brain showed there had been spread to her liver, her spleen, her brain. My mom would be told not to blame herself for the delay in seeking treatment; most ovarian cancer patients, as in her case, don't get the diagnosis until the cancer has progressed considerably.

The doctors would describe the treatment, the chemotherapy, and possibly the "debulking" surgery—to remove the ovaries and the pelvic organs. She was told that radiation wouldn't be used because of the widespread distribution of the cancer. Molly knew the chemo would make my mom lose her hair, and vomit, and become very weak—prone to serious infections.

Once treatment began, Little Ray wouldn't be able to manage by herself; she would need what Molly called "a fair amount of care."

"What do you mean, Molly?" I asked the old ski patroller.

"Ray realizes she's not going to get out of this, Kid. You know her—if she's going to die, she'll do it on her own terms," the trail groomer told me.

I knew what Molly meant. My mother would refuse all treatment; the treatment might prolong her life, but she knew the treatment would make her suffer and wither, with no hope of a cure. Her doctors advised her against this decision; almost no one refused *all* treatment, the doctors told her, although they admitted there was a less than fifteen percent chance of a cure. "Zero is less than fifteen percent, you know," was Little Ray's response.

"It's the diaper man reaction—you can't blame her, Kid," Molly said.

I didn't blame her. I knew what Molly meant. My mom wouldn't let herself become incapacitated, dependent on Molly or the snowshoer for her most intimate and degrading needs. Little Ray wouldn't be remembered as sick and pathetic.

As with other enigmatic matters, Mr. Barlow managed to be mysterious and emphatic at the same time. "You know your mother, Adam," Elliot said. "She can accept that she's going to die, but not that her ending isn't in her hands."

"What does *that* mean?" Em and I asked the little English teacher.

"Molly knows what I mean," the snowshoer said. "The end of it is in Ray's hands, as it should be—that's all I'm saying." We could see the snowshoer was crying. Molly wrapped her big arms around the little English teacher, hugging all four feet nine of her.

"It's in Ray's hands and in *yours*, snowshoer," the trail groomer told her. My mother had gone off to bed, in one of the guest bedrooms.

"I don't care if we spend the night here, or if you go home without me," she'd said to Molly, kissing her good night. By mid-September, my mom didn't look or feel ill, but her energy and appetite had declined, and she continued to hold her lower abdomen and pelvic areas accountable for "still growing."

Over the next four months, we would notice her progressive decline—people who didn't know about her cancer would ask her if she was okay.

"Little Ray is your rescue job now, Elliot. I'm fine on my own—you know that, don't you?" Em asked the snowshoer, who was crying.

"I know!" the little English teacher told her, engulfed in Molly's embrace.

"Here's what I know," Grace said to me, but loudly enough for Em and Molly and the snowshoer to hear her. "Em should stay with you and Matthew, when I'm in New York. You both have novels to finish—you can take turns with Matthew. When I'm home, Matthew will have the three of us taking turns with him—he'll love that," Grace told us. It's good to remember these moments, when the people you care the most about behave at their best.

That night, when Molly went home, she took Mr. Barlow with her—the two of them leaving my mom asleep upstairs in our house. When I was getting into bed with Grace, she said she was sorry she ever used the word *weird* for anyone in my family. "Em is alone tonight—I doubt she's sleeping with your mother," Grace told me. "You should go find Em and sleep with her—I know you would rather be in bed with Em than with me, anyway," Grace said, but she said it nicely. There was no edge to it. "Just don't sleep with your mom," Grace added, as I went looking for Em. That had an edge to it.

I found Em in the guest bedroom I'd moved my clothes to. "You have enough clothes for the rest of your life," Em said to me. "I'm sorry about your mom," she said, holding me while I cried. "You're my rescue job now," Em told me. A little later, she said, "I've not thought about two writers living together—I'm trying to imagine it."

"I've thought about it—I can imagine it," I told her. My hand inadvertently touched her breast. I hadn't meant to touch her there. I put my hand somewhere more neutral, like her hip—a bony part of her hip, I think, but I'm not sure where my hand ended up.

"You imagine things faster than I can—as a writer," Em said.

"Imagining things faster isn't necessarily a virtue—not as a writer," I said.

"The idea of two writers living together—I'm trying to imagine it," Em repeated. Very slowly, but deliberately, she took my hand from her hip, or wherever that bony part was, putting it back on her breast. We fell asleep this way—two writers, trying to imagine what was possible.

In the morning, around the time Matthew usually came looking for me, Em reminded me that my mother was alone in one of the guest bedrooms. "You should be with her, I think—I'll bet Ray would like that," Em said.

I went looking for my mom, who was pretending to be asleep when I found her. "Is that my one and only?" she asked me, but there was nothing tentative about the way she threw an arm and a leg over me. My history of being in bed with my mother was not something Grace could ever take away from me. "Oh, don't cry, sweetie," my mom said. "Look how lucky I've been. I have the best husband and the best wife—I have the two best wives, really—and I get to be with my one and only. There's nothing to cry about, sweetie—I've had a pretty long run, too," the old skier told me. The former slalom racer was not given to complain about finishing off the podium, but it made me cry that my mom would not complain about dying. To Little Ray, the ovarian cancer was as fair an outcome as the competition she hadn't measured up to as a slalom skier.

Matthew was excited to find me and his grandmother together. "Found you, *and* Grandma!" he cried, climbing into bed with us. "And Em is in *your* bed!" Matthew exclaimed—to a four-year-old, a morning of wonders. He didn't stay long. "Going to see Em," he told us, as he was leaving.

"I've been thinking about you and Em, sweetie," my mother said, when we were alone again. "I know Nora thought everything was about sex," my mom began.

"Sex was all-important to Nora," I agreed.

"Sex isn't that important—not in the long run, sweetie," my mother told me. "You and Em should try living together—you might like it." We could hear Matthew shrieking in the guest bedroom—the one with my lifetime supply of clothes, the one Em chose to sleep in.

"It sounds like you've decided everyone is awake, or that everyone should be awake," we could hear Em saying to Matthew.

"I know Grace can be a pain in the ass, sweetie," my mom was whispering, "but isn't everyone happy that Em is speaking?"

Given the absolute certainty of the ovarian cancer, it was unrealistic to say that everyone was happy, but I didn't hesitate to whisper back: "Everyone is happy that Em is speaking."

"Me, too, sweetie," my mother whispered, notwithstanding that she was dying—with an arm and a leg thrown over me.

Molly told me that my mom had requested a "rescue medication"—those were the night groomer's words. It was just something to have on hand, "to use at her own discretion," Molly said—meaning, my mother's.

"If or when it's needed, it'll give her a *boost*—that's all," the snowshoer said.

It wasn't clear to me what good a *boost* would be for my mother. They gave her Prednisone, the fifty-milligram tablets, telling her that, if anything could, it would give her a rapid surge of high energy. It remained a mystery to me what my mom would want with a sudden surge of high energy. For what?

"It'll make her feel very good, even euphoric, Adam," the little English teacher told me—a little testily, I thought. Out of character.

The doctors had told Little Ray that this *burst of energy* would not last long; it could actually *hasten her ultimate demise*, Molly was told, with my mother nodding her head the whole time.

"That's exactly what Ray wants and needs, Kid," Molly confirmed. I could tell the trail groomer and the snowshoer were in cahoots about having the Prednisone on hand.

"What does she have the Valium on hand for?" I asked the two of them. It was a tranquilizing muscle relaxant in the benzodiazepine family, I had read somewhere; I'd always thought Valium was used chiefly to relieve anxiety.

"A sedative is a sedative, Adam," Mr. Barlow said—dismissively, which was also out of character.

"We know your mom is going to have some rocky days, Kid," was all the night groomer would say about having the Valium on hand.

Bromley was a family ski area, a small mountain. When Little Ray resigned before the start of the 1995–96 ski season, her fellow ski instructors and all the patrollers knew she was a goner. Molly was forewarned of a goodbye party in the works for Little Ray.

My mother pooh-poohed that idea. "I'll plan my own goodbye party—when the time is right, sweetie," my mom said.

"We know, Ray—that's what we're afraid of," the trail groomer told her.

"Smarty-pants, Molly," my mother said, but Molly and I knew her. My mother liked drama, and she was good at it. Molly and I knew what we were dealing with in the case of the little English teacher, too—as a man, and as a woman, the snowshoer was inscrutable.

Grace was sad that my mom wouldn't be Matthew's ski instructor. Molly had not taken to becoming a ski instructor—not as much as my mother might have hoped—but Molly liked teaching little kids. At the start of that ski season, I saw how Molly took charge of teaching Matthew to ski. I thought the old ski patroller was also working with the new patrollers. It was my impression that Molly ran the meetings on patrol protocol for the first-timers, but I wasn't paying close attention to the business at Bromley

Mountain. I'd stopped skiing with my mom, again; she'd stopped skiing at Bromley altogether.

"Ray is getting her exercise with the snowshoer now," was the way Molly put it. I saw what those two were doing, as soon as there was snow. There were trails on the mountain uphill of my house, off Dorset Hill Road; they weren't ski trails, but the old logging roads, and the trails to an abandoned quarry and the bat cave, would suffice. Elliot Barlow kept her snowshoes and her ski poles in my basement; that was where my mother kept her telemarks, and her boots and poles. Ray was back to skiing the way she'd learned— putting the skins on her telemarks and skinning uphill, before she skied down.

"Your mom can almost keep up with me when we're climbing," the snow-shoer said. "Naturally, I can't keep up with her when she takes the skins off and she's skiing down."

"I don't know for how much longer she can keep up with the snowshoer, or ski down, Kid," Molly said.

Around the house, in my house or hers, I saw no slowdown in my mother's lunges, her squats, her wall sits, but come that December, her familiar piggybacking with Mr. Barlow underwent a subtle change. She stopped carrying the little English teacher around; the snowshoer did all the piggyback-ing. This wasn't a detail Molly would miss.

"The snowshoer is seven years younger than your mom, Kid," the old ski patroller said. *And the snowshoer isn't dying,* I refrained from saying, but I almost said it.

I understood why Molly kept herself busy at Bromley Mountain. The old patroller didn't want to hover over my mother every minute—not that Molly would ask my mom how the dying was coming along. I'll just say we were all aware that my mother was touchy about our *hovering over* her.

"Stop *hovering over* me, Molly!" she'd more than once said to her beloved patroller.

"I love you, Ray!" Molly would say, sometimes bursting into tears.

Around our house, only Matthew was behaving normally; Matthew didn't know his grandmother was dying.

The winter months were just beginning, but the maniacal telemarking and snowshoeing on the mountainside above our house had an irreversible permanence about it. "They look like religious fanatics," Em said. I shuddered to think how the nonspeaking Em might have pantomimed my mom's and Mr. Barlow's devotions to their tortuous exercise. Em would occasionally

go for a walk, but working out wasn't her thing. And it was deer-hunting season in Vermont when my mother and the snowshoer started their mountain-
climbing workouts on the old logging roads and trails uphill of my East
Dorset house; there were no other skiers or snowshoers in those woods, just
deer hunters.

"If you two want to make sure you'll be shot, Ray, you ought to attach
antlers to your ski hats," the old patroller said.

"Smarty-pants, Molly," my mom said.

"If they survive till December, only the muzzleloaders can shoot them,
and the season for muzzleloaders is over before Christmas," Grace reminded
Molly and Em and me in her matter-of-fact fashion. Grace didn't care about
the fanatical telemarking and snowshoeing on the hillside above our house.
But Little Ray and Mr. Barlow's après-workout activities troubled Grace; like
the abundance of our guest bedrooms, the sauna had been my mother's idea.
Little Ray and Molly bemoaned not having a sauna in their little Manchester house; their bathroom was so small and poorly insulated, the town fire
marshal told them they would burn the house down if they put a sauna in it.

I thought the fire marshal might have been kidding, or he'd had a few
beers and misjudged Molly's masculine capabilities. Molly knew better than
to burn down a house, unless she meant to. "Why didn't we just insulate the
shit out of the sauna?" my mother had belatedly asked the fire marshal, after
years of not having a sauna. The fire marshal had long since retired.

Hence the sauna in our house off Dorset Hill Road was well insulated,
and the adjacent room had four showers. "A four-man or four-woman bob-
sled crew could shower together after their sauna—as I suppose such people
do," Grace had observed, of having four showers in the same room. She was
no less judgmental when my mom and Mr. Barlow took showers together,
after their sauna, or when Molly took a sauna and a shower with them—even
when Molly took a sauna by herself, after skiing, because Matthew loved
taking a shower with Molly, which Grace was the most judgmental about. So
much depends on the way you grow up. Why wouldn't Matthew love taking a
shower with the old ski patroller, who was his very own ski instructor? Molly
turned on all four showers, and she and Matthew splashed each other and
screamed like crazy. There was a red light that was on when the sauna was
on, and (even with all the insulation) you could smell the cedar benches
when they were hot, and you could hear the hiss of the water on the hot
rocks. Matthew was always checking out who was in the sauna.

"Grandma and the snowshoer, in the sauna—naked!" he would announce. (Or he would report on who was in the shower—they were always naked—and Matthew would never fail to count how many showers were on.) "Molly is like two naked people!" was Matthew's complimentary assessment of the old ski patroller, his very own ski instructor. Matthew had no interest in taking a sauna; he just wanted to see for himself who was in there. "Too hot!" was all he said about the sauna itself. Grace thought the communal showers and the sauna were for Europeans and hippies.

Em said saunas were "strange"; she also called them "too sweaty." Yet the sauna and the shower room gave our house the atmosphere of a gym, as the winter months were getting started. Like a lot of former wrestlers, I associated saunas with cutting weight; I had mixed feelings about them. But I loved taking showers with Matthew in the shower room, where we turned on all four showers, screaming and splashing each other. I'm sure Matthew had more fun in the shower with Molly, who was definitely like two naked people.

I should have known better than to tell Grace that Matthew had more fun in the shower with Molly than he did with me. "Of course he does!" Em cried.

In our five (going on six) years of less than marital bliss, Grace didn't see the cause for mirth in Matthew's having fun with Molly in the shower. "I know you—I don't doubt that *you* would have fun with Molly in the shower," Grace said.

"Of course he would—I know *I* would!" Em told her. The way Grace left the room—in a huff, leaving Em and me alone—you would never have guessed that Grace was the one responsible for getting Em to take up talking.

"There are only so many times you can leave a room in a huff and expect it to have an *effect!*" I called after Grace.

No matter how busy she was on the mountain, Molly made me ski with her; she found the time. My skiing didn't amount to half a day a week; I didn't take more than two or three runs with Molly. "It's enough to keep your hand in, Kid—you're going to want to ski with Matthew, until he's so much better than you that he won't want to ski with you," the old patroller told me.

Molly would warm me up on a couple of blue runs—we'd take Twister to Yodeler, to the base of the Blue Ribbon Quad. Then the trail groomer tested me on two black diamonds—we took Stargazer or Havoc the whole way.

I met up with Molly after one of her lessons with the little kids, while Matthew was having cocoa in the base lodge with a bunch of ski schoolers, or I would catch up with her after one of her training sessions with the newbie patrollers. One time, I was hanging out with a couple of veteran patrollers; I was half listening to Molly, who was finishing up with the newbies in the ski patrol's first-aid room at the base.

"Alcohol gives you a sensation of warmth, but it enlarges your blood vessels—alcohol actually speeds up the loss of heat from your body," Molly was telling the new patrollers. "Normally, the cold makes the blood vessels to your skin constrict—to preserve body heat—but alcohol blocks this mechanism of self-preservation," Molly continued. The two veterans I was hanging out with knew the gist of Molly's message by heart; they knew exactly what the old ski patroller was going to tell the newbies next. "Imagine there's a bunch of college kids, in their twenties—these boys have been knocking back the beer in the base lodge," Molly was saying.

"I like this part, Kid," old Ned confided to me; he'd been on patrol almost as long as Molly. The old and young patrollers called me *Kid*, because that was Molly's name for me, and all the patrollers revered Molly.

"Ned is morbid, Kid—this part gives me the willies," Meg said. She was younger than me, and much younger than Molly, but she was almost as big as Molly; Meg had to lean down to me when she whispered in my ear, exactly the way Molly would have.

"Imagine these college boys come looking for you patrollers, because one of their buddies is missing—he was taking a last run, over an hour ago, and his car is still in the parking lot. The lost boy hasn't gone home," Molly was saying more solemnly.

I could imagine Matthew as a *lost boy*. This part gave me the willies. "You see?" Meg went on whispering in my ear, leaning over me. I could see the old ski patroller's doomsday scenario unfolding, with my dear son in the imaginary *lost boy* role.

The college kids, redolent of beer from the base lodge, find the patrollers lined up for the last chair to the top of Number One. The lift will shut down soon, when these patrollers get off at the top. Then patrol will be starting sweep. "What do you ask these college kids about their missing buddy?" Molly asked the new patrollers.

"It's always a girl who gets it," Meg was whispering in my ear.

"We should ask which trail their buddy was taking his last run on," a young man said.

"What else?" Molly asked.

"We should ask if their buddy has been *drinkin'*," a young woman piped up.

"You see?" Meg whispered in my ear.

"And why do we need to know if the lost boy has been drinking?" Molly asked. She sounded a little impatient or tired, or both; this time, she didn't wait for one of them to answer her. "Because we need to know how much time we have to find him," the old patroller answered herself. "The lost boy has veered off course. He's hit a tree. He's lying in the woods, where we won't see him when we sweep. Alcohol will facilitate his freezing to death in a comfortable and peaceful fashion—he'll freeze to death faster if he's been drinking. That's why we need to know," Molly told the new patrollers.

"Here comes the paradoxical undressing—I love this part, Kid," old Ned said.

"You are *sick*, Ned—sick *and* morbid," Meg said. "I hope you never find me undressed, paradoxically or otherwise."

"At my age, Meg, if I found you undressed, there would probably be something paradoxical about it," Ned said.

"You are *sick*, Ned," Meg told the old-timer again.

"Paradoxical undressing is not uncommon with hypothermia deaths," Molly said outright, just for starters. "Paradoxical undressing most often occurs in the throes of moderate to extreme hypothermia—if you're freezing to death, you become increasingly disoriented, confused, and combative. But if you start taking off your clothes, you'll lose more body heat—much faster," the old patroller said.

"If you're freezing to death, aren't you already cold? Why would you take off your clothes?" one of the young men asked Molly.

"That's why it's called *paradoxical*, honey," Meg went on whispering in my ear.

"Meg doesn't see the humor in life-threatening situations, Kid," Ned said.

"It could be a cold-induced malfunction of the hypothalamus, the part of your brain that regulates body temperature," Molly was explaining.

"Your *hyper-what-a-mus* must be out of whack, Ned—if you were freezing to death, you would probably get a paradoxical boner," Meg said, not in a whisper.

"Young women didn't used to be vulgar, Kid. And it's *hypo-*, not *hyper-*, Meg," old Ned said.

"Another explanation is that the muscles contracting your peripheral blood vessels become exhausted, just fighting the cold. If those muscles give out, or just relax, you're going to get a surge of blood and heat to your extremities—you'll still be freezing to death, but you'll feel overheated," the old patroller explained. "On ski patrol, we're supposed to know things about mountain survival—we shouldn't be surprised by paradoxical undressing," Molly was saying. "If you die from hypothermia in a city, someone finding you might assume you were sexually assaulted—that's all I'm saying," the old ski patroller said. Knowing Molly, I knew she was done explaining. One of the young men among the new patrollers laughed.

"It's always a guy who laughs, Kid," Meg said; she was done whispering, but she leaned over me, glaring at old Ned.

"You have to admit this part is funny, Kid," Ned said, but the way Meg was leaning over me, I knew better than to laugh.

Besides, now there were new, young faces looking at the old guy everyone was calling *Kid*, and Molly was motioning me to follow her. "Let's go skiing, Kid," was all she said. Small talk wasn't the old patroller's thing; Molly wasn't one to linger after a patrol meeting. We were riding the old Number One chair, to the top of Upper Twister and the Blue Ribbon runs, before I told the trail groomer that, from what I'd overheard, it sounded like an interesting meeting she'd had with the new patrollers.

"I like the new kids, and I like our volunteer patrollers, but some of them think protocol is just an outdated system of rules—the truth is, if you're looking for someone who's lost, you have to ask the right questions, Kid," Molly said, in her seemingly perfunctory but proficient way. I wasn't qualified to contribute to this conversation, and I could tell the old patroller was predisposed to say nothing further about freezing to death, or paradoxical undressing. We rode the old chairlift the rest of the way in silence.

When Molly kept her thoughts to herself, I knew she was thinking about my mother. We all were, but—like Little Ray—we hadn't said much about it. The way my mom and the snowshoer were working out, they looked like they had a plan, but they were keeping it to themselves—the way Molly kept her thoughts.

Come Christmastime, we noticed how tired my mother was; she would often go to bed right after dinner. One night, we were still eating dinner when Little Ray slipped away to one of the guest bedrooms. When Em was putting Matthew to bed, he wandered off—he was supposed to be brushing his teeth—and he discovered my mom, who was sound asleep. Molly and Mr. Barlow would stay for the night, too.

"It's a good thing there are adequate guest bedrooms in this house—we can play musical bedrooms, à la musical chairs. Let this be a lesson to you, Adam—you should always listen to your mother," Mr. Barlow said. Molly and Em and I laughed; it was the kind of thing the snowshoer could say, and we could laugh about, because Grace was Christmas shopping in New York and Matthew had gone to bed.

The next morning, Em and I were asleep—in the guest bedroom I'd made my own—when my mom climbed into bed with us. Em was sleeping with one arm around my waist; I could feel her stop breathing on the back of my neck when she saw my mother over my shoulder. "Please stay with us, Em," my mom said; she'd never before gotten in my bed when anybody was with me.

"Okay," Em said, but I could feel her hide her face between my shoulder blades. I could see my mother clearly in the predawn light; she lay facing me, with her head on my pillow, and one leg thrown over me for old times' sake. Em would tell me later that Little Ray had grabbed hold of her arm, the one around my waist; my mom didn't let go of Em's arm the whole time we were talking. These days, my mother and the snowshoer were often wide awake and wandering around before dawn; some mornings, I would wake up to the teakettle whistling in the kitchen, where the snowshoer was making herself some tea. Molly was an early riser, but not as early as those two—not these days. Most mornings, Molly was among the earliest of the ski patrollers to show up in the first-aid room at Bromley, but getting up at sunrise was early enough for the old patroller.

"Listen to me, you two: there's something you should know—you especially, sweetie," my mom was saying in her wide-eyed way.

"Breathlessly, like a little girl," Em would say later.

"You know Grace—she's always telling me things she won't tell you, sweetie, because she knows *I'll* tell you, and she wants you to know," my mother went on. I could feel Em's head nodding against my back. Em had this same experience with Grace. When Grace wasn't satisfied with being Em's publisher—when Grace wished she was Em's editor, too—Grace told Elliot Barlow, knowing Elliot would tell Em Grace's thoughts *as an editor*. "Grace wants to take Matthew skiing in Aspen—she's booked the Jerome for all three of you, sweetie," my mom told me. I could feel Em thrashing around, shaking her head between my shoulder blades.

"Jesus," I said.

"You don't want to stay at the Jerome too many times, sweetie, or you might end up there," my mother said. Em was holding her breath, or she'd died against my back. I held my breath, too; I could tell Little Ray had more to say. "This is supposedly to celebrate Matthew's fifth birthday, but it's Grace who's interested in Aspen and staying at the Jerome. I suggested another hotel, sweetie—I hear The Little Nell is nice," my mom told me. At the base of Aspen Mountain, The Little Nell was brand new when I'd been in Aspen. "When I die, if you don't see my ghost around, you'll have to see if I'm at the Jerome—you'll have to get me out of there, sweetie," my mother said. Em made a sudden exhalation and inhalation, more near-death imitations.

"What?" I asked my mom.

"You know I don't want to end up at the Jerome, sweetie—just get me out of there! If I'm going to be a ghost, I want to be around my one and only," my mother told me. At first, I thought Em was whistling, but it was Mr. Barlow's teakettle. "If the snowshoer's having tea, I want a cup of coffee—go back to sleep, you two," my mom said. Em and I listened to her going downstairs. All this before sunrise.

"Jesus," Em said. I knew she wasn't a ghost person, but Em foresaw the unlikelihood of my convincing my mother's ghost to leave the Hotel Jerome, if Little Ray *ended up* there.

I asked Molly to tell me her thoughts on this predawn conversation, but I should have known the old ski patroller was decidedly not a ghost person— more decidedly not than Em. "Where your mom *ends up* is the farthest thing from my mind, Kid—it's the here and now that matters to me," Molly said.

When I asked Elliot Barlow her opinion of my mother's determination not to *end up* as a ghost at the Jerome, the little English teacher took a literary view of the afterlife—of ghosts in particular. "I know you and your mom have a thing for ghosts, Adam, but ghosts have a credibility problem," Mr. Barlow began. I knew where she was going with the credibility theme; in my *Loge Peak* screenplay, the ghosts were a *writing* problem, the snowshoer said. She thought the characters who were alive were more believable than the ghosts—not to mention, more badly behaved. As with Molly, the here and now were what mattered to the snowshoer.

I remembered after the avalanche in Wengen, when we were inside the train car, with our flashlights on the little Barlows' frozen faces. I saw how their little noses were flattened against the window, and how their skin was whitened by the cold. But the little English teacher would read more into her parents' "enraptured" expressions than I could see; their "rapture" came from knowing that their only child would not predecease them or die with them. Now that I was a father, and knowing Matthew would be my only child, I could see what the snowshoer saw in her parents' dying faces. "For once, they were happy that I wasn't skiing with them," the snowshoer had said.

She'd taken her time saying goodbye to her parents—the way someone who doesn't believe in ghosts would know it was her last look at them. That frigid night in Wengen, in the derailed car, our breathing fogged up the window where the snowshoer knelt and cried. The little Barlows' faces were disappearing in the foggy window, which their loving daughter wiped clear with her ski glove.

I saw how hard my mother and the snowshoer were working out, like they had a plan to live forever. Elliot Barlow didn't concern herself with where my mom's ghost might *end up*. I'd seen the little English teacher take a long last look before. I thought the snowshoer was taking what she believed was a long last look at Little Ray. I should have known what those two were up to. They didn't have a plan to live forever, but they had a plan.

The old ski patroller knew it; Molly knew better than to interfere with it. "I've told you, Kid—you know what I'm going to say," she said, when I asked her what she thought was up with my mother and Mr. Barlow. "I'll bet your mom and the snowshoer last the longest—I'm betting they go the distance," the trail groomer told me.

"Jesus," Em said, when I repeated this to her; she'd heard Molly say this before, too. "But what does Molly mean?" Em asked me.

"Search me!" I said.

There was no hanky-panky between us, but Em and I were sleeping together every night. In this way, we went through Christmas and New Year's, not knowing what was up with my mother and Mr. Barlow, except they went to bed earlier and earlier, and they were up before dawn every day.

"Now what's *rrr-rong*?" Em would whisper in my ear, when we were lying in the predawn light—listening to the whistling of the teakettle in the kitchen, where we could also hear the snowshoer's serious voice and my mom's more girlish exclamations.

It was January before I asked Grace if she was planning to tell me about our upcoming family trip to Aspen and the Hotel Jerome. "I can't confide in your mother anymore—she tells you everything," Grace told me.

"I hear The Little Nell is nice," I said, but Grace had heard this before; she wasn't buying it.

"I want to stay at the Jerome," Grace said. "If Paul Goode is there, you can introduce us. He'll remember you, won't he? I know you don't think much of him as a screenwriter, but maybe he's got a book in him—a Paul Goode memoir would be huge," Grace told me, speaking as a publisher.

"Jesus," Em said later. "That would have been the time to tell Grace he's your father, for starters."

At first, the snowshoer was in favor of telling Grace everything. "It doesn't matter where you start, Adam. I know you—once you begin, it'll all come out," the little English teacher told me. "If you tell Grace everything that happened in Aspen, she might not want to stay at the Jerome—not with Matthew, let's hope—but I think there's no getting around her wanting to publish Paul Goode's memoir, even if she knows he's your father," the snowshoer said.

"Jesus," Em said. "On second thought, *don't* tell Grace that Paul Goode is your father—then she'll *definitely* want to publish his memoir. Just tell her everything else," Em told me.

Grace didn't believe in ghosts, but if I told her about the ghosts, maybe Grace wouldn't want to take Matthew to the Jerome.

"If you're going back to the Jerome, you should leave Matthew with us, Kid," the old ski patroller said.

"You should begin by telling Grace about the ghosts—you *definitely* don't want to take Matthew to the Jerome," Em told me. Em said Grace's trip to Aspen and the Jerome was not about Matthew's fifth birthday. Grace had booked the Jerome for mid-February—Matthew's birthday was in March.

"Leave Matthew out of this craziness," the little English teacher told me.

Molly and Em and the snowshoer agreed: Little Ray only knew the news accounts of what happened in Aspen.

"Don't tell Ray anything more, Kid," Molly said.

"What happened to *you* in Aspen isn't a story for *mothers*," Em told me.

"Leave your mom out of this, Adam—she shouldn't be in your movie," the snowshoer said.

I couldn't make any headway with Grace. I told her about the ghosts, but she was such a disbeliever—she refused to believe a ghost could frighten Matthew. "You damn fiction writers—you can't distinguish between what you make up and what's real," Grace told me. "This will likely be our last trip together, as a family—we know we're no longer a couple. It won't kill you to introduce me to Paul Goode, will it?" she asked me. That was when I realized Grace knew Paul Goode would be staying at the Jerome when we would be there—that was why she'd made the reservation for mid-February, irrespective of Matthew's birthday. "If your mom is at death's door, Matthew and I will go, or I'll go alone—I know how to introduce myself to a movie star, if I have to," Grace said. I understood then. Going to Aspen and staying at the Jerome was all about her meeting Paul Goode, as a publisher—as Em would say, *for starters*.

"Don't tell her anything else—Grace doesn't need your help to put her heels in the air," Em said.

"Stop with the ghosts—that's enough to tell her, Kid," Molly said.

"Maybe now's not the time to tell Grace that Paul Goode is your father. She might think you're just making it up—you damn fiction writers," the little English teacher told me.

Come mid-January, the snowshoer and my mother were trekking up the mountainside above my house before first light; they had come down the mountain and were in the sauna by sunrise, when Molly was making her breakfast. Matthew was ecstatic; our house was full of people he loved who were up before he was. "Grandma and the snowshoer, in the sauna—naked! And Molly gave me one of her pancakes," Matthew reported, when he climbed into bed with Em and me. We weren't waking up to the sound of the snowshoer's teakettle, not now. Those two were up and out of the house before their breakfast; they weren't even making tea and coffee till they were out of the sauna, often after Molly had left for Bromley.

It was the last week of January when my mother climbed into bed with me, right after I'd gone to bed and Em was still brushing her teeth. My mom had gone to bed hours ago; I'd assumed she was fast asleep. "*Shh!* Don't say anything—just listen, sweetie," she whispered in my ear. "Don't tell Molly or the snowshoer, but you're not just my one and only—you're the love of my life!" my mother told me, giggling like a little girl. Then she was gone, back to her own guest bedroom—back to Molly or the snowshoer, I could only guess.

There was a certain comfort, and a no less certain sadness, in hearing I was the love of my mom's life. I didn't doubt that she was the love of Molly's life, and the snowshoer's, but I wondered if my mother would be the love of my life, too; at the time, it seemed unlikely that this position could conceivably be occupied by anybody else. I was still crying when Em came to bed, and we talked about it. Nora was the love of Em's life; Em said she had no higher expectations, no other prospects. Upon saying this, even in the dark, Em must have sensed I was ever hopeful I might be a lowly prospect. "You're still stuck on me?" Em asked me. I couldn't speak. I just nodded my head against her, as I'd felt her do to me. "Well, now is not the time, but we'll have to consider what we can do about that," Em said.

It was still dark when Molly shook me awake in the morning, waking up Em, too. "Get your ski clothes on, Kid, though we're not going skiing—any warm boots will do," the old patroller told me. She'd seen the headlights and heard the car, as *those two* drove out the driveway. Molly knew—she must have known for a while—where my mom and the snowshoer were going.

It had stopped snowing the afternoon of the day before. By five the following morning, when Molly woke me, the night groomers would have gone home—they were long gone. The lift-maintenance mechanics would show up at six, Molly told me, as she drove us to Bromley; it was still pretty dark. "It was right around midnight when I saw the headlights and heard their car in the driveway, but I thought I was dreaming and went back to sleep—I've been dreaming about this for so long, Kid," Molly said.

The snowshoer and Little Ray would have started their climb after midnight, when the night groomers had already gone. There had been sufficient moonlight, Molly knew. "Ray could find her way up Twister in the dark, Kid," the old ski patroller said. It was a mile, straight up Twister, to the top of Bromley. Molly drove to the maintenance shed, where she started up one of the snowmobiles that were parked there overnight. The lift-maintenance mechanics used the snowmobiles for their morning opening routines. Molly drove the snowmobile up Lower Twister. In our single headlight, the fresh tracks were easy to see in the corduroy the groomers left behind—a snowshoer and a telemark skier, on a mission. There was no one around. We passed the first steep part of Twister, with no sign from the tracks that the telemark skier was slowing down or had lagged behind. "Your mom must be running on Prednisone, Kid," Molly said.

I understood this was what the Prednisone was for—this *burst of energy* that wouldn't last long. It could actually *hasten her ultimate demise*. "It'll make her feel very good, even euphoric," the snowshoer had told me.

Near the top of Upper Twister, Molly gunned the snowmobile—to get over what she called the Rock Garden. That was where we noticed how the climbers' tracks changed. My mother must have had some trouble on the second steep part of Twister. We saw only the snowshoer's tracks, the rest of the way. Elliot Barlow had carried her piggyback to the top. Little Ray must have held her skis and poles. "At the end, Ray would want her skis on, Kid," Molly said. We got to the top of Bromley just barely ahead of the sunrise, but my mom and Mr. Barlow were way ahead of us; they'd been there for five hours, or more, in the freezing cold. The old ski patroller knew exactly where she would find them.

Little Ray liked the Number Ten chairlift, the Blue Ribbon Quad, the best. My mother also liked drama, and she was good at it. In the predawn light, we saw my mom and Elliot Barlow sitting together in the foremost downhill-facing chair of Number Ten. They'd had a six-pack between them, a lot of beer for those two. The empties were lined up on the east side of the unloading platform, the sunrise side, between the sign that said NO DOWNHILL LOADING and the drop-off edge of the platform—where the safety net was.

"I'm guessing the Valium was for both of them, Kid," Molly told me. The sedative would increase the effects of the alcohol, making it easier and faster for them to freeze to death—comfortably and peacefully, the old ski patroller explained. "I'll bet it wasn't exactly a suicide pact," Molly insistently said. She meant that my mother probably didn't know the snowshoer intended to die with her. In the chairlift, my mother was fully dressed for skiing—her parka zipped up to her chin, her gloves on, her ski hat covering her ears. Not the snowshoer, who was paradoxically undressed; her parka, gloves, and ski hat were strewn all over the unloading platform; she'd frozen to death somewhat undressed.

"The snowshoer assisted your mom's suicide—I'll bet that was the pact between them, Kid," Molly explained, as she was dressing the snowshoer. "But Mr. Barlow always meant to go with her—she just helped Ray go first," the old patroller said. This was what Molly meant about my mom and the snowshoer lasting the longest—"I'm betting they go the distance," the trail groomer had always said.

I was searching for a note in the pockets of my mother's ski parka, but she'd left nothing in writing for me—not even a familiar quip. "When the time is right, sweetie," she might have written, but I couldn't find anything. I asked Molly to take a look in the snowshoer's pockets. Surely the little English teacher would have written something, I thought, but the ski patroller said the snowshoer's pockets were empty.

There was fresh snow all around; nothing was written in the snow. "What are you looking for, Kid?" Molly asked me.

"Writing in the snow—one of them might have written something," I said.

"Look at them, Kid—they left room for you to sit with them, for the ride down the mountain," the old patroller told me. "You're supposed to ride with them, Kid—clear as written in the snow," Molly said. "You sit between them, so they don't slump in the chair, and I'll bring you down—that's what I'm supposed to do, Kid," she said.

She went into the lift-station shack. God knows what went on in there; I never knew. Molly said she would make sure the safety gate on the unloading platform was set in the right position. "I'm also checking the stop button," she called to me. I saw her check the bull wheel for ice. I watched her leaving me, over my right shoulder. I saw the rising sun strike the left side of my mom's face, but her face was the same grayish white as the hoarfrost on the seats and the safety bar of the chairlift; I put my arm around her shoulders, and the snowshoer's, but it was hard to look at them.

I could hear Molly's snowmobile; she didn't gun it, going downhill. I knew she would go down Twister to Yodeler, to the base of the Blue Ribbon Quad. It wouldn't take her more than five minutes to get down the mountain. I had only a vague idea of what she had to do at the base of Number Ten. She would climb up the ladder to the motor room and start the drive motor; then I think she had to go into the lift station and turn on the safety system. I sat with the snowshoer and my mother for ten or fifteen minutes; it was a peaceful time.

That chairlift was a four-seater, and we were three small people. I sat close between my mom and Mr. Barlow, holding them tight. To the east, where the sun had risen, was Mount Monadnock in New Hampshire, but I wasn't squinting into the sun. I made myself look at my mother and the snowshoer. It was a wonderful, uninterrupted time. I admired the life they'd made together, and how they'd chosen to end it. I admired Molly for not interfering.

The chair started moving, without warning. It was a quiet ride, going down. You feel exposed on a chairlift going down a mountain; some people feel queasy. But I just held tight to my loved ones. The ride couldn't have been long enough for me—I had so much to say to them. "You're my one and only, too—you know that, don't you?" I asked my mom. "You really are *the only hero*, you know—not just because of the Gallows Lounge shooting, not to me," I said to the snowshoer. They were just enjoying the ride; they were done explaining.

Molly was there to stop the chair at the bottom. I saw one of the lift mechanics barreling down Peril in a snowmobile. Molly and the mechanic must have been talking on the radio. You can see the Blue Ribbon Quad from the top of Number One; the lift mechanic had probably noticed that Number Ten was moving.

"I've got two bodies in the chair, Willy," Molly told the mechanic. "I need the Spryte to take them the rest of the way to the first-aid room."

"Is that Ray and the snowshoer, Molly?" Willy asked her.

"It is, Willy," Molly said. "And Ray's son, Adam, is with them—the Kid's okay," Molly assured him.

"I'm glad you're okay, Kid. I'll go get the Spryte for you, Molly," the lift mechanic told her. The Spryte, I knew, was an ugly thing—a flat-nosed pickup truck on two caterpillar tracks.

In the first-aid room, Molly and I would wait for the ambulance to arrive. The patrollers working that day would start showing up in the room at seven—just a couple at first, half a dozen by eight, a dozen by eight-thirty. The patrollers were "a nosy bunch," Molly warned me. "They'll be asking questions, Kid. We'll be glad when the ambulance gets here—it'll be coming from Londonderry," the old patroller told me. "The state police will be involved," Molly was saying, but I tuned out the rest. I didn't need to know how the coroner had to "release the bodies"—*Release them where?* I wondered. The Blue Ribbon Quad, Number Ten, wouldn't be open for business till nine, Molly was saying—just to hear herself say something. Being alone with their silent bodies was killing her. I just hugged her. Molly recited the protocol, but she knew the rest of the details didn't matter.

48.

FIVE YEARS, FOUR MOVIES

The end of January is the coldest time of the year on Bromley Mountain; those two had picked a perfect night to freeze to death. I wasn't wrong to imagine the little English teacher would leave me something *in writing,* in addition to what my mom and the snowshoer had written in the snow—the scene those two so artfully composed in the chairlift at the top of Number Ten.

My mother and Mr. Barlow had been gone only a week when Grace said she saw no reason why all three of us couldn't go to Aspen now; she kept our reservation for a suite at the Jerome.

"Tell Grace to go to Aspen by herself, but if she insists on taking Matthew, you should go with them," Em said. Without generalizing about ghosts to Em, I suspected it was too soon for my mother's ghost to show up—wherever Little Ray might make an appearance. Em hadn't forgotten my mom's heartfelt plea—to get her out of the Jerome, if she ended up there—but Em had made Matthew her priority. "Tell Grace to reserve a second room. Grace can do her Paul Goode business, you can do your ghost business. Matthew and I have our own room—no ghost gets near that boy if he's with me," Em said.

"It's weird enough with Em already," was Grace's first response to Em's idea about traveling with us. "Besides, it's too late to book a second room at the Jerome."

With my mom and Mr. Barlow gone, a pall was cast over our East Dorset house. We'd all asked Molly to stay with us, but the old patroller was keeping to herself in the Manchester house. It was Em's theory that Molly was going through Little Ray's things, as Em had gone through Nora's. "What you should do, Longhand Man, is go back to your writing—that's what the snowshoer would tell you to do," Em said.

I hadn't been at my desk—I'd not even looked at my writing notebooks during the first week my mother and Elliot Barlow were gone. As Molly had said, what was written in the snow was clear, but it was like the snowshoer to have more to say; it was like the little English teacher to let a literary quotation speak for her.

The notebook I'd most recently been writing in lay open on my desk. In the blank space below the last sentence I'd written, in the small but perfect penmanship of the experienced copy editor she'd become, Elliot Barlow had quoted Herman Melville—an excerpt near the beginning of a long sentence, one the snowshoer knew I would know. It was one of the passages my grandmother had repeated when she was reading *Moby-Dick* to me—a passage she'd later asked me to read to her. "Death is only a launching into the region of the strange Untried," was all Mr. Barlow had written in my notebook; there's more about "the immense Remote, the Wild, the Watery, the Unshored."

I showed Em what the snowshoer had written, not bringing up anything remote, wild, watery, or unshored. For a writer like Em—who was waiting for an *upheaval* of some kind before she finally read *Moby-Dick*—I thought "the region of the strange Untried" might be enough of an upheaval.

"I intend to read that novel someday," was all Em said; she was not sufficiently upheaved to start reading Melville.

Like me, Em imagined that the snowshoer might leave her something *in writing*. The little English teacher, it turned out, had left more than a literary quotation for Em, who was contacted by a lawyer representing Elliot Barlow's estate. Em was a beneficiary of the snowshoer's will; Mr. Barlow had bequeathed her the late writing team's apartment on East Sixty-fourth Street.

Grace declared that Em was "property rich"; she'd inherited real estate in midtown Toronto and on the Upper East Side of New York. "If your new novel isn't the breakout book for you that I believe it will be, you can unload the house in Toronto—the snowshoer's apartment is small, but people would kill to be given a *closet* on the Upper East Side," Grace told Em in that sure-of-herself, New Yorker way. Grace had never been to Toronto, but she was confident that New York was superior to any other city in the world—and Em had been *given* a pied-à-terre on the Upper East Side.

To be fair, Grace wasn't alone in believing Em would never move to Canada—as Em occasionally threatened to do. It seemed stubborn to me that Em refused to sell the house in Toronto, but she insisted she wanted a place to go if she ever left the United States. It had been a while since I'd seen Em do her seagull thing—her arms spread like a seagull's motionless wings, which sometimes meant she was thinking about drifting back to Canada. Yet a drifting seagull was also Em's way of pantomiming Ronald Reagan's laissez-faire abstention from interfering with the AIDS epidemic—this was what Em's seagull thing had meant to most of the regulars at the Gallows Lounge. To be fair, Grace was ever the champion of Em's writing.

When my mom got sick and the snowshoer and Em left Manhattan to come to Vermont, Grace introduced Em to the booksellers at the Northshire. Grace saw to it that the bookstore had Em's backlist in stock before she got to town. Grace had been telling the booksellers that Emily MacPherson's new novel would be her breakout book.

"You should live with Em," Grace kept telling me; she kept telling Em we should live together, too. "You two fiction writers are nomads—it doesn't matter to you where you live," Grace told us. "If you tried living together, you two might actually be happy for a change," Grace said in that sure-of-herself, New Yorker way.

My soon-to-be-ex-wife had inserted herself as a matchmaker for Em and me. "If you and Em are together, that would be the best transition for Matthew—he knows and loves you both—and, at your age, it doesn't really matter that you and Em don't have sex, or if one day you manage to find a way to do it," Grace told me. "Em is over sixty, you know, and you're fifty-four," Grace said. Grace was going on forty. She didn't seem to be concerned about her own circumstances—I mean, regarding what would be *the best transition for Matthew*. While we agreed we would sell the East Dorset house, Grace was evasive about where she and Matthew would live—whether they would stay in Vermont or move to Manhattan. "You and Em might as well live in New York—you'll probably end up there, eventually," Grace said; she sounded more certain about what Em and I *should* do than she did about her and Matthew.

"I also have to think about Molly," I reminded Grace.

"Molly is seventy-five, almost seventy-six," was all Grace said about Molly, as if the old patroller were too old to bother about.

Em and I were worrying about Molly when we invited ourselves and Matthew to an early dinner at the Manchester house, one night when Grace was in New York. "I'll bet Molly has surrounded herself with your mother's clothes—she's probably sleeping with your mom's clothes. A week after Nora died, you can bet your ass I was sleeping with her clothes," Em told me.

Molly told us to come ahead of dinner time—then I could help her with the cooking. When Em and Matthew and I arrived, we saw neat piles of Little Ray's clothes on the futon in the TV room and on the bed in Molly and my mom's bedroom. The piles were well organized—the pants with other pants, the long-sleeved jerseys and turtlenecks together, the blouses separated from the skirts and sweaters. If the old patroller had been sleeping with my mother's clothes, she was over it. The clothes were for Em to try on. While Molly and I were in the kitchen, Matthew had fun dressing Em—or, as Matthew put it, "helping her" try on his grandmother's clothes.

"I found a photograph of your mom—it was under some old ski pants she never wore," Molly told me in the kitchen, where the photo was displayed in a bowl of apples on the counter, a safe distance from the stovetop and the chopping block.

In the black-and-white photo, I recognized the sweater and the matching ski hat, but the sweater was too tight on my mother, and the pom-pom on the ski hat was too feminine for the jock look my mom had most admired in her late teens and early twenties. In the shabbiness of the dark Victorian bedroom with the tall windows, I could discern what would become the restored Hotel Jerome. Molly hadn't found the photo under the ski sweater my mom was wearing in Aspen in 1941—when Little Ray was eighteen, almost nineteen.

I'd seen the sweater before; it was too big for the shoulders of the small snow shoveler, and the pom-pom on the hat was too girlish for a boy, although my mother had told Molly and me that the boy who couldn't take his eyes off her would have been a pretty girl.

"I'm guessing it was the ski sweater and the hat your mom gave to that boy who was a little smaller than she was—the one she didn't say she slept with, not at first," Molly reminded me. "You remember, don't you, Kid?" the old patroller asked me.

"I remember," I said.

"I'm just guessing, Kid, but if you showed Paul Goode this picture, he would remember Ray—and her sweater and hat," Molly said.

In the black-and-white photo, my mother is the smallest and youngest of her fellow skiers crowded into one bedroom at the Jerome; a teammate must have snapped the picture. Little Ray is the only skier looking at the camera; she's smiling, as if she were posing for a portrait in the chaos of her teammates' disarray.

At eighteen, my mom's calmness and the naturalness of her smile made Molly and me imagine that my mother had already made up her mind. "Aspen—March 1941," Little Ray had written on the back of the pic.

"Look at her smile—she's already met him, Kid," the old patroller told me in the kitchen. We could hear Matthew shrieking, while Em tried on

Little Ray's clothes. Molly meant that my mom had spotted the kid who could be my father, she'd seen that boy who wasn't yet shaving—the one who would give her what she wanted, her one and only, with no strings attached.

Molly had more to show me, not about my mother. The old patroller didn't need me to come ahead of dinner time to help her with the cooking. Molly was roasting a chicken in the oven; the potatoes and onions and carrots were already in the oven, too. She'd prepared our dinner before we arrived; Molly knew Matthew would be entertained "helping" Em try on my mother's clothes. The old ski patroller wanted to be alone with me in the kitchen. Perhaps ski patrollers are a family; they pay attention to what happens to other people on ski patrol. Or maybe Molly was unique among patrollers—she kept a close eye on the news, not only the news about boot-packing and running sleds.

"Those two patrollers were killed with your friend Monika—if you haven't heard, Kid," Molly said, showing me a news clipping. "Monika was driving—they make cars with hand controls for paraplegic drivers."

The headline was objective and succinct.

HWY 82 CRASH KILLS THREE

They had hit a snowplow head-on. The three women were coming from Woody Creek in a winter storm. They were driving back to Aspen on Highway 82—nighttime driving, whiteout conditions. Monika had just passed the Aspen/Pitkin County Airport when her car strayed into the oncoming lane. The driver of the snowplow wasn't seriously injured. The state police said the three women weren't wearing seat belts. Monika was described as "the Austrian downhill racer and an Aspen resident"; Nan and Beth, longtime ski patrollers at Aspen Highlands, were referred to as "Aspen natives." It was a local newspaper; the three friends were treated respectfully. "Perhaps alcohol was a factor"—this was as much as the reporter ventured to say about the women's well-known drinking habits. There was a photo of the crumpled car; in the one of Monika Behr with Nan and Beth, the three friends were younger than they were when I met them.

The sports television networks would not be kind to Monika Behr. With hindsight, the seeds of Monika's reckless driving could be seen in her crash on the women's downhill course at Cortina—the ceaseless replay of her career-ending, slow-motion fall. The video footage of Monika's lifeless-looking body being airlifted from the piste would be perceived as a harbinger of her dead body being taken from the wreck in the whiteout on Highway 82.

"When I die," Monika had told me, "I want to lie in the sheets at the Hotel Jerome—I won't care if the sheets are clean."

"I wonder if there are rules for ghosts," I'd written in the *Loge Peak* screenplay.

I was remembering what Monika Behr had said about children. "Personally, I hate children," Monika told me, at her gym in Aspen.

"You mean as skiers," I replied, because we'd been talking about the skiing at Buttermilk.

Monika Behr had made herself clear. "I mean in general," she said. The gym rats in The Last Run were laughing; they knew Monika wasn't kidding.

Molly knew about my bad behavior in Aspen at the Hotel Jerome. I'd not shown her my *Loge Peak* screenplay; Molly wasn't much of a reader. The old patroller knew I'd connected with Clara Swift in the breakfast room at the Jerome; this made Molly look prescient. "You couldn't get me to go there for breakfast," she'd always said.

Meanwhile, Matthew was having a better time than Em, who didn't enjoy trying on my mother's clothes. Molly might have been ready to get rid of them, but Em wasn't comfortable wearing them. I knew Em had been dreading going back to New York, to the apartment she'd inherited from the snowshoer. Em remembered her life with Nora's clothes, after Nora was gone. In New York, Em knew, the little English teacher's clothes awaited her.

Between the photo of my mom in the ski sweater and hat she gave to Paul Goode, and the news about Monika Behr's fatal car crash, I was in an Aspen frame of mind. I could tell Em wasn't feeling much better. Among my mother's clothes, Em found some winter items to take with her. We drove Matthew home and put him to bed. When Em and I were going to bed, I showed her the snapshot of my mom in the tight sweater and the ski hat with the pom-pom; I also showed her the news clipping about Monika Behr.

One day, I would think of Monika Behr as my most unmarriageable girlfriend—ever. But, at the time, I hadn't met her ghost. I was just guessing that Monika Behr would be a bad ghost.

"At the time, I couldn't imagine what would ever bring me back to Aspen and the Hotel Jerome," I'd written five years before I knew I was heading back.

That was the last voice-over I'd written in my unfinished *Loge Peak* screenplay. "How'd you know *that*? That's creepy," Em told me, when we were lying in the dark.

"It just sounded good in voice-over," I said.

"That's a *writing* answer—I wasn't asking you about your screenplay," Em told me. She meant I must have *known* I might be going back to Aspen and the Hotel Jerome.

"I don't know how I knew," I told Em.

"Even creepier," Em said.

As for *even creepier*—in the first two weeks of February, before we went to Aspen, Grace was watching Paul Goode movies on our bedroom TV. The VHS cassettes were stacked on her night table. Grace made a point of replaying Paul Goode films only at night, when she was going to bed.

In the five years since Clara Swift had jumped from the Loge Peak chair-lift at Aspen Highlands, four Paul Goode movies would be released in the-aters. *Ocean Avenue* was in postproduction and *Every Other Weekend* was in preproduction when Clara Swift jumped to her death. At the time, Paul Goode also had a deal to make *Forgetting Nebraska;* he'd already written it. Then there was *Rim Shot,* which had recently been released.

The closet and the chest of drawers in the guest bedroom I'd adopted weren't big enough for my winter clothes—even though the clothes Em had brought from New York and the winter items she'd taken of my mother's were in another guest bedroom. I kept going back to Grace's and my bed-room to get more clothes; I tried to do this when Grace was away, or at least when she was awake. It was disconcerting to see her sound asleep with a Paul Goode movie going ahead on the TV screen. This was why I watched once more the small but disturbing scene from *Ocean Avenue*—the flashback near the end of the film, when the doomed couple reconcile their marriage, which leads to their killing each other. They were a couple careening out of control, a relationship like a runaway sled on a mountain.

There's a long shot of the Santa Monica Pier, looking south along the beach, which is crowded in the late afternoon. We're in Paul Goode's point of view as we come closer to the former bombshell redhead, now a little the worse for wear; she's sitting on the sand with her knees hugged to her chest, facing out to sea. Paul Goode comes into frame and sits behind her; he scut-tles toward her on the sand, like a crab. The redhead knows he's there; she reluctantly reaches for him, behind her. He moves closer to her, until they're like two people on a sled—clinging to each other, as the imaginary sled picks up speed and the music rises. The scene gave me the chills; my father must have been sixty-five, old enough to be the wrecked redhead's father.

"What do you want?" Grace suddenly said, either to me or to someone she was dreaming about; she was sound asleep. I went back to the guest bedroom, where I got into bed with Em. I told her what had happened. Em knew the flashback scene in *Ocean Avenue*.

"You'll get another shot at a normal life—my life with the snowshoer was normal, compared to this," Em said, hugging me.

"Every creature wants a normal life—even an octopus!" Little Ray had said.

That night of the flashback in *Ocean Avenue*, I told Em I was worried about Molly—alone in the Manchester house with all those guns. "Molly won't shoot herself—she wouldn't leave a mess for one of us to deal with," Em assured me.

That February, one night when Grace was awake, we watched the end of *Every Other Weekend* together. I had an armload of clothes and was leaving when Grace told me to stay.

"You must see the ending—worst scene ever," Grace said.

"I've already seen it," I reminded her.

"You should see it again—every writer can't see this scene enough," Grace told me.

From a partially open door, the tired-looking blonde stares at the car parked in the driveway. A love song is fading in as Paul Goode gets out of the driver's side of the car; he opens the back door for a little girl. Paul kneels down in the driveway and kisses the little girl goodbye; she is fighting back tears as he helps her put on her backpack. Paul walks the child halfway to the open door. The blonde doesn't come outside. The little girl runs inside the house without looking back at her father. The woman never looks at Paul; she just closes the door after her daughter. It takes Paul Goode a couple of seconds to compose himself; the love song is fading out as he gets back in the car.

"That'll be us," Grace told me.

"That won't be us—we've agreed to joint custody," I reminded her.

"That'll be us—that's how we'll feel," Grace said.

Grace never used to watch the terrible Paige what's-her-name, the movie journalist for the Hollywood gossip show, but Grace was watching her every night now. My father's love life was of interest to Paige, and to Grace. And Toby Goode was nineteen now, a boy prone to get into trouble; Paige took an interest in Toby's troubles, too.

There was the night Grace was riveted to an awards show at a film festival in Europe; it wasn't one I'd heard of. God knows why Paige was there, but so was Paul Goode. He was with a girl in a dress that had a décolletage for miles; you could get lost in that cleavage. My father must have been seventy, or he soon would be. The girl with her boobs spilling out of the dress was young enough to be his granddaughter.

"It's Paul Goode," Paige whispered to camera. "Get a load of *the nymph* that's with him!"

My father had a tight-lipped smile when Paige called out to him. "Paul! Talk to me, Paul!" Paige was calling, but my father and *the nymph* made their way along the red carpet—not pausing for Paige, or the photographers, or the TV cameras.

Another night, Grace was no less transfixed by the breathless reporting of Paige from a comedy club in West Hollywood, where the underage Toby Goode had been busted by a bouncer for having a fake ID. Toby was with what Paige called "an older woman"—she was not that much older, as it turned out. Toby's date was over twenty-one; at least she was old enough to drink. "Like father, like son," Paige crowed.

"She doesn't have children," Grace said. *The poor kid—the scum journalists should leave Paul Goode's kid alone,* I was thinking. I didn't want to know what Grace was thinking. Imagining, as I knew she was, a Paul Goode memoir— maybe she was thinking the more dysfunction in the family, the better.

I saw Otto and Billy one night, albeit briefly. The two bodyguards made an appearance on Paige's Hollywood gossip show. The paparazzi were block- ing the entrance to a Santa Monica restaurant as the limo pulled to the curb. Otto got out of the driver's seat; Billy held the back door open for Paul and Toby. It was night, but father and son were wearing dark glasses. Otto was clearing a path through the paparazzi. "Here come the bad boys now, and I don't mean the bodyguards," Paige was chirping, when Billy spotted the TV camera; his hand covered the lens—then blackness.

"Are those two thugs always with him?" Grace asked me.

"It seems so," I said.

When you write screenplays that don't get made, you lose your sense of humor about the bad movies that do get made—like *Forgetting Nebraska.* Grace slept through the end of that movie—good judgment on her part. Masochist that I am, I always watch the end.

The camera crosses the open porch of a run-down farmhouse in the prai- ries. Through a screen door, we see the supper dishes being cleared from a kitchen table. Two small children come out the screen door, climbing on the porch rail. In the distance, something catches the children's attention. One of them just stares, but the older of the two runs back inside, bringing an elderly man back out. The old man stares into the distance, then sits down in a chair on the porch; he collapses into the chair as the music fades in. Off a blacktop road, a straight line through farmland, a dusty car turns in to the dirt road leading to the farmhouse.

An elderly woman comes out the screen door, sitting down in a chair next to the old man. The kids sit on the porch rail, waiting. Last, a stunning brunette comes out the screen door and down the porch steps. (She was supposed to be Clara Swift, but that didn't work out.) The brunette looks more worn out than the wrecked redhead in *Ocean Avenue*—as if living with Paul Goode, or merely missing him, takes a toll. The brunette is wringing out a wet dishcloth before she realizes what everyone is watching—the approaching car. As if an unseen hand has pushed her, she sits down hard on the porch steps. She wipes her hands on her apron and gives a passing thought to her hair, then she doesn't bother. She sits there as if she's given up on her appearance, and on everything else. The old woman gets out of the chair. She urges the old man to get up, too; she pushes him back through the screen door, into the kitchen. Then the old lady gets the kids to go inside—they complain, drag their feet. The worn-out brunette is left alone on the porch steps as the music rises.

As the car stops, we see the faces of the soldiers inside; they are trying not to gawk at the stunning but worn-out brunette. Only one of them gets out of the car; he takes a duffel bag from the trunk. Paul Goode is the returning soldier. The worn-out brunette just sits on the steps, wringing the dishcloth in her hands; she stares at the ground, not at the soldier. (Is that because Paul Goode went to the war as a young man in his twenties, and—after two tours of duty in Vietnam—he came home looking like a guy pushing seventy?)

Paul Goode nods goodbye to his younger-looking buddies; they know better than to hang around. As the car leaves, Paul sits down beside the brunette on the porch steps. He puts his hand in her lap, palm up, not looking at her. Maybe he thinks she's too worn out, but she looks thirty or forty years younger than he does. The brunette drops the dishcloth and takes his hand in both of hers. Her head falls on his shoulder. The old faces and the faces of the children are at the screen door, watching them. Grace slept on; the TV in our bedroom faded to black; the end credits to *Forgetting Nebraska* rolled.

Now a new Paul Goode movie would be playing in Aspen, when I checked into the Jerome with Grace and Matthew. It was wishful thinking to hope that *Rim Shot* was a gay porn film, or that Paul Goode was belatedly coming out—no such luck. *Rim Shot*, of course, is a basketball movie. It's more credible to think Paul Goode could be gay than it is to imagine he was ever big enough to play basketball. It's ridiculous to imagine my father could coach basketball—even a high school girls' team. The concept of a little squirt like Paul Goode as a basketball coach is condescending to high school girls—not to mention demeaning to *disabled* high school girls. (This was my first impression of *Rim Shot*, when I'd seen only the trailer.)

49

NOT A GHOST

EXT. ASPEN SIDEWALK, ISIS THEATRE, E. HOPKINS. NIGHTFALL.

The red brick of the Isis is reminiscent of the Jerome. The movie poster for *Rim Shot* strikes a discordant note—the clash of contemporary culture with the façade of the old building.

>   ADAM (V.O.)
>   Five years later, my father was back at the
>   Isis.

In the poster, Paul Goode has his arm around a teenage girl in a basketball uniform. They could be father and daughter—more credibly, grandfather and granddaughter— but if they're related, how did the girl get so tall? The top of Paul's head is level with the girl's broad shoulders.

>   ADAM (V.O.)
>   In the trailer, it's clear that Paul Goode and
>   the girl are coach and player. But the trailer
>   is misleading—the girl is in a wheelchair! It
>   looks like Paul Goode is coaching basketball to
>   disabled girls.

The worn-out brunette in the poster—Paul Goode's romantic interest—must be the basketball player's mother. The mom is as tall as the teenager.

714

Burdened with too many shopping bags, GRACE stops to rest on the E. Hopkins sidewalk—she's sizing up the *Rim Shot* poster.

> ADAM (V.O.)
> It was dark when we got to the Jerome on our first day in Aspen. Matthew was excited to explore the hotel, but Grace would go shopping anywhere—as late as the stores were open. She shopped; I gave Matthew a tour of the Jerome.

PULL BACK: Otto and Billy have paused on the E. Hopkins sidewalk, watching Grace struggle to pick up her shopping bags.

> OTTO
> Should we help this lady carry her stuff?

> BILLY
> If she's goin' to the Jerome, we'll help her carry her stuff.

As Grace moves on from the Isis, the bodyguards follow her.

> OTTO
> This lady looks like Clara.

> BILLY
> She just looks worn out.

> OTTO
> Clara looked worn out.

> BILLY
> Clara looked dead.

                OTTO

Jeez . . .

                BILLY

Clara looked forty-five—with women, forty-five
is worn out.

                OTTO

This lady looks forty, doesn't she?

                BILLY

With women, forty is worn out.

                OTTO

Jeez . . .

Grace drops a bag; trying to pick it up, she drops
another one. Otto rushes ahead to help her; Billy
reluctantly follows.

                ADAM (V.O.)

Grace recognized the bodyguards—from watching
Paige what's-her-name. I'm sure she talked
their heads off, all the way to the Jerome.

Otto ends up carrying most of the shopping bags—
Billy has only one or two. Grace is talking or asking
questions nonstop, but we hear only Adam's voice-over.
Starting softly, we also hear the country music playing
in the J-Bar.

INT. ANTLER BAR, HOTEL JEROME. NIGHT.

Adam is showing MATTHEW the stuffed heads of the
animals: a mule deer, a buffalo, an elk, a Rocky
Mountain bighorn sheep. The country song is a little

louder, but we don't hear what Adam and Matthew are saying—only the song and Adam's voice-over.

> ADAM (V.O.)
> Grace told the bodyguards they had the least boring job in the world. But what about all the crazy *women*? she would have asked them. Lots of crazy women—mostly *young* women, Grace would have guessed.

EXT. HOTEL JEROME, E. MAIN. NIGHT.

At the intersection of E. Main and Mill St., Grace and the bodyguards are waiting for the walk light. Otto is bashful, not saying anything but nodding his head to whatever Grace says. Billy is trying to be suave, but he's telling Grace everything she wants to know.

> ADAM (V.O.)
> *Mostly young women, definitely*, the bodyguard who did all the talking told her.

Carrying nothing, Grace's hands are free to search her purse for a couple of business cards, which she gives to Otto and Billy as the walk light signals the go-ahead. Otto is carrying so many bags that he doesn't have a hand free; he accepts and holds Grace's business card between his teeth.

> ADAM (V.O.)
> Knowing Grace, she told them she was a publisher—one who wanted to acquire Paul Goode's memoir.

At the entrance to the Jerome, the bodyguards will not give Grace's shopping bags to a COWBOY DOORMAN, who

remains outside with nothing to do. The doorman doesn't
see the tall hippie girl wearing a ski sweater over a
turtleneck; she is kicking a snowbank by the entrance,
but she loses interest in it. She stalks the cowboy
doorman, who doesn't see her; she lifts her sweater
and the turtleneck, showing him her bare breasts. He
doesn't react at all.

> ADAM (V.O.)
> I saw that tall hippie girl when we got to
> the hotel. She's a ghost now. Not everybody
> sees her.

The hippie girl keeps prancing around the cowboy
doorman, showing him her unappreciated breasts.

EXT. POOL AND HOT TUBS, HOTEL JEROME. NIGHT.

Adam and Matthew aren't wearing outdoor clothes;
they don't linger long in the steam rising from the
hot tubs and the heated pool. It's cold outside. No
one is swimming, but Lex Barker is looking anxious
in the hot tubs. Adam closely watches Matthew, to be
sure his son doesn't see ghosts, but Matthew doesn't
notice this ghost; the boy is oblivious to the half-
naked Tarzan, who is prone to expect the worst in the
water.

> ADAM (V.O.)
> I kept my fingers crossed, hoping that Matthew
> didn't see ghosts. So far, so good—that's all
> I was thinking. But I remembered what Monika
> said: "Not every ghost is seen by everyone."
> She said that was the only safe generalization
> about ghosts she knew.

INT. ELEVATOR, HOTEL JEROME. NIGHT.

Grace and the two bodyguards carrying her shopping bags don't see the forlorn cowboy carrying his saddle or the other ghost riding with them. Clara Swift is dressed as she was the morning she met Adam in the breakfast room of the Jerome—the same skirt and sweater, the sweater she couldn't decide about untucking or tucking in. Her ghost has decided to tuck in the sweater. Clara can't look at Otto and Billy.

> ADAM (V.O.)
> "Aspen was never an easy town for cowboys,"
> Monika had told me. I was sorry to see Clara
> Swift riding the elevator with the cowboy. She
> was sorry to see me, too. Aspen was never an
> easy town for Clara. It seemed perverse that
> she would hang out with the misplaced cowboy,
> and she would always wear what she wore when
> she hooked up with me.

INT. LOBBY, HOTEL JEROME. NIGHT.

The long-dead companion of the 1887 Aspen volunteers is still seated, in a propped-up fashion, in an overstuffed chair by the fireplace—still bleeding from his long-ago wounds. The country song has changed, to a sadder one. Adam is showing Matthew the mule deer heads, mounted on either side of the big mirror over the fireplace. There's no one else in the lobby; Matthew doesn't see the still-bleeding Aspen volunteer.

> ADAM (V.O.)
> I was trying to keep Matthew awake until dinner
> time, but the poor kid was jet-lagged.

INT. J-BAR, HOTEL JEROME. LATER THAT NIGHT.

There's an angry, reverberant beat to the country
song in the uncrowded J-Bar. Those two miners—
the ones who were blown to bits, setting black-
powder charges in the 1880s—are still standing at
the bar, the one with the sledge and his pal. THE
SKIERS, a few hangers-on from the après-ski mob, are
outnumbered by the ghosts. The guests at the Jerome
must be dining elsewhere in town, or in one of the
hotel's fancier dining rooms.

> ADAM (V.O.)
> A quick dinner in the J-Bar seemed like a good
> idea our first night.

When Adam enters the J-Bar with Grace and Matthew, he
recognizes the regulars among the ghosts; they know he
can see them. The miner at the bar raises his sledge.
The invisible Indian-fighters—those heavily armed Aspen
volunteers sitting at a table next to some clueless
skiers—give Grace a coarse once-over. At a corner
table, the stoic Ute is unsmiling—still bitter about
the 1887 uprising. Jerome B. Wheeler is keeping the Ute
company; the good hotelkeeper gives Adam and his family
a gracious nod.

> ADAM (V.O.)
> I should have known there'd be new ghosts to
> consider. I regret Monika got a look at my
> family.

ANOTHER ANGLE: Monika Behr and her fellow downhillers,
Nan and Beth, have their own table—as usual, except
they're ghosts. In their late thirties when Adam met
them, five years ago, they look younger, fitter, more
jockish now—being dead becomes them.

ADAM (V.O.)

Those downhillers were knocking back the beer;
becoming ghosts had enlivened them. Death
rekindled their glory days, when they were
in competition. I wondered where Monika's
wheelchair was. Were wheelchairs not allowed in
the afterlife? I'll never learn the rules for
ghosts.

Monika has little interest in Adam; she gives him a
cursory glance. She is more interested in Grace—most of
all, in Matthew.

MATTHEW

Do they have hamburgers?

GRACE

Of course they have hamburgers.

MATTHEW

I want a hamburger!

ADAM (V.O.)

Knowing how Monika felt about children, it was
unnerving to see how she looked at Matthew. A
hamburger would wake up Matthew, who was fading
fast.

INT. HALL, HOTEL JEROME. LATER THAT SAME NIGHT.

In the first-floor hall, near the elevator and the doors
to the pool and hot tubs, is the ghost of a NAKED BOY,
shivering with cold. The country song is now an elegy.

ADAM (V.O.)

The drowned ten-year-old was one of those
ghosts Monika had called "just tourist

attractions"—they were "the ones you hear
about," she'd said, but I hadn't seen the naked
boy before.

PULL BACK: Adam and Grace, with Matthew, are
approaching the elevator, as the drowned ten-year-old
wanders away down the hall. It's clear that Grace and
Matthew see the shivering boy; they just don't realize
he's a ghost.

>   GRACE
>   It's irresponsible to let a child that age go
>   to the swimming pool alone—especially at night!

>   MATTHEW
>   Where is his bathing suit?

>   GRACE
>   We should call the front desk.

The elevator door opens; Adam and his family step
inside.

INT. ELEVATOR, HOTEL JEROME. CONTINUOUS.

Curled up in the corner of the elevator, using the
cowboy's saddle for a pillow, Clara Swift is in the
arms of the cowboy. Matthew and Grace don't see them.
Clara ignores Adam and Grace, but she looks lovingly at
Matthew.

>   ADAM (V.O.)
>   It was creepy how Monika had looked at Matthew.
>   But Clara Swift had been a mother. I knew she
>   must miss her son. There was nothing creepy
>   about the way Clara looked at Matthew. It made

me want to confess everything—not to Grace, but
to my father.

The elevator door opens; Adam and his family step out.

INT. HALL, HOTEL JEROME. CONTINUOUS.

In the third-floor hall, one more of Monika's "tourist
attractions" is passing—the ghost of a SOBBING SILVER
MINER. The miner's dishevelment is more apparent
to Grace than what links him to an earlier century;
Matthew sees the miner, too. Like his mom, Matthew
doesn't know the miner is a ghost. The elegy CONTINUES
OVER.

> GRACE
> (to Adam)
> From what you've said about the Jerome—not to
> mention the way your mother went on about it—I
> expected a more upscale clientele.

Coming toward them in the hall is the ghost of a
SOAKING-WET MAID. Grace and Matthew let the wet ghost
pass, withholding comment. The elegy is coming to its
mournful conclusion.

> ADAM (V.O.)
> It was the hotel maid who died of pneumonia
> after falling through the ice on a pond—she
> still showed up to turn down the beds.

> GRACE
> They send a soaking-wet maid for turndown
> service?

> MATTHEW
> Why is she wet?

ADAM

Maybe she turned on a shower by mistake.

GRACE

We should call the front desk.

INT. BEDROOM, HOTEL JEROME. LATER THAT NIGHT.

Matthew is asleep in a rollaway—a single bed, but a big bed for a small boy. He's holding a teddy bear.

PULL BACK: in a king-size bed, Grace and Adam are sleeping; their bed is alongside Matthew's rollaway, which is on casters.

ADAM (V.O.)

Matthew wanted his rollaway in the bedroom,
next to us—not in the living room of our suite,
where I also left a light on for him.

The door to the living room is open, as is the door to the bathroom, where another light has been left on—providing the bedroom with enough light to make Matthew feel safe. Adam is sleeping on the side of the bed nearest Matthew's rollaway. Separating the two beds is a narrow aisle of carpet, serving as a path to the bathroom or the living room.

ADAM (V.O.)

The jet lag affected us all.

CLOSE-UP: on Adam's face, asleep. We hear a bouncing ball, a basketball being dribbled.

ADAM (V.O.)

The trailer for *Rim Shot* replayed itself in my
sleep.

INT. BASKETBALL COURT, SMALL GYM. DAY.

There's no music, no dialogue—no sound, except
the basketball. A TEENAGE GIRL in a wheelchair is
practicing her dribbling. Before she can take a shot at
the basket, she dribbles the ball off the footrest of
her wheelchair. The ball rolls off the court. The girl
looks too discouraged to go get the ball. Then we hear—
she also hears—a ball being dribbled.

> ADAM (V.O.)
> Grace had read reviews of *Rim Shot*. The
> basketball player isn't permanently disabled.
> She has a spinal injury from a car crash.
> She'll miss the basketball season of her senior
> year in high school, but she'll completely
> recover. You wouldn't know this from the
> trailer.

The bleacher seats are empty, but the girl in the
wheelchair isn't alone in the gym; she sees Paul Goode
coming toward her, dribbling a basketball. Paul is in
his coaching outfit: basketball shoes, shorts, T-shirt,
a whistle around his neck.

> ADAM (V.O.)
> The girl's drunken father was driving the car—
> he was killed in the car crash.

The WORN-OUT BRUNETTE, the girl's mom, enters the gym
and takes a seat in the bleachers. Paul bounces the
ball to the girl, a pass the girl handles better than
we might have expected. The girl dribbles once or
twice, taking a shot at the basket. The ball bounces
off the glass; it doesn't touch the rim. Paul retrieves
the ball, noticing the widow as he dribbles back to the
girl.

> ADAM (V.O.)
>
> The tall widow will fall in love with her
> daughter's basketball coach—anyone will know
> this from the trailer, if not why the widow
> wants to be with a guy who barely comes up to
> her boobs.

Paul passes the ball to the girl—a hard pass, which the
girl handles just fine. The girl takes her time—more
dribbling, with more determination. The girl's widowed
mother can't bear to watch; she hides her face in her
hands.

> ADAM (V.O.)
>
> Grace read more than the reviews; she also read
> the Hollywood gossip. Paul Goode and the young
> woman who played the teenage girl were now "an
> item," Grace read. The young woman wasn't a
> teenager, but she was only in her twenties—an
> age difference of more than forty years.

The teenage girl in the wheelchair puts up a shot; it
swirls once or twice around the rim, then falls in. The
little coach and the big girl in the wheelchair high-
five each other. Even sitting down, the girl is almost
as tall as Paul Goode.

> ADAM (V.O.)
>
> You wouldn't know they were *an item* from the
> trailer, either.

INT. BEDROOM, HOTEL JEROME. THAT SAME NIGHT.

CLOSE-UP: on Adam's face, asleep.

> ADAM (V.O.)
>
> When I wasn't seeing this trailer in my sleep,

I was seeing that woman with the baby carriage
in *The Wrong Car* in black and white.

EXT. GETAWAY CAR, MOVING. DAY.

At a city intersection, the driver stops for a WOMAN
WITH A BABY CARRIAGE in the pedestrian crosswalk.

> ADAM (V.O.)
> My father was thirty when he played the getaway
> driver. The woman with the baby carriage was
> not much younger. In the years I thought she
> was a ghost—when she was haunting or stalking
> me—was it only in my imagination that she
> hadn't aged?

INT. GETAWAY CAR, STOPPED. DAY.

In a hail of gunfire, the gangster in the passenger
seat and the three thugs in the backseat are shot.

EXT. GETAWAY CAR, STOPPED. DAY.

The woman with the baby carriage has paused in the
crosswalk while the ongoing gunfire riddles the
getaway car; all four tires are shot, the car appears
to slump, and gas and oil (and maybe blood) leak into
the street.

> ADAM (V.O.)
> At my book signings, she wasn't with the baby
> carriage; she didn't wait long enough to get to
> the front of the line.

CLOSER ON: the little driver sits unharmed and relaxed at the steering wheel, as if waiting for the light to change.

>   ADAM (V.O.)
>   The woman had stalked Paul Goode—in real life,
>   she'd spied on every woman who ever knew him.

PULL BACK: the woman pulls a sawed-off shotgun out of the baby carriage; she approaches the getaway car as Paul Goode gets out of the driver's-side door. He tips his duckbill cap to the woman, leaving the car door open for her. She shoots the slumped-over bodies of the dead passengers, just to make sure. Paul Goode nods to camera as he exits frame, as if the camera were one of the marksmen who ambushed the getaway car. Loose bills float through the blown-out windows of the car. Camera stays on the woman, transferring the satchels of money to the baby carriage, where she also stows the shotgun.

>   ADAM (V.O.)
>   When she showed up in the attic bedroom of my
>   grandmother's house, the crazy woman was spying
>   on *me*. I should have known this woman wasn't a
>   ghost—she couldn't be bothered to disappear.
>   When I woke up with her sitting at the foot of
>   my bed, she just walked away.

INT. BEDROOM, HOTEL JEROME. THAT SAME NIGHT.

CLOSE-UP: on Adam's face, asleep.

>   ADAM (V.O.)
>   The woman with the baby carriage wasn't
>   credible as a ghost.

PULL BACK: from the open door to the living room, the
ghost of Monika Behr enters the bedroom with catlike
stealth and purpose. She walks fine; for a big woman,
she moves with athletic poise and quickness. She's
feeling the sheets—on the bed where Adam and Grace are
asleep, and on the rollaway, where Matthew is sleeping.
There's more room for Monika with Matthew. She slips
off her parka, her turtleneck, her sweatpants; Monika's
ghost is in her bra and panties when she gets in bed
with Matthew.

> ADAM (V.O.)
> Do ghosts make their own rules? It should have
> occurred to me that Monika's ghost wouldn't be
> paralyzed; she didn't need a wheelchair. Dead
> or alive, she had a thing about the bedsheets
> at the Jerome.

CLOSE-UP: on Matthew, hugging his bear to his chest;
Monika lies facing him, her head on the same pillow.
She tries to take his bear away from him; Monika is
amused that, even when the boy is sleeping, he holds
the bear tighter. Monika holds Matthew the way the boy
is holding his bear, hugging him to her chest.

> ADAM (V.O.)
> How Monika had looked at Matthew gave me the
> shivers.

ANOTHER ANGLE: Monika, hugging Matthew, looks at Adam—
wishing he would wake up and see her now. Adam goes on
sleeping; he's stuck in 1956, hearing Sam Cooke sing
"You Send Me."

> ADAM (V.O.)
> I was dreaming about that woman with the baby
> carriage. I knew I didn't want to see her—not
> anymore.

"You Send Me" CONTINUES OVER.

ONSCREEN, CLOSE-UP: in black and white, a doorknob
turns—first one way, then the other—but the door
doesn't open.

> ADAM (V.O.)
> I was more afraid of the woman with the baby
> carriage now that I knew she was not a ghost.

PULL BACK: beside the door is a hat rack with four or
five duckbill caps, all the same, hanging from the
hooks.

A WIDER ANGLE: the gun moll and the getaway driver
are undressing on a bed, dropping their clothes on the
bed or flinging them onto the floor of a small studio
apartment. There's a radio on the bedside table. In her
bra and panties, kneeling on the bed, the moll manages
to take off her bra and turn off the radio—no more Sam
Cooke. The getaway driver is wearing only his boxer
shorts, which the moll swiftly yanks down; for half a
second, we see his little bare ass.

> ADAM (V.O.)
> And how would I recognize her now? The woman
> with the baby carriage would be in her late
> sixties.

CLOSER ON: the door to the apartment, as the driver's
boxers are flung onto the floor. The door opens, and
the woman with the baby carriage pushes the carriage
ahead of her as she comes inside, the door key clenched
in her teeth.

> ADAM (V.O.)
> If the woman with the baby carriage was
> stalking Paul Goode, would my father recognize
> her now?

On the bed, the moll tries to cover herself, as does the little driver. The woman wheels the baby carriage up to the bed, staring down at them.

> GETAWAY DRIVER
> You coulda knocked, ya know.

> WOMAN WITH THE CARRIAGE
> You coulda put a note on the door—sayin' you was busy, or somethin'. You gave me a key, ya know.

> GUN MOLL
> (to the driver)
> You're *married*? You have a *baby*?

> WOMAN WITH THE CARRIAGE
> (to the driver)
> It's your turn with the baby, little fella.

FADE TO BLACK. "You Send Me" suddenly starts playing again.

INT. BEDROOM, HOTEL JEROME. THAT SAME NIGHT.

As the Sam Cooke song abruptly stops, Adam's eyes pop open. He's staring at Monika, who's holding Matthew in her arms.

CLOSER ON: Adam sits bolt upright in bed.

A WIDER ANGLE: Adam sees that Monika has disappeared, leaving Matthew uncovered in bed—still sleeping, still hugging his bear. Adam gets into the rollaway, pulling the sheet and blanket over himself and his son. Adam lies staring at Matthew.

                    ADAM (V.O.)
I was trying to convince myself that I'd only
imagined the woman with the baby carriage in
my attic bedroom, and at the back of the line
at my book signings—just as I hoped I'd only
imagined Monika in bed with Matthew.

SUPER: BREAKFAST AT THE JEROME, 1996

INT. BREAKFAST ROOM, HOTEL JEROME. NEXT MORNING.

CLOSE-UP: at a table for two, Otto and Billy are
talking; they're keeping their voices down.

                    OTTO
Has he given her the plane ticket?

                    BILLY
He's goin' to give her the ticket—that's why we
packed her suitcase.

                    OTTO
I know—it's under the table.
         (he looks under the table)
Why do it at breakfast?

                    BILLY
It leaves the rest of the day free—for skiin',
or somethin'. And there's lots of flights, if
she misses the first one.

CLOSE-UP: at a different table for two, Paul Goode and
the tall young woman who was the basketball player in
Rim Shot are in a standoff; they're not talking to each
other when Paul hands her a plane ticket.

                OTTO (O.C.)

This is a big girl—she won't be easy to carry.

                BILLY (O.C.)

You won't be carryin' her far, just through the
lobby and outside—the van to the airport will
be there.

            TALL YOUNG WOMAN

A plane ticket?

              PAUL GOODE

First class—back to L.A.

            TALL YOUNG WOMAN

You can't tell me where to go!

              PAUL GOODE

Your suitcase is packed. Just go.

A WIDER ANGLE: Billy has her coat over his arm; her
suitcase is in his other hand. Otto is hovering nearby.

            TALL YOUNG WOMAN

Your bodyguards touched my clothes!

She throws the plane ticket on the table as she stands.
Paul picks up the ticket. When he stands, Paul barely
comes up to her boobs. Otto picks her up—a low bear
hug, at her waist, slinging her over his shoulder. A
big girl.

Paul Goode gives Otto the plane ticket; opening his
mouth, Otto takes the ticket between his teeth. The
choreography of the exchange is too smooth for it to be
the first time.

                    TALL YOUNG WOMAN
            (to Paul)
      You bastard!

INT. ELEVATOR, HOTEL JEROME. CONTINUOUS.

Clara Swift won't look at Adam, who doesn't look at
her; Clara can't stop looking at Matthew. The cowboy
carrying his saddle eyes Grace.

                    ADAM
            (explaining, to Matthew)
      You and your mom will go skiing in the
      afternoon. You and I will go to my book signing
      this morning.

                    MATTHEW
      Not a book signing.

                    ADAM
      It won't take long—not many readers!

                    GRACE
            (to Adam)
      I'm going to that dead skier's gym—I'm just
      curious.

                    MATTHEW
      She's dead? She has a gym?

                    GRACE
      It's not her gym anymore, Matthew.

                    ADAM
            (to Grace)
      It was a shrine to Monika Behr when she was
      alive—I can't imagine what it's like now.

You won't like it, Grace—there's no aerobic
equipment. It's strictly a gym for weight
training.

INT. BREAKFAST ROOM, HOTEL JEROME. CONTINUOUS.

As Otto is carrying the tall young woman away, with
Billy following, Adam and his family arrive for
breakfast.

> TALL YOUNG WOMAN
> (screaming)
> Bastards! You're all bastards!

Billy and Otto recognize Adam; they nod to him as they
pass. The bodyguards recognize Grace, too; she waves to
them, breezily introducing herself to Paul.

> GRACE
> I met your bodyguards.
> (offers her hand)
> Grace—Grace Barrett. I use my maiden name as a
> publisher.

INT. LOBBY, HOTEL JEROME. CONTINUOUS.

As Otto carries the tall young woman through the lobby,
with Billy following, some LA-DI-DA GUESTS are having
coffee there. Jerome B. Wheeler, pouring coffee for the
still-bleeding Aspen volunteer, gives Otto and Billy a
reproving look.

> TALL YOUNG WOMAN
> Pricks! You're all pricks!

INT. BREAKFAST ROOM, HOTEL JEROME. CONTINUOUS.

Adam and his family have joined Paul at a larger table.
Grace has what she wants, an introduction to Paul
Goode.

                    GRACE
          (to Paul)
Was she your co-star in *Rim Shot*?

                    TALL YOUNG WOMAN (O.C.)
          (distant screaming)
Pricks and bastards—all of you!

                    PAUL GOODE
She wasn't having a good time here—L.A. is more
her kind of town.
          (he keeps looking at Adam)
You were on the Loge Peak chair.

                    ADAM
          (offers his hand)
Adam—Adam Brewster. I didn't want to remind
you . . .

                    PAUL GOODE
          (changes the subject)
Well . . . who's this good-looking boy?
          (to Matthew)
You must be five, maybe almost six?

                    ADAM
This is Matthew.

                    MATTHEW
I'm almost five!

> PAUL GOODE

Good for you, Matthew.
>> (to Grace)

The boys told me about you. I don't know if
I'm a memoir writer—so far, I've only written
screenplays.

Matthew finds the writing subject disheartening.

> MATTHEW

I have to go to a book signing.

> PAUL GOODE

How awful!
>> (to Adam)

You're a writer?

> ADAM

I write novels.
>> (a pause)

None of my screenplays has been made as a
movie—not yet.

> PAUL GOODE

There are more unmade movies than anyone knows.

> GRACE

That's a good first line, or a last one—for
your memoir.

Paul changes the subject.

> PAUL GOODE

>> (to Matthew)

When my son was your age, he loved the
blueberry pancakes and the hot chocolate here.

CLOSER ON: Adam—he's enjoying his father's company.

> ADAM (V.O.)
> I decided I liked him, but it only made me want
> to tell him everything. How could I ever know
> him, as a father, if I kept anything from him?

EXT. ENTRANCE, HOTEL JEROME, E. MAIN. CONTINUOUS.

A cowboy doorman holds the door open to the Jerome van,
but the tall young woman isn't ready to go. Otto has
set her free, and Billy has helped her into her coat,
but she won't take the plane ticket from Otto, who
holds it out to her.

The tall young woman slips on the snow and falls,
trying to bat the ticket out of Otto's hand. Otto
puts the ticket back between his teeth; when he lifts
the young woman to her feet, she hits him. Otto looks
wounded to his core. He wipes the ticket on his sleeve
before holding it out to her. This time, she dissolves
in tears, but she takes the ticket.

Circling them is the ghost of the tall hippie girl;
she's wary of the angry young woman, who is taller than
she is. The hippie girl shows her breasts to Billy and
Otto, who don't respond.

> BILLY
> (to Otto)
> Did you see that guy who was ridin' on the
> chairlift with Clara?

> OTTO
> He's with the lady who looks like Clara!

BILLY

Yeah, the publishin' lady.

OTTO

Why did that guy come back? If I was on a
chairlift with someone who died, I wouldn't go
back.

BILLY

It'll drive you crazy to think about the
motives of other people.

OTTO

The motives of other people?

Otto looks pained, thinking this over.

The tall hippie girl is still showing her breasts and
getting no response. As the Jerome van drives away, the
angry young woman is giving the bodyguards the finger
out her open window.

TALL YOUNG WOMAN
(screaming)
Pricks! Asswipes!

The tall hippie girl gives the finger to the
bodyguards.

INT. THE LAST RUN GYM. THAT SAME MORNING.

The muscle-bound trainer we saw on the night shift
in 1991 looks like he's in charge. Also working as
a trainer is the really ripped woman we saw doing
bicep curls, the one who was wearing a tank top
with a bikini bottom. She's still in a tank top

that shows off her upper arms, but she's wearing
sweatpants now.

VARIOUS LIFTERS are using the free weights and the
weight machines, but Grace is riding a stationary bike,
and a SKINNY GUY is running on a treadmill. Damaged Don
PLAYS OVER.

>   DAMAGED DON (V.O.)
>   Your worst nightmare is knowin' Louise. She'll
>   drink all your money and give your dog fleas!
>   It's bad news just knowin' Louise.

>   ADAM (V.O.)
>   Grace said they had bikes and treadmills in The
>   Last Run now—Monika wouldn't have approved. And
>   Monika would have hated the music. There used
>   to be only the grunts of the lifters and the
>   clank of metal.

>   DAMAGED DON (V.O.)
>   (repeats)
>   It's bad news just knowin' Louise.

Grace on her bike and the guy on his treadmill are
watching skiing highlights of Monika on the TV.

>   ADAM (V.O.)
>   Grace said The Last Run had TVs. The TVs were
>   soundless, and there were no remotes—you
>   couldn't change channels. The VHS cassette kept
>   repeating itself—all Monika Behr highlights,
>   over and over, including her crash at Cortina.
>   Monika would have hated that.

Grace and the runner wince as they watch Monika's slow-
motion, career-ending fall.

INT. WOMEN'S LOCKER ROOM, GYM. SOON AFTER.

Grace thinks she's alone in the locker room, where
she has wrapped herself in a towel and is going to the
sauna. She sees women's workout clothes discarded on
some benches, and two ski patrol jackets are hanging on
a couple of open locker doors.

> ADAM (V.O.)
> Grace said the women's locker room was empty
> but a mess.

> DAMAGED DON (V.O.)
> Don't think it gets better with Gwen. She'll
> run over the kids and fuck your best friend!
> It's bad news the day you meet Gwen.

INT. WOMEN'S SAUNA, GYM. CONTINUOUS.

Grace thinks she's alone in the sauna, but Monika and
Beth and Nan are there—topless, with towels covering
their laps. The three dead downhillers know who Grace
is. Grace loosens her towel, letting it fall to her
waist. Monika and Beth and Nan are amused; they point
out their breasts are bigger.

> ADAM (V.O.)
> Grace said the sauna gave her the willies. She
> said the dead skier somehow haunted the place.

INT. EXPLORE BOOKSELLERS, E. MAIN. SAME MORNING.

FICTION READERS are seated in a Victorian house—a
bookstore of interconnected rooms. Although Adam is
reading to his audience, there is NO SOUND except
Adam's voice-over.

> ADAM (V.O.)
> Matthew loved it when anyone read aloud to him.

A WIDER ANGLE: Matthew has been browsing in the children's section, where a FEMALE BOOKSELLER takes his hand and leads him to the back of the audience at his dad's reading.

> ADAM (V.O.)
> But Matthew didn't love my readings, or my book signings.

People in the audience stand and applaud; a line forms of the readers who want Adam to sign their books. At the end of the line is a STERN-LOOKING WOMAN WITH GRAY HAIR. We may or may not recognize her as the woman with the baby carriage in *The Wrong Car*, because she is wrinkled and gray. Matthew wouldn't recognize her, anyway, and she's not with a baby carriage.

ANOTHER ANGLE: on Adam, seated at a table, signing books. Given the labyrinth of rooms, Adam can't see the end of the line.

> ADAM (V.O.)
> I love Explore Booksellers, but the end of the line was in another room—where the woman with the baby carriage would be, if she was there.

PULL BACK: Matthew, bored, has wandered away from the book signing. The female bookseller is keeping him company. They both see the gray-haired woman, who has left the book signing; the woman is leaving the bookstore without a book.

> ADAM (V.O.)
> I was thinking how I might find a way to be
> alone with my father.

The female bookseller draws imaginary circles around
her ear with one index finger, indicating that the
stern-looking woman with gray hair is cuckoo. Matthew
imitates the cuckoo gesture.

EXT. POOL AND HOT TUBS, HOTEL JEROME. NIGHTFALL.

Adam is treading water in the pool, alongside Matthew
in his Schwimmflügel—his German water wings. They're
talking to each other, but we hear only Adam's voice-
over.

> ADAM (V.O.)
> At bedtime, I was reading *My Father's Dragon* to
> Matthew. It's about a little boy who runs away
> from home. He's a stowaway on a ship; he goes
> to an island of wild animals to rescue a baby
> dragon.

ANOTHER ANGLE: Tarzan is as wary as ever in the hot
tubs, where he maintains a watchful distance from Grace
and Paul Goode, who are talking to each other. Lex
Barker is listening to them, but we hear only Adam's
voice-over.

> ADAM (V.O.)
> Grace had struck up an animated conversation
> with my father—about skiing, she told me later—
> but she'd managed to tell him we were getting
> divorced, whatever that had to do with skiing.
> I don't doubt she made it clear that she was
> the skier in the family—notwithstanding that my
> mom had been a ski instructor.

CLOSER ON: Adam and Matthew talking—we hear their conversation in the pool.

> ADAM
>
> All the chapters are short, and they have titles.

> MATTHEW
>
> Like "My Father Meets the Cat."

> ADAM
>
> And Chapter Two—"My Father Runs . . ."

> MATTHEW
>
> ". . . Away."

> ADAM
>
> And Chapter Three—"My Father Finds . . ."

> MATTHEW
>
> ". . . the Island."

> ADAM
>
> And the author's name is . . .

> MATTHEW
>
> I don't know.

> ADAM
>
> Ruth Stiles Gannett. If you love a book, Matthew, you should remember the name of the person who wrote it.

> MATTHEW
>
> I can remember Ruth.

> ADAM
>
> Ruth is just fine.

CLOSER ON: Grace and Paul Goode in the hot tubs, where
Tarzan is listening to their conversation.

> GRACE
>
> But you go back there, to Loge Peak—you ride
> that chair?

> PAUL GOODE
>
> That old two-seater is gone—it was a Riblet
> double, built in the sixties. You took four
> lifts to get to the top of Loge Peak.

> GRACE
>
> There's a quad now, isn't there?

> PAUL GOODE
>
> A high-speed Poma quad. You take only two lifts
> now, and the new chairlift follows a different
> line to the top.

BACK ON: Adam and Matthew in the pool.

> ADAM
>
> Do you like your Schwimmflügel?

> MATTHEW
>
> My what?

> ADAM
>
> Your water wings are German—they're called
> *Schwimmflügel*.

> MATTHEW
>
> They're water wings!

> ADAM
>
> Water wings are just fine.

INT. ELEVATOR, HOTEL JEROME. A LITTLE LATER.

Adam, Grace, and Matthew are wearing their hotel
bathrobes and slippers—their hair is wet from the pool
and hot tubs. The cowboy is used to them. Clara Swift
avoids looking at Adam or Grace, but she is fixated on
Matthew.

> GRACE
> (insistently, to Adam)
> Paul said he skis at Loge Peak, but the new
> quad doesn't pass over that gulch where Clara
> jumped out of the chairlift.

Adam sees that Clara Swift is upset to hear this; the
cowboy is trying to comfort her.

> MATTHEW
> Who jumped out of a chairlift?

> GRACE
> Matthew—it was no one you knew, and it was a
> long time ago. No one jumps out of chairlifts
> anymore—you have to be crazy. I shouldn't be
> talking about it.

> ADAM
> (looking at Clara)
> No, you shouldn't . . .

> GRACE
> I would love to ski there—with Paul, I mean—but
> I don't want to be pushy. I can't just invite
> myself to ski with him.

> ADAM
> I have to talk to him—there are things I should

explain to him. I'll say you're an expert
skier—I'll say he should ski with you.

The cowboy gives Adam a *what-the-fuck* look. Now Clara
Swift looks more closely at Grace. Adam tries to change
the subject.

> ADAM
> (to Matthew)
> Chapter Four—"My Father Finds . . ."

> MATTHEW
> I don't know Chapter Four!

> ADAM
> "My Father Finds the River."

> CLARA SWIFT
> (to Matthew)
> That's where the dragon is tied up.

Only Adam and the cowboy hear what Clara says.

> THE COWBOY
> (to Clara)
> What dragon?

Clara is embarrassed that she spoke. Adam knows she
must have read *My Father's Dragon* to her son, when he
was Matthew's age.

> GRACE
> (to Adam)
> What do you have to talk to Paul about? What
> *things* should you explain to him?

> ADAM
> I'll tell you . . . later.

> MATTHEW
> (repeats, to himself)
> "My Father Finds the . . ."

> ADAM
> ". . . River."

> MATTHEW
> ". . . the *River*."

Clara Swift is crying on the cowboy's shoulder.

INT. BEDROOM, HOTEL JEROME. MATTHEW'S BEDTIME.

CLOSE UP: on Grace's face on the pillow, eyes open, listening to Adam read *My Father's Dragon* to Matthew.

> ADAM (O.C.)
> "The jungle began just beyond a narrow strip of beach . . ."

Grace rolls over, showing us the back of her head.

> ADAM (V.O.)
> Grace and I were trying to go to bed at Matthew's bedtime. Paul Goode got up early for breakfast, because he was a serious skier.

ANOTHER ANGLE: on Adam in Matthew's bed, reading to Matthew.

> ADAM
> Chapter Five—"My Father Meets Some Tigers."

> MATTHEW
> How many tigers?

> ADAM

I don't know.

CLOSER ON: Grace, covering her head with her pillow.

> ADAM (V.O.)

If Grace and I were going to take turns skiing
with my father, we had to get up earlier.
Matthew had no trouble getting up early. In my
mind, I was already rehearsing my confession to
my father.

DISSOLVE TO: Grace is asleep, the covers thrown back.

> MATTHEW (O.C.)
> (whispers)

Mommy is asleep.

> ADAM (O.C.)

That's why we're whispering.

BACK ON: Adam reading to Matthew in Matthew's bed.

> ADAM
> (whispers)

This is the last chapter tonight.

> MATTHEW
> (whispers)

I know . . .

> ADAM
> (whispers)

Chapter Six—"My Father Meets a . . ."

Adam points to an illustration in the book.

> MATTHEW
> (loudly)
". . . a *Rhinoceros*."

> ADAM
> (whispers)
Shh!

> MATTHEW
> (whispers)
". . . a Rhinoceros."

INT. ELEVATOR, HOTEL JEROME. NEXT MORNING.

Adam, Grace, and Matthew are dressed for skiing—the cowboy and Clara Swift are dressed as usual. Clara glares at Grace.

> MATTHEW
> (to his mom)
You were asleep. You missed Chapter Six—"My Father Meets a . . ."

> GRACE
> (as Clara glares)
What did I miss?

> MATTHEW
> (to his mom)
You missed the *rhinoceros*!

> GRACE
I'll have to catch up.

> ADAM (V.O.)
I saw the way Clara Swift was looking at Grace. Clara knew Grace was one of those women who

would try to sleep with my father—not just ski with him. I'd been too busy preparing my confession to think about what Grace was preparing to do.

INT. BREAKFAST ROOM, HOTEL JEROME. CONTINUOUS.

Paul Goode is being seated at a table set for four, but he's with only one other person—the beautiful Chinese woman who was his co-star in *Leaving Hong Kong.* He is dressed to ski; she isn't. They're already seated at their table when Adam and his family arrive in the breakfast room and are seated at an adjacent table.

> ADAM (V.O.)
> It was hard to get to breakfast before my father. Grace was taken aback that he wasn't alone.

> GRACE
> (whispers)
> She's not here to ski.

> ADAM
> (whispers)
> The woman with the tattoo in . . .

> GRACE
> (whispers)
> I know who she is!

Paul Goode waves to Adam's family; Grace is agitated.

A WIDER ANGLE: Otto and Billy are seated together at a nearby table. Otto waves to Grace and her family, too.

The CHINESE MAN and his LITTLE GIRL enter the breakfast
room, joining Paul and the Chinese woman at their
table—the woman's husband and daughter. They're dressed
for skiing.

> GRACE
> (embarrassed)
> Two skiers in the family.

> PAUL GOODE
> (to Adam and Grace)
> Otto can take the kids to see the animals in
> the Antler Bar. It's a long wait for their
> pancakes.

Otto likes little kids; he holds the kids' hands as
they leave the breakfast room.

> GRACE
> (calls to Otto)
> Thank you!

Grace points to Adam when she speaks to Paul; she
is trying to sound casual, but *casual* doesn't come
naturally to Grace.

> GRACE
> He's a blue-run skier—take it easy with him
> today. You can save the harder stuff for me,
> tomorrow.

> PAUL GOODE
> As you wish . . .

The way the Chinese woman regards Grace is not unlike
the look Clara Swift gave Grace in the elevator.

>   ADAM (V.O.)
> Here was another woman who knew my father; she
> was familiar with the kind of women who slept
> with him.

Grace and Adam are alone at their table, not speaking
to each other; in their awkward silence, they look
estranged.

>   ADAM (V.O.)
> I knew I had to tell Grace everything—not
> because it felt virtuous to confess, but
> because it was the right thing to do.

SUPER: FIVE YEARS AGO

EXT. LOGE PEAK CHAIR, ASPEN HIGHLANDS. FLASHBACKS.

The lift line is a little busy: couples ride together;
singles pair up. Clara, a distraught mom, gets her way.
Toby is paired with Billy; just ahead of them, Clara is
a single, about to merge with a short line of singles.
Clara and Adam don't recognize each other until they
get on the same chair.

>   ADAM (V.O.)
> Not every confession is the right thing to do—
> not if you're just confessing to make yourself
> feel better.

Clara caroms off a tree, then a rock or two, as she
slides down the gully. From Adam's POV, as the stopped
chair sways in the wind, Clara's motionless body is
marked by the bright colors of her ski clothing; the
colors stand out against the snow and rocks at the
bottom of the ravine.

CLOSE-UP: on Clara's lifeless face. Strands of her hair, from under her ski hat, blow over her open eyes, staring at the sky. Gentle hands enter frame, tucking Clara's hair under her hat; careful fingers close her eyelids.

WIDER: kneeling next to Clara is the ghost of a UTE WARRIOR. He stands, looking up at the chairs high above him.

> ADAM (V.O.)
> I was crazy to imagine I might help Toby, my half brother, by reaching out to him.

On Adam in the windblown chair, looking down at Clara and the ghost. The chairlift starts to move again.

> ADAM (V.O.)
> How would it help Toby Goode to know his half brother had slept with his mother?

EXT. ENTRANCE, HOTEL JEROME, E. MAIN. AFTER BREAKFAST.

A cowboy doorman is putting Paul Goode's and Adam's skis and poles on the Jerome van. Paul is talking nonstop to Adam, but there is NO SOUND. We hear only Adam's voice-over. The ghost of the hippie girl can't stop showing her breasts to Paul—only to him—but he doesn't see her.

> ADAM (V.O.)
> I had doubts about my confession to my father. How would it help him to know who I was or what had happened? Even the ghost of that hippie girl gave me doubts. When she was alive, she never showed her breasts to me—she just gave me the finger. Now she ignored me, but she showed her boobs to everyone else.

EXT. EXHIBITION LIFT, ASPEN HIGHLANDS. SAME MORNING.

Paul and Adam are on the four-seater chairlift from the base of Aspen Highlands with TWO OTHER SKIERS. Paul is still doing all the talking; we hear only Adam's voice-over.

> ADAM (V.O.)
> I let my father talk on the Exhibition quad,
> a ten-minute ride. I was hoping there would
> be just the two of us on the new quad to Loge
> Peak.

ANOTHER ANGLE: on the chair passing over Prospector Gulch.

> ADAM (V.O.)
> If we were alone on the Loge Peak quad, I would
> have seven minutes to tell him everything.

EXT. LOGE PEAK QUAD, ASPEN HIGHLANDS. CONTINUOUS.

The lift line is sparse. There's ONE COUPLE behind Adam and Paul. Adam pretends to have a problem with the binding of one ski, taking the ski off and putting it back on; Adam waves the couple ahead, so that he and Paul get on the next chair by themselves.

CLOSER ON: Adam and his father on the moving chairlift; Adam is the one doing the talking now.

> ADAM
> I should have told you five years ago, when I
> slept with your wife. That's why Clara was so
> upset I was on the chairlift with her—she'd
> slept with me the day before. She hated it. She
> hated herself for doing it. She never wanted

to see me again. She couldn't stand to look at me. It was just an awful coincidence that we ended up on the same chair—we weren't skiing together. But it was *not* a coincidence that Clara was upset. Do you see?

Paul Goode listens.

> ADAM
>
> I was alone for breakfast when Clara said point-blank she wanted to sleep with me, but she didn't mean it. I don't know why she did it—I'm guessing, because of you. She was repelled by what she did. I hated myself for doing it, too. She wasn't herself when she did it. She wasn't herself when she saw me again on the chairlift—she was upset, and not thinking clearly, before your son fell. *Do you see?* What happened wasn't entirely your fault—it was my fault, too.

A view of the gulch the old two-seater passed over.

> ADAM (V.O.)
>
> We were at six minutes when I told him he was my father.

CLOSE ON: Paul's disbelieving expression.

> ADAM (O.C.)
>
> I should have told you before. I should have told your wife you were my father. That might have stopped her, but I didn't tell her. I haven't even told *my* wife that you're my father.

A WIDER ANGLE: the lift station at the top of Loge Peak. Paul and Adam unload and ski away from the chairlift.

               ADAM (V.O.)

Broadway was a blue run. My father had listened
to Grace about my limitations as a skier.

CLOSER ON: Paul and Adam stop at the top of Broadway.
Adam removes his gloves, taking a photo from his parka
pocket.

               PAUL GOODE

Why should I believe you?

               ADAM

I saved my mother's photo until we were off the
chairlift. I'm sure you'll recognize her; maybe
you'll remember her ski hat and her sweater.

CLOSE-UP: the black-and-white photo of Adam's mom, Ray
Brewster, in Aspen, March 1941.

               ADAM (O.C.)

My last name, Brewster, didn't ring a bell
with you.

PULL BACK: Paul Goode looks away from the photo. He
sees Adam wring his hands.

               ADAM

My mom was Ray Brewster. She died recently—
ovarian cancer. She didn't want anything from
you—she got what she wanted. She wanted me,
with no strings attached.

               PAUL GOODE

She gave me her ski hat, and her sweater.

               ADAM

I know.

                    PAUL GOODE
          (angry)
How can you *know*? How do you know *that*?

                    ADAM
I can't explain it.

                    PAUL GOODE
What do you want?

                    ADAM
Nothing. I just want you to know who I am, and
what happened.

                    PAUL GOODE
          (still angry)
Let me see you ski. You first.

Adam pushes off. Camera stays on Paul, watching his
son ski.

On Adam, as he stops skiing. Adam watches Paul ski up
to him.

                    PAUL GOODE
There must not be a skier gene. How could Ray
Brewster's kid ski as badly as you do?

                    ADAM
I tried hard not to learn.

                    PAUL GOODE
You succeeded, but you have your mother's
hands. Ray was always wringing her hands.
          (pushing off)
I'd rather ski with your wife.

> ADAM
> (calls after him)
> I wasn't *giving* you the photo!

There's no point in calling. Paul Goode is quickly
gone.

> ADAM
> (quietly, to himself)
> I was just *showing* you.

INT. THE LAST RUN GYM. MIDDAY.

In the middle of a ski day, the gym is almost empty; the
sound of clanking metal rises above the country song
that's wailing. The two trainers are standing together—
the muscle-bound man and the ripped woman in a tank top.
They look disconcerted by what they're seeing.

PULL BACK: a barbell, loaded with flat weights, is
going up and down—all by itself—over a weight bench.

ANOTHER ANGLE: the lat machine looks like it's on
automatic—an unseen force is doing the pull downs, the
weights miraculously rising and falling by themselves.

> ADAM (V.O.)
> The trainers at the Last Run must be used to it
> by now. They can't see Monika or Beth or Nan,
> but they know when those three downhillers are
> working out.

CLOSE ON: Adam riding a stationary bike.

> ADAM (V.O.)
> I was done skiing with my dad at Loge Peak.
> Grace and Matthew were still skiing at Aspen

Mountain when I got back to the Jerome from
Aspen Highlands.

A WIDER ANGLE: what Adam sees from his stationary bike.
Monika is doing bench presses; Beth is assisting her
with the heavy barbell. Nan is the ghost going nuts on
the lat machine.

> ADAM (V.O.)
> Those three downhillers were the same
> troublemakers they'd been when they were alive.

INT. EXPLORE BOOKSELLERS, E. MAIN. SOON AFTER.

Adam is looking at VARIOUS AUTHOR PHOTOS on his own
novels in the bookstore. He chooses one book, returning
the rest to the shelves.

> ADAM (V.O.)
> I wanted to give one of my novels to my
> father. Which one didn't matter to me; I
> chose the novel with the author photo I liked
> best. I wondered what Paul Goode thought
> about a *writer* gene—if he believed there was
> one or not.

**EXT. ASPEN SIDEWALK, ISIS THEATRE, E. HOPKINS. LATE
AFTERNOON.**

The poster for *Rim Shot* has new meaning, now that we
know about Paul Goode's relationship with the young
woman who plays the teenage basketball player. Paul
has his arm around the tall girl. We see the worn-out
brunette who plays the girl's mother.

> ADAM (V.O.)
>
> When Grace and Matthew came back from skiing,
> Grace went to the matinee performance of *Rim
> Shot*. I took Matthew to the swimming pool and
> hot tubs. Matthew loved the heated pool at the
> Jerome, but you can get cold in a heated pool—
> if you stay in the water too long.

INT. ISIS THEATRE, E. MAIN. THAT SAME AFTERNOON.

PAN: like the gym, the theater is almost empty.

STOP ON: Grace is sound asleep, the light from the
screen flickering on her. Except for Adam's voice-over,
the sound of a basketball is the only sound—there's no
dialogue, no music.

A WIDER ANGLE: Nan and Beth enter the row of seats
where Grace is sleeping, sitting on either side of her
in a predatory way. Monika has slipped into the row
behind Grace, leaning over her.

> ADAM (V.O.)
>
> From what Grace described to me, I could
> imagine Monika's mischief.

Nan and Beth unbutton Grace's blouse. Monika manages to
remove Grace's bra, exposing her breasts while she's
sleeping.

ONSCREEN: tear-jerking scene from the trailer, after
Paul passes the ball to the girl in the wheelchair.
The girl takes her time—more dribbling. The girl's
mother can't bear to watch; she hides her face in her
hands.

ADAM (V.O.)
You wouldn't know from the trailer that you
were watching the end of the movie, not that
Grace saw the end that afternoon in the Isis.

The teenage girl in the wheelchair puts up a shot; it
swirls once or twice around the rim, then falls in. The
little coach and the big girl in the wheelchair high-
five each other.

FADE TO BLACK. END CREDITS ROLL. MUSIC PLAYS OVER.

The house lights come up on Grace with her blouse
unbuttoned and her breasts exposed. There are only
A FEW MOVIEGOERS who notice, as Grace struggles to
conceal her breasts and button up her blouse. Grace
searches for her bra, but it's gone.

**EXT. ASPEN SIDEWALK, ISIS THEATRE, E. MAIN. LATE
AFTERNOON.**

The three downhillers are laughing. Monika is fooling
around with Grace's bra—it's too small for Monika.
They are bumping and shoving one another, the way
jocks do.

**EXT. POOL AND HOT TUBS, HOTEL JEROME. SAME LATE
AFTERNOON.**

Matthew and the little Chinese girl are in the pool,
paddling around in their water wings; the kids are the
same age. Adam and the Chinese actress and her husband
are talking, while they keep an eye on the kids. NO
SOUND—only Adam's voice-over.

                    ADAM (V.O.)
I couldn't get Matthew out of the pool, now
that he had someone to play with. I was
enjoying the Chen family. Grace didn't tell me
she and Matthew had skied a few runs on Aspen
Mountain with Mr. Chen and his little girl.

A WIDER ANGLE: a distraught-looking Grace, in her hotel
bathrobe and slippers, is disrobing by the hot tubs.
Grace gives a wave to her husband and the Chens. Grace
makes it apparent that she prefers the hot tubs to
joining them in the pool.

                    ADAM (V.O.)
I could tell Grace was upset about something.
The Chens sensed this, too. Mrs. Chen assured
me that she and her husband would watch
Matthew, if I wanted to join Grace.

CLOSER ON: the hot tubs, where Grace thinks she's
alone. Adam joins her. We don't hear what Grace is
saying, but it's clear that Lex is listening. It's
also clear, from the way Grace's hands are all over
her breasts, that Grace is telling Adam about waking up
in the movie theater with her bra gone and her boobs
hanging out of her blouse. Tarzan can't conceal his
dismay.

                    ADAM (V.O.)
Her bra removed, her breasts exposed, while
she slept through *Rim Shot*—the downhillers had
done it. I told Grace this was the twisted work
of "three dead skiers," meaning Monika and her
friends. I told Grace I had slept with Monika
Behr—hence Monika had it in for me.

Now Grace *and* Lex Barker are dismayed.

> ADAM (V.O.)
> This is the way confessing works—once you
> start, you can't stop. I told Grace I'd slept
> with Clara Swift, too—I said I'd told Paul
> Goode about it. I admitted to Grace that I
> should have told her and Paul before now.

Tarzan looks like he would rather wrestle a Nile
crocodile than hear more confessing—Grace, too.

> ADAM (V.O.)
> As for telling Grace that Paul Goode was my
> father, I sensed I'd said enough in the hot
> tubs—enough for now, anyway.

PULL BACK: there is Mrs. Chen, holding Matthew's hand.
Matthew is shivering in his hotel robe and slippers.

> ADAM (V.O.)
> I was saved from more confessing by Mrs. Chen.
> Matthew needed a hot shower or to put on warm
> clothes. Matthew just wanted to watch his
> favorite movie—*The Little Mermaid*.

Adam and Grace get out of the hot tubs. Grace looks
in shock. Tarzan, alone in the hot tubs, looks in
shock, too.

INT. ELEVATOR, HOTEL JEROME. CONTINUOUS.

Matthew is still cold; Adam is rubbing the boy's back
and shoulders. Grace is untouchable and inconsolable.
Clara Swift is looking at all of them with new empathy;
Clara knows what a family on the edge looks like.
Matthew, still shivering, can't remember the words to
"Part of Your World"—one of Ariel's songs in *The Little
Mermaid*. Matthew hums the tune, not bothering with

the words. Clara Swift hums along with him. She hums beautifully; Clara can carry a tune.

The cowboy and Adam are stunned by Clara's humming. Matthew, not hearing Clara, just keeps humming the tune to "Part of Your World." Grace is distraught; she looks crazed.

INT. BEDROOM, HOTEL JEROME. SOON AFTER.

The door to the living room is open. We can hear *The Little Mermaid* from there. Grace is talking to Adam in a whisper. Adam is getting dressed. Grace paces around, still in her bathrobe and slippers from the hot tubs.

> GRACE
>
> You slept with Monika Behr *and* Clara Swift—a busy trip. I don't suppose you would object if I slept with Paul Goode. I mean, how *could* you object?

> ADAM
>
> (quietly)
>
> There's something you should know.

> GRACE
>
> Something *else*?

> ADAM
>
> (more quietly)
>
> Paul Goode is my father.

> GRACE
>
> (derisively, in disbelief)
>
> *Now* you tell me!

> ADAM

If you don't believe me, ask him.

> GRACE

I don't believe you.

> ADAM
>> (softly)

I know.

> GRACE

You can take Matthew to the J-Bar—get him a hamburger. I'll just do room service.

> ADAM

Okay.

> GRACE

Paul Goode isn't old enough to be your father.

> ADAM
>> (more softly)

I know.

INT. LIVING ROOM, HOTEL JEROME. CONTINUOUS.

Matthew, warmly dressed, is on the couch watching *The Little Mermaid*. He is riveted to Ariel, who is singing her song. Adam enters from the bedroom.

> MATTHEW
>> (points to his chest)

Ariel wears seashells for a . . .

> ADAM

. . . a *bra*.

> MATTHEW
> > (nods)
> . . . a *bra*.

> ADAM
> Lots of seashells, under the sea.
> > (a beat)
> How about a hamburger?

Adam pauses the video, holding up *My Father's Dragon*.

> ADAM
> I can read to you in the restaurant, if it's
> not too noisy.

> MATTHEW
> > (nods)
> Okay!

INT. ELEVATOR, HOTEL JEROME. CONTINUOUS.

Clara uses the cowboy's saddle as a headrest; the
cowboy lies with his head in her lap, face up, his
Stetson on his stomach. Clara is humming "Part of Your
World" to him when the elevator door opens—Adam and
Matthew step inside. Matthew clearly has "Part of Your
World" on his mind. He is already humming the tune.
Clara hums in unison with him. Adam and the cowboy
react as if the spontaneous duet is weird. Clara stops
humming. Matthew just hums the tune.

INT. J-BAR, HOTEL JEROME. CONTINUOUS.

The usual ghosts are in the J-Bar, with a few HOTEL
GUESTS and SKIERS. Monika and Nan and Beth are at their
usual table.

ANOTHER ANGLE: a WAITER is seating Adam and Matthew. Adam sees how close their table is to those three downhillers.

               ADAM (V.O.)
Regarding the rules for ghosts: Jerome B. Wheeler is the guy in charge of the ghosts at the Jerome. Mr. Wheeler has *his* rules.

Monika is flaunting Grace's bra. Monika and Nan and Beth pass the bra around, holding it up to their bigger boobs. There is NO SOUND—only Adam's voice-over and a country song.

CLOSER ON: Monika's rowdy table, as Jerome B. Wheeler is suddenly standing over the three women downhillers. He holds out his hand. You don't have to read lips to know what he's saying: *Give me the bra.* Beth hands it over. Jerome B. Wheeler is speaking to Monika, who keeps shaking her head.

               ADAM (V.O.)
The Hotel Jerome is not a bad place to be a ghost—a good ghost is watching over things.

PULL BACK: the unsmiling Ute is standing there, backing up Wheeler; the Aspen volunteers have surrounded the table. Wheeler is pointing to the door to the street; he's telling Monika and her friends to leave. Jerome B. Wheeler also points to Matthew—a gesture not lost on Adam. Wheeler makes it clear that children are out of bounds to ghosts. Monika is pissed off, but she does what she's told—she and Nan and Beth leave.

               ADAM (V.O.)
My mom had begged me to get her out of the Jerome if she ended up here as a ghost. My

mother wasn't here, but there must be worse
places.

Jerome B. Wheeler considers what to do with Grace's
bra—he looks uncomfortable holding it. The Ute refuses
to look at it. The Aspen volunteers want nothing to do
with it.

> ADAM (V.O.)
> I appreciated Jerome B. Wheeler's rules—
> children should be out of bounds to ghosts.

**INT. LIVING ROOM, HOTEL JEROME. SAME NIGHT, SAME DINNER
TIME.**

Eating her room-service dinner, Grace is watching *The
Little Mermaid*. She is unresponsive to Ariel's dilemma.
The sound is off and it's the hundredth time.

INT. J-BAR, HOTEL JEROME. AFTER DINNER.

Only TWO SKIERS are riding the barstools at the bar.
The volume is turned down low on a country song; we can
barely hear it. What we hear more clearly is Adam's
voice-over.

> ADAM (V.O.)
> After dinner, I was reading Chapter Seven of *My
> Father's Dragon* to Matthew—"My Father Meets a
> Lion."

A WIDER ANGLE: surrounding Adam and Matthew's table are
the ghosts, who've pulled up chairs to listen to the
story. Jerome B. Wheeler and the Ute are listening,
as are the two miners who were blown to bits setting

black-powder charges; the miner with the sledge grips
his hammer. The two miners don't have a good feeling
about meeting a lion.

> ADAM (V.O.)
> I didn't think the ghosts would be
> interested in a children's story, but maybe
> the ghosts didn't know it was a story for
> children.

ANOTHER ANGLE: the Aspen volunteers have their
doubts about the story; they look at one another
in disbelief. You need weapons to deal with a lion,
they're thinking.

> ADAM (V.O.)
> I could tell the Aspen volunteers were getting
> restless with the story—*My Father's Dragon*
> isn't for heavily armed white men.

NO SOUND, as Adam keeps reading to Matthew.

CLOSE-UP: on Jerome B. Wheeler, holding Grace's bra in
his lap.

PULL BACK: Jerome passes the bra to the grim-faced Ute.
Without looking at it, the Ute passes it to one of the
miners—the one not holding the sledge. The miner stares
at the bra, then nudges the miner gripping the sledge.
The miner with the sledge is the closest to Adam.
There's an awkward exchange of the bra between the
miners. The miner with the sledge passes the bra under
the table to Adam.

CLOSE-UP: on Adam, still reading, glancing at the bra
in his lap.

**INT. ELEVATOR, HOTEL JEROME. SOON AFTER THE J-BAR
READING.**

Clara Swift is asleep, her head on the cowboy's saddle;
the cowboy sleeps with his head in Clara's lap, his
Stetson on his stomach. The ghost of Paulina Juárez,
the Mexican maid who is Paul Goode's mother, stands
protectively over Clara. When the elevator door opens,
admitting Adam and Matthew, Paulina holds an index
finger to her lips, cautioning Adam to be quiet.

> ADAM
> (whispers to Matthew)
> Only whispering on the elevator.

> MATTHEW
> (whispers)
> Why?

> ADAM
> (whispers)
> To practice being quiet—your mom might be
> asleep when we get back.

> MATTHEW
> (whispers)
> Okay.

Paulina whispers to Adam. Matthew doesn't see or hear
her.

> PAULINA
> (one hand on her heart)
> Lo siento. Tu madre.
> (repeats, in English)
> I'm sorry. Your mother.

Adam nods to her. Paulina is smiling at Matthew.

                    PAULINA
              (whispers to Adam)
     ¿Tu hijo? Your son?

                    ADAM
              (whispers back, nodding)
     Matthew.

                    MATTHEW
              (whispers to his dad)
     What?

                    ADAM
              (whispers)
     Just remember to whisper.

                    MATTHEW
              (whispers)
     You just told me!

Paulina is beaming at her great-grandson.

                    ADAM (V.O.)
     Who knows the rules for ghosts—why was my
     grandmother's ghost a younger woman, in her
     early thirties? She'd been forty-eight when she
     died.

The elevator door opens. Adam and Matthew step out.

                    PAULINA
              (whispers to Adam)
     Tu abuela. Your grandmother.

                    ADAM
              (whispers back, nodding)
     Sí.

>   MATTHEW
>   (whispers to his dad)
> See what?

The elevator door closes. Clara Swift and the cowboy go on sleeping. Paulina sees Grace's bra on the floor of the elevator; she hides it in the apron of her uniform.

>   ADAM (V.O.)
> When the lies of omission unravel, so does the story.

INT. LIVING ROOM, HOTEL JEROME. CONTINUOUS.

Adam and Matthew enter their suite. The TV in the living room is on—a close-up of Ursula, the sea witch in *The Little Mermaid,* is paused on the screen. Ursula is grotesque and purple; the living room has a purple hue. Adam is wearing a flannel shirt; he is unbuttoning the shirt and feeling around inside it, searching for Grace's bra. Matthew is disquieted by Ursula.

>   ADAM (V.O.)
> The missing bra didn't matter—the bra was just the beginning.

INT. BEDROOM, HOTEL JEROME. CONTINUOUS.

Grace is asleep in bed. There's a light on in the bathroom; the door is open. Matthew and Adam undress for bed. Adam takes off his flannel shirt. He's searching the sleeves—no bra.

>   MATTHEW
>   (whispers)
> What are you looking for?

> ADAM
> (whispers)
> Good boy—keep whispering.

> MATTHEW
> (whispers)
> I know!

Matthew goes into the bathroom to brush his teeth.

INT. HALL, HOTEL JEROME. CONTINUOUS.

Adam peers down the hall from the open door to his
suite. No bra. He closes the door. The bra is looped
over the doorknob on the exterior of the suite door.
Paulina must have put it there.

INT. LIVING ROOM, HOTEL JEROME. CONTINUOUS.

Ursula on the TV—her purpleness tints the living room.
Adam gives Ursula a look as he passes through.

> ADAM (V.O.)
> Ursula, the sea witch, isn't important, but
> she's like the bra—these are the details you
> remember when the worst things happen.

INT. BEDROOM, HOTEL JEROME. CONTINUOUS.

Adam is tucking Matthew into his rollaway.

> MATTHEW
> (whispers, pointing to the living room)
> Is Ursula still on, in there?

> ADAM
> (whispers)
> Would you like me to shut her off?

> MATTHEW
> (whispers)
> Shut her off.

> ADAM
> (whispers)
> Okay.

INT. LIVING ROOM, HOTEL JEROME. CONTINUOUS.

In the purplish light, Adam regards Ursula; she stares balefully at him.

> ADAM (V.O.)
> Looking back, so many small and unimportant
> things look like signs.

Adam aims the remote at Ursula, turning the TV off.

FADE TO BLACK. FADE IN.

INT. HALL, HOTEL JEROME. NEXT MORNING.

Grace's bra has spent the night on the doorknob of Adam's suite. Passing the bra are a familiar threesome. Billy goes by first, followed by Paul Goode—Paul is the only one dressed to ski—with Otto coming last. They see the bra.

> ADAM (V.O.)
> Grace wouldn't wait for Matthew and me, to go
> down to breakfast. We were too slow getting our
> ski stuff on, and Grace was ready to go.

Grace, dressed to ski, comes out the door, sees her bra on the doorknob, clutches her breasts, grabs the bra.

INT. BEDROOM, HOTEL JEROME. CONTINUOUS.

Adam is helping Matthew put his ski pants on when Grace comes into the bedroom, holding out her bra.

> GRACE
> (to Adam)
> Why is my bra on the outside doorknob of our suite?

> ADAM
> I have no idea.

Grace drops her bra on the bed; as she leaves, Adam is helping Matthew put his ski sweater on.

> MATTHEW
> Do seashell bras feel funny?

> ADAM
> I have no idea.

ANOTHER ANGLE: on top of a chest of drawers is the copy of his novel Adam bought to give his father; Adam's author photo is looking up at him as he finishes getting his ski stuff on.

> ADAM (V.O.)
> I knew Grace and Paul Goode were going skiing. It was not a good morning to give one of my books to my father. I'd not inscribed my novel "To my father"—I'd just signed it. Maybe I would add "For Paul Goode." Maybe just signing it was enough.

INT. LIVING ROOM, HOTEL JEROME. CONTINUOUS.

Matthew, dressed to ski, points the remote at the
TV, turning it on. PRESIDENT BILL CLINTON is on TV;
he's talking, but the TV volume is off. Adam looks
at the TV.

> MATTHEW
>
> Ursula is gone.

> ADAM
>
> We like Bill Clinton.

EXT. ENTRANCE, HOTEL JEROME, E. MAIN. CONTINUOUS.

A cowboy doorman is loading up the Jerome van with
the Chen family's ski equipment and luggage. The tall
hippie ghost, forever unnoticed, is showing her breasts
to Mr. Chen.

> ADAM (V.O.)
>
> The Chen family was leaving. Matthew and I
> would ski at Aspen Mountain, while Grace and my
> father were skiing at Loge Peak.

INT. BREAKFAST ROOM, HOTEL JEROME. CONTINUOUS.

As Adam and his family are being seated, Paul Goode—
alone, at a table for two—gives them a wave. Grace
waves back. Adam and his father exchange nods. Otto
and Billy are sitting at their own table. Otto stands,
waving to Matthew.

> MATTHEW
> (to his mom and dad)
> Can I go see the animals with Otto?

                    GRACE
Yes, Matthew. Thank you, Otto.

                   MATTHEW
         (as Otto takes his hand)
Thank you, Otto.

                    ADAM
         (calls, to Matthew)
We'll order your pancakes.

Adam gets an icy look from Grace.

PULL BACK: we see Adam and Grace from Paul Goode's
table, as Paul would see them. Grace is doing all the
talking.

                    GRACE
    I'll tell you how the rest of this trip is
    going to go.

ANOTHER ANGLE: of Grace talking to Adam, from Billy's
POV. Billy is curious about Grace, but Billy has a
wandering attention span.

                    GRACE
    I'll finish my business with Paul—after skiing,
    or later tonight, after Matthew has gone to bed.

INT. ANTLER BAR, HOTEL JEROME. CONTINUOUS.

Otto is imitating the expressions on the faces of the
mounted animal heads, entertaining Matthew.

                 ADAM (V.O.)
    "Your business," I said. "Don't interrupt me—
    Paul's memoir is the main thing," Grace said.

"And don't tell me you have *no idea* about
my bra," she said. I didn't explain. Grace
wouldn't have believed what I could tell her
about her bra among the ghosts.

INT. BREAKFAST ROOM, HOTEL JEROME. CONTINUOUS.

Paul Goode sees the one-sided conversation Grace
has with Adam. The dissolution of their marriage is
apparent to him.

> ADAM (V.O.)
> Grace told me she and Matthew were leaving
> Aspen the next day. She wanted to be alone
> with Matthew, to explain to him what was
> going to happen when she and I separated. "I
> won't blame you—for Matthew's sake," Grace
> assured me.

ANOTHER ANGLE: Billy is pondering the mysteries of
a magazine, paying no attention to Grace's ongoing
lecture to Adam.

> ADAM (V.O.)
> Grace explained that I would stay in Aspen by
> myself, for another day and night. When I got
> back to Vermont, I would have my turn to be
> alone with Matthew, Grace said.

A WIDER ANGLE: Otto brings Matthew back to the table,
where Grace stops talking to Adam.

> ADAM (V.O.)
> Making Matthew the priority, as Grace and I
> agreed he should be, made me accept Grace's
> plans.

Adam's POV of his father alone at his table. Paul Goode is smiling at Adam's family, but Paul's thoughts are unreadable.

> ADAM (V.O.)
> I didn't care if Grace slept with my father—I just wanted her to know who he was, if she was going to sleep with him.

INT. SILVER QUEEN GONDOLA, ASPEN MOUNTAIN. THAT MORNING.

In the six-person gondola, with FOUR OTHER SKIERS, Adam and Matthew sit back-to-back. They turn their heads to talk.

> MATTHEW
> It's like being in an egg.

> ADAM
> What is?

> MATTHEW
> *This* is!

> ADAM
> Being in a gondola?

> MATTHEW
> It's like being in an *egg*!

The four other skiers are troubled by this thought.

EXT. SILVER QUEEN GONDOLA, ASPEN MOUNTAIN. CONTINUOUS.

From a blue run, Silver Dip, we see what would be a skier's POV of the gondola eggs, passing overhead.

                    ADAM (O.C.)
You know what an egg becomes?

EXT. EXHIBITION LIFT, ASPEN HIGHLANDS. SAME MORNING.

Paul and Grace ride the four-seater chairlift from
the base of Aspen Highlands with TWO OTHER SKIERS, a
married couple.

                    GRACE
          (ignoring the couple)
You've had an interesting life, growing up
here, becoming an actor, and a screenwriter.
You're a war veteran, you've suffered a
personal tragedy, but people are interested in
your first experiences—the *formative* ones.

The married couple, riding with Paul and Grace, are
interested—they're eager to hear more.

                    PAUL GOODE
I don't think I want to write about those first
experiences—the *formative* ones.

                    GRACE
But most movie stars can't write. You're a
writer.

                    PAUL GOODE
My first sexual experience was with your
husband's mother. I suppose it was *formative*.

Like the eager couple in the chairlift, Grace wasn't
expecting this—the two other skiers are riveted now.
Notwithstanding his offhand manner, Paul knows exactly
what he's doing. As Grace says, he's a *writer*. Whether
you like his writing or not, Paul Goode knows how to
tell a story.

EXT. COPPER BOWL, ASPEN MOUNTAIN. SAME MORNING.

Copper Bowl is a blue run. Adam and Matthew are
passing under the Silver Queen Gondola—skiing
cautiously, talking happily. We hear only Adam's
voice-over.

> ADAM (V.O.)
> When a marriage is falling apart, when there's
> a child involved, and the separation lies ahead
> of you, that's when you have to be better than
> you've ever been. That's when the story isn't
> about you.

EXT. LOGE PEAK QUAD, ASPEN HIGHLANDS. THAT MORNING.

In the lift line, Grace is trying to get away from
the married couple who rode with her and Paul on the
previous chairlift. Paul is talking to Grace in the
lift line. The couple who rode with them are listening,
but we hear only Adam's voice-over.

> ADAM (V.O.)
> The best of adult intentions notwithstanding,
> couples who are breaking up behave badly.

Grace is wary of TWO DRINKERS—two young guys, sharing
a pint of tequila, in the lift line ahead of her and
Paul. Grace doesn't want to get on the Loge Peak chair
with the two drinkers or the married couple.

> ADAM (V.O.)
> I don't blame Grace, and my father would blame
> himself for everything.

The two drinkers look behind them in the lift line as
the chairlift approaches; one of the young guys beckons

to Paul and Grace to join them on the chair. Paul
doesn't hesitate to move ahead in the lift line. Grace
has no choice; she gets on the chair with Paul and the
two drinkers.

CLOSER ON: the ascending chairlift. The drinkers are
lighting cigarettes in the wind. Now we hear what Paul
says.

> PAUL GOODE
> On this chair, your husband told me he slept
> with my wife.

Hearing this, one of the smokers burns his eye when the
lit end of his cigarette is blown into his face. His
buddy burns his fingers on his cigarette, cupping it in
his hands.

> PAUL GOODE
> Clara was repelled by what she did—she hated
> it; she hated herself for doing it, your
> husband said. I believe him, but what happened
> wasn't your husband's fault.

The smoker who burned his fingers drops the lit
cigarette in his lap, where it's lost in the folds of
his parka. The wind has picked up. The other smoker
rubs his sore eye.

> PAUL GOODE
> It was my fault that Clara did it—she did it
> because of what I did.

Grace is distressed that the tequila drinkers are
hanging on every word. Paul is as insouciant as the
noir characters he plays in his films.

PAUL GOODE

Your husband meant well—I know he was trying to
make me feel better. "It was my fault, too," he
told me.
(as Grace nods)
No, you don't understand. What Clara did—sleep
with your husband, jump off the chairlift—is
all my fault.

As the chairlift climbs, the wind blows harder. As
the drinkers pull up their face masks, plumes of smoke
rise from the parka of the smoker who dropped a lit
cigarette in his lap.

PAUL GOODE
(to the smoker)
Your parka is on fire.

The one on fire unzips his parka and takes it off,
as the parka bursts into flames. We see his burning
parka fall from the chair. It falls to the ski slope,
alarming THE RIDERS in the following chairlift and SOME
SKIERS on the piste under the lift.

PAUL GOODE (O.C.)
(to everyone)
Anything that's burning likes the wind. Fire
loves the wind.

Moments later: Paul points off to the right. Grace and
the drinkers see the gulch the old chairlift passed
over.

PAUL GOODE
(to Grace)
The old chairlift went over that gulch—Clara
jumped off the lift, over there.

The drinker is shivering without his parka.

> PAUL GOODE
> (to Grace)
> We were right about here when your husband told
> me I was his father.

> GRACE
> He should have told your wife he was your son!
> Clara wouldn't have slept with him—not if she
> knew!

> PAUL GOODE
> Clara would have slept with someone else. She
> was going to sleep with someone—with *anyone*.
> (a beat)
> Your husband showed me the photo when we got
> off the lift.

One drinker whispers to the other drinker.

> DRINKER
> Who took a photo? Of *what*?

Grace is perturbed how the drinkers have inserted
themselves into the conversation, but Paul doesn't
care.

> PAUL GOODE
> (to the drinkers)
> It was a photo of her husband's mother—at
> the age she was when she slept with me. She
> was eighteen, almost nineteen—I was fourteen,
> almost fifteen.

The lift station at the top of Loge Peak is
approaching. Paul, Grace, and the drinkers prepare to
unload.

EXT. THE WALL, ASPEN HIGHLANDS. CONTINUOUS.

The Wall is a black double-diamond run that crosses under the Loge Peak quad. TWO SKI PATROLLERS examine the smoldering ashes of the drinker's parka.

> ONE PATROLLER
>
> What the fuck?

> THE OTHER PATROLLER
>
> A skier on fire on the chair?

EXT. A BLACK RUN, ASPEN HIGHLANDS. CONTINUOUS.

On a black diamond, or a double diamond, Grace and Paul are skiing hard, matching each other's turns and cuts. When Paul stops sharply, Grace pulls up and stops beside him.

> GRACE
>
> Show me the photo.

Paul takes off his gloves, unzips a pocket in his parka, and shows Grace the photo of Adam's mom. Paul and Grace are looking at the photo when the drinkers pull up beside them. The drinkers are better skiers than we might expect, but they're not as good as Grace and Paul; the one without a parka is freezing. To Grace's dismay, the drinkers stare at the photo.

> PAUL GOODE
> (to Grace)
> I don't think your husband meant to give me the photo—he just wanted me to see who his mom was. Please give the photo back to him.

CLOSE-UP: the black-and-white photo of Ray in Aspen in 1941.

PAUL GOODE (O.C.)
She gave me her ski hat, and her sweater.

PULL BACK: Grace is zipping the photo into her parka.

PAUL GOODE
Under the circumstances, I was smitten—I loved
her sweater, even her hat. I wore them until
they didn't fit me. I never threw them away.
During the war, my mom gave them to a girl who
worked in the kitchen at the hotel.

GRACE
(she pushes off)
Okay, okay—I get it!

Paul gives her a head start before he goes after her.
The drinker without the parka is shivering and shaking;
he starts to moan. The drinkers push off—not trying to
keep up, just to survive.

ADAM (V.O.)
Grace said my father was reprising his role as
the getaway driver in *The Wrong Car*—Paul Goode
was imitating the cocksure confidence of the
little driver.

In black and white, from *The Wrong Car*—in the getaway
driver's apartment. The door opens, the woman with the
baby carriage pushes the carriage ahead of her as she
comes inside, the door key clenched in her teeth.

On the bed, the moll tries to cover herself, as does
the little driver. The woman wheels the baby carriage
up to the bed, staring down at them.

GETAWAY DRIVER
You coulda knocked, ya know.

EXT. STILL A BLACK RUN, ASPEN HIGHLANDS. CONTINUOUS.

Paul and Grace are skiing fast in a steep, narrow chute. They have to pull up and stop as they merge with a new trail.

> ADAM (V.O.)
> Grace understood there would be no sex with Paul Goode—only skiing.

Paul is talking again. We hear only Adam's voice-over.

> ADAM (V.O.)
> The drinkers were gone. Paul Goode had stopped acting. His son had slept with his wife, but my father wasn't going to sleep with Grace. Point taken.

INT. SILVER QUEEN GONDOLA, ASPEN MOUNTAIN. THAT SAME DAY.

In the six-person gondola, Adam and Matthew sit back-to-back, bent over their knees.

> ADAM (V.O.)
> What good are you, as a father, if you can't be a good example? Matthew said we were in an egg—we were going to hatch, or be born, when we got to the top.

The FOUR OTHER SKIERS on the gondola are disconcerted by Adam and Matthew in their pretending-to-be-born positions.

> ADAM (V.O.)
> Matthew was the one who mattered, my father told Grace.

EXT. LOGE PEAK QUAD, ASPEN HIGHLANDS. SAME DAY.

Grace and Paul have the four-seater to themselves. Paul
is talking as the chairlift climbs; Grace is nodding as
she listens to him. Adam's voice-over is all we hear.

> ADAM (V.O.)
> Regarding the unraveling of my father's
> marriage to Clara Swift, Paul Goode said he and
> Clara had paid insufficient attention to their
> son, Toby. Point taken.

EXT. PROSPECTOR GULCH, ASPEN HIGHLANDS. SAME DAY.

The two patrollers who found the drinker's burnt parka
have found the drinkers themselves, on a blue run under
the Exhibition lift. The freezing drinker without a
parka is huddled under a blanket on the patrollers'
toboggan; the other drinker is acting out the fire
on the chairlift. We can't hear what the drinker is
telling the patrollers, but we know the story.

> ADAM (V.O.)
> It was not the kind of ski day Grace or I had
> expected.

**EXT. LIFT STATION, SILVER QUEEN GONDOLA, TOP OF ASPEN
MOUNTAIN. SAME DAY.**

Adam and Matthew imitate the hatching or birthing
process as they unload from the gondola. REPULSED
SKIERS move away from them.

> ADAM (V.O.)
> It's hard to pretend to be born without causing
> offense.

EXT. UPPER STEIN, LOWER STEIN, ASPEN HIGHLANDS. SAME DAY.

Paul and Grace, just skiing. When they pause, they're
talking back and forth like old friends. They're skiing
down two double diamonds, the Upper Stein to the Lower
Stein. Adam's voice-over is all we hear.

> ADAM (V.O.)
> My dad would not be writing a memoir, he told
> Grace. Our Matthew and Paul Goode's son, Toby,
> would be spared from reading such a story,
> Grace told me.

**EXT. POOL AND HOT TUBS, HOTEL JEROME. LATER THAT
AFTERNOON.**

Adam and Grace and Matthew are in the hot tubs, where
Lex Barker is listening to their conversation.

> ADAM
> (to Matthew)
> We have three chapters to go in *My Father's
> Dragon*—we won't finish.

> GRACE
> (to Matthew)
> You and I will be back in Vermont tomorrow
> night, but your dad won't be home till the
> night after.

> MATTHEW
> (to his dad)
> What three chapters?

> ADAM
> The gorilla, the crocodiles, and the dragon.

Tarzan knows apes and crocodiles, but the dragon
worries him.

> ADAM
>
> I can handle the gorilla tonight. Your mom can
> deal with the crocodiles on the plane.

> GRACE
>
> I can read you the dragon chapter at home,
> tomorrow night.

> ADAM
>
> And when I get home, we can start the story all
> over again.

> MATTHEW
> (startling Tarzan)
> From the beginning!

INT. J-BAR, HOTEL JEROME. THAT EVENING.

Adam, Grace, and Matthew are eating dinner. There's
no acrimony between Adam and Grace; they're talking
to each other, and Matthew joins in, but we hear only
Adam's voice-over and a country song. Without Monika
and her pals, the ghosts are unthreatening—the two
miners at the bar, the Aspen volunteers at their usual
table, Jerome B. Wheeler in conversation with the
Ute. From the street, the tall hippie girl peers in a
window.

> ADAM (V.O.)
>
> I knew it was the last time we would go
> anywhere together as a family, but that night
> felt as much like the beginning of something as
> like an ending.

INT. LIVING ROOM, HOTEL JEROME. THAT NIGHT.

Grace is alone in the living room, watching TV.

ONSCREEN: Paige what's-her-name, on her movie gossip
show—Paige is interviewing Juliette Leblanc again. It's
been only five years, but Juliette isn't aging well.
They're in a hotel somewhere.

> PAIGE
> Paul Goode is gonna be *seventy*?
> (Juliette shrugs)
> He doesn't *look* seventy.
> (Juliette shrugs)
> And Clara Swift—if she were still alive—would
> be *fifty* this year.

A YOUNG MAN wearing only a towel walks into the living
room of the suite, from the bedroom.

> JULIETTE
> (to the young man)
> I told you, I'm having an interview—I didn't
> mean tomorrow.

The young man shrugs; he goes back to the bedroom.

> PAIGE
> (whispers)
> And who is *that* gorgeous guy?
> (Juliette shrugs)
> Back to Paul Goode. Do you think it's a wonder
> he hasn't been killed by a woman he slept with?

> JULIETTE
> (not shrugging this off)
> *Or* a woman he didn't sleep with.

Paige, at a loss for words, hadn't thought of this.

> PAIGE
> (to camera)
> I'm with Juliette Leblanc—we're at an
> undisclosed location!

BACK ON: Grace, turning off the TV. She can hear Adam
reading aloud in the bedroom.

> ADAM (O.C.)
> "A beautiful lioness paraded past . . ."

Grace covers her ears with her hands—not her kind of
story.

INT. BEDROOM, HOTEL JEROME. CONTINUOUS.

Adam is with Matthew on the rollaway, reading the
gorilla chapter of *My Father's Dragon*. Grace drifts
through the bedroom on her way to the bathroom.

> ADAM
> ". . . she was much too occupied looking
> dignified to see anything but the tip of her
> own nose."

INT. BATHROOM, HOTEL JEROME. CONTINUOUS.

On Grace, looking at herself in the mirror.

> ADAM (O.C.)
> "It was the lion's mother . . ."

INT. BEDROOM, HOTEL JEROME. A LITTLE LATER THAT NIGHT.

CLOSE-UP: on Matthew, asleep in his rollaway.

ANOTHER ANGLE: on Adam and Grace, asleep—not touching, on their respective sides of the bed.

> ADAM (V.O.)
> ". . . there was no dragon anywhere in sight."

CLOSE-UP: on the night table, on Adam's side of the bed—nearest the bathroom door and Matthew's rollaway—is *My Father's Dragon* with the cover illustration of the baby dragon on a cloud.

FADE TO BLACK. Sam Cooke's "You Send Me" PLAYS OVER. FADE IN.

EXT. ASPEN SIDEWALK, S. MILL. EARLY NEXT MORNING.

It snowed overnight. The S. Mill sidewalk has been sporadically shoveled. The small wheels of the baby carriage find the snowy sidewalk slow going. We see the GLOVED HANDS pushing the baby carriage, but not the baby. It's a cold morning.

We are in the POV of the woman with the baby carriage, but we don't see her—only the SKIERS, coming toward us on the S. Mill sidewalk. We pass E. Cooper, moving toward E. Hyman, as Sam Cooke's "You Send Me" CONTINUES OVER.

INT. BREAKFAST ROOM, HOTEL JEROME. THAT SAME MORNING.

Flanked by Otto and Billy, Paul Goode arrives for breakfast—early, as always. "You Send Me" PLAYS OVER.

INT. LIVING ROOM, HOTEL JEROME. SAME TIME, SAME MORNING.

Grace watches one of the cowboy porters load a luggage cart with her stuff and Matthew's. Adam is writing in the copy of his novel for his father. Matthew watches him.

>   MATTHEW
>   What are you writing?

>   ADAM
>   It's what I write when I sign one of my books to someone I don't know well. I write, "With my appreciation."

>   MATTHEW
>   Oh.

We still hear Sam Cooke singing "You Send Me," more quietly here.

EXT. ASPEN SIDEWALK, S. MILL. CONTINUOUS.

The baby carriage is passing E. Hyman, on its way to E. Hopkins. TWO SKIERS come toward us, on their way to Aspen Mountain. Sam Cooke keeps singing "You Send Me."

INT. BREAKFAST ROOM, HOTEL JEROME. CONTINUOUS.

"You Send Me" is the only sound. Adam, Grace, and Matthew are being seated. Grace and Paul wave to each other. Otto stands, leaving his and Billy's table—again offering to show Matthew the stuffed animal heads in the Antler Bar—but Grace stops him, pointing to her watch. She explains to Otto that it's travel day.

Adam gives Otto the copy of his novel he signed for
his father. Otto brings the signed book to Paul Goode,
who reads the "With my appreciation" inscription on
the title page. There is a nod of recognition between
father and son.

Matthew would rather be in the Antler Bar with Otto.

EXT. ASPEN SIDEWALK, S. MILL. CONTINUOUS.

The baby carriage has passed E. Hopkins and is waiting
for the walk light on E. Main. We see the gloves come
off the older woman's hands, as she tucks them under
the blankets in the carriage. Sam Cooke sings "You Send
Me" like it'll never end.

EXT. ENTRANCE, HOTEL JEROME, E. MAIN. CONTINUOUS.

The ghost of the hippie girl is ignoring the cowboy
doorman, but someone off camera gets her attention.
It's a relief that "You Send Me" is fading.

ANOTHER ANGLE: the cowboy doorman sees the woman with
the baby carriage coming. The tall hippie approaches
the carriage and peers inside; she seems puzzled by
what she sees, as the woman wheels the carriage past
her, going inside the Jerome.

She is the older, gray-haired woman Matthew saw at
the bookstore. She has aged more noticeably than Paul
Goode, since their time together in *The Wrong Car*. She
is *that same woman,* but she's almost Paul's age. Unlike
Paul, she looks seventy.

INT. LOBBY, HOTEL JEROME. CONTINUOUS.

Jerome B. Wheeler sees the woman with the baby carriage cross the lobby. Wheeler regards her with regret and resignation. It's as if he knows everything that's going to happen, just as he seems to know everything that has happened.

Jerome B. Wheeler returns his attention to the still-bleeding Aspen volunteer—as the woman with the baby carriage passes through the lobby, and Sam Cooke's "You Send Me" FADES OUT OVER.

INT. BREAKFAST ROOM. HOTEL JEROME. CONTINUOUS.

Adam and Grace see the gray-haired woman in profile—just her head and shoulders, as she walks by. From where they sit at their table, Adam and Grace don't see the baby carriage.

> ADAM (V.O.)
> Usually, a ghost won't kill you—more often,
> it's not a ghost.

Matthew not only recognizes the gray-haired woman from the bookstore; from where he's sitting at the table, Matthew sees the baby carriage, too.

> MATTHEW
> (to his dad)
> She was at your book signing.
> (he whispers)
> She's *cuckoo*.

Matthew draws imaginary circles around his ear with one index finger. With his other index finger, Matthew points to the older woman who walked by their table. Adam must be daydreaming.

> ADAM
> (whispers back)
> Who's cuckoo?

> MATTHEW
> (still pointing)
> The woman with the baby carriage.

Adam stands up, seeing the woman with the baby carriage from behind. She is standing at Paul Goode's table.

> MATTHEW
> She didn't bring the baby to the bookstore.

A WIDER ANGLE: Billy and Otto are engrossed in a *Playboy* centerfold.

ANOTHER ANGLE: Paul Goode looks up from his breakfast at the woman with the baby carriage. It's been forty years. Paul doesn't recognize her—not until she speaks, reprising her dialogue from *The Wrong Car*.

> WOMAN WITH THE CARRIAGE
> It's your turn with the baby, little fella.

She pulls the sawed-off shotgun out of the baby carriage, shooting Paul Goode point-blank.

CLOSE ON: the woman with the double-barreled twelve-gauge. She puts both barrels under her chin, shooting herself.

CLOSE ON: Grace covering Matthew's eyes with her hands.

CLOSE ON: Otto and Billy, standing paralyzed at their table.

A WIDER ANGLE: on Adam, standing over his father's body.

CLOSER ON: the blood-spattered author photo on Adam's novel.

CLOSER ON: the body of the woman with the baby carriage; one of her arms blocks our view of her head, or her head is gone.

> ADAM (V.O.)
> Like something Paul Goode would write—more noir than noir.

INT. ELEVATOR, HOTEL JEROME. MOMENTS LATER.

Clara Swift is pounding her head against the elevator. The cowboy holds her, letting her pound her head against his chest. Marty Robbins, singing "Streets of Laredo," PLAYS OVER.

> ADAM (V.O.)
> Noir is the new Western.

EXT. ENTRANCE, HOTEL JEROME, E. MAIN. MOMENTS LATER.

Three of the usual cowboy doormen keep the entrance clear for the arriving police cars and an ambulance. COPS and EMERGENCY MEDICAL TECHNICIANS rush past the tall hippie girl, who is showing her breasts to no one now. "Streets of Laredo" CONTINUES OVER.

INT. J-BAR, HOTEL JEROME. CONTINUOUS.

The Aspen volunteers and the Ute are looking out the windows of the empty J-Bar, together—as Marty Robbins keeps singing.

> ADAM (V.O.)
> For melodrama, noir has replaced cowboys and Indians.

INT. LOBBY, HOTEL JEROME. CONTINUOUS.

As the cops and EMTs rush through the lobby, where Jerome B. Wheeler and the still-bleeding Aspen volunteer are having coffee, "Streets of Laredo" PLAYS OVER.

> ADAM (V.O.)
> Cops and EMTs are the new Aspen volunteers. My father might have appreciated what Juliette Leblanc told Paige what's-her-name: maybe a woman he slept with, *or* one he didn't, was going to kill him.

INT. BREAKFAST ROOM, HOTEL JEROME. CONTINUOUS.

NO SOUND but Marty Robbins. Grace is holding Matthew's hand, while she talks to one policeman. Both Grace and the cop agree that the crime scene is no place for Matthew. The policeman escorts them out of the dining room.

ANOTHER ANGLE: a POLICE PHOTOGRAPHER finishes taking pictures of the two bodies, which the EMTs cover. The photographer takes pictures of Paul Goode's breakfast table, before he allows Otto to pick up Adam's novel.

Billy is talking to another cop, while Otto takes a clean napkin from an unused table; he dips the napkin in Paul's water glass, wringing the napkin out in the glass. Otto wipes the bloodstains off the author photo, before giving Adam back his book. Adam lingers, to talk to the cop who's been talking to Billy. The cops are nodding. What happened is incontestable. Marty Robbins keeps singing.

> ADAM (V.O.)
> Like the Western, there is no mystery about what's noir—what happens is what was always *going to* happen; it's what *always* happens.

EXT. ENTRANCE, HOTEL JEROME, E. MAIN. MOMENTS LATER.

The tall hippie girl watches the EMTs carry the bodies to the ambulance. The cowboy porter, with the cart holding Grace and Matthew's stuff, has to wait for a police car or the ambulance to leave. For a moment, there's no place for the Jerome van to park. Adam and Grace and Matthew wait. The hippie ghost sees Grace take the photo from her parka pocket and give it to Adam, who puts the photo in the copy of his novel. The tall hippie is interested in the novel. Adam is wary of the inquisitive ghost.

As the ambulance leaves, the Hotel Jerome van takes its place at the curb. Adam says goodbye to his family. Marty Robbins's "Streets of Laredo" CONTINUES OVER.

Adam is shivering with cold—he's not dressed to be outside, and the hippie's curiosity about his novel is weird and annoying. Adam goes back inside the hotel, while Grace and Matthew wait for the Jerome van to be loaded. The tall hippie girl is upset that Adam has taken the book away.

INT. ELEVATOR, HOTEL JEROME. MOMENTS LATER.

The cowboy is still consoling Clara when Adam gets
on the elevator. Clara is distraught to see him, but
she's curious about the book. Adam holds it up, showing
her his author photo. He points to himself. Clara is
unimpressed that he's a writer—likewise the cowboy.
"Streets of Laredo" FADES OUT OVER.

INT. BEDROOM, HOTEL JEROME. CONTINUOUS.

Adam drops his novel on the bed. The photo of his mom
falls out. *My Father's Dragon* is on the night table. He
grabs it and runs out of the room.

INT. STAIRCASE, HOTEL JEROME. CONTINUOUS.

Adam running down three flights of stairs—it's faster
than waiting for, and riding on, the elevator.

EXT. ENTRANCE, HOTEL JEROME, E. MAIN. CONTINUOUS.

Adam runs out of the hotel. There are no cowboy
doormen. Two police cars are parked at the curb, but
there are no cops. The Jerome van is gone. Matthew
will not be able to hear the last two chapters—not on
the plane, and not at home in Vermont. The tall hippie
ghost is the only one there. She is as interested
in *My Father's Dragon* as she was in Adam's novel.
Reluctantly, Adam shows it to her. The hippie girl
smiles, pointing to herself.

                    ADAM
        I don't understand.

The tall hippie girl stomps off. Adam goes back in the hotel.

INT. ELEVATOR, HOTEL JEROME. CONTINUOUS.

Clara is reading the first sentence of *My Father's Dragon* to the cowboy. Adam watches and listens.

> CLARA SWIFT
> "One cold rainy day when my father was a little boy, he met an old alley cat on his street."

Clara finds it hard to stop reading, but she forces herself to close the book—handing it back to Adam. The cowboy is hooked on the story; he is more forlorn than usual.

> CLARA SWIFT
> (to Adam)
> I love this story—I read it to my son when he was a little boy.

Adam nods; he looks guilty about taking the book back.

> ADAM (V.O.)
> It hurt that Clara Swift and the cowboy were more interested in *My Father's Dragon* than they were in my novel, but writers have to accept readers like this.

INT. BEDROOM, HOTEL JEROME. CONTINUOUS.

When Adam enters the bedroom, his grandmother Paulina Juárez is sitting on the bed beside his untouched novel. Paulina is looking closely at the photo of Little Ray. Paulina holds the photo to her heart when

she sees Adam. Paulina must know her son has been
killed.

> ADAM
> Lo siento. I'm sorry.
>> (Paulina nods)
> The photo is for you.
>> (she's surprised)
> Your son's ski hat and sweater.

Paulina is smiling and nodding.

> PAULINA
> ¡Sí! ¡Muchas gracias!

> ADAM
> De nada. You're welcome.

Adam picks up his novel, showing her the author photo.
Paulina is polite, but she's not dying to read it. Adam
puts his novel on the night table, under *My Father's
Dragon*.

EXT. POOL AND HOT TUBS, HOTEL JEROME. LATER THAT DAY.

At a distance, Adam and Lex Barker in the hot tubs.

> ADAM (V.O.)
> No one thinks of Tarzan as a big reader. But
> Lex Barker must have been a reader. Maybe not
> novels for children—Lex didn't have a stellar
> reputation with children. Not knowing what to
> expect, I began at the beginning. *My Father's
> Dragon* isn't a long novel—a little over eighty
> pages, counting the illustrations.

CLOSER ON: Adam reads to Tarzan in the hot tubs.

ADAM

"My father and the cat became good friends but
my father's mother was very upset about the
cat. She hated cats . . ."

Tarzan nods; he hates cats, too.

INT. LOBBY, HOTEL JEROME. LATER, SAME DAY.

Adam reads to the still-bleeding Aspen volunteer.
Jerome B. Wheeler is listening in. We hear only Adam's
voice-over.

ADAM (V.O)

I decided to begin at the beginning with all of
them, but not everyone believes in dragons.

INT. J-BAR, HOTEL JEROME. LATER, THAT EVENING.

The Aspen volunteers, at their usual table, are not
listening to Adam's reading, but they observe—from a
safe distance.

ADAM (V.O.)

Readers vary, when it comes to having the
imagination to enjoy a story outside their own
experiences.

A WIDER ANGLE: on Adam reading to the Ute and the two
miners who were blown to bits underground; Jerome
listens in.

ADAM
(reads)
". . . a baby dragon fell from a low-flying
cloud onto the bank of the river. He was too

young to fly very well, and besides, he had
bruised one wing quite badly, so he couldn't
get back to his cloud."

EXT. J-BAR, HOTEL JEROME, E. MAIN. CONTINUOUS.

The ghost of the tall hippie girl is looking in the
windows of the J-Bar from the E. Main sidewalk.

> ADAM (V.O.)
> Some readers and writers don't look like
> readers or writers.

EXT. POOL AND HUT TUBS, HOTEL JEROME. A FLASHBACK.

NO SOUND. As Adam reads, Tarzan is nodding off. Lex
Barker falls asleep—he falls face-first into the water.
He wakes up coughing and snorting, waving his arms and
beating his chest.

> ADAM (V.O.)
> Some can't go the distance.

INT. LOBBY, HOTEL JEROME. A FLASHBACK.

NO SOUND. The still-bleeding Aspen volunteer looks
dead, again—or he's asleep. Jerome B. Wheeler puts an
index finger to his lips. Adam understands; he stops
reading.

INT. J-BAR, HOTEL JEROME. MUCH LATER, THAT NIGHT.

PAN the J-Bar. The Aspen volunteers sleep, their heads
on their table. The bar is closed; no one's at the bar.

CLOSER ON: Adam, still reading to the Ute, the two
miners, and Jerome B. Wheeler. There is NO SOUND, only
Adam's voice-over.

> ADAM (V.O.)
> I thought the two miners might make me stop at
> the crocodile chapter—a bridge of crocodiles,
> across a river, is hard to believe—but the
> Ute and the miners made me read to the end. If
> Jerome B. Wheeler already knew what happened,
> he was too polite to say. Jerome had been
> around longer than *My Father's Dragon*.

INT. LOBBY, HOTEL JEROME. LATER THAT SAME NIGHT.

The still-bleeding Aspen volunteer still looks dead
or asleep, as Paulina Juárez comes through the lobby,
holding hands with her son, Paulino; Paul Goode, as a
ghost, is fourteen. He's wearing the ski hat with the
pom-pom and the sweater Little Ray gave him.

> ADAM (V.O.)
> I knew why Paulina was a younger ghost than she
> was when she died. Paul Goode was a kid again.
> At fourteen, Paulino was the age he was when he
> met my mom.

The actor who plays Toby Goode at fourteen is the same
actor who plays Paulino at that age. Paulina Juárez is
happy to see Adam, who's glad to see his grandmother
reunited with his father—at a time they once enjoyed
together.

> ADAM (V.O.)
> It was evident that Paul Goode's ghost didn't
> know who I was. Maybe his mother would explain
> to him, one day, but I could see that my

grandmother was in no hurry to talk to him
about grown-up matters.

INT. HALL, HOTEL JEROME. CONTINUOUS.

Adam stands in the first-floor hall, waiting for the
elevator. He stands with the reunited mother and son,
Paulina and Paulino Juárez; they wait for the elevator
together.

> ADAM (V.O.)
> The rules for ghosts confound me. Why was the
> ghost of Clara Swift forty-five, the age she
> was when she jumped off the chairlift? It was
> out of order that Clara's ghost was older than
> the ghosts of Paul Goode and his mother.

The elevator door opens. Before anyone can step
inside, Clara steps out. She and Paulina Juárez are
old friends, always glad to see each other. Clara and
the fourteen-year-old Paulino are happy but shy about
being "introduced." Paul Goode's ghost looks like he's
meeting Clara for the first time.

Paulino wanders off down the hall, in the direction of
the Antler Bar, while Paulina and Clara follow after
him, smiling to each other. They look like they were
waiting for this.

INT. ELEVATOR, HOTEL JEROME. CONTINUOUS.

The cowboy is kicking his saddle when Adam gets on the
elevator. Alone with his saddle again, the cowboy must
know that Clara has made new friends, or she's found
an old one. The cowboy sees that Adam is carrying *My
Father's Dragon*.

> ADAM (V.O.)
> It was late, I was tired, but I'd been a writer
> long enough to sense when someone has the soul
> of a reader—like a poor cowboy, who's not had
> much opportunity to read.

DISSOLVE TO: eighty pages later. Adam is reading to the
cowboy. The two of them are lying down—propped up by
the saddle. Adam's voice-over is the only sound.

> ADAM (V.O.)
> The bridge of crocodiles wasn't a barrier
> to the cowboy's imagination. We would get
> through the final chapter, "My Father Finds the
> Dragon." I felt badly for the cowboy. Clara had
> been his friend. Now Clara would be hanging out
> with Paul Goode and his mom. As Monika told me,
> "Aspen was never an easy town for cowboys."

INT. HALL, HOTEL JEROME. MUCH LATER, SAME NIGHT.

In the third-floor hall, a tired-looking Adam is
unlocking the door to the living room of his suite.

INT. BEDROOM, HOTEL JEROME. CONTINUOUS.

CLOSE-UP: we see the clothes of the tall hippie girl—
we are familiar with her sweater, which she is always
lifting to show her breasts. Her clothes are strewn on
Matthew's rollaway bed, her boots next to the rollaway.

PULL BACK: the ghost of the tall hippie girl is under
the covers, on Adam's side of the bed. She is reading
Adam's novel, which she found on his night table, when
Adam enters the bedroom.

> ADAM (V.O.)
> Even I knew better than to sleep with a ghost.
> And it was the wrong time for a moral dilemma.

A WIDER ANGLE: as Adam undresses, leaving on his boxer shorts. Before he goes in the bathroom, he puts *My Father's Dragon* on the night table next to his side of the bed.

CLOSER ON: the hippie girl puts down Adam's novel; she picks up *My Father's Dragon,* thumbing through pages.

> ADAM (V.O.)
> Not every dilemma is a moral one.

INT. BATHROOM, HOTEL JEROME. CONTINUOUS.

CLOSE ON: Adam in the mirror as he brushes his teeth.

> ADAM (V.O.)
> It was okay with me if she read all night. I
> just couldn't read all of *My Father's Dragon*
> aloud—not so soon, not again.

INT. BEDROOM, HOTEL JEROME. CONTINUOUS.

The tall hippie girl has moved to the far side of the bed, where she reads *My Father's Dragon*. Her reading light is on the night table on that side of the bed. Adam's novel, with the author photo facing up, is on his night table when Adam comes out of the bathroom and gets into bed.

> ADAM (V.O.)
> Writers simply have to accept readers who
> prefer other writers.

CLOSER ON: the two of them in bed. Adam takes a look at her, but the hippie girl keeps reading. Adam turns on his side, away from her, closing his eyes.

FADE TO BLACK. FADE IN.

CLOSE ON: Adam's sleeping face, as his eyes open.

PULL BACK: in the foreground is the empty side of Adam's bed, where the copy of *My Father's Dragon* lies on the dented pillow.

ANOTHER ANGLE: fully dressed, the ghost of the tall hippie girl is sitting on Matthew's rollaway, reading Adam's novel. Adam faces her. She looks up from the novel at him.

                    ADAM
     It's for you. Did you see where I signed it, on
     the title page? There's also an inscription,
     just the usual "With my appreciation"—because I
     don't know your name.

She finds the title page, seeing his signature and the inscription. She gives him a disbelieving smile, holding the book to her left breast. With a sense of humor, she lifts her sweater and turtleneck, giving him a look at her right boob—the hippie girl's way of showing him her appreciation. Adam understands.

                    ADAM
     You're welcome.

DISSOLVE TO: Adam has dressed and packed; he surveys the bedroom, looking for anything he's left behind. This time, he doesn't overlook the copy of *My Father's Dragon*.

> ADAM (V.O.)
>
> It was easy for Grace or me to get a new copy
> of *My Father's Dragon*, to finish reading it to
> Matthew. I knew who might like to have her own
> copy at the Jerome.

**INT. ANTLER BAR, HOTEL JEROME. MOMENTS LATER, THAT
MORNING.**

NO SOUND, except Ian and Sylvia singing "Four Strong
Winds"—the Ian Tyson song. Paulina Juárez and Clara
Swift are talking to each other and watching Paulino,
who is having fun imitating the expressions on the
faces of the mounted animal heads. We know who showed
Otto how to do this.

> ADAM (V.O.)
>
> Paul Goode wanted Otto to show Matthew the
> animals in the Antler Bar before breakfast. As
> a kid, my dad must have loved the animal heads
> on the walls of the Jerome.

ANOTHER ANGLE: on Adam entering the Antler Bar. Paulino
sees him—a quick wave, then back to the stuffed heads.
Clara tightly holds the book Adam gives to her; Paulina
wants to see it.

A WIDER ANGLE: Clara is showing Paulina the
illustrations, just the first few pages, when Adam
slips away. Paulina blows him a kiss as he leaves.
Clara waves goodbye.

INT. LOBBY, HOTEL JEROME. CONTINUOUS.

The still-bleeding Aspen volunteer is curious about the
new reader in the lobby. The tall hippie girl is on the

couch; she doesn't look up from Adam's novel as Adam walks by. Jerome B. Wheeler gives Adam a salutation as Adam passes through the lobby. Adam pauses to bow, showing his respect for Wheeler.

Up the volume on Ian and Sylvia's "Four Strong Winds," as Otto and Billy come through the lobby, followed by two luggage carts and two cowboy porters.

INT. FRONT DESK, HOTEL JEROME. CONTINUOUS.

Adam and the two bodyguards are checking out at the same time—cowboy porters coming and going, as Ian and Sylvia keep singing.

> ADAM (V.O.)
>
> The Hotel Jerome is real—it's a great hotel. If you ever go to Aspen, you should stay at the Jerome, if you can afford it.

EXT. ENTRANCE, HOTEL JEROME, E. MAIN. CONTINUOUS.

An army of cowboy doormen and porters is loading the Jerome van, as Otto and Billy and Adam wait together. The three of them are talking to one another, but we don't hear what they're saying—only "Four Strong Winds," now fading, and Adam's voice-over.

> ADAM (V.O.)
>
> It seemed suitable that my father's bodyguards and I would share a van to the airport. We had more in common than our flying away from Aspen and our experience at the Jerome.

**INT. HOTEL JEROME VAN, THE FIRST ROW OF BACKSEATS.
CONTINUOUS.**

Billy gets in the sliding door first, slipping across
the seat to the spot behind THE DRIVER. Adam gets in,
expecting Otto will choose the second row of backseats
for himself, but Otto crams himself into the same row
of seats with Billy and Adam—squeezing Adam between the
bodyguards.

In the front seat of the van, the driver adjusts his
rearview mirror. We see Billy's face first; tears
stream down Billy's cheeks. Then we see Otto's big
face—he is sobbing. Last, the mirror shows us Adam—he's
crying, too.

> ADAM (V.O.)
> We had all lost someone important to us—someone
> who, for different reasons, had always been
> separated from us, someone we understood only
> at a distance. Yet my father's importance to
> us—as removed from us as Paul Goode was—would
> be irreplaceable.

A WIDER ANGLE: on their three faces as the van lurches
ahead.

FADE OUT "Four Strong Winds" as the Jerome recedes from
view.

50.

EM AS ISHMAEL

I heard about the snowstorm in the Northeast at the Aspen airport. My Chicago connection would be canceled. To Albany, or to Hartford—it doesn't matter that I don't remember. I wasn't going to get back to Vermont from Chicago—that was clear. I decided to fly from Denver to New York. I knew Em was at the snowshoer's pied-à-terre on East Sixty-fourth Street. It was her apartment now.

I called Molly from the Denver airport. I thought the old ski patroller would know everything about the snowstorm, but she didn't care about it. "It's just snow, Kid. By the way, we're done hearing from Jasmine," she told me.

A nurse at a home for assisted living in New York had called Molly. (The nurse was calling all the numbers Jasmine called most frequently.) Jasmine had passed away peacefully in her sleep, the nurse wanted Molly to know. "I told the nurse I was sorry about the *peacefully* part," the old patroller said.

I called Grace from Denver, too. Given the good bookstore in Manchester, Grace had already bought a new copy of *My Father's Dragon*. Grace said she would read Matthew the last two chapters while I was in New York, waiting out the snowstorm in New England. Em had delivered her novel—"based on her life with Nora," as Grace put it. I thought *her life with Nora* was a vague way for Em's publisher to describe the novel. This meant Em and Grace couldn't agree on a title, I was thinking. "Em sent two copies, one for you," was all Grace would say.

I asked Grace what Em was calling her novel. "You're seeing Em tonight—she'll tell you. Maybe you can talk her out of it—Em won't listen to me," Grace said. I could tell Grace was done talking about it. I knew she'd rejected *Two Dykes, One Who Talks* as a title. I'd already imagined Grace's grievances against the *Dykes* word.

Em told me Grace had suggested *The Gallows Lounge Shooting* as a title, but Em was opposed to a title with the "Gallows Lounge" in it. Em didn't want her novel to sound like nonfiction, but a title with "Two Dykes" in it was unacceptable to Grace. What I could sense—long-distance, in the Denver airport—didn't bode well for *peacefully* resolving what to call the novel.

Of course I called Em from Denver, too. Paul Goode's shooting was big news in New York, but other news was in the mail. Em called the letter, from someone at the archdiocese, "kind and compassionate—not at all perfunctory, beyond pro forma." It was only the hierarchy of the Catholic Church she hated, Em told me. "I have nothing against all the rest of the Catholics," she said; she sounded worn out. Em had been busy boxing up Mr. Barlow's things; not that long ago, I knew, she'd been boxing up Nora's. It was upsetting enough for Em to be putting away the snowshoer's stuff, but Em was angry and crying because she came across a box of Nora's writing. Knowing Elliot Barlow had been her rescuer, Em understood that Mr. Barlow was both saving the box for Em and protecting her from seeing it. "Nora's box," Em called it, pun intended.

To say it was a box of Nora's writing doesn't cover it. Em wrote what Nora said onstage at the Gallows. Em put in writing what she knew how to pantomime and had rehearsed, but Nora was known to ad-lib her lines onstage—a subject of much disagreement between the two of them. Nora was also known to rewrite, in her own words, what Em had scripted for her to say. Dear Mr. Barlow would have known that *Nora's box* contained a ton of contention between Nora and Em. Bernard ("Bonkers") Nathanson had been a sore subject at the Gallows, where the cowardly management wouldn't permit Nora and Em to ridicule Nathanson for his being a turncoat to abortion rights and the pro-choice cause.

A former pro-choice activist, Dr. Nathanson was a licensed obstetrician and gynecologist in New York. One of the founders of the National Abortion Rights Action League (NARAL), Nathanson had worked with Betty Friedan for the legalization of abortion in the U.S. He was also the former director of New York City's Center for Reproductive and Sexual Health, but Bonkers Nathanson became a right-to-lifer. In 1984, Nathanson was the narrator of *The Silent Scream*—an anti-abortion film that included an ultrasound video of a fetus sensing it was about to be aborted.

I remember the row between Nora and Em concerning what Nora had written for Em to pantomime about *The Silent Scream*. Em knew there was no way for her to pantomime a threatened fetus and be funny. Nora was incensed that Nathanson had called himself a "Jewish atheist." In Nora's opinion, Nathanson gave Jews and atheists a bad name—he was bad-mouthing both groups. But Em knew there was no way for her to pantomime a Jewish atheist and not look like she was anti-Semitic. Their differences of opinion didn't matter; their Bonkers Nathanson skit never made it to the stage. The Gallows management wouldn't allow Nora and Em to make Dr. Nathanson a target of their political comedy. *Bonkers* was Nora's name for Nathanson, naturally.

"We shouldn't mock a doctor who repents his killing unborn babies," one of the cowards managing the Gallows had whined. But I was only beginning to understand why Nora's box was a Pandora's box for Em to have opened. There might be more in that box than Em's writing, and Nora's—that's what I was worrying about.

I asked Em if it seemed contradictory of the snowshoer to save Nora's box for her, but to keep her from seeing it. "No!" Em cried. "It makes perfect sense." Grace couldn't restrain herself from editing every reference to Bonkers Nathanson out of Em's novel, Em now told me. I only knew that Grace and the snowshoer had been seeing Em's novel in piecemeal fashion, as Em wrote it—whereas Em had wanted to finish her novel before showing it to me.

"It's okay that Bonkers Nathanson changed his mind about abortion— that's his choice," Nora had always said. "What's not okay is that Nathanson won't let other people make that choice for themselves."

As for the sea change in Nathanson's abortion politics, what got to Em was the part about his becoming a Catholic. Nathanson's newfound belief in God would have riled up Nora, Em said. But what would get to Nora, Em knew, was not just Nathanson's finding God. "Bonkers Nathanson is a former abortionist groveling for forgiveness from the Catholic Church," Em said.

I knew how this was relevant to the epigraph Em had chosen for her novel, long ago—the quote from Nora, the one with such a moderate or reasonable tone that it didn't sound like Nora. "There's no stopping the Catholic Church," Nora had said. "You shouldn't try to stop them; all you can do is try to control the damage they do."

Grace, I knew, had objected to the epigraph from the beginning. And now Em was hopping mad because Grace was opposed to anything in Em's novel that sounded like, or could be perceived as, anti-Catholic. Em's whole novel could be perceived as anti-Catholic—this was Grace's editorial opinion. "The snowshoer and you were my editors—now it's just you, kiddo," Em told me.

Speech was relatively new to the formerly nonspeaking Em. I'd noticed she would experiment with how she wanted to sound—the way a teenager would try out different attitudes and voices. In her experiments, Em often spoke like Nora—*kiddo* was what Nora had called me.

"You and Nora were a stand-up act in a comedy club—your foremost objective wasn't to offend no one," Mr. Barlow had written Em. "Don't let Grace make offending no one be the objective of your novel. Remember why you wanted to write *Two Dykes, One Who Talks* in the first place—not as nonfiction, but as a novel," the snowshoer wrote. "In a novel, your foremost objective isn't to offend no one," the little English teacher told Em.

In the Denver airport, I was forever on the phone. Em had finished reading Mr. Barlow's advance galleys of Bernard Nathanson's *The Hand of God*. I knew Grace had got hold of the advance galleys, too. My chief concern was that Em would try to read aloud the entirety of Chapter 15, the last chapter in *The Hand of God*—the Catholic chapter. It would be a bad way for me to miss my flight to New York—hearing all about Bonkers Nathanson's conversion to Catholicism. He wrote that he'd been having "lengthy conversations with a priest . . . for the past five years, and it is my hope that I shall soon be received into the Roman Catholic Church."

God help Cardinal O'Connor if the son of a bitch baptizes Bonkers Nathanson, or some other craven convert to Catholicism—God help His Eminence if the son of a bitch gives Communion to another former infidel and repentant sinner, like my hateful father! I was expecting Em to say, but she didn't.

"If Cardinal O'Connor baptizes Bonkers Nathanson, I might throw up," was all Em said. She reminded me about one night at the Gallows when we were backstage—Damaged Don was there—and Nora was having one of her First Amendment fits.

The Roman Catholic Church was riding roughshod over the Constitution, Nora was railing—that bit about "Congress shall make no law respecting an establishment of religion, or prohibiting the free exercise thereof." Nora was reiterating what had been Mr. Barlow's mantra—the snowshoer's way of saying that freedom of religion wasn't a one-way street. We were free to practice the religion of our choice, but we were also free from having someone else's religion practiced on us. Nora and the snowshoer sounded like a broken record—the way they never stopped saying that freedom of religion also meant freedom *from* religion.

Damaged Don, who we didn't know was listening—Don just kept strumming his guitar—spoke up. "Those Catholics—they'll beat you up about *their* freedom of religion, but they don't give two shits for *yours*," the Damaged Man declared.

Well, we know what became of Don. The Damaged Man was gunned down in a parking lot in Montana, after Reagan's reelection, when the gay boys Don had been singing about were still dying, and Don was still singing his plague song.

> Don't give Ronald Reagan
> eight years.
> He talks tough to commies,
> he kills all the gay boys,
> but that does fuck-all
> for our fears.
>
> Please don't give the Gipper
> eight years.
> No, don't give the Gipper
> eight years.

If there was a Damaged Don box in the snowshoer's pied-à-terre, I knew it wouldn't have been easy going for Em. After Don was killed, and for as long as Ronald Reagan was our president, Nora had closed out every performance of *Two Dykes, One Who Talks* with a Damaged Don song. As Nora said, she couldn't sing, but neither could Don. Em, crying, hugged Nora while she sang.

In the Denver airport, I decided that singing the Damaged Man would be better than hearing more of *The Hand of God*. I started with the chorus of Damaged Don's plague song. Em, crying, sang with me on the phone.

> It's time to head back to
> Great Falls.
> I'm lackin' the talent,
> I can't stand the sadness,
> I don't have big enough balls!
>
> It's time to head back to
> Great Falls.
> I'm just goin' back to
> Great Falls.

The Damaged Man was with us; he'd managed to make Em and me feel less alone. Later, we sang "No Lucky Star" to each other.

That was when Em told me she'd barely glanced at Elliot Barlow's notebooks. She had filled two boxes with the notebooks; we would read them together, she told me. All she'd read was a short passage about the snowshoer's last visit to St. Vincent's—in the 1990s, after Ronald Reagan was no longer in office. The snowshoer had written about Reagan—just one sentence, after seeing her friends who were dying of AIDS.

"If or when there's another plague, I hope America has a better plague president than Ronald Reagan," the little English teacher wrote.

Em still had to get to the bottom of Nora's box, she told me, but she promised she would be done with it by the time I got to New York. When I boarded my flight in Denver, I felt closer to Em than ever before, but I knew she would keep surprising me.

I began to realize that I'd overlooked Em's earliest, unspoken seagull imitations—signifying her going back to Canada. Nora had observed I was slow to notice more of the world—she meant politically. "It took you long enough, kiddo," my older cousin had told me—meaning for me to get out of Exeter, literally and figuratively. In Nora's opinion, Exeter was not only a cloistered school and a small town; Exeter was a cloistered state of mind.

Zim had died in February 1968. Elliot and I had gone to his memorial service in March. But I was still out of it, politically, two years later, when Nora and Em went to hear Kurt Vonnegut speak at Bennington College's commencement. I loved Vonnegut's writing—he'd been my favorite teacher at the Writers' Workshop in Iowa City. Kurt and I continued to have a correspondence; when I was in New York, we often had dinner together. But I don't know where I was, literally and politically, for Kurt's speech to the graduates at Bennington in 1970—I wasn't there. It was Nora who told me Vonnegut was a socialist—Nora said she was one, too. Em just did her seagull thing, which didn't only mean she was thinking about going back to Canada, but sometimes it did.

Of course I remembered when the craven management of the Gallows Lounge had complained about the *Canadian*, meaning Em. She'd been born in Canada, she had a Canadian father, but her early childhood was the only time Em had lived in Canada; then she'd moved to Massachusetts with her mother. Thereafter, Em visited her father in Toronto only once a year, over the Christmas holiday.

I hadn't heard Em talk about "social democracy" in Canada—not until

I came back from Aspen and the Hotel Jerome the second time. I don't remember seeing Em do a socialist pantomime at the Gallows, where the cowardly management surely would have blamed the *Canadian* for anything remotely resembling anti-American politics—even though it was Nora who started calling herself a socialist, and only after Vonnegut's speech at Bennington. *Vogue* magazine published the speech, and Nora made me read it. Nowadays, all I remember is the end of Kurt's speech—the socialist part. But I'm embarrassed that I skimmed over the socialism when I read the speech the first time.

"I suggest that you work for a socialist form of government," Vonnegut had told the students. (Their parents and grandparents must have shit their pants over that idea, Nora said.) "Free Enterprise is much too hard on the old and the sick and the shy and the poor and the stupid, and on people nobody likes," Kurt had continued. The speech sounded like Kurt; reading it was just like listening to his voice. "So let's divide up the wealth more fairly than we have divided it up so far," he went on. He talked about people having enough to eat, and a decent place to live, and medical help. "It isn't moonbeams to talk of modest plenty for all. They have it in Sweden. We can have it here," Kurt said to the students.

Elliot Barlow had voted for Stevenson in 1956; Mr. Barlow liked what Vonnegut said about Eisenhower. "Dwight David Eisenhower once pointed out that Sweden, with its many Utopian programs, had a high rate of alcoholism and suicide and youthful unrest. Even so," Vonnegut said, "I would like to see America try socialism. If we start drinking heavily and killing ourselves, and if our children start acting crazy, we can go back to good old Free Enterprise again." I liked the speech because it was funny, but the socialist part slipped away.

Em had been paying attention to Canada, politically—more than I knew. Though the homophobe, her dying father, had left Em the house in midtown Toronto, Em had refused to sell it. Em had even refused to rent out half the house, as her father had. She was a dual citizen, of Canada and the U.S. I knew she wanted to have a place to go if she ever left the United States, but I didn't know Em had been reading about democratic socialism or socialist democracy—not to mention social democracy in Canada. That part slipped away, too. From my American perspective, Canada was more socialist than the United States—that was all I knew.

In the Denver airport, we didn't talk about socialism, but before we got off the phone, I asked Em about the title of her novel. I let her know that

Grace wouldn't tell me the title. "Grace hopes I can talk you out of it," I told Em.

"You can't—the title was the snowshoer's idea. You won't talk the *two* of us out of it—Elliot Barlow isn't listening anymore," Em told me. She was calling her novel *Come Hang Yourself*, Em said. I would never have tried to talk her out of it, not even if the only hero hadn't had a hand in it.

If you ever went to the Gallows—even if you went there only once—you would remember the hangman's noose above the bar, where a sign said, COME HANG YOURSELF.

I remembered the night when I ran into Prue, the Tongue Kisser and her husband at the Gallows. Prue was happy to show her husband where she'd once had an all-noir act. This was during the AIDS years. Prue must have been forty. Her husband was appalled by *Two Dykes, One Who Talks*—then Damaged Don did a dirge onstage, and the tongue kisser's husband looked at the hangman's noose above the bar in a welcoming way. In the AIDS years, the Damaged Man wasn't funny at all, and the dickless management at the Gallows considered taking down the noose above the bar, or at least removing that sign. In my years of going to the Gallows, the tongue kisser's husband was one of the few who looked noir enough to hang himself on the spur of the moment from the noose above the bar.

When I got to East Sixty-fourth Street, Em was raging around the apartment in her pajamas; she was in the kind of rage that made me think an old injury had come back to hurt her. "Was it something in Nora's box?" I asked her. Nora had hurt Em's feelings before, but this wound had nothing to do with Nora's writing or Bonkers Nathanson. An old magazine had been hiding in Nora's box.

It was a familiar-looking issue of *Vogue*—August 1, 1970. On a dog-eared page, I recognized Vonnegut's Bennington speech. I'd since read it many times in *Wampeters, Foma & Granfalloons*—a collection of Kurt's short works, mostly essays and reviews and speeches. I'm sure Elliot Barlow had all of Vonnegut's books. I know I did; I thought Em did, too. I saw no harm in Nora's saving that old issue of *Vogue*—I knew Nora had loved that speech.

"Nora was getting off on the *photograph*—she wasn't saving the speech!" Em wailed. On the page facing Kurt's speech was a black-and-white photograph of the eighteen-year-old Isabella Rossellini. At that age, with those eyes and that mouth, Isabella was Nora's type. "I know what Nora was doing with this magazine!" Em cried.

After all these years, to be jealous of a girl in a magazine—even if she was a girl Nora might have been masturbating over—amazed me. I tried not to be jealous of how much Em had loved Nora, but it made my heart ache. The photo was a full page—a close-up of Isabella Rossellini's face and throat, with her dark hair falling over her shoulders. Twenty-five years before, I might have masturbated over such a pretty face in a magazine, but it wouldn't have helped Em to know my thoughts. All I could do was hug her while she raged. If there were more mystery boxes, we would open them together—we would pack up the snowshoer's stuff together, too.

That night, when I was lying in bed with Em, it occurred to me that it had been about a month since my mother had climbed into bed with me. "*Shh!* Don't say anything—just listen, sweetie," my mom had whispered. She'd giggled like a little girl and said I was the love of her life. Those were her last words to me. Then my mother was gone; she had plans to keep, after midnight. It was a mile, straight up Twister, to the top of Bromley. Little Ray and the snowshoer had some serious climbing to do. I knew I would hear my mom whispering to me, and giggling like a little girl, for the rest of my life.

That was the same night Em had asked me if I was still stuck on her. I couldn't speak, but we both knew I was. "Well, now is not the time," Em had said, "but we'll have to consider what we can do about that."

My first night at the snowshoer's since the apartment had become Em's, I sensed it was still not the time for us to consider what we could do about my being stuck on her. We were lying in bed, holding hands. Em was telling me I couldn't let Grace *edit* the way we separated and divorced, or allow her to *edit* where and when I was going to be with Matthew. I just listened. Em had more experience rejecting Grace's edits than I did. Even knowing she wasn't Em's editor didn't stop Grace from trying to edit Em.

I didn't know that Em had been talking to Molly about what would be best for Matthew. Molly knew Grace was looking for a larger apartment in New York. Grace wasn't planning to be a divorced woman living in Vermont. Her parents had a house in Manchester; one day, it would be Grace's house. Grace and Matthew would come to Vermont—for weekends or school vacations, and to ski—but Matthew would be going to school in Manhattan, Molly pointed out. The old patroller was paying particular attention to the new skiers at Bromley; she kept an eye out for potential buyers of a second home.

"With all those bedrooms, it'll have to be a whole family of skiers or a sports team," Molly told Em.

"Matthew's going to be a New Yorker, you know," Em said to me in bed, squeezing my hand. "If we're living here, it'll be easy for him to stay with us—Matthew is used to us being together."

"Okay," I said. I was afraid of saying the wrong thing, or sounding too excited about the prospect of my living with Em.

It was no big deal to me how the Gallows pulled the plug on the *Two Dykes'* skit about things to do with a penis. What I couldn't forget was Em's pantomime—how she would put an imaginary penis between her boobs or between her thighs, but nowhere else.

More recently, Em implied there were other things she could imagine doing with a penis—just not in her vagina. When Em was a kid, she had a feeling—"not as strong as a conviction," was the way she'd put it—that she didn't want a penis in her vagina. Was it wishful thinking, on my part, to imagine Em might not be adamant about what to do with a penis? She didn't sound unwavering. "A penis is just a funny clitoris," I'd heard Em say to Molly when they were washing dishes.

Em would be sixty-one in the coming year; I would be fifty-five. Because she was six years older, maybe Em could read my mind. "Molly and I have been talking about penises," Em told me. It was not a conversation I could imagine lasting very long. "A clitoris is smaller than a penis, but a clitoris has almost eight thousand nerve endings—twice as many as a penis, kiddo," Em said. I guess it was a longer conversation than I'd imagined. "A clitoris gets a hard-on, you know," Em told me.

"Okay," I said. I didn't know what to say. It was Molly who told me a penis doesn't have any muscles. Everyone knows a penis doesn't have a brain. Em had stopped holding my hand.

"Well, now is not the time," Em said again, "but I'm working on things to do with your funny clitoris."

"Okay," I said. There are these moments when you see the course of your life unfolding, and you feel powerless to alter it.

"And we'll have to talk about your writing," Em said.

"Okay," I said. You see the road ahead, and you know you'll follow it—your future feels as unalterable as your childhood, and you know how childhood works. You go along with it.

"You write about sex, you know—you describe having sex, in detail," Em told me. "But whatever we decide to do with your penis, you won't write about what *we* do—you won't describe how *we* have sex, okay?" she asked.

"Okay," I said. You are never over your childhood, not until you are under the train—unter dem Zug.

In the morning, I was still asleep when the phone rang. I woke up hearing Em talking—not knowing, at first, she was talking on the phone. "She shit in bed, you know—nothing peaceful about it," Em was saying. "Her pussy was a subway station—it never slept," Em said. "Do you have the wrong Jasmine?" Em asked the nurse at the home for assisted living, who was still apparently calling all of Jasmine's contacts. "We called her Rush Hour Pussy—if she didn't shit in bed when she died, you have another Jasmine. I'm sorry, but we don't know her," Em told the nurse. I was lying in bed with my whatchamacallit, looking forward to many mornings of waking up with Emily MacPherson.

Matthew's fifth birthday—March 2, 1996—was my last night in the East Dorset house. I would miss the sauna and the guest bedrooms. When Grace and I had no more wall space for hanging Matthew's pictures in the rest of the house, we hung them in the guest bedrooms. Wherever I would live, for the rest of my life, I would never have enough wall space for pictures of Matthew. For his fifth birthday, Molly spent the night in one of the guest bedrooms; Em and I spent the night in another one. Before that house was sold, Molly would spend a few more nights there, but Matthew's fifth birthday was the last night in that house for Em and me.

Grace and I weren't the only ones who got to spend time with Matthew alone, telling him how things would be when his mom and I separated and divorced. Matthew got to spend time alone with Em, and with Molly, too. Matthew was very particular about the details. He asked you to repeat yourself; he corrected you if you contradicted yourself. We went over the details again and again. Repetition isn't comforting only to children.

I felt like a five-year-old when Molly went over the details with me. For as long as Matthew was in preschool in Manchester, he would be welcome to stay with Molly when his mom had to be in New York. Matthew had the most fun with Molly and with Em, and there was no knowing when the East Dorset house would be sold. If Matthew started kindergarten in Manchester that fall, there would always be room for Em and me *and Matthew* to stay with Molly. "For a few more years, Kid, Matthew won't mind the communal sleeping arrangements," the old patroller said.

I said I still didn't mind the communal sleeping arrangements.

Molly knew I hadn't seen my mother's ghost in Aspen, at the Jerome. I didn't expect my mom to make an appearance in the vicinity of East Sixty-fourth Street, but I admitted to Molly I was disheartened not to have seen Little Ray and the snowshoer in Vermont. "Where are they?" I asked her.

"Where they are isn't a place, Kid," the old patroller told me. "I see those two all the time, right here," she said, touching her heart. I knew Molly wasn't into ghosts; I didn't doubt she saw *those two* in her heart. "The main thing, Kid, is that you're going to be seeing only half as much of Matthew as you're used to—if you're lucky—and Matthew knows he'll be seeing only half as much of you," Molly said.

"I know," I said. Em had warned me about this.

"Matthew can follow the seasons of the year, you know—he gets it, about the passage of time," Em said.

"Matthew understands the sequence of time, Kid," was the way the old patroller put it. Matthew understood what happened first, and what came next. He knew the order of events; he could follow stories, from their beginnings to their endings.

"When you're alone with Matthew, don't be sad—he knows when you're sad, like I do," Em told me. "Don't let him know you're sad because you'll miss him, or that you're thinking about how it'll be for him to miss you," Em said.

"I know," I said. Naturally, the next time I was alone with Matthew, he asked me why I was sad. "I miss my mom and the snowshoer," I said. We were lying on the futon in the TV room of the Manchester house, after dinner. I didn't like to think about Molly's intention to leave the Manchester house to me; she'd already told me. Matthew and I could hear Molly and Em talking in the kitchen, where they were washing the dishes.

"Grandma and the snowshoer look a lot younger than they were," Matthew whispered.

"You've seen them?" I whispered back.

"Grandma and the snowshoer, in the sauna—naked!" Matthew whispered. "They're still fooling around—they're just much younger now," he assured me. This was what Em meant about Matthew's following the passage of time—his understanding the sequence of time, as Molly put it—even when time seemed to be working in reverse.

After Matthew fell asleep—in Molly's big bed, where he loved to sleep, leaving the futon in the TV room for Em and me—I told the old patroller and Em what Matthew had told me. "He's seen his grandma and the snowshoer—they're still fooling around in the sauna, but Matthew said they look a lot younger now." I didn't say Matthew had seen the ghosts of those two. I knew Molly and Em weren't ghost people. I knew ghosts could be younger than they were when they died, but what I'd learned about the rules for ghosts was that I knew nothing.

"When I see those two, they're the age they were when they met—of course they're still fooling around," Molly said. "They're the way they were when they both wore Ray's clothes, Kid—when your mom and Mr. Barlow were the only ones who knew the snowshoer was meant to be a woman," the old patroller said.

Em knew I was wondering why my mother hadn't shown herself to me— why I hadn't seen her. Nora had told Em how I missed my mom when I was a child—how I'd always wanted to see more of my mother than I did. When I was with my mom, I never doubted her love for me. Even now, I trusted I would see her—when the time was right, as she used to say. Em knew Nora exaggerated, at times. I'd learned what Nora also told Em—that my mother was the love of my life. As far as Nora knew, this was true.

When Em spoke to me, she was trying to make me feel better. "Your mom and the snowshoer know Matthew comes first—you'll be the next to see those two, kiddo," Em said, giving me a hug.

I tried to make Em feel better about the review of Bonkers Nathanson's *The Hand of God* in the March 15 issue of *Kirkus Reviews*. It was such an overcautious review, so noncommittal in tone, it came to no conclusions. In the end, what were we to make of Nathanson himself? "He is clearly not at peace with his past, and he states that he is seeking admission to the Catholic Church"—that was putting it mildly, to make what Bonkers was *seeking* sound as innocent as applying to a school.

"What a limp-dick review!" Em was screaming, while I hugged her. In Em's opinion, *The Hand of God* was a proselytizing call for a theocracy. "In a social democracy," Em said, when she calmed down, "I wonder if you can count on the separation of church and state—I mean, if you can count on it actually working."

I could count on the separation of church and state to get Em's attention. I knew Kurt Vonnegut wanted to see America try socialism. But this was when I learned that Emily MacPherson, the author of *Come Hang Yourself*—the formerly nonspeaking member of *Two Dykes, One Who Talks*—was thinking about giving a little socialism a try. This was the beginning of my paying attention to Em's interest in social democracy in Canada. From this moment, I was on the lookout for Em's seagull imitations. Even the way Em watched the seagulls floating over Manhattan got my attention. I knew her seagull thing hadn't always meant she was thinking about going back to Canada. A seagull's seemingly directionless drifting had been Em's way of pantomiming Ronald Reagan's laissez-faire approach to AIDS; her seagull thing had been her way of portraying President Reagan as the Pontius Pilate of the AIDS epidemic, but Reagan wasn't in the White House now. Even when Em was asleep, I watched her for signs she was drifting back to Canada—her arms spread like a seagull's motionless wings, a faraway look in her eyes when she woke up.

It's hard to write about how much I missed Matthew. Every time I said goodbye to him was hard—no matter how soon, or how long, it would be before I saw him again. By the fall, the East Dorset house had still not been sold. Matthew was going to kindergarten in Manchester, but Grace and I were in agreement that he would be starting first grade in Manhattan the following fall. We were in agreement about the things that mattered. The part about missing Matthew was the hard part—also for Grace—but Matthew was always excited to see me, and Molly and Em, too.

One night in Manchester, when Matthew and I were watching TV on the futon, I overheard Em and Molly talking in the kitchen; they must have been continuing their conversation about penises. I heard Em say it wasn't complicated to take care of a thing with no muscles and no brain, just nerve endings. "It sounds like it's easier than taking care of a dog," the old patroller said. I can't imagine what else they could have been talking about. Em and I were in agreement about the things that mattered, too.

Grace tried hard not to insert herself as an unwanted editor of Em's *Come Hang Yourself*, which would be published in the spring. Em tried hard to ignore what was written about *The Hand of God*. Nathanson himself was not the reason Em would drift away to Canada. In December 1996, Bonkers Nathanson was baptized by John Cardinal O'Connor at St. Patrick's Cathedral in New York. No, Em did not show up at St. Patrick's with a box for Cardinal O'Connor; she'd not been invited to the private Mass, where Nathanson also received confirmation and First Communion from the ass-kissing cardinal. When Nathanson was asked why he'd converted to Catholicism, he would say that no religion matched the special role for forgiveness provided by the Catholic Church.

"I'll say," was all Em said. It was not Nathanson who would eventually compel Em to do her seagull thing—nor would it be John Cardinal O'Connor himself. O'Connor's pro-life advocacy was a given; the cardinal relegated women to the childbirth role, and O'Connor's relegations of the gay community were similarly dogmatic and doctrinaire. Cardinal O'Connor and the Catholic Church did not believe in the separation of church and state. As Nora knew, all you could do was try to control the damage they did.

That said, had Nora been alive—if she'd survived the Gallows Lounge shooting, and the comedy club were still kicking—Nora would have relegated Cardinal O'Connor's baptizing of Bonkers Nathanson to "The News in English" part of the *Two Dykes* stand-up act, the part Nora referred to as "shit in the offing." It certainly was a shit show, but Em didn't move to Canada because of the private Mass O'Connor provided for Nathanson in St. Patrick's Cathedral. The *shit in the offing* part happened later.

Soon after Bonkers Nathanson's baptism, Em took what she called a "reconnaissance trip" to Toronto—this was in January. I knew the story of Em showing Nora the exterior of the house on Shaftesbury Avenue; she'd not shown Nora the inside. In her *reconnaissance trip* to Toronto, Em made plans to gut the interior of the house. She arranged to have her hateful father's furniture and his dingy curtains carted off. She found someone to strip and sand and polish the old floorboards, and someone to paint the walls white. Em was away from New York for only a week, but it felt to me like the start of something longer; she'd taken a step toward making the house more fit to live in. "The Realtor told me it'll make the house more sellable," was what Em said about the renovations.

I didn't doubt Em's determination to try living with me, nor was I kidding myself; I knew Matthew was a big part of why Em wanted to try. "Don't worry, I'm not leaving you guys—I'm just playing house," Em told Matthew and me, about the renovations in Toronto. "I'm just thinking I might like to try a little socialism," Em would say later, just to me.

That winter of 1997, there was a lot of driving to and from New York. With Matthew in preschool in Vermont, there was a lot of staying with Molly in the Manchester house, too. I was grateful to my mom for teaching me to ski, and grateful to the old patroller for making me keep skiing. Although I would never be better than an intermediate skier, Matthew and I would have fun skiing together for a few more years.

With all the driving back and forth between Vermont and New York, Em and I were often alone together in the car. I was usually the driver, because Em wanted to practice reading aloud. In the coming spring and summer, there would be public readings to promote *Come Hang Yourself*. "As a writer who is relatively new to *speaking*, you'll have to find your reading voice," Grace had forewarned Em. There was no mention of *Madeline*.

While Em and I had been taking turns reading the snowshoer's notebooks aloud to each other, this was usually at night, when we were in bed. Mr. Barlow's notebook entries were not linear in nature—they weren't sequential.

The little English teacher wasn't keeping a diary; her notebook entries were her observations, not necessarily connected to one another. This was not ideal for reading aloud on long trips in a car—no narrative momentum.

I knew Em had been waiting for a certain moment when she would finally read *Moby-Dick*—an *upheaval* of some kind, as she'd put it, signified (in Em's nonspeaking days) by her tipping over a coffee table. Between Em's urgency to find her reading voice, and the renovations to her house in Toronto, Em had found the *Moby-Dick* moment she'd been waiting for. *Lucky me*, I was thinking—someone I loved would read *Moby-Dick* aloud to me again.

"You can see why the third-person omniscient voice is a safer voice for Em to be in," the snowshoer had said.

I'd admired the third-person, deadpan omniscience of Em's narration when I read *Come Hang Yourself* and gave Em my notes. I knew we were each other's editors, for the foreseeable future—given that the little English teacher was gone. Before long, Em would find her reading voice in *Moby-Dick*—she was channeling Ishmael, the antithesis of a deadpan narrator. In those long car rides, listening to Em as Ishmael—giving voice to her most ferocious first-person—I thought Cardinal O'Connor was lucky. If the son of a bitch had baptized Bonkers Nathanson after Em's long voyage on the *Pequod*—I mean, all the way to the doomed ship's encounter with the white whale—Em as Ishmael might have held the ass-kissing cardinal accountable. Yet Em *seemed* to have let her grievances against Cardinal O'Connor go. A benign gesture—like Ishmael imagining that Queequeg *seems* to be saying to himself, "We cannibals must help these Christians." *We'll see*, I was thinking.

Ishmael's first-person voice, as expansive as the sea itself, would affect more than the way Em read aloud. The pitch and timbre of Em's speaking voice began to change. Even as a beginner, she'd spoken with intensity—as if she'd been channeling Nora. Since she'd met Ishmael, Em was channeling a sailor; her voice was lower and less strident, but she was no less intense. In fact, she sounded more forceful—more masculine than Nora.

"First-person *male*," Grace called Em's newfound reading *and* speaking voice. It seemed wrong to Grace that Em, who was so feminine in her appearance, should sound like a sailor, but I felt differently about the change in Em. She'd not just found her voice in reading *Moby-Dick* aloud; aboard the *Pequod*, Em had found and embraced a bigger world.

In the strong, low voice in which she read aloud to me—"'It was the whiteness of the whale that above all things appalled me'"—Em also said, "Stop the car, I have to pee." (No wonder—with all the reading aloud, Em was drinking a lot of water.) And when Em read *Moby-Dick* to me, I thought of Emmanuelle—the high school student who'd been charged with exposing herself, mooning and flashing her titties on the Swasey Parkway.

The "Police Report" had cited "an outrage to public decency," but I was just embarrassed. At thirty-eight, I'd not known Emmanuelle was a high school kid. She'd been reading *Moby-Dick* to my grandmother. Emmanuelle was the one who found Nana—dead in bed, with that big book. I still wondered if Emmanuelle had noticed Nana's thumb between the pages—if Emmanuelle knew *where* in *Moby-Dick* my grandmother was reading when she died.

In 1980, when Nana died, Emmanuelle might have been as young as sixteen—she couldn't have been older than eighteen, I was thinking, when Em interrupted her reading in the car. "You're thinking about Emmanuelle, aren't you?" Em asked me.

"You could probably go to jail for sleeping with Emmanuelle—*Moby-Dick* is not an excuse, sweetie," my mom had told me.

"I don't think Emmanuelle is *that* young, Ray—I don't think it's illegal to sleep with her," Molly had said.

I told Em I wasn't thinking about Emmanuelle "in that way." I just wanted to ask Emmanuelle *which part* of the *Pequod*'s voyage had been the last part for my grandmother; I wanted to know what Nana was rereading to herself when she died. I knew Em would have said it was okay, if I'd been thinking about Emmanuelle *in that way*.

We'd talked about this. "We're too old to sleep with young women anymore, but it's okay to think about them—*in that way*—and it's okay to look at them," Em had told me.

"Okay," I'd said.

Once, when Em saw me looking at a young woman—in that way—she said, "I saw her first." This had since become what we said when we caught each other just looking. In truth, we didn't look at other women a lot.

It was a long winter, with a late spring, in 1997. There were uncounted hours of reading *Moby-Dick* in the car. Em had just finished Chapter 111, "The Pacific," when she woke me one night—crying out in her sleep, as Captain Ahab cries out in his, "'The White Whale spouts thick blood!'" When I woke her up, and she'd calmed down, there was another matter on her mind. "You know, kiddo—she would be in her thirties now," Em said.

"*Who* would be?" I asked her.

"Emmanuelle—she's thirty-three, maybe thirty-five," Em told me.

"I know," I said.

"I'm just thinking out loud, kiddo. If Emmanuelle finished reading *Moby-Dick* to herself, she's a real reader. Emmanuelle will show up at one of your readings," Em said. I repeated that I wasn't thinking about Emmanuelle *in that way*, but Em said it didn't matter what I thought about her. "If Emmanuelle kept reading *Moby-Dick*, she has staying power—she'll show up one day," Em said.

I was learning that Em as Ishmael made herself clear. But Em was still learning about six-year-olds. Matthew took what you said literally. Em had told us she was *playing house* in Toronto. Matthew pressed her for more details. To a six-year-old, playing house sounds like fun. But where was Toronto, and how did you play house? Matthew wanted to know. Em's explanation of playing house to Matthew was a revelation to me. She sounded like Em as Ishmael, or maybe she was Em as a fiction writer—or both.

"Toronto is in Canada, a foreign country with a different kind of government. For some reason, the Queen of England is also the Queen of Canada," Em began. Not a word about social democracy, so far.

"But where is it?" Matthew asked; he didn't care about the kind of government, or the queen.

"If you drive to an airport and go in an airplane, it only takes as long to get to Toronto as it takes to drive to Vermont from New York. My mystery house isn't far away," Em said.

"Why is it a mystery house—what's the mystery?" Matthew asked. Now maybe we would get somewhere, I thought.

It would take a while for Matthew to imagine the house Em had in mind. It would take me a while, too, whereas Em was the kind of fiction writer who was good at foreshadowing—she always knew where she was going; she saw the path ahead of herself. Em's house in Toronto was no mystery to her.

"Imagine an empty house, no furniture. The rooms don't know what they are—no one has told the rooms what they're for," Em said. "Imagine you're a room, but you don't know if you're supposed to be a bedroom or a living room or a dining room," Em went on, creating sympathy for the rooms.

"The poor rooms!" Matthew cried, a compassionate child.

"Well, the bathrooms know they're bathrooms—what toilets are for is no mystery—and a kitchen knows what it's for," Em said. "But this house has two kitchens—one is upstairs—so the kitchens are kind of confused, too," Em told us.

"Why is there a kitchen upstairs?" Matthew asked her.

"There used to be two families living in the house," Em explained, "but the family living downstairs never saw the family who lived upstairs. The family living downstairs only *heard* the upstairs family—when someone was walking around, or when someone went up or down the back stairs," Em told us.

This wasn't the best story to tell a six-year-old, Grace said. Matthew had nightmares about an unseen family living above him. Matthew swore he could hear them, although there was no one walking around above the five upstairs bedrooms in the East Dorset house—and there was no upstairs in Molly's Manchester house, where Matthew occasionally had the same nightmare.

One night, when Matthew and Em and I were at Molly's, Matthew slept with me on the futon in the TV room. I knew he liked sleeping with Molly, in her bed, better. I thought Matthew might be worrying about the upstairs family, but it turned out he just wanted to tell me what was up with my mom and the snowshoer. "Those two don't hang out at the house anymore—I only see them at Molly's," Matthew told me. "They must know the house is for sale, and that you're not there anymore," Matthew said.

"I see," I said, wishing I could see them.

"They're not getting any older—all those two do is goof around," Matthew assured me.

Matthew must have talked to Molly and Em about seeing them, because both Em and the old patroller spoke to me. "Where they are isn't a place, Kid," Molly had already told me, touching her heart. Now Molly made it more clear; those two must be hanging out at her house because they could see all of us there. It was Matthew and Molly and Em and me that mattered to those two—not where we were, the old patroller said.

I just wished I could see my mom and the snowshoer, I admitted to Em. "You know those two—they'll figure something out," Em told me. "Those two know how to make a plan and stick to it."

There was more evidence of stick-to-itiveness in the snowshoer's notebooks, not that we needed more evidence; Em and I stopped reading for the night when we came across Elliot's entry about the Rock Garden. "I can carry Ray out of the Rock Garden, if she can't make it," the snowshoer had written.

Near the top of Upper Twister was what Molly also called the Rock Garden, where the old patroller and I had noticed how the climbers' tracks changed. My mother must have had some trouble on the second steep part of Twister. Molly and I had seen only the snowshoer's tracks the rest of the way. Elliot Barlow had carried Little Ray piggyback to the top.

"Those two are always piggybacking each other everywhere," Matthew had said of their younger ghosts.

"That's just what those two do—they love each other," was all I could say to Matthew about their piggybacking.

I had almost everything I wanted, I was thinking. I had Matthew's love, and Em was seriously trying to live with me. I just wished I could see those two—I missed them, and their fooling around.

51

"O CANADA"

Mr. Barlow was right, as usual—the little English teacher had predicted that a book about *Two Dykes, One Who Talks* would appeal to the reading audience. Readers who'd never been to the comedy club had heard about the Gallows Lounge shooting. And before the Gallows went bankrupt—before the comedy club's holdings were taken and disposed of, for the benefit of creditors—Grace had the foresight to buy the film archives of Nora and Em's onstage performances. It was Grace who had the idea of licensing the rights to these crudely filmed performances to Em's foreign publishers.

Grace was right, too—the novel would be a breakout book for Emily MacPherson, a literary bestseller. *Come Hang Yourself* was translated into more than thirty languages; those cheaply made films of Nora and Em onstage were used for publicity purposes worldwide. The management at the Gallows had been born cheap, Nora said; the film archives of the onstage performances were barely better than home movies, shot by student interns. Em could remember when the management complained about the upgrade from the eight- to the sixteen-millimeter format—eight millimeter was the standard format for home movies, and the cheapest. All the footage was in black and white; the camera was handheld and the sound erratic. The management at the Gallows told the performers that their work was being filmed to preserve the history of their onstage artistry, or some such crap, but Nora said it sounded like a lawyer's idea. In case the comedy club got sued, there would be a crude record that the offense was the performer's fault—as no one knew better than Nora, who was always ad-libbing.

Until *Come Hang Yourself* was published, Em had never seen so much of herself onstage. Nora had viewed only one of their earliest performances at the Gallows—this was way back in 1973. "Amateurville," Nora labeled the cinematography. Nora and Em were thirty-eight. This was the skit about Em at the dinner party with Simone. Nora called Simone a slut, because Simone had sucked the sleeve of Em's blouse at a previous dinner party. This time,

Simone hooked pinky fingers with Em under the dinner table. Em stabbed Simone's arm with a salad fork.

In the film archives that Grace's New York office licensed to Em's foreign publishers, Grace had edited out the dinner-party conversation about *Bat Pussy*—the porn film that was a parody of porn films. Nora and Em—in their jeans and T-shirts, jock-walking around onstage—were sexy and tough in their lesbian-looking way. The cinematography was amateurish, but Em's pantomime and Nora's deadpan monologue about the blouse-sucking, pinky-hooking Simone was a record of a rare relationship. It was Nora and Em's relationship that readers of *Come Hang Yourself* would remember best. Those film clips—those glimpses of Nora and Em when they were hot—would break Em's heart all over again. And despite their clumsy camerawork, those student interns never neglected to get a shot of the hangman's noose above the bar and the COME HANG YOURSELF sign.

The first public readings or onstage interviews would be difficult for Em. They would screen a film clip from the Gallows to the audience before she came onstage. Where she was waiting, offstage, Em could often hear Nora's deadpan voice; sometimes, she could hear Nora clearly enough to know which pantomime she'd been performing. "I've had enough of the damn déjà vu, kiddo," Em would say to me. I was usually backstage with her. I went to Em's readings; I was her onstage interviewer when that was the format the venue chose.

A black-and-white still from the archive footage made an atmospheric book jacket for *Come Hang Yourself*. The hangman's noose is in focus in the foreground of the frame, but the empty barstools are out of focus, and the lights from the stage are a blur in the background. At the Gallows, there was usually no one at the bar when Nora and Em were onstage. I told Grace that the book jacket was a nice touch, but some of the women who came to Em's public readings or her onstage interviews were disturbing. They were younger women, for the most part in their thirties or forties. They were women who identified with Nora and Em. These women were deluded to think they could replace Nora, Em assured me, but the Nora look-alikes were scary, and the ones with a hangman's noose around their necks were worse. When *Come Hang Yourself* was published, Em was in her early sixties and I in my mid-fifties. These women who imagined they might substitute for Nora were younger than we were.

The New York book launch for *Come Hang Yourself* was in the Barnes & Noble with the escalators on East Seventeenth Street in Union Square. I loved that bookstore; I'd read there a few times. The authors' readings were on one of the upper floors. From where you faced the audience, you could see people riding up the escalator—as if someone in the seated crowd had imagined them. The divine souls on the escalator were looking right at you; they appeared to be ascending to heaven, leaving you behind. I was explaining this optical illusion to Grace, while the booksellers kept Em out of sight in a back room. I told Grace I wanted to forewarn Em about the "levitating apparitions" on the escalator.

"You and your *apparitions*," Grace said. I shouldn't have shown Grace my Aspen screenplay—both the *Loge Peak* beginning and the *Not a Ghost* ending. Either *Loge Peak* or *Not a Ghost* was a good title, but I knew no one would make the movie—no matter what I called it. It wasn't just too long. "The first-person voice-over is passé—*Jules et Jim* was third-person voice-over, you know. And *The Little Mermaid* is Disney—the rights to Jodi Benson's singing 'Part of Your World' would cost you a fortune," Grace told me.

I'd overlooked the expense of clips from "Part of Your World"—I'd been thinking how Toby Goode would feel, seeing his dead mom hum that song to a cowboy ghost. I didn't say this to Grace. I'd told her that I knew my Aspen screenplay would never be made. Eliminating my passé voice-over wouldn't fix it. To begin with, everyone would know who the Paul Goode and Clara Swift characters were, no matter what names I gave them. When I'd shown my Aspen screenplay to Em, she said: "Not only should Matthew never read this—he should never *know* this. The same goes for your half brother, Toby Goode," Em told me.

"I know," I said. Matthew was only six. I was thinking I didn't have to hide or destroy my Aspen screenplay, whatever I decided to call it—not just yet. Matthew wasn't reading screenplays.

At six, Matthew was fixated on Em's house in Toronto—he had no interest in unmade movies. "I wish I could *see* the house with the rooms that don't know what they are—the poor rooms!" Matthew kept saying. Em had succeeded in making Matthew interested in her mystery house before he'd seen it. There'd even been talk of a sightseeing trip to Toronto at the end of the school year. I was the one thinking about unmade movies.

"There are more unmade movies than anyone knows," my father had said, in the same way he had said I had my mother's hands: "Ray was always wringing her hands."

At the Union Square Barnes & Noble, with the audience for Em's book launch ascending on the escalator, I tried to change the subject with

Grace—the *apparitions* word wasn't a wise choice with her. "The way people just *appear* on that escalator—the first time you read here, it can be a little unnerving," I was saying, when a wild-eyed woman with a hangman's noose around her neck came up the escalator.

"I told you to talk Em out of that title," Grace said. I just watched the escalator. I knew the fangirls would keep coming, not only the Nora look-alikes but the women wearing the nooses. I tried to change the subject again, by asking Grace how she'd managed to edit out the *Bat Pussy* part. "One student intern deserves another," was the way Grace explained it. She said some film students at NYU had done the editing. Grace also instructed them to edit out the night of the Santas—when the tall Santa had shot Nora, after he'd taken aim at Em. Em would never forget that Trowbridge intended to kill her first; she didn't need to see it.

That night in Union Square, I slipped away from Grace, who was preoc-cupied with the film clip from the Gallows—she'd selected it, of course. The projectionist was already screening it for the early arrivals in the audience. This was how I got a glimpse of what Em's public appearances would be like. You could count on Em's fangirls to get there ahead of time. The Nora look-alikes and those women with the nooses wanted front-row seats.

In black and white, from more than twenty years ago, I was watching and hearing Nora ask Em where she'd been last night. More than twenty years later, Em still looked contrite and fearful. "You got home so late, I was asleep. You hit your head on my knee, getting into bed," Nora was saying—when I snuck off to the back room where the booksellers were hiding Em. I wanted to let Em know about the fangirls, but she'd had sufficient forewarning in her mail. Em said the hang-yourself women were new to her, but many of the Nora types who'd written Em had enclosed photos. These women—including a bunch of the early arrivals that night in Union Square—had managed to read *Come Hang Yourself* in galleys. Grace said she'd sent out an unprecedented number of advance galleys for this largely unknown author.

Not unknown for much longer, I was thinking, when Em and I were fac-ing those scary women in the front row. We were waiting for the audience to settle down, but the latecomers couldn't find a seat in the crowd. That was when I saw Emmanuelle, ascending to heaven on the escalator. "I saw her first," Em whispered to me, covering her microphone with her hand. I covered my mike accordingly, whispering to Em that Emmanuelle must have finished reading *Moby-Dick*. I whispered that her showing up at Em's reading, not one of mine, must mean that Emmanuelle was what Em called a *real reader.* "She definitely has staying power, kiddo," Em whispered back, still covering her mike with her hand.

Two of the hang-yourself women had been saving a seat for someone in the front row; their nooses were a forbidding deterrent in the chair between them. "No one wants to sit on a hangman's noose, or next to a woman wearing one," Em would tell me later. At the time, Em simply asked the hang-yourself women to put their nooses around their necks and give the empty seat to Emmanuelle. I'd beckoned to Emmanuelle to join us. She seemed mildly surprised to see me. On second thought, perhaps the only thing that surprised Emmanuelle was to see me with Em.

An attractive woman in her thirties, Emmanuelle was married with children. She'd meant to come with her husband, Emmanuelle told Em and me, but their babysitter got sick; it was only fair that her husband stayed home with the kids, because Emmanuelle had finished reading *Come Hang Yourself* and he hadn't. Em and I just nodded, but we couldn't look at each other—we were dying to ask Emmanuelle if she'd read the entire novel, in order. We were both thinking that Emmanuelle had turned out to be a book nerd—an Emily MacPherson reader, not a stalker. We'd not imagined that Emmanuelle might be ordinary, neither a Nora type nor a hang-yourself woman—not even, as the "Police Report" had cited, "an outrage to public decency."

It's hard to explain why it meant so much to Em and me, but Emmanuelle seemed to have turned out okay. I was relieved to see the *principled young woman* I'd once imagined her to be—before I learned she was a high school student who'd been charged for mooning and flashing her titties on the Swasey Parkway. Maybe Emmanuelle had just been bored to death, growing up in Exeter. "Nora hated growing up in Exeter," Em reminded me, after she'd met Emmanuelle. That night in Union Square, it was Emmanuelle's normality that meant the world to Em and me. Don't forget, Em and I were trying to imagine the rest of our lives together as being normal—or as normal as we could make it.

Em had stopped wearing Nora's SILENCE=DEATH T-shirt to bed. I took this as a positive sign. It was an oversize nightshirt on Em—her boobs were lost in the pink triangle. "Please put it with your T-shirts, but don't wear it unless I ask you to," Em said.

She'd also stopped singing "Goin' Back to Great Falls" in her sleep, another positive sign, and even Grace approved of Em's and my onstage routine for *Come Hang Yourself.* Em and I tried to have a conversation—one that would set up her reading.

"When I first met Emily MacPherson, she was my cousin Nora's girl-friend," I told the audience. "You were always Nora's girlfriend, and nobody else's," I said to Em. She'd written out the *nobody else's* part for me. Em wanted to make sure I started with that. The first few times I said it, I had some difficulty looking at those scary women who were always in the front row, but I would get used to them.

"I met Adam Brewster at his mom's wedding, when he was only fourteen—I don't think he'd started shaving," Em told the audience. "You didn't know how to dance with a girl—you just stared at my boobs," Em said to me.

"I think I was shaving once or twice a week," I told her, trying not to stare at her boobs.

"He still stares at my boobs, but I'm getting used to him," Em told the audience.

"Why did you want to be a writer—what made you start writing?" I asked her.

"When I stopped speaking, all the words didn't just disappear—I had to do something with them. The writing and the pantomime started together," Em said. She told a story about being a pantomime student—later, a panto-mime teacher—in what Em called "workshops" in Italy. Until I read *Come Hang Yourself*, I hadn't understood that these *workshops* were part of a festival for pantomimists in Barolo—where the wine comes from.

The Disastri Festival was short-lived. *Disastri* means *disasters* in Italian, Em explained. She said Barolo looked like an expensive town; the panto-mime festival was a financial *disastro*. "Maybe only pantomimists are inter-ested in pantomime," Em told the audience.

Em and I agreed that Disastri was an appropriate name for a pantomim-ists' festival, or for a writers' festival—both pantomime and fiction writing are good at disasters. "Especially the kind of disasters you can see coming—fiction writers and pantomimists have to know how to set up disasters," Em told the audience. That was my cue to ask her to read from *Come Hang Yourself*. I knew the excerpt Em was going to read.

I refrained from making a *Moby-Dick* joke. I didn't say, "Call her Ish-mael," or make a similarly smart-assed remark about Em's reading voice sounding like a sailor's on a doomed ship. I didn't think the Nora types in the audience—not to mention those women with the nooses—were likely to be Melville readers.

There were two chairs behind the two lecterns, also facing the audience and the escalator, reserved for Grace and me. While Em was reading from *Come Hang Yourself*, we kept an eye on the escalator, on the lookout for a woman with a noose—the one who was late. A front-row seat had been saved for her, but Emmanuelle was sitting there. Whoever the missing woman was, she never showed up. A woman wearing a hangman's noose could get in trouble around Union Square, I was thinking, while Em read the part about Nora's onstage monologue in Barolo being dubbed into Italian.

An Italian filmmaker—not an amateur—made a feature-length documentary about the Disastri Festival. The title of the film, *Disastri*, was both deadpan and tongue-in-cheek. The festival performers—mostly pantomimists, but including Nora—had signed releases. At a festival for pantomimists, most of the performers didn't speak onstage; there's no need to dub a pantomimist's performance. What made *Two Dykes, One Who Talks* a comedy act was the juxtaposition of Em's pantomime with Nora's monologue. It was also what made Em and Nora original at a pantomime festival. When Nora signed the release, she didn't know what a big deal dubbing is in Italy. Some of the same families have been in the dubbing business since the 1930s, and dubbing is an art form; they take pains to make the Italian translation match the lip movements of the onscreen speaker. I remembered watching *High Noon*, dubbed into German—a different movie on Austrian television. Gary Cooper's lips were out of sync with the German.

Em wrote that she'd never seen dubbing done better than the way Nora was dubbed into Italian, but Nora had hated it. Her lips were perfectly in sync with the Italian. The voice actor, who was a big deal in the dubbing world, sounded exactly like Nora. But Nora didn't like it because the voice actor was a guy. There was nothing homophobic intended—both the filmmaker and the voice actor were sincerely trying to match Nora's voice. "The dubbing wasn't dykey," Em had written. "He just sounded like Nora, if Nora spoke Italian."

Nora said she sounded like Anthony Quinn in Fellini's *La Strada*; Quinn played Zampanò, the circus strongman, who is cruel and abusive to Giulietta Masina. Until I read *Come Hang Yourself*, I hadn't known that onstage at the Disastri Festival, Nora and Em had reprised their Sturm und Drang about other girlfriends. When we were alone once, I'd innocently asked them if lesbians stayed friends with their former girlfriends. At the time, I didn't know that Em had never had a girlfriend before Nora. And Em seemed to shrug off the question—she just did a sexy little dance. Em's shrug and dance rubbed Nora the wrong way.

"What do you mean—*you don't know?*" Nora had asked Em (in Barolo, Anthony Quinn had asked Em in Italian). "If you left me, and I saw you with another girlfriend, I would tear off her tits and dance on her dead pudenda!" Nora told Em, who started to cry. Both in Barolo and when this was unrehearsed—when I was their only audience—Em kept doing her little dance, but she went on crying. "If I left Em, and she saw me with another girlfriend, Em would just cry," Nora had told me and the audience at the Disastri Festival, but I would remember how Em was dancing. It was not exactly a dance on anyone's dead pudenda; it was more tender and complicated than that.

Nora and Em didn't do their dead-pudenda dance at the Gallows; it wasn't funny enough for a comedy club. What Em read aloud to the audience, that night in Union Square, was that she never considered having another girlfriend. There'd been no one before Nora—there would be no one after her. The idea of *another girlfriend* always made Em cry. There was nothing evasive or ambiguous about her crying, or about her little dance— not to Em. That night at Barnes & Noble, the excerpt Em read wasn't only meant for those scary women in the front row; it was meant for me, too. I knew how the excerpt ended, of course—before I heard Em end it that night in Union Square. "It still makes me cry that Nora didn't know she was my one-and-only girlfriend, but Nora never believed me when I told her I would rather be with a penis than be with another girlfriend," Em read aloud. "It's pretty clear I'm not inclined to penises, isn't it?" was the way Em ended it.

There was a Q and A after the reading. I suppose it was inevitable that one of the Nora look-alikes or a woman in a hangman's noose would ask Em about me. "What is your relationship with Nora's little cousin?" a dead ringer for Nora asked Em that night in Union Square.

"It's pretty clear he's not a girlfriend, isn't it?" was the way Em always answered that question. She would be asked about me a lot.

"You're still stuck on me?" Em kept asking. "I'm just checking, kiddo—I would still rather be with a penis," she assured me.

Em would one day put what she meant about being with a penis another way. "Nora was my collision course—I'm done with collision courses, kiddo," she said.

That night in Union Square, after the Q and A, the booksellers set up two tables for the book signing. Grace sat with Em at the table where Em was signing copies of *Come Hang Yourself*. Grace gave herself the job of asking

Em's readers to write out their names so Em could spell them correctly, but I knew Grace was poised to intervene if one of the Nora types or hang-yourself women wanted Em to autograph her bra, or something.

Emmanuelle sat with me at my signing table. I was signing copies of my backlist titles, mostly paperbacks, for a smaller lineup of readers. It turned out that Emmanuelle and I were done before Em. That was when I asked Emmanuelle if she knew which chapter of *Moby-Dick* my grandmother was reading when she died. "When I found her, she'd closed the book on her thumb—her thumb was a bookmark," Emmanuelle said.

I should have known my grandmother had been reading "The Blacksmith," the gloomy Chapter 112, because Nana knew nothing as comforting on the subject of death as the line she loved in that dark chapter—that bit about "Death is only a launching into the region of the strange Untried." It was a line my grandmother had repeated when she was reading *Moby-Dick* to me—one she'd often asked Emmanuelle and me to read to her. It was the line Elliot Barlow had left for me in my writing notebook, before she trekked up Bromley Mountain to die with Little Ray.

Melancholy had always comforted my grandmother; I remembered how she'd left her door open, although this was frowned upon at River Bend. But I couldn't think of anything to say to Emmanuelle—a young wife and mother, who kept glancing at her wristwatch. She must have been thinking of her husband, at home with the kids. Emmanuelle wasn't thinking about death; she would have taken no comfort from that bit about "the region of the strange Untried." Emmanuelle, who had a life of her own, thought of other things; not everyone wants to think about death. And Em and I had our writing to think about, and—above all—there was Matthew to make happy, and to entertain.

When we took him to Toronto to see Em's mystery house, Matthew loved playing the game of imagining what the empty rooms were for. Em and I knew Matthew's nightmares about the upstairs family had been dispelled when he immediately said the long, narrow attic on the third floor should be his room—a boy after my own heart. I wondered if there was a gene for being drawn to attics.

Em's home was a tall, skinny, red-brick townhouse in a string of similar row houses. There was an attic window under the apex of the steeply pointed roof; in a side alley, I saw a fire escape from the third floor. It was a neighborhood of neat, traditional houses that were well maintained—even the trees were cared for. Shaftesbury was a short street that ran parallel to the train tracks. As Em had pointed out to Matthew and me, the Summerhill subway station was at one end of the street.

Matthew hadn't hesitated to choose the third floor for himself, but he soon changed his mind. There was no bathroom in the attic, and Matthew didn't like the look of the fire escape—an iron ladder. "Someone could climb the ladder and get in—a monkey could do it," Matthew said. Like many children his age, he'd seen *The Wizard of Oz* and had nightmares about the flying monkeys.

"There are no monkeys in Canada, and no flying monkeys anywhere," Em assured him, but Matthew had decided the third floor was off-limits for sleeping. So much for being drawn to attics. Before Matthew chose his bedroom, he wanted to know where Em and I would be sleeping. Thus Em and I were playing the game of imagining what the empty rooms were for. Matthew was in no hurry to determine the fate of the rooms in the house; prolonging the game was the fun of it. To divine the use of Em's bare rooms was an ongoing mystery, and Em had other plans for Matthew and me in Toronto.

When you're new to a city, the landmarks you latch on to may seem peculiar to the natives, but Em and I were hell-bent on keeping Matthew entertained. Em had done her Toronto tourism research for six-year-olds. The top attraction for Matthew was a Gothic Revival castle called Casa Loma. There were about a hundred rooms—copied from Austrian, English, Scottish, and Spanish castles. There were a couple of towers, scary passageways, secret panels. There was a stable made of mahogany and marble; Matthew didn't like the underground tunnel you took to the stable, but he loved everything else about Casa Loma. There were opulent chandeliers in the dining rooms and the ballrooms; there was a white pipe organ. Matthew wished Em's house had stained-glass windows. There were military uniforms, displayed under glass—Matthew wanted one of the uniforms. Matthew wanted the moose head he saw in the billiards room, too. Matthew wanted a canopy bed—a funny thing for a six-year-old to want, but Em explained Matthew's reasoning. The canopy was protection; the flying monkeys came from above.

It was our first trip to Toronto together, but I knew this was only the beginning. Em hadn't limited her research to six-year-olds. We stayed in a hotel in Yorkville; we could walk from there to Em's house, or we could take the subway two stops north to Em's street. Summerhill Station, on Yonge Street and Shaftesbury Avenue, was on the Yonge-University subway line. From Em's street, we could take the subway one stop north—then the St. Clair streetcar to Spadina. It was an easy walk to Casa Loma from St. Clair and Spadina; Em had also explored some interesting but longer walks to Casa Loma.

Matthew and I loved the subway in Toronto. (Matthew's mom was one of those New Yorkers who eschewed the subway.) One day, Em took us on the subway one stop south from Bloor-Yonge to Wellesley Station. She wanted us to walk around Wellesley and Church Streets—an LGBT neighborhood called the Gay Village, or just the Village. With every subway or streetcar we took, Em knew where to get on and when to get off. No walk was too far; with Em as our guide, we were never lost. "You've been busy here, not only with your mystery house," I told her. I saw shades of her nonspeaking days—the way Em nodded her head, like it was going to fall off, not saying a word.

In the coming years, getting to know Toronto, I grew tired of Casa Loma—until Matthew was old enough to be tired of it, too. Parents of younger children had to leave their strollers on the first floor. I used to look longingly at the left-behind strollers, wishing I could stay on the first floor with a book I was reading, pretending to guard the strollers. I felt some sympathy for Sir Henry Pellatt, the soldier and financier who had commissioned Casa Loma. Pellatt lost his dream house to the taxman—the way another soldier and financier, Jerome B. Wheeler, lost his hotel for back taxes. Those long-ago big spenders had an air of fascination about them. In spite of the lost hours in Casa Loma, Em made Toronto magical for Matthew and me.

Schools were in session in Toronto over American Thanksgiving; it was late November, 1997. For Matthew and me, this was our third time in Toronto that year. Canadian Thanksgiving was in early October, Em had explained. For Matthew and me, it was the first time we saw those girls in their uniforms from the Bishop Strachan School, where Em had gone when she was a little girl—Matthew's age, or a little younger.

Em remembered certain girls at Bishop Strachan, but she only dimly remembered herself as a little girl in a BSS uniform. When Em and Matthew and I arrived to see the school, it was the time of the afternoon when the day girls were going home; the little ones were leaving with a parent or a nanny, the big ones on their own. Matthew was mesmerized by these girls of all sizes, wearing identical clothes. Their short pleated skirts and their knee-highs were gray; they wore burgundy blazers or sweaters, matching the burgundy stripe on the sailor collar of their white middy blouses. The girls' neckties had regimental stripes of gray and burgundy. Matthew stared at all the girls, but Em was fixated on the little girls; she still hoped to remember herself as one of them.

Matthew really liked the uniforms; he was attracted to the uniformed girls, but intimidated by the big ones. Most boys would be. For Matthew and me, our third time in Toronto marked the first time Em's house was sufficiently furnished for the three of us to stay there. The furniture was sparse, but the designation of the rooms was to Matthew's liking—so far. Em gave Matthew a grown-up bedroom with his own bathroom on the second floor; the king-size bed served to compensate Matthew for the lack of a canopy. It was a big bed for a little boy, but Em assured Matthew it would always be his bedroom; when he was "all grown up," she told him, perhaps all the rooms on the second floor would be his. I could see it was strange for Matthew to imagine himself *all grown up*. Those big girls in their school uniforms were the clearest images of *all grown up* in Matthew's mind. Em was just thinking like a fiction writer; she knew how to construct a plot, even for her house.

For now, Em chose the kitchen on the second floor for her workspace. She used the kitchen table for her writing desk; in a desk chair, with casters, she could cruise the length of the table. She kept cold drinks in the fridge; she had a coffeemaker and boiled water for tea on the stove. "When your father and I are too old to climb stairs, this can be your kitchen—if you end up living in Canada," Em told Matthew. "I'll find a room to write in downstairs."

My writing room and our bedroom were on the ground floor. When Matthew woke up in the morning, Em and I could hear him coming down the stairs to our bedroom. Our first time sleeping in the house on Shaftesbury Avenue, Matthew and I loved lying in bed and listening to the trains; we weren't thinking about my being too old to climb stairs, or when Matthew would be old enough to decide for himself to try living in Canada. Em was the one who was good at imagining the future. In every family, even in a makeshift family, someone should be good at foreseeing the future.

Not only as a writer, I felt more at home in the past—the longer ago it was, the more sure I was about it. Em was a fiction writer who had done stand-up; she was good at reacting to the present. We can all see hatred when we're confronted with it, when it's in our faces, but Em was good at seeing what was coming; she could see the hatred and the backlash ahead. Em saw Ronald Reagan coming—at a time when no one was worried about Reagan, not even Nora.

The past has a certain finality; the past isn't subject to change. Em had decided that the house she'd restored on Shaftesbury Avenue would be her last house, even before she'd moved in. She was blunt about it, from the beginning. "Listen, kiddo," Em said. "When you start sleeping somewhere you know will be the last place you'll get to make your home, that's when the future has a certain finality, too."

"Okay," I said. Not only politically, I would always be Nora's little cousin. Nora and Em went somewhere first; I got there later.

The fourth time Matthew and I were in Toronto that year, it was the week between Christmas and New Year's—the first time we were riding on the subway by ourselves. There was no school that week in Toronto; Matthew was disappointed not to see girls in BSS uniforms. On the subway, we would look at various girls and try to imagine them in those school uniforms. "Not her," Matthew was the first to say.

Em was too busy playing house to play with us. There were furniture sales that week, Em told us. Matthew and I were exploring on our own. We took the subway to St. Patrick Station and found our way to Kensington Market; we took the subway back to Summerhill Station from Queen's Park. It was our tentative way of seeing the city. When Matthew and I were getting to know Toronto, the subway was our new best friend. We took the subway to Osgoode Station and walked around Queen Street West. We took the subway to St. Andrew Station and saw some big theaters on King Street West.

It was when we were taking the subway back to Summerhill from St. Andrew that we saw *those two*. They were horsing around, as usual, in the car next to ours, but they were headed our way. We'd just left Rosedale Station, where I thought they probably piggybacked onto the train, but Matthew said I was wrong—those two had been with us the whole way.

"They were fooling around in the station at St. *Somebody*," Matthew said.

"At St. Andrew?" I asked him.

"That's where those two piggybacked onto the train," Matthew told me. The next station was Summerhill. Those two had piggybacked into our car, just before the subway stopped. They were out the door ahead of Matthew and me, racing each other up the long flight of stairs in Summerhill Station—the snowshoer waving to us, my mom blowing us kisses. Then they were gone again. "All those two do is fool around—they just goof off," Matthew said, both fondly and with exasperation. I couldn't speak. I was so happy to see them.

"Where they are isn't a place, Kid," Molly had told me.

"You should listen to Molly, kiddo," Em said, when I told her I'd seen them on the subway. "Those two must be happy to see you—maybe they were waiting for you to be where you belong," Em told me.

"I belong with you," I told her. I was remembering what the former maid of honor told me on my mother's wedding night.

"There's more than one way to love people, Kid," Molly had said.

As I lay in bed with Em—hearing the train go by, listening for Matthew's footsteps on the stairs—Em was describing the book tours we would take together. We were both good at writing in hotels, Em said. She would go with me on my book tours; she would get a lot of writing done. I would go with her on her book tours. Em was most interested in the translation trips to Europe. We had many of the same European publishers; we were represented by the same international literary agency, in London. When Matthew was still little, we would take a babysitter on our translation trips, Em was saying. Later, when he was older, Matthew might want to bring a girlfriend with him—"or maybe a boyfriend," Em whispered, because we could hear Matthew coming down the stairs to climb into bed with us.

For a moment—imagining our future together, dreaming about the years ahead—I'd forgotten that Matthew was only six. There would come a time, I was thinking, when I'd be lying in bed with Em, waiting for a six-year-old to climb into bed with us, but Matthew would be sleeping upstairs with a girlfriend—or maybe a boyfriend—or Matthew wouldn't be sleeping upstairs.

Some days, when I'm lying in bed with Em, I'm in the singles' line for the Loge Peak chairlift—about to be paired up with Clara Swift again. Some days, I'm seeing that tall hippie girl; she's still kicking a chunk of frozen snow in circles on the sidewalk in front of the Jerome. She's disinclined to show me her breasts; she just gives me the finger, again and again. How many times do I have to say it? Unrevised, real life is just a mess.

I keep saying it and saying it. They publish your novel, they make your screenplay—these books and movies go away. You take your bad reviews with the good ones, or you win an Oscar; whatever happens, it doesn't stay. But an unmade movie never leaves you; an unmade movie doesn't go away.

One of my novel-to-film adaptations, the one with the fourth director, finally moved forward; it had taken fourteen years. So one of my unmade movies went away. In 1998, we shot the film in New England. We showed it at a couple of film festivals in Europe—at Venice, and at Deauville. Toronto was the last festival where we screened it, before we opened in theaters in late 1999. In 2000, I lost at the Golden Globe Awards, but I won an Oscar. Em went with me to the Golden Globes. Em was so upset that I didn't win, she refused to go with me to the Oscars. "Fuck the Hollywood Foreign Press!" Em said. This was all because of one journalist from the Hollywood Foreign Press who spoke to Em in the women's room. She mistook Em for an actress who had once been famous. Em wouldn't tell me who the has-been film star was. "An old bag," was all Em said. I knew the entire Hollywood Foreign Press would be blamed. "I'm a jinx—I jinxed you," Em said. "Take Molly to the Oscars—she'll bring you better luck," Em told me.

Molly had her doubts about going to Los Angeles in the ski season. It was late March, 2000. Molly was almost eighty. The old patroller was still working—albeit part-time, and mostly as a ski instructor. Molly and I were thinking that my mother was the one who should be going to the Oscars with me; we knew my mom had been the one who believed everyone looked like someone in the movies.

"I don't see a lot of movies, Kid—and by the way, I don't have the right clothes for the Oscars," Molly said.

Em tried to explain that Armani was dressing me for the Oscars. "Armani will dress you, too," Em told Molly.

"Nobody's dressing me—I can still get my ski boots on and off, by myself," the old patroller said. Armani would need more explaining.

We had a three-bedroom suite at the Four Seasons in Beverly Hills. Molly and I flew to L.A. with Em and Matthew. He had just turned nine. Molly and I had given our measurements to Armani beforehand. We'd just checked into the hotel, when the three tailors from Armani came to our suite with Molly's dress and my tuxedo. "We're here for the fitting!" one of the tailors told Em, who'd heard the doorbell and let them in.

"Nobody's fitting me," the old ski patroller told the tailors.

"We do adjusting on the spot!" one of the tailors told Molly.

"Nobody's adjusting me," Molly told the tailor.

Nothing went wrong with our clothes at the Oscars, which were at the Shrine Auditorium that year—maybe the last year the Academy Awards were there; I can't remember. I just remember being on the red carpet with Molly. I saw Paige what's-her-name coming our way, with a cameraman in tow. "This woman is a ditz," I warned Molly. In the press release, I'd said I was bringing my mother's best friend to the Academy Awards. Molly hadn't liked the sound of that.

"Best friend sounds like *old girlfriend* to me, Kid—it's nobody's business to go there," the old patroller had said. "And I'm not your *stepmother*—everyone thinks stepmothers are evil," Molly said. Paige what's-her-name was such a moron, I was hoping she wouldn't remember Molly was my mom's best friend—if Paige had even read the press release.

"You brought your mother's best friend—more of the nominees should do that!" Paige what's-her-name exclaimed. "Is that a writer's thing?" Paige asked me, or maybe she asked Molly. It was hard to tell if Paige was speaking to you, because her eyes always roamed around—looking for someone more important to talk to.

"I'm more like his second mom," the old patroller told the idiot.

"His second mom!" Paige cried. She was one of those interviewers who breathlessly repeated what you said when she didn't know what else to say.

"I'm not a writer's *thing*," Molly told Paige, but Paige had spotted a movie star on the red carpet; Hollywood's what's-her-name and her cameraman were moving on. Paige knew people didn't watch the Academy Awards to see the *writers*. "If I had to spend more time around that woman, I might break her femur—or her tibia, or something," the old ski patroller said.

Molly and I were sitting in the sixth row of the front orchestra. All the nominees had aisle seats—so we didn't have to climb over people, or push past their knees, if we won. Molly and I looked closely at the older actresses who had once been famous, but we didn't see one who resembled Em. "There's no old bag who looks like Em, because Em isn't an old bag and she doesn't look like anybody else," Molly told me.

"Fuck the Hollywood Foreign Press!" I said, knowing this was what Em would say.

At the after-parties, Molly and I took turns carrying Oscar around, holding his lower legs. That was when the penis jokes started. I'd read that Oscar was supposed to be a knight, holding a sword. "Oscar looks like a naked gold man, holding his imaginary penis—he's holding what he *wishes* was his penis, Kid," Molly said.

We thought the Oscar statuette might have been modeled on a penis. I'd read that the Oscar weighed eight or nine pounds, and it was thirteen or fourteen inches tall. "A big penis," I told Molly.

"The statuette looks like a big dick to me—not that I would know, Kid," the old patroller said. We couldn't wait to hear what Em thought about the Oscar—not that Em knew a lot about penises, comparatively.

There was a predawn light in the sky when our limo drove us back to Beverly Hills. We knew Em and Matthew had watched the Oscars in our suite; they'd called room service and had their dinner in front of the TV. There was a chocolate Oscar on the TV console. Someone had eaten Oscar's head. Molly and I guessed that the Four Seasons gave chocolate Oscars to the hotel guests with children. Even with a head, the chocolate Oscar had been only five or six inches tall. I didn't doubt that Matthew must have eaten the head. "If you'd lost, Kid, Em would have bitten off Oscar's ass, or something," Molly said. I didn't doubt this, either.

I went to bed, careful not to wake Em. Matthew woke us in the morning, when we heard him asking Molly where the Oscar was—the real one. "It's by the TV, next to the chocolate one," Em and I heard Molly respond.

I don't remember how old Matthew was when he stopped climbing into bed with Em and me in the morning. Maybe seven? I just remember how much I missed it when he stopped. "Oscar doesn't have any clothes on," Em and I heard Matthew say in the living room.

"Tell me about it," the old patroller said.

"Bring me Oscar—I want to see him!" Em called to Matthew.

We were in bed when Matthew brought Oscar to us. "He's really heavy, and I have to pee, but I'll be back for him," Matthew told us. Em was looking over Oscar, very closely. We could hear Matthew peeing in the bathroom, because he'd left the door open. I don't remember how old Matthew was when he learned to close the door. "Oscar has a cute ass, but his head looks like a penis," Em whispered to me. The likeness to a penis was inescapable.

The rest of our time in L.A., and on our flight back east, Matthew was the one who carried Oscar everywhere—in a white athletic sock. "The cock in a sock," Em called it—just not around Matthew. It was one of Molly's athletic socks; the sock was long enough, but it wasn't wide enough to fit around the base of the pedestal.

A little more than a month after I won an Academy Award, Cardinal John O'Connor died in the archbishop's residence in New York. He would be interred in the crypt beneath the main altar of St. Patrick's. A bunch of political bigwigs—from both sides of the aisle, as they're always saying—showed up for the funeral on a hot and humid afternoon in May. Em was up early that Monday morning, rummaging around in my T-shirt drawer in the East Sixty-fourth Street apartment. "Holy crap," I heard her saying to herself, or to no one in particular. I could only faintly hear what sounded like a news channel, on the TV in the kitchen. There must have been something on TV about the cardinal's funeral, because Em was riled up about the dignitaries attending O'Connor's service in St. Patrick's. Em was stomping around, naked, before she put on Nora's SILENCE=DEATH T-shirt. "Don't wear it unless I ask you to," Em had said when she'd told me to put it with my T-shirts.

"What's going on—what's wrong?" I asked her.

"Fuck the Democrats who go to O'Connor's funeral!" Em was raving.

It made sense to Em that Republican politicians would attend Cardinal O'Connor's funeral, and they would be there, in St. Patrick's—former president George H. W. Bush, Texas governor George W. Bush, New York governor George Pataki, and New York City mayor Rudolph Giuliani. Of course they showed up, but what were the *Democrats* doing there? Em kept asking. Em was incensed at President Bill Clinton and First Lady Hillary Clinton. The Clintons supported abortion rights and gay rights. Why did they go? Em was asking. I hoped she would put on a few more clothes, if she was planning to go to St. Patrick's. I didn't understand why Em was removing the shirt cardboards from my dress shirts back from the dry cleaner's.

And why would Vice President Al Gore and his wife, Tipper, go? Em was asking. Or two former New York City mayors, Ed Koch and David Dinkins, both Democrats? Cardinal O'Connor had opposed legislation prohibiting discrimination based on sexual orientation—legislation supported by the *three* mayors at the cardinal's funeral, including Mayor Giuliani. "I get why Giuliani is going—he's a Catholic *and* he's a *Republican*!" Em wailed. I realized what Em intended to do with the shirt cardboards she'd put on the kitchen table. With a black Sharpie, Em was making protest signs.

GOOD RIDDANCE

That sign would suffice, I was thinking. I imagined Em in Nora's SILENCE=DEATH T-shirt, carrying the GOOD RIDDANCE sign among the thousands of mourners lined up behind the police barricades on Fifth Avenue—listening to the service on the loudspeakers, while the invited dignitaries paying their respects to Cardinal O'Connor were inside the cathedral.

FUCK THE DEMOCRATS

This sign was unwise. With the political bigwigs expected in St. Patrick's, there would be an army of Secret Service agents around—and all the cops. *Stick to* GOOD RIDDANCE, I was thinking—in the context of O'Connor's funeral, the GOOD RIDDANCE message was the only one that made sense. "I wish you wouldn't do this," I was saying to Em, when Grace called to tell me I should keep Em away from St. Patrick's—or I should go to the cathedral with Em, if I couldn't keep her away. "That's my plan," I told Grace, hanging up the phone.

I was fed up with Grace's interfering in our lives, but you shouldn't complain if your ex-wife is on your side, and even Em agreed that Grace's interference with the Oscar in our lives had been a good idea. As a means of toting Oscar around, Grace had replaced Molly's athletic sock with a drawstring dust bag for shoes. Typical of Grace, it was not just any shoe bag; it was a Manolo Blahnik bag, for a pair of high-end heels.

"Cold water, air-dry, and it won't shrink," Grace said—her washing instructions for the designer shoe bag.

Molly was relieved Matthew wasn't carrying Oscar in her sock. "The sock can slip off, Kid—if Matthew drops the big dick on his foot, it'll break a toe, or something," the old patroller said.

Matthew thought the shoe bag was a better idea than the sock. All of Oscar fit in the Manolo Blahnik bag, even the pedestal; it was much easier for Matthew to take the naked gold man everywhere. When Matthew was staying with his mother—or with Molly, or with Em and me—the Oscar stayed with Matthew. He'd been asked to bring the Oscar to his school, so that all the kids could see an actual Oscar. Matthew might have wished that Manolo Blahnik's name was not so prominent on the shoe bag. A smart-assed kid in Matthew's class had teased him. "That's not an Oscar—his name is *Manolo*. You just have a stupid *Manolo*," the kid teased Matthew.

When Matthew was alone, he played with Oscar—as if the naked gold man were an immovable kind of action figure. Oscar wasn't a posable soldier or superhero—Oscar had no jointed limbs—but what mattered most to Matthew was that Oscar had no uncertainty about his name. "Your name is *Oscar*," Em and I heard Matthew tell the statuette. There was no mention of *Manolo*.

As for Em's protest plans at St. Patrick's, I not only said I would go with her—I volunteered to carry the more inflammatory of the protest signs. If I was the one holding FUCK THE DEMOCRATS, maybe the cops or the Secret Service would arrest me first. Maybe a woman in a SILENCE=DEATH T-shirt—even if she'd brought a GOOD RIDDANCE sign to Cardinal O'Connor's funeral—would be perceived as less of a threat to our fragile democracy. And while Em was putting on her shorts and her running shoes, I reread to her the snowshoer's repetitious notebook entries on the subject of the First Amendment—knowing Em was as sick of hearing about the First Amendment as I was.

I recited the clause Mr. Barlow had loved best: "'Congress shall make no law respecting an establishment of religion' "—that was the clause the Catholic Church ignored. The First Amendment's protection of "the free exercise" of religion was not in jeopardy, the snowshoer always said. Our freedom *of* religion was assured. What was at risk, in America, was our freedom *from* religion, I was saying—when Em kicked off her running shoes, which I had just watched her put on.

"I *know*," Em said. I wanted to spare her the pointlessness of her protesting at St. Patrick's, and she knew it. I followed her into the bedroom, where she took off and kicked away her shorts. Before she got in bed, she took off Nora's T-shirt. She didn't have to tell me to put it back in the drawer. "I've had enough of the damn déjà vu, kiddo," Em was saying.

"I know," I said, sitting beside her on the bed. "I'm still stuck on you, you know," I told Em.

"And I'm still of the opinion that I would rather be with a penis—with *your* penis, anyway," Em replied. "It's a good thing you don't have an *Oscar*, if you know what I mean," she added.

"I know what you mean," I said, holding her hand.

When Em fell asleep, I went into the kitchen and decided what to do with the protest signs. I would regret getting rid of FUCK THE DEMOCRATS. Our fellow Democrats would do something to disappoint us again. I had sufficient common sense to keep the GOOD RIDDANCE sign, although I put it on a high shelf—above one of the kitchen cabinets, where Em would need a stepladder to reach it. *Maybe that'll make her think twice about it*, I was thinking. But I didn't doubt that someone would surely die—someone who had it coming. I didn't doubt that Em would find another deserving candidate for the GOOD RIDDANCE sign.

Along with my not having an Oscar for a penis, it was another good thing that Em was depressed for a few days following the funeral. She wouldn't watch TV; she didn't read the newspapers. By the time Em heard the news about Cardinal Bernard Law, she was over her inclination to protest. Cardinal Law was the archbishop of Boston; he delivered the homily at O'Connor's funeral. To be fair, many of the mourners in St. Patrick's didn't know how bad Cardinal Bernard Law would turn out to be. Law got a standing ovation for praising O'Connor's "constant reminder that the church must always be unambiguously pro-life." The TV cameras in the cathedral had focused on the Clintons and the Gores, who at first remained seated. They eventually stood, reluctantly—or so it was reported. In more than one account I read, the Clintons had refrained from applause, but I was worried Em would have a shit fit because our fellow Democrats had not stayed sitting down. Yet there were no cries to bring back the FUCK THE DEMOCRATS sign—not then.

It would be a couple of years before the scandal of child molestation by Catholic priests implicated the archbishop of Boston. For years, Cardinal Bernard Law had transferred abusive priests to other parishes; he never told the parishioners or informed the police. He'd protected the priests, not their victims. Cardinal Law was vilified in Boston. At the end of 2002, the discredited archbishop flew to Rome, where the pope accepted his resignation. In 2003, Cardinal Law was taken to task by the Massachusetts attorney general. Over sixty years, a thousand children had been abused by more than two hundred priests in the Boston archdiocese. Cardinal Law had known about it; the former archbishop of Boston had suppressed any publicity about it.

The Vatican did more for Cardinal Law than kick him upstairs. In 2004, Cardinal Bernard Law would be appointed as high priest of the Basilica of St. Mary Major—one of Rome's most prestigious churches. Law would serve on the Vatican committee in charge of advising the pope on the assignments of bishops, notwithstanding that the former archbishop of Boston had been disgraced for covering up the child abuse of priests. His disgrace didn't matter to the Vatican, where Cardinal Law was rewarded for his staunch defense of church orthodoxy.

What would Nora have said? "Holy crap," was all Em said about it. *Holy crap*, I thought.

By 2004, Em and I were spending more time in Toronto—we were learning to be more like Canadians. Or we were learning to let go of the things we couldn't change; we just did our best with those things we could do something about. At least this was what Em said we were doing. It did seem to me that we were *trying* to be more like Canadians, because we both liked Canada—and we liked being in Toronto—but it also seemed to me that Em and I were demonstrating we were the little English teacher's students. Mr. Barlow had been more than our copy editor. As writers, Em and I were the snowshoer's disciples. More and more, the writing was the only thing that mattered—besides Matthew.

When you get older, you find out how good (or not) your teachers were. Elliot Barlow had taught Em and me to care about the writing, not only about *our* writing. Melville had listened to Schiller: "Keep true to the dreams of thy youth" was good advice for a writer. As fiction writers, Em and I had our own gods to listen to, but the snowshoer gave us a manageable rule: what applies to fiction is relevant to other writing. You have to be truthful to time and place; you can't leave out anything important. Lies of omission count as lies, right?

In June 2004, Em and I knew Ronald Reagan had died—it was a while before we got around to reading his obituary in *The New York Times*. Em and I were in no hurry to read about him. Reagan had been secluded from the public since 1994, when it was learned he had Alzheimer's. His death didn't mean much to Em and me; we'd never liked him. By the time Reagan died, he was long dead and gone to us. We'd hated him enough when he was president. We didn't run to get the stepladder when we heard he died. The GOOD RIDDANCE sign stayed put, but there was no forgiving Reagan's willful silence about the AIDS epidemic. "Government is not the solution to our problem; government is the problem," he'd said. How easily he abdicated his responsibility.

Reagan's aw-shucks, nice-guy demeanor had belied his moral absenteeism. A lot of Americans didn't care about the gay men who died of AIDS. Like Ronald Reagan, those Americans who didn't care about those gay men already seemed dead to Em and me.

Reagan's obituary in *The New York Times* made Em miss the Gallows Lounge; she said his death deserved a political comedy club. The obit was laden with Reagan's backstory; Em and I took turns reading it aloud to each other. Em began, but she got bogged down in Reagan's radio career. It made Em cry to imagine we might have had a president who cared about the AIDS victims, if Reagan had *stayed* in the broadcasting business. It was my turn to read, Em said. She'd gagged on a phrase in one of the opening paragraphs—a line about Reagan's promising America "a return to greatness." Nora said Americans were obsessed with their own greatness. Many American politicians ended their speeches by telling us how great we were—the ideologues always assured us we could be great again.

I read aloud for a long time; it seemed to me I was reading forever, but I only got as far as the Republican National Convention in Detroit, where Reagan was first nominated for president. I told Em it was her turn to read when she was swearing over Reagan's acceptance speech. It was 1980, when Reagan exhorted us to "recapture our destiny." Nora would have said that *destiny* was just a bullshit synonym for *greatness*. At that point, we weren't even halfway through the undying obit. Em was getting angry, all over again; she was shouting her way through Reagan's opposition to government financing of abortions for poor women, and his pushing for a constitutional amendment to prohibit abortion. There was more heavy breathing when Em read about Reagan's call for "a return of God to the classroom"—this meant bringing back prayer in schools. And Reagan was against limitations on buying and owning guns. As tedious as it was to read Reagan's obituary, Em and I were reminded of the reasons we'd disliked him; we thought the *Times* had left no stone unturned. The four short paragraphs about the botched assassination attempt were enough; after all, not much had come of it. We tolerated how much there was about "Reaganomics," considering it was just another name for the standard Republican policy of lowering taxes on the rich. Em didn't make it past the start of President Reagan's second term, when the Gipper said the nation was "poised for greatness." I knew Em—she'd had it with America's *greatness*. I knew I would be the reader for all the rest. I was dreading the Iran-Contra scandal, and the back and forth with Gorbachev; I had to get through Reagan's speech at the Brandenburg Gate, the Berlin Wall business. Em made more coffee and tea; we needed caffeine to make it to the end of the obit.

There was spontaneous cheering only once, when I read what Tip O'Neill said about Reagan—"he was an actor reading lines," the former Speaker of the House had said. O'Neill was a Democrat from Massachusetts. Tip O'Neill also said "it was sinful that Ronald Reagan ever became president"— prompting a moment of sadness between Em and me, because Tip O'Neill had died a decade before.

Near the end of Reagan's obituary, *The New York Times* quoted a college professor who said "the Reagan presidency was lacking in moral leadership, an essential quality for greatness." The obit ended strangely. Reagan just talked about himself; a journalist had asked him how he thought history would remember him, an uninspired question.

"That's it—that's all there is?" Em asked me.

"That's it," I said.

"What about AIDS—did you skip the AIDS part?" Em asked. I'd skipped nothing; maybe Em had missed the AIDS part, when it was her turn to read. We'd blown most of the morning, reading the ceaseless minutiae of that obituary to each other; now we had to reread the whole thing. "How could we have missed the AIDS part?" Em kept asking me. But we hadn't missed it. For those of us who knew the writing mattered, *The New York Times* had left out the AIDS part. There was no mention of it in Reagan's obit.

"Holy crap," I could hear Em saying. She was in the bedroom, rummaging around—more shirt cardboards were coming. The GOOD RIDDANCE sign would stay put—GOOD RIDDANCE wasn't good enough. This was a *writing* matter.

"I don't give a shit that the Gipper is gone! Do you?" Em was screaming in the bedroom. I just guessed this meant the writing was the only thing that mattered.

I thought Em's first protest sign missed the mark; out of context, it might have been misunderstood.

WHAT ABOUT AIDS,
YOU ASSHOLES?

In Times Square, if we were carrying that sign on the sidewalk, no one would know which assholes we meant. You may remember that *The New York Times* used to be in an eighteen-story, neo-Gothic building on West Forty-third Street—dark and gloomy.

FUCK ALL THE NEWS
THAT'S FIT TO PRINT

Well, okay—that one was more clear. But I didn't see us getting that one past the revolving glass doors at 229 West Forty-third Street—that one was strictly a sidewalk sign. I went into the bedroom to put on my running shoes. I was feeling fatalistic about protesting. Either the writing mattered or it didn't. You have to be truthful to time and place; you can't leave out anything important. *Lies of omission count as lies,* I was thinking, when I heard Em tearing up the shirt cardboards in the kitchen. "Holy crap," she was saying softly—just in resignation. "More damn déjà vu, kiddo," she said sadly, when I found her at the kitchen table with her head on her arms. The pointlessness of our protesting *The New York Times* in Times Square was apparent. It's not easy to hold lies of omission accountable.

That was when Em started singing in her sleep again—only humming, at first, just the tune. I didn't recognize "O Canada"; I just knew it wasn't "Goin' Back to Great Falls." The lyrics would come later. When Em was just humming in her sleep, I didn't realize she was still learning the lyrics. I didn't know the significance of the song.

52.

THE LESBIANS' CHILDREN

In 2004, when Ronald Reagan died at ninety-three, Molly would have been eighty-three or eighty-four. Working part-time, mostly as a ski instructor, had not served to broaden the old patroller's interests. More than ever, with my mom gone, Molly's whole world was Bromley Mountain. At Bromley, the Sun Mountain Express Quad had replaced the old Number One chairlift in 1997, but Molly still called the new lift "Number One."

I tried to explain to the old patroller that this wasn't the same as what Em and I meant by the damn déjà vu we found so depressing, politically speaking.

"It sounds the same to me, Kid," Molly said. "The new lift takes you to the same old place. It's the same trip, just a faster ride—it's no more or less depressing than it ever was," she added.

I was confused by Molly's response to my telling her how the obituary in *The New York Times* let Reagan off the hook for AIDS. The old patroller just didn't get it. Em said it could be challenging to talk about a political matter with Molly—not to mention a *writing* matter.

Since she'd learned the lyrics, it was clear Em was singing the Canadian national anthem in her sleep. I don't know why I didn't recognize the tune. About the only things I'd watched on TV in Toronto were hockey and base-ball games, but I wasn't familiar with "O Canada" when I was in bed—with Em's arm, or her leg, thrown over me—as I heard her sing:

O Canada! Our home and native land!
True patriot love in all of us command.

I got the feeling Em wasn't actually asleep when she was singing; the grinding of her hips against me was not meant in a patriotic way. I was the one who was asleep. Em was singing *to me* in my sleep.

With glowing hearts we see thee rise,
The True North strong and free!

From far and wide,
O Canada, we stand on guard for thee.

It's strange how the subliminal effects of my hearing "O Canada" in my sleep were coincident with more meddling on Grace's part—she'd decided Em and I should be married, for Matthew's sake. Em and I were pretty sure it didn't matter to Matthew whether we were married or not.

"It's for *your* sake that we should be married, kiddo," was all Em said about it, at first. This would become clear. The singing of the Canadian national anthem was intended to indoctrinate me. In her own way, Em was an old-fashioned fiction writer—a plot-driven storyteller. My becoming a Canadian citizen was part of the plot.

Em would shepherd me through the immigration process. She knew the steps I had to take, en route to my applying for Canadian citizenship. My first step was to marry her, Em said. Em was already a Canadian citizen; she had a Canadian passport. If we were married, Em could sponsor my immigrating to her country of birth. Like me, Em would have to go through the business of becoming a permanent resident of Canada.

I don't remember the rules and regulations, because Em kept track of them for me. I would have what was called a "record of landing"; Em kept this and my "record of travel" for me. I think there was something about my living in Canada, and filing taxes in Canada—for three of the next five years—but Em would remember this for me. When you have someone to guide you in a foreign country, you're not responsible for the details. I just knew my moving to Canada began with my marrying Em.

"We have to be married before you can start immigrating, kiddo," was the way Em put it.

"Okay," I said. We doubted the zither man was alive. Given how Em and I had met, and the surrounding events of my mother's wedding, how could Em and I get married without an Austrian zither-meister? Em imagined the old Austrian with kids and grandkids, only because she remembered his name for me. *Son of the Bride*, the edelweiss man had called me. Em searched the phone books for Manhattan and Brooklyn. There were businesses beginning with *Son of*, and *Daughter of*, but no musicians—not a *Son of Zither Man* or a *Daughter of Zither-Meister*, as Em imagined. We searched together for "The Third Man Theme" or "The Harry Lime Theme," and for just plain zither players. There was no one.

"You can find anyone you're looking for in New York, Adam," Uncle Martin once told me. Em had an idea.

"How do you say *The Third Man* in German?" Em asked me.

"*Der dritte Mann*, and Anything Else on a Zither." This was what Em found in the Brooklyn phone book—this was what an unnamed zither player was promising. Even Elvis?

There was no trace of an Austrian accent in the recorded message Em and I listened to; the voice on the zither player's answering machine was all Brooklyn. He sounded like an emotionally disturbed high school student, the kind of kid who eventually commits a violent crime—he shoots his teacher, or all the girls in his class.

"I do private parties, but nothin' religious. I'll do a weddin'—the more secula, the betta," the zither kid began. "I gotta big repertoire, for a zitha—no band, just a zitha. If you don't know what a zitha is, you betta call somebody else," the zither kid concluded. In the background, we could hear "The Harry Lime Theme"—the familiar strings, plucking away. I will hear this song forever, whether that's a good thing or not. Em and I couldn't speak. The Brooklyn boy's vernacular was unexpected, but the emotional wallop of "The Third Man Theme" surprised us more.

The boy in Brooklyn would turn out to be the grandson of the old Austrian zither-meister. When Em and I had recovered sufficiently to meet him, he told us his grandfather never stopped talking about a wedding in New Hampshire, where an old man in diapers was killed by lightning. "My grandfather—it was my mom's wedding," I told the zither kid. We met the boy in a coffeehouse of his choice on the Lower East Side; the walls were covered with black-and-white photographs of the Brooklyn Bridge. The kid brought his zither, though we never said we were auditioning him.

"*Son of the Bride*," the zither grandkid said, almost reverentially. "I hear there was orgasms goin' on—long-lastin' ones, all weekend," the zither man's grandson told us, in hushed tones. "My grandfather neva got ova the orgasm girl."

That makes two of us, I thought of telling the kid, but not with Em there. Em and I hadn't delved into the details of my overhearing her orgasms. Knowing Nora, she would have said something to Em—on the subject of Em's orgasms having a life-changing effect on me—but Em and I had not discussed her orgasms in detail.

I was remembering how the zither man had taken his time, getting up the nerve to tackle Elvis, when Em just started singing in the coffeehouse on the Lower East Side. Well, out came the zither; the grandkid hadn't hesitated. The old edelweiss man, in his lederhosen and the Tyrolean hat with a feather, had to work up the courage to give us the zither version of "Heartbreak Hotel" and "I Forgot to Remember to Forget," but the zither-meister's grandson knew his Elvis cold, the way the kid knew his Harry Lime. They must have known the zither boy in the coffeehouse. Everyone in the place was happy to hear him play; our waiter looked like he'd been waiting for the zither.

There would be no mention of Em as *the orgasm girl,* as the zither kid referred to the legendary character. Em didn't identify herself, and I wasn't going to blow the whistle on her. The zither kid had idolized *the orgasm girl;* she was the most desirable girlfriend imaginable, in the kid's estimation. "She neva speaks, and she neva stops comin'—there's no beatin' that," the talented grandchild assured us. We didn't want to disillusion him, now that Em was speaking. And the zither boy's segue from "Heartbreak Hotel" to "I Forgot to Remember to Forget" was seamless. Em and I wanted his music at our wedding. Em's way of demonstrating that she couldn't possibly have been *the orgasm girl* was to keep singing.

The kid knew the zither-meister's liveliest and most lugubrious numbers. He serenaded us, and the other patrons of the coffeehouse, with "The Café Mozart Waltz" and "Farewell to Vienna." I let Em do the talking for us; she wanted to keep speaking as soon as she stopped singing. I thought of the old Austrian musician, taking Em's orgasms to his grave—as I would take them to mine. Em just kept talking.

Em told the zither man's grandchild we were having a civil marriage—"the most secular wedding you can imagine," was how Em put it. Molly's Manchester house was small, and there would be no guests to speak of—only Molly and Matthew were invited. Em explained that Matthew was my kid, and Molly had been the maid of honor at my mom's wedding. The zither grandkid remained calm; the old Austrian must not have talked about my mother and Molly.

I remembered telling the zither-meister about the complications of my mom's wedding dress—how the maid of honor had to wrestle the dress on and off her. "That's not for us to think about, Son of the Bride," the old Austrian had cautioned me. Em and I tried to be discreet with the talented grandson. We did not get into details about the justice of the peace. Elsie was a local Vermont magistrate, and a ski instructor at Bromley—a somewhat younger friend of Molly's and my mother's.

"Elsie is not a clergywoman—I doubt she ever goes to church," was all Em told the zither boy about the justice of the peace.

"Cool," the grandkid said. I can't remember his last name, but his first name was Ernst. "Ernie sounds betta in Brooklyn," he said, so we called him Ernie.

"It may turn out to be an oversight not to tell Ernie more about Elsie—if the kid tries to hit on her, or something," Em said.

It was a warm summer day. Em and I said our marriage vows in Molly's driveway, where the opportunity to shoot Zim—to spare him from the Vietnam War—had long ago been lost. I was careful not to say the word around Em, but it was *anticlimactic* that the old patroller's driveway was once the site of more memorable drama than what would happen at our wedding. No one would come close to choking to death, or otherwise need saving with a lacrosse stick. No one would be struck and killed by lightning. Manchester, Vermont, would not reverberate with prolonged orgasms. In the kitchen, where Em was helping Molly prepare dinner, the old patroller said she doubted Manchester generally experienced orgasms of an unforgettable kind.

I'd been in the driveway with Matthew and the zither boy. I came into the kitchen without hearing how the enviable orgasm conversation had started. Em may have been joking about her orgasms at my mom's wedding. Em later confirmed she told Elsie and Molly how the zither-meister's grandson had heard about the orgasms that went on and on. Elsie and Molly were relieved to learn we'd kept the zither kid in the dark. They agreed it was best if the boy didn't know Em was the perpetrator of the enviable orgasms—"back in the nonspeaking days," as the old patroller put it.

My coming into the kitchen caused Elsie to change the subject—only slightly, as it would turn out. Elsie wanted Em and me to know we were the first straight couple she'd married in several months. For the last few years, she'd been busier doing civil unions. Vermont was the first state to introduce civil unions, in the summer of 2000—too late for Em and Nora to do it. "Not that Nora would have wanted to do it," Em always said.

It made Em sad when Nora put down marriage and monogamy—"heterosexual hang-ups," Nora called them. It was my impression there were more gay men who said this, though some gay women felt the same way. Not Em—she definitely didn't feel this way.

"If we're together, kiddo, no fucking around," Em told me.

"Got it," I said.

In Molly's kitchen, immediately after Em and I were married, I didn't see where Elsie was going with the civil unions. There'd been a backlash to the legislation; opponents of civil unions put up signs and covered their cars with bumper stickers saying, TAKE BACK VERMONT. The Roman Catholic bishop of Burlington, who'd testified against the civil-unions bill, also sent out mailings. "How Would Jesus Vote?" one of the bishop's mailings asked.

"Thank God Nora is dead—it would kill her to see this shit going on," Em had said. She didn't mean it, but I understood her point. By the end of 2004, more than seven thousand couples had entered into civil unions in Vermont. Civil unions would be a boost to Vermont's economy; many same-sex couples came to Vermont to get them. In 2009, the success of civil unions encouraged the Vermont State Senate to approve same-sex marriage. Governor Douglas, a Republican, vetoed the legislation, but the Senate and the House overrode the veto.

Em and I knew what Nora would have said, because my cousin never tired of saying it: "You can count on the Catholic Church and the Republicans to be the assholes they were born to be."

Over the years, Em shortened this. "The assholes they were born to be," was all Em would say.

As Nora had also said, "Nothing will change." She meant the Catholic Church and the Republicans, but—according to Em—the Republicans would get worse.

Even on our wedding day, civil unions were Elsie's chosen conversation. I would not have called Elsie a Nora look-alike, but she was definitely a Nora type—masculine-looking, big and strong. A gay woman in her late forties or early fifties, she'd known Nora and Em for as long as they'd all been around Manchester together. Em was right to assume she didn't have to tell Ernie more about Elsie. Ernie was a savvy Brooklyn boy; he knew better than to hit on a lesbian who was twice his age and double his size.

Molly's chicken chili was Matthew's favorite—hence our wedding dinner. We could hear him singing "Puff, the Magic Dragon" in the driveway, for the umpteenth time. The zither kid had won us all over. In the car, en route to Vermont, the Brooklyn boy had entertained Matthew on the zither. They sat in the backseat; Ernie had a wooden lap desk for his instrument. The zither kid knew Matthew's favorite songs. Matthew loved "Puff, the Magic Dragon"; Em had taught him the words. I'd listened to the two of them, all the way from New York—Em and Matthew singing "Puff," with Ernie on the zither. Ernie and Matthew were still at it in the driveway.

Three or four hours of "Puff" had depressed me, but not Matthew. At thirteen, he was on the threshold of growing up; Matthew was moving on from make-believe. His time for dragons was running out; Matthew would soon be into more worldly things. Yet I could hear how happy he was, singing "Puff, the Magic Dragon" in the driveway—a song about the end of childhood. "Doesn't Matthew know it's a sad song?" I asked Em.

"Don't cry, kiddo. Matthew will still love us—we'll have fun in other ways," Em said, hugging me. We could hear Matthew singing:

A dragon lives forever, but not so little boys
Painted wings and giants' rings make way for other toys

"It'll be okay—you two are going to be fine together," Elsie said, squeezing my hand. She must have noticed I was crying. I'd been wishing Elsie would stop talking about civil unions, not realizing she was working her way back to the orgasm subject. "Same-sex couples have better orgasms, and more of them—I'm just telling you what I hear," Elsie said, giving my hand a harder squeeze. "But it'll be okay—you two are going to be fine together," the justice of the peace repeated.

"Adam is crying because of the *song*, Elsie—he's crying because Matthew is growing up," Em said, holding my other hand.

"Fuck—I thought we were having an orgasm anxiety moment, or something," Elsie said, letting go of my hand.

"As for same-sex orgasms, kiddo, we're the exception that proves the rule," Em told me.

"Enough of *Puff*—no more dragon!" we heard Molly yelling in the drive-way. Matthew stopped singing; Ernie didn't touch the zither's strings. "The chili's ready," the old patroller told them.

There was no screened-in porch, no backyard, but there was a breeze-way between the house and garage with a picnic table and benches. It was a pleasant place to eat on a summer night, if the mosquitoes weren't too bad and there were no bats. Matthew loved it when there was a bat; what he loved best was to hear the women shrieking. It was an enjoyable but uneventful wedding among warm-hearted people—provided you were able to overlook the eternal sadness of the dragon in the song. And during our dessert—after Matthew had mangled our wedding cake when he was feeding it to us—a bat swooped into the breezeway. It was wonderful to hear how Matthew laughed; he was so happy, and he was only thirteen. Molly and Em, and even Elsie, shrieked—all for Matthew's benefit, not really because of the bat. These three women were not inclined to shrieking—not counting Em's earlier orgasms.

Matthew was spending the night at Molly's; he was already asleep by the time Ernie and Em and I walked back to the Equinox, the hotel where we were staying in Manchester. It wasn't very late at night when we left the old patroller's; Molly and Elsie were just starting to do the dishes. Em and I understood it was too early for the Brooklyn boy to go to bed; we led Ernie to the hotel tavern, leaving him there with his zither. The Equinox was a resort hotel; in the summer, it was popular with golfers. It seemed cruel to abandon the zither kid among men in lime-green pants and pink polo shirts; the women were wearing culottes, or something worse. But Em reminded me that it wasn't Ernie's wedding night—the Brooklyn boy could deal with the golfers. We had no doubt the zither kid would be taking requests and playing for the fashion mavens.

"Sinatra songs, or something worse," Em said, when we were alone in the bridal suite. I took some comfort from the certainty those golfers weren't a "Puff, the Magic Dragon" crowd. Besides, the tavern was too far away for us to hear the sing-along.

"Don't take it personally if I tone down the orgasm, kiddo—I don't want to give myself away to Ernie, who's in the same hotel," Em told me later, when we were lying in bed in the dark.

"Got it," I said. I was happy she was happy.

I was almost asleep when Em rolled closer and took hold of my penis. "Seriously, I stopped having the projectile orgasms when I was with Nora—it'll kill you to keep having the orgasms you're supposed to have and get over when you're a kid," Em said. I appreciated her sincerity, though I would wonder how Em—in the nonspeaking years—might have pantomimed the *projectile* part of her early orgasms. (Not to mention the part about the lethality of the orgasms you're *supposed to* have and get over when you're a kid.)

"Got it," I said. Em and I had been the kind of kids who couldn't wait to grow up. Our childhood felt like an eternity to us. But why? What was so great about being adults? Loving a child, especially living with one—even if you live with a child only part-time—makes you realize how fleeting childhood is. There's not enough eternity to childhood. And now that Em and I were older, we were aware how little eternity was left to us. It wasn't only how fleeting Matthew's childhood would be. Em's time and mine would also slip away.

"Carpe diem, kiddo—fuck the future," Em said, holding me in a seize-the-day kind of way. I hugged her back—the bridal suite silent, no Sinatra, no zither.

On our wedding night, one of us would be singing in our sleep. I was sure it was Em. "It was you, kiddo—I kicked you twice, but you just kept singing," Em told me in the morning. We could only agree on which couplet we'd heard someone singing—the one about poor Puff, despairing in a cave.

"It was you, kiddo—you're the one who identifies with the dragon," Em said; she had a point.

In the car on the way back to New York, I was thinking there would be no honeymoon on the cliff for Em and me. Em and I would have no honeymoon at all. In the car, Em asked Ernie and Matthew not to play or sing "Puff." She said what happened to Puff made me sad; Em said the song compelled me to sing it, and to cry, in my sleep. I hadn't heard about the crying till we were in the car.

"It's a bummer about Puff—Matt and I will think of somethin' betta than endin' up alone in a cave," the Brooklyn boy said. No doubt the zither-meister would have been proud of his grandson.

I could see Matthew's serious expression in the rearview mirror. He hated it when kids at school called him *Matt*, but he was having so much fun with Ernie, the zither grandkid could have called him anything. "Don't be sad, Dad. Puff isn't real—he's just a made-up dragon," Matthew assured me.

Em was watching me closely in the front seat; she saw how I'd gripped the steering wheel harder. I knew Matthew was trying to make me feel better, but it was such a grown-up thing to say. Imagining the years ahead, I saw how swiftly the time would fly.

"You want me to drive?" Em asked me.

"Got it," I said.

It bears repeating. Like the Western, there is no mystery about what's noir—what happens is what was always *going to* happen; it's what *always* happens. I've said it seemed suitable that my father's bodyguards and I would share a van from the Hotel Jerome to the Aspen airport. The three of us had lost someone important. Paul Goode would be irreplaceable. Yet I'd underestimated the importance of my half brother, Toby Goode—not only to me, but to Otto and Billy.

I spied on my half brother, reading everything about him and looking at all the photos in *Variety* and *Vanity Fair* and *The Hollywood Reporter* and the footage of him on TV. His career as an emerging writer-director was of more enduring interest than the women he dated. In interviews, I liked how my half brother answered the least imaginative but most repeated question. Given Toby Goode's movie-star parents and his good looks, why wasn't he an actor? "I'm first of all a writer, then a director—I'm behind the scene, not in it, by choice," he answered. I didn't doubt he owned the writer gene. Toby would have made our father a believer in the writer gene. I hoped for the best for Toby Goode.

I don't presume to speak for Toby, regarding his seeming reluctance to get married and have children. I don't speculate on his reasons; I won't add to the Hollywood gossip on this subject. Usually, the paparazzi don't bother screenwriters or directors, but they hounded Toby because of the actresses he went out with. Whatever his reasons were for not getting married and having children, I was glad I got to see more of him than I might have, had he been a family man.

I was glad I got glimpses of Otto and Billy, too. I should have known those bodyguards wouldn't be left out of the picture; their loyalty to Toby was recognized and rewarded. The two bodyguards became Toby Goode's guardians. From the outset, Otto and Billy felt more than legally responsible for looking after him.

I wasn't surprised to hear my half brother had no tolerance for what he called "the bodyguard misnomer," in reference to Otto and Billy. "They're not my bodyguards; they're my backup fathers—I love them," Toby had told the Hollywood press. "Otto and Billy have always loved me and looked after me—when they get old, I'm going to look after them," my half brother said. Nor was I surprised to hear how much Toby Goode liked going back to Aspen and the Hotel Jerome. "The Jerome is my home away from home," he said. Our grandmother, Paulina Juárez, had to be happy to see him, and how it must have pleased Clara Swift to see her son again—whether Toby could see her or not, and notwithstanding that she only saw him at the Hotel Jerome. I see my mother and the snowshoer only on a subway, or in the vicinity of Summerhill Station. I'm not complaining—I'm just happy to see them. And when I think of my father, I imagine Paul Goode as reunited with his family.

As Otto and Billy got older, you could have mistaken the former body-guards for Hollywood royalty. Toby Goode's backup fathers were chauffeured around L.A. in the backseat of the car; Toby took them everywhere. "I'm just returning the favor," my half brother had said.

Em and I were on a book tour in 2012 when we heard about Otto. That

November morning in Munich was part of Em's translation trip for *The Lesbians' Children*, her novel about a lesbian couple who are very particular about the way they have children. Each woman chooses a different sperm donor. It is a first-person novel, and the daughter (also a lesbian) is telling the story—about her straight brother and their two gay moms. *Wir Lesbenkinder* was the German title—literally, *We Lesbian Children*. Given the time difference in Munich, Em and I had gone to bed the night before—not knowing the Obama-Romney election results in the U.S.

Em and I woke up early to the sound of singing. We got out of bed and looked out the window. There were young men and women singing in the street; they looked like German university students. I turned on the TV.

"Don't worry, kiddo—those students aren't singing for Romney," Em said. She was always ahead of me—not just politically, not only because she was older. I was a hindsight man; I only got what was going on after it happened. Em was prescient about Romney twice. Em would say later, "The two guys Obama beat, McCain and Romney, might be the last honorable Republicans who'll be nominated for president for a while." Em's low opinion of Republicans was prescient, too. Once again, it was only with hindsight that I would get it.

When the station had exhausted its election coverage, I saw the news about Otto on the TV. Toby Goode had his arm around the gray-haired Billy, who was sobbing—Billy's head had fallen on Toby's shoulder. Notwithstanding the simultaneous translation—the German anchorwoman was speaking—I could hear my half brother's voice. "I saw Otto in the rearview mirror—how he'd slumped in the seat, the way Billy had to hold him upright, but I saw Otto's eyes," Toby tried to say. Then he stopped speaking; he couldn't say the rest.

The German anchorwoman said everything else. Toby Goode and his backup dads had been at a party; they'd left early. Otto had the heart attack in the backseat—"der Herzanfall," I heard the German anchorwoman say. The video wasn't clear. It looked like the paramedics were moving Otto from Toby's car to the ambulance—"zu spät," the German anchorwoman said. That was clear—the ambulance was *too late*.

I went back to the window, where Em was watching the German students. Em could see I was crying; she knew I wasn't crying for Romney. It was good news that Obama won, but that wasn't the only news. We just went on watching the happy German students—they were still singing.

That November in Munich, I was almost seventy-one; Em was already seventy-seven. Maybe we went on watching those German students because the inexorable march of time had caught up to Otto; maybe Otto's mortality made Em and me imagine our own. That November in Munich, when we heard Otto had died in L.A., Toby Goode was thirty-five. Matthew was twenty-one.

There was no time difference in Toronto, where Em and I watched the 2016 U.S. election results on TV. In immigration terms, I'd become a permanent resident of Canada in 2015. I would be eligible to apply for Canadian citizenship in 2018. Em was already a dual citizen of Canada and the United States and I would become one in December 2019. Em and I had voted in the 2016 U.S. presidential election, via absentee ballot, for Hillary Clinton. Matthew was with us in Toronto for that election night; he'd voted for Clinton in New York.

A former girlfriend of Matthew's watched the election results with us. Matthew had met Carol on the subway when she was a Bishop Strachan student; Em and I agreed that Carol looked cute in her BSS uniform, in that short skirt with her knees showing. "Nice knees—I saw her knees first," I remembered Em saying to me. I used to wonder, when Matthew and Carol were no longer dating each other, if Matthew missed seeing her in the BSS uniform. "*You* miss seeing Carol in the BSS uniform, kiddo—I know *I* do," Em told me.

Carol was Matthew's age, twenty-five, when we watched Hillary Clinton lose to Donald Trump; we'd not seen Carol in a BSS uniform for six or seven years. I was almost seventy-five and Em eighty-one. On that election night, I might have wished that Em was still not speaking, but Em was making up for lost time.

"Trump is a pussy-grabber," Carol repeated, for the fourth or fifth time. In her BSS uniform, or not, Carol was angry about a self-described pussy-grabber going to the White House.

Em was angry at our fellow Democrats *and* about Trump's pussy-grabbing. In 2012, Obama got more votes than Hillary. Who were those Democrats who didn't show up for Mrs. Clinton? "All of them weren't crybabies for Bernie," Em was saying. I was a registered voter in Vermont; I'd always voted for Bernie. We'd all wanted Bernie, but Bernie hadn't been nominated. The Democrats who wouldn't vote for Hillary were like the ones who didn't vote for Humphrey in 1968, Em was saying. "Those Democrats gave us Nixon, these Democrats gave us Trump!" Em was raving.

At two in the morning, in the Trump headquarters in New York, there were yahoos in coats and ties and MAKE AMERICA GREAT AGAIN baseball caps. They were chanting for Hillary to be locked up. Em essentially said Trump didn't win the election. "Our fucking fellow Democrats lost it—we gave it to him!" Em was screaming.

"It's a good thing you two moved to Canada, so you can get away from shit like this," Matthew said, giving Em a hug.

"We can't get away from shit like this, Matthew—there's no getting away from this shit," she said, not letting him go.

"I know," he told her.

"Pussy-grabbers!" Carol was calling the yahoos in baseball caps on TV, where the chanting to lock up Hillary just went on.

I remembered what the snowshoer had written in a notebook. Mr. Barlow was quoting Alexander Hamilton, who called the voting public a "great beast." The *great beast* had spoken, I was thinking, while Em and Matthew went on hugging each other, and Carol kept watching the celebration at the pussy-grabber's headquarters in New York. The way Matthew had to bend over Em when he hugged her made it appear he was whispering in her ear, but he spoke loudly enough for me to hear him, and Matthew was looking at me when he said what Em and I were only thinking to ourselves—we couldn't have said it.

"I don't really mean this, you know, but it's a good thing Molly isn't around—the pussy-grabbing would piss her off," Matthew said, bursting into tears. All I could do was hug him and Em; I would have lost it if I'd tried to say anything. The three of us knew Molly had loved Bernie, but the old patroller wouldn't have been a crybaby about it. Poor Carol. She knew what wrecks we were whenever one of us mentioned Molly. Carol had heard about my mother and the old patroller—"my two grandmas," Matthew called my mom and Molly. Carol muted the volume on the Trump headquarters in New York, where the yahoos in coats and ties were still chanting for Hillary to be locked up. We could only imagine what Molly might have thought of Trump and his pussy-grabbing supporters.

In the summer of 2019, Em would be back in Barolo, where she'd last been at the Disastri Festival with Nora. We were both invited to the Collisioni Festival—the *Collisions* Festival was for writers and rock bands, but the damn déjà vu was in the air for Em. One night, for old times' sake, it was expected we would attend a special showing of the *Disastri* documentary. "If old age doesn't kill me, kiddo, the nostalgia could do it," Em said. That July in Barolo, Em was almost eighty-four; I was seventy-seven. Some of Em's pantomime fans were at the *Disastri* screening, where Em had to see and hear Nora as Anthony Quinn, talking about the dead-pudenda dance in Italian.

Matthew, who by then was twenty-eight, had flown with us to Milan; he had his own room where we were staying, at the Albergo dell'Agenzia in Pollenzo. He liked writers and rock music. The writers' onstage interviews and the book signings were daytime events, the rock concerts at night—all in Barolo. The parties and dinners were in the surrounding area; everywhere we went, we were driven from and back to the Albergo. Our driver, Bella, was a beautiful young woman; she was a good driver. "I saw her first," I whispered in Em's ear, just to tease her—Em was usually quicker to say it than I was.

"Matthew saw her first, kiddo," Em whispered back. We were in the backseat of Bella's car. Matthew sat up front, in the passenger seat—riding shotgun next to the beautiful Bella.

"What are you two whispering about?" Matthew asked us. "It's embarrassing—they still behave like newlyweds," he said to Bella. The three of us loved to hear her laugh; for such a pretty girl, Bella had a hee-haw like a donkey.

"Matthew says he's too old for Bella," Em told me later. I couldn't imagine Matthew as *too old* for anyone. Had Bella said she was too young for him? I was wondering.

At our book signing after the *Disastri* screening, a tall and gloomy guy, a pantomime fan, told Em he'd liked her better before she started speaking. "It's a compliment, kiddo," Em said, because she saw the way I was looking at the guy. The women wearing the hangman's nooses—not to mention the Nora look-alikes—were older now. The hangman's noose was not a welcoming look for an older woman. For the *Disastri* audience, Em was mostly signing Italian translations of *Come Hang Yourself*—in Italian, *Vieni ad impiccarti*—although some of the Nora look-alikes, and just normal-looking readers, were asking Em to sign *Noi figli di lesbiche*. The literal translation, *We Offspring of Lesbians*, made Em cringe. The beautiful Bella had translated the title in the car. I'd thought Em was going to barf in the backseat, but the way Matthew laughed made Bella start hee-hawing. Our pretty driver's hee-haw had won us over.

At our daytime events in Barolo, in Em's onstage interview and in mine, we were asked if *The Lesbians' Children* was autobiographical. "It's a mixed bag," Em said.

"The autobiography part isn't what matters," I began, before I got bogged down in all the amalgams. The fictional lesbian couple was based on an amalgam of my mom and Molly, but also of Em and Nora. The first-person narrator, the gay daughter, was what Em meant by *a mixed bag*. The gay daughter was definitely an amalgam of Em and Nora. "I suppose I'm the model for the straight younger brother—his tendency to be the last to get what's going on sounds like me," I told the interviewers. This usually got a laugh, at least from Em; even the Nora look-alikes were warming up to me, but not the older women with the nooses. Those women would never like me.

Our next-to-last morning at the Albergo, Em and I distinctly heard a hee-haw from Matthew's bedroom; he had the room next to ours. Our next-to-last night in Barolo, we were invited to a party at the palace of the marchese of Barolo—the handsome twenty-three-year-old was the heir to the Barolo winery. We liked him.

"The marchese looks gorgeous but doomed," Em told me.

"Are you thinking of someone else?" I asked her.

"A young JFK Jr.—before the plane crash, kiddo," Em said.

From the terrace of the palace, we overlooked the town of Barolo—we could see the throng that had gathered at the biggest outdoor stage, and could hear the music from the rock band on the loudspeakers. Matthew was singing along with Thirty Seconds to Mars—the Leto brothers' band was the one onstage. There was an older Italian woman who was coming on to Matthew, but he just kept singing.

"Those guys aren't Pink Floyd," the older Italian woman was saying about the band.

"No, they aren't," Matthew said. That was when the waiter with the tray—a huge tray with many bowls of olives—collided with one of the palm trees on the terrace.

It could have been "The Kill" or "This Is War"—I don't remember which of their songs Thirty Seconds to Mars was playing—when the partygoers started stepping on the olives. When you step on olives with pits, they feel like live beetles. Matthew said later he was sure he was singing along with "A Beautiful Lie" when the older Italian woman started screaming about the beetles. We were walking on beetles, she wanted everyone to know—in English, and in Italian.

Em said later she was saved by the olives underfoot. In truth, the irrational dread of walking on beetles was what rescued Em from a conversation that had gotten her all riled up. Giuseppe, a pushy journalist, was pursuing the same question he'd asked us at our onstage interviews; he hadn't liked our earlier answers. The politics in our novels could be considered anti-American, Giuseppe had told us. Why wouldn't we admit we were "political refugees from the U.S."—wasn't that why we were living in Canada? Em had reminded Giuseppe that we'd moved to Toronto before Donald Trump was a Republican candidate; we'd begun the immigration process when Obama was president, and we loved Obama.

"It was a personal decision, to go back to where I was born—politics was only part of my decision," Em had already told Giuseppe. "And *he* only thinks about politics after everything has happened," Em had said, pointing at me.

"I would go anywhere *she* went—I would move to Italy if *she* moved here," I'd told Giuseppe, pointing to Em.

"Republicans were bad and getting worse before Trump was their guy—Republicans will be bad after him," Em pointed out to Giuseppe, but Giuseppe ignored what he didn't want to hear. Our being dual citizens didn't interest him. Em told Giuseppe that she and I intended to keep voting in future U.S. elections; we just liked living in Toronto, she said, but Giuseppe wouldn't listen. Giuseppe wanted to make our story all about the pussy-grabber.

Pantomime originated in Roman mime, Em had told me; this was why she'd first come to Italy, to the Disastri Festival. On the terrace, while Thirty Seconds to Mars was playing, I heard Em saying to Giuseppe: "You are too focused on Trump—you should be more aware of his *enablers*." Em put the blame where the blame belonged—on chinless Mitch McConnell and dick-less Lindsey Graham, and the craven Senate Republicans—as I'd heard her do a hundred times.

"Marcus Aurelius was the only Roman emperor who was also a philosopher—you're familiar with the *Meditations* of Marcus Aurelius, aren't you?" Em was asking Giuseppe. I knew this was going where it always went—it didn't matter to Em that Marcus Aurelius had died in AD 180. Giuseppe said nothing. He didn't know anything about Marcus Aurelius.

"How much more grievous are the consequences of anger than the causes of it," Marcus Aurelius had written, but this would be lost on Giuseppe.

"Chinless Mitch and dickless Lindsey will still have their jobs after Trump is gone," Em was telling Giuseppe.

"Where is Trump going?" I heard Giuseppe ask. I knew where Em hoped Trump would end up; she had a Shakespearean ending in mind.

"Al Capone went to jail for tax evasion," Em was saying to Giuseppe.

"Trump is just another criminal—he's going to end up in jail, where he'll be killed by his fellow inmates," Em told Giuseppe, who was writing this down. It sounded like what would happen in a novel—or what *should* happen, I was thinking. "Trump is just another tyrant, more despotic than presidential— think of Shakespeare's wicked kings," Em was saying. "Macbeth was born to feel sorry for himself—all he does is whine. 'Life's but a walking shadow,' and more self-pitying shit," Em was saying, but Giuseppe had stopped writing this down. "Losers never stop whining—'a tale told by an idiot, full of sound and fury, signifying nothing'—all Trump will end up doing is whining," Em went on. Giuseppe was confused about Macbeth; he might have thought Macbeth was like McConnell, one of the craven Republicans.

I was waiting for Richard III—I knew Richard, the murderous coward, would be coming. Em was working herself up to him. "And there's fucking Richard—'Now is the winter of our discontent,' the scumbag begins, but he ends up sniveling," Em told Giuseppe, who looked lost. Giuseppe was wondering if *fucking Richard* was like *dickless Lindsey,* one of the Senate Republicans. "The chickenshit ends up crying—'A horse! A horse! My kingdom for a horse!' Fucking Richard is begging," Em was crying. That was when the older Italian woman started screaming about the beetles. Em had more to say as we were leaving the terrace, but only Matthew and I could hear her over the shrieking. Giuseppe was stomping on the olives.

In the car, on our way back to the Albergo, Em kept talking; she was saying something about a plague. Matthew and I were wondering what plague she meant, but Em only meant that Trump would be a bad plague president— even worse than Ronald Reagan—if there ever was another plague.

"Not to change the subject, but Bella knows something about Giuseppe," Matthew told us.

"My girlfriend went out with him. She calls him Pino, which means 'pine tree'—she says he has a little penis!" Bella said. She was gripping the steering wheel with both hands, but she wiggled the pinky finger of her right hand. "The littlest one she's seen, since she saw her baby brother's—he's no pine tree!" Bella cried, her pinky still wiggling. Em and I were happy to hear Bella's story, and her hee-hawing.

In December of that year, 2019, I would obey the notice to appear at the government office for Immigration, Refugees and Citizenship Canada in Scarborough—this was for my swearing-in ceremony. As an old Yankee from New England, I wondered what my grandmother might have said—to hear me swear to be faithful and bear true allegiance to Queen Elizabeth II.

The same day I was sworn in, I took the Oath of Citizenship with eighty-three new immigrants, from thirty-five countries. I'm guessing there were families who'd been granted Protected Persons status by the Immigration and Refugee Board of Canada. There must have been families who'd suffered hardships—they'd endured a more dangerous life than mine, before getting to Canada. A young girl spoke to me; she was only twelve or thirteen, wondering what my story was. "What about you, Mister?" she asked me. "What are you running away from?"

That July night in Barolo, our last night at the Albergo, Em and I were just lying in bed. We weren't in need of Protected Persons status. We were just feeling old. We weren't *too* old—we were just too old to be roadies. I almost said we were too old to be writers, still singing for our supper, but I didn't.

"There are German students somewhere, kiddo—they're still singing," Em said. I hoped she would keep saying it. I almost said the nostalgia could finish us off, but I didn't. From the bedroom next door, we'd heard Matthew and Bella—they'd been singing Thirty Seconds to Mars songs to each other.

Now even the hee-haws had stopped; everything suddenly seemed more serious. I thought Em was asleep when she rolled closer to me, holding my penis. "You know, kiddo—we're both lesbians' children," Em said.

"I know," I said. This I didn't hesitate to say.

53

THE VOICE ON THE SUBWAY; THE SILENCE IN THE ROCK GARDEN

Henrik hadn't written Em when Nora died. I had written him after our cousin's death, but he hadn't responded. Henrik had always been wary of Molly; when the old patroller died in January 2006, Henrik's inner writer was unleashed. He wrote me at the snowshoer's East Sixty-fourth Street address, and he wrote Em twice, sending the same letter to Em's Toronto address and in care of her New York publisher; that was why Grace saw it.

Henrik wrote that he was going to rent a U-Haul truck and come to Manchester to get his guns, or he was sending a couple of "college boys" to get them for him. Henrik offered no condolences for Molly. When we heard about the old patroller, Em and I were in Canada. We came back to the States and went through Molly's Manchester house, with Matthew and Grace. Naturally, there were things of sentimental value. Each of us took things we wanted. We could have taken a gun or two, before Henrik or the *college boys* drove my uncles' arsenal of weapons down to Dixie, but Em and I were done with guns, and Grace had never wanted one. Like most boys, Matthew wanted to have a gun, but he was fourteen; he was too young to have a say in the matter.

"We're just keeping the guns for Henrik, sweetie—we're not going to start a war or anything," my mom had told me, but there were more guns hidden away in the Manchester house than I'd imagined. The old patroller had left the house to me. I knew my mother had arranged this. Except for Molly's twenty-gauge, the guns had belonged to Uncle Johan and Uncle Martin. Henrik was champing at the bit to have them.

"That's a shitload of lethal weapons, kiddo," Em said, when she saw the guns gathered together. "Everyone in Vermont—not to mention, the deer—will be safer when these guns are down in Dixie." Em and I never said the name of the southern state where Henrik had gone to college, just to play lacrosse—the same state Henrik served in the U.S. House of Representatives. Not saying the name of Henrik's state was almost as good as forgetting it. We wished we'd never known Henrik in the first place.

Em reminded me that Henrik had married a second time, when he was in his forties; he'd had no children with his first wife, and only one with the second. Nora had hoped Henrik's kid would be a girl. Henrik would have nothing to do with a daughter, Nora said—she meant a girl might have a fighting chance to be herself. If Henrik had a boy, Nora said, the poor kid would be like his father.

The boy was twentysomething when he and a lacrosse teammate took turns driving the U-Haul truck all the way to Vermont. Henrik had named him Johan, after his father, but the kid was a Johan in name only—he lacked the Norwegian's good nature. I'd told Matthew the stories—how Henrik had bullied me, how Nora had bullied him back. Matthew was dying to meet Henrik, but Em and I doubted the old congressman would do the gunrunning himself. We wondered if young Johan might be one of the *college boys*. Henrik had written once more, only to me. "We call him Johnny," Henrik wrote. "The Johan didn't go over big, not down here." That was the last I would hear from Henrik—not counting the consequences of his party's policies.

Johnny called Grace's number when the gunrunners got to Molly's driveway. Grace's parents had passed away; their house in Manchester was Grace's now. Arthur Barrett had beaten the ball drop in Times Square; he'd permanently put his pajamas on before the ball could drop again. Grace and Matthew met the two lacrosse teammates in Molly's driveway. When the old patroller died, I just knew I was done with Vermont and that driveway, where my mom's mission of mercy was tragically averted.

Grace said the southern college boys were the worst male jocks imaginable. "They're from a subculture of misogynist insouciance—women make them slouch," Grace said.

"Lax bros," Matthew called the gunrunners. Johnny sounded like he was a hundred percent Henrik.

"The chill attitude, the backward baseball caps—those boys would have beaten up Matthew if I hadn't been there," Grace went on.

"They would have raped you if I hadn't been there!" Matthew told his mom.

"Don't go there, Matthew—raging puberty is ahead of you. You'll be there soon enough," Grace said.

Em and I were staying away from the *raging puberty* business. We were in the East Sixty-fourth Street apartment, trying not to think about what had happened to the old patroller. We'd been moving to Toronto in a part-time fashion, mostly because we wanted to see as much of Molly in Vermont as possible. Em and I wanted to divide our time between Toronto and the snowshoer's pied-à-terre for as long as Matthew was in school in New York.

"You two almost-Canadians will go the whole hog now, I imagine," Grace had said to us. We knew the *raging puberty* business was Grace's version of what was about to wreak havoc in her household. She'd met "someone serious," as Grace put it. Jeremy was a younger man; he was also in publishing.

"You should definitely try a younger man—I like it better than I thought I would," Em had told Grace.

Jeremy had two young daughters, not a lot younger than Matthew. "They soon will be starting puberty," Grace had forewarned Matthew. For now, Matthew liked the girls, and he liked Jeremy. Matthew admitted to Em and me that his mom had made him anxious about his own puberty; the onset of the girls' puberty sounded worse. Grace was projecting her experience with puberty onto the girls. She'd told me stories of her painful periods; she'd had terrible tampon problems. Poor Matthew was imagining these girls he'd met and liked—how they would be changed by their excruciating bleeding.

"The girls will soon be over puberty, as you will soon be over it," I tried to assure Matthew, but he remained wary; his mother made it sound like puberty would be raging all around him. It was Em who got through to Matthew, by being funny about it.

"When you can't put anything anywhere without getting blood all over it, that's a good time to come see us in Toronto," Em told him. "Or you can bring the girls to Toronto, and they can bleed with us for a while—it may be your mom who'll need a break from all the puberty that's happening," Em said. Then Em did a little puberty pantomime; it wasn't too explicit for Matthew. Em just danced around, like she had her period coming on. She was singing her own version of the Jerry Lee Lewis song—"a whole lotta bleedin' goin' on," she was singing—when Matthew started laughing, and he sang along with her. For now, the *raging puberty* wasn't a problem.

Em and I had met Jeremy, and his girls. We liked them, too, and we wanted Grace to be happy. I knew the only song Em was seriously singing. Em really meant what she sang to me in my sleep, when she was brainwashing me—and now I was the one singing it. It's not hard to learn "O Canada," but I was trying to learn both the English and the French versions. I knew one day I would have to sing it. At my swearing-in ceremony, when I took the Oath of Citizenship, I would also sing my new national anthem.

For now, the old Norwegians' guns had gone down to Dixie, but the old patroller was gone forever—not just down south. "In America, kiddo, the guns don't ever go away—they just turn up somewhere else," was the way Em put it.

When it came to missing Molly, there would be no fooling around about it; there was only the missing part, or the part about seeing her in my heart. Molly was all business, no fooling around; in the old patroller's opinion, ghosts were just fooling around. When I missed Molly, if I wanted to see her, I had to look in my heart.

Sometimes in my sleep, or in my dreams, I'm standing at the top of the Blue Ribbon Quad on Bromley Mountain. I'm looking at the foremost, downhill-facing chair on the lift—the chair closest to the edge of the loading platform, where the safety net is. It's too early in the morning for the chairlift to be running. I can see the sign that says NO DOWNHILL LOADING when I look east—in the direction of Mount Monadnock, in New Hampshire—where the sunrise is. But I'm not in this dream to see the sunrise. The chairlift is a hearse, a waiting hearse; all that's missing are the bodies.

Sometimes the old patroller and I are climbing up Bromley Mountain. We're near the top of Upper Twister, where what Molly called the Rock Garden is—that was where we noticed how the earlier climbers' tracks changed. My mother had some trouble on the second steep part of Twister. The old patroller and I saw only the snowshoer's tracks the rest of the way. That was when we knew Elliot Barlow, the only hero, carried her piggyback to the top.

Loved ones leave us and we go on—ghosts or no ghosts, my way or Molly's, we still see them. As Matthew and I knew, the dead don't entirely go away—not if you see them on the subway, or in your heart.

Matthew and I knew that all the Christmas trees in Canada were blue to Em. We understood that the blue Christmas trees were "psychologically" true—"in Em's mind," was the way we put it. In the last week of January 2006, when we lost Molly, Matthew was fourteen—almost fifteen. He was beginning to be comfortable with words like *psychologically*.

Some confusion was caused by the appearance of an actual blue Christmas tree in Toronto—a big one. Matthew said the blue tree was part of a neighborhood program called the Cavalcade of Lights, but everything about the giant blue Christmas tree would remain a mystery to me. I just remember the first Christmas season we saw it, the Christmas and New Year's of 2005–2006, because that was when I heard about the old patroller.

"The tree is fifteen meters, almost fifty feet, and they're talking about making it taller," Matthew told us. He knew Em and I were too old, or too American, to learn the metric system. We would never know how to tell the temperature on the Celsius scale; Em and I were Fahrenheit people. The sculpture of a Christmas tree with blue lights looked even taller on the Canadian Pacific Railway overpass at Yonge Street, just north of Scrivener Square—an enormous blue Christmas tree, atop the trestlework of a railway bridge in midtown Toronto. Matthew and I loved the blue tree, but Em scarcely noticed it.

"Another Christmas tree—it must be almost that time of year," was all Em said, when she first saw it.

"It's blue," I pointed out, but Em just shrugged and scuffed her feet—in Little Ray's indifferent, jock-walking way.

Those two ghosts took some interest in the blue Christmas tree. Above-ground, my mom and the snowshoer didn't venture far from the Summerhill subway station, but the big blue tree captured their limited attention for a while. I saw them occasionally in the underpass, beneath the railway bridge, where the noise of the traffic on Yonge Street was exaggerated. Those two seemed to like the whooshing sound, or the heightened roar of the engines. They were piggybacking each other around, in their juvenile fashion; when they saw me, they just waved and disappeared, or they went back to the subway.

It was early one morning, the third week of January 2006—bright and cold in Toronto. I'd brought my old ski clothes to Em's house on Shaftesbury Avenue, because Toronto was a good city for winter walks. I was out walking, a bit after sunrise; I went north on Yonge Street, heading into a northeast wind. The wind was getting to me at Eglinton, where I took the subway back to Summerhill Station. It was crowded and warm on the subway, standing-room only—the morning rush hour on the trains going downtown. I had no idea what my mom and the snowshoer thought about rush hour, or if they thought about it. I didn't know if they thought about anything—all those two did was fool around. At first, I didn't see them on the crowded train.

The standing-room only must get in the way of their piggybacking, I was thinking—their single-leg lunges wouldn't work at rush hour. I was about to get off the train when I saw them. Little Ray was curled up in Mr. Barlow's lap; they were huddled together in a seat by the door. My mom was sobbing, but the little English teacher was looking straight at me. I could read her lips before the door closed: *Go home*, the snowshoer was telling me before I got off the train. I was frightened, not knowing what was wrong. My foremost fear was for Matthew. It was a school day in New York; something could have happened there. I imagined Em was still in bed, or she might be making her breakfast when I got back to the house. Maybe something had happened to Em, I was thinking, as I ran along Shaftesbury Avenue.

As we grow older, we learn how memories work. The people we miss know where to find us—on the subway, or in our hearts. When I got home from Summerhill Station, Em was on the phone.

Willy would find Molly in the Rock Garden, in the steeps of Upper Twister—near the top, where Little Ray, running on Prednisone, couldn't keep going. Mr. Barlow had carried her piggyback the rest of the way, but there'd been no one to carry the old patroller to the top of Number Ten.

As Molly had told me on the dark morning we drove to Bromley to look for my mom and the snowshoer, the lift-maintenance mechanics showed up at six, before anyone else. That was why Willy was in Upper Twister on a snowmobile before sunrise; in his headlight, he saw the old patroller lying in the Rock Garden. Willy was on his way to the lift stations at the top of Number One and Number Ten. Willy would have known the one and only chairlift Molly was headed for when her heart stopped—the foremost, downhill-facing chair of Number Ten, my mom's favorite, the Blue Ribbon Quad.

Willy wasn't a patroller, but the lift mechanic knew the old patroller had died where she'd fallen. Out of respect for Molly, Willy wanted her fellow patrollers to take her where she'd been going. Willy said he might have made Molly look like she was lying more comfortably in the Rock Garden; he said he tried to make her appear to be merely resting.

Willy would have been talking on the radio to a few of his fellow lift mechanics in the maintenance shed. The patrollers working that day wouldn't start showing up in the first-aid room before seven, but I'm sure some patrollers were called at home—the ones who'd known Molly the longest, the ones who loved her the most.

Old Ned and Meg had called me in Toronto—the two of them, together. Em had answered the phone. "It's someone named Ned—he's with a woman named Meg. It's for you, kiddo," Em told me, her voice breaking. I knew Molly must be gone.

Ned was working only part-time as a patroller now, the way Molly had been a part-time ski instructor; Ned was almost as old as Molly. "The old girl got as far as the Rock Garden, Kid—she almost made it all the way, but she was carrying some extra weight in her backpack," Ned said.

"What was she carrying?" I asked him; I was pretty sure I knew.

"A six-pack of beer, and enough Valium to do the trick—she was as cold as the beer cans, Kid. Our coldest night of the season—the end of January is as cold as it gets at Bromley, you know," Ned said.

"I know," I told him.

"Ned is morbid and tactless, Kid. You know that, too, don't you?" Meg asked me.

"I know that, too," I told her. I was fond of them; I wouldn't have wanted to make the call they were making. I was already imagining how to tell Matthew about Molly.

I could see the rest of it—as Ned and Meg kept talking. The ski patrol had taken Molly to the top. Willy was with them when they settled the old patroller into Number Ten; the first chair headed down the mountain would be Molly's last chairlift. Willy was the one who went inside the lift-station shack. He made sure the safety gate on the unloading platform was set in the right position; he checked the stop button, and looked over the bull wheel for ice.

While Willy drove his snowmobile to the base of the Blue Ribbon Quad, where he started the drive motor and turned on the safety system for Number Ten, Meg sat with her arm around Molly in the chairlift. Meg was almost as big as Molly; she was strong enough to hold Molly upright in the chair. Meg made one of the new patrollers sit on the other side of Molly for the ride down.

"She was a young woman who worshiped Molly—one of those solitary girls Molly went out of her way to look after," Meg told me.

"You know Molly, Kid—she wouldn't have wanted a guy riding down the mountain with her, even when she was dead," Ned said.

"You're sick, Ned—sick and morbid *and* tactless," Meg told him.

"I know—I'm sorry, Kid," Ned said.

Since she'd been working part-time, Molly told me she still woke up early, maybe earlier. The old patroller said she liked putting skins on her telemarks and skinning up Twister. She liked skiing down before the lifts were running; she liked skiing on the freshly groomed corduroy, before other skiers had skied on it. But I knew Molly. The old patroller wouldn't have *trained* for skinning a mile up a mountain. Unlike my mom and Mr. Barlow, Molly didn't *train*.

Molly was going on eighty-six. The old patroller was a big woman to be skinning a mile up Twister to the top of Bromley. I find it hard to imagine her heart stopping, but old Ned and Meg were amazed that Molly made it as far as the Rock Garden.

I thanked the two of them for their call, and for telling me what happened; then Em and I had to talk about it. If the snowshoer had been there, we said, Molly might have made it all the way. Elliot Barlow had gone the distance with my mom. Em and I said Molly shouldn't have been by herself in the Rock Garden. If Mr. Barlow had been with her, even as small as the snowshoer was, she could have lugged the old patroller the rest of the way. Speaking as two of Elliot Barlow's rescue jobs, Em and I believed the only hero could have done it. There's no question the snowshoer would have tried.

Sometimes Em gets angry with me when she catches me "screwing around" with my Aspen screenplay—as she usually puts it. I can't make up my mind about the title. I have two titles; they seem interchangeable to me. *Loge Peak* or *Not a Ghost*. Either they both work, or they both don't. "If the film can't get made, it won't matter what you call it, kiddo," Em reminds me. But an unmade movie never leaves you; an unmade movie doesn't go away.

Sometimes I hear the voice of the woman on the subway, except that I'm not on the subway when I hear it—and it's my mother's voice I hear, not the voice of the woman who makes the underground announcements. I'm usually in the underpass, beneath the Canadian Pacific Railway bridge, when I hear my mom's voice. Every sound is amplified there; kids riding their bicycles like to shriek, just to hear the echo. My mom thinks it's funny to startle me.

"The next station is Summerhill—Summerhill Station, sweetie," I hear her say. It scares the shit out of me, every time. Or there's this one—the other stop announcement on all the older subway trains, on the Bloor and Yonge and Sheppard lines. "Arriving at Summerhill, sweetie—Summerhill Station," my mother will say, in an echoing voice. Then I'll hear her and the snowshoer laughing; I only occasionally see them in the underpass. Usually, when I see those two on the subway, or in Summerhill Station, they don't speak at all.

As for the actual woman's voice on the subway, she doesn't say *sweetie*—I can't imagine her saying it. I wouldn't know who she was, if Matthew hadn't told me. It was Matthew who noticed when the voice on the subway changed. It was sometime in 2007, Matthew said—when a new voice was prerecorded for the announcements on the older underground trains. I didn't notice, but my mother must have noticed, and Matthew really liked the woman's voice on the subway.

It would be some years later, in 2013, when Matthew told me her name. It was spring in Toronto. Matthew and I were watching some dumb game on TV. Matthew was scrutinizing his cell phone, too. He was twenty-two; I had the impression there was always something interesting on his phone. Em and I were in our seventies; we were dependent on Matthew to demystify the technology in our lives. Matthew showed us what we were doing wrong with our laptops and our cell phones; Matthew made the Internet more manageable.

That April evening, Em was watching the TV on a different channel in the kitchen. Obama was still president, but Em had been riled up since the 2010 midterm elections, when the Republicans retook control of the U.S. House of Representatives. Em hated the new Republicans more than she'd hated the old ones; she said the new ones hated Obama more.

"Tea Party assholes!" Matthew and I heard Em screaming; she must have been watching CNN.

"I'll bet it's Ted Cruz or Michele Bachmann," Matthew told me.

"She said *assholes,* plural," I reminded him.

"It's Ted Cruz *and* Michele Bachmann—they're both assholes," Matthew assured me.

That was when his cell phone spoke to us; the voice on the subway was on his cell phone. "The next station is Bathurst—Bathurst Station," the woman on the subway said.

"Her name is Susan Bigioni," Matthew told me, handing me his phone. A short film was on Matthew's cell phone, a Toronto Transit Commission film. *Voices of the TTC,* it was called.

Susan Bigioni speaks on camera for only ten seconds. "Arriving at Bathurst—Bathurst Station," the bright-eyed brunette says, more sincerely than my mother, no fooling around.

"She works as a TTC communications assistant," Matthew said.

"You're *our* communications assistant," I told him.

"I know," Matthew said.

"It won't be an aw-shucks, seeming nice guy—not the next time, you assholes!" Em was screaming at Ted Cruz and Michele Bachmann—or at everyone in the Tea Party, or at all the Republicans. Em had a point. There was an angry bullying about the patriotism *down south*—as we say in Canada, when we mean the United States. Matthew and I knew what Em meant— the next bad Republican president, whoever it was, wouldn't have Reagan's B-actor charm.

Matthew and I just went on watching the same dumb game. We kept replaying Susan Bigioni's ten seconds about Bathurst Station; I don't know why it held our attention. Maybe that was when I saw where I belonged—where the voice on the subway told me all the stops. It's such a clear voice.

As Em and Matthew know, I hear the silence in the Rock Garden no less clearly.

I can tell when Em is thinking about Nora or the snowshoer—the way she lowers her eyes when she is cast down. I never know what to say. "There's a reason we're fiction writers, you know—real life sucks; make-believe is our business," I try to tell her.

Em does a better job with me when she knows I'm in the Rock Garden. "There are German students somewhere, kiddo—they're still singing," Em keeps saying.

We were living full-time in Toronto when Trump was elected president and Em blamed those Democrats who didn't vote for Mrs. Clinton. If there was ever a time for a FUCK THE DEMOCRATS sign, I feared this was it. But Em already knew a sign like that could be misunderstood; she didn't want to be mistaken for a Trump supporter. Besides, our dry cleaning in Toronto was returned to us on hangers—no more shirt cardboards. I should have known. You can't have enough GOOD RIDDANCE signs.

In December 2017—two days after my seventy-sixth birthday—I found *The New York Times* in disarray on our kitchen table, where Em had abandoned her uneaten breakfast. Enough time had passed since the Reagan obituary—Em was reading the *Times* again. (I was reading the *Toronto Star*; it was a good way to learn about the city.) I saw that the *Times* was open to another obituary. Cardinal Bernard Law had died in Rome. The former archbishop of Boston, the cardinal who covered up all those child molestations by priests, was gone. If there was ever a time for a GOOD RIDDANCE sign, here it was.

I saw the torn-apart cardboard carton on the kitchen floor—a box from Blood Brothers Brewing; she'd taken one of the cardboard panels for her sign. I had an idea where Em would go with her message.

There was a six-story building on Yonge Street, on the corner of Shaftesbury Avenue. Em and I had talked about it. Both the shield and the name of the Archdiocese of Toronto were inscribed above the glass doors, where the words CATHOLIC PASTORAL CENTRE were written. The building didn't look like a cathedral could be contained inside it. We never saw nuns coming or going—not a single priest with a collar, not that we could remember. Matthew must have gotten tired of hearing us wonder out loud about the place. He'd gone online, which only added to the Catholic mystery. There were archives, collections, artifacts; researchers could book an appointment, after consulting with the reference archivist. "Usually, or often, there is a photo of Pope Francis by the glass doors—he looks very nice, in a beneficent way," Em had said.

This was where I found her, one December morning—in front of the beneficent-looking Pope Francis, or someone with the pope's generous smile. I'd read only the last sentence of Cardinal Law's obituary—the part about the pope's presiding over the cardinal's funeral rites in St. Peter's, "an honor accorded to all cardinals based in Rome."

I suggested to Em that she move away from the photo of Pope Francis. It isn't always the pope who is pictured there; the photos change. But I'm pretty sure it was Pope Francis this December morning. "Someone might think the pope has died, and you're saying *good riddance* to him," I said to Em. The longer we stood on the Yonge Street sidewalk, the more we were in the way of people headed for the subway—or people coming from the subway station on Shaftesbury Avenue. That was when the young priest suddenly appeared, as if he'd been born with his hand holding Em's arm in her warmest winter parka. He had the unflagging enthusiasm of an assistant coach on an athletic team, or like someone new to his job.

"You look unhappy—*good riddance* to what, or to whom?" he asked her. We'd not seen him emerge from the glass doors of the archdiocese building. Maybe the young priest had nothing to do with the Catholic Pastoral Centre; he could have been coming from the subway, or he might have been on his way to it. He'd appeared so suddenly, it was as if he descended from heaven.

"Cardinal Bernard Law is dead—good riddance to *him*," Em said, almost shyly. "He knew about those sexually abused children—he protected the pedophile priests," Em told the young priest, slightly more assertively. His scarf was knotted loosely, his overcoat unbuttoned, as if the winter weather didn't affect him; the whiteness of his priestly collar stood out on the gray sidewalk. "The Vatican rewarded Cardinal Law—they made him a high priest of some big-deal basilica," Em said, more boldly.

"The Basilica of Saint Mary Major," the young priest assented, nodding grimly. This would go nowhere, I was thinking. I took hold of Em's other arm, pointing across Yonge Street to the Boxcar Social—a coffeehouse she liked.

"You didn't eat your breakfast—would you like a croissant?" I asked Em. She nodded—in the fierce way she used to nod when she wasn't speaking. When Em nodded this way, it made me afraid she could revert to nonspeaking without warning or explanation.

"Croissants are sinful!" the young priest cried; he came with us. The walk light takes forever when you're trying to cross Yonge Street there, but the light seemed to change for us as soon as the young priest pressed the button. "Mind you, croissants are not as sinful as Cardinal Law," the priest was saying. "Cardinal Law isn't in Rome anymore. 'It is a fearful thing to fall into the hands of the living God.' Hebrews 10:31, I think," he told us. Em and I just looked at each other. This might go somewhere after all, we thought.

Each of us had a croissant. We were drinking our tea or coffee when Em got up the nerve to ask the young priest if he meant that Cardinal Law would face "harsher judgment"—where the evil cardinal was going.

"Romans 12:19, maybe. 'Beloved, do not avenge yourselves, but *rather* give place to wrath'—this is where the *'Vengeance is Mine'* bit comes in," the young priest told us. Em had unzipped her parka, but she'd kept it on; this was when I noticed she was wearing her pajamas and her fleece-lined slippers.

"The *'Vengeance is Mine'* bit," Em repeated, in the deadpan way Nora would have said it at the Gallows.

"Deuteronomy, definitely—32:35. It's more of the 'says the Lord' bit—the good old 'heap coals of fire on his head' bit," the young priest explained to us, making us almost feel sorry for Cardinal Law, given everything that was in store for him. "Proverbs 25:22, if I'm not mistaken," the young priest modestly added. I liked him. He was doing his best to make Em feel better—with the "coals of fire on his head" part, and all the rest of it.

When I got up from our table to pay the bill, Em was telling the young priest we were writers. I could see him writing down our names and the titles of our books. The priest was writing on the GOOD RIDDANCE sign. When I found out the priest had paid for everything, I went back to our table. Our heaven-sent priest had departed. Em told me he'd left the way he came—a young man in a hurry. "It's a heap of the 'says the Lord' bit, if you ask me," was all Em would say about it. At least she was still speaking.

Outside, on the Yonge Street sidewalk, the young priest had disappeared— if he really was a priest, if we actually saw him. Em was annoyed that he'd taken her sign, whoever he was. I saw our reflection in a storefront window.

I was wearing a pair of my Roots sweatpants, what I usually wrote in—we were just an old couple, still able to walk. Em saw us reflected in the window. "It's a good thing we're fiction writers, kiddo, or they might make us retire," Em said.

Our reflections in the storefront window were transparent—we could see through each other. We knew we wouldn't retire; writers can't stop writing. But one of us would die first. I hoped it would be me—my head on my desk, in the middle of a sentence Em would finish for me. She knew me well enough. I didn't want to find Em with her head on her desk. I couldn't imagine finishing Em's last sentence. There are no mountains to climb in Toronto—no last chairlifts for Em and me, only last sentences.

What do we want most when we're children, and crave more when we're old? Consistency is what counts the most. We want the people we love to be consistent, to stay the same—don't we? I can't really tell Em what I feel about my mom, because Em has no reason to love her awful mother—nor should she. We're alone in the way we love our mothers, or in the way we don't.

When I see Little Ray on the subway, when she and the snowshoer are just fooling around, I miss her when she was even younger than that—before she met Molly or the snowshoer, when I was a child and I was already learning to miss her. Now that my mom is gone, I miss what was constant about her—or the most constant thing about her. When I was a child, my missing her was the most constant thing in my life. You are never over your childhood, not until you are under the train—unter dem Zug.

The older I get, this is what I remember best about my mother. I'd told her I didn't like the dark. Kids generally don't like the dark, do they? I said I didn't like the dark, or words to that effect.

"Hug the dark, sweetie, and the dark will hug you back," my mom said. "But the dark has other dates to make, sweetie—if you don't hold her tight, she won't wait around all night."

"The dark is a *she?*" I asked her, but my mom was gone. Little Ray didn't wait around. She just vanished, like a ghost.

I try not to think about the vanishing.

ACKNOWLEDGMENTS

Tom Best

Kristin Cochrane

Dean Cooke

Emily Copeland

Giustino De Blasio

Amy Edelman

Kay Eldredge

Gail Godwin

Ron Hansen

Khalida Hassan

Brendan Irving

Colin Irving

Eva Everett Irving

Janet Irving

Jonathan Karp

Bayard Kennett

Gen. Charles Krulak

Jon O'Brien

Anne Tate Pearce

Dick Peller

Anna von Planta

Theo Salter

Dr. Martin Schwartz

Anna Scott, Aspen Historical Society

William Scoular

Jackie Seow

Nick Spengler

Cleve Thurber

Grant Turner

Martha Turner

Dr. Abraham Verghese

Kate Wells

Edmund White

Kip Williams

Bill Wolvin

And all the good times at the Hotel Jerome

ABOUT THE AUTHOR

JOHN IRVING was born in Exeter, New Hampshire, in 1942. His first novel, *Setting Free the Bears*, was published in 1968, when he was twenty-six. He competed as a wrestler for twenty years and coached wrestling until he was forty-seven. In 1992, he was inducted into the National Wrestling Hall of Fame in Stillwater, Oklahoma.

Irving has been nominated for a National Book Award three times, winning in 1980 for *The World According to Garp*. In 2000, he won the Oscar for Best Adapted Screenplay for *The Cider House Rules*. In 2013, he won a Lambda Literary Award for *In One Person*. Internationally renowned, his books have been translated into more than thirty-five languages. *A Prayer for Owen Meany* is his bestselling novel, in every language.

A dual citizen of the United States and Canada, John Irving lives in Toronto. *The Last Chairlift* is his fifteenth novel.